E

CW01432704

Radiant Dark J

ISBN: 9781070752310

A SPARK OF DISCORD

Book one of
An Age of Stars

Antoni Krupski

The mainlands **Southeast**

Heavia Valley

Boventos

Fort Flum

Vetiti Wall

Fort Praes

Walk of Exile

Merchant's Bay

Merchant's Road

Sanscar

Desert's End

Deadswood

Redmawr

Golden Road

Ignis

The Canicule

Waveless Sea

Brinkshold

Litore

Lake Ignis

Moat Calor

Slipstorm

The Endless Open

The Celestial Complex

Lutum

Fort Foxtrake

Punchbowls

The Solar Auditorium

Lunarpass

Lunar Hills

Ruins of Lignum

Arbor

Ashgrove

The Red Hills

Ausdive Town

Litdun Peaks

Lynxrock

The Red Sierra

The Arm of Jupiter

Dam of Sangis

The Auburn Pole

Solis Bridge

Road of Lignum

Lunar Path

Deadaxe Road

Sangis

Brunnock

Liglock

Auburn Road

Saa's Crossroads

Sagswood

Regal Road

Negal Wall

Fort Diolus

Diolus Isles

Auburn Lake

Kittsvale

Trade Ridge

Auburn Oak

Goattreath

Negal Town

Fort Angel

Negal Forest

Hydwick

Centaur's Grove

Antrum Lookout

Centaur's Lagoon

Vaswick

Artis Bay

Deniswater

Trader's Dock

Antrum Bay

Aquarmare

Mount Taigis

Dog's Paw

Taiga Isles

Fort Deus

Sagwhel

Tower of Spears

Watchpoint Illiero

Foxies

Seden

Refien

Three Goats

Trader's Sea

Sangis Waterway

Northeast

The lostlands

Triplex Ocean

Twin Islands

Mount Rugg

Cautus

Fort Lux

Brimstone

Tideless Sea

Sanctum Animo

Caligo

Murbereka

Whitefin Bay

Temple of Mind

Mea

Whitefin Sea

Enigma Towers

Geminport

Crexpath

Ram's Haven

Serpent's Hand

Nebulus Plains

Temple of Soul

Enigma Path

Mea Minor

Selerborn

Tharnham Keep

Serpent's Tower

Fort Nebula

The Encula

Ramsport

Salempath

Baldreck

Ceto's Cove

Lirhold

Lucehold

Lushwood

Salem

Medra

Heavia Rainforest

Lucewatch

Bullshorn

Aangmouth

Gulf of Venom

Cornhold

Heavia Valley

Venom Bay

Boventos

Fort Flum

Ram's Plains

Vetiti Wall

Fort Praes

Kamicar

Desert's End

Deadswood

Redmawr

Walk Exile

Merchant's Bay

Merchant's Road

Golden Road

Waveless Sea

The Canicule

Ignis

Brinkshold

Moat Calor

Slipstorm

The Endles Open

Litore

Lake Ignis

Fort Foxtrake

Dunshoali

The Celestial Complex

Lutum

Ruins of Lignum

Airdrive Town

Litaun Peaks

The Solar Auditorium

Lunarpass

Lunar Hills

The Red Hills

Ashgrove

Lynxrock

Arbor

The
Venusian
Archipelago

The Celestial Complex

Mount Mortis

Fort Creo

Mortis Valley

Fort Wextry

Watchpoint Inretio

Somerdock

Dam of Sangis

Oretown

Arkdale

Erthal Keep

Moat Stilo

Judicium

Sangis

Iustitia

Civitas

Westreen

Kinhal Peak

Penny Harbour

Frisen Keep

Saturnian Mountains

Templebay

Baerston's Hearth

Tantum Monastery

Waterkee

Hydwick

Sangis Waterway

Vaswick

Drogstone

Fort Longrey

Taefa

Galeheart

Aquainare

Bloomwood Rock

Ormar Reef

Moaning Rock

Boxroso Bay

Orris

Castlecross

Aspatch Keep

Flixo Keep

Frozenfall

Windtune

Forsten

Darwin

Fort Harbere

Thorlorn Dock

Lslydore

Winterdam

Southbay

Westrick

Tower of Spears

Kipway

Eel's Skerry

Fort Copalt

Halton

Brasstal

Tower of Waves

Smoker's Holdfast

Brightpool

Teal Islet

Tower of Tridents

Situla

Mount Fluctus

Nameless Isle

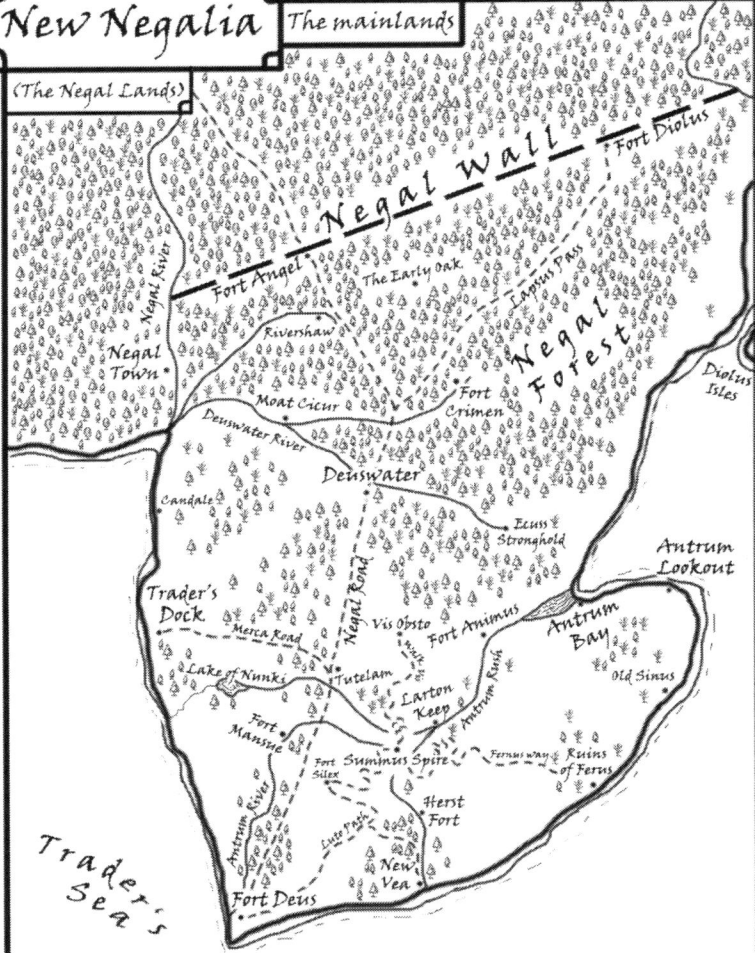

New Negalia
(The Negal Lands)

The mainlands

Negal Wall

Fort Diolus

Fort Angel

The Early Oak

Lapsus Pass

Negal River

Rivershaw

Negal Forest

Negal Town

Moat Cicur

Fort Crimen

Diolus Isles

Deuswater River

Deuswater

Candale

Ecuss Stronghold

Antrum Lookout

Trader's Dock

Merca Road

Negal Road

Vis Obsto

Fort Animus

Antrum Bay

Lake of Nunki

Tutelam

Larton Keep

Old Sinus

Fort Mansue

Fort Silex

Suminus Spire

Antrum River

Fernus way

Ruins of Ferus

Antrum River

Lute Pass

Herst Fort

Trader's Sea

New Vea

Fort Deus

Refren

Fort Deus

The mainlands

1. Gate Yard
2. Middle Bailey
3. Main Barracks
4. Cheval's Quarters
5. Soldier's Quarters
6. Main Armoury
7. Main Stables
8. Storehouses
9. Barbican
10. Main/Upper Bailey/Courtyard
11. Royal Forge
12. Royal Stables
13. Royal Armoury
14. Royal Castle
15. The Blue Spire
16. Centaur Mausoleum
17. Lower Bailey
18. Infirmary
19. Tavern
20. Market
21. Sect
22. Negal Road
23. Luto Path
24. Storm Tower
25. Cliff Bunker
26. Docks
27. Taiga Watchtower

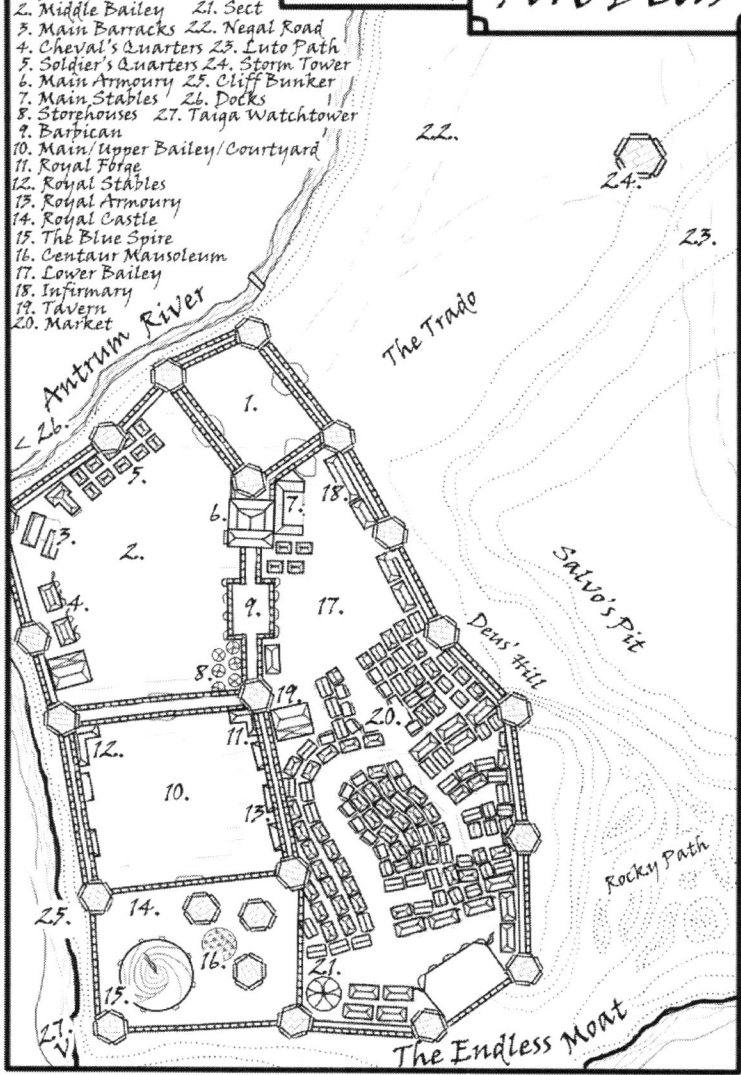

Antrum River

The Trado

Salvo's Pit

Deus' Hill

Rocky Path

The Endless Moat

Selerborn | The Lostlands

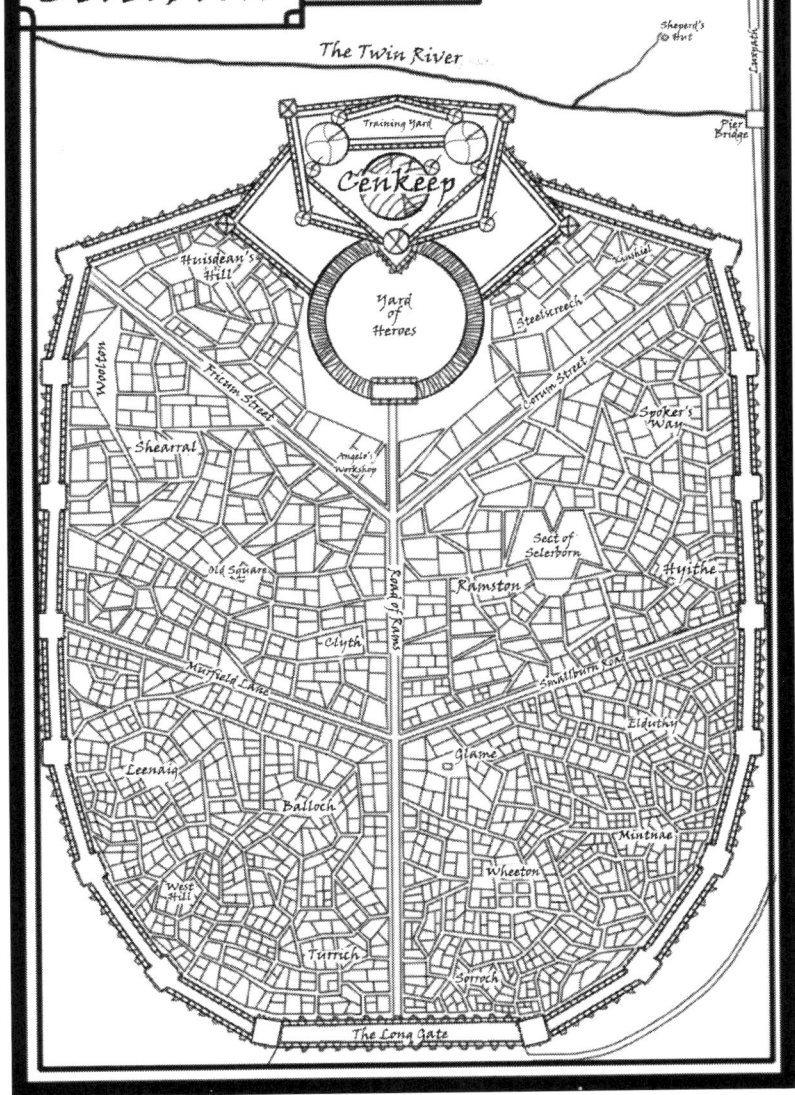

The Twin River

Shepard's Hut

Lasspath

Pier Bridge

Training Yard

Cenkeep

Yard of Heroes

Huisdean's Hill

Ennhia

Steelscreech

Woolton

Fictum Street

Carun Street

Spoker's Way

Shearral

Angeir's Workshop

Sect of Selerborn

Huithe

Old Square

Ramston

Murfield Lane

Clyth

Road of Rams

Smallburn Kirk

Elduthy

Leenaig

Glame

Mintnae

Balloch

Wheeton

West Hill

Turrich

Sproch

The Long Gate

PROLOGUE

Good fortune, my brothers," Elder Marcarius declared with a sharp grin on his face.

A booming thump echoed around the marble dome as the elder released a hefty book upon the midnight table. Marcarius carefully opened the tome, the only source of light being the sunbeams piercing through the glass ceiling. Thirteen pairs of eyes were fixed on him as his index finger found the words on the page. It was difficult to catch said words, since they still morphed into different shapes and symbols with no signs of slowing down. It was customary to wait for what Deus Caelestius had to say, but as the moments dragged into minutes, a breeze of impatience wandered the Auditorium.

The fourth solar meeting, Marcarius thought as they waited. He could remember the first like it was yesterday. *We were so young back then.* The first meeting was five years after he had met his new brothers. *Look at us now,* furrowed and old, the toll of age making its mark on each elder.

"Is something the matter, Marcarius?" Elder Ezekiel asked, breaking the silence.

Marcarius paid his brother no heed. He squinted harder. *Give us something, Deus. You're making me look a fool.*

"If the words don't manifest themselves, perhaps Deus has nothing to say," Elder Jericho suggested eventually.

"He's always had a say," Elder Ulrich frowned.

"Evidently, not today," Marcarius sighed, closing the tome. "Check it again later, if we must, but if silence is what he sends, then it shouldn't delay our duty."

"How peculiar," Elder Yuval said dryly, leaning back in his chair.

"So," Marcarius began, pushing it to one side, "which one of you fools has the most important issue to propose?" Most elders only smiled, dropping their gaze. "Really? I knew this past century was a still one for most, but-"

"Solomon?" Elder Sage interrupted. "Perchance you might share what troubled us."

The balding elder looked up in bemusement. "What? Uh, are we not waiting for Deus? I thought we commenced meetings... like that."

Nothing was said in response. The elders glanced at each other, sharing dubious faces. Solomon wiped the droplets of sweat that sat on his forehead. "Forgive me, brothers. I must confess, my mind is elsewhere."

"Good," Marcarius smiled. "Then we have found our foremost topic."

"I... um... I had hoped to discuss it lastly. It's... not a topic we should begin with."

"Nonsense, it is troubling you," Marcarius insisted.

"What is it, Solomon?" Elder Ignatius pushed.

Solomon nervously cleared his throat. "Very well... The food trade, although superb, has been... waning. Crops in environments they should thrive in are quicker to whither than usual, and yields are descending with it." Boredom was in the air. Some elders yawned; some plucked their long beards. "Brothers, be it as it may, the farms haven't been this weak since... well, since the *Pause*."

Stillness infected the hall like a plague. The mere mention of that word was enough to make the men quiver. Marcarius broke the silence. "Are you suggesting that's what will come of this, Solomon?"

Solomon inhaled, letting it known that was the case.

Elder Colbert was quick to speak up. "We... must evacuate to the Complex. What are we doing sitting here-" The Piscean stood.

"Colbert, I..." Solomon choked on his words. "Sit. It's not as bad as it seems. It is only a *slight* change. With any luck we will be able to identify the problem and keep the climate how Deus left it-"

"And if we don't? Deus and his magic have been gone for centuries-"

Elder Ulrich cut in before any more worry was sewn. "Nonsense. Abundance or lack of, a problem is here to be solved and we are here to solve it." The elders agreed in unison by ceasing all movement, reminded of their place and why they were there. "Have you identified any causes,

Solomon? What could be changing our climate now?"

"W-well, we have noticed that one of the leading causes could be from the changing ocean currents."

"And what would be the solution to this dilemma?"

"The logical approach would be to cease any activity affecting the currents... Forgive me, Ezekiel, but it is rumoured that, as ridiculous as it sounds... the excavation of citrine has had a say," he said carefully, plucking at his turquoise robes, clearly not wanting to step on the Scorpion's tail.

Ezekiel squinted, slowly standing. "What have you been smoking?" His tone cut through the air. "Don't you dare even *ponder* ceasing the mining, brothers. The Scorpions will *not* give up their bond of blood for an obscure threat of a third *Pause!*"

"Control yourself, Ezekiel. Who's to say a different mineral wouldn't imbue your ancestors?" Elder Yuval chipped in calmly.

Ezekiel's aged hands slammed on the desk, shaking his dark red robes. "A different mineral! Have the years deranged you? Even if we *wanted* to, no one alive can practise magic."

Elder Ignatius frowned. "Deus was a paranoid man, Ezekiel. The stones might mean nothing."

"Would you truly take that wager, Ignatius? Or had you a fly in your ear when you took your vows?" Ezekiel's furrows cut so deep that it didn't look like much of his face was left. "You all know damn well what the stones mean. You're asking for the death of a race."

"We're asking for the *prevention* of a *Pause,*" Ignatius continued. "I'm afraid ensuring the people's survival holds a little more importance than keeping a single house's name alive."

"Tell that to your precious Sigmund. How many men has he lost over those foolish raids in the jungles?"

Ignatius stood with fury. "Watch your tongue, Scorpion-"

"*Enough!*" Marcarius bellowed, standing before Ezekiel could fire back. Ezekiel and Ignatius sat in compliance as Marcarius's gaze shifted to Solomon. "Are you positive this is the only solution?"

"The mining has been proven to change the tides, and lately, the changing tides have shifted warmer currents to cooler places and vice-versa. From what I know, this is the only thing we can act upon."

Marcarius was suspicious. "The mining has been proven?"

"Yes, from traders, ferries, travellers. The Archipelago is notorious for irregular currents-"

"You want us to place our trust in traders?" replied Ezekiel, his wrinkly face turning as if he had bitten into something sour.

"I said enough," Marcarius repeated calmly. "Solomon excels in his field, as we all do, Ezekiel; I will hear no more objection." He turned back to Solomon. "What you describe as a slight change, are you sure it will tip the balance into another *Pause?*" he asked the elder of balance.

Solomon shook his head. "It's difficult to know. Prior solutions only seem to be temporary. If people paid attention to the first *Pause* earlier than they did, Deus could have saved a lot more people."

"Better safe than sorry," Elder Lyman agreed. "I say that if the mining is ceased and the temperature is not restored, or worse, then it's our duty to sound evacuations."

Elder Aldous nodded. "Any chance we get to give us more time would be worth it, even if it might mean... the... temporary exposure of a people." Ezekiel wore daggers in his eyes.

Marcarius stood. "Brother Ezekiel is right; none of us can practise magic. Therefore, if another *Pause was* to occur, we'd have no way of saving ourselves and our people... If we see something we can do, we should do it. I call for there to be a termination to the mining come three moons. All in favour?" The room went quiet. Ezekiel's eyes were fixed on Marcarius. Hands slowly rose. First was Ulrich, then Ignatius, soon the rest of the elders joined in with clear uncertainty. Elder Colbert and Elder Jericho abstained, probably in an effort to create no conflict, as the Pisceans and the Cancerians were largely sworn to Scorpius. "Then it is settled, three moons and you will discontinue the mining. Or action may be required," he said. "Any queries?" The great marble hall fell silent once more.

A moment passed, and the next sound that echoed around the elegant walls was the sound of screeching marble as Ezekiel pushed back his chair to get up. "Brothers," he bowed as he took his leave. Words almost formed in Marcarius's mouth before Ulrich gently touched his arm and shook his head. The room was tense. No one knew what to say. Following a deep sigh, Marcarius returned his vision to the book and turned the page. He needed to continue. The meeting could not end just because one elder was being stubborn. After all, the elders had all pledged to Deus Caelestius to serve the realm. *We can't break that vow,* he knew.

Ulrich placed his hand on Marcarius's shoulder. "Fear not, brother. If Ezekiel still has wits, he will learn there is no other way," he said softly.

Marcarius gave a nod of reassurance. "Forgive me, brothers. I would take comfort in seeing a different host. Ulrich? If it's not a trouble?"

Ulrich nodded, fetching the tome detailing all of the realm's needs. Talk was quick to return to a steady flow.

Marcarius had never been so distracted at a meeting, almost every word flew right over his long, grey hair. *Thank the gods it's not Eldric Scorpius who is to receive that news from Ezekiel*, but Marcarius didn't know if Eldric's son frightened him more. He knew nothing about the new Lord of the Stingers, and hoped for that to remain the case. *The path within one's blood is the path they're doomed to follow*, was the common saying, so Marcarius hadn't much hope for the blood of the Scorpion beyond that.

It felt like years had passed by the time his attention returned to the meeting; Elder Yuval was speaking of the seers of Sanctum Amino.

"My men give me word of serpents," Yuval began, the other elders already half asleep. "They say 'the bearer of serpents will poison the sea'."

"False soothsayers and prophets have existed for generations. I need not fret if I were you," Ignatius reassured, closing his eyelids in a know-it-all manner.

"I would if I were *you*. They say 'the serpent will first strike the north'," Yuval added without breaking eye contact, provoking a scowl from Ignatius and Ulrich.

The elders exchanged uncomfortable glances as Ulrich turned the page, opening his mouth to talk of the next issue, until Marcarius cut off his non-existent words. "Are your seers in Lunarpass at this time?"

Yuval looked startled at the question. "You're interested?"

"Why wouldn't I be?" Marcarius smirked. "They've chosen a curious time to preach this. Perhaps this *serpent* is connected to the climate."

Ignatius sniggered loudly. "And if the seers said that bread would soon fall from the sky, you'd think that connected too?" he quipped, making the other elders chuckle. "Seers preach folly, Marcarius. You know this."

"Might be I would," Marcarius said calmly. "It's no folly when lives are at stake."

The room fell into silence again, as if reminding them of the *Pause* was reminding them of a huge monster in the room. Elder Yuval cleared his throat. "Seer Junius is who you want, Marcarius. I'll arrange a meeting."

"That would be of utmost help, brother," replied Marcarius as he performed a grateful nod. Marcarius didn't know what caused him to ask, nor did he know why curiosity got the better of him. The magic that once bound him is similar to the arts the seers practise, although all trace of it was lost to the world in the *Pause*. Still, something about the phrase was intriguing to the old man. *The bearer of serpents will poison the sea.*

◄▬▬▬▬●

Hours passed and the meeting had concluded. The Solar Auditorium lay empty once more. It would be a hundred years until the elders returned, sitting in their seats exactly how they left them. The rest of the elders were already back at Lunarpass, the capital city east of the Auditorium. Marcarius, however, stood at the edge of the island, brooding, as the waves crashed against the rocks, soaking his ocean-blue robes.

"Brother," a familiar voice called out from behind. Marcarius didn't flinch; he only stared out to the ocean. He smelt a familiar lemony essence as Ulrich walked up next to him, his golden robe glistening in the sunlight. He stood for a moment, taking in the scenery. "We should go back, get some rest," Ulrich said. "Today has been a long day."

"I can vouch for that," Marcarius added.

Wearing a concerned face, Ulrich turned. "What troubles you, brother?" he spoke softly.

"The Scorpions," he confessed. "Deus Caelestius promised us safety with each ancient gemstone. Ezekiel has a right to be melodramatic. We cannot know what awaits us when the gems all fade."

Ulrich smiled. "Deus was a dexterous man. I'm sure if the stones do fade, he would have intended for them to."

"But supposing he didn't... perhaps not seeing us last this long, keep our word; what fate is to come of us? *Safety* has a broad meaning."

"The fate of any man, I expect," Ulrich said grimly. "But nevermind that, I'm quite curious in the ghost stories you're so keen to hear."

Marcarius made himself smile. "I will not be much longer. Only coming here every century makes me forget how beautiful it is," he said, still gazing out onto the Waveless Sea. It was called Waveless for a reason. Water was as still as death around the Celestial Complex, even though the waves were violently crashing against the rocks of the island he stood on. The closer the water was to the Complex, the stiller the life.

Ulrich held his smile as he turned to walk to the stone dock. Although, Marcarius was scarcely worrying about the Scorpions, neither was he admiring the view. The most cordial few decades ever to grace Austellus were coming to an end, and he could feel it closing like a chapter in a book.

ESMOND I
-Farewell-

A re you sure you must leave so soon?" asked King Esmond Centaur with an arm around Lord Sigmund's shoulders and a half smile on his face.

"Past certain, ma dear friend," Sigmund Horncurve replied. "The solar meetin's peace treaty buys us time, aye, but not enough. I'd love to stay 'n celebrate, but wars don't lead themselves."

Don't they? How inconvenient. "Damn the war. I wish we could spend more time together," Esmond cursed.

War was a slippery word; the Horncurves and the Haussciers were doing no more than back and forth raids for their race's gems over the lush forests in the Heavia Isles, a ram and a bull constantly butting heads at the top of the world. Still, Esmond granted the old man his impropriety, not caring to offend by telling him what it was.

"Do you and your men need any more supplies?" Esmond asked as they arrived at the royal stables. "From here to Selerborn is at least a moon's ride. That's a long time to be on horseback..."

"Yer supplies, I need not, my king. We're only a troop of a dozen. Yer kindness will be wasted on us," Sigmund smiled as he tightened the saddle on his amber horse. "Now where are ma damned grandchildren?"

"Keep the head, da'," Riley Horncurve smiled from where the other horses grazed. "They're ready for the journey, I made sure o' that before they started playin'." Esmond looked over to the thick northern accent.

Riley trotted toward them on his hazel horse, his short, blood-red hair glistening in the sun. He held his proud posture, despite how the wind tugged fiercely at his mahogany fur cape. "Well, what are ye waiting for, the bloody snows to come?" Sigmund winced. "Go get them!"

"Don't trouble yourself, my lord. I'll find the youngsters," Esmond offered as Riley dismounted.

"Yer too kind, my king, but let us walk together. We're not in a hurry, are we?" Riley responded, taking the lead before Esmond could protest.

The courtyard of Fort Deus was a spacious square, with dummies and little stalls for blacksmiths and armouries. Short, brown grass underfoot sat with bits of residue from frost left the night before. It was cold enough to see one's breath, yet the sun shone as bright as ever; even the great orange flame in the sky couldn't heat up the Auburn Pole.

Esmond followed Riley through the wooden door to the castle, revealing a hallway of cobblestone walls paired with a dark, wooden floor. The castle was vast. Even from the entrance could the echoes of shrieks and laughter be heard. Dead in front of them, there was a prodigious hall, the home of Esmond's glistening throne. It was engraved with the mark of the Sagittarius, and was encrusted with zircon gems, as blue as the sky.

"This week has been fantastic, Esmond." Riley smiled to the king. "It's good to get the kids oot, let them see more of the world. The fact they get along so well with yours is great too."

Esmond agreed with a nod. "It is. It's also the first time in history we can say that *friendship* held the kingdoms together."

"Aye. Makes a nice change from the fear and terror the Caelestius dynasty offered."

"You shouldn't even say that in jest, Riley," Esmond smirked. "That dynasty was loved. One bad word about Deus, and the people want to see you quartered. Three hundred years of Centaur reign, and we're still 'usurpers' in their eyes."

Everyone knew the tale of how Deus Caelestius created the Celestial Complex, using his powerful magic to fend off *The Great Pause*. Erland the Escaper, the first Centaur king, had a story that couldn't compare to that, in the same way a peasant couldn't compare to a deity.

Riley let out a chuckle. "Common folk never lack imagination. *A bloody usurper?* Of who? The last Caelestius died centuries ago, thanks to the cursed ram."

Esmond couldn't give an answer. He smiled to his feet as he walked.

"Do you mind it?" Riley asked.

Esmond wanted to think that he didn't. "Not as much as I should, I admit, in both senses. My councillors tell me I don't do enough. Often. You'd think they'd understand by now," Esmond replied.

Riley painted a grin. "Da' hates it with a passion. Suppose going for that long is gonnae do a number on ye."

"Not surprised your da' hates it, you northern folk can be quite a handful," Esmond mocked, mimicking Riley's accent and sparking a laugh from him. It was sad for them to both admit, but Sigmund was ancient, bordering the wise age of eighty, despite how impossible that might be to construe from his lively behaviour. It was a miracle that his sixty-year reign had proven the ram to be so immortal. Although inheriting the solar throne at fifteen, King Esmond Centaur had only ruled for half that time, sometimes even being intimidated by the ram's refusal to die.

Their conversation led them through the castle, all the way to where their children played. Esmond and Riley peered into the chamber.

"My love." The sweet voice was owned by Esmond's queen, Semira, sitting in her beautiful navy garb next to a gentle woman dressed in gold. Queen Semira got up to peck Esmond on the cheek. "May I offer you tea, my lord?" she beamed, adjusting her long, black hair.

"One more tan before I ride north won't hurt," Riley replied as he took the already filled teacup into his hand.

"You've met Lady Elayne, I take it," Esmond said, inclining his head to the golden woman.

Riley smiled at her. "My lady has eluded me, but aye, I have."

"Eluded?" Elayne's frown was full of laughter. "If only I could join you two in your midnight roisters. But it's no place for a baby," she said, caressing the back of her daughter's head with her thumb.

"I beg to differ," Riley muttered under his breath.

"That being said, Ayla likes it here. She might never want to leave."

Esmond couldn't help but smile as he crossed his arms. "An old soul, Elayne. Must be to have so much hair," he smirked, Ayla staring up at him with her radiant, grey eyes, and hair so much like her mother's dirty blonde.

"Takes after her mother," Semira Centaur agreed, taking a sip of tea.

"It's a shame your husband can't be here to wave us goodbye, Lady Elayne," Riley said.

"I'm sure you'll meet him on the road."

Esmond wore a wounded frown. "Reynold should be back by now..."

Elayne glanced at the king. "Perhaps he got lost?"

Semira sniggered. "In the Negal Forest? That'd be a first."

"Reynold is duly capable of such things," the lioness smiled.

As the conversation lulled, more and more did the grunts and cries of Riley's twin sons fill the room. Their father winced in response. "Are you two *tryin'* to embarrass yerselves in front o' the king?"

"Eh?" Cadmus frowned, distracted from his brother's sword, which quickly knocked him to the floor. "Agh!"

"The king ay the tourney!" Marcus announced triumphantly.

"The arse ay the tourney," Riley corrected. "Fletcher, go on, show me kids what for. They need a Centaur to knock some sense into them."

Fletcher smirked and uncrossed his arms, picking up Cadmus's sword.

Cadmus walked in between the two boys, holding the stomach Marcus had just whacked. "Begin!" he announced, signalling the start of the duel by waving his bruised arm. Almost immediately, the boys clashed swords again as Fletcher's little brother sat on the floor, watching in awe, banging his fists with excitement. *Arse ay the tourney.* It made Esmond chuckle.

"I hear there's been a squabble at the solar meeting," Queen Semira said, reminded by the fake fight. "Allegedly, it concluded with Elder Ezekiel storming out," she continued in her typical, expressive fashion. "Or so I overheard from Lord Casteron. A raven came to him last night."

"Yikes," Riley commented, raising his dark brows.

"You say it as if it's difficult to vex a Scorpion, Semira," Elayne said, rocking baby Ayla gently.

The queen shrugged. "I wouldn't know. I've never tried to vex one."

"You wouldn't even need to try," Esmond smirked. "They get pissed off at their own shadows."

Riley exhaled a sharp *tsk.* "Arians get pissed off for less. Ye don't see us startin' *rebellions* over that, though."

"A shame, really. You're the only kingdom who'd put up a decent fight," said Esmond, making a smile tug at Riley's lips.

Semira sipped her tea and frowned. "They'll always hate us, Esmond. You're the son of the man who executed their future."

"*That's* their gripe? Something that happened *decades* ago?" Riley snickered. "The Aries curse me if I'm ever that spiteful over justice."

The four took a breath of silence, punctuated by the sound of Marcus and Fletcher's dramatic duel. Eventually, Elayne said, "Hate all they want, they can't touch us. And a squabble is a long way from fully-fledged war."

"A shadow away, perhaps," Esmond smirked. "In any case, I'm sure Elder Marcarius might enlighten us." The castle was less than a moon's ride southeast of Lunarpass, and the meeting had concluded a few days ago. Elder Marcarius still had to traverse down the Negal Road before being safe in the arrow-shaped lands of New Negalia where Fort Deus lay, *a road full of brigands and thieves, as I know all too well. I hope Reynold is ok...*

Before they had time to ponder more about Venusians, in jogged Riley's brother, Luther, out of breath. "Riley, could you not leave father waiting? I don't fancy dealing with a grumpy Sigmund all moon."

"Does anyone?" Riley tittered. "Where's Athena?"

"She's already in the courtyard, brother," Luther continued testily. "Come on."

Riley knocked back his cup, finishing the last of his tea. "My queen," he said, taking Semira's hand and kissing it gently. "Lady Elayne." He inclined his head.

Marcus and Fletcher were still sparring when Riley crept up behind his son. He nudged his arm as Fletcher Centaur swung. The sword clattered on the ground.

"Ow!" Marcus howled. "I was winnin' that!" he yelled angrily at his father, holding his sore arm.

Riley snickered, grabbing him by the head and directing him to the door. The Horncurves ran out, laughing and shouting all the while.

Esmond shared a mocking look with his son as they followed the Horncurves. *"You* were winning that, for the record."

Fletcher grinned. "I know."

"There ye are!" Lord Sigmund bellowed as the group entered the courtyard. "Any longer and I wouldae passed of auld age."

"Sorry, father. Marcus was being a wean," Riley jested, acquiring a thump to the chest by Marcus's fist. Riley leapt to try and grab Marcus before he ran off, his stomach in more pain due to his laughter. Accepting his defeat, he turned to Esmond. "My king," he said, clasping the Centaur's hand before putting him into a hug.

"I will see you when I see you next," the king said.

"That'll be a good day," Riley smiled. The two faced their sons.

"Ye were good, Fletch. A little more practice and ye might be able to win against me," Marcus Horncurve said with a smirk.

"Shut up, Marcus," Cadmus laughed at his twin. They definitely *looked* like twins, sharing their father Riley's crimson hair. "Ye were shite."

"Do yer dinger!" Marcus disagreed, preparing to fight.

Cadmus set his hand on Marcus's face, pushing it back while he held his hand out to Fletcher. "See ya later, pal. Happy birthmoon for tomorrow tay," he said before they shook hands.

Riley grabbed Cadmus by the head as he did Marcus. "You were both shite," he jested, shoving them to their horses. "Now come on, saddle up."

"We'll be siblings soon, Eleanor!" Marcus called to the young lion. "Send my love to yer sister, would ye?"

Eleanor Lyrderyn frowned. "Lyssa finds you repulsive, Marcus."

His face feigned delight. "Her sweet words move me. I'll remember them when we get married."

Riley grabbed his head again. "I said saddle up," he repeated, throwing him towards Cadmus as a grin crept on his face.

"You will have to come visit Selerborn one day. There's so much I want to show you," Athena Horncurve said to her gang of girls, trying her best to ignore her noisy brother.

Eva Centaur twirled her long, curly, brown hair with her fingers. "I wish I could go. There's nothing to do here," she said, clearly envious of Athena's rousing stories.

"I'm sure your father will let you if you asked," Athena smiled as she hopped onto her pony.

Leta Centaur took her sister under her arm, glancing at Esmond. "When we're old enough, Eva."

"I *am* old enough," Eva snapped, jerking Leta's arm away.

Leta laughed in response. "I'm two years older than you and I can't even go into the Pole," she said.

"In any case," Athena interrupted before a fight began. "I look forward to see you beautiful princesses soon."

Esmond thought Athena was so sweet. *I shouldn't need to cripple my children. I shouldn't forbid them from exploring.* He knew his daughters hated it. *I don't do it because I don't trust them, but would they know that? Would they know how much I care?* Unchained, his family would desert him, leaving the hive to hunt and live. Twelve was too young for that, yet he hated it all the same.

Lord Sigmund embraced Esmond tightly. As they pulled away, he was the last Horncurve to mount his horse. "Thank ye for your hospitality, King Esmond. Yer kindness will not go unpaid."

"You need not pay me for kindness, Sigmund. You might need it again when fighting that silly war," Esmond mocked.

Sigmund held his smile as he turned his horse and trotted out to the middle bailey, his family and his wards following close behind, waved adieu by the Centaurs. A veil of quietness fell over the keep when they were gone. It would have been silent if not for Fletcher, who sat sharpening a wooden sword with a rock. Esmond knelt beside him, offering his hand. "Did you make this?" The blade was sharp, almost giving Esmond a splinter as he tapped the end with his index finger.

"Yeah," Fletcher smiled, admiring his work. "It's my first time trying to craft a sword. Marcus showed me how they make them in the north."

"Stick to arrows, Fletch," Leta japed as she sauntered back into the fort with her sister Eva and Eleanor Lyrderyn.

Esmond was surprised; the quality of the sword was finer than most, despite its wooden make. "It's pretty good, nice work," he said, returning it to Fletcher and turning back to the castle.

"Why do you refuse to train your men with swords?" Fletcher asked, catching his father's attention. "Nowhere else in the world do *chevals* and *equos* exist."

Fletcher's ignorance was almost charming. "It's not that I refuse," he smiled. "We are Centaurs. We are blessed with the blood of the Sagittarius. Gods give us and our men strength as long as we have a bow in hand."

His son was still suspicious. "Do you really believe in those myths?"

"I only believe in what I see," Esmond smirked, taking back and flourishing the blade. "But when I see, I don't need to believe, and I've seen my men triumph over rotten odds many a time. All because of a bow? All because of a gem? That whole world is so much bigger than ours that it's impossible to fathom if that's really the case." He offered his son the splintered sword. "I don't know what's out there, probably won't until I'm dead, but that's no reason not to wonder."

Fletcher took back his blade, running his finger along like Esmond had. "It is if you never get an answer."

The king chuckled. "Answers are everywhere. It's just the wrong ones you need to worry about."

"It is if you never get the *right* answer," he corrected with a smirk.

Esmond nodded. He could see Fletcher's face thinking, cogs turning. It made him smile. "Don't waste your time wondering, then."

MARCARIUS I
-Vision-

A ccording to brother Yuval, his seer should be through these doors," Ulrich loudly whispered to Marcarius, standing outside the Blue Tavern. Nightlife in Lunarpass was always dynamic. Live music and laughter could be heard in every inch of the city. Lanterns and torches were littered in almost every building, although they were hardly required; nowhere in Austellus did the moon shine brighter than in Lunarpass.

The racket grew to an unpleasant level as Marcarius carefully pushed the door, the heat and smell of alcohol lining the cool night air. "Why for Deus's sake did brother Yuval choose such an acoustic place?" he winced, trying to keep his voice above the noise.

"So our matters stay of privacy," a husky voice sounded from behind. The two elders turned to see a hooded figure unapologetically push past them. Marcarius sent a peeve-filled glance to Ulrich. *Do manners not exist in Sanctum Amino?* They reluctantly followed, keeping a suspicious eye on the seer's bare feet. Junius seated himself at the very corner of the tavern, out of view, and mostly out of light. Marcarius and Ulrich pulled out wooden chairs and seated themselves at the round, wooden table.

They sat in silence. The tavern was still full with fresh faces lingering from the celebrations, laughing and chattering and drinking. "You come for a reason?" the seer spoke. Despite his whisper, the seer's words found a comfortable place amongst the babbling.

"Knowledge," Marcarius uneasily confessed.

"Such is my strength," Junius said. "Tell me, what in particular do you wish to know?"

"Your recent... tellings... of serpents," said Marcarius, his face stone-cold as his eyes locked onto the shadowed lips of the hooded man. A wide grin broke out on Junius's face, seemingly for no reason. With a lightning reaction speed, the seer swooped to the right as a bottle of ale hurtled towards them, smashing where his head would have been. Shards of glass scattered across the room like juice from a squeezed fruit. "*By Gods!*" Marcarius cried, his vision fixed from where the bottle had flown.

Grabbing his arm and pulling him close, the seer whispered quickly, "I trust you. You speak truths. Your friend not though."

"I-I assure you, I know my brother *completely*, like a knight knows his horse. Any secret is safe with-" Marcarius matched his harsh whisper before he was interrupted.

"Your sight is weak and your brother is shallow, come." He dragged him along, acting as if he had planned the whole ordeal. *My brother is shallow,* he thought, uncomfortably agreeing.

After being yanked through a door of dark red curtains, Marcarius found himself on a balcony, one that kept the same cobblestone aesthetic of the tavern. "You want to hear of serpents?" The seer asked.

"Tell me everything you've seen, Junius," he sighed, already exhausted, stepping to the stone railing that looked out to the city.

"The serpent you seek is all," he began in his raspy, hushed voice. "The King of Light is who will judge," Marcarius slowly turned. "Set too close to the sea, and the oceans will carry poison. Set too close to a man, and he shall own again. But if it should placate, no longer should it be feared."

Great. Riddles. Marcarius's hope of a clear explanation flew off the balcony.

"It will make the brightest stars weep, and-" the seer cut himself off. "Junius will say no more."

It was nonsense. *I'll need more than just time to be able to untangle this... divination?* "How do I know you are a seer and not a madman?" he asked candidly.

The seer slowly pulled back his dark hood, revealing his grotesque face. Chills coated Marcarius from head to toe. His eye sockets were an abyss, slits cutting into his eyelids where wrinkles used to live. The stains of wine-coloured blood on his skin, making it clear where each droplet of blood fell from his face, swollen tissue in the shape of a U under each eye due to lack of sleep. After giving him enough time to observe, the seer pulled his hood back up, working a twisted smile. What Marcarius had just seen, he couldn't unsee, and he had seen a great deal. He repeatedly blinked to make sure that if it was a dream, he would wake up.

"I lost my sight long ago... I was given a new one," he mumbled. "That is all you need know." Junius turned for the exit, leaving Marcarius speechless. Before the elder could stop him, he vanished from sight, seemingly fading into the darkness. It felt like trying to decipher one of the old sorcery books the elders had to crack when they were children. *Except those sorcery books weren't written by madmen.*

Ulrich could have been scanning the tavern for the millionth time. His eyes were squinted and his mouth open. Marcarius held three goblets of wine in his hands, trying not to spill them. Ulrich got up to confront him as he approached. "Where in the world have you been?"

"Forgive me, the bartender was... verbose," Marcarius calmly replied to an already fuming Ulrich. "The seer appears to be gone?"

"How observant of you," Ulrich said sarcastically.

"A pity," Marcarius acted. "Would you help me with these chalices, brother? They are rather heavy."

Ulrich sighed, wearing a heavier face as he took the goblets from his hand and placed them on the table along with a silver coin. "Forget this folly, let's go back. I'm not waiting for a bloody seer while this tavern falls into lunacy," he insisted, Marcarius making no point of objection as he nodded and headed straight to the door. The walk back to their inn was silent, good that it was only a small street away. Both had many a thing to think about. Ulrich was suspicious, without a doubt, glancing at Marcarius every few moments. *How many times have I helped that man?* Marcarius thought, hoping to give rationale to his actions. *How many times has he been on the brink of breaking before I have come and helped him up? Shallow* wasn't the word Marcarius would have used, though. *Maybe he is. Maybe it's not worth telling him of the prophecy. Maybe he would never understand.* But nor did the old elder of Centaur.

Marcarius took to his room when they arrived at their inn, anxious to remember all that was said. He grabbed some papyrus and a quill to print the seer's words. *The serpent you seek is all,* he recited in his head. And then he stopped. *But if not Ulrich, who else can I tell this to?* Part of him hoped for Ulrich to walk in on him, so he didn't have to choose...

"I've never known you to lie, Marcarius," a tired voice said from the crack in the slightly-open door.

Marcarius's heart leapt from his chest. "Brother," he flinched as he held the papyrus behind his back. "This? Oh, this is nothing. Folly, like you said."

"If I am truly your brother, then you have nothing to hide," he said with sadness in his eyes. Marcarius released his tight squeeze on the papyrus as he gave it to Ulrich. His eyes watched nervously as Ulrich unfolded the crumpled document. "Is this what you spoke of with the seer?" Ulrich guessed.

"Yes," Marcarius admitted. He stared at Ulrich as his eyes scanned back and forth along the page.

Ulrich lowered the page to his side, looking betrayed. "You would have a mug of ale hurled at my head to prevent me from hearing this? Why would you keep this nonsense from me, brother?" he said, paying more attention to what Marcarius had done than what was actually written down.

Marcarius remained embarrassed, looking at the papyrus to see if it had ripped in his violent attempt to hide it. "Because it is just that, nonsense," he eventually spoke up, trying his best to speak in his regular wise tone.

Ulrich sighed. "We leave at first light."

He carefully shut the door, leaving Marcarius in the dark, and for the first time in a while, he yearned to be elsewhere. Staring at the scribbles on the papyrus, he wished that the week had been a bad dream. He wished that he was back at Fort Deus, his only duty telling the Centaur children of the great wars their ancestors had to lead for them to exist. He wished he had defended and saved himself from Ulrich's judgement. Then again, there was no easy way of saying that you trusted a stranger over your own brother.

SIGMUND I
-Blood-

R ise and shine, up and oot." Sigmund Horncurve patrolled around
his troop, prodding everyone once or twice with a wooden stick he
had found before returning it to the ground.

Marcus rolled over to face Sigmund, desperately trying to rub the crust
out of his tired eyes. "Ugh. It's still dark, grandpa. A few more moments."

"A few more moments *ye will not have* once we are starving in that
damned desert. Now up, up, up!" A deep mist hung in the air of the Negal
Forest, obstructing vision immensely. It was a struggle to see no more than
ten feet in every direction. Lanky, amber trees dangled overhead eerily, only
to vanish when consumed by the dense fog. The sky was a navy blue, and
at one glance, it seemed like dusk, but it was in fact the antecedent of dawn.

"I think we should wait for first light, our vision is pretty skewed,"
suggested Riley, sitting up against a tree.

"Do ye think a ram will wait for the bloody fog to clear? It charges
face down for heaven's sake, our sight doesn't matter in the slightest. Either
the air changes for us, or we storm through it. Now stop whining," he
scolded, leaving Riley to his weightless suggestion. *They're fools to argue.*
After respite, Sigmund would only ever resume travel in the infant hours
of the day, believing that travelling at any other time would bring ill
fortune. When ranging down to the Pole, he postponed their ride by an
entire day after he clumsily overslept, missing the birth of the day. His
party had no choice other than to deal with it; in the time they had woken

and prepared for the journey, Sigmund often was already yards ahead.

After stomping out the dwindling embers of their fireplace, he leant over to recover his dark red scabbard, his magnificent longsword safely cased within. Shofar was his most prized possession, its black steel tattooed from head to toe with battle scars, accompanied with a wine-coloured, worn leather hilt with a guard and pommel in the shape of twisted ram horns, topped off with his race's jewel, the Diamond Horn, embedded at the rear end of the grip. There was no separating Sigmund and his Shofar, not even when they were safe, not even when he was sleeping.

After everyone had clambered sluggishly onto their horses, they advanced into the dark, foggy nothingness. Marcus spoke up snidely. "I'm too *hungry* to ride, grandpa."

"What did I say about *whining*?" Sigmund snapped, turning on his mount. *Look at yer siblings. Be more like them,* he might have said. Athena and Cadmus were just quietly getting along with it, though their eyes were half closed. He let a moment pass and spoke softer. "We will break fast at Fort Angel. Until then, discipline your damned appetite." If he wasn't mowing down men on a battlefield, or out of his mind with a goblet of ale in hand, Sigmund was often a miserable old man, and he knew it. Despite that, he had a great deal of enthusiasm when it came to protecting his family and his people. For them not to see that was almost insulting.

Riley raised his hand well above his head while riding, ripping a fresh persimmon from a branch, making dozens of brown leaves fall from the tree above. "Here," he said, tossing it to his son who barely caught it. After a while of careful trotting, they came across a river bank where the fog lifted slightly. The lake was at the very end of its route, the sun barely peeking over the horizon while the moon and stars still glistened like fireflies on the surface.

"Campers?" Cadmus noticed, spotting a troop of sleeping men surrounded by trees. The man who looked like he should have been keeping watch, in his yellow and brown fur coat with a sword in hand, had his head resting against the foot of a large tree, mouth wide open and eyes shut peacefully.

"Well spotted, Cadmus," Sigmund smiled, as he noticed the fiery gold lion sigil of Lyrderyn sewn on the man's coat.

"Their huntin' party?" Riley realised in a barely audible mutter. "Are these ghastly forests Reynold's idea of a good time?"

"Why don't we ask?" There were five men awake, dressed in different black, shredded rags, tiptoeing around the bodies of the dozing. *"You there!"* Sigmund thundered, startling the men. The Lyrderyns awoke, dazed and confused. Simultaneously, the other five unsheathed small daggers, three lunging at the rising Lyrderyns as two bolted away in different directions clutching valuables.

One of the men plunged a dagger into the side of Reynold Lyrderyn. Athena screamed. He stabbed thrice before a sword spiked through his head. Sigmund kicked his horse into a gallop after Riley, unable to assist as Riley dismounted and felled a bandit. Reynold's brother knelt next to him as he squalled in shocked pain, sword still wedged in the bandit's head. Sigmund frantically twisted his head, trying to grasp what was happening.

He turned to the sound of Cadmus kicking his horse into a gallop as he became veiled in fog.

"Fitz! Son! Watch out!" Reynold's brother yelled, unable to aid.

Another thug thrust a dagger into the dirt, barely missing a Lyrderyn boy. Sigmund's effort to help the boy left him stunned when Fitz rolled away, faster than a cat, opening the bandit's throat in a clean swipe of a katar dagger. He kicked the body back and darted towards Reynold and his father. *"Uncle!"*

"The other one's getting away!" Cadmus yelled back to the camp. Sigmund looked over to his grandson; he sat atop his horse, sword in hand as he dragged a trussed, fallen bandit, blood spilling from his open leg.

Sigmund leapt on his horse to chase the other bandit, followed by two of his ram's guard. A katar hurled into the bark of a tree Sigmund rode past, startling him. He looked back to see Fitz biting his lip and wrinkling his nose as he steadied his arm to throw his next blade. He launched the weapon and it dug itself into the back of the bandit's foot. Stumbling, the bandit let out a cry of pain, pulling it out and throwing it on the floor to continue his now limp dash. Sigmund slowed his horse as the bandit grew weak, watching out for if Fitz was to throw another katar. His ram's guard kept their pace though, and a moment before they could slice at the bandit, an audible *crack* sounded as the katar tunnelled into the back of the bandit's head. He let out a final cry of pain before plummeting headfirst into the ground with all his momentum. The golden helmet he had been carrying tumbled out of his hands as he fell, and Fitz jumped on his horse to retrieve it and his blades. Everyone let out a silent sigh of relief after the last bandit fell, pausing to catch their breath. Sigmund was slightly amused to see Marcus and Athena stunned on their horses as he rode back.

"What a, h-healthy coincidence, y-you were travelling through," Reynold painfully managed a small smile as he held his stomach, shivering from the shock and the chilly air. "Off so soon, are you? I-I would have liked a few more drinks with you-"

"Save ye breath, Reynold, you old fool. What were you thinkin', lying open in the forest like this?" Sigmund winced as he returned his clean sword to his scabbard. "Can you stand?"

Sir Goldwyn helped his brother up. "J-just about," Reynold confirmed, his quaking legs barely supporting his body.

"Milord," Cadmus called as he threw the body of a tied-up bandit at Reynold's feet. The young man had blood running down his legs from where Cadmus sliced, and pain in his eyes, seeming on the verge of tears.

Sir Brendan of the lion's guard knelt beside him and took the man by the neck. *"Who the fuck do you think you are?!"* the knight roared.

He desperately clawed at his throat. "We're no one, sir. A-a-assassins. W-we were sent here, sir."

The knight's grip tightened as he slammed the bandit onto the floor again. *"Who sent you?!"*

"T-the Khavars, sir, they only let five of us through the gate, sir, the others are going to the Lunarpass, sir. They want the king's cousin," he wheezed, feeling the life drain from his leg. Fitz trotted over with the recovered helmet in his hand, staring at the bandit.

"There are more? How many?" Sir Goldwyn challenged in his soft voice, with the arm of Reynold around his shoulder.

"At least six dozen, sir. You can't catch them, sir. They'll be gone when you look, sir," he whimpered apologetically.

Sir Brendan tightened his grip and pushed him against a tree as he stood. "Tell those pious Khavar bastards who sent you that if they send more men, all of your worthless hearts will be ripped out from your pathetic bodies for endangering these people. Do you understand?"

"Y-yes sir, right away sir."

"Do you understand?!"

"I understand! I do, I do!" he wept, as he was flung violently from Sir Brendan's tight grip. The bandit bent over to recover gold that had fallen from his pockets. As he reached out, Fitz stood on his hand, pointing a katar at his throat. The bandit sent a terrified look before scrambling to his feet, falling into a lame jog.

"Help me, would you?" Sir Goldwyn pleaded breathlessly as the other lion's guard rushed over to put Reynold's other arm around his shoulder. They carefully lifted Reynold onto his horse. "Son, ride for Rivershaw with Sir Cedric and Sir Brendan. Follow the river. See that your uncle is treated as soon as possible," Sir Goldwyn urged. Fitz gave a sharp nod as he climbed the horse Reynold sat on, the Lord of Ignis still holding his stomach as the blood stained his hand. They broke into a gallop straight away, the two knights following close behind. Goldwyn turned to the Horncurves with astonishment. "*Gods*, I thought we were done with Khavars. Why would they send *assassins* after us?"

"The solar meeting's peace treaty is still active. Whatever the reasonin' be, it is at the height of crime to attack during this period," Sigmund declared, pointing his finger to the ground.

"Whatever the reasonin' be?" Riley laughed in a bitter tone. "If the Khavars *did* assemble this attack, there's nae chance that they meet their justice." He gave a pause to look around the group, his dark brows raised and half a smile on his face. That stupid, know-it-all face angered Sigmund even more. *Haughty little ram.* "Our evidence is a hole in the stomach of Reynold Lyrderyn. Not only could that wound be of anyone's doin', charging a powerful family like that with poor evidence is a death wish."

"The lord has a good point," Sir Ardin of the ram's guard turned to Sigmund.

"If we can't take action, what are we supposed to do?" Sigmund replied aggressively, the words grinding through his teeth.

"We can't do nothing, nor can we accuse them; that bandit could have lied," Goldwyn suggested, raising his broad shoulders. "If word gets around that this is Venusian work, done at a time as sacred as this, then we'd spark a fire that we cannot put out. I say we keep this private, try to hang the others in Lunarpass before Lord Thaddeus is brought to any harm."

"Let's not forget that the Khavars and all of those damned criminals are exiled," said Riley, leaning on a tree with his arms crossed. "Any exiled races still in the realm come three days will be outlaws anyway."

"It's nae *death wish* to accuse them then, ye numpty," Sigmund frowned. "They have no *power* here. The world needs to know that. Let them come, and they'll be crushed at their first taste o' battle."

"You're not the one who decides that, da'," Riley sighed, sliding his sword back into his scabbard. "King Esmond is."

Sigmund spat. "Cancerians are liars, oath breakers. If there's any left in the realm come three days, I will kill them myself." It wasn't the first time the Venusians broke a vow of peace; it had happened roughly two centuries ago, when the seasons stopped for a second time. King Archer the Brave hadn't expected company when fleeing with his people south to the Auburn Pole, let alone the company of the infamous Oquinteus line. *The Oquinteus: the damned rams who bloodied our Arian hands until the end of time. They deserved every bit of grief when I shoved Shofar into Jaakko's stomach.* That made Sigmund smile to this day. Still, the Centaurs couldn't have known that then, and King Archer arranged a treaty of peace with the Oquinteus so they could both rebuild the kingdoms they lost in the pause.

After learning that the Oquinteus had rebelled and murdered Deus Caelestius, the furious Cancerians sent assassins to murder the cursed rams, to avenge their king, the very assassination to spark the *War of the Wastelands*, before the Cancerians fled with the Pisceans to the Archipelago. *Assassinations are in their blood, and they're doomed to follow that,* Sigmund thought spitefully. *If another war is what they want, they'd have better fortune wanting something else.*

"Either way, my lord," Sir Goldwyn began, adjusting his saddle before looking toward Sigmund. "It looks like conflict is on the horizon. I bid you a safe journey on your way back to Selerborn," he added, climbing onto his horse. Sigmund managed a near smile at Goldwyn as he also mounted his, getting ready to ride in the opposite direction.

"Keep your brother alive," said Riley, exchanging the courtesy with Goldwyn as he turned and cantered away into the thick fog.

Marcus took a gulp of air as he stared at the blood soaking into the brown grass underfoot. "I almost killed that man," Cadmus said as he trotted over to Marcus's side, his eyes also fixed on the blood.

"It happened so fast," Marcus commented, still staring, not blinking. "Any one of us could have been killed."

FLETCHER I
-Change-

H ow many do you think there are?" Fletcher Centaur asked, staring out of his chamber's window.

"Hundreds," his eldest brother Asher smiled, their shoulders in line as they both gazed out onto the upper bailey of Fort Deus. The yard was littered with men and women laughing and conversing. Music played by a band of four echoed throughout the fort, the bards smiling at the people tossing coins at their small stage. Stalls were set up offering free refreshments and food, and people danced in joy and drunkenness around them. Fletcher and Asher had their attention stolen by the roar of a small crowd as Lorimer Centaur's arrow pierced a target, joining three others in the bullseye. Every time Fort Deus held a tourney, it seemed like Esmond and his brother were the only ones contending, both matching each other's skill, and exceeding everyone else's.

The head of events rang a bell on a raised platform next to the shooting range. "The victor is Lord Lorimer of Centaur's Lagoon. Please come here to receive your prize." Lori stepped up to the podium, slipping a blue and silver ring on his finger. He looked quite pleased with himself.

"You were close, brother," Lori smiled at Esmond as they locked hands in good faith.

"I didn't realise you wanted me to try," Esmond smirked playfully. The crowd roared for a second time as Esmond raised Lori's hand.

"Come on, Fletch," Asher turned and put his hand on Fletcher's back.

"The feast should've started already; we can't have you not there." Fletcher smiled and nodded as they sauntered to the door.

Scents of onions and spices filled the hallways as they got closer to the throne room. Families that had come from all over the Arm of Jupiter were flooding into the castle, taking seats and claiming tables. Fletcher and Asher met their father and uncle at the wooden door of the keep as they were turning to go into the hall.

"Ah, there's the ancient man," Esmond smiled at Fletcher as he rotated him by the shoulders to face the hall.

Fletcher was shy of words as he gazed upon the room full of people. If there were hundreds in the courtyard, there must have been thousands here. People Fletcher had known since he was small, and those he had only heard of in stories alike filled the hall, watching his every movement. Sigils from all over Austellus lay embroidered on the coats of most: the golden lion of Lyrderyn, the green twins of Kalyx, the brown hammer of Sculptor, the auburn pony of Equuleus, even his uncle Lori had his own sigil: a centaur veiled in water like the lagoon he lived in.

Fletcher climbed the steps and stood in front of the throne of zircon, turning to the flock of people who were waiting for him to commence the feast. *"Right, you lot!"* Esmond bellowed as he hammered on the high wooden table. *"A speech from the birthmoon boy himself!"*

The room cheered and stood. It almost overwhelmed the boy. He waited for the hooting to die down. "A speech? I don't have much else to say other than there's so bloody many of you," he smiled, sparking laughter from the audience. "Enjoy the night everyone. Let's get pissed." He raised a cup from the table beside him, the joyful clamour returning after another round of cheers. Esmond, Semira, and their siblings seated themselves on the high table in front of the throne of zircon, the Centaur children scattering themselves out to sit with their friends from other families. Asher and Fletcher joined their little brother and Jovian Reade, Esmond's squire, at a smaller table to the side. "I'm quite moved by that speech, Fletch. I think I teared up," Jovian said dryly.

"The first of many, Jovian," Asher returned. "I plan to use at least eight words in *my* speech."

The squire shrugged. "If I don't weep, I'm disappointed."

Hew wasn't paying attention to the jesting. His eyes were locked on the door. Waiters poured into the room carrying mahogany platters packed with food: meats, soups, potatoes, fruits, bread; the menu seemed endless.

Asher poured a goblet of wine for himself and Fletcher, handing the wine jug to Jovian. "You're a man now, Fletch," said Asher, passing Fletcher's goblet. "How is it?"

"A man? I'm not a man yet; I don't feel any different," Fletcher replied, staring into the dark red wine.

Asher chuckled. "You'll need change to happen to feel different. Your age simply marks how long you've spent in Austellus."

Fletcher smiled. "I know. I was just under the impression that becoming a man was such a huge leap," he said as he ran his fingers through his short, wavy hair.

"A leap that begins now, perhaps?" Asher smirked, nudging his brother's goblet towards him. He raised his goblet. "To change."

Fletcher looked up with intrigue. "To change," he said, gently bumping his cup with Asher's.

◄————◼

The banquet was in full swing: Warmth from breath and hot food filled the hall, some were already beginning to faint from the alcohol, others sang and danced around a young bard and his fiddle. Only a few royal families had detoured from Lunarpass to attend the celebration, the first, of course, being almost all of the Lyrderyns; they had stayed for a week before the event to reunite with the Centaurs and for Elder Ulrich to attend the solar meeting. *I wonder how their hunting trip is going.*

The food was amazing; the best Fletcher had ever tasted. Even Hew seemed to adore it, Fletcher and Asher chuckling at the way sauce was smeared over the boy's face as he looked up from his bowl. He was only ten, and would often lose his days listening to Elder Marcarius's many great stories, if not consumed by books. He wasn't much of a fighter like his brothers, and only Fletcher seemed to care about that. *The outside world will swallow him whole. He has to learn sometime.*

Fletcher overheard Eleanor Lyrderyn from the other table. Her worried tone carried over the feast's hubbub. "My father said he would be back for the celebrations. I haven't seen him all day," Eleanor said worryingly as she played with her food.

"Don't worry Ells, father always returns. He went hunting with all of his lion's guard, I'm sure they'll keep him safe," her sister Lyssa reassured, her and Asher's eyes locking for a brief second before she blushed and smiled down at her food. She tucked a tress of blonde hair behind her ear.

"Hey, bud. Mind if I excuse myself?" Asher asked, keeping his playful blue eyes on Lyssa.

"Go get her, Asher," Fletcher winked.

Asher put his hand on Fletcher's shoulder as he got up to walk over to their table, smiling. *I probably shouldn't encourage him*, he thought. When they returned to Ignis, Lyssa was meant to marry one of the Horncurve twins. *Still, Asher would respect that...*

Before he had time to overthink, Asher's seat was replaced with a short, slim, youthful man. Fletcher turned to see Todd Kalyx of Mea, casually placing his legs on the table. "My lord," Fletcher greeted, slightly startled, pretending to only just notice his presence.

Todd smiled with his brown eyes. "You knew I was a lord? That's a skill I wish I possessed."

Fletcher smiled and looked at his dinner, surprised at how open Todd was. "I know you're a lord from how confident you are. And, we are in a hall half full of lords."

Todd chuckled. "Confidence can be found in peasants, too, can't it?"

"Only the brave ones."

"And still you know the difference with me? With what rags I wear?"

"I do," Fletcher smirked. "By the way you talk, you have more than proven that you are, Lord Todd." He took another sip of wine.

Todd's grin grew. "Well played," he said, his skinny hand reaching out to tear a piece of bread from a loaf. "Wit will be a virtue when you're king."

Fletcher turned to look at the ash brown haired lord, eyebrows frowning. Asher was heir to the solar throne. When he ascends it, all Fletcher would have to inherit is his family's seat at Fort Deus. "You say it as if I will."

"My seers tell me a great number of things, and your rule over this castle at least is sooner than you think. Not all kings need to sit on fancy chairs, you know," Todd smirked before tossing the piece of bread into his mouth. The Lords of the Twin Islands were well known for their myths of seers and clairvoyants. Supposedly, they were superstitious to the point that they only named twins to lead them, so as to complement their Geminian roots. Hew had told Fletcher that, and called them crazy, but still, the prince was intrigued.

"How will it happen?" he asked, confusion taking root in his face.

"The seers never tell me how. If they told me how, anyone could prevent the inevitable, prevent their fate," Todd stated, looking into

Fletcher's curious eyes before turning to face forward at the people drinking and laughing. "Your father dies and your brother renounces his claim, you kill them both to take the throne, your brother and father renounce their claim and bestow it on you, anything can happen. Anyway, asking *why* would be a far greater use of your time."

"Why then?" he asked without thought, pausing to shake his head. *You're an idiot, Fletcher.* He turned back to his half empty plate. "Well I only believe in what I see," he said, mimicking his father's tone with hopes to seem wiser than he was.

Todd turned to face Fletcher once again, a smug smile stretching across his face. "But when you see, you don't need to believe." He winked at him before getting up from the stone bench and leaving Fletcher in a stunned silence. It seemed to amuse Jovian; all he could do was grin while Fletcher stared at Todd in awe. He glanced anxiously at his brother, the four princesses watching attentively as he told stories. *What hope do I have to be a better ruler than you? You've always been better, more caring.* Fletcher then shifted his troubled blue eyes to his father who stood across the room, laughing and joking with his arm around Blaine Casteron, Lord of the Tusks. Fletcher caught Esmond's gaze for a brief second before he said something to the guests and walked over to Fletcher's table.

Esmond saw Hew using both of his hands to drink the last of the wine from a goblet. "I hope that's your first cup." He smiled as Hew looked up, a little startled. Hew nodded quickly as Esmond gave a small chuckle and ruffled Hew's already curly brown hair. Esmond faced Fletcher. "Come with me, Fletch," he said. Fletcher frowned, stood, and followed his father out of the hall.

A chilly gust of air and darkness rushed into the castle as the guard opened the exit for King Esmond. As the door was closed behind them, the music trailed into a muffle and was replaced by the distinctive *clank* of metal clashing, ringing out across the empty courtyard. Bits of food and pieces of silver were littered all over the yard, and the stalls and events that lay thriving a few hours ago had been relocated. A young man wearing violet, fitted with the dual swordfish sigil of Casteron was the only person in the whole yard, sitting next to a raven in a cage and writing on a slither of papyrus. All of this was illuminated by the new Rose Moon that twinkled in the sky, a pink sheen gently coating everything it could coat. Esmond led his son to the forge, where he noticed that the sound was coming from the hammer of he who was called 'Blackfist', the fort's smith.

The artisan looked up to see the king and his son standing at the entry. "My king," he bowed as Esmond stepped forward to look upon his work. "I made it exactly how you asked."

Esmond took the outcome of the smith's work and inspected it, his body obstructing it from Fletcher's vision. "It's perfect, you will be rewarded greatly," Esmond smiled at him.

"Only the finest work for the finest king," Blackfist beamed back.

Fletcher was gazing back to the door, wanting to return to the feast. "Son," his father said from behind.

Fletcher turned to lock eyes with his father before he noticed the gift he was carrying. Just by *looking* at the bow Esmond held, cold, sticky fingers crept down Fletcher's spine. He took it into his hands, the steel warm to the touch. It was ornate with engravings of patterns and had complex twists in the bow head, resembling bird wings. Sagittarian jewels glistened in the pink moonlight as he tilted the bow to admire them with all of their blue majesty. The gems were resting in the grooves of the bow, expertly forged by only the most masterful of hands. Fletcher lowered the weapon to his side, and embraced Esmond rigidly. "Thank you, father."

"You've always wanted to be a smith," the king said. "Who better than for Blackfist to show you how?"

It was the second time that night Fletcher had been lost for words. "Can I fire it?"

Esmond presented his hand to the tourney target, untouched from earlier. Fletcher beamed as he darted across the courtyard to retrieve a shaft of arrows he had crafted in his spare time. He excitedly nocked and drew the arrow into his bow. On release, he let the arrow fly into the target, hitting the second circle from the bullseye. "It's amazing," he said, gazing at the bow once more.

"Keep that safe, it's no toy," Esmond said. "They say that with zircon in hand, a Sagittarian's blood runs blue as the sea and the holder has the stamina of a horse," he said, also mesmerised by the blue gems.

"I thought my blood felt bluer." Fletcher mocked. A harsh creek echoed over the courtyard as the keep door was opened, revealing Blaine Casteron, his two eldest sons, and his *First Avail* walking towards them.

"Prepare to leave for the docks," Blaine told the men following him as he advanced to Esmond and Fletcher. "King Esmond, you have been a fantastic host."

They locked hands with affinity. "You're leaving?" Esmond asked incredulously. "So soon? Why? You're only a troop of four. I value your company, you know."

"It pains me to refuse, but our sail to the Archipelago is treacherous, come a moon and the tides will be too violent," Blaine replied, matching Esmond's sad eyes. His sorrow was understandable, as Esmond had grown up with Blaine and Reynold Lyrderyn over in the Venusian Archipelago, when his brother, Ivor Centaur, was heir to the throne. After the passing of his father, Ivor only ruled for two years before renouncing his claim and bestowing it on Esmond, fleeing for a reason that was still a mystery. Thus, Esmond was ripped away from Blaine to rule over the Auburn Pole. Esmond hated Ivor for that, for abandoning his family and leaving forever. *Perhaps that's why he keeps us all so close. He's never seen Ivor since.*

Blaine wore a sorry simper across his face. "And there's something else, Esmond." He took a moment before wincing and shaking his head. "I really shouldn't tell you. You don't need any more stress."

"What is it, Blaine?"

He hesitated before confessing. "Scorpius has wed into Khavar, merging the two families and doubling their forces. And the Scorpions will *always* have animosity for you, my king, ever since your father called for the head of their heir."

"I'm not the one who did it," Esmond said sternly.

"Do you think it makes any difference to them?" Blaine asked softly. He frowned at the floor, as if the dirt was offending him. "I don't want this to be the last time we meet as allies, Esmond. We grew up together; you're a brother to me... but... but..."

Esmond slid his gaze to the floor. "I understand; you have oaths to keep, just like me." Fletcher looked at his father for relief, engulfed in fear as he thought back to what Todd had told him, toying with the devil to draw his bow and fire at Blaine, putting an end to it before it began.

Blaine managed a painful smile after tying the last straps on his stallion. "Esmond," he said, making Esmond's head rise to face him. "Whatever the Khavars decide to do, we Pisceans are still pledged to serve them. Whenever the time comes that we must kill you or your men..." He sighed. "Then Venus will harbour another traitor. I'll never let that happen."

"Your home is within finger's reach of them, Blaine," Esmond grimaced. "I won't have you endanger your family for my sake."

"You don't have a say in this, my king," he muttered. "They'll have to bring us both down before they're rid of enemies."

ESMOND II
-Threat-

S eventeen golds?!" Esmond Centaur winced at the thought.

"Yes, my king. The expenses for the provisions and events this week totals seventeen golds and four silvers." The head of gold and events paused to rub his delicate hands together. "I should fear not, my king. Once Lord Reynold returns from his coursing, I'm sure our costs will be covered."

The king doubted that. The expenses were more than a fortune, enough to hire twenty assassins of the highest calibre. Regardless, the currency had already been spent.

Esmond was still nauseous from what Blaine Casteron had told him last night. He was grateful that the wealthy Lyrderyn family were sworn to them, but if a time came that Austellus falls into war, a vast desert still stands between the Centaurs and the great banks of Ignis; without the funds, the crown had little more power than a merchant. *My head hurts too much for this.* "Fine, we'll take on these matters when Lord Lyrderyn and Elder Marcarius return. Anything else?"

The rest of the king's council were as inert as the king himself. Sir Orion Reade, Esmond's *First Avail*, looked particularly rough, his long black hair tied back lazily, his face a milky pale. The three eldest men, the heads of gold, trade, and law, looked as if they were on the verge of falling asleep. Only Galloway Malone and Sir Roswell Dart seemed to be present.

"Has everyone departed safely?" Esmond continued.

"I believe so, my king," Sir Roswell answered lethargically. "Only Lord Todd Kalyx seems to be here still."

"I'm aware," the king tittered. Earlier that morning, as he was tiredly stumbling through the wreckage of last night, Esmond had found the Lord of Mea lounging in the throne room, next to one of the three roaring hearths that never failed to keep the room a pleasant level of toasty. "Lord Kalyx," he nodded. "It seems you're the last one standing."

Todd chuckled. "If you can call this standing."

"Well, if you're ready to crack open another skin, you're more than welcome to," the king jested.

"I'd love to, Esmond, but next time. I can't leave my brother in charge of the Twin Islands for too long." He stretched his arms out. "I just need to find some energy before I head off."

Esmond nodded. "Stay however long you need."

Todd then stood abruptly, as if he had suddenly found all the energy he needed. "Thank you," he smirked knowingly. "I would keep those fires well lit, Esmond. Snow always finds a way to let the cold creep in." With that, he left, and Esmond hadn't seen him since. *The day snows fall on Fort Deus is the day the world goes mad,* the king thought with a smile.

"Very well, until our elder returns, you are all dismissed. Thank you, my lords." Esmond was the first person out of the six to leave the tattered assembly hall. He walked slow, head down, his rough hand grazing over the smooth cobblestone walls while he collected his thoughts. Not that there were many thoughts to collect; the lingering shadow of alcohol made his mind spin like a wheel. He wondered if Asher was still alive, the boy still being deep in song by the time Esmond went to bed. He wondered if *anyone* was alive; Fort Deus had been silent all morning.

"Open the gate! It's Lord Reynold!"

Thank the gods. Esmond lunged to the nearest window to see the castle gate being unlatched. His stroll turned into a scurry as he met the winding staircase down to the hallway. Esmond drove the door open, not letting the guard open it for him. His eyes locked with young Fitzroy's as he galloped into the courtyard. Esmond couldn't help but beam, but the boy wasn't smiling back. There were scratches all over his face, dried yet still bloody. His gaunt face was somehow gaunter, and his wavy oak hair was tangled and knotted, like an animal had made its home there. *Something's not right.*

A moment later, the inanimate body of Lord Reynold flopped from

Fitz's horse, striking the red ground. Esmond's smile was snuffed like a flame. *Please no.* He ran over to Reynold, his fingers meeting his long, golden hair, trying to lift his head to not touch the dirt. Suspicion was raised in the yard, soldiers and blacksmiths halting work to see what the hubbub was about. A scream from little Eleanor Lyrderyn fell out of one of the fort's windows, adding more chill to the bitter air.

"Orion, take him to his chambers," Esmond commanded as the knight rushed to his side. Reynold's eyes were heavy, dark, but somehow smiling. "Get him food and warm fur immediately."

Sir Orion nodded obediently. *"Guards!"* he called, sending men running to his aid, lifting Reynold carefully.

As the men took Reynold away, Esmond looked to the young boy shivering next to his horse. He took off his fur coat to put around the thin shoulders of Fitzroy. "What the hell happened?" The king cursed, escorting Fitz into the warm castle.

"B-bandits, my king. Five of them," Fitz trembled.

"Bring him soup," Esmond told a young serving girl, seating Fitz down on a bench in the cosy throne room. "Where are the lion's guard? Did they all fall?"

Fitz stretched his pale, bony hands out to the hearth. "We would have if the Horncurves didn't wake us. The guard told me to get to ride ahead." He winced, like the warmth was hurting him. "They're not far behind."

Esmond turned to the sentry who stood next to the exit. "Keep the gate open," he ordered, provoking a nod from him. The serving girl hurried in with a steaming pot of leftover soup used for the morning meal, and a wooden bowl on top of the lid. "Three more bowls," he said softly as she placed the containers on the stone table, before nodding and rushing to get more. "Horncurves? They left days ago, how far did you travel?" Esmond asked as he filled up the bowl with soup scented with onions and herbs.

Fitz took the bowl with both hands, taking a careful sip to warm his hoarse throat. "From the river bank near Fort Angel. We've ridden without stopping."

The serving girl jogged in with three more bowls. "Thank you," Esmond said before turning back to Fitz. "You didn't stop to camp?"

"No, my king. Uncle was stabbed three times in the stomach. We had to keep moving. We got bandages at Rivershaw and Deuswater, but Sir Cedric said we shouldn't stop," said Fitz, cold sweat running down his face.

"Stabbed three times?" Esmond winced. "How the hell is he alive?"

A muffled "This way, sirs," could be heard outside, the door opening to reveal the three leftover Lyrderyn knights, all shivering in their ripped fur coats and frozen gold armour.

"This way gents, come get warmed up," said Esmond, trying to be calm as he filled up the other three bowls. The men sat on the same bench, as close as they could to the crackling fire, Sir Goldwyn even touching it.

"W-where's my brother?" Sir Goldwyn stuttered.

"He rests in his chambers. Drink up, tell me what happened," said Esmond, handing out the bowls to the damaged knights.

"A boar attacked us, my king," Sir Brendan claimed, his raspy voice even more gravelly than usual, covering for the other two who attacked their bowls like the hungry lions they were.

Esmond crossed his arms and smiled. "A boar, was it? Those assassins must have been pretty fat for you to come to that misapprehension."

Goldwyn glared at his son. "Fitz was meant to keep that to himself."

Lady Gina, Goldwyn's wife, scampered into the room, lifting her skirt so she could run. "Fitz!" She cried as she snatched him into an embrace.

"These men, did they wear a sigil? Colours of a family?" Esmond questioned the knights, trying not to be irritated by the lie.

Gina cried. *"What men? Goldwyn, what have you done to him?!"*

The king frowned. "Gina, please."

"Please what? My son was attacked!"

"Mother," Fitz winced, "it's fine. I'm fine."

"No, you're not," she protested. "You're coming with me. We need to get you cleaned up." The boy was dragged away, too exhausted to object.

Sir Cedric sighed when he left. "They dressed in black rags, my king. One bandit said they were sent by Khavars."

"Khavars?" Esmond echoed. "Why would they want Lyrderyns dead?"

"Lord Casteron might know," Sir Cedric said. "Is he still here?"

Esmond could feel the alcohol stirring in his stomach more than ever. *He should be. He should have never left.* "Bandits have nothing to gain by slaying the lion," he frowned.

Sir Goldwyn looked up at Esmond. "An act of rebellion. Perhaps they were enrolled." Esmond returned the look to Goldwyn, his face coming to a cold conclusion as the notion built. *'The last time we meet as allies'.*

"I need to check on Reynold," Esmond stood and said. "My men are at your service, sirs," he nodded before leaving them in the homely throne room. Fort Deus was so huge, not a sound could go unheard, and as

Esmond drew closer to the guest chambers, the constant weeping of Princess Eleanor was growing louder and louder. He went down at least ten long corridors of the maze of a fort before it was loudest. He reached out to carefully push Reynold's chamber door. Eleanor was gripping the sheets Reynold lay on with tears in her eyes. Asher stood next to Princess Lyssa with his arm around her, trying to comfort her, Lady Elayne standing next to them. Sir Orion slid next to Esmond in the narrow doorway with a bowl of soup in one hand.

Reynold opened his eyes feebly, looking towards the king. "E… Esmond." The lion's hand flailed in the air. "Let me see the king alone," he grumbled. The Lyrderyns nodded and slowly left them. "I-I feel weak."

Esmond pulled a small grin. "I doubt being stabbed three times would make you feel strong."

Reynold responded with a failing chuckle. His veins were scarcely visible through his pale skin, yet a fiery ember still glowed in his blue eyes. "We're not as safe as we once were, Esmond. Not as the wounds of war heal." Reynold steadily turned his head to the window. "They… came from Lunarpass. And if… this is Venusian work, you know they won't stop at me. You know there'll be more coming."

Esmond's face turned. Elder Ulrich and Marcarius were in Lunarpass for the meeting. Surely, they would have reached the Negal Wall by now, but thoughts of their great elders already being assassinated at the city still spiked his mind. *They wouldn't kill elders. However low people would stoop, never would they go there.*

"Promise me you will keep my daughters safe from them," Reynold muttered. "Don't let them go back to Ignis."

They can't stay here forever, he thought. Esmond looked up to Reynold, after staring at the floor. "Fort Deus is impenetrable. They are safer here than anywhere in the realm."

Reynold hardly managed a smile. "That is all I ask." He closed his eyes. "Leave me… I need sleep."

You better not die on me, Esmond squinted. Out of all the lords in Austellus, he knew Reynold the best; to see him with an open stomach was just as wounding to the king. He walked to Sir Orion, who stood in the doorway. "Get Lord Vesta to enforce a new edict." Sir Orion stopped himself from turning to listen. The king shook with fury at the concept. "Until the rest of the bandits are disclosed, no one is passing through the wall alive." *Threaten me, you've made your move.*

SIGMUND II
-Wrath-

Y ou are mistaken. I command you to let us through," an aged voice
exclaimed from the other side of the wall.

"No mistake in this, old man. King's orders. Now scoot
along," a rough looking man replied from the gateway that stood under the
Negal Wall, taking another bite out of his deformed apple.

Sigmund Horncurve and his troop trotted towards the wall, observing
the man who was shaded and protected by two giant metal portcullises on
either side. He was as thin as a bone, yet had a plump round face, and wore
a torn, black rag the colour of death. His walk was skewed.

The man turned to Sigmund. "You too fellahs, piss off."

Sigmund scowled in outrage. "You have no right," he grumbled. "Do
you know who you speak to?"

"I don't know. Some lord from gods know where." Bits of apple flew
out of the man's mouth. "Law is law, and no one is to go through this wall.
Now piss, off," he repeated. There were towers on either side of the
gateway, and a line of armoured men on the wall's battlements.

"I am Elder Marcarius, the Centaur's own servant, and I demand you
let us through, or you shall regret it." The voice echoed behind the two
gates again. *He denies Elder Marcarius? Has this cretin lost his wits?*

"Are you stupid, eldah mark-areas? You're not coming through this
gate. No one is until those filthy bandits are found!"

Sigmund dismounted his horse and calmly walked over to the gates, his family cautiously sat on their horses. "I have a royal excuse," he claimed, pulling out a crumpled piece of paper from his red furs.

The gatekeeper turned around again, limping over to Sigmund while he held his crudely bandaged leg. "Alright, let's see," he said, thumbs digging into his belt.

Sigmund's old hands fumbled around with the paper before he reached through the gate and grabbed the gatekeeper's throat, pulling him forward. "I am *Lord* Sigmund *Horncurve* of Selerborn, and you better let us through before I *smash* yer head against these bars," he snarled.

"L-Lord Sigmund, sir. I can't do that, sir. It's the king's orders, sir," the man panicked, clawing at his throat.

Sigmund tightened his grip. "How do you think your king would react to his elder, and most trusted advisor being turned away by some low-life peasant? Because I strongly doubt he would reward you with anything less than a sharp blade," Sigmund leered.

"I'll let them through. I'll let them through," he gave in.

The old man stared the gatekeeper in the eyes, before releasing his grip, making him scuttle across the gateway. Grabbing the handle that lifted the portcullis, the man wound the two gates open for the elders. By now Sigmund had already remounted his horse, waiting to kick it into a walk as soon as it got high enough.

"Our thanks, Lord Sigmund. We must have this keep's lord educate his gatekeepers so this doesn't happen again," sighed Ulrich as he approached the Horncurves. "I assume you're returning to Selerborn now?"

Sigmund grinned rigidly. "Aye. Back home."

"I would watch yourself if I were you," Marcarius said, his grateful smile becoming neutral.

His grin died. "Was that a threat?"

Marcarius closed his eyes modestly. "It was a warning. Brother Yuval's seers speak that 'the serpent will first strike the north'."

Sigmund responded with a wheezy guffaw. *"Seers!"* he exclaimed, resuming his laughter. "I appreciate your concern, Marcarius. But the day a serpent kills a ram is the day the great bells of Lunarpass chime for a thirteenth hour. It just won't happen!"

"Very well, then I wish you good fortune, my lord. I hope your ride back fares well." Marcarius bowed, keeping his composure as he and Ulrich resumed their journey.

"Seers," he repeated, unable to shake off his chuckling. Unable, at least, until it was abruptly halted as the iron portcullis burrowed into the dirt, slamming down inches in front of him.

"Not you," The gatekeeper mumbled spitefully.

Fury met Sigmund's face once again. "What do you think you're doing?" Marcarius and Ulrich stopped in their tracks to turn around.

"The deal was, I let those old blokes through, 'cause they work for th' Centaurs. You're a foreigner. You could've planned the attack."

Sigmund was beginning to tilt over the edge. *"Ye glaikit!* If it wasn't for us, the Lyrderyns would be dead!"

Riley pulled up next to his father, placing his hand on his shoulder and shaking his head. "Let's go back. There's nae need to fight. We can wait until the bandits are found."

"We wait for no one," Sigmund hissed at his son. "We don't have *time* fer this. The longer we delay, the more we *endanger* our people-"

"And why would I trust a filthy ram who just threatened me? Handling weapons here is an arrestable offense. Drop your swords, and I might let you eat some grass in your cell," the gatekeeper said.

That's when he realised. *You're no gatekeeper.* Pushing Riley's hand away, Sigmund snarled and unsheathed his longsword.

"Guards!"

Six armed guards rushed out of the doors on either side of the gate. "Drop your weapons in the name of the king!" one of the men said. *Do they know who they're talking to?!* Sigmund dismounted, Riley following, trying to keep the peace. Sir Ardin and Sir Gerard of the ram's guard dismounted after Riley. His children and the elders backed off.

"Please father, don't," Riley said with his hands in the air.

"Listen to your son... King of the sheep," the gatekeeper smirked.

His fire didn't need any more fuel, not after what the crabs had done. Sigmund boiled with fury, driving his longsword over his head and meeting one of the guard's blades. Three of the guards leapt to attack Sigmund, his ram's guard lunging in front to protect him. The guard wasn't so lucky when Sigmund swung his sword for a second time. Like a bat to a ball, he cut him in two from the waist up. As the boy cried in pain, another sword flew from behind him, Sigmund turning to counter it with a swift reaction. It didn't matter who wielded it, he'd cut down anyone who stood in between him and that gatekeeper. His face scowled when he saw that he couldn't do that. *My own son.* Riley lowered his sword and dropped it; Sigmund, still frozen in shock, made no move to. He looked around to his ram's guard, who had also settled their swords. *The bloody bampot,* he fumed, staring daggers to the gatekeeper who cowered safely behind the portcullis. Sigmund groaned as he fiercely cast his sword down, wedging it deep into the dirt, the guards jogging over to confiscate the weapons. The rest of the party sat on their horses, meters away, speechless.

Finally, the gatekeeper spoke proudly. "Take 'em to the dungeons."

"No!" Athena cried, the five leftover guards seizing the four defenceless Horncurves.

Riley struggled to turn to his children as a guard dragged him away. "We'll be fine. Go with Luther and the elders. They'll keep ye safe," he managed to yell.

The children watched as their father, grandfather and knights were violently dragged off to Fort Angel, tears filling Athena's pretty, grey eyes.

While being escorted by the guards, his hands behind his back, Sigmund wriggled for a more comfortable position. "Ye will rue this," he murmured in a dark tone, barely audible. The guards didn't respond, the man escorting him shoving him forward. They passed through a stone archway, entering the fort.

Although Fort Deus was ten times as large, Fort Angel still spanned a healthy portion of the Negal Wall, possessing a similar architecture. The stronghold was commanded by Lord Madoc Reade, father to Sir Orion Reade, honoured by Esmond himself. The wall itself stood leagues higher than the other buildings in the fort, cobblestone layered on cobblestone for hundreds of yards. *A petty excuse for a wall,* Sigmund thought bitterly. *The Vetiti Wall is twice as big, and actually serves a purpose, keeping exiles out of our land. What is this piece of shite doing? Heavia is much worse than the Auburn bloody Pole.* The more Sigmund looked at it, the more he wanted to knock the Negal Wall down.

Lord Madoc briskly descended the steps that led to his family's chambers. "What is the meaning of this?" He asked the guards. "Lord Sigmund, I'm terribly sorry, it's been havoc here the past two weeks…"

Two guards jogged over, carrying the body of the boy Sigmund had sliced open. "They tried to get through, my lord," one said.

Madoc's eyes examined the body. He was a fit, young boy, not an age above nineteen. The wound spanned his whole chest, thick blood concealing what lay under his skin. Madoc hesitated for a moment. "Oh, no, no, no, no," he said, cupping his face. Madoc hid his quivering lip with his finger, before placing his thumb on the green Reade sigil the boy wore:

a large oak tree with twenty arrow shafts sticking out of it. Sigmund didn't so much as feel sorry for the boy, but he remained quiet nevertheless. Lord Madoc took a gulp of air before talking. "I shall send a raven to Fort Deus asking the king what is to be done with you." He turned to the guards, tearful. "The dungeons," he said.

Sigmund winced, but still stayed silent. He knew better than to object at this time. *I've already dug too deep.* The guards led them down some aged cobblestone steps into the dank prison. Sunlight still shone down from the steps, so there was no need to light a torch. The cells were eerily empty, the only inhabitants being the occasional rat scurrying across the dusty stone floor.

A guard held his arms out to two cells. "You two in that one, and you two in the other," he said, pushing Sigmund and Sir Gerard, and Riley and Sir Ardin in two cells respectively. Slamming the cells shut, the guard left the Horncurves in the dungeons, planting himself at the head of the steps.

"If only ye had swallowed yer damned pride," Riley uttered, moodily.

Sigmund marched towards the bars. "We were *repulsed-*"

"*You killed a boy!*" Riley snapped, doubling his aggression. Silenced, Sigmund walked over to a bench that was chained to a wall, his violent heartbeat beginning to steady.

"Hostility is the last thing we want," Sir Gerard said from where he sat on the cold ground. "You need to control your temper, my lord." Sir Gerard knew full well what Sigmund could do to punish him for saying that, yet he said it regardless. Staring at the floor, Sigmund bit his lip, real life hitting him like a battering ram as he struggled to accept the blame. Murder committed in the lands before the wall was seen as a great crime, and even though King Esmond was a close friend, Sigmund didn't know what he would do.

"Did you not see who he was?" grumbled Sigmund.

His son winced. "What are ye talking about?"

"He was the bandit, the one that fool Sir Brendan set free." He ground his teeth just thinking about it. "Somehow, the wee bastard fooled Lord Madoc and got himself-"

"It doesn't matter who he was," Riley turned to face a seething Sigmund. "Yer not as invincible as you once were, father. You'll be lucky if you're not hanged for this."

EVA I
-Tap-

*C*ome on, I don't bite, Eva Centaur whispered to herself. Her arm was beginning to stiffen up. *That's it.* As she relaxed her hand, an arrow propelled forward, piercing a bunny through the skull. Two other rabbits scurried away when she ran over with a smile on her face. Eva knelt beside the dead animal and tugged at the arrow, removing it on the second attempt. After gently kissing the arrowhead, she twirled the shaft around before returning it to her quiver. She may as well have planted it in her hair, as the quiver drowned in the untamed, frayed, brown locks that fell down her shoulders. Raising her prey by the throat, she stuffed it into a leather satchel before throwing it over her back.

The trees that lay in front of her were those of the Negal Forest, and the deep morning fogs that lay a few hours ago had been lifted. Sunbeams shone radiantly amongst the mahogany branches, making the golden leaves seem even browner. Her father didn't want her to go out; he had probably sent dozens of men looking for her by now. *I should go back before I cause any more headaches.* She already had her fix of hunting for today, so going back didn't seem *too* bad of an idea.

Before she could think to turn, the blue horse-and-arrow sigil of Centaur caught her eye as she spotted two men riding down the Negal Road. She leapt behind a tree. "And what will I gain out of this?" A deep voice asked the man he rode with. The voice belonged to Galloway Malone, the head of war, and council to her father. She could recognise the faded northern accent a mile away, despite how time chipped away at it.

"Other than safety from the wars to come… lands, riches, you will be a hero amongst our people." The man he rode with replied. This voice, Eva didn't recognise. He was presumably some knight she had forgotten the name of. He certainly dressed that way, in his steel plated armour, boiled leathers underneath. *What accent is that, though? Where is he from?*

"And what do you mean for *me* to do?" asked Galloway. As the voices faded, Eva crept to the next tree, being overly cautious of her footing, making sure that the sticks underfoot didn't crack or rustle.

"Just how the note said - keep all the armies on the other side of the wall," the foreigner replied again. "Come a moon and they'll be as meek as a lamb." Confusion pulled Eva's mouth into a frown. *Are they talking about father's armies?* The parties that Lyrderyn, Horncurve, Sculptor, and Casteron arrived with certainly weren't large enough to be considered armies. *Why would father want the armies behind the wall?* After all, it had been built specifically to protect them. Eva needed to know who the man Galloway spoke to was, or at least see his face.

"I don't know if I want to go through with this. I'll be known as a turncoat for the rest of my days… I just want peace," Galloway said with his head down. Eva placed her hand on the rough bark belonging to a tree, leaning outwards to look at the men. They were a few feet in front of Eva, their royal blue robes flapping in the gentle breeze, trying to escape from the armour gripping it in place. The knight Galloway travelled with was definitely foreign. He had a heavy head of black hair, with what looked like a beard from behind. His skin was a slight tan, even though he didn't have so much as a goosebump on his exposed right arm. Eva was used to the bitter cold, yet sometimes she still felt the nibble of autumn through her scarce, tattered silks and furs. How this man let off nothing close to a shiver was strange to her.

"And peace is what you'll get. Yes, you can be one of those valiant knights who fights beside his king until his last breath, or you could die for something you care about like your family, in the process, making a decision that could save millions. Make no mistake, Galloway; there will be no peace for your family, nor any… death is coming for the Centaurs." Eva's heart missed a beat in her chest, before it sunk down into her stomach. *What have I just heard?* She no longer cared who this man was, she just wanted to run back into the warm arms of her father. "If anything, we are doing them a favour. If we don't wield the knife, then it will be-"

Crack! Eva shot her gaze down. Blood was running through her fingers. Wide-eyed, she pivoted on her foot to put her back against the tree. She could feel the gaze of the men behind her. She didn't realise how tightly she was gripping the bark. Her eyes met the missing chunk of tree smeared with her own blood. *Breathe*, she said to herself, eyes closed tightly. It was like purgatory, an eternity of waiting before she could hear the swallows chirping and the faraway crashing from the Antrum River's water over her heartbeat. Against her own will, she tilted her head from behind the tree to look upon the road ahead. The men seemed to have not noticed; they had doubled the distance from Eva in the time she spent cowering.

Not even allowing a sigh of relief, Eva slid down the edge of the land, and as her feet hit the muddy road, she broke into a sprint down Luto Path. The men rode on the Negal Road. If she was quick, she could make it behind the castle unnoticed and before the men arrived at the gates. They were too far away to hear the fragile, strong patting left by her shoes as she ran. Regardless, she slowed down slightly as she came closer to the road's fork. Eva had travelled through the rocky path a thousand times; it was a shortcut to the castle only she knew about. Anyone else would be an idiot to try and traverse it. The fall would surely kill a man. Without thinking, she leapt down onto the rocks, only just landing on a stone that looked like a fingernail, preparing to jump to the next one. A gasp left her mouth when she lost her footing, slipping down to the next rock prematurely. She lunged to the stone face, holding a scream in her throat as she dug her slashed fingers into the mud. If the men hadn't heard the first slip up, they definitely heard this one. She winced at the pain, but didn't let a sound come out. By waving her legs manically, she managed to find another rock, letting a moan out as she released her fingers and fell down to it. Eva didn't even care if the guards saw her at this point, she bolted down the rocky valley before she was presented with another rock face to climb. Her adrenaline was still at peak, not realising that she was on the verge of exhaustion. She clumsily scaled the hill until she saw the refreshing sight of Fort Deus, standing as tall as ever over the crags around it.

She turned her head toward the entrance to see where the men were. For a second, it seemed as though Galloway was staring right at her, but after a blink, he faced forward again. Eva couldn't quite see the foreigner yet; Galloway and his companion rode side-by-side, so all Eva could see was half of Galloway's rough face. He had a scar cutting through his left brow, making the hairs there unable to regrow. Wearing the face of a man who had seen many battles and fought many wars, he was born and raised in Selerborn during the latter half of *Sigmund's Uprising*, even playing the role of a ram's guard before being relieved to advise for the king. It made no sense to Eva why he would want to see more death. She let her breathing steady before hoisting her weight over the rocks.

There was a small area of land that surrounded the castle before it gradually fell down into the ocean. 'The Endless Moat' people called it, anyone surviving the fall being washed away by the river into the Trader's Sea. Merchants delivering or buying goods would often find missing knights floating near the coast on their voyage to Trader's Dock, presumably slipping off the cliff during their watch. Luckily for Eva, the land was peppered with trees and shrubbery high enough for her to sneak past unseen. She slowed into a jog as she reached the castle wall, holding out her hands to prepare for the climb. They were still trembling, blood and dirt smeared all over.

Firmly grasping two cobblestone blocks, she ascended. Rocky slabs that were cold to the touch soothed her pain somewhat, making her red fingers less and less functional. The wind vigorously attempted to blow Eva off, but she clung with all the strength she had. The casual clank of steel echoed from inside the walls. A grey shimmer of a helmet uncovered itself when the battlements came into view. Normally, she would wait for the patrol to walk past, but it didn't even cross her clouded mind as she kept climbing. Scaling the final few slabs was when her muscles tired, and by summoning what energy was left, she lifted herself up and over the wall.

The startled guard halted his saunter in shock. *"Hey-!"*

Before he could grab the princess, she pushed him away and bolted along the battlements. The rampart led into a tower decorated with a winding staircase and blue banners. She ran down the stairs like a hand around a clock, unintentionally smearing dashes of blood on the walls as she held her hand out for balance. Her leather satchel thumped against her back, making her run swifter.

Lord Ellys Dart, who was strolling in the hallway, looked up from his scroll as Eva came careering down the stairs. "There you are, my lady, we have been looking everywh-"

Before he could finish his sentence, Eva was already in and out of the room, beelining through the corridor. She ran past many puzzled people, not caring enough to look up and see who they were. After revolving around a final bend, she found herself pushing the wooden and metal door belonging to the throne room. She charged straight to the small back room, her father's business chamber.

She propelled the door open, almost striking Sir Orion who stood on the other side, to see her father jotting text down with a quill. Not letting a word escape Esmond's mouth as he stood in astonishment, Eva galloped into his arms.

"My sweet Eva," Esmond managed to say. He pulled away from the hug, holding her shoulders. "What happened? I have many men searching for you."

Tears that Eva had fought off earlier materialized. "I'm sorry, I should never have gone." She held her elbows whilst she shook. "They want to kill you, father, they want to kill us."

Esmond's face grew cold. "Who?"

"Galloway. I mean the man he was with. They're going to kill us," Eva said, trying to stop her tears from drowning her words.

It was clear through Esmond's perplexed face that he still didn't understand. *He has to understand.* He took her head into his hand and gently pulled it near his chest. "It's okay," he said softly. "You're safe now."

"We're *not*," she cried. "He's *conspiring* with some... some *foreigner,* and... the armies, he wants-"

"Shhh, shh, shh, it's okay." Esmond stroked her hair gently. "Don't be scared, Eva. Lord Malone has been loyal all his life." She winced. *He doesn't believe me.*

"You found her, then?" Asher Centaur had appeared in the doorway, a persimmon in hand. Jovian Reade was next to him.

Esmond nodded. "Go clean her up."

"No, you have to believe me," Eva frowned, shaking off the tears. "I know what I heard."

Her father's blue eyes pondered hers. "Clean your sister up, Asher. Get bandages for these cuts."

A servant apprehensively walked in next to a stunned Sir Orion. "Begging your pardon, Lord Malone has returned," he whispered to Orion before glancing at Esmond. "Also, a raven," he said before handing a rolled-up note to Sir Orion.

She felt light-headed. "Come on," the prince said, holding his hand out. She gripped Esmond even tighter.

"Esmond," Orion said, opened scroll in hand. "You might want to read this."

Esmond glanced, the annoyance ruling his face. He stood from his kneel and walked over to Orion, taking the scroll from his hand. It had cost a few seconds for Esmond to comprehend what lay on the page. "Sigmund?" Esmond twisted in confusion. "Is this true?"

"Sealed with the mark of our elder, my king," Sir Orion said, holding out the merlot wax seal of Elder Marcarius.

Esmond took a moment to scratch his stubble before looking up at Asher. "It's Sigmund. He's been arrested at the wall."

Asher frowned. "Why?"

"Killed a boy, allegedly." He ran his fingers through his brown hair before continuing. "I'll need you to hold the fort in my stead."

"No, you can't go up! Please stay!" Eva exploded, running towards her father.

Sir Orion turned to Esmond. "We could send a rider to speak for you. I could go if you want."

Esmond looked down at the note. "No, I must go. I need to speak with Sigmund. They won't trust the word of a rider anyway."

Asher bit into the half-eaten persimmon. "Ok," he said. "Come on, Eva. You're getting blood all over father's furs."

Esmond slipped his head down to see Eva grasping around his waist. He cupped her face into his palm. "I'll come back soon, don't worry. Promise me you won't leave the castle again."

Her tears froze on her face as her head looked to the ground, nodding. Esmond managed a smile before ruffling her messy hair and turning to Sir Orion. Eva followed her brother out of the room until her walk was halted by Galloway entering the fort, not even shedding a smile before glancing at her and marching down the corridor. He was alone, and his companion was nowhere in sight. *They must have seen me. One, if any.*

"Are we to prepare to leave, my king?" Sir Orion asked, taking back the scroll into his hand.

"Summon the guard and my brother, we leave as soon as possible."

ESMOND III
-Deuswater-

Y ou honour us with your presence, your grace. We have reserved the royal suites for you and your companions." A nod from Esmond Centaur was all it took to please the chubby man behind the counter. "May I suggest a whore to lie with tonight? We have the finest available for your grace."

Esmond painted a smirk on his face. "That won't be necessary..." he turned to face Lori. "...but perhaps for my brother."

Lori strolled up to the counter placing a small stack of silver coins on the wood. "You know me too well," he said, prompting a nod from the man as he rushed behind to fetch out two young wenches.

Although he was fit and handsome, Lorimer wasn't married, nor betrothed to anyone like his two brothers were. King Ivor had Semira Jade betrothed to him before he fled, the throne and his bride-to-be bestowed upon Esmond. And since then, there was little more land and wealth to inherit by marrying into other families without travelling across half a world to see them. There was once the possibility of a match between Asher and Lyssa Lyrderyn, but Reynold's interest was piqued at Sigmund's offer of either of the Horncurve twins for her hand. Reynold had much more to gain from the fertile lands of Ram's Haven than the desolate equivalent of the Auburn Pole. As for Lord Lori, he had many suitors in Centaur's Lagoon, all willing to kill each other to be his bride, but Esmond could never see the man finding one he liked well enough... *He'll never love anyone as much as his bastard's mother.*

An early dusk lay on the city of Deuswater, and a chilling cold filled the air as Esmond and Sir Orion stepped out of the inn-brothel-hybrid. Although the city was dwarfed compared to the brute that was Lunarpass, Deuswater was still relatively lively. It was the number one destination for soldiers and knights to come after a week's training. Beyond that, Deuswater was home to the sect of Deuswater, built atop the lake, with people attending to pray to their god(s); this part of the realm normally being the Sagittarius, where people can admire its mark on the sky through a long telescope. Otherwise, Deuswater would be a relatively forgettable town with its enchanting wooden cabins and pretty lakes.

"Are you sure he said they'd be here?" Esmond asked, looking up at the blackening sky.

"You read the same words I did," Sir Orion exhaled while his eyes scanned around. "We should go to the gate, we have a better chance of seeing them there," he said, receiving a nod from Esmond. Deuswater was one of the few cities without a wall built around it, and even though the Negal Wall stood from bank to coast, an odd raider would sometimes get past unnoticed, either being quickly shot down by archers on the wall or fought off by the villagers themselves. These forlorn raids were often conducted by tribes from the Red Sierra north of the wall, many attacking to try and make a name for themselves, or maybe to return home with plunder. All for a mediocre effort at most, a much greater use of their time being to raid the many villages north of the wall, which they did a great deal regardless. Esmond chuckled as he was reminded of the tribesman that called himself 'Eluf of Red tooth', who had taken Fort Diolus for an entire day, before no more than fifty Reade soldiers marched along the wall from Fort Angel to sweep them out; that was the highlight of his year.

"You been brought any Khavar bandits yet, Esmond?" Sir Orion asked him as they walked through the muddy, moonlit streets.

Esmond took a second to adjust his thoughts. "Not yet, no. I asked for any suspects to be brought to Fort Angel. It's still strange to me why they'd do this."

"They were gold in the woods waiting to be grabbed. For all we know, the bandits could have been peasants. Even in the Negal lands, Reynold should've known better than to let his guard down so much."

Esmond sighed. "Yes, but either way, Cancerians would have their reasons: revenge, ambition, hatred-"

"Stupidity," the knight smiled thinly. "If they were wise enough to learn from their previous attempts, they would learn that rebellion in any form has always ended badly for those who oppose the crown. The *Oquinteus Rebellion*, the *Scorpius Rebellion*... they're just reminders to what happens. If another war is what we need to show them, so be it."

Esmond couldn't help but grin seeing his *First Avail* speak so passionately. "Yep. How am I meant to hold the realm together if everyone's at each other's throats?" he replied, smiling sarcastically.

Sir Orion and Esmond approached the archway - a stone centaur statue to mark the entrance to the city. "Well, you've done well by holding ten kingdoms together under one crown for such a long time. Before the *Pause*, fifty powerful families were at each other's throats, and before those kingdoms were brought to heel, there were... I believe eighty-eight that needed to be tamed."

Esmond released a chuckle. "Don't patronise me. It was my ancestors that did all the work. I am no great ruler."

"You're not a bad one, though. People like you. Men rallied by your father's side to crush the *Scorpius's first rebellion*, and rallied again the second time they threatened to."

"That was out of love for my family and loyalty, not for me. In my thirty-year reign I have built no great wonders, led no great discovery, won no great wars."

Sir Orion frowned in his efforts to defend him. "You think people don't respect you?"

Esmond crossed his arms and leant on the statue. "I think people don't fear me." A sly smirk spread across his face in response to what he thought. "Perhaps a war wouldn't be the worst thing," he jested, looking up to the stone stallion.

A flickering light bounced off the trees from the Negal Forest, slowly edging towards the town, catching Sir Orion's vision. "At long last," he remarked. Esmond looked down to the road, spotting the blues of his house and the reds from the Horncurves. He slowly walked towards them, a smile on his face to be reunited with Elder Marcarius.

"You took your time coming," Esmond called as they trotted closer.

Marcarius looked exhausted, his forehead wrinkles more prominent than ever, and low bags under each eye, yet him and his shoulder length grey mane was never a more welcome sight. "The road has not been kind," he said with a smile. "We took respite at Fort Angel for a couple of days."

Esmond helped Marcarius dismount his horse before embracing him.

"It's good seeing you. Your counsel was missed," he said, muffled by the slightly discoloured blue robes. When they pulled away, Esmond looked to the rest of the troop. Athena, Marcus, and Cadmus sat cautiously on their horses, Luther and Ulrich already dismounted. "I'm sorry to see you all again so woeful."

Luther led his horse by its reins. "At least we learned to not test father's resolve," he said bitterly. Luther didn't even make eye contact with Esmond as he walked his horse, nephews and niece into the city.

"What mouths have spoken of Reynold..." Esmond turned to a worried Ulrich. "...Do they speak truly?"

Esmond looked to the ground, substituting his smile. "Must have sickened you as much as myself. Poor old fool collapsed from his horse as he rode into the fort. A moment I don't wish to live again..."

"And of his health?"

"He lives, and by Guy's judgement he should be healthy by the week."

Ulrich let go of his breath. "Oh, that is comforting."

Esmond managed a saddened smile. "Come, you must hurt after your travels." Esmond took Marcarius's horse's reins into his hand, nodding to Sir Orion to take Ulrich's.

They walked together to their detached segment of the brothel, a small private inn big enough to house all twelve persons, erected for royal visits exclusively. Esmond and Orion led the horses into the stables before joining the Horncurve party inside the inn. The inn seemed not part of Deuswater: almost a noble building without housing for a few meters in all directions, lit with flashing lanterns from within. Wooden beams stretched high along the inn, and cobblestone steps led up to the plank door. Inside lay a cosy hall, not big enough to be a tavern, but not small enough to be a chamber. Barrels full of ale and wine covered the wall, and a toasty fire crackled as Riley's children huddled close. It seemed like the inn had not been used in a while, the air almost colder than it was outside.

Marcarius was sitting at a bench, both delicate hands cupped around a steaming beverage. "Where are the king's guard?" he asked.

Esmond smiled. "You doubt the king's ability to travel his own country unaccompanied?" he said, walking towards the bench. "...they're at the brothel."

Marcarius rolled his eyes as Esmond and Sir Orion took their seats, Esmond reaching for the urn the elder had used for his drink. Marcarius held out his hand. "You don't want to drink that, lord." He said. "It is an acquired taste."

Esmond pretended to be offended. "First you doubt my competence, now you doubt my tastes? The gods have returned a different man." He grabbed a cup and filled it with the brew, not even letting it cool before knocking it back. Instantly after hitting his tongue, Esmond sent tears of ale shooting from his lips. "What sort of *barbarian* drinks this for pleasure?"

Athena couldn't stop giggling along with the room's smile.

"Watch how you speak to your elder," he responded with a smirk. Esmond took his and Sir Orion's cup in both hands with a grin on his face as he walked over to an open keg. "We have many things to discuss, Esmond," Marcarius continued.

"Delightful," said Esmond dryly, wine pouring from the barrel and overflowing into the cups he held. "Tell me about this *squabble* at the auditorium."

Ulrich looked confused. "You have word?"

"My lady wife did. The Pole spreads rumours faster than fire," Esmond replied, placing the dripping cups onto the table.

Marcarius took a swig from his drink before speaking. "Solomon predicts we are on the verge of another *Pause*." That single word stole the room's attention.

"What? How?" Esmond asked.

Ulrich stood to look out of the window. "It is true. Tides have changed and thus, the weather."

"The mining of citrine is believed to be the cause," Marcarius added.

Luther released a single laugh from where he sat sharpening his sword on the other side of the room. "Gods save us all."

Cadmus turned to Luther. *"Uncle,"* he scolded. Luther didn't seem to pay attention, continuing to whet his blade.

"Did you call a cease?" Esmond asked again.

Marcarius nodded. "Yes. Ezekiel wasn't too happy."

"I can imagine," Sir Orion said before taking a gulp of wine.

"Gods," Esmond cursed, "are the seers preaching this doom too? Do they think the sky will fall down like they thought a few years ago?" Esmond mocked, but Marcarius's cold stare didn't seem to deny it. "No way," he muttered.

"I fear the seers speak of graver matters," Marcarius admitted.

Sir Orion chuckled. "What could be graver than a *Pause?*"

"At least we know what a *Pause is*, Sir Orion," Marcarius replied cryptically. Ulrich continued to stare out the window, ignoring everything. Esmond frowned. "A war?"

"A serpent," said Marcarius. "However, it seems we will know when it comes," he continued, reaching into his robe and pushing a crumpled piece of papyrus across the table.

Esmond took the scroll, unravelling it in his hands, Sir Orion peeking over his shoulder. They scanned the paper, both pulling the same perplexed face. "Stars will weep? What is this nonsense?" Esmond smiled, tossing the note back to the table.

"What the seer speaks of. Like I said, it will be difficult to miss if this serpent is 'all'," Marcarius repeated. Esmond wanted to believe it a lie, even though he didn't know what it meant in the first place. His son, Hew, loved to remind him of the most famous tale of seers, no more than two centuries ago, when the Auburn Pole was ruled by Archer the Brave. Seers professed to Archer how a war was coming, and to prepare. Sure enough, one year later, Achilles Oquinteus rebelled after his father, Percival Oquinteus, was assassinated by Khavars, and by having that extra year to prepare for a war he had not seen, Archer scarcely triumphed in the *Battle of the Wastelands* with half the numbers of Achilles's armies. If it wasn't for that slither of crucial advice, the Centaur dynasty would have died then and there.

Esmond shook his head. "I'm too tired for this, I have too much on my plate already," he said, finishing the last of his drink before standing. "We should all get some rest, long journey on the morrow."

He turned to Sir Orion. "Don't let the guard get too drunk, I intend to arrive at the wall before the week's end."

"Goodnight, your grace," Athena smiled from the roaring fireplace. Her innocence both warmed and broke Esmond's heart. She reminded him so much of Eva. All he could do was smile as he climbed the stairs.

◆━━━━━━━◗

Although they had ridden for days, leaving Esmond exhausted, his sleep was interrupted. The bed was warm and cosy, enough to knock any man out, and the muffled cheers and chatter of the town wasn't loud enough to disturb him. It was worry that stole his sleep: questions like *what is this serpent? We would never be able to survive a Pause should it come again. What must I do to Sigmund when I reach Fort Angel? What's Galloway doing behind my back?*

After what felt like minutes of trying to sleep, the early morning lights fell into his chamber. A thick mist lay upon the houses as it did the forest, creating a sea of white and brown. Esmond crept out of the inn silently, so as to not wake anyone. The streets were just as quiet, if not for a single merchant carrying goods bound for Trader's Dock. They seemed to not recognise the king, as they too had their heads down with heavy eyes, a change almost welcomed by Esmond. He would only come to Deuswater as a respite to travel elsewhere, so when he spent time there, he tried to admire the winsome town as much as he could.

As he walked, houses became scarce, orange trees grew common, and the sound of crashing water got louder. He could spot the majestic dome head of the sect of Deuswater from behind at least four tall houses. It was painted with stars, and those stars fell as shadows within the sect. The stream was so peaceful, another welcome change to the yells and crashes of Fort Deus. The only reason Esmond liked to hide away at Fort Deus rather than rule over in Lunarpass was because the coast was so much more peaceful anyway.

His councillors, including Marcarius, would always tell him that it was optimal if the king ruled in the capital, but he stayed in Fort Deus regardless, allowing his beloved cousin, Thaddeus Centaur, to look over Lunarpass, to sit the solar throne, Thaddeus often being mistaken as the current king. Fort Deus was the ancestral home of the Centaur line, distant cousins or brothers to the current head of the family normally taking the zircon seat. As for Esmond, despite how much he denied it, he still experienced the bitter taste of a usurper when he sat on the solar throne, opting for the castle that his ancestors held long before the *Pause*, and bearing the much friendlier throne of zircon. Not that he thought he *usurped* it; it just didn't feel like *his*. But on that thought, no one could truly *own* the solar throne.

The sect was beautiful as Esmond remembered, towering over the Deuswater River as it wound its way around. The morning made it quieter than normal, only a few pastors dithering around. It was huge, almost every sound amplified due to its echo. A detailed ornament of constellations hung from the ceiling, and the famous golden tube shot out of the window into the sky.

"Sorry, sir. The stars will soon not be vi-" a tired pastor who stood in front began, before opening his eyes. "K-King Esmond. I am terribly sorry. Please, stay as long as you wish," he said before walking briskly away, embarrassed. The other pastors didn't notice at all that the king was in their presence. Esmond walked towards the golden tube, placing his eye against the glass ring. Sure enough, the mark of the Sagittarius sat in the sky, faded by the clouds and darkened by space. Esmond was not one to believe in gods, but knowing that something was out there was enough to make him speculate. After admiring it, Esmond took one last look at the great sect before leaving the way he came.

"Good morning," a voice called as he stepped out of the sect. He raised his drowsy head to see Elder Marcarius, looking a lot more refreshed. "I've been looking all over for you. I trust you slept well?"

"I won't let bad sleep bother me," Esmond smiled, his throat hoarse from the night.

Marcarius smiled back. "Ulrich and I are about to leave, be safe on your way to the wall."

Esmond frowned. "You're not coming with us?"

"I'm afraid our paths must be divided once more; me and Ulrich must return to Fort Deus. I trust you will make the right decision regarding Sigmund," he said, holding his arms out for a hug.

Marcarius's body was warm as it pressed against Esmond's. "I hope so," Esmond whispered under his breath. "I don't think there *is* one, though."

LYSSA I
-Cub-

"Father is going to die, isn't he?"

Lyssa Lyrderyn opened her sleepy eyes to see her sister pacing around their shared chamber. "Eleanor, go back to sleep," she said, tugging at her sapphire quilt to cover her cold shoulders.

"You didn't say no," Eleanor said, perching on her bed while she grabbed the shredded fibres that came from her quilt.

Exhaling, Lyssa dragged her right arm to her face to rub her blue eyes. "Guy said he'll get better in a fortnight-"

"A week ago. He's not getting better."

Lyssa released a moan as she stretched her body, bending her back before holding her arms out. Eleanor crossed the stone gap betwixt the beds, falling into Lyssa's arms. Every day, Reynold had been getting worse. He spent more and more time in a sweaty sleep, waking up in the night to screams and shivers, despite how warm his solar was. By the day, when he *was* awake, he'd be muttering words to himself, like 'wounds', and 'winter', and 'wilted'. *He's becoming less like father the longer he's in that bed. If he lives, he won't be the same man.* Lyssa wanted to sleep through it, and not only because she was tired.

Knock, knock, knock. "Lyssa," an exhausted voice said from the other side of the door.

Placing her hand on Eleanor's shoulder, Lyssa rose from her bed and padded barefoot towards the wooden door. She pulled it open, revealing her mother holding a sealed note. Lady Elayne's blonde-brown hair was wiry with grey sprouting all over, her eyes dried puddles and her skin a milky white. She walked into the room, leaving the door open behind her.

"Father?" Eleanor asked nervously.

Elayne cupped Eleanor's young face, stroking her cheek with her thumb before returning it to her side. "You'd best come see for yourself."

The fort was uncannily dark, even for first light. and the surrounding cliffs howled as if they were in mourning, a result of the strong winds gusting through the crevices. The girls left the chamber, walking down the chilly corridor. Lyssa peeked into her father's chamber, the bed he had lain in for weeks empty, only a few serving girls inside the chamber as they peeled the sheets from the bed. Indentations clearly showed where her mother sat every day, and where her father had lain. Ayla lay in her ornate crib beside the bed, fast asleep and curled up like a cub.

Lyssa was surprised that her mother wasn't nagging them to get properly dressed, appearance and manners normally at the height of Elayne's concerns. All that Lyssa managed to grab before leaving the room was her silk gold gown, messily worn over her sleeping cloths. However, she dared not remind or even talk to her; Elayne looked like she hadn't slept in years.

Lyssa and Eleanor were led into a stark section of the castle; windows becoming scarcer and light becoming absent. It was at the end of the hallway where a double door lay, metal hatches and chains unlocked, and a man to guard it. He effortlessly pushed the door, revealing steps down to a rounded dome with a glass ceiling. It was reinforced with metal at the edge of each pane, casting shadows in the shape of small arrows. The rounded walls were lined with statues of dead Centaurs, a piece of their race's gem sitting in their stone hands. The names were familiar to Lyssa, told a thousand times in stories and songs: Erland the Escaper: led the first people out of the complex; Archer the Pioneer: led his people north to inhabit the free lands; Esmond the Sickly: died of a plague caught from his travels to the east; Jovian the Cruel: buried with his kingdom of Lter in *The Second Pause;* the names went on forever.

Lyssa's thoughts were interrupted by a shriek from her sister, rushing to the centre of the room. There stood the podium of what was normally used to honour the latest Centaur to fall, yet King Palmer II was not in his place. What lay in the middle of the room was a grey stone table with a lifeless Reynold atop.

She thought she'd be prepared for this. She thought ever since he started to change that he would have preferred to die *as* himself, before he lost too much of his mind. Asher Centaur had said that, and she trusted him more than she should for a boy she had just met. But there was something different in thinking about a dead father and having a dead father. Unwelcome feelings crept in - ones of confusion, anger… tiredness.

Sir Roswell Dart, son of Lord Ellys Dart and Esmond's *Second Avail* stood in front of the body, whispering to a pastor who cleaned the corpse. Sir Roswell was quite a bit younger than Esmond, with short black hair resting on his head and a face free of a beard, much like his father. Another pastor held Eleanor back as she tried to leap towards her father, resisting his hold for a brief moment before losing energy to swing another fist.

"Our greatest sympathies, we are all at a loss for words," Sir Roswell replied, turning and making the light twinkle off his grey and blue armour. Eleanor returned to her mother, clutching her with both arms; Lyssa just watched, wishing it was a dream. "Did he name an heir before his pass?" Sir Roswell continued.

Lady Elayne nodded, lifting the sealed note. "He kept insisting that Lionel was his rightful heir and will take his place."

Sir Roswell gasped. "He's been found?"

"Poor thing must have been deluded by his final moments. Lionel hasn't been seen since… since…" Elayne covered her mouth, head shaking and tears forming.

Sir Roswell looked to the ground mournfully before lifting his head again. "You are to be liege lady then?"

"All I know is that he wanted a male heir-" Lyssa couldn't figure out if Elayne paused to chuckle or to cry. *Don't be stupid, she's crying.* "His brother, Sir Goldwyn is the next male heir," she managed to say, stuttered by her tears. "Please excuse me." She pulled herself from Eleanor and briskly left the mausoleum. The room fell silent, the only sound being the echoes of Eleanor sniffling. Sir Roswell apprehensively inclined his head to the Lyrderyn princesses before walking out.

Lyssa wrapped her arm around her sister, escorting her out slowly after Sir Roswell. It was the first time in a while that Lyssa had heard her brother's name; only a few years had gone by since he was lost to the world. Part of her always wondered if Lionel was still alive, somehow stumbling his way through the vicious dunes that surrounded Ignis, but there wasn't much hope for a boy of twelve to survive alone in the desert. He was

Reynold's only male heir, ironically taken by his own lands.

As Lyssa turned the corner, she spotted Queen Semira tugging at her blue sleeves nervously, appearing to be looking for them. "Ladies... I am... so sorry," she began. "If it's not impudent of me, we have been breaking fast for a time, and you two must be hungry."

Lyssa was warmed by the offer. "Not impudent at all, my queen," she smiled, as best she could. She and Eleanor followed the queen through the hallways, Lady Elayne nowhere in sight, not even in her chambers.

The queen led them to a dining room. It had two benches atop the stone floor, one littered in used bowls and cups, and the other seating Fitz, Lady Gina, and Sir Brendan. To the left of the room, crockpots bubbled and bread baked in warm furnaces, more than half of the leftovers most likely to be sold to the residents of the lower bailey. Semira held out her arm to the table their family sat, Lyssa and Eleanor taking their seats.

"Sir Cedric has just gone looking for you," Sir Brendan said in his gravelly voice.

Semira seemed not to notice the knight's statement. "Please tell me if you need anything," she said to the girls before taking her leave.

Fitz sent a scathing glance at Lyssa as she reached for drinks for herself and Eleanor. "Not a single tear?" he hissed.

"What?" Lyssa replied, wincing in confusion.

Fitz repeatedly stabbed his fork into a sausage on his plate, yet he seemed to be grinning. "Your face is dry. You haven't a single tear to mourn your father."

Lyssa's face instead twisted with rage. "And where were you when Reynold was getting stabbed? I have half a mind to think you sat and watched."

Fitz skewered the sausage violently for a final time, sending sauce splattering across the table.

"*Lyssa!*" Lady Gina scolded.

"He was a father to me as much as he was to you!" Fitz spat.

Lyssa smiled in shock, looking from Fitz to Gina. Eleanor and Sir Brendan didn't want to be involved. Lyssa threw her wooden plate back and stormed out of the room, a faint "Milady!" called out by Sir Brendan. That was just what she needed to send her over the edge, as if waking up to a dead father wasn't enough. Her march turned into a jog the further she advanced into the hallway, eyes slowly becoming puddles. By the time she arrived at her chamber, her vision was clouded by tears. Lyssa rushed to her bed and sank her face into the pillow, letting her cry soak the bed. It was strangely relieving to her, it felt like she hadn't cried in years, yet she couldn't stop it. She had been so drained of emotion the past week that she forgot what it felt like. She cried for a while.

The next thing she heard was the creek of her chamber's door.

"Go away!" she yelled into her pillow, not caring to look who it was.

She didn't expect the warm voice who replied. "Your cousin's a prick."

Lyssa paused her sobbing to look to the door. The man who stood in the doorway was Prince Asher, a bowl of soup in one hand and the door latch in the other. "You heard?" Lyssa asked, composing herself despite her embarrassment.

Asher closed the door behind him. "Fitz yells like a baby who needs milk... Of course I heard," he said as he perched on her bed.

She couldn't help but smile. Lyssa was silent as she moved up to sit beside him, using her fingers to sweep away the tears.

"You need to eat," Asher said softly, holding out the bowl to her.

"Why are you so kind to me?" she asked, cupping the bowl gently.

"Well someone has to," he smirked. "You're my guest, and if you were to starve... I can't imagine a better way to start a war."

Lyssa giggled before taking a sip. The soup warmed her throat; she didn't realise how cold she was. Asher smiled solemnly at Lyssa as he stood, heading to the door. "Don't go," she blurted out, causing Asher to stop in his tracks. He seemed surprised as he turned to face Lyssa, leaving a moment before retracing his steps next to her. "Everyone loves him," she sighed. "They love him because he can work a katar like he can work his breathing. How come I'm the only one who can see how much of a bastard he really is?"

"He's only fourteen. I doubt he knows what he's saying," Asher replied, looking to the floor.

"He's an idiot," she laughed. "And Lord of bloody Ignis after Goldwyn, you know that? That won't make him act any better."

Asher frowned. "If he is, so be it," he said. "You'll want to be on the right side of him if he does."

Lyssa agreed with a sigh, interrupted by a chuckle, still not believing her cousin's audacity. She apprehensively placed her head on Asher's shoulder. His warm arm coiled around her like a snake. "I don't care," she whispered. "Fitz can do as he likes, Goldwyn too... I'm leaving Ignis as soon as I get back."

Asher rubbed his thumb on her bare shoulders. "Leaving where?"

She pondered it. *Here's nice, if it wasn't so cold. Maybe somewhere far away... like the Venusian Archipelago. That would be ironic.* "Somewhere away from death," she said. "Maybe I'll go wandering in the desert, join my dead brother."

"You know you can't do that."

"Why not?"

"Because I won't let you leave if you say stuff like that."

He made her smile again. It turned into a smirk. "Maybe you should come with me then, make sure I don't."

"Yeah," he tittered. "I'd have to."

"Yeah," she sighed. "You would." Lyssa closed her eyes, letting her tears roll down her cheeks. He stayed until they dried.

◆———◙

Later that day, it was time for Reynold to have his true send off. Winds howled louder near the Antrum River, and carried the cold breeze as if needles were in the air. The entire Lyrderyn troop stood by the bank, wearing noble golden clothes that didn't suit the weather, as Sir Brendan and Sir Goldwyn carried a boat onto the water. Reynold's corpse lay atop, dressed in his armour as he had wished, a fragment of the Lyrderyn's peridot gem safely in his cold hands. Eleanor was clutching her mother tightly as the boat slowly floated on the river. Lyssa stood next to them in her golden robes similar to Eleanor's.

"Are you sure we should do this without Ulrich?" Lyssa whispered to her mother.

Elayne stared out to the river. "I wish we didn't have to, but we can't leave him rotting in the Centaur's crypts," she replied, devoid of emotion.

Sir Cedric kindled a torch before passing it to Goldwyn. It spat vigorously as Goldwyn lifted it for the aggressive winds, creating a near-bonfire on a stick. He carefully slid down the bank, holding the torch back. With one swing of his arm, the beacon soared through the air, landing on the boat before it floated too far. And with that, the late lion of Ignis became a blaze, sailing out to the Trader's Sea.

ESMOND IV
-Supply-

K ing Esmond, you are welcomed," greeted Lord Madoc. The party Esmond Centaur had travelled with certainly seemed to startle the lord, perhaps only expecting half the number.

"It's been too long, my lord," smiled Esmond, locking hands with him after dismount. Madoc Reade's grin didn't mask the stress well; wrinkles of pain spanned his forehead from ear to ear, and Esmond could swear that his number of long, grey hairs had doubled since the last time they met.

"Father," Sir Orion saluted, taking the old man into his arms. "I hope you are well."

His returning smile had a hint of sadness. "No worse than always." Madoc's sight was caught by the Horncurves. They were all tired, Marcus seeming close to falling from his horse. "My lords, my lady," he bowed, turning back to Esmond. "I wish to speak alone."

Esmond looked behind him at his party. Athena was by far the least weary, beaming down as he studied the quail. "See them to chambers," Esmond whispered into Sir Orion's ear before turning to walk with Lord Reade. Fort Angel appeared greater in the day; like Deuswater, Esmond would only spend time at the fort during dusk and first light. Soldiers paused their sword strokes as the king walked past, bowing before they returned to their training.

"About the bandits that you asked to be captured," Lord Madoc said to Esmond.

"Ah, yes. Have you received any?" The king asked, grateful to be stretching his legs after his long ride.

Madoc hesitated. "About that, my king." He scratched the back of his neck. "One of the bandits behind the attack on Lord Reynold had come here for refuge. He murdered two gatekeepers in the dead of night and took the position for himself. No one thought to question their absence."

Esmond nodded solemnly. "It's good you found him."

Madoc dithered again. "I regret to inform he managed to escape."

"Escape?" Esmond winced, stopping their walk. *How could someone escape the Negal Wall?* He couldn't help but sigh. Another day might have found him angrier at Madoc Reade. "Find him."

"We will, my king," Madoc promised. "We've sent our best riders on the case. A price on his head won't go unpaid for long."

Oaf, he thought. *A loyal oaf, I suppose.* "Good. Any more?"

Lord Reade shook his head. "We've been brought peasants and soldiers for the most part. Not at all matching your description. Most have returned to their homes and compensated in full."

Esmond let a grin go. "I may need to elaborate on the meaning of suspicious. But yes, it's a far worse crime to keep innocents locked up." Esmond found himself thinking of the Horncurves. "Speaking of innocence: Sigmund?"

"Proven guilty, it grieves me to say. Reputedly, his blade cut through the boy like a knife through butter."

It was something he could see Sigmund do to shield his pride, although still not wanting to believe it. "The boy; did you know him?"

Madoc cleared his throat. "This fort is small, Esmond. No doubt everyone knew him."

It was evident that the lord was uncomfortable. He tenaciously rubbed his aged hands together, blinking at an abnormal speed. Esmond didn't press the issue. "I wish to see Sigmund," he eventually replied.

Lord Madoc nodded. "This way," he said, holding his arm out to the steps down into the dungeon.

Esmond turned to face the stables. Sir Orion was reaching into his pockets, retrieving a copper coin to buy their horse's housing. His attention was stolen by a whistle from Esmond's lips, the knight placing the copper into the stableman's hand before following Esmond down the steps.

"Esmond, ye are not a more welcome sight," Riley rejoiced, hands pressed against his cell bars.

Esmond simpered meekly. "Let the innocents free and leave us," he said to the two guards.

The guards nodded woodenly, turning to unlock the cells. Riley was the first out, placing his hand on Esmond's shoulder. The ram's guard gave a nod to the king as they passed. "Are ma children with ye?" Riley asked.

"They travelled with us to the Fort, yes. We met the elders on the road," Esmond was pleased to say. Riley's face gleamed with relief as he patted the king's shoulder excitedly and jogged up the steps. Sigmund sat in the darkest corner of his cell, staring down to the worn cobblestone. Esmond walked over to the wide-open cell door. "What have you done, my friend?" he asked, leaning into the entrance. The ram didn't flinch, nor care to give a glimpse. Esmond wanted to know what was going through his mind, but didn't want to force it. He stood there in silence for a while, hoping for a response. Following a sigh, the king spoke again. "There-"

"Make the trial tomorrow," Sigmund interrupted, still as a rock. "I've waited long enough."

Esmond nodded, backing out of the cell. *Ideally, you'd be waiting forever.* He gave one last look at the old man before turning to the steps. This wasn't the closure he had hoped for, but Esmond thought it best to leave him alone. He shared a concerned glance with Sir Orion as they walked up the stairs, the daylight blazing their eyes. "It seems all my friends are being torn away from me," the king said.

Sir Orion replied with an exhale. "You don't have to *sentence* him tomorrow," he said.

"And rob the family of their justice? That's one line I'll stay happily behind," Esmond said. Desperately clawing for a solution would only worsen his judgement. "I know you would not stand by and do nothing if it was either of your sons killed."

The knight nodded. "A foolish suggestion." Sir Orion had two sons: Jovian Reade and Isben Reade. He had told Esmond numerous times that he would have liked to have more children, but baby Jovian was all his wife, Emma Dart, could manage before passing on her mothering bed. Although a tragedy, her death opened doors to Orion and Esmond that were closed before, one of those giving Orion the chance to swear off women and join the king's guard. That was what occurred for a time, until Esmond decided that he favoured the knight as a *First Avail* instead. Jovian turned out a good lad nonetheless, a squire for Esmond, never too far from Orion's care and sight. Isben, however, squired for his grandfather, Lord Madoc Reade.

The prospect of seeing them reunited was about the most joyful thought Esmond could draw from the cloudy fort.

A wooden cart rolled into the yard, portcullis shutting behind it. Lord Madoc rushed over to the man who pulled it.

"Fresh stocks, my lord," he said, unveiling the cart as Esmond and Sir Orion walked over. The king's presence startled the short man. "My king," he bowed, falling to one knee.

"Is this it?" Lord Reade asked as he examined the cart. The cart was loosely packed with fresh fruits and vegetables, but Madoc was still troubled. "This is less than a quarter of what we normally receive."

The trader stood frantically, placing his hands on the cart. "I assure you, my lord, this is no less than a third of the arrow's supplies for this moon. I counted myself: one third to Fort Deus, one third to Deuswater."

This sorry stack of food was meant to provide meals for everyone in Fort Angel and Fort Diolus combined for the next moon. It looked like it could barely fill up one castle for a single week. "There must be a mistake," Lord Madoc insisted.

"I do admit, my lord, farmers are saying their yields are low. And the persimmons are in a sorry state, my lord. Not even the pigs eat half of them. Too cold for thems to grow properly, they say."

"Too cold?" Esmond frowned.

"I dunno, your grace," he said, fumbling with his hands.

It wasn't as much of a surprise to Esmond as it was worrying. *A change in season... Predictions of a pause... Does this mark the beginning?* "What about meat? Did you not receive meat from Aquamare?"

"No such shipments from there, your grace. All there was at Trader's Dock was this here cart. And the other two, of course."

The Tridents would send regular shipments of meat to everywhere in the Pole, Aquamare being one of the hearts keeping trade pumping in the whole of Austellus. The Centaur's supplies would first arrive at Sagwhel; the southernmost city in the Pole, then to Centaur's Lagoon, then to Trader's Dock. The most common reason for Aquamare's shipments to not arrive at Trader's Dock would often be either a misrouting, or a sabotage conducted by the exiled people of the Taiga Isles. Thus, it wasn't uncommon for the Centaur's shipments to be suspended, but with already a lack of food...

"I will speak to Lord Jade," Esmond reassured Madoc Reade before turning to Sir Orion. "Don't let me forget." Madoc shooed off the trader, letting him enter the castle.

Allowing another sigh, Esmond turned to see the stubbled goatee belonging to his brother near the wall, fiddling with the saddle on his horse. *What is he doing?* "Brother," he said as he walked closer.

Lori glanced over as he tightened the straps. "Esmond," he smirked. "I should be ready to leave soon."

Esmond was confused. "Back to the Lagoon? Half the day has already passed; you'll need three full days before you reach the Crossroads."

His mischievous smirk grew larger. "Who said anything about the Crossroads?" he said, letting go of the final strap attached to his white stallion. "I'll spend the night at Negal Town. If I'm quick, I could make it there before any trouble." He stroked the horse's muzzle softly.

Staying in Negal Town would imply that Lori wanted to go the coastal path, through the Sagswood, then through Centaur's Grove. This path was risky, especially due to the recent incidents regarding bandits, but Esmond knew better than to talk sense into his brother. "Would half of the king's guard be enough to get you there safely?" Esmond proposed.

"Safely? I can't promise that." His smirk grew into a grin.

Esmond saw through it. "Do you want them, or not?"

He shrugged. "They might slow me down."

"Lori."

His brother chuckled. Esmond couldn't help but smile as well. "I was hoping you'd offer," he said. "I want to get there sooner rather than later. I left my children there."

Esmond raised one brow. "Your bastard children."

"Gods be good, Esmond, they're still my children," Lori replied.

"I didn't mean offense by it. It's just…" he paused to scrape the beard on his face, his fingers following down the neck. "You know tradition. I know how much you love them. Gods know I do too. But allowing them to… inherit, say, like you were asking about… it's unwonted. People won't take kindly to it."

Lori tilted his head like a dog. "You've never cared about being unwonted."

Esmond took a moment to collect his thoughts. "Tomorrow I'll be forced to make an unpopular decision. If the north doesn't hate me for it, the Horncurves will. If the Horncurves don't hate me, the south will. I lose either way."

"Oh. About Sigmund?" Lori asked.

Esmond replied with a nod, blowing into his fist to heat his frozen fingers. It was true; if Esmond was forced to cut off Sigmund's head, that would be something the north wouldn't forgive, let alone his family, and if he was to refrain from punishment, his own people would chastise him for lack of justice. There was an option to send the Horncurve into exile, that recourse beginning to seem more and more like the right choice, despite the fact that his father, Palmer II, was the one to free Sigmund from exile in the first place. *Maybe I should just lop my own head off and save me the trouble of choosing.*

"I don't know. I see a ruler in Feliks. I know fifteen may be an age too young to recognise, but..." Lori looked up to the Negal Wall, struggling to finish his sentence.

Esmond smiled. "I understand," he said, thinking of Asher. *He must be thriving in his new position.*

"And as for Vesta." A smile led his face when he thought of his daughter. "Oh, sweet Vesta."

"All I'm saying is that we need to be careful, Lori. The country is frail. One blunder could send the world into war."

"Brother," Lorimer said, his playful smirk returning, placing his hand on the back of Esmond's neck. "If fate brings a sword to your hand the next time we meet, then we will both remind Austellus why the Centaurs sit on the solar throne."

ASHER I
-Sight-

One step at a time, Asher Centaur traversed the beautiful cobblestone path, enveloped with moss and veiled in mist. The mist was dense, he could barely see how far the fall was, let alone how long the path stretched. His vision was blurry, yet what was further down the path pulled him closer. There were sheer drops on either side, the only thing to guide Asher being the bright light in the distance. He didn't question why he walked. He didn't question why he was warm and not cold. The light was more important than anything. Even the stone was warm to his barefoot tread. The rags he wore, not princely at all. Bugs hid from him as he followed the path, leaping behind rocks and hiding in moss as if a giant was in their presence. When he arrived at the end, he could finally see. The path he had followed was now winding down, embedded in the mysterious cliffs, what lay at the bottom still concealed with haze. Although, now it was cloaked with smoke rather than fog, at least that's what it seemed. Asher felt as though he fell instead of walked down; before he knew it, he had descended. The rounded floor was made from smooth stone, and water sat as still as death inside the obscure engravings. They seemed to mean nothing, yet so much at the same time. He could hear a waterfall, but the water remained still. He could hear echoes bounce around the cliff walls, yet no words were spoken. The light in front of him was brighter than anything he had ever seen, yet he was not blinded. Asher squinted to try and discern the silhouette that walked towards him.

"Prince of Ash is his name," the voice said to him in a raspy tone.

"King of Light is his fate."

As Asher blinked in confusion, a force pressed against him, stopping him from stepping forward. There was no wall, nor wind, just pressure. "Who are you?" he asked, the light beginning to hurt his eyes.

"I am none, yet I am some. The serpent that comes is all," the silhouette said.

A slight breeze brushed against Asher's exposed forearms. "What serpent?" he asked, his wavy black hair caressed by the wind.

"The Serpent of Stars." The calm breeze slowly turned into a gust. "And you must find him, Asher Centaur, as you must find the prince." The rough gust whirled into a fierce gale. Asher's ears were surrounded by air, his clothes flapping rapidly. "For it will poison... realms... complete," was all Asher could interpret as he blew back, struggling to hold his footing. Instead of falling flat on his back, he slid across the floor, like a boat on the sea. If he didn't stop, he would crash into the rough cliff with tremendous force. Thankfully, he landed into the arms of a man, face concealed with a dark hood. A moment before he had time to thank the stranger, he unsheathed a dagger, slashing the Centaur's throat. He clawed at his neck as blood rushed out. The man had vanished. Light grew brighter. Wind became ferocious. His world collapsed.

Asher ejected from his bed, clawing at his throat the way he did in the dream. A cold sweat fell from his hair, stroking his cheeks as it dripped on the bed. *It was a dream*, he thought breathlessly. Terrified to rest his head on the pillow, he drew his sheets, sitting on the side of the bed. He grabbed his head as a sharp pain surged through it. All over in an instant, yet he couldn't help but worry. He shook his head in denial and stood. The light that poured into the room was dull, a day no different from the last. Asher slipped on his royal blue robe, adjusting it before opening the door. Two guards bowed deeply as he stepped out, almost taking Asher by surprise.

"My prince, food is being prepared in the kitchen," one of the guards reported.

Asher didn't respond, just giving a smile and nod as he walked through the corridor. A trickle of sweat fell from his forehead. Asher swept his wet head with his sleeve as a second drop fell. The prince wasn't hungry in the slightest, but he went nonetheless.

Chef Giorgio scurried up to the prince, bowing deeply. "Our finest bread, fruits and oats to break your fast this morn, my prince," he spoke with a foreign accent. "Please, take as much as you desire."

The chef rushed off behind the counter, pushing a board of food out on the stone.

Remaining silent, the prince took a handful of bread and a persimmon like usual, the lack of variety draining him.

"Oh, no, no, that is not food fit for a prince," the chef frowned, "Please, please, we cannot have you starve." Without giving time for Asher to protest, the chef showered him with food, enough to be a feast.

"Thank you," was all Asher felt comfortable with saying, not wanting to be cruel. The chef nodded excitedly as he disappeared into his palace of bread. *Gods, can this headache get any worse?*

Asher entered his father's throne room, plate in hand. His original plan was to sit alone and brood about the dream, though that intention was quickly shattered when he saw Jovian Reade, passed out and leaning against the throne of zircon. He laughed at the squire's gormless sleep. "Is ale that much your enemy, Jovian?" he said, poking him with a loaf of bread.

Jovian barely opened his eyes, smiling as he woke. "How is your tolerance so high?" he said, rubbing his eyes.

"The same reason why gods are called gods," Asher smirked, seating himself on a bench next to the throne. The smell of alcohol still pervaded the air, drawing a wry smile to Asher's face. *Too much of the stuff probably made me have that stupid dream.*

Jovian dragged himself sleepily to the bench, plunging into the seat next to Asher. A yawn escaped his mouth as he gazed at the food, his brown curly hair shooting off in all directions. "Lyssa was getting comfortable with you last night," the squire remarked playfully.

Asher turned to face his inebriated friend, smiling in curiosity. "What of it? Can I not comfort a girl? Poor thing just lost her father."

Swallowing the bread he had chewed and grabbing a leftover cup and jug from the night before, Jovian poured a drink for himself. "There's a difference between solacing a girl and drunkenly singing *'The Maid of Mea'* while you both nestle in each other's arms," he jested before bringing the cup to his lips.

"I really did that?" The prince laughed, quickly snapping out of it. "Don't let me do it again, she's betrothed to someone else." *Don't let me do it again? What are you thinking, Asher?* Jovian scowled as the liquid touched his tongue, ripping the cup from his mouth abruptly.

Jovian's face told Asher everything, the prince trying to contain his laughter as Jovian winced. "I should perhaps have water," he said, standing.

"Perhaps," Asher repeated as Jovian headed for the corridor. Jovian Reade had played a key part in Asher's life for as long as he could remember. Sir Orion and Esmond's friendship spanned long before Asher even existed, being a king's guard for all of Asher's life, and a knight for much longer. A thought of the Reades was never a sour one, their loyalty to the Centaur dynasty meeting no ends.

Now that he was alone, Asher could brood about the dream like he wanted, but he soon found that there wasn't much to brood about. *I was somewhere north, there was a man, he said some words, and I died.* It wasn't necessarily *scary*, but the fact that it was so vivid could only make Asher wonder. *If it is true, and it's in the north, maybe I can see where. Maybe Lyssa would know. Maybe she could show me.* He snickered at himself. *Listen to yourself, Asher. It was a dream. Dreams aren't real.*

Lyssa Lyrderyn was, though. She was more real to Asher than he ever would have wished for. Every time she was around, he'd feel all tingly and nervous. He tried to shut off the thought of her. *You can't. She's betrothed. She can't. Don't. Betrothed. Don't.*

◆━━━━●

A short time passed while the Fort awoke. Asher was joined by his siblings to break fast, notwithstanding his empty plate.

"Why is the concept of Guy being wrong so foreign to you?" Fletcher asked as he ate with his family.

Leta Centaur took a drink before replying. "Maybe because he hasn't been wrong before?" She smirked dryly. "Think what you will. I've heard that the Scorpions in the Archipelago coat their weapons in poison. I think Lord Reynold was poisoned."

"You may be right, but they were Khavar bandits. Like you said, it's the Scorpion warriors who coat their weapons," Asher said.

Fletcher placed his fork on his plate. "Khavar and Scorpius have joined houses. They wed into one another."

Everyone shifted their gaze to Fletcher. "Since when? How do you know?" Asher asked.

"Blaine Casteron. He told our father when he was here on my birthmoon."

Leta had even more reason to be right now. Asher didn't know what to say, or who to accuse. *Does it matter? The culprits must be from the Archipelago by now.*

A guard marched into the hall, the echo of his chainmail rustling as he moved. "My prince," he said. "The elders have returned." Asher stood immediately, following the guard out of the Fort.

Marcarius had a big smile on his face as he trotted into the bailey, made even bigger as Hew bolted past Asher, leaping into the elder's arms during his dismount.

"I've missed you, Hew," Marcarius grinned.

"Elder Marcarius, welcome back," Asher said, embracing the old man. "Come inside, join us, we were just breaking fast."

Marcarius seemed offended. "At this hour?" Asher raised his eyebrows, seeing through Marcarius's jesting. The elder smiled, placing his hand on his stomach. "Nothing would delight me more."

That was the answer Asher had expected; both the elders must be starved from their ride. Asher nodded to them, taking a glance at Ulrich's indifferent expression before turning to lead them into the castle.

"Father has made me in charge of the fort," Asher said as they walked. "He's had to go north for some business with Sigmund."

"I'm aware, I met him on the road," Marcarius smiled. "I always thought you would do well ruling. You'll need me not when you are king."

Asher shrugged. "It's piss easy. I don't know what father's always complaining about," he chuckled. "We'll always need an elder, though. If you're that keen to go, I'm sure Elder Ulrich would allow me his service."

The lion smiled at the jest. "Perhaps if the Pole became a bit warmer."

"Ah," sighed Asher. "That's a no then."

There was a strange silence. "Maybe not," Marcarius muttered.

"What?"

The elder glanced at the boy. "Nothing to fret about, my prince. Mere rumours. Ah, who do we have here?"

Mere rumours? No way. If the Pole's getting warmer, that would mean... No, it can't be. Asher regarded the man suspiciously as his siblings took turns hugging him tightly, no one looser than the last. "How was the meeting?" Fletcher asked.

"We've had better," Marcarius said, taking a seat and tearing a loaf of bread. "But alas, you may rest easy. The kingdoms are not yet in shambles."

"What's a shamble?" Hew asked.

"A mess," Leta smiled. "A big one." She tickled him, Hew responding with a dismissive push.

"Speaking of which, do you happen to know anything about poison?"

Asher was the first to ask.

"I believe so, Asher," Marcarius nodded, glancing at Ulrich. "What about it do you wish to know?"

Asher was about to speak, but Fletcher interrupted. "Our sister thinks that Lord Reynold was poisoned. She thinks it was the Scorpions, not the Cancerians," he said.

"What?" Ulrich grimaced. Everyone who wasn't Ulrich and Marcarius traded fraught glances.

Prince Asher cleared his throat. "Lord Reynold passed in his slumber... We thought you would have word by now," he said to Ulrich. "Guy thought he would recover, yet... I'm sorry."

Ulrich was distraught. He placed his fork on his plate and stopped eating. "May I see his body?" he asked eventually.

There was another awkward pause. "He..." Asher attempted to say. "He's... gone."

The lion's elder was clearly at a loss for words; it looked like they were trapped in his throat. "If you would excuse me," he said, standing up and traipsing out of the hall.

"Gods, Fletcher," Asher moaned.

"I'm sorry, I didn't realise."

Dolt, he thought. Asher hoped his father knew, not wanting to be the one to break it to him. Reynold was a brother to Esmond - a true friend. Asher knew that. Their bond was an unbreakable one, since all the king would reveal of his childhood would be the days he and the lion would jump around the canyons of the Tusks.

After his brother had left, Marcarius was apprehensive to ask about the lord. "What was Reynold like in his final moments?"

"Sir Roswell said he was... shaking," Leta explained. "That he was having amnesia and delusions. Skin as white as snow. Cold sweats. He kept mumbling words like 'wounds' and 'wage' and 'wind'."

Marcarius's face turned as he looked down in reverie. "Nothing about this leaves the castle, do you all hear?" he frowned. "Doubtless it's poison... the sting of a Scorpion."

SIGMUND III
-Time-

Abiding in his black cell, Sigmund Horncurve sat alone, wide awake as the dawn of his trial awoke. He had neither slept, nor moved his position. Light spilled into the dungeon as the trapdoor opened, revealing a kingly figure descending the steps. Sigmund moved his head for the first time in days to look at who came to visit. The figure was King Esmond, almost looking divine as the sunlight shone behind him.

"Everything is organised, it will begin in a few hours," Esmond said tiredly. The king placed his hands on the bars, in a way that made it seem like he wanted to enter and speak.

"The penalty is death, I suspect?" Sigmund asked, returning his gaze to the floor.

The king gave a deep sigh as he joined Sigmund in the cell, closing the bars after him. "There is another option," he said. "You could be banished from my realm. You'll be free to live out your days in permanent exile."

Sigmund sniggered. "Live oot me days," he repeated, massaging his old hands. "Yer a fool if ye think there's anything left to live. Come the Frost Moon, I'll have seventy-eight bloody years."

The king nervously approached Sigmund, clearly not knowing what to say. "You're one of my greatest friends, Sigmund," his whole face frowned as he spoke. "I don't know if I can live a life knowing that I put an end to yours."

Sigmund responded with a smirk. "You wouldn't have put an end to my life; *I* put an end to my life as soon as I chopped down that boy... I can see that now." His smirk dried like a tear on skin. "I was still so angry about Reynold, about what those Venusian bastards had done to him. He might have been your best friend, Esmond, but he *saved* us, he *saved* me and my family. Had it not been for Reynold, we'd still be in exile. Your father would've never made us part o' the realm again if Reynold hadn't convinced him to." He sighed lightly. "All you can do for me now is grant me the peace I need. Gods know how noisy this life has been fer me." Sigmund fumbled with his hands once more, his eyes dropping to the floor. The talk of exile reminded Sigmund of long ago, when Selerborn was still under Oquinteus rule, making all residents of the city banished from the realm. His tone turned spiteful. "Before I killed that bastard Jaakko, my family were hunted like animals. It's a braw miracle that we Horncurves still exist; if it wasn't for your father, and Reynold... it probably widnae'. I don't want to live through that again, Esmond... and I'd rather you kill me now than a random wean with a pitchfork."

Esmond smiled at his jesting. "What about your sons? Your grandchildren?" He asked.

"What aboot them? I've played my role for the Horncurve line. I restored us to heights we have never seen before." Sigmund hesitated, afeared to admit. "It's time for a new ram to lead the storm, eh?"

Esmond seemed to respect his wish, stepping back. "Very well. If it's what you want..." Sigmund could feel Esmond grow colder, only giving a nod on his way out of the cell.

Exile was so much messier back then, Sigmund thought. When he was a victim of it, banishment meant running to the corners of the world, hoping that in ten years, a lord from Austellus didn't wish to root you out of his freshly pioneered lands. Nowadays, there were two much cleaner options: exile to Heavia, safely protected behind the Vetiti Wall, forfeiting any sort of luxury as the beasts of the jungle try to tear you apart, or, of course, choose from the many islands of the Venusian Archipelago. Neither seemed particularly appealing to Sigmund, especially since he had spent his entire life fighting one and despising the other. *Was it worth it? All of the bloodshed over shores?* The loss of great knights and warriors; even loved ones. *Especially loved ones,* he winced. It still wounded him deeply when he thought about his wife. Scarlett Hastem was the bravest woman he had ever known; even great knights were no match for her. He wished he had been there when she fell, just to see her one last time, or perhaps save her if it wasn't impossible. At least if there was an afterlife, Sigmund would finally be able to join her again.

It must have been difficult for Riley and Luther to grow without their mother. Sigmund never thought of it like that. The Sigmund that his sons saw was always the grumpy old git with immoderate spite. That's not who he wanted to be. That's not who he *was* before Scarlett died. Sure, they must have seen the true Sigmund when he was inebriated out of his mind, but for a good part of those times, so were they. *It's too late to change.* He was one of the oldest men in Austellus. He had been ready to face death for a long time.

Coming to terms with his fate, it saddened him some to know that he wouldn't be able to see his grandchildren grow up, yet it was the first time in forever Sigmund felt so tranquil. *I probably wouldn't even live long enough to see that happen,* he smiled. When the guards came to take him to his trial, he almost hated the disruption of peace more than what he had to face. Walking for the first time in days proved a challenge, the first few steps causing the ram to stumble around, but he quickly found his footing. The day was calm, yet the sun was engulfed with black clouds. Sigmund was led towards Fort Angel's hall, noticing that his son stood outside the door. He ambled up to an offbeat Riley, who watched him timidly.

Sigmund was the first to speak. "Whatever Esmond has to do today, don't blame him."

Riley avoided eye contact. "I know ye would go for death rather than exile. He doesn't deserve any blame."

"Good," he said, continuing his walk. There was a certain sorrow in Riley's eyes that Sigmund hadn't seen before. A sorrow he didn't even share when he heard the news that his mother had fallen at Heavia. A sorrow he wouldn't describe as sorrow, but it still made the boy's eyes well up.

"Father." Riley said before the door was pushed. "I... will keep your legacy alive," he uttered reluctantly.

Sigmund smirked, descending the steps he had just climbed. He looked into Riley's hazel blue eyes, darting all over the place. "Look at me, son," Sigmund said, grabbing Riley's attention. "You're a good man." He took a gulp of air before continuing. "Be... better than me." Riley seemed nonplussed to hear that, and Sigmund left him that way, returning to climb his fate.

Since the day was clouded outside, the hall was as shadowed as ever. Sigmund had a huge stone floor to stand on whilst he was watched by judging eyes. The first thing that caught his heed was the casket of the squire that put him into this position. Sir Orion Reade gripped the leathers the boy wore, his eyes red with sadness. The knight's loathsome look he gave to Sigmund unsettled him. The Horncurve's family stood on the opposite side of the hall. His terrified grandchildren watched with their uncle Luther, Riley walking in to join them shortly after. Finally, at the head of the hall stood King Esmond and Lord Madoc, both conveying more woe than hatred.

"There will be no need for a trial," Esmond announced to no one in particular. "Lord Sigmund has confessed and pleaded guilty for the murder of Isben Reade." The king looked as if he didn't want to continue. He looked to the Horncurves, all of their eyes begging for mercy. He looked to his *First Avail*, his eyes begging for justice. The king dropped his eyes. "Take him outside."

"No!" Athena cried, running in front of the king. "Please, mercy! He didn't mean it! I swear he didn't mean it!"

Esmond was shy of words. Sigmund placed his hand on his granddaughter's shoulder. Athena turned to face him, her eyes balling. "Go to yer father, little Athena. Ye don't want to see this," he smiled down at her. "I'm going to see yer grandma," he said before turning to be escorted out by Madoc's men.

The sky darkened at the pace Sigmund walked. People stopped their work to understand what was happening. A man released a tree stump in the middle of the yard, *thumping* the ground on its impact. It had clearly not been used often, yet a sickly spatter of blood still coated the stump, and slashes from where swords swiped lay engraved in the wood. King Esmond was the last person to leave the hall, nervously fumbling the pommel of the sword still encased in his scabbard. Sigmund dropped to his knees next to the stump, looking up to the sky. Black clouds grew more and more common as the moments drew on.

Esmond stepped beside Sigmund, looking down at him dolorously. He wasted no time. "I, Esmond Centaur of Lunarpass, King of Caelestia, sentence Sigmund Horncurve of Selerborn to pay in blood for his committed crimes, the confessed murder of a noble." Esmond seemed to scarcely believe he had just said that. "Will you speak a final word?"

Sigmund thought for a brief moment about what to say. *A final lesson for my grandchildren? A proverb for poets to sing about? A fable speech to wrap up my drawn-out life?* He opted for none of them, and looked up to Esmond. "Give me my rest," he said.

He couldn't tell if the king abhorred or admired that Sigmund gave his last breaths to him. Either way, Esmond closed his eyes once again, unsheathing his sword to make an unbelievably harsh *screeching* sound. The sword was Shofar. Sigmund could recognise the dark steel of his baby from miles away. He smiled sadly. "May you never die, my friend," Esmond murmured under his breath as he primed his swing.

Time slowed as the king veered the sword. Sigmund looked up to his family. Riley held Athena as she cried on his chest. Cadmus dared not look, while Marcus watched resentfully. Luther watched in sorrow. Sir Ardin and Sir Gerard had their swords unsheathed, laying the pommel against their chins to pay respect. The three leftover ram's guard were still in Lunarpass with Elder Ignatius. Sigmund wished he could see them all again, especially Sir Harold Smyth, just to thank him; one last night of drinking in honour of himself. Still, he was content, lowering his head over the block.

A sudden bolt of lightning lit up the sky in the distance as Esmond came to the arch of his swing, making an icy rain shower from above. Sigmund shut his eyes for a final time, and the last thing he felt was the cold, damp steel of Shofar meeting his neck.

HEW I
-Promise-

"Ready?" Fletcher asked.

Hew Centaur nodded, shielding his body with a blue buckler half his size. Breathing in, he threw an aggressive overhead swing. Fletcher effortlessly raised his sword, nullifying the attack. Hew doubled the power into his next overhead slash, sure that it would at least stagger his brother. Instead, Fletcher slipped behind him and swept his leg like a broom, knocking Hew to his back.

"Ow!" Hew yelped on impact. "That's not fair, you cheated!"

Fletcher smiled down at him, holding his hand out. "Stop whining, people won't care about cheating when they want to kill you."

Hew took Fletcher's hand and brushed himself off as he stood.

"Come on, let's go again," Fletcher continued, kicking Hew's sword back to his reach.

Hew picked up his sword, examining Fletcher's confident posture to find a weakness. *He used his body as well as his sword*, Hew thought. With a small run-up, Hew threw himself at Fletcher, leaping off the grass and ramming his brother with his shoulder.

Fletcher lurched back, chuckling, but not falling like Hew wanted.

Breathlessly, Hew lunged at Fletcher with his sword, his buckler slipping from his hand. He was met with a parry knocking him to the ground once more. Falling face first into the dirt, Hew struggled to rise. He felt his lungs collapse, holding his chest as he grasped a tuft of grass.

Fletcher dropped his sword and shield, falling to his knees next to Hew. "Ma!" he called out.

On the other side of the bailey, Queen Semira tossed away her artwork to run over to her son. "It's ok, steady now," she said calmly, holding Hew by the chest. "Think of Elisii." Hew nodded, his world turning from a battlefield into a pacific meadow. He dreamt that he was lying down, the sun stroking his skin, and the brown grass prickling his back. "That's it, good boy." As his lungs opened up, he returned to the chilly breeze of Fort Deus, opening his eyes to see his mother smiling at him.

The queen softly struck Fletcher on the back of the head, hard enough to make him sway. "Be careful."

Fletcher couldn't help but smirk at his mother as she walked away. He stood and held his hand out to Hew once again. Fletcher kicked the sword closer, and Hew just stared at it. *I hate this,* he thought. "I don't want to."

Fletcher sighed. "You have to learn sometime… weapons win wars, not stories."

"And how would you know?" Hew snapped.

"Stop it you two," Queen Semira interrupted, her attention wavering.

"Tomorrow, then," Fletcher replied, shaking off Hew's response.

Hew nodded unenthusiastically, leaving Fletcher to collect the weapons. Hew hated combat; even Elder Marcarius said that his place is on no battlefront. Even though Hew took a deep interest in war, battles hardly excited him. Hew wanted a mind for strategy, a mind he hoped that would destroy enemies without swinging a sword. But he was only ten, and some of the wars he studied lasted longer than his entire life.

◄━━━━━━►

Dusk was quick to set on Fort Deus, and Hew's favourite part of the day grew ever-closer. He crept down the corridor to Elder Marcarius's athenaeum, tiptoeing so the castle wouldn't hear. Since both his father and Marcarius were gone, he was free to take any book he wanted, losing sleep just so he could read them all. Gently pushing open the door, the nostalgic smell of aged books filled his nose. Tomes and scrolls nestled against the walls, Hew scanning them to choose which to read. He snuck to an unfamiliar section, brushing dust on the side of a book to see the title. 'The sorcery and malediction of Caelestia', it read. Hew thought magic was ponderous, though he was interested in the city of Caelestia. His hand found the next book: 'The twelve ancient deities of old Caelestia'. Close, but gods were still not what he was looking for. He reached for the next.

"The illustrious city of Caelestia." Hew spun around, startled by the voice. It belonged to Elder Marcarius, a different book in hand and a smile on his face. "An absorbing read."

"Please don't tell father," Hew uttered, hating himself for forgetting that Marcarius had returned days ago.

"Your mind is curious. His grace won't scold you for that." Elder Marcarius took Hew's book into his hand, dusting off the cover and revealing a red and blue tome with ornate patterns. The old man smiled sadly as he looked into the book, as if he was reminiscing. "Come on then," he said, taking the book over to a candlelit corner of the athenaeum.

Hew's face lit up, his expectation of a rebuke turning false. He smiled excitedly, slotting the book he had borrowed the night before to its home before scampering after the elder. Hew leapt on a chair, unveiling the many pages of his ancient book. Inside lay a detailed map of a perfectly symmetrical, spherical city, filled with extravagant buildings, majestic domes, and regal citadels. It was strangely familiar, almost abnormally so.

"So, what do you know of Caelestia, Hew?" Marcarius asked, sitting

Hew could only think about the constant praise the city received from all the songs and legends. "It was the greatest city ever built?"

"It *was* the greatest city ever built," Marcarius agreed. "Yet it started just as a tiny settlement of the humble Caelnes, eventually conquering half the world with their magic and unstoppable legions." The Caelnes were a people founded by King Caelulus: a refugee from the Jupitan War, where unceasing barbarian raids eventually led to the sacking of his home of Jupiter, forcing Caelulus and his people to flee. He was said to have killed his brother Caelus after they quarrelled over where to found their new capital. It was also believed that Caelulus was first to practise and use magic, learning its ways when he was left to die in the wilderness. Marcarius would never let Hew forget, that being the elder's favourite topic to teach. Not that it was a very *useful* topic. *It's all legend. It might not even be real.*

"Here," Marcarius said, pointing his finger at the lower half of the map. The elder dragged his finger along a district, outlining a border. "This is all that is left of Caelestia... the city of Lunarpass."

Hew's recognition of Lunarpass woke him from his déjà vu, yet it was strange to think that the city was once more; the Lunarpass Hew knew always seemed complete. "Where's the rest of it now?"

"Some say the land was swallowed by the sea along with half of

Austellus during the *Pause*."

"Half?" Hew addled. "Austellus used to be twice as big?"

"Closer to three times bigger, little one," Marcarius laughed. "But now the land has wandered away, and the rest of Caelestia with it."

Hew was awestruck, thinking that the world he lived in currently was immense enough. "Have you ever seen it?" Hew asked. "...the rest of Caelestia."

"Only with younger eyes than yours. It was where I was born." The sad smile returned to the elder's face.

"Do you wish you could go back?"

Elder Marcarius looked down, shedding his smile. His eyes grew cold and hateful, a side Hew had never seen. "No." The elder stared out a window, the moon reflecting off the rocks that surrounded Fort Deus. A gust out in the dark night brought the old man back into the real world. "You are young, Hew. When you age, you will come to realise that time moves quicker and quicker. Soon death would be..." He stopped himself. "I'm sorry. You don't need to hear about death and misery. You still have a long-"

"What were you going to say?" Hew interrupted.

Marcarius looked into Hew's searching eyes. "People desire eternal life until they have it. That is all I'll say."

Hew was confused. What was the point of life if you didn't live as long as possible? He would sometimes even dream of becoming an elder, albeit an idle hope due to the total loss of magic and those who practised it to the world.

"You must be tired; you've trained all day." Marcarius closed the book.

"I'm not tired," Hew insisted, reaching for the tome.

"Hew, I've been generous. Don't push your luck," the elder affirmed. "Take the book, read it tomorrow if you must."

Hew hung his head, clutching the book and nodding before quietly walking out. Although it had time to set, the idea of a bigger world still sounded foreign to Hew. All he had ever known was the Negal lands behind the wall, and Hew believed that alone to be huge, taking several days to travel from Fort Deus to the Negal Wall. The only world he knew outside of the Negal lands was the Lunar Path and Lunarpass itself, though his visits were too few to remember in great detail.

He could scarcely recall the last time he went to Lunarpass. It was his fifth birthmoon when he arrived, and the streets were lined with people welcoming King Esmond with cheers and toasts. Hew had almost felt claustrophobic when he traversed the streets in his oversized chariot. Even the stallions flinched at each bouquet thrown their way. But although the reasons for his visit were lost in memory, the wonders of the city still lay engraved in Hew's head: the deafening, yet dulcet chime of the Lunar Bells, their sound reaching to the far corners of the world, the way the columns twisted and turned in a display of unparalleled sculpting and architecture, the love that went into crafting such a perfect city as harmony blustered with the wind. If he ever ascended the solar throne, Lunarpass was without question where Hew would want to rule, not at a Fort on the edge of a cliff, but a prestigious city, packed with memories, tales and myths.

Arriving at his chamber, Hew was slow to open his door. Slow enough for his attention to be caught by a muted chuckle down the hallway. Curiosity got the better of him as he tiptoed down the hallway, the moans of weakness and laughter echoing against the walls. The sound led Hew to Asher's room, which was lit up with candles. The laughter undoubtedly belonged to a woman, but it sounded like she was in pain. *He wouldn't be hurting her, would he?* The door didn't make a sound as Hew apprehensively pushed it wide enough to peek through. The girl sat upright, her bare back tensing as her head lolled slightly. Long, golden hair tumbled down her side, a strong hand clutching it in a firm grip. A giggle escaped her mouth as she was tossed down, weakly rocking back and forth.

Hew saw her face, and she saw his. She was wide-eyed as she vaulted under the blanket. Asher jerked up, shirtless and astonished, grabbing a robe to swiftly swathe his exposed legs. He was heading straight for Hew, though Hew wasn't quick enough to escape before his older brother grabbed his shirt.

"What did you see?" Asher questioned, pinning his brother to the cobblestone wall. The book fell from his hand. Hew was too afraid to answer. The words trapped in his throat. *"What did you see?!"* Asher repeated.

"You and Lyssa," he cried.

Asher let his grip go, sliding his hand down his face in remorse. "Promise me you won't tell anyone." Hew let his breathing steady. *"Promise me,"* he repeated, gripping Hew's shirt once again.

"I promise," Hew swore.

FELIKS I
-Eye-

Centaur's Lagoon was packed to the gate with people to welcome the return of their lord. Feliks stood at the centre of the road, his dark blue cape beating in the wind as the folding drawbridge stretched out. Beside him, his sister struggled to stay afoot, holding herself tensely to make sure the wind didn't carry her away, though that was one of the costs of living in such a miraculous place. Still, Feliks would pay any cost to live in a place like Centaur's Lagoon, *especially as its lord...*

It always took an eternity for the great drawbridge to unfold to the mainland; sometimes it would seem faster to paddle over on a raft. Though, there were no rafts in sight, and Feliks had to wait for the great wooden slug to crawl all the way to the other end of the lagoon before he could see his father again. As soon as it did though, Lori galloped onto the bridge, Sir Devon Thorneton, Sir Arter Whyte, and Sir Ellis Lovell following closely behind. He had a warm smile on his face as he approached the city, people cheering for his arrival.

Feliks had *mostly* been in command of the lagoon during his father's absence, and though he savoured that time, he was happy for the rightful lord's return - only *mostly* because although he was acting lord, it may as well have been his father's councillors that sat the lagoon's seat, as the bastard had next to no say on the few issues brought to his attention. That was the one thing he hated of his heritage; it felt like him being born a by-blow shielded him from genuine judgement. Not sharing his father's last name was another thing that irked him, Feliks's surname taking the now extinct scion of Centaur, 'Sagitta'. It was a curse of a name, only ever granting him a restriction of power and a loss of dignity as nobles sneered behind his back. The idea did appeal to him: owning a grand castle or city such as Centaur's Lagoon, not being looked down on as a mistake, having authority and power for once. *A stretched hope if I've ever known one.*

Feliks was cruelly woken from his daydream when an arrow punctured his father's leg. The cheers to greet the lord turned into gasps of stupor. His father let out a grunt of pain. It came from nowhere, yet more followed. Another arrow was on course to hit his head, Lori luckily falling from his horse for it to miss.

"Attack!" yelled a man from afar.

Feliks couldn't blink. *"Cover me!"* Sir Ellis yelled, dragging Lori from the floor whilst Sir Devon and Sir Arter shielded the incoming barrage of arrows. Warriors flooded the bridge, charging and howling.

Finally, Feliks was able to move again, comprehending what was happening. *"Raise the bridge, raise the bridge!"*

Panic fell in the lagoon. Traders and workers abandoned their posts, civilians ran and screamed, nobles retreated to the higher part of town. Each second that passed, Feliks feared more and more for his father's life. He could only watch. The drawbridge wasn't quick enough to stop the attackers from crossing, nowhere near so.

Please, please, please. They were slowing down. His father collapsed again. Sir Ellis winced and grunted, struggling to move the limp body. Sir Arter noticed, lowering his shield to help them up. Lori and the king's guard barely managed to enter the city, one of the many arrows they had been feathered with finding its way into Sir Devon's shoulder. Sir Ellis carried Lori before Feliks, awaiting his orders. Lori smiled up at his children, ignoring his completely pierced leg.

"Find him aid!" Feliks shouted at no one in particular. Brandon and Ollie of the city's garrison came running to Lori, lifting him by the arms and carrying him away. Feliks looked around the panic. *There's no one to lead the defence. I have to.* He leapt to a nearby pillar, standing on elevated land so he could be seen. *"Anyone who can hold a sword, fight!"* he yelled, his shock morphing into fury, *"don't let these fuckers see tomorrow!"* He looked to his hands. They trembled like webs in wind. *"Sir Arter, the peace treaty,"* Feliks called as he jogged up to the knight. "We haven't got the garrison. They're not here because of the bloody treaty."

Sir Arter was snapping off the arrows wedged in his hedgehog-like shield. "The eye," he said calmly. "Does it still work?"

Feliks nodded. "It needs time to open, though."

"We can hold them back until it can," he said. *"Shields!"* ordered Sir Arter, causing a timid wall of bucklers to form at the entrance.

Feliks unsheathed his sword, joining the wall. A gang of archers managed to reach the gate's battlements before the attackers reached the city, instantly firing on the enemy before being taken out one by one by foreign arrows.

Sir Devon knelt in a corner, gritting his teeth as he pulled the arrow from his shoulder. Yellow gunk mixed with blood oozed out of the wound, making Feliks cringe, turning him to look elsewhere. To his horror, he realised that to the left of him stood Vesta, a sword and shield in hand. "What are you doing? Go back! Run to safety!"

"I can fight," his sister replied stubbornly.

Oh gods, no. She was only ten. There was no way she could fight. *"Callum!"* Feliks yelled as his close friend caught his sight, firmly holding his position in the wall. "Get her out of here, now!"

Callum nodded, prying Vesta from the wall. She wailed and screamed, thumping Callum repeatedly as he dragged her by her waist.

In the time Feliks had spent to look forward, the foe seemed to have doubled their force. They were outnumbered two to one, but that made no matter. *I don't deserve a home I can't defend.*

The attackers seemed fearless, holding their swords into the air as they closed in on the gate. The first foe failed his attempt to break their formation, yet the second man wasn't so luckless, sliding into the shield wall and making the troops scatter back like waves crashing on rocks. Before Feliks knew it, swords were clashing and blood was spilling. His heart raced, parrying an attack he had scarcely reacted to before cutting the man down. *This is real. This is happening.* Feliks didn't think he would be frightened; he disproved himself as his sword trembled with his next parry. *Relax. You won't die today,* he told himself, before plucking up the courage to slice another down. He spun his blade around, blocking and dodging attacks as he returned their attempts with blood.

Sir Arter was just as impressive at felling his foes, chopping through one after another. He and Feliks seemed to be the only ones putting up a fight, the peasants and guards trading their lives with the enemy.

"On the walls!" a guard alerted.

Feliks's eyes shot up, noticing that men had used grappling hooks to climb over. Some of those who jumped into the fray were met with the raw end of a pike, skewered like meat. Others dodged the pikes completely, killing the peasants who wielded them. They were now surrounded; the only exit was the gate to the city. He could hold them off for a little longer, enough time for more archers to come.

The defenders were gradually backing towards the door without any command needed, forced back by the attackers.

"Fall back!" Feliks commanded with a woozy shout. His eyes shot all over the battlefield, making sure he wasn't taken by surprise. As they backed into the corner, the doors opened for them, letting the wounded fall into the city. Feliks turned around to run to safety.

"Feliks!" a voice called behind.

His heart missed a beat as he heard his sister. Someone managed to disarm her, holding a dagger to her throat. Callum lay next to them, lifeless as blood leaked from his stomach. Feliks ran towards her, but it was too late, it had happened too fast. Blood gushed out of Vesta's throat as she fell to the ground. He couldn't do anything. He should have forced her back. A heartbeat later, Feliks cast his sword to the murderer, with a force so strong that it could have brought down castles. The amount of fury he put into his throw caused his sword to completely impale the head of his sister's killer, but it wasn't enough. He darted over to the faceless man, unsheathing a dagger to repeatedly stab him. His stabs were brutal and tenacious, one after another after another, ripping open the man, but it wasn't enough. Tears streaked down his face the more he stabbed, making him stab more. His vision was clouded. His mind was clouded. *This isn't real. This can't happen.*

A hand grabbed Feliks to drag him into the city before he was killed, his body now limp and exhausted. He fell to the floor, curled up and soaked with blood and tears.

"We need to move," Sir Arter said softly as he crouched next to Feliks.

He nodded weakly, allowing Sir Arter to carry him. A new shield wall had been built in the crossroads of the city, the last handful of the lagoon's defence valiantly standing their ground. Archers had found the gate's battlements, using their new cover to shoot down the attackers. For all that, they were overwhelmed. Feliks would have been content with joining his sister, but it wasn't over for him yet. If it wasn't Centaur's Lagoon they were defending, perhaps it would have been.

"Now!" Sir Arter signalled to a man on the city gate's battlements. He nodded as he yanked back the lever on the wall. The sound of ropes snapping echoed under the wooden ground the raiders charged on. The floor opened like an eye, sending most of the attackers below into the sea, drowning or dying on impact against the rocks. The last few were shot down by the archers as they either tried to escape, or make a null attempt to kill one last man.

The fall of the last attacker wasn't met with any cheer, nor any sigh. The civilians of the lagoon cautiously came out of hiding, still in shock.

Feliks fell to his knees, running his fingers through his brown hair. He gripped it so hard he could have pulled all of his roots out, but he didn't care. He rocked back and forth as he squeezed his head, letting the tears fall down his face. It was all his fault. No doubt the whole of Austellus heard his cry.

ESMOND V
-Fish-

It was good to be home. The road was long and tough but it was finally over. On his journey, Esmond Centaur had plenty of time to brood, plenty of time to assess if he had done the right thing. He decided that above all his power, it was Sigmund's desires that came out on top. Perhaps he may not have had those desires if he hadn't been captured in the first place, locked up in his cell to think about life and the role he had played. It was a stupid way to go, and Esmond hated him for not holding his tongue, or rather his sword, but that did not diminish his respect for Sigmund. In the end, the old ram had lived up to his name, charging down anyone who stood in his path; that's what rams did best after all. As for Sir Orion, he had been quiet the entire journey, enough to have Esmond share his pain. He didn't know Isben as well as he would've liked, but from what Esmond knew, he was a good squire, an excellent swordsman too, according to his grandfather. All of Fort Angel mourned for him. His father insisted for him to be buried where he died - at the gate of the wall, to judge those who would pass through and haunt those he disliked.

One spark of hope, however, came from a lion; hopefully, by now, Reynold had returned to good health. *Together, we can finally get to the bottom of the food crisis, before it claims any lives...* The king wanted nothing more than to bring to bear the dilemmas that engulfed the realm, and to squash all of them like bugs before more came. It was certainly a change of pace, but Esmond was determined not to become overwhelmed.

He trotted into Fort Deus with his party of Sir Warrick Mayne and Sir Connell Atlee, and the cold air was never sweeter. It was around midday, a time which normally had the higher bailey bustling; but it was empty, and so was the castle. Esmond peeked into the throne room, noticing that his office door was closed. He propped himself up to the door and knocked.

"Ahem, I wish to see the king," he said into the door, smiling. He heard the drop of a quill from the other side.

"The king is busy, he would not like to be disturbed," the voice replied.

Esmond chuckled as he opened the door. Asher was already standing, grinning and holding his arms out. "Welcome back, father," he said, before they embraced tightly.

Esmond walked over to his desk, looking down to see what Asher was doing. "How was being king?"

"It was great. Don't know why you hate it so much," the prince said.

"Is that what it seems like?" Esmond asked. "I happen to quite enjoy being king, I'll have you know."

Asher smirked. "Was that what I was meant to believe when you said, '*I fucking hate this job. Whoever picks up this bloody crown can have it*'?"

Esmond couldn't help but smile. "That was an exception," he said. "It's the people you choose to help you rule that make it more difficult than it needs to be. You'll know the feeling one day."

The prince shrugged. "Maybe you haven't chosen the right people."

In reality, Esmond had only chosen a few people to be on his council, those being Sir Orion, Sir Roswell, and Tobi Sparks, who was in Lunarpass with Thaddeus Centaur. The rest had been hand-me-downs from his father, King Palmer, or taken on just because Elder Marcarius said it would be 'beneficial' to. "I'm sure you'll have better luck," Esmond said.

That made Asher smile. "Do you have a moment?" he asked, growing sombre. "I need to talk to you about something."

"I will after the council meeting. Come along if you want."

Asher smirked at the prospect. "I mean, sure, but-"

"Good," Esmond smiled. "I won't start without you." He walked to the door smugly. *That was easy*, he thought excitedly. *Finally, my son at a meeting.* He stopped himself on his way out, reminded by the empty castle. "Where is everyone? Your siblings?"

Asher looked up, holding a hazy face. "Oh, they're by the coast, fishing."

"Fishing," Esmond repeated, unconvinced.

The prince replied with a shrug. Esmond dreaded to think that the paucity of food had stung Fort Deus too, though it would make sense since Fort Angel and Fort Deus were part of the same trade route, but if the entire castle had to go and fish, it must have hit harder than he thought.

That was it. Esmond couldn't wait any longer, he had to get things straight. He waited in his council room for what seemed like hours for his advisors, impatience pumping through him.

"Welcome back, King Esmond," Elder Marcarius meekly greeted upon entry. He didn't seem himself; he was shy and uneasy. The king grimaced at the pile of scrolls the elder cupped in his arms, letting them tumble onto the table when he took his seat. Sir Orion was the last to enter, taking his seat next to Sir Roswell at Esmond's right hand.

Esmond stood. "As you can see, my son and heir will be joining us today. If we could hold off on politics today, that'd be great; another heated debate about Larton Keep would be just the thing to scare him away," he smirked, holding out his arm to Asher.

"Your opinion shall prove invaluable, my prince," Ellys Dart warmly spoke. The rest of the council didn't say anything, if not for the courteous smiles they exchanged with the young prince.

"Elder Marcarius," Esmond began. "Whenever you're ready."

Marcarius nodded. "As we all know, countless... occurrences have shrouded the past moon. To begin our meeting, I shall go over a brief list of edicts that must be enacted in the following days." Marcarius unravelled the scrolls to jog his memory. "Firstly, succeeding the dreadful death of Lord Reynold Lyrderyn, the title of Lord Ruler of Ignis shall pass to his brother, and heir, Sir Goldwyn Lyrderyn, without intercede."

What? Reynold died? First Sigmund, then Reynold? If he knew he would die, Esmond wouldn't have left. He had known him as a boy, loved him like a brother. His muscles tensed as if he had been struck.

"Truly dreadful," Ellys Dart agreed.

"Also, following the execution of Lord Sigmund Horncurve, the title of Lord Ruler of Selerborn shall pass to his rightful heir, Riley Horncurve, without intercede," the elder continued. He had his scrolls piled in sections, seals from all over Austellus broken upon them.

"They are the rightful heirs, there will be no need to intercede," Esmond said coldly.

Marcarius seemed to agree, slipping his gaze back to his scrolls. "I have received glum word from Iustitia: Lord Daryl Venulaes has passed in his slumber due to sickness. Without intercede, the title of Lord Ruler of Iustitia will pass to his requested, and rightful heir of Kenneth Venulaes."

Lord Daryl too? That marked three wounded kingdoms. Esmond admired Daryl, often calling him the grandfather of the realm. He was as charming as he was tactful, the kind the realm needs more of. But he was also aged, some say forgetful in his senility.

"Kenneth?" Sir Roswell queried. "He is a boy of fifteen."

Esmond ignored him. "Grant him his wish. Write to Iustitia and offer condolences and blessings to the new lord."

"My king," Wye Vesta objected. "I agree that fifteen is too young to be burdened with such responsibilities. Perhaps send one of our own to govern until the heir comes of age."

"Yes, one of our own," Sir Roswell agreed.

"I'm not going to respond to years of service and loyalty by dishonouring his last request. Kenneth will claim his title and I will hear no more of it," Esmond answered, scarcely raising his voice yet still silencing his councillors. He shot a look at Marcarius.

The elder nodded. "I will do as you ask, my king," he said, dropping the scroll to let it join the others. "Lastly, an edict has been enforced to prevent passage through the Negal Wall until Lord Reynold's murderers are identified."

Esmond shuddered. He was stupid for imposing that. The king was too blinded by Reynold's attackers. *Sigmund's death was my fault, despite what he said.* "Withdraw that edict," Esmond said. "I was foolish to not seek counsel."

"I will see to its withdrawal, my king," Wye Vesta bowed, exposing his receding hair, grey as ash.

"Very well. That concludes the edicts passed," Marcarius said. "We may begin discussion."

"I believe the issue surrounding a lack of food is of paramount importance," Kaus Jade stated before anyone else could. The old lord felt his grey, pointed beard. "Harvest yields are at a record low, farmers report. And our trade routes with Aquamare have been plundered. As it stands, we've been unable to recover the food consumed in the recent celebrations."

King Esmond couldn't dismiss it as coincidence that the two major sources had failed at the same time. He felt like he was being gamed, those who might want to attack the realm weakening the king's position as much as they could before striking. "Have you adjured supplies from elsewhere?"

"That I have, my king," Kaus Jade affirmed. "With luck, suppliers from Lunarpass and Sangis will be with us in just over a fortnight. However callous this moon may be, I have made sure we do not go hungry again."

Esmond nodded silently. "How will we fare this moon?"

"If all the ocean's fish don't die, we may barely scrape by. It will be a hungry few weeks, my king."

"Still better than an empty few," the king said, placing his fist to his mouth.

Galloway Malone stirred. "Plundered by whom, Lord Jade?"

Kaus frowned. "One can only assume the peoples of the Taiga Isles, if not raiders from the Pole."

The king sighed. "Make sure they are monitored. If we can't grow our own crops, we can't afford to forfeit another shipment."

Galloway nodded. "I shall see to it, your grace." Esmond didn't know if he entirely trusted Lord Malone after what his daughter told him. He couldn't let that prohibit his duty though.

"How many cargo ships are set to sail?" Sir Orion asked calmly.

"Six, I believe."

"And how many arrived at the dock?"

Lord Jade looked unsure. "One, if at all."

The knight scowled. "Why would they stop at five? There were six to be sabotaged and I doubt those cargo ships were heavily armed."

Sir Orion had a point. The council silently contemplated, trying to deduct the possibilities. King Esmond sighed. "We can't know who did it and why, not by discussion. The least we can do is make sure these ships have more guards for next time," he said. The council was useless. They sat there, thinking in a puddle of ignorance. "What of the costs, Lord Ellys. Will we at least be able to cover the expenses for the celebrations?"

Ellys Dart looked as if he had fallen asleep, awoken by the call of his name. "Yes, my king. Sir Goldwyn has agreed to cover the expense upon his return to Ignis," the old man said warmly.

"Excellent. There's a positive to end on," the king smiled. "Are there any more issues?" The council traded glances with one another.

"It seems not, my king," Elder Marcarius observed.

That can't be it, that was too short; it seemed like so much had happened this moon. "Very well. You may all leave." Each lord bowed on their way out, leaving only the king and the prince in the chamber.

"You can speak, you know," Esmond smiled.

Asher slumped back into his chair. "I should have told you about Reynold."

"Eh, forget it," Esmond sighed, taking the seat next to his son. "I made a mistake in going. I should have been here."

"I know you loved him. It was a shock for all of us."

Esmond nodded as he brooded. He didn't like being hung up on the topic. "What was it you wanted to talk to me about?"

"Um." Asher readjusted himself. "I know this might be weird, but... I want to go and squire for Sir Goldwyn. I want to see more of the world."

Esmond didn't believe it. "Squire, is it?"

Asher frowned. "What?"

"Squiring... it's inventive."

"Inventive?" Asher repeated.

"Yes. An inventive lie," the king smirked.

The prince's face dropped like a boulder. He raised his palm to his brow. "Hew told you didn't he?"

The king smiled curiously. "Your brother hasn't told me anything. I just don't see you wanting to become a knight in a land foreign to your own."

"You'd be surprised what I want," he smirked, before remembering his place. Asher hung his head in his hands, sighing and grasping his wavy black hair. "I'm sorry, I-"

"I'll let you go," Esmond said in an icier tone.

The prince was stunned as he looked up. "Really?"

"I was Fletcher's age when I ran away with your mother. I'm not saying this is the same, but that decision ruled my life for decades to follow."

"But you were the king."

"As might you be," Esmond smiled. "There's nothing I want more than for you to carry on what I leave behind. I just want you to know what leaving here *truly* means. I want you to know that you *truly* want to."

"I do," he begged. "I can do anything Sir Goldwyn requires of me, I can write to you and tell you how everything is, I can see-"

Esmond conjured a sorry smile. "I said you can go." The king shifted his chair to stand. "You don't deserve to be locked away in this castle. Go see the world if that's what you want to do."

An ember sparked in Asher's blue eyes. He stood and met his father with a hug. "Thank you," he whispered. "Thank you so much."

RILEY I
-Oat-

For almost the entire journey, the Horncurves sat in a sullen brood upon their horses, mourning for their loss. In body, Sigmund hadn't left them yet; he was carried in a lightweight casket, Riley Horncurve intending to bury him back at Selerborn. But in soul, Riley didn't know when Sigmund left him. In his final hours, he seemed like a different person. *Death would make any man mellow*, he thought, despite mellow and boisterous being such a large leap apart. *It wasn't his time. It couldn't have been.* Simply carrying his longsword was a tricky concept for Riley.

Sometimes, it would seem like Sigmund loved Shofar more than his children, though he supposed the sword had been around longer. It was the same sword Sigmund used to dice up Jaakko Oquinteus, putting an end to that corrupt dynasty. He'd said that ever since, he could feel his blood pumping through his veins when he held it, and that his blood pumped through the sword too. Riley could scarcely believe that his father was the same age as Cadmus and Marcus back then; neither of them were as skilled as Sigmund was in his prime. He must have been a phenomenal swordsman to fell every man from the gates of Selerborn to the Cenkeep, only accompanied by his militia of two hundred. The battle lasted long after the king died, well into the eve against those who were still loyal to Oquinteus. That day, all memory of the Oquinteus dynasty was obliterated, not by tricks and manipulation, but by a storm led by sheer force.

There was a lengthy song written about the events of that day, and

Riley smiled each time he heard it. Soon after Sigmund's victory, the song went on to become legend, printed in the memory of every Arian.

Riley felt like the bringer of bad news as the great city of Lunarpass peeked over the horizon. He was excited to see his wife again, but the news he had to break dampened the feeling. He dreaded even more so how his people would react when they heard of Sigmund's death. *He saved them from a tyrant, brought them honour, riches. How can I be better than that?*

Lunarpass never failed to send a shiver down Riley's spine, or anyone's for that matter. The entrance was a powerful arch, almost a tunnel with how vast it was. Brown grass underfoot had transformed into a fine stone, possessing a mystical feel. Lunarpass was alive and friendly: traders, nobles, merchants, and peasants all sharing the same floor, smiling and bowing to each other as they passed. It seemed unreal, utopian even. Even the city's garrison sauntered around, taking tastes of merchant's goods. The city's garrison was a peculiar thing; they wore almost no armour and carried only a spear, and a rounded shield that seemed to be attached to their arms. They cared not of who came into the city, nor of those who left. *They must place a lot of trust in Lunarpass's defences and scouts to let their guard down this much. If only it was the same in Selerborn.*

It took an hour or so to reach the inner city, doubling the majesty and mystery the outer parts presented. Here, the marble was fascinating, bending in such ways that didn't seem possible. Above them stood the Sphaera - a colossal, rounded building where only the elders and the noble families they served could enter. The Sphaera was big enough to be a city on its own, one of the few sections of Caelestia still intact after the *Pause.*

The concept of a sectioned-off city separating nobles and lowborn was foreign to Riley. In Selerborn, highborn and lowborn alike dined at the same table, tasted the same air, saw the same sights.

The Horncurves trotted without a care past the Ulcus Basilica - a long, gracious hall where the solar throne lay. They didn't come to exchange small talk with Thaddeus Centaur. Riley just wanted to get home.

Approaching one of the eight entrances of the Sphaera, Riley itched more and more for a drink. Lunarpass was where the bitter colds of the Auburn Pole and the scalding heats of the Canicule met, creating a climate neither hot nor cold. It made Riley feel strange, always used to one extreme or the other almost everywhere else in Austellus. Two guards stood, propped up against the gate, fitted with gear of the city's garrison.

"State your name and business," one said, stepping forward.

"Riley Horncurve. L... Lord of Selerborn," he stuttered, unable to say. "My *business* has got nothin' to do with ye."

The two guards backed off, whispering to one another and exchanging confused glances. Eventually, the same guard who spoke stepped forward. "Sigmund is Lord of Selerborn. We can't let you through without him."

"Sigmund is dead," Riley revealed without hesitation. Sir Ardin and Sir Gerard, who began carrying the casket over, froze as Riley held out his hand. He heard steps echoing from inside the Sphaera.

"Let them through," a strong, aged voice said from within. "They're with me," Elder Ignatius said as the light hit his face.

The guards cautiously stepped aside, letting the Horncurves dismount and enter the exalted entrance hall.

"You took your time coming," the elder said, giving Riley a brief hug.

"You got word of Sigmund?" Riley asked as they walked.

"Yes. This morning," the old man responded. "Not the word I had hoped to wake to."

Riley nodded. "Join me for a tan. The road has been long," he said, taking the lead.

Their footsteps rang through the rounded marble ingress as they walked, filling the empty Sphaera with echoes and life. Last time Riley was there, it was booming with movement and people, but now, not even the sunbeams moved from their rigid glare. It seemed such a waste that only fourteen of the eighty-eight sections of the Sphaera were used throughout the solar celebrations. Riley wondered if anyone used it during the century in between. *If not, that would be even more of a waste.*

"So, you're to be the new Lord Ruler of Selerborn?" Ignatius asked as he caught up to Riley's power walk. "By your father's wish?"

"Aye," he said rigidly, stroking the diamond on Shofar's pommel with his thumb. Riley had nothing else to add, slipping his gaze to the floor.

Ignatius nodded after a while of walking in silence. "I don't know if you know, my lord, but the ceasefire ends tomorrow. We have no chance of making it to Selerborn before-" The elder's speech trailed off as Riley stopped walking and stared him down. His bitter glare made Ignatius sink his head into a bow.

Lord Riley took a lengthy inhale, followed by an exhale twice as long. "I know." He turned to walk again.

Riley's reunion with his wife was met with little more enthusiasm. Athena bolted into the room where Lady Emily sat, leaping into her arms.

The three other ram's guard were nowhere in sight, presumably getting drunk in a brothel.

"Welcome back," she giggled sadly. Riley held aside her brown hair and pecked her on the cheek before he sat next to the closest jug. They were on a balcony which looked out onto what seemed like all of Lunarpass, yet it seemed so much smaller from up there. "So, when are we headin' back?"

"First light," Riley said bluntly, making his cup overfill with ale.

Lady Emily stood and brushed dust off her red dress. "We better get ready then. Dusk is almost here." She strolled out of the room, followed closely by an excited Athena, her word-vomit trailing off into an echo.

Riley drained his cup with the first swig, grabbing the jug for another.

"Slow down, father," Cadmus said as he watched.

The Horncurve looked up to his worried sons. "Sir Gerard, four more cups. And we'll need more ale than this."

Before he knew it, the morning was young and one drink turned into twenty. Ignatius was unconscious in his seat, mouth wide open as he snored peacefully. Marcus and Cadmus were out cold, leaning against each other in a drunken manner. Sir Ardin was asleep too, crouched in the corner.

The rest were lost in song, coming to the last verse and accompanied by a piper Sir Egan had grabbed from the brothel.

> *Your reign is done, you no-good loon!*
> *Take our freedom, lose your moons!*
> *With sword and flame, he slew him through,*
> *The ram who brought our light,*
> *'Twas just a boy who felled him so,*
> *His shine made from the night.'*

"To Sigmund!" Sir Harold cheered, raising his cup.

"Sigmund!" They all toasted.

"See? He's good, innae?" Sir Egan said as he put his hands on the shoulders of the bard.

"Aye!" Riley smiled. "Where did ye learn to play our song, boy?"

"I'm a traveller, my lord, a *trouper*. There's not a song I don't know," The bard known as Upilio grinned.

"I would be honoured if you were to come back with us, traveller. You'll be famous among our people! I can see you inspiring a great many."

Upilio was dumbstruck, bowing down to the Horncurve. "I am the one who is honoured, truly."

"They'll love ye back home," Riley slurred, raising his cup of wine.

Sir Egan placed his empty cup on the marble table. "Well, I must be off now, don't wanna fall off my horse tomorrow," he said, leading himself and the piper out of the room.

"Make sure ye don't fall down the stairs first," Riley called, by way of goodnight.

The breeze that entered the terrace was cool and refreshing, gently brushing over Riley's red hair and blooming beard. Lights from the city could still blind Riley from where he sat, the great bells illuminating the night with a thousand lights in the shape of stars.

Luther Horncurve sighed gently. "It wasn't father's time," he said. "He should have died in battle, with blood on his sword and fight in his heart."

"He should have," Riley agreed. "No one could ever kill him in battle, though." His room was spinning. The ram could barely speak sentences. "Do ye remember when he used to take us hunting?" Thinking back gave Riley a vast smile. "Every day at the crack of dawn."

"I'll never forget waking up to those buckets of icy water," Luther slurred as he looked down.

Riley laughed. "We were both so shite. We'd use our entire quiver on the first bunny."

"I remember well," Luther smiled. "I couldn't help laughing at that face he always pulled when we missed."

"I bet it encouraged you to miss more," Riley jested.

"Aye," Luther said, reaching to gulp more wine. As he sipped, purple pellets spewed from his mouth. His entire body shook with laughter.

"What is it?"

"That time neither of us wanted to go," he continued to chortle. "We hid in the wardrobe and hoped he wouldn't find us. You felt too ill to hunt."

Riley's smile grew. "We wouldae gotten away with it if ye didn't fall for his trap."

"He put oot an oatcake, brother. I'm a simple man," Luther smirked as he tried to drink again. "It was a bloody good oatcake, mind ye."

"It bloody well better have been. I retched on my horse an hour later," Riley reminded as he looked to his goblet. His brother and he were the only ones in the room. Sir Harold had fallen asleep as they talked. Riley's smile returned sullen once again. "Life was so much simpler back then. So much simpler when…" He trailed off, not knowing how to finish.

"…When mother was alive," Luther said.

He was right. "Aye," Riley agreed. "Her death forced us to grow up."

His brother emptied his cup before standing to stretch. "As does Sigmund's," he said. His back cracked as he pressed on it, making the ram exhale with relief. Luther put his hand on Riley's shoulder as he came to the end of his yawn. "Let's make sure he didn't die for nothing, eh?"

Riley nodded, slipping his gaze. "Night, little brother."

Luther replied with only a smile, staggering out of the room soon after, and leaving Riley the last awake. He sighed as he sat back, rubbing his eyes, until something odd pricked his side. *Shofar*, he smiled. The sword must have been too big for the scabbard; whenever it was unsheathed, it made a horrible scratching noise. Luckily, it wasn't loud enough to wake anyone. Riley placed it on the table in front, running his finger along the fine black steel. *This is mine now, somehow*, he thought. *I don't deserve it.*

"I'd rather you don't play with that thing in your state."

Riley whipped his head to face the door. It was Emily. "What state? I'm in no state," he said, doing a poor job at concealing his slur.

Emily stared at him, unconvinced. "Your finger's bleeding."

She was right. Blood was dripping onto the sword. "Ah, balls," he cursed, sucking his finger dry.

Emily Horncurve wandered over to sit next to him, all the while examining Riley with sullen eyes. "There are better ways to deal with loss than drinking yourself into an early grave," she sighed. "Athena says you've been at it since you left Fort Deus."

"Deal with loss? I drink because I want to, Emily. I'm a grown man."

"Then why does a fourteen-year-old know better than you?"

He dragged his palm down his tired face. "I'm not dealing with loss."

Emily frowned. "Your father just died, Riley."

"Aye, my *father*," he growled, stumbling into a stand. "It's not my loss. I didn't love him. I *never* did."

Emily just stared back.

"I *don't*," he continued, a strange pressure attacking his eyes. "He treated me like a sack o' shite. Why would I love him? Why would I…" He winced.

"Shh," Emily said, hugging him. Riley couldn't hold it back then. His eyes would hurt even more if he tried. He wept until the sun rose.

ASHER II
-Lock-

I t's not going to work, Sem," Asher Centaur claimed as Queen Semira
attempted to stuff a new-born tin breastplate into Asher's leather case.
"It can, it will," she insisted, struggling to press down on it. With
a heavy elbow-slam, Semira closed the case and fastened the latches as
quickly as she could. "See?" She smugly turned to Asher, a moment before
the latches burst off the case.

"Just leave it," the prince laughed. "I can protect myself with a sword
and bow well enough."

"Fine," the queen resigned, taking the plate out of the case. "Just don't
come crying to me if you get loaded with arrows."

"The one thing more dangerous than a barrage of arrows is your
concern for me," Asher smirked, packing his final cloth shirt into a second
bag. "The Lyrderyns will keep me safe. I won't cry for you if they don't."

"If you say so," Semira added as she excused herself from his chambers.
"Be done soon, they've waited long enough," she added on her way out.

A peculiar breeze floated around Asher's room after his mother left.
The room was completely empty, everything that belonged to him packed
in sacks and containers. He savoured every moment he could that morning,
especially when he was eating his warm breakfast, not knowing when he
would taste the flavour of home again. Before that, whilst the castle slept,
he went walking along the jagged hills on which his home lay, scaling down
to the Antrum River as he reminisced over the countless years' worth of

memories the land had sewn.

Jovian Reade accompanied him, letting Asher leave with a clear conscience. Asher told him everything: from Lyssa to Hew to Reynold. Well, not everything... enough, at least. Instead of replying with a droll chaff like he normally did, Jovian listened intently, digesting every word. Although, not long suffering his brother's death, chaffing had taken a hiatus from Jovian's personality. He never liked talking about it, despite Asher believing it would help him move on. Shutting himself away and dealing with it on his own terms seemed the best course for Jovian regardless, all too familiar with tragedy since the loss of his mother at such a young age. It made Asher see him in a brighter light when he was more than open to receive Asher's troubles atop his own.

"You *do* know what Goldwyn will do if he finds out - his already betrothed niece having her virtue stolen by a Centaur," Jovian had said. "Let alone what the Horncurves would do."

"I didn't tell you to be reminded of the reasons why it's a bad idea. I know it's a bad idea," Asher replied. "Besides, Cadmus and Marcus have no interest in the princess, it's obvious."

"Why did you tell me, then?"

"Because you're the only one I can trust," he frowned angrily.

Jovian was silenced. "Me? What about your brothers?"

"Hew knows."

"Exactly, so tell Fletcher. Can you not trust him also?"

"I can, I..." Asher paused to think of a warrant. "I don't know. I didn't mean for Hew know. I don't trust Fletcher to keep his mouth shut." The prince shook his head. "Jovian, please."

"What do you want me to do, Asher?" Jovian shrugged.

Asher rubbed his eyes. "Do what you need to," he sighed. "I can deal with not telling my brothers, but I'd regret it if I didn't tell you."

As the prince sat on his bed, his brother appeared in the doorway, as if summoned by his thought. "I have been ordered to help you with your belongings," Fletcher jested in a posh voice.

Asher looked up with sombre eyes, still half stuck in the past. He stood to place his hand on one of the many cobblestones lining the walls of his chamber. "You've always wanted this room."

Fletcher replied with a nod as he glanced around the walls. "Yeah, it's always been bigger than mine." The cobblestones were pleasantly cool to Asher's touch, chilled by the morning fogs. "How are you feeling?" Fletcher asked, knocking him out of his daydream.

"Good," he smiled. "Excited."

Fletcher nodded. "Come on, best not keep your new family waiting," he said, using two hands to lift one of Asher's heavy cases.

The prince's eyes tracked his brother on his way out, wondering whether Fletcher was genuinely happy for him. "Fletcher," he blurted out, not knowing what to say. "Do you... mind?"

His brother wore a smirk as he turned in the doorway. "Do I mind?" he snickered. "Do I mind that everything we'd ever talk about is happening without me? Do I mind that I won't be by your side to experience it with you?" he said, so calmly it hurt more. "No, I don't mind," he muttered bitterly on his way out.

Asher sighed, grabbing a clump of his long black hair as he looked down. It *was* everything they talked about. It was something to wake up for. Something to look forward to the future for. And Asher was doing it alone, and worse, not for that reason. *Maybe I should tell Fletcher. Maybe, then, he would understand.* But the thought of anyone other than Jovian knowing about Lyssa sent shivers down Asher's spine.

The courtyard was filled with the sound of farewells and laughter. The king leant against Asher's horse, joking with Lord Goldwyn, Lady Gina, and Lady Elayne. Goldwyn Lyrderyn was a lord now, not a sir, and everyone had to remember that, all being so used to the latter. Leta and Eva were saying their goodbyes to Eleanor. The three girls seemed to be inseparable during the Lyrderyn's stay, Asher not finding one without the others. Finally sat Fitz, atop his horse and holding a sour face, clearly wanting to leave. Asher tried not to notice Lyssa, sitting prettily on a maroon stallion as she trotted gently around.

"Ah! Here he comes now!" Lord Goldwyn smiled warmly, as he held his large arms out. All eyes fell on Asher as he dragged his case on the brown ground to his cart. Asher replied with a faint grin to the applause, his concerned attention mostly on his brother.

"Are you ready?" Esmond asked.

"Just about," he answered.

Asher's entire shoulder was swallowed by Lord Goldwyn's hand, the new lord smiling down at him. "If you ever want or need anything, all you need to do is ask. 'Tis a long time to hold your tongue if you don't."

"I will, my lord."

"Good lad," he uttered. "I'll let you say your goodbyes then. We won't go too far ahead," he affirmed, climbing on his horse and starting the journey.

"Have you got everything you need?" The queen smiled as the cart containing Asher's belongings trotted out of the Fort. She cupped his face into her soft hands.

"Yes, mother," he assured. Semira pulled her son's head closer, kissing his forehead. Hew waited for him, almost getting teary as he stood beside his brother. "Be good, ok?" Asher said, embracing him.

"When will you come back?" he sobbed.

"I'll make it back for your birthmoon, that much I know." His brother's birthmoon was plenty of moons away, but even Asher doubted if he could keep that promise. *How long will I be going for? Why am I even going? Is Lyssa really worth this much? I've just met her.* "Don't you want to travel the world with me, Asher?" she had asked him, so wickedly it made him stiff just thinking about it. "I'd be all alone at Ignis."

Hew nodded, pulling his head from Asher's tear-soaked chest. "Don't cry. You won't even know I'm gone," he said, as Eva shyly crept towards him, also teary, before leaping into his arms. "Smile, Eva," he smirked, making his sister muster a grin as she backed off.

"Hold out your wrist," Leta ordered, hiding something behind her back. Asher did so, letting Leta plant a rope-like zircon bangle on it.

"A bracelet?" he asked.

"It's magic," she promised, revealing an identical armlet on her wrist as she pulled back her sleeve. "It'll keep you safe."

"I'm sure it will," he smiled, tickling her as she was grabbed. "I'll miss you," he whispered to her, not loud enough for the others to hear. She tightened her grip as soon as she heard that, her unbreakable smile beginning to crack.

Last was Fletcher, the hardest goodbye. His sulky eyes were locked on the ground. "Write to me," he said. "Tell me if the world is worth seeing."

Asher sighed before gently touching Fletcher's chin. "When I come back, I promise you we'll see it together."

"You promise?" he echoed.

"I swear," he vowed. "By every single god."

Fletcher couldn't help but smirk as his excitement was rekindled, embracing his brother tightly. Like Asher had wished, Fletcher didn't wear a face of spite as they pulled away, but a face of hope. He contently followed his father through the portcullis to the middle bailey, waving farewell to his family. The people of the lower bailey clapped and cheered to celebrate the new dawn, tossing gifts of good fortune and favour. Amongst the applause, Asher spotted a hooded figure, neither clapping nor cheering. He was fixed on the character as they walked past, seemingly vanishing in the air succeeding a blink or two. His eyes were frantic to relocate, only to be disappointed by the empty crowd.

"Well, this is it," said Esmond when they arrived at the Trado.

"Yeah," Asher sighed, eyes ricocheting like a ball between the rackets of his old life and his new.

"Look, Asher," the king spoke, in a tone not heard before by his son. "Is there anything you want to... or need to tell me? You can trust me."

There were lots of things to tell him. Things that would be best to tell seated. "No."

"Good. Fantastic," he stuttered. "Remember what I said, Asher. If you think it a mistake, you can come back whenever you want."

"I..." Asher began, tripping on his words. "I promise it's not a mistake."

His father smirked. "You're thinking like a king already," he said.

Asher smiled before giving Esmond a tight embrace. After, Asher climbed his horse and began a steady trot forward, looking back. The king waved his son away.

Asher continued his silent trot, smiling to his father. As he turned, he felt something cold spike his hand. Then another. Then another. Before long, flakes began falling, only to melt on his warm person. *Is this a dream?* The cold snowflakes seemed to prove it wasn't. This couldn't be. Asher looked to the sky, the fluffy clouds making more and more flakes fall. He wasn't dreaming. It was snowing. It hadn't snowed in Fort Deus for centuries.

FELIKS II
-Stone-

H e had never seen a gem like this before. It was a pale orange with perfect cuts, almost delicate. He handled it in his closed palm, feeling the smooth yet deadly make of the gem. Lori was beside him, drawing long, deep breaths as he slept. His father's purple veins branched out like tree roots under where his pale skin was swathed with a grey dressing. Feliks was the one to tell his father about Vesta, that being the first thing he heard after he awoke from his day-long slumber. Lori didn't seem to be as distraught as Feliks thought he would, though. His father definitely hurt more than he let on. If he hid his feelings to make Feliks feel safer, it wasn't working.

Although it was much like Lori to do something like that, Feliks couldn't help but feel as if his father was different. Not just in thought, but in mind and body too. Lori would often wake in the night in puddles of sweat, shaking in a pale shock and unable to move. He told Feliks of vivid dreams he would have. A recurring one was a dream of drowning: "It's like I'm sinking, drowning. But not in water. It's too thick to be water. I felt like I could breathe through it, but when I tried to breathe in, I grew colder," Lori said when he awoke in a chilled sweat a day ago. Feliks reassured him that it was just a dream and to get rest, especially because of his festering leg, but when he'd fall asleep again, the same dream would wake him. Feliks worried if Lori had fallen ill from something - that would explain his boundless sweats and pale skin at least - but it made more sense for Lori to be grieving his daughter, his loss sending him mad.

Life didn't feel right without his sister, almost like a dream in itself. It happened too fast for Feliks to do anything, but he still hated himself for not being able to. Vesta would have grown to be a great woman. Lori would often say how much she resembled the queen, with her long black hair and rigid attitude. *She would have been safe in the city*, he thought, safe in the loch keep where the bandits couldn't reach. *I didn't do enough,* he whispered under his breath.

"It's not your fault," Lori weakly uttered from his soaked bed.

"Morning," Feliks mumbled, lowering his head with embarrassment. "How are you feeling?" Lori tried to sit up, groaning with pain as he held his leg. "Does it still hurt?"

The lord sent a haughty gaze. "I wouldn't have mewled if it didn't." He bared his teeth as he dragged his leg up, grabbing a pillow so he could rest his head on the wall. "Are you coping?"

"Mmm," Feliks acquiesced, nodding once, rubbing the stone he held.

His father caught sight of it. "What's that?"

"A gem," Feliks told him. "The garrison are back. They found a bunch on the raider's bodies."

"Really?" Lori winced. "Gems?"

Feliks tittered. "Raiders with wealth is a scary thought, isn't it?"

"Let me see?" Lori held out his hand as he readjusted again. His hand was coated with open scratches, cutting in different directions. Giving one last look, Feliks dropped the stone into his open palm. *"Ah!"* Lori yelped, dropping the stone on the floor.

Feliks fell to the ground and grabbed it before it rolled out of reach.

"What was that?!" Lori shrieked as he held his hand in pain.

"You should put a bandage on that," Feliks observed calmly.

"No, no, look." Lori dabbed his thumb on his palm. "It doesn't hurt when *I* touch it. Give it to me again."

Cautiously, Feliks passed the stone into Lori's shaking hands, his father prying it with two fingers. He slowly moved the stone to his palm. He made a toothy wince as the gem touched his skin, retreating it almost instantly. "You are sure this was on the body of a bandit?" Lori asked nervously.

"Yes, Sir Arter said so."

The Centaur raised his quivering fist to his stubbled chin, rocking in his bed as his sweat coalesced with his black curls. The look of a terrified boy was in his eyes. He shook his head. "Get me a saw."

"A saw?"

"Yes, a saw, a knife, a sword, anything." Feliks was apprehensive. Lori blinked sporadically. "To the Whare. Go to the Whare!"

The bastard stood slowly. *Has he gone crazy?* "What do y-"

"This is citrine! I've been poisoned!"

Feliks's eyes widened as he saw into his father's realisation, stumbling into a sprint out of the room. *No, no, no, not you too.* Pushing past the guards, Feliks flew down the staircase in seconds. *Bloody Scorpions.* His heart pounded a million times a second. It would give out if he lost his father too. He almost slammed into the wall at the bottom, pushing himself away and bulldozing through the door of the loch keep. Cold auburn air hit Feliks's face as he ran. Waking citizens watched as the boy rushed through the city, almost gliding face-first into some. He saw the Whare at the end of the street: a small hut that seemed isolated from the Lagoon. *He's going to be a cripple,* he realised, *Lori the unhorsed will be a joke.* He continued to evade pedestrians with powerful dodges, slowly draining his breath. *Forget that, Feliks, you're being an idiot. Just get the saw and save him.* When he made it to the Whare, he flung the door open. Alchemist Cuthbert rose from his seat, lowering his eyeglass.

"Excuse me," Feliks apologised, before dashing through to the back room, making sure not to knock the countless vials and vessels that laced the shelves. The rear room was a cluttered mess, packed to the door with tools and materials. He didn't know where to start, so he leapt in, pots and metal crashing as if he were on a battlefield.

"Can I help you, my lord?" Cuthbert asked from the door.

"A saw, I need a saw!" Feliks barked. A sickness caught up with him.

Cuthbert seemed perplexed, yet he still wanted to help. The alchemist's pensive walk irked Feliks, making him grow impatient. Feliks saw the blade looming out from beneath a pile of scrap, grabbing it before Cuthbert had a chance to bend over. "Thank you," he said, running out to the street.

This time, instead of needing to evade the people, the people evaded him, almost instantly leaping out the way when they caught a glimpse of the fang-like blade. Feliks worried if it was sharp enough for a clean cut, let alone if the amputation would deterge the poison. He could only hope.

"Good, come here," Lori anxiously said as Feliks breathlessly entered the room. The lord pointed at a part of his leg almost reaching his thigh, hands trembling more so than before.

"That high?" Feliks asked in shock.

Lori shook his head nervously. "There's no telling how far it's spread."

Feliks nodded obediently, resting the saw's teeth on his father's thigh. He knew he had to saw, but couldn't bring himself to do it. "How do you know you were poisoned?" he asked anxiously. "What if they were raiders, not assassins. Maybe this one stole the citrine."

"Just do it, Feliks!" Lori snapped, taking a moment to calm himself. "What have I got to lose if I'm right?"

"A leg, maybe?" Feliks grimaced, worry still coating his face.

"Would you prefer my life?" Lori shook his head, lowering his jaw on a cloth, clamping it with his teeth. "Do it quickly," he murmured.

He seemed like he wouldn't change his mind, and Feliks would rather a legless father than a dead one. Feliks apprehensively went along with his father's unhinged plan, tightening his grip on the saw, holding Lori's leg in place. *Why do I have to do it?* Feliks thought, desperately trying to temporise. "Can I not get Cuthbert to do it? He's done amputations in the past. He'd make a cleaner cut."

"Feliks!"

"Fine! Fine!" He took a gulp of air as he moved the blade. Lori let out a grunt of pain as the saw's fangs dug into his leg, dark blood beginning to leak and squirt.

"What by gods are you doing?!" Cuthbert exclaimed as he burst into the room.

The bastard was almost relieved, snatching a brown rag to absorb the red liquid that drizzled down his father's leg. Cuthbert seized the saw, tossing it to the ground.

"Gods! Cut it off Feliks," Lori squalled in agony.

"What? Nonsense! I said it will heal!" the alchemist insisted.

"It won't get better!" Feliks contended, trying to keep his hand still as he held up the orange jewel. "This is citrine, right?"

Cuthbert's glower transformed to a sceptical frown, his old eyes examining the gemstone, his pupils dilating with knowledge. "You think he was poisoned?" he asked, making Feliks do a brisk, yet unsure nod. It was common belief that citrine had some sort of link with certain poisons, since citrine was the stone of the Scorpio, but the topic wasn't Feliks's strongest. "Come, Feliks," Cuthbert ordered, leading him out.

"What? No! Come back!" Lori shouted as Feliks followed the alchemist down the stairs.

"Do you have something?"

"I'll show you," Cuthbert assured. The lines of people in the street had multiplied in number, Feliks trying and failing to cover his blood-stained clothes. "I do admit, my time in the Archipelago has been limited, but I did spend a great deal of that time studying their poisons," said Cuthbert upon entering the Whare. "I am embarrassed that it hasn't taken sooner for me to realise." He carefully scrambled through his vials, twisting them to read their obscure labels of letters and numbers.

"So, you know the poison that was used on my father?" Feliks repeated.

"Judging by the symptoms, I believe the effects point towards a venom named the 'kiss of the vectem'. Most alchemists are killed before they get the chance to examine it, for even the most prudent of those succumb to the toxin. I wouldn't blame your lord father for acting so hastily."

"How? Is it contagious?" Feliks asked, shuddering.

"Not contagious, my boy," Cuthbert laughed. "They say it can enter through the skin itself. All that is required is a mere drop of the poison to be lethal. But I was lucky," Cuthbert said as he squinted to read his sprawled letters. "Ah!" The alchemist gently extracted a green potion from his shelf, enthusiastically lifting it to Feliks as if he'd know what it was.

"Is that a cure?" Feliks asked eagerly.

A mad grin washed over the alchemist's face. "We'll find out soon enough."

ESMOND VI
-Kid-

It was late. Esmond Centaur could barely walk straight, crust beginning to form in his eyes. His candles were lit in his bedroom at the blue spire, despite it being at such a late hour. Semira was still awake, reading.

"The king shows his face," she remarked. "I'm beginning to think you're forgetting about me."

"Never," the king smirked. "Actually…" He reached into his blue cloak, revealing a withered purple petunia.

"For me?" Semira chuckled lightly.

"Well, it was in a better state when I picked it at the wall."

"I didn't want a living flower anyway," she jested, taking the petunia and slipping it into her bedside vase.

Esmond sniggered at his own heed. "I'm sorry."

"It's ok, just come to bed."

The king nodded tiredly, slipping out of his clothes. He placed his blue and gold crown on a hook embedded in the wall like the thousand nights before, and collapsed next to Semira. It was the first time in a while he had felt the luxury that was his bed, often falling asleep at his desk, tending to the overwhelming amount of complaints regarding food and crime. Today, however, was different.

"There was a raid on Centaur's Lagoon," he said, "a few days ago."

"My gods," Semira gasped, closing her book slowly.

"Lori didn't trust the word with a raven, that's why I didn't know until now."

"He was attacked! Why wouldn't he want you to know immediately?"

"That's Lori for you. My king's guard arrived this afternoon."

Semira was at a loss for words. "Was anyone hurt?"

Esmond sighed. "My brother: an arrow through the thigh, Sir Devon: an arrow through the shoulder, and Vesta..."

The queen took the silence as she dreaded. She clasped her golden pendant, rotating it nervously. "Such a sweet girl," she muttered. "Sometimes the world is so cruel."

Esmond hadn't told his daughters yet, he daren't. Vesta was as close to them as any who had the pleasure of meeting her. Even at the young age of ten, she was always so polite. One time, she and Eva had snuck out of the castle during a feast, playing in the nighttime woods. When they were caught by Sir Devon, Vesta stepped forward admitting it was her idea, even though Esmond knew Eva was guilty as error. Despite the punishments, despite the shame it might have caused, she still took the blade for Eva.

"What will you do?" the queen asked.

"What?"

"Your brother has been attacked and his daughter murdered. You need to do something."

"*I* need to do something?!" the king snapped. "Do what, exactly? In case you hadn't noticed, Semira, I've been awake day and night trying to figure out why this is all happening. My best friend was taken from me not even a moon ago, and I still don't even know who took him. Everyone I know are dropping like flies and you don't think that it haunts me every second? Daryl Venulaes, Reynold Lyrderyn, Sigmund Horncurve-"

"Sigmund was different-"

"Was it? He was still taken!" Esmond ran his fingers through his ever-growing hair.

"I'm sorry... I..."

"No, Semira," Esmond winced, "I'm sorry."

Semira rested her hand on her husband's. "There isn't a soul alive who didn't love Reynold. I'm willing to bet the entire country would rise up to avenge his murder," she claimed. "And you're the king. If you wanted to change it so people are punished for what they bloody wear, then you are free to do so."

Esmond bit his tongue behind his shallow smirk. "Where should I start then?"

"That bandit from the Lyrderyn ambush said the rest of them were in Lunarpass. If you want to get anywhere, you'd have to start there."

"Stroll straight into their den? That's probably what they want. Surely it's better to starve the wolves than feed them."

"By not doing anything, you're feeding them anyway. You just said yourself that everyone is dropping like flies. Who's next? Oberon? Lori? Goldwyn? ...Asher? And it's *your* capital for goodness sake. If you're saying it's their den, you've already lost."

"You're right. The longer I sit here, the bigger the target on everyone else," he sighed. "I almost didn't let the Lyrderyns go, let alone Asher." *But that was for a different reason. I'm sorry Reynold, if you're still watching.*

It was a while since the king had seen Oberon Trident last. Come to think of it, it was during a food crisis like now. There's not a man in Austellus who doesn't know the Lord Ruler of Aquamare's name, some saying he is the greatest fisherman ever to have lived. Some even say he could bend water, whatever skills he has proving vital for the survival of many of the people in the Auburn Pole not even twenty years ago. *Though, that food crisis wasn't as bad as this one. It was barely an inconvenience compared to this one.* The thought made him titter. *I may need to visit Oberon again.*

Semira's eyes searched him, reading his face. "It wasn't your fault."

"What wasn't?"

"Sigmund's death. You didn't kill him, not truly."

"May as well have. Like you said, I'm the king." He fiddled with his nails, snapping them as he flicked.

"He was a good man. A great man. Whatever cracked inside him that day, wasn't Sigmund at all. He'd never *intend* to kill anyone who wasn't holding a knife to his throat."

Of course he wouldn't intend to kill him, Esmond felt like saying. There must be something more to this. *Maybe I didn't know Sigmund at all? It was like him to snap so easily, though.* He exhaled. "That's the saddest part of this world: we get punished for our actions, not intentions."

Semira mimicked the king's sigh, turning to lie on her back next to the king. "But could you imagine a world without law?"

"Imagine or prefer?" he smirked. "Do you remember when we met?"

The queen thought back, a smile leading her face. "You had just been coronated at Lunarpass."

"I was fifteen, and you fourteen. The first thing I said to you was-"

"Let's not wait, waiting is boring," she giggled. "We ran away, right here."

"Yep. We were lost long enough for my councillors to give up and come to Fort Deus instead of waiting at the capital. I said I would never budge from here; do you know why?"

"Why?" The queen smiled curiously.

"Because hiding away with you, at the edge of the world where no one could find us, breaking all laws out of boredom... was the happiest I have ever been," he said, his grin fading. "I wanted to hold on to the feeling of being lost until I was dead. The feeling of not following the laws of kings. The feeling of doing it *my* way."

Semira crawled up to Esmond's chest. "I prefer your way," she smirked, gently kissing him. For a brief moment, Esmond was taken back twenty-five years. *If there was any one moment to be frozen in*, he thought, *I would choose this one*. What would the realm have been like if Elder Marcarius didn't have the bright idea to seek them at Fort Deus? Surely it would be in shambles: the recently crowned king and his betrothed becoming lost to the world. It humoured if it didn't sadden him - the thought of society coming to a halt because of one runaway boy.

As they broke away, the king felt his current self sliding back into him. "I can't be a kid anymore... it's time to be a king."

"Meaning?" Semira looked up, her crystal blue eyes flickering.

"I'll go," he said. "I'll go to Lunarpass."

EVA II
-Owl-

No, you can't go! Not without me!" she cried, clutching her father's waist. Tears streamed down her cheeks like a leaky bucket.

"I must go, Eva," Esmond replied sadly. "Your mother will still be here, Fletcher will look after you."

"I need to go with you! If we stay here, we'll die!"

"You won't. I need to go alone, Eva. It's too dangerous out there."

It was infuriating beyond sense that her father didn't believe her about Galloway. Eva Centaur had seen it with her own eyes and still, no one trusted her. She bolted out of her father's office, almost tripping on the few steps that followed out into the throne room. She pushed past the guards without a care, streaming down the hallways like water in a river. As she arrived at her and Leta's shared chambers, she slammed the door, rushing for her bed.

She and Leta had spied on Galloway the entire week, and despite their persistence, all they were rewarded with was hours of wasted time watching the old lord be as mute and prosaic as he always had been. The girls were completely fruitless, and it left Eva feeling like an idiot. Although Leta said she believed her, Eva had her doubts. She even doubted herself. It didn't matter now, anyway. Esmond was going to follow Asher to safety come nightfall, whilst the rest of the Centaurs wait for a slaughter at their own home... *He's leaving come nightfall*, she thought again, halting her tears.

She had an idea.

Without hesitation, Eva tore a large portion of cloth off her bedding, laying it flat on the cobblestone floor. Her eyes scanned the room, looking for the essentials. *I need clothes,* she thought as her half-opened drawer came into view, *everyone needs clothes.*

Eva liked dressing up, despite what everyone else thought. She had a mound of fur coats and tunics and leggings; it all made choosing whether to take something or not harder than it needed to be. *Those* clothes were fine; it was the gowns and dresses most ladies would swoon at that Eva loathed. Any she would receive from birth moons and such, she would give to her sister, although Leta also preferred a tunic to a garb. Leta would wear anything, though, and Eva always kicked up too much of a fuss for either of her parents to bother.

Before long, she had all the clothes she'd need, tightly bundled in a little sack. She sat on the floor, pondering what else she'd need when she barely heard the furtive footsteps that only her sister could do. At first, she froze, but soon leapt to her bed and forced herself to cry again.

"Eva," Leta knocked from the other side, inviting herself in. She held her arms out, allowing Eva to fall into them. "Shh, don't cry."

Eva looked up with her helpless blue eyes. "Do you still believe me?"

Her sister glanced around. "Close the door," she muttered, moving towards her bed.

Eva nodded, not knowing how to feel about the unanswered question. She peered left and right in the hallway before silently closing the door. Her sister sat on the bed, pulling an agitated expression as she examined the scroll she held. Eva slipped next to her, intrigued by what it was. "Is it a letter?" she asked.

Leta cleared her throat. "My dear friend," she read, "I hope everything is well. It has come to my attention that a decision is required for the coalition to continue. As of yet, it appears the plan has been running smoothly, though I fear a hollow has appeared in the road. It grieves me to report that King Esmond has made plans to travel and resolve to Lunarpass, and thus, will see to our inability to coordinate further. However, in doing so, the role you have given me can still be resumed without backfire or collapse. Best wishes in your endeavour, Galloway Malone, head of war." She passed the note to Eva. "Shot the raven down a few minutes ago. I think it was on course for the Taiga Isles."

Eva speechlessly stood, following the words on the page again. "He'll finally believe us," she grinned, taking the note.

"No," Leta contested, thwarting her sister's march to the door.

"What do you mean? We finally have evidence. He'll believe us-"

"No," she repeated, snatching back the scroll. "If we give this to father, all we're proving is that I was shooting down Galloway's letters, some of which are important, just for the sake of finding one out of the ordinary. Besides, the note is only showing that they're *working* together. They could be working on *anything*. We can figure this out together, then tell him."

Or they could be working together to murder us. "How are we supposed to figure it out? Galloway is going with father. You can't shoot down any more birds."

"Like I said, this note was flying to the Taiga Isles... That would be a good place to start." She slotted the note back into her girdle. "Look, I just wanted to show you, because now I *do* believe you." Leta left the room as quietly as she came in, silent enough to let even bugs sleep.

The man Eva had seen with Galloway, he must be from the Taiga Isles. It was regrettably one of the few places in Austellus Eva knew little about, despite the islands being so close. *Maybe Elder Marcarius knows about them*, but he was going with Esmond as well. Not much seemed to be known about those taciturn isles. They were one of the many lands formed via *The Great Pause*, breaking off from the Auburn Pole it had been tethered to. Even the people there were a mystery, outsiders believing there to be a fully thriving, independent kingdom while others assuming they were inhabited by savages like those in the Red Sierra. Eva hoped she'd know soon, for her family's sake.

The longer the day dragged on, the more restive Eva became. And worse, the more restive she became, the slower time moved. She was torn between staying and going. If she stayed, her mother *might* let her and Leta explore the islands, and figure out what Galloway was up to. If she escaped, she *would* be safe from what she knew she heard. She might even find out what Galloway was up to anyway, in turn protecting her father from him. *But Fletcher and mother and Hew are staying. They're just as much in danger. They need to come too, but how the hell do I convince them? Mother and Fletcher don't believe me, Hew thinks I'm crazy... If I told them, they'd just stop me, and if they stop me, father dies too.*

Her final evening meal with her family was greeted with nothing but silence, that being the case by all of her siblings. It was harsh how empty the dinner table felt without Asher. She dreaded to think what it would be like without her father as well, who made her feel a prang of guilt every time he'd glance at her, or attempt to quell her moodiness with jests. He must have said goodbye to everyone properly excluding Eva. *It doesn't matter though*, she knew. Her father wasn't going to leave her yet.

The sky was indigo, the castle prepared for sleep, and Eva was wide awake, on her side whilst her sister slept. *Now is a good time. I've waited long enough,* she thought. She slithered out of her bed, reaching underneath for her prerequisite gear, all folded into a bulky sack. After flinging her exalted satchel over her shoulder, she crept over to Leta's bed.

"Leta," she softly whispered, touching her arm.

Her sister heavily opened her eyes. "Eva, what are you doing?" she asked, her voice thick with disbelief.

"Leaving," she blurted.

"What about Galloway? We have a thread now. We might know what he's doing if we go to the isles."

"Galloway's going with father. Please come with me, Leta."

Leta knocked her gaze away, contemplating. She looked how she did when she meditated: a look Eva wished she could pull off when she thought. It made her look ten years older. "No," she turned. "I want to stay here... I have to stay here. If there's people coming for us, I want to be by our family for when they do."

Eva's confidence fell to guilt. She looked to her feet. "You all might die if you stay."

"Next to no one has died within these walls for almost a century. If you're right you can laugh over my grave." There was a sharp sting in her voice.

All Eva could do was nod softly. "Ok," she muttered, turning to begin her shameful plod towards the door. The sack she carried seemed heavier as her adrenaline leaked out of her.

"Eva," her sister called out. Eva turned to see Leta elegantly jogging over on the tips of her toes. Dropping her satchel, Eva wrapped her arms around Leta as tears took their form. "You're an idiot," Leta chuckled.

"I know," she smirked through her sorrow, burying her face in Leta's soft bedclothes. The embrace was long. Long enough for Eva's confidence about her decision to plummet further.

"Go on, then," Leta mumbled as she pulled away. "They'll leave soon."

She was right. Outside the window set a soft sun, the steady hoot of tawny owls beginning to sound to greet the moon. It would be too late soon. Eva nodded, throwing her satchel over her shoulder once again as she broke into her silent sprint. She looked back to Leta as she got to the door. All she did was smile behind her avoiding eyes.

The shadows were her friend as she ran down the hallways, the rising lunar lights unable to spot her. She looked down to the higher bailey from a window, the guards half asleep as carts full of luggage littered the courtyard. None of the lords who were travelling seemed to be present yet. This was the perfect chance.

The air was freezing, and the ground slightly moist still from the freak snowfall a few days ago. Eva was glad she packed blankets. She spotted the king's carriage from a mile away, noticing the blue zircon wedding ring calling like a beacon. *Why isn't he wearing it? He never takes the thing off.* She was pulled towards it, sticking to the dark cobblestone walls like resin. She got close enough to the cart to jump in, yet it was guarded by two plump guards. If she somehow managed to sneak past, she would be heard instantly by the creaking wood the luggage lay on.

There was a closer cart. A smaller one. It had a cloak covering it, with different shapes bulging out over the top. Eva peeled the sheet from the cart, managing to slip in and conceal herself. She shivered as she stared into the stained white cloth for a while, until finally sleep took her as the train moved into a steady trot.

ATHENA I
-Retail-

Unpleasant would be the best way to describe their journey so far. With barely any rest due to the noisy and slurred songs sung well into the early hours of the morning, days were dragged out and tiring, not only for Athena Horncurve, but for everyone. She was past the point of grieving, now exhausted with the feeling of languor. No one smiled or joked anymore. Conversations were full of lassitude, void of any sort of enthusiasm.

Well actually, thinking about it, Athena believed she may have made Cadmus crack this morning. It was while they broke fast: she took too big a bite out of a giant redcurrant, spattering juice all over her grey clothes. As everyone else groaned at the wasted food, Cadmus sniggered from the back, shaking his head. It was an improvement, at least.

The sight of civilisation was also very welcome. The last time the party had seen any sort of life was at the large settlement of Litore: an outpost town on the very edge of the Canicule, and a prime destination to stock up on supplies before tackling the vast desert.

Athena was amazed at how different each part of the world was. Only a week's ride away from the humid heats of Litore sat the icy Auburn Pole, Lunarpass seeming to be the paste that stuck the climates together as they met. As the sand grains underfoot gradually lessened in number, more and more could Athena feel the northern spell of home.

Along the rocky coast where they rode, the trading behemoth known as Merchant's Bay came into view. The sound of people almost took the party by surprise, everyone being so used to the soft crunch of sand and the gentle howl of wind for the past few days. The metropolis was alive with salesmen advertising their wares. *"One copper a crab! One copper a crab!"* the loudest merchant boomed over the noise. *"Ginger and cinnamon! Fresh in from Heavia!"* another yelled. *"Thoroughbred stallions to the highest bidder!"* announced another to a gathering crowd. *Is there anything this city doesn't have?* Athena thought as she smiled.

When they were travelling south, Merchant's Bay wasn't half as busy as it was now, perhaps because their stay was greeted with a murky downpour of rain. Now, as the party admired the commerce thriving, a mellow, bright sun fell on the bay, albeit a late sun, slowly setting after the long day. However warm, it wasn't uncomfortably so; the stifling heats were cooled by the zephyr carried from the Waveless Sea. If Athena should ever sweat, the breeze would wipe it from her head.

Riding through the many stalls and past the docks, the party found themselves approaching the tents and seaside inns as the beach's sand made its way onto their horse's hooves. The tumult of trade was almost drowned by the swinging tide, rocking back and forth in its majestic form. The Horncurves entered the same inn they had stayed in before: a homely wooden cabin, its plank floors peppered with the beach's sand.

"My Lord of Horncurve," the receptionist recognised immediately as they entered the cabin. It was hard not to recognise the red locks of a Horncurve. "Would you like to reserve the same rooms?"

"Aye," Riley grinned rigidly, glancing around his family. Only his kin stood inside, the rest of the ram's guard waiting by the entrance, clearly eager to begin carousing.

"Fabulous," the receptionist smiled as he lay down the rounded keychain on the desk. "I trust you know the way by now?"

Riley nodded, gesturing to his family to get a move on.

After heading out to collect their luggage, the Horncurves took to their rooms. Athena felt bad taking the single bedroom for herself as she always did; her brothers always had to share, and she knew they would butt heads from time to time, even if they didn't mean it. *I guess they'll have nothing to talk about, anyway,* she sulked, preparing for the sound of silence.

Knock, knock, someone tapped on her chamber's door. Lady Emily invited herself in, curiously excited. "Are ye settled?"

"Yeah," Athena replied dryly from her bed.

"Good," Emily smiled, "come with me."

Athena obeyed, following her mother down the wooden hallway towards the twin's room. "Boys!" she called as she knocked.

Marcus was the one who opened the door, looking as tired as ever. Cadmus was lying on his bed, knees up as he stared to the ceiling.

Athena and Marcus edged towards their mother as she strolled into the centre of the room, shutting the door behind her. She pulled out a pouch, and untied it. "Come on, Cadmus," she called before he lifted his head, wondering what this was about. The Horncurves traded addled glances at each other.

Before she unknotted the last string, she held the pouch close to her chest. "Now, I understand... that this has been a hard time for everyone. So tonight, ye can all have a treat."

She tugged gently on the last string, revealing numerous silver coins piled in the pouch. "Take two silvers each, and get anything ye want from the market."

The room brightened with excitement, the Horncurves diving in to grab their share.

"Thanks, ma," Athena smiled as she took her five before running out with the boys.

"Be back before midnight!" she yelled before the thundering of footsteps in the corridor ceased.

Cadmus nudged his twin playfully as they ran on the sand, huge grins covering their faces. Athena couldn't keep up with their charge, yet was happy that they smiled nonetheless.

"Athena!" Cadmus waved to her as they came before the markets. She ran up to her brothers, panting lightly. "Alreet," he smiled, "let's all meet back here in an hour and show each other what we've got." Everyone agreed in their huddle, nodding and rushing off in different directions.

The market was a mess, in a good way. There was no organisation to the stalls, everything from food, to jewellery, and weapons being scattered all around the bay, sometimes all next to each other. Athena was excited to spend her small stash, each silver coin being the equivalent of twenty-five coppers. There was almost too much choice.

Sure enough, the hour passed like it was a minute, and the sun wanted to duck behind the horizon. With her left over one silver and twelve coppers, Athena made her way to the spot Cadmus said they'd meet. Cadmus was sitting on the dock, his legs dangling into the tepid water.

"Where's Marcus?" she asked as she strolled over, hauling her sack of goods over her shoulder.

Cadmus had the cheeks of a chipmunk, white powder veiling his mouth as he chewed. "I don't know," he replied, sending dust fleeting from his mouth. "Want one?"

He held a long, red, powdered thing in his hand, unlike anything Athena had ever seen. "What is it?" Athena smirked as she edged closer.

"Go on, try it!" Cadmus insisted, planting it in Athena's palm as she took a seat next to him on the dock.

Fear wasn't a thought that ran through Athena's head as she took a huge bite into the soft goo. Luckily for her, it wasn't the taste she should have been fearful of. The world around her morphed like it was jelly, breathing with patterns and distortions. Colours seemed brighter, her senses heightened intensely, all the while overcome by a powerful feeling of weightlessness, and levity.

She couldn't have said how long it lasted. The sun hadn't moved much, though. She stared blankly into the setting sea. "Woah."

"I know," grinned Cadmus as he excitedly edged towards his sister, clapping his hands together.

Athena struggled to regain her bearings, half of her body still part of the clouds. "We... we need to tell Marcus about this," she said, letting a smile lead her face.

"Aye, let's go find him," Cadmus smiled as he raised his sister by his hand, entering the market once again.

Athena could barely react to the countless obstacles Cadmus almost ran her into. Everything seemed to move a thousand times faster. She was too much in shock from what just altered her reality, yet there was still a feeling that wasn't her own. She felt lighter on her feet. She had never felt more inspired to create. "Where did you get that?" she asked her brother when she decided to rejoin the living.

"Sis, I got it from the ocean, where did you think I got it?"

"How much did they cost? I have some left-over nicks," she fired back, Cadmus's lordly comment flying past her head.

"Really? He stopped in his tracks. "It might be enough, aye." Cadmus glanced around to gather his bearings.

"Do you remember where it is?" She giggled at his gormless face. "It was on the very edge of the market, I kinda just wandered there, though," he admitted, finally choosing a direction.

After a while of searching, Cadmus led her to a barren corner of the market, stalls scattered far from a lone tent, as if they were afraid. Athena's face twisted at the lack of life. "How did ye *wander* here? This would be the place I'd go to murder someone a chuck 'em in the sea."

A smirk swept Cadmus's face. "The most disparate places are always the most interesting, sister. They're always worth explorin'." They stopped in front of the tent. Cadmus stared at it. It was dark green and black, tattered, shredded cloths falling down the sides. The nails that kept it standing looked rusted and used, while the dirt it was pinned in slushy and muddy, unlike anywhere else in Merchant's Bay. It was as if the gentle breeze kept the entrance flap closed, the red rag sucking inward tightly.

"Are we gonna go in?" Athena asked as her impatience grew uncomfortable.

He continued to analyse the tent in a confused guise. "Last time I didn't go in the tent. He had a stall set up."

"Oh... maybe he's gone?"

Cadmus winced. "I don't know."

"Well just try anyway. He's clearly not gone."

Cadmus nodded uneasily. He peeled back the entrance of the tent, unveiling two figures, a dagger to separate them. The figure receiving it span around like a compass. "Cadmus!" Marcus spat in surprise. "What are ye doing?!"

Without time to breathe, the figure snatched Marcus, holding the flashy blade to his throat.

"Hey!" Athena yelped, barely processing.

Cadmus dove towards his brother, walloping the black-hooded figure with his closed fist so hard, it would have easily defaced the recipient, if he even had a face. He tumbled to the floor, as did the dagger and Marcus. The figure found his footing immediately to exit out the back of the tent. Athena and Cadmus gathered what breath they could to chase after him, leaving in the manner the man did.

The outside was cooler and quieter than before, an added chill from the fact that the man had vanished. Marcus carefully followed them out, equally as bemused.

"What the..." Cadmus uttered as he scanned the horizon.

Athena's stomach sank. "Guys..." she swallowed, leading their attention to the black robe that sat atop the sea.

ASHER III
-Pass-

The dream he had was recurring, almost vivid. The only time he could get a night's rest was when he was too tired to ride further. Luckily for them, the Lunar Path was forgiving. Days were long and productive, and nights were short and refreshing, for most. A frequent number of nights were shared with Princess Lyssa, who would sneak into Asher's tent and warm his bed until dawn. They couldn't tell if they were ever spotted by the early scouts, but Asher Centaur didn't care. It was the only shred of happiness he could muster from the night time, and he swore to her that he'd get violent with anyone who tried to compromise that.

That's why Lunarpass was such a welcome place, the city that never slept to keep Asher company as he brooded. He sat with his newly acquired company atop a marble balcony belonging to the Sphaera, sweat still cold from the dream that haunted him. The air wasn't uncomfortable though, it was as if the gods themselves tailored the winds to be at a perfect temperature.

"It's a beautiful sight, isn't it?"

The voice took Asher by surprise. He whipped his head round to be met with Lyssa, walking slowly in a gorgeous silk red and gold dress. "You just gave me a better one," he said, admiring her person.

She smiled down at her feet, her dimpled cheeks sending Asher off the planet. She perched herself on a seat next to him, helping herself to a flagon of wine that Asher had a half empty glass of. "Couldn't sleep again?"

Asher sighed, returning his eyes to the lights of the city. "It's bad, Lyssa. I can't remember the last time I got a full night's sleep."

"It helps if you close your eyes," she smirked piquantly.

Asher grabbed the nearest pillow to throw at her. "I'll close *your* eyes in a minute."

She giggled. "I'd like to see that."

He returned his passive stare to the city. "It's always the same; the same dream. I'm walking down a cliff face, like no cliff face I've ever seen before. There are light blue and green vines all over the rocks. And there's a mist, always a thick mist. So, I head down, it's the only place to go, and I make it to this... this..." he paused to think. "I don't know how to describe it."

"Try," Lyssa asked, placing her hand on his knee.

The place was difficult to imagine, even though he had seen it not more than an hour ago. "Okay, well... the floor's a big round stone with marks on it, and there's water sat in between the markings, but it's not wet, in fact, it's completely still. I can never make it past half way, there's always this wind that blows me back before it happens. It's when this man starts saying weird shit to me."

"Well, what does he say?"

"He tells me to find the Prince of Ash; the King of Light, the Serpent of Stars."

Lyssa raised her eyebrows. "All three?"

He rolled his eyes under his smirk. "He always says something about a serpent. The Serpent of Stars. And that I must find it. To poison it? I don't know, it starts to get hazy there."

"Hazy?"

"Yeah, there's too much noise to hear what he says. That's normally when the wind sends me flying back and my throat gets cut open by another one. That's when I wake up..."

Lyssa was taken aback again. She twirled her golden locks with her finger. "Have you tried doing anything?" she asked as the thought waned.

Asher shook his head. "The wind is too strong; you can't do anything but flail your arms around."

"I don't mean that. I mean the whole dying thing. Why don't you just slap this man to the afterlife?"

"He's got a knife, Lyssa," he laughed.

"And you've got infinite attempts if this dream keeps coming back."

She had a point. "Okay," he resigned, "next time I'll beat him up for you. Might be I'll take his head off too."

Lyssa smiled as she placed her empty wine glass on the marble table. "Or, you might need a girl to do it for you." She ambled over to him with a smirk on her face. "It would be embarrassing if *Prince Asher Centaur* can't kill an imaginary man."

Asher couldn't decrypt what her eyes told. "I've told you this because I trust you, if you tell an-"

Her index finger trapped Asher's words on his lips. She placed herself on his lap. "You can tell me anything." A kiss was planted on his cheek. "But if we die of sleep deprivation then you'll never get to," she smiled, taking his hand.

Asher chuckled. "I yield."

"Good," Lyssa whispered as she and Asher leant in for a kiss.

From then on, the night was smooth. The dream didn't care to visit again, and Asher woke peacefully to the sound of the Lunar Bells, sounding the start of the day. For such a loud noise, they were oddly calming, as if granting a certain safety.

<hr />

Asher looked to the other side of his king-sized bed, expecting to see a dent where Lyssa had slept, yet she was still there, fast asleep like the cub she was. He gently touched her arm. "Lyssa... wake up..." he whispered.

Her tired eyes adjusted to the daylight pouring into the room. She shot up like an arrow, covering her nude body with the royal bed sheets. "Crap, I fell asleep."

It was more amusing to Asher than it was stressful.

"Asher, help!" she yelled, not shaking off the embarrassed smile from her face.

"Okay, okay," he laughed, taking his time fetching her clothes that were passionately spread across the floor.

The door burst open. In his panic, Asher threw what clothes he carried under the bed whilst Lyssa vanished under the covers.

"Can you believe my cent's guard?! *Twenty-five* of the city's garrison watched you and the Lyrderyns stroll into this city and not *one* bothered to tell me! If I were any less than a Centaur, I'd have them all thrown into the dungeons!"

"Thaddeus! It's good to see you!" Asher smiled. *Have you ever heard of bloody knocking?*

"Likewise, nephew," Thaddeus echoed, embracing Asher tightly. "How was your trip? I hope the Lyrderyns are a lot less barbaric than knights here."

"They've been great to me." Asher thought he was doing a pretty good job at masking his panic. *Please just get out.*

"I expect nothing less from lions," he said. "I got word from your father this morning, you know. He's leaving the nest. Should be here by the moon's end."

"Really? Why?" the prince asked, discreetly pushing some clothes under the bed that were sticking out.

"Realm matters, I'm guessing," Thaddeus sighed. "You know, food, the passing of some lords, tensions in the Archipelago. He says 'the wounds of war are healing', whatever that means."

"Interesting," he said. "You'll get kicked off the throne."

Thaddeus gave a hearty laugh. "I plan to put up a fight first."

Asher nodded. "My coin is on you."

"Why?" he smiled curiously. "Has my cousin gotten fat?"

"No," Asher replied. "But your barbaric knights might have toughened you up a bit."

"That they have." Thaddeus performed another laugh as he inspected the room. He edged dangerously close to Lyssa. "Well, for however-"

"Wait!" Asher dashed in front of him. "Sorry... I... the bed isn't..."

Thaddeus frowned, even more curious to see what Asher was hiding. "What's wrong, comrade?"

Asher closed his eyes as he sighed. *What have I done?* "Please don't tell anyone," he muttered. Thaddeus's jester eyes faded, becoming serious. All Asher could do now was step to the side and hope he wouldn't go crazy. He closed his eyes again.

He opened them to see a wide grin painted on Thaddeus's face. He reached behind Asher, prying Lyssa's black knickers that lay on the bed. "Nothing to be ashamed of," he beamed, dangling them before Asher's face. "You're a man now, boy! Well before I leave you two alone, just know that you can ask if you want anything."

Asher could barely get words past his thumping heart. "Will do-"

"Except the throne, I'm beginning to quite like it," he smugly added on his way out, carelessly closing the door behind him.

Asher picked the pants from his face. Lyssa couldn't stop giggling as she resurfaced on the bed. "Do my knickers smell nice?"

"Get out," Asher leered playfully.

He couldn't help but see the funnier side to it, despite just being embarrassed in front of his infatuation. Nevertheless, Asher was slower to get ready than normal, fairly over action for the rest of the day.

Breakfast was the best he had had since Fort Deus, the flavours of the food holding that distinct touch of home. Thaddeus had told him that the persimmons were fresh in from Deuswater, ordered especially for their visit. It was so thoughtful of him, increasingly so to go out of his way for them. It must have made them taste better.

Beyond that, the entire party had a day to kill, to relax, as the closest settlement of Litore stood leagues away from Lunarpass.

The plaza was alive and booming as it always had been, not a single frown in sight. Asher and Lyssa had managed to get away from their guard, becoming part of the horde of citizens that roamed the streets. He doubted the lion's guard cared that much; there hadn't been any sort of crime committed successfully in this city for almost fifteen years, and those almost achieving so struck down before they could carry out the act. *The city must have come a long way for that to be the case*, Asher thought. Either that, or Thaddeus was just that brilliant of a ruler. Regardless of what was done, it was clear that Lunarpass had surpassed a fellowship when it came to its residents.

"It hasn't changed one bit since the last time I was here," Asher commented.

"Nor for me," Lyssa teased.

"I think five years is a slightly longer gap than a moon," he chuckled.

"I wouldn't know, you're the math expert," she smiled, clutching his arm tighter.

Almost on cue, Asher could only squint at the sight of a familiar figure at the back of the crowds. It was the same one from Fort Deus, he was sure of it. The one that wasn't smiling. He felt a tingle down his spine.

"What's wrong?" Lyssa asked.

"Hang on," Asher let go of her, eyes fixed on where the figure stood.

"Wait, where are you going?"

He didn't notice Lyssa struggling to keep up as he effortlessly walked through the crowds. It was like they opened as he walked, making a clear path. The figure moved slowly, but it felt like he was still going faster than Asher's power walk.

It took a time for them to catch up with the figure, but they did so eventually, leading them to a shaded, yet noisy alley way. Asher felt like they were the most obviously suspicious people in the city, yet no one batted an eyelid, as if they were shielded from sight.

The figure took a low bow as they caught up. "Asher Centaur," he whispered, "your presence was seen."

Lyssa held onto Asher's arm as soon as she could, ready to pull him back as the fear piled on for them both. "Who are you?" he asked.

"My name is Seer Junius, yet I am merely a servant of the realm, and the Prince of Ash has a cosmic role to play."

Asher clocked where he had heard that name before. "You know about my dream?"

"Know? Junius only sees. Your dream is not a dream, Asher Centaur, but part of your journey."

"My journey?" *It better be my journey with Lyssa.*

"Come the day you arrive at Merchant's Bay, an associate will offer a boat excursion. You will accept, and so will be of sense."

"A boat where?"

"Any more words will put you and your loved into danger," he bowed as he did before. "This is not farewell, Asher Centaur." Junius prowled deeper into the unlit alley.

"Wait!" Asher called. He and Lyssa tried to chase him, but as they turned the corner, Junius was gone.

"That... wasn't a *man* in your dream," Lyssa uttered, weak of breath.

"I think I gathered that," Asher replied, in awe of the single dove that pecked around in the empty alley.

EVA III
-Vectem-

Being small was a massive asset for Eva Centaur's journey. If she were any bigger, it would be a struggle to merely survive. She was glad to have made it past the Negal Wall no less than a day ago, but now that it was the Auburn Pole they had to navigate, and not the safe cloak that was the Negal lands, she had to be more careful. She knew security would double in response to being in the open Pole, since it was clear that Esmond didn't seem the safest of people to wander through it without a heavy arsenal. The added danger didn't take away from the harsh beauty of the outside world though, if anything, the risk complimented it. *I wish I could feel like this every day. Life would be so much more exciting.*

Although it was unpredictable, daytime seemed to be the best time for Eva to sneak out of her stuffy wagon to get food and air. She had tried both day and night, but the party preferred to travel during the night for a reason unexplained to her. Even so, it was easy to get food, as the wagon storing all of it was only two away from hers. Luckily, her wagon was only there to transport spare laces and satchels and replacement goods for if something broke on the journey, so it wasn't touched thus far.

At present, the dawn was new and the camp was settled. Eva had a difficult time sleeping through the night, the change to the Auburn crossroads being unpleasantly bumpy compared to the refined roads of the Negal lands. She had an aching pain of hunger, becoming more and more prominent watching the party sup earlier. Not all were asleep now, but she was too hungry to wait any longer.

Carefully lifting the cart's cloth, Eva tried to get a bearing of her surroundings. She felt sick to see that the food wagon, that'd never been guarded before, had Sir Devon sitting right in view of where she had to go. She reached for a stone on the path, throwing it to try and get the knight's attention.

The pebble was loud, compared to the silence of the dawn, but all Sir Devon did was open his eyes to the sound. "Sir Connell," he called weakly, "check out what that was, will you?"

"On it, champ," Sir Connell Atlee responded, holding the hilt of his sword as he walked.

Sir Devon chose to close his eyes again, leaning his head against the post. Eva bit her cheeks. *What now?* Sir Devon had the sharpest ears in the guard. He would definitely hear Eva stealing food from the wagon; the wood always made a loud creek when she stood on it.

She was getting desperate. If she were to hunt, which was seeming like her only option at that point, she didn't know if she could even hold the bow still, the lack of food making her hands shake. *Damn it.* She picked up her beloved bow and slipped out the other side of her wagon. She crept from tree to tree, using all her sneaking skills to do so. The oak was rougher than it was behind the wall, but trees are trees, and if Eva was hidden by them, they were good enough. She got more careless the further she strayed from the camp, her steady sneak turning into a lethargic slump. She was ready, though. With a tight grip around her bow and arrow, she could put a quick end to anything that would show itself.

Crunch! A twig snapped to her right. It sounded like something big. Her mouth watered at the thought. She drew her arrow, pointing at the noise. It was getting closer. *Crunch... crunch...* Her fingers were tingling. The large shadow grew closer.

"Woah, don't shoot!" The curly haired boy who turned the corner dropped his sword and put his dirty hands up. "Eva?!" Jovian Reade's face twisted as he recognised her.

"Shh," she sounded, surrendering her draw to put a finger to her lips.

"What are you doing here?" he whispered, edging closer.

"Don't tell anyone you saw me," she ordered.

Jovian was still confused. "How did you... were you hiding in a wagon? I thought I heard breathing."

"*Don't* tell anyone you saw me!" she repeated, practically hissing.

The confliction shone through Jovian's face. "Eva, you don't know what you're doing. It's dangerous out here, what if you fall out? What if we're ambushed?"

All Eva could do was grit her teeth.

"Look, I'm sorry, but the king needs to know-"

She drew her bow again, aiming it at the squire's head, trying her hardest to fight off the hungry tears. Jovian looked at her, a disappointed sparkle in his eyes. "He'll... send me back home if he knows."

"Where you'd be safer..." he frowned, taking no heed to the bow as he continued to walk.

Tears crawled down Eva's cheeks. "It's not safe at home! People are coming to kill us!"

Jovian continued to shake his head whilst Eva had to catch up to his march. "Whatever you might have heard, that's where your lord father wants you. It's the safest place for you."

"Lord Malone is a traitor!" The sleeping birds fluttered away at the sound. Jovian halted his walk. He turned around. "He's been sending ravens to the Taiga Isles. He wants to kill us. They're... going to wipe out our families."

Jovian studied Eva's eyes. "If this is true... It's a crime to falsely accuse someone," he said anxiously.

"Yes! It is true!" she cried. "I heard him talking; me and Leta shot a raven down, but I *need* to be here to get evidence first."

The squire hesitated, though he remained stubborn. "I can watch Lord Malone. Trust me, Eva, you'd be *much* safer around your family."

"You *can't* watch Lord Malone! You *can't* leave father's side; you're his squire."

Jovian paused to think. "A squire can have a lot of power, you know," he said emptily. "I'm the king's word. I can set up guards to watch Lord Malone. I can tell Marcarius to fetch his letters."

"You'd risk that?" Eva muttered, her tears finally clouding her vision of the boy. "You'd be caught in a day." She let the tears fall. "Please. It's more dangerous to go *back* now. I might be safer at home but why would you think I'd make it that far?"

Jovian scratched his untrimmed stubble, head darting all over the place. He had a nervous smile on his face. "What are you doing to me, Eva?" he whispered under his breath. The squire exhaled. "Did you come out for food?"

She nodded timidly.

Jovian sighed once more, raising his brows as he dubiously felt them. "I can sneak you some food when the party sleeps, we can't risk you being seen by anyone else." He picked up his sword to sheath it back in his scabbard. "I'll still keep an eye on Lord Malone. So long as I'm here, he won't touch your father." Eva lowered her bow and cleared her nose. "Go on, now. I'll distract them."

She nodded and crept back to the camp after Jovian, with double the caution than before. It was easier to slide back into her wagon than it was to slide out. It also felt safer. And now she never had to leave; Jovian slid a piece of bread and a persimmon when his patrol permitted, letting her build a small stash. Eva couldn't have been gladder that it was Jovian who caught her and not any of the others, whom she may not have had the chance to sway, despite how close it came. Still, she had to be more careful now.

Was what I said right? she pondered, thinking back to what Leta had told her. It *was* a crime to falsely accuse someone. A grave crime. *I mean, Jovian is trustworthy, right? He won't tell anyone.* It was too late now to think of Galloway as an innocent man, especially since she painted him in such a criminal light, but she couldn't help but have a slither of doubt.

"Sir Devon? Sir Devon! Wake up, big man."

Eva stopped eating to see what was happening. Sir Connell was touching his shoulder, shaking him gently.

"Guys, there's a problem," he called to the sleeping camp.

Jovian came jogging over and knelt down next to Sir Connell whilst the rest of the party slowly emerged from their tents.

"Jovian, help me lay him down," Sir Connell requested calmly.

He did so, letting the lifeless body of Sir Devon lie on the ground. His skin was completely pale; there was definitely something wrong with him. Eva squinted to try and get a better visual. His purple veins were defined and webbed, almost bulging out of his skin. Sir Connell dithered with what to do. Sir Devon shook as he sweated profusely, and a black substance seeped out of his mouth. Eva's eyes were wide, but she couldn't look away.

"Guys! Help!" Jovian yelled.

King Esmond rushed over. "Woah, woah, what's wrong with him?" People gathered around.

"I found him like this, my king. He was just a bit tired but I thought nothing of it…" Sir Connell panicked.

"Let me see him," Elder Marcarius ordered, making the crowd part.

He knelt down and checked the knight. "His pulse is rapid," he said. "Help me take off his armour."

Sir Connell began unlacing. Others dropped down to help.

"Come on, don't die on us, Dev," Esmond pleaded.

His breastplate was lifted, and his cloth was torn, exposing a wide chest. His toned stomach was moving up and down in a stuttered fashion, struggling to breathe. The arrow wound was revealed, turned completely black, pulsating like it was alive. Jovian gagged and looked away. Eva still couldn't stop watching.

"Eughh, gods!" the king cursed.

"It's too late," Marcarius said in dread as he felt his beard. "All we can do now is ease his pain, pass me his cloth."

"What's the cause?" Sir Arter asked.

"This is the work of a poison out of my field, I'm afraid. The arrow that penetrated his skin must have carried it. Even if I had seen the wound earlier, I doubt I could have saved him," he muttered, letting Sir Devon bite down on the cloth as he twitched.

Esmond held his hair back as he paced. *"Damn Khavars!"* He kicked a carriage, sending it rocking.

Like a torch, Sir Devon's life extinguished, all movement ceasing as fast as a blink. A wind of silence blew around the camp. Eva couldn't believe it. Sir Devon was one of the few that had been around since the start. He was the body of Fort Deus, the strongest knight in the king's guard. And he had gone so quickly, out of the blue.

"His like will be missed, may you wait for us in the next life," Elder Marcarius honoured, closing Sir Devon's eyes with his palm.

"We need to get some sleep, everyone, tonight's ride will be tough," King Esmond sighed, slumping next to Eva's wagon. With that, people hesitantly returned to their tents, shock still stirring every soul.

"What should we do with him?" Sir Ellis asked.

"Send his bones to his family. Tell them he died protecting mine."

Sir Ellis nodded. "Boys." He gestured for the remaining king's guard to help carry Sir Devon away.

"Jovian, have the day off, kid, I'll keep watch now," Esmond said to his squire, slipping his head into his hands.

"My king," Jovian bowed before slowly making his way to his father's tent.

Marcarius came over and sat beside Esmond as the last few people cleared away. "You're doing the right thing, my king. We need to get to the bottom of these tasteless murders."

"I know," he sighed again. "Like you said, the moment that arrow pierced his shoulder, his decline was sealed. It just pains me to think *that* was the same fate Reynold and Daryl suffered."

"A sickening way to go, but we must stay strong, my king," Marcarius said, trying his best to comfort the lost man.

He took off his zircon crown and twirled it around his hands. "You know, that day, my brother had two of those arrows shot in his leg."

"We must pray for him; he is likely to be afflicted too…"

"I swear to you… If he dies like that… I *will* kill every last man on that damned archipelago."

FELIKS III
-Couth-

S o, you're telling me you were attacked?" Feliks asked the sobbing
man, trying to discern what he was saying.

"Aye milord, pitchforks 'n all milord. Burned most huts to the
ground, they did," he wept, kneeling on the cool stone floor.

Feliks adjusted himself to have a comfier sit on the lagoon's throne.
"Tell me what they were wearing again?"

The man wiped himself down. "Same as a common man, milord.
Cloths and rags."

The bastard tried to hold back a yawn. "We'll send builders to repair
your homes, and weapons to arm yourselves-"

"I would advise against that, my lord," Lord Oliver Patel whispered in
his ear. "This attack was like to be of their own: peasants trying to take
advantage of the weak position that the lagoon is in."

"We'll send builders to repair your homes, and extra guards to stop
such an outbreak if it were to happen again. Will that be sufficient?" Feliks
corrected himself jadedly.

The man's face lit up. "Absolutely milord! Absolutely! I thank you!"
He galloped down the steps.

Feliks had near had enough. He relaxed his neck, letting his head fall
back so he could see the sky.

"Should I call in the next enquiry, my lord?" Oliver asked.

"Give me a moment, Lord Patel," said Feliks. Centaur's Lagoon was one of the few places in Austellus that had an open-roofed throne room, and despite sitting there all day, every day, for a fortnight, the sight was the only thing that didn't bore Feliks. The room had stone pillars on each side, stone steps coating the floor, and a small waterfall from the Trader's Sea flowing in from behind, keeping the Lagoon's water level at a surplus. The waterfall would sometimes make it difficult to hear quiet enquiries, but frankly, Feliks would rather hear the calming water than the fiftieth notification of attacks on Artis Bay. *I'd rather fight myself than send people to fight for me. The pricks organising these attacks deserve a bloody enough end, taking my family away.* He thought back to the day his sister died, and her killer whose face he maimed with his dagger. *He deserved worse. He might have felt a few seconds of pain, but he's dead now. I have to live the rest of my life without a sister. That's not justice,* he knew.

He hoped more than anything that his father would wake and release him from this hell. Alchemist Cuthbert kept assuring Feliks that his father *was* sleeping, and not dead, but still, being asleep for two weeks was long enough for any man to doubt. If Lori was to go, he'd have no one left. Feliks couldn't see his friends anymore, as they were close by their families, and Feliks's duty was called on as Acting Lord of the Lagoon. He couldn't even keep the lagoon if his father passed, Feliks's bastard name not giving him the right to inherit the lands. The future was all up in the chilly air.

There was a rickety wooden bridge connecting the room to the rest of the lagoon. Feliks looked up to the sound of it rattling.

"Feliks! Feliks! Good news!" Cuthbert ran in, smiling and waving his hands in the air. "Your father is awake! Lord Lorimer has woken up!"

He almost thought he had dreamed it. The acting lord was ejected from the throne, running after the alchemist as smiles lifted the lagoon. He ran through the busy streets as fast as he could, overtaking Cuthbert and heading straight for his father's chambers.

From his bed, Lori looked as healthy as ever. His skin was a normal colour, his muscles strong, not shrivelled anymore. It was as if his sickness had been bled out of him in the form of sweat on his mattress. *Maybe gods do exist. My prayers have been answered.* "Feliks," he smiled, holding his arms out. Feliks leapt at him, gripping him tightly. "Did I miss much?"

A laugh came over Feliks. "A fair bit," he said, pulling away.

Lori pulled the cover to see his leg, creasing his face in preparation. His wince turned into confusion. "What?"

"What?" Feliks asked, unable to match his father's confusion due to his unbreakable smile.

"We were getting ready to cut off my leg. I thought I..." Lori scratched his shaggy beard. "I thought I passed out from the pain."

"No, we didn't have to," Feliks shook his head enthusiastically. "Cuthbert found a cure."

"That's a shame," he sighed. "Lori the Legless has a nice ring to it, don't you think?"

Even mere minutes after waking from a coma, he had jest in him. Feliks's cheeks hurt from grinning.

Cuthbert emerged from the staircase, out of breath.

"Ah, there's the magic man!" Lori cheered.

"I did no magic, truly, my lord," Cuthbert smiled, pressing his back. "You, however, should be honoured to know that not a man in Austellus has survived what you have. Truly, you have exceeded favour, my lord."

"You're lying," Lori posed.

Cuthbert giggled. "If I were lying, you'd be dead, my lord. I was lucky enough to encounter the poison ashores. Truthfully, I had no understanding whether my cure would work."

Lori seemed to respect the gamble; his eyebrows raised in a flummoxed manner. "Well it seems I owe you my life, Cuthbert of Redmawr. Name any keep, any castle, and it's yours."

Cuthbert's appreciation widened with his smile. "I am contented to serve, my lord," he bowed.

"Really? Nothing? Can't I grant you anything? Redmawr perhaps. It's your home, is it not?"

"I'd rather not return to Redmawr, my lord. I am fully satisfied with my place here," he repeated, slightly colder.

"Very well. You will instead have my eternal gratitude," Lori nodded.

Cuthbert bowed in response. "That will suffice, my lord."

"Good," he smiled. "How long before I can walk again?"

The alchemist stroked his short beard. "I'm not sure, my lord. Your leg seems to have healed enough to do so. Not having used them in a moon may add unwanted imbalance."

"A *moon?!*" Lori staggered. "How long have I been asleep?"

"Just over a fortnight," Feliks claimed. "You can honour *me* with a castle, if you want. It's hard as balls to sit that seat."

His father tittered, still overwhelmed. "Well, you couldn't have done a worse job than me," he said, sitting up. "Feliks, help me stand, will you?"

Lori wrapped one arm around Feliks, clutching the bedside desk with the other. "Three... two... one!" He gritted his teeth as he put his weight on his fragile legs. There was no pressure on Feliks's shoulder for a moment, piling on all at once when Lori began to wobble. He sat back on the bed.

"Do you want me to get a stick?" asked Feliks.

Lori shook his head. "I'll be fine." He attempted to stand again, Feliks just watching in amusement. He instantly fell back again.

"I'll get a stick," Feliks insisted, a smirk on his face.

He walked reasonably well with his new wooden cane. Navigating the winding stairs was troublesome, but other than that, Lori was fine.

"You look like a magnus with your beard and staff," Feliks commented when they surfaced on the street.

Lori responded with a loud chortle. "It would explain how I survived. I must see to casting hexes on some Scorpions," he smiled. "Speaking of which, Cuthbert, do we know who was accountable?"

"Not any more than you know, my lord. Scorpius is an enormous house now, to even get close enough to inspect would be a death wish."

Lori was maddened by the response, his cheeks hollowed in. *He wants Vesta avenged as much as I,* Feliks observed. *He can't do that with a limp.* "Ah! Lord Patel! Good to see you!" Lori smiled as Oliver came into view.

"No less for you, my lord," Oliver Patel bowed. "We all prayed for your safe awakening."

Lord Patel seemed young for his age. He must be in his early thirties or so, as Feliks could remember him looking exactly the same from when he was a child. He was also very elegant despite his indigent background, carrying himself as if he was a nobleman since birth.

"Thank you, Oliver. It clearly worked," Lori beamed. He looked around him. "Is this what's left of my council? Have I been asleep for so long that the rest have abandoned me?"

"Lord Lott and his son set off to Artis Bay this dawn, my lord," Oliver informed. "There have been numerous miniscule revolts in the surrounding towns."

Lori didn't seem surprised. "I take a nap and the realm falls into chaos. Thank the gods I didn't pass," he smirked. "And of Lord Carr?"

"Fort Carr was one of the destinations subject to attack. He is there with his family," said Lord Patel.

A chuckle infected Lori. "There're some four thousand men stationed under Fort Carr, why would they attack there?"

"All dispersed, I'm afraid. The *pennons* wouldn't come at the command of Lord Lott. Lord Carr had to send his own men to keep the peace," sighed Oliver as they arrived at the rickety bridge.

"My *pennons* wouldn't summon at my military advisor's request?" Lori spat. "Gods be good, they're all witless! What would it take? Did they not even listen to you, Feliks?"

Feliks glanced at Oliver, then Cuthbert, not quite knowing what to say. He shook his head.

Lori was smarter than the character he played. He took the silence as he knew, restraining himself from sending dirty looks to the other two. They arrived at the draughty council chamber next to the throne room, and Lori's suspicions were confirmed when he saw the mountain of unbroken scrolls. He glanced at his son again. "Feliks, a word," he said, pulling the bastard to one side. "You were the acting lord, don't tell me you let these dolts walk over you."

"They said I was too young," Feliks muttered through his teeth.

"You know that's not true," Lori frowned angrily, not raising his whisper. "If it happens again, remember who you are."

Feliks squinted sceptically. "A bastard."

"A Centaur." Lori turned and walked back.

Feliks didn't need reminding of how sour the council was towards him. Esmond was the same age when he became king, so it *was* a doltish lie. *Maybe I wouldn't have this problem if you had just married my mother,* he winced. Though, it wasn't right to cast the blame on his father, and he knew that. *It was my fault I was trampled on.* He had given up arguing his rights as acting lord fairly quickly. *If I did make orders, who would listen to a bastard anyway?*

"Sorry about that," Lori said, slumping down in his chair. "Shall we get through this mound, then?" He didn't bother checking what the letters read; all he did was check the seal to see if it was worth his time. "Kramer, nope. Orr, nope." A pile of tossed scrolls fabricated behind him. "Treath? What? No! Go bother my brother." He threw that one harder. The council grew comfortable with boredom. "Sculptor... hmm, maybe," he put that to one side. "Branch, nope. Cen-" He leaned forward to double check that his eyes weren't playing tricks. He unravelled the scroll.

"Who is it?" asked Feliks.

The council watched as Lori's eyes followed the page. "Oh no," he whispered under his breath. "What are you doing, brother?"

"My lord?" Cuthbert asked also.

"My brother is on his way to the capital," he sighed.

The councillors were confused. "And why is that a bad thing?" Oliver asked.

"Because the wounds are healing," he spat. He held himself back in the chair. "How do I know that?" Lori asked himself. He began to shake. Feliks edged closer. "I think I… just need a glass of water-" he tried to stand, but collapsed and yelped in pain. They ran towards him. "The Serpent of Stars. It will poison the city, flooded by-" he trembled, before he abruptly stopped his shrieking, closing his eyes and fainting back into a slumber. No one knew what to do. It was as if he was possessed.

MARCUS I
-Heart-

He tried to kill me, Cadmus," he continued to argue as they rode. "The man held a knife to my throat. A seer of Sanctum Amino wouldn't do that."

"Well, who else *could* it be? The man disappeared into thin air," Cadmus frowned.

"Maybe he swam away," Marcus Horncurve shrugged.

"Oh, don't deny what we all saw, Marcus," Cadmus winced. "He *vanished.*"

"Well, do you know seers to vanish in the first place?" Marcus lashed. "Have ye ever seen one?"

"Look, we all saw it, there's no point fighting," Athena sighed.

"Thank you," Cadmus groaned.

"-But Marcus has a point, a seer wouldn't want him dead."

"Thank you," Marcus snickered.

"Ok, so, what did he *actually* say to you?" Cadmus asked bitterly.

Marcus sighed. "What I've told you. He said he *had* somethin' for me. He called me by my name, so I followed... I didn't know what else to do."

"There," Cadmus muttered stubbornly, "he knew yer name: a seer of Sanctum Amino."

"He *wasn't!*" Marcus protested.

"Oh, whatever," Cadmus shrugged, riding ahead of them so he didn't have to hear.

"Is that all he said?" Athena asked softly.

Marcus nodded, rubbing his leather reins.

Athena sighed. "Cadmus said he bought a weird food from the guy," she said. "I tasted it, and it wasn't like any food I've ever tasted. It made me *feel* different. It made me feel *great*, actually."

"What's your point?" Marcus asked tiredly.

"My point is: Cadmus is wrong. Why would a seer sell that shit?"

"Aye, he's wrong," Marcus leered. "Why would a seer try to kill me?"

Athena couldn't think of an answer. "He's foreseen something terrible you're gonna do," she jested.

Marcus smirked at his sister. "Aye," he muttered sharply.

That question plagued him day and night. Even with all the facts he couldn't so much as come to a guess. *Telling them what happened after wouldn't help either. They wouldn't understand. No more than I do.* "A heart warmed by fire, Horncurve," the mysterious man had said in the tent. "A fuel for life… or a fuel to end." That was when the man held out the knife. "You know what you seek…"

Now, because of Cadmus, what the man was going to do was still a mystery. *Would he have killed me? He was giving me the knife.* And almost embarrassingly, he somehow knew why. *Revenge.* It wasn't a thought that brushed his mind too much, but still, like a snake, it coiled and squeezed his mind until his wounds grew in pain. It made Marcus lose sleep just by thinking of what he could have done with that dagger.

Esmond wasn't guilty. He knew that. Sigmund was, and his crimes were paid for. That's what everyone else believed, so it must have been true. But still, part of him denied it. Part of him wanted to think there was another way, a way where the whole north wasn't shamed.

It wasn't like Marcus could do anything, regardless. It wasn't like he knew what to do if he could. *I don't seek anything*, he reminded himself while he sat alone near the Ramscar while his camp slept. *I don't need anything.* He threw another stone into the river, before deeply inhaling the Canicule's summer air.

If any other thought was in his mind, Marcus would be fast asleep like the rest of them. His legs and back ached badly, and tingled when he didn't move them. It never was *this* bad riding down, but was forgivable due to the circumstances. They had stopped at the small trader's town of Jugum, mostly populated by travellers. If Marcus was in control, he would put more guards out; Heavia lay not that far down the Ramscar, and even though a wall separated them, the stress of past raids still tugged at his mind. *The exiled of Heavia,* he thought. *The savages that took my grandmother.* He frowned, his boiling blood clashing with the calm night.

Snap! Marcus's head whipped to the sound. The tall, dead jungle trees with their sandy vines blocked all vision of what made it. He slowly rose, feeling the pommel of his sword. He listened for another sound, but was met with nothing. Carefully, he advanced, parting the crusty vines so he could pass through. He heard the trickle of water. *They're in the stream.* He crept closer and closer. The final few vines parted in front of him. He leapt out, drawing his sword to his twin as he held a defensive stance. "Oh, it's just you," Marcus sighed.

Cadmus chuckled, shaking his head and sheathing his sword. "Thought you were a raider or something."

"Same," Marcus smirked. "Can't sleep either?"

Cadmus shook his head again, this time sadder, as he and his twin sat. "I keep expecting to see grandpa when I wake up. Every time, I think it's *his* boot hitting my side, not da's."

"Yeah," Marcus sighed. "He's been gone for too long…"

Cadmus frowned at him. "He's not coming back."

"I didn't say he would."

"No, but you trailed off… as if *hoping* he would."

His twin had a way of irritating him like no other. "Of course I bloody hope that. I looked up to the man, we both did!"

"Keep the head, Marc, I'm tryna help you," he sighed. "It does us no good, keeping our minds on it, hoping for the impossible."

Marcus frowned "How do you know what's good for us? Our grandpa was executed. It's hardly gonnae be peaches and cream after that."

"Of course not, but that's not what I'm saying," Cadmus leered, raising his voice. "You need to learn to stop fighting, to sit back and let things be. It wasn't King Esmond's fault, and it's not your place to hate him."

It came as no surprise that his brother knew. Marcus deflated slowly.

"I'm sick of *bickerin'* with you," he groaned. For a while, Cadmus picked at his nails, his jaw visibly tensing through his cheeks. Eventually, he tittered. "It's the only thing we've done since he left."

Marcus agreed with a nod. "I'm glad some things don't change."

Cadmus gave a familiar look back, one with a subtle smirk and glittering eye. It was the twin look, the one exclusive to those two, the one that guaranteed the murder of boredom, the one that reminded them how identical they were.

"Thank you, by the way…" Marcus said, "…for savin' my life."

"Took you long enough," Cadmus smiled. "You know I'd kill for you, pal," he said, ruffling Marcus's scruff of auburn hair. "Nothing matters when we fight, ya know that?"

Marcus nodded, losing his eyes to the night. "I'd kill for you too, Cad."

He could feel Cadmus's smile even when he wasn't looking.

"Come on," Cadmus grinned, standing.

"What?"

"Look, we both can't sleep, I know a tavern, let's get pissed."

Marcus smirked, shaking his head. "Lead the way," he said.

The town was a strange bit cooler than the riverside, the Ramscar constantly offering a sultry stream. It almost gave Marcus a shiver, though he didn't mind it; he knew shivers meant that they were closer to home.

With just over half a moon in the sky, the shine made the tavern stand out like a sunbeam in the woods. It was the only building in Jugum that had torches aflame inside. Cadmus confidently pushed open the door, meeting a sorry bunch of people, slumped and drunk in opposing corners of the wooden room. The door made a *creak* loud enough for the few people inside to draw a gaze, so when they noticed Elder Ignatius was part of that crowd, it made the twins wince.

"Nice one, Cad," Marcus whispered sharply.

"Boys," Ignatius said tiredly, "over here."

Cadmus sighed, making his way. "Elder Ignatius, me and Marc were-"

"Two more cups, please, Roes," Ignatius called to the serving girl.

She nodded, bringing two huge cups in front of the twins.

"What's on your minds, lads?" The elder asked, taking a sip.

"A lot," Marcus said, reaching for his cup before Cadmus.

"Well do tell," the elder said unenthusiastically. His eyes looked half closed. "Nothing could possibly make this journey any longer."

He'd know if the man was a seer, Marcus realised, *he practically grew up with them.* He sent his twin a knowing look. "Don't," Cadmus winced.

Marcus faced the elder. "What do you know about seers, Ignatius?"

Cadmus sighed, leaving.

"Seers?" Ignatius frowned. "Ah, ye mean those creepy fuckers across the sea? I know enough… what do ye need to know?"

He took another deep swig of ale. "At Merchant's Bay, I found a lad who knew my name. He took me to his tent, told me some things… He tried to kill me."

Ignatius slowly put his cup down, eyes finally awake. "Say that again?"

"He held a knife to my throat. Cadmus saved me and tried to grab him but he had already vanished in the water."

The elder took a moment to process. He winced. "Yer saying this lad tried to kill a Horncurve?"

Marcus was getting annoyed, and it shone through his voice. "Was it a seer, or not?"

"Well, wha' didae say to you?" he slurred.

"A heart warmed by fire: A fuel for life or a fuel to end, you know what you seek."

Ignatius took an age to reply. "And do you?"

Marcus was flabbergasted. "It's not a *joke*." Sighing, he tossed his cup. "*Cah*, I shoulda known you're pissed. You're not even gonna remember this."

He started to walk away. Ignatius grabbed his arm. "And do you?" he repeated, suddenly seeming completely sober. "Sit down and tell it true."

Marcus blinked. "I don't... what?"

Ignatius turned to the counter, looking down. Marcus slowly sat. "Let me tell you about a man, who many people looked up to. He was the greatest warrior of our time; he saved many people, brought justice to those who needed it, gave hope to those most doubtful, evinced love and happiness when it seemed like things would only get worse... Everything seemed better when he was around, until the woman he loved more than anything died, and a part of him with her... Slowly, so slowly, the hope faded, the love faded, the happiness faded... soon the only thing left was his swing of *justice*. Somehow, he thought things would go back to normal once enough people had paid. He sent thousands, upon thousands of good men to the grave, all because he was *so obsessed* with the idea of it. All that was left of him was anger, and I don't even think he realised that come his last breath." Ignatius searched Marcus's eyes. "The fury of a broken man... always fighting with the fuel to end," he muttered bitterly. "So, tell me again, how do you feel now that he's gone? How do you feel now that he's dead, and you can never bring him back? How do you feel about the way he died?"

"Angry," he admitted flatly.

"There you go, Marcus," Ignatius sighed. "That's why a seer wanted to kill you."

FLETCHER II
-Steer-

For the past fortnight, Fort Deus was too quiet for comfort. Having half his family missing didn't help, but the silence that plagued the walls was more down to the silence of uncertainty. Leta came clean with what Eva had done a day or two ago, to ease the stress of their mother. If it didn't ease the stress, it only made it worse, as Leta didn't reveal the whole story to her. She did with Fletcher Centaur, though. Fletcher always admired Galloway, growing up hearing of his tales of battle from the wars he had fought in, so it was a shock to learn all that he planned to do. Well, he still didn't know *what* he planned to do, no one did, but he trusted the word of his sister too much to dismiss it.

Hew was all but noisy most of the time. They had slowed down on training together, Fletcher's new flood of responsibilities making it difficult to tailor the time. Hew obviously didn't care, though. If anything, it was better for him, the endless books he could read becoming more of a coping mechanism for his family's absence than a hobby. It was the only thing that would stop him crying.

Fletcher only wished he got that kind of happiness from ruling. He thought it would be different to what it was. He thought he would have bidding servants, willing to do whatever he wished at the drop of a quill. In a way, he *did* have that, but it was nothing like the stories. He was lucky if he had *anything* to do some days, as most of the tedious and important issues were already handled by Sir Roswell, or just referred to the capital now that Esmond was heading there. Sometimes, Fletcher would join Sir Roswell in his tedium, in tasks such as counting coins, distributing their ever-shrinking food supply to the other forts in the Negal lands, helping the knights with organising their weapons and armour. *It's not the worst,* he thought. *But it's not where I should be either.*

It put his mind at ease that this is what Todd Kalyx probably meant on his birth day, ruling over the castle that is. But he couldn't help but wonder why Todd thought he would make a good king in the first place. He would much rather be in Asher's position: exploring the world and experiencing things most people don't. *That's where I belong. Not on a dusty throne in the middle of nowhere.*

He was sitting at Esmond's desk, twiddling his feather quill between his fingers like most days. Come to think of happiness, he hadn't smithed a good arrow in ages. Maybe it was time.

Knock, knock! "A visitor has come to see you, my lord," called Sir Roswell from the other side of the door.

Fletcher jumped up, straightened his garnet tinted leathers, and headed out to the throne room. "Thank you, Sir Roswell," he smiled as he passed.

Fletcher entered the throne room, where stood a man in the centre. He had tanned skin, a steel breastplate to cover only his pectorals, and worn boiled leathers underneath. A heavy head of black hair was what fell down his shoulders, in a style completely foreign to Fletcher, and a wiry beard to accompany it, even though the face underneath the beard seemed young, not too far from Fletcher's age. His heartbeat grew in pace as he realised who he was. He could be wrong, but it was unlikely… Eva's description was verbatim. *It seems the bunny has hopped into the wolf's den,* he thought. *Let's see if you're brave enough to conspire to my face.* "Lord Fletcher, it is an honour to meet you," the man said, falling to one knee.

"And what am I to call you, my lord?" he asked, sauntering to the throne of zircon.

"It is generous you think me of a lord, your lordship," the man humbly corrected.

"Are you not? You sure dress like one. But still, you must have a name."

"Tyran Capra, if it please, your lordship. Son of Nero Capra, King of the Three Goats," he bowed.

Fletcher noticed Leta peek her head out from the hallway, eavesdropping. "I didn't think *Capra* sounded familiar. How has it come to be that you have strayed so far from exile, my prince? Should I call you a prince? You're technically a prince, correct?" he smirked.

"I come before you *as* a man of exile, nothing more. This is your realm," he assured. Tyran's face soured with confusion.

"Very well..." he replied, not giving a cue for Tyran to continue.

"I come before you today to-"

He was interrupted by the sound of heels hitting stone. Queen Semira entered the room. *Perfect.*

"You must be the queen," he said, falling to his knees again. "It is also a great-"

"Please continue, Tyran," Fletcher insisted, Semira's queenly stride taking her to the seat next to him.

Tyran stuttered. "I... uh... come before you today not as an enemy as we are most commonly painted, but a-"

"What do you come as then?" Fletcher chaffed. It almost amused him how annoying he must have seemed. *You can waste our time, but we'll waste yours too.*

"...But as a possible ally," he continued in a composed tone, making Fletcher worry a little. "We are in a very tight knit, us people of exile, and it has come to our attention that the Cancerians are to plan another attack focusing here, on Fort Deus, while your lord father is elsewhere."

"So, you'd deceive us?" asked Fletcher, a smirk and a frown connected in growth.

"I'm sorry?" Tyran winced.

"A very tight knit, you said. What's to stop you from stabbing us in the back?"

Tyran was taken aback. "Even for men of exile, we would not stoop to such-"

"Answer the question," he demanded, in a tone so icy, that even the roaring hearths had to shudder.

"Lord Fletcher," he addressed, evidently holding himself back. "If you were to let me speak, and not think to dismiss my enquiry before I say it, then perhaps you will surprise yourself, your lordship."

Fletcher leant back and glanced at his mother, who almost seemed disgusted by the way Fletcher spoke to him. He waved in a manner to have Tyran speak again, although against his wish.

"Thank you," he sighed. "I know our families have had discord in the past, but we think that the days are done for unquestioned killing and bitter raids. Khavars sail our way with boats so big they could swallow castles, and we recognise that they will stop at no one when it comes to murder."

"Even people in a tight knit?" Fletcher asked, more hesitantly, a part of him wondering if he were telling the truth.

"Look, I know you will have a difficult time trusting us, but we're not asking you to trust us. We wouldn't have come to you if we didn't fear for our people's lives," he insisted. "All we ask of you, is that you accept an agreement of alliance, and that you aid us in protecting both of our homes as we will aid you. And afterwards, when the fighting has waned, we will return to our islands and continue to live in exile from your father's realm like we have done for hundreds of years. Even if you despise us throughout, more soldiers to your army can never hurt."

Fletcher was stumped. He genuinely thought an essence of truth was involved in his constitute. He put his fingers to his mouth while he sat back, pondering. *If he's lying, what could they do anyway? The armies here probably outnumber them three to one. If he's not, then we will have men to fight whatever is coming. It'll be more men to feed, though. We're only just getting by on fish.* Fletcher stood. "Ok, Tyran. We *will* accept your alliance." Leta and Semira straightened their postures in distress.

"Thank you, Lord Fletcher. This is the right-"

"Under the conditions…" he added, "…that the raids on our shipment boats are to cease immediately, and stock that you have plundered will be returned."

"Of course, your lordship. We will control our envoys." *Got you. So you did plunder the cargo ships.*

"That we must be fully notified of the numbers your army consists of, where they are stationed, and when you are due to move them."

"A fair request. We will oblige."

"And…" he continued, shifting his gaze to a worried Leta. "On the morrow, you will take my sister and the queen to visit the islands. Leta here has always wanted to see them."

Tyran turned his head round to see Leta. "Don't be shy," he smiled. "That can be done also, your lordship," he faced Fletcher once again.

Fletcher walked down the throne stairs in a powerful poise. He held out his hand. "Then we have an alliance, my lord."

They shook hands, and the serendipity was sealed.

◆———◗

"I'm going to the islands?! Why didn't you tell me?"

"You accepted the alliance, Fletcher! Are you mad?"

Fletcher held his hands in the air as he strolled around to his desk. "I accepted because I had to, Leta."

"Didn't you notice? Eva's description matched the traitor *word for word!* It *was* him; I *know* it!" she yelled.

"What?" The queen winced.

Leta and Fletcher shared a mutual look of despair. "That's why Eva left," Fletcher sighed. "She overheard him and Galloway conspiring." His sister pulled the letter from her breeches and handed it to the queen.

Semira was even more confused. "Then, why didn't you tell me? We could have had that man locked up by now."

"We didn't know for sure," claimed Leta. "We figured that we'd try and get more evidence before we started telling people… so it would be more believable."

"But at least if we knew, we could keep an eye on them," she said. The queen seemed to accept it for a moment, before her wince returned. "Wait, so why *did* you accept the alliance?"

Fletcher toyed with his father's quill again. "I realised he was Galloway's man as soon as I walked in. I thought I'd push him for a bit to see what kind of man we're dealing with, but the more he talked… He's the only eyes we've got on the eastern Trader's Sea. If this Khavar attack happens, we'd have never known; they would have crushed us."

"Why would you believe him?" Leta said, raising her voice. "He's going to betray us the first chance he gets."

"That's why I was surprised by myself," he chuckled, putting his legs on the table. "I thought from the start I wouldn't believe him. But lo and behold…"

Semira remained confused. "So, you said yes because…?"

"Think about it, ladies. We get more food, as he agreed to stop plundering and to share what he had. Gods know the whole fort is getting tired of grilled eel and cod," he began, counting the reasons on his fingers. "If what he says about the Khavars coming turns true, we will have more intel, *and* a fresh army at our back, and if he decides to march against us, we will have the *exact* numbers of what their force consists of, and full control of what they do with them, so we could prevent it entirely."

"Full control of what they do?" The queen quizzed. "He agreed to tell you how many, not to hand over his armies to you."

"Yeah, I know, but that's half the battle," he assured. "We'll know *exactly* what he does with his armies, down to a single man. And if we at least know the number of men who have the *potential* of marching on us, then we could prepare accordingly - match them in numbers, lean the odds in our favour if we must."

The girls just stared at him, as if to say: he could just as easily lie to you. *If he lies about anything, he won't keep his life for long.*

He rubbed his eyes. "I don't trust the man, okay? I don't think I ever could. But if what he's saying is true about the Khavars, and he is genuine, then we've got nothing to lose. If not, then we'll have an enemy on our doorstep, knowing every move they make before they make it," he smirked, beginning to enjoy himself.

"How?" Leta asked in a more intrigued tone.

"That's the final reason," he smiled as he stood. "Leta, you *did* say you wanted to see what was going on at the islands... Tomorrow you will. You will find out as much as you can about their intentions: read their letters, ask questions to those who'd answer, befriend those who'd care to do so. You might even find something that incriminates Galloway. Maybe you could bring a few Centaur spies with you as well, plant them just where they'll be needed." A confident, sly grin grew on Fletcher's face. "By the end of this week, the Capras will be an open book."

EVA IV
-Stallion-

Shh, if you make any more noise, you'll wake her."

"How do you know it's a girl?"

"It's too small to be a boy, you idiot. Now let's just grab that fancy bow she 'as and let's go!"

"Go? If she's a girl we can sell her to the tavern. They'll pay a fortune for the little slut."

She woke up in an awkward position. Her left arm and neck were stiff with a needle-like pain. A cloth was over her head, the world pitch-black to her. Wherever she was now, she knew it wasn't in the wagon. She slowly reached for her bow as the footsteps around her grew closer.

"Stop, Ollie! I think she moved!"

A man started nudging Eva Centaur with his foot. "You can't scare me, Rob. The bitch is as good as dead."

Ollie yelped like a dog as a leg was swept underneath him, knocking him to the floor before an arrow plunged into his throat by a quaint hand. Eva vaulted up, pulling the arrow out of his neck and throwing the cloth from her head. The daylight was bright, but she soon adjusted.

"This one's dangerous, lads. She'll sell for a fortune!" One of the four rugged looking men said, unsheathing a knife.

Before he could think to move, Eva ejected an arrow into his head, flinging his body as his head hurtled back. The three others ran towards her. She reached for her quiver, still attached to her back, and unloaded an arrow into the heart of another with ease. He squealed, clutching his chest as he fell. She reached for one more arrow, only to have her hands waving in the air at the empty quiver. To her horror, all her arrows were scattered all along the muddy, auburn ground, but the men were too close for her to fetch them. She rolled back as one man lunged, the other man pouncing atop of him and stabbing him in the back by accident. He quickly pulled the knife out and lunged for Eva again. She dodged to the side, removing the massive boot the dead man wore, and clobbered the last one over the head with it. To make sure they were dead, she slit their throats.

She fell to the ground, catching her breath, adrenaline shaking her body. Her hands were coated in blood. *Just like hunting rabbits,* she whispered to herself. *We're nothing more than animals.* She controlled her breathing to calm herself like Leta had taught Hew.

Eva felt like she'd just had the best sleep of her life, and must have done to not wake up from falling off the wagon. *Shit.* Looking around, all she had on her person was her bow and satchel, suitcase nowhere in sight. That case had *all* of her clothes. *All* of her memorabilia. Everything she needed to survive was on a wagon heading to Lunarpass, and she didn't even *know* where she was.

Still in stupor, more so now that she recognised the situation, she went to gather her arrows on the floor, returning them to where they belonged. She wasted no time, immediately picking a direction to get some sort of idea of where she was. She thought it best to follow the road. Whipping her satchel to her front, she wanted to check what little things she did have, if any. All that remained in her open satchel was an empty water bottle, the last drop used to quench her morning thirst.

This isn't so bad, she told herself. *This is just like the Negal lands. Just like home. I just killed three oversized bunnies. That's all they were. Bunnies.* A sharp pain pricked her. The pain grew thicker as she saw the huge gash across her forearm. It must have happened when she rolled away. Her efforts to remain calm were failing, a sickness running over her. Who could she fool? Her stomach was growling. Her throat was dry. Blood was rushing out of her arm. She had just killed five men. She had never killed a man before. She felt more ill the more she walked. A wave came over Eva, closing her eyes as she fell into the mud.

She dreamt that the bunnies came back, that endless hordes of them were running to steal her. Her quiver wasn't empty any more, but nor was it full. Every time she'd reach for an arrow, she'd find one. And every time she'd have an arrow, she couldn't waste any time with firing, or she'd be grabbed. Her arm ached more and more, but there was no way to stop, no way for respite, no way to run. There were too many of them. She still wanted to fight them back when she was overwhelmed…

◆———————◆

Eva opened her eyes to feel feathers massaging the back of her neck as a toasty hearth roared in the corner of a small wooden room. Her belongings were neatly leaning on the side of her bedside table, and silky bandages hugged her right arm. As soon as she noticed the cup of clean water by her bedside, she tried her best to awkwardly stretch across to reach it, knocking over a couple of unlit candles.

"Let me," spoke a calming voice that entered the small room. He had a slight tan of the skin, and was curiously under dressed for a man of the south. A short, brown head of hair sat beneath the brown cloth tied around his head, and large muscles scaled his body. "You know how many drunken fools I had to fight through to get you safely in this room?" he smiled, strolling towards her. "Every man and their dog in this damned tavern had their eyes fixed on you. If I had turned my head for one minute… Even *I* couldn't save you from that many hungry wolves."

As she was passed the cup, Eva grabbed it with both hands and necked the water. After the liquid hit her stomach, she realised it wasn't water, wincing appropriately.

The man chuckled. "They only deal rum here, I'm afraid. Don't worry, it was the weakest I could get."

"Where am I?" she asked eventually, taking a few more swigs before doing so.

"Must have had quite a fall to forget where you are," he said. "Judging by your arm, I'm willing to bet it wasn't just a fall, though."

Eva stayed quiet, holding her injured arm closer to her chest.

"You're at the Crossroad Inn. I found you about a mile off from here as I was riding down the Lunar Path," he smiled warmly, taking a woolly chair next to the bed. "You're lucky I found you. Most men would've walked right by, especially after seeing those five corpses you made."

"Why did you help me?" she asked, caressing her wounded arm.

"I thought you might have an interesting story: a girl that doesn't look past thirteen, cleanly murdering five men and escaping with only a tear on her arm."

"They tried to kill me. They wanted to sell me to the tavern."

"And you didn't let them," he smiled. He picked an arrow from her resting quiver, examining it, "These arrows are the finest I've ever seen. How did you get them?"

"My brother made them," she replied.

"Oh, really? A smith, is he?" he said, raising his eyebrows before slotting it back in the quiver. "He's a talented lad."

Eva agreed with a nod, reminded of home by the thought of Fletcher and the soft, warm bed sheets that lay atop her. *I don't want to be here anymore,* she thought. *I don't want to go to Lunarpass. I want to be back home in my bed. I shouldn't have left.* "Are you a lord?" she asked.

"Will you kill me if I am? You seem like a dangerous girl," he smiled.

Eva matched his smile, looking down at the woollen sheets.

"My name is Idris Equuleus, eldest son of Doran Equuleus, Lord of Lutum. You can just call me Idris, though," Idris declared. *Thank the gods he's on my side,* she sighed to herself. Equuleus was a distant scion of Centaur. Distant enough for some to say the connection is irrelevant, but their attitude towards the crown for as long as the Centaurs have held it has always been steadfast.

The connection stemmed back to King Jovian the Cruel, as he wed Lady Camilla Equuleus. Granted, King Jovian was the least liked of the thirteen kings that followed Erland the Escaper, hence the name, but a link through blood was still present. Some say he would make miscreants run through the streets of Lter with a flaming arrow in their back; if the offender made it to the other side of the enormous capital - which was borderline impossible - Jovian saw it as an intervention of the gods, granting them their life, if they would even live long enough to be treated. Though it was cruel to do so, it might be unfair to some for Jovian to earn that name, as he would only be cruel when people were on the wrong side of his justice. Either way, Jovian met his retribution eventually, *The Second Pause* taking his life, and the Kingdom of Lter.

Idris's clothing now made sense, though, Lutum situated right on the edge of the Canicule; he didn't seem to have an ounce of southern in him.

"Why are you so far south?" she blurted out.

"You know where Lutum is, do you? The more I learn about you, the more I'm starting to believe you're highborn yourself," said Idris, squinting.

Eva fell quiet again, looking down at her rough hands.

"I like to explore," Idris explained. "Too many of us like the comfort of our own home too much. I just want to get out as much as possible before I'm tied to the chair where I was born for the rest of my days."

Eva had always thought a similar thing. Even though she'd never sit on any throne, all Eva could remember wanting, before the Galloway situation, was to explore. The thought sent her back to when the Horncurves were leaving Fort Deus, Athena promising to take her to Selerborn one day, one day far in the future because of her age and place. She was teething with excitement as much as frustration, never knowing *if* it would happen. Yet only a moon later, she lay in a bed right in the heart of the Auburn Pole, with the ability to go anywhere she wanted. "I agree," she muttered, fiddling with her bandages.

He smiled before standing up. "Well, I'd better leave you to rest. Don't worry, I won't abandon you until your arm is better… and you have some sort of idea where you're going."

She was staring into the crackling fireplace. *Will I ever have an idea? Everywhere I go, I want to be somewhere else.*

Idris smiled once again as he reached the door. "Oh, what should I call you? I almost forgot to ask."

"A girl?" she smirked.

He chuckled. "I was more thinking of a name."

"My name is Eva," she twinkled, "just Eva."

ESMOND VII
-Heed-

It was difficult to remember when he was in Lunarpass last. It must have been roughly five years ago, when they visited the capital for Hew's fifth birthmoon treat. In truth, Esmond Centaur was necessitated to go after threats of a second *Scorpius Rebellion* spawned. That was when Eldric Scorpius ran the Archipelago, his madness fortunately claiming him that same year before anything unravelled, letting the throne of citrine fall atop his son Vincent, already of senior age and seasoned in battle. Luckily, Vincent hadn't been *as* eager for bloodshed as far as Esmond could see.

Come to think of birthmoons, a few days ago came the new Thunder Moon. None of the party - apart from Elder Marcarius and Sir Orion - remembered it was Esmond's. He was past the age to receive gifts, regardless. *Forty years old.* It seemed so old, yet so young.

The city seemed timeless, not a day older than when he was born into it. All the same, he was grateful he wasn't raised there, believing that growing up at the Tusks with Reynold and Blaine made a much different man out of him. Some of his fondest memories ensued from that island: playing in those massive caves and having every sound echo back a thousand times, running and jumping through and over huge ravines, Reynold always lagging behind while Esmond and Blaine raced ahead, never a step before each other. That was why it pained Esmond so to come to the capital for the reason he did. He didn't want another war; he wanted peace. Peace for his family, for the realm.

Gods knew both needed it. But gods also knew that Esmond wouldn't draw the line at war in order to get said peace. "The wounds are healing. Esmond must know," Reynold had said on his deathbed, according to Sir Roswell. "He must undo the stitches. He must tear it open to fester..."

Esmond's welcoming to Lunarpass was resplendent in every sense of the word. The party were showered with confetti with each step the horses made, whilst people clambered on each other to get so much as a wave from the king. Powerful words and names were repeatedly thrown at him, such as 'Saviour' and 'Champion', yet as much as Esmond loved the praise, being damn near humbled by it, he didn't come all this way to be eulogised.

Thaddeus waited for him roughly a hundred meters from the Lunar Gate, arms wide open to greet his cousin. "It's been too long, Esmond!" he called, booming over the crowd.

"That, it has, Thaddeus," he beamed down, marching to the acting king, embracing him strongly.

"You will be pleased to know that living quarters and accommodations for your party and your supplies by your request have been fully seen to, your grace. Should there be any problems, then just tell me and I'll have the culprits flogged in the streets," he chortled as they walked.

"Have the years made you so dissimilar, cousin? Your grace? Don't call me that shit," he chuckled, poking Thaddeus. "I'm Esmond to you."

Thaddeus replied with a smile. "I feared that the years had made you so," he was relieved to confess. "I have been proven wrong once again."

Esmond put his arm around his cousin. "This Esmond isn't going anywhere," he assured. They walked for a length, waving to the endless crowds of citizens. "How soon can you get a council meeting arranged?" he asked eventually. "My appetite for justice grows by the second."

His cousin could only frown. "You have just arrived, Esmond. Your councillors are like to be worn from travel. How about we open a barrel of wine to celebrate your arrival?" he suggested, a smile on his face.

The smile was not reciprocated. "Wine comes after. If we drink as much as we normally do, then we won't be able to walk straight, let alone think," he said contently, a smirk returning to his face.

"Very well," Thaddeus nodded, "does within the second hour sound reasonable?"

"Reasonable enough," he accepted, knowing it would take an hour to even reach the higher city.

"Good, well I'll leave to inform the rest, if you don't need help navigating yourself around."

"I believe I can manage," Esmond averred, already feeling lost as he looked around the ever-expanding city.

"Excellent," Thaddeus smiled warmly. "I'll herd up the sheep then," he said, patting Esmond on the back before taking his leave.

It wasn't like Esmond to not meet his cousin with wine flowing and songs playing. He was all but over his grief, and it made him exhausted.

Esmond's company for most of the trek north had caught up to his side, the *First Avail* sighing on his arrival. Sir Orion looked beaten and worn down, his grief clearly battling with him too. They talked *this* journey, quite often actually, the knight's state of deeper thinking proving insightful for Esmond. He *did* have more of a sense of humour, but Esmond couldn't help but feel it was tainted by the sorrow, always not far from Sir Orion's thought.

Fortunately, because of how much both had lost over the past few moons, their grief was shared, being on the same wavelength throughout. Esmond couldn't ask for better company.

The knight was smiling, a smile faked for the people as they continued to hang out of their high windows and flood the city grounds. Despite its falsity, Esmond still felt good to see it. "Don't you think it's wise to rest before the meeting?" he asked. "Not just for us, but for yourself too."

"No," Esmond assured, "my thoughts are clear. It's as if throughout our journey they have piled and piled; I can't wait any longer before they spill," he frowned, still clamping his smile in place. "Do *you really* think it would be wise to?"

"No," Orion confessed, a genuine smile breaking through the facade, "Ellys Dart told me to ask you. Give the man a break, Esmond, he's got to be nearing seventy birthmoons by now." They continued to trot through the streets, before the silence was broken again by Sir Orion. "I thought it best to ask too; I wasn't sure if your mourn for Sir Devon had passed."

Esmond looked down to his reins, massaging the shabby leather with his thumbs. He could still remember the day he joined the guard. No one could believe the size of the young man, a head above every other man at the tourney. It was held at the Crossroads, celebrating... something or other. The reason for the tourney slipped Esmond's mind. He would hold tourneys and carouses for no reason other than to do something sometimes. This one must have been about his twentieth birthmoon; he remembered being as old at least. Anywise, the tourney was vast, being the first one he held allowing any applicant to join. That was why men shook to see the fit young brute that was Sir Devon saddling his horse. He unseated many great knights, including the likes of Sir Warrick Mayne and Sir Arter Whyte, but his elimination was met when he was put against Sir Brendan Gryfford, matching his size and age. It made for a phenomenal joust, the duel going on for almost fifteen rounds, yet Sir Brendan prevailed, the knight proceeding to join Reynold's lion's guard that same day. Despite their efforts, no one was a match for Lorimer Centaur, the king's brother securing the tourney, getting ever-nearer to his renown of being *almost* undefeated upon his retirement. Still, Sir Devon had impressed Esmond so much, that his request to become a part of the king's guard was accepted without a second thought.

"Sir Devon was a good knight, possibly the strongest in the guard, in more ways than one. He fell protecting a Centaur, like he pledged he would the day he joined, and I would owe him my life for doing so… but do you know what's weird?" he winced. "The more people you lose, the less it affects you. It's like each loss takes away another part of you, and when there's nothing left to take, you're just empty."

Sir Orion frowned for the king, remaining silent.

"I've lost my family to Fort Deus because of my stupid adolescent decisions. My eldest marches to Ignis, as good as lost too," he said grimly. "You're the closest thing to family I have in this damned city."

"…Thaddeus?" the knight pouted.

"I don't know the man, Orion," he sighed. "I *do* love him, though. I owe him a lot for taking the position that he has, but it pains me that I barely see him. It makes me a stranger to him."

"That doesn't make him any less a Centaur," Sir Orion grimaced.

"You're right, I shouldn't have said that," he surrendered, regretting.

"I don't blame you," the *Avail* groaned, "but remember, Esmond, even if you're immune to loss now, it doesn't mean that everyone in this realm is fine with their loved ones being taken. It's going to be hard to keep having to hear this, but you are no longer a father, or a husband, or a cousin; you're a king, and these people won't stop looking to you to help them."

Esmond's eyes were pulled to the endless crowds, still cheering and saluting his arrival. Semira's words kept echoing in his head: *be a king. Be a king. Be a king.*

From then on, their time to the Sphaera was silent, both of the warriors reflecting. Esmond didn't spend much time in the goliath building, only heading to the king's chambers at the top for a change of clothes. There was an obscene number of steps in the Sphaera; it seemed unfair that the king had to climb the most.

The higher city wasn't empty by the time dusk approached. Esmond grew tired from greeting the thousandth lord once again, and before he could even get to the Ulcus Basilica, the council meeting had already been postponed by three hours. He still arrived before everyone else, allowing himself to be reunited with his throne alone.

The Ulcus Basilica was a prodigious hall of cool stone and marble. Ornate pillars spanned all the way to the throne, above a glossy marble floor bursting with patterns and illustrations spanning aeons back. The glass ceiling reflected the moon perfectly as it rose from its slumber, like most of Lunarpass. It added a new, beautiful decoration to the room, unmatched by any piece of furniture, however grand. It was said that Solaris, Lunarpass' lost twin, broken off during the first *Pause*, did the same with the sun, the lunar throne that sat there sparkling with a thousand stars as it rose. Yet as much as the myths of Caelestia praised both thrones, the words on the page could never do it justice.

The solar throne was of another world entirely, as if almost every structure in Lunarpass didn't make Esmond feel dwarfed enough. It was said to be indestructible, made of a compound so condensed, that not even the most powerful of magic could move or dent it. Books said it was made of steltrium: an ancient, magical and forgotten alloy, capable of bringing down civilisations. It spanned up half of the huge back wall. Beams of what men would call light sprawling in different directions, twisting in the air. It looked like stars floated around the throne, the seat emitting the lustre, accompanied with other types of red and orange glow so mesmerising, some say people have starved to death for how long their stare had remained unbroken. As for the actual chair, the black-grey metal twisted so intricately, sprawling in ways that mortal smiths could not work metal, yet somehow transpiring to be the most comfortable seat in the realm. Inside the metal sat something deeper. A bright, honey coloured energy flowed through every inch of the chair, the arcane substance pulsating as if it were alive. What *this* was, was unknown. The scriptures say it held the energy of the sun. Elders said it was a living essence of magic, trapped and never to be released. Some folk also believed it to be a star, locked inside the throne, to extinguish if an unworthy king was to ever sit on it.

No matter what it was, to Esmond, it was the most beautiful thing he, or any man, would ever see. He put his hand on the beguiling armrest, on touch, glowing brighter and warmer as if it were speaking to him. "I've missed you, you know. Even if you don't believe it," he whispered.

Reverberating footsteps filled the room. Esmond didn't bother himself to turn around; he knew that whatever he turned to see wouldn't be as breathtaking as the solar throne. He let the hasty footsteps make it all the way to his side.

"It never gets less enchanting," the voice of Galloway Malone found Esmond's ears.

"It doesn't, does it?" Esmond agreed eventually. He stared a while longer. "Well, the meeting should start soon," he said, making his way to the staircase that led down under the throne, "a lot we need to work through, Lord Malone."

"Actually, I hoped to catch you early," he admitted, letting Esmond stop and turn before continuing. "This has been on my mind for a while, and... I can't help but feel... a distrust coming from you, my king."

"Why would that be, my lord? Have you done something to make me distrust you?" he asked playfully, being careful to not let any of his knowledge show.

"Sometimes... the reality of situations may not show their true light to eyes that only catch a glimpse," he said, expressing with his hands.

"You knew Eva saw you."

Galloway was taken aback. "I was hoping to be-"

"To beat around the bush?" Esmond frowned. "If there's something you want to tell me, then say it to my face, and not with interpretation. You always have before."

"My king," he said, dropping to his knee, "I'm nothing but loyal to you, and the fact that the princess has depicted me in such a way is almost insulting. I would ask your forgiveness."

The king scratched his beard. "It came from my daughter's mouth," he said after weighing up the old northman. "What reason would Eva have to lie?" Galloway seemed to accept that, furrowing his scarred brow and nodding. "But... like you said, it can be misinterpreted. Whatever business you may have with the Capricornians can stay between yourselves. You *have* been loyal for so long, so I will continue to heed your advice until you give me another reason to distrust you."

"Thank you, my king," he bowed. "It might put you at ease to know that business is concluded; the act is like to be carried out already. I promise you, it's all for peace in the future."

"It might," Esmond agreed, cupping his bearded chin. "Now come on, we have a lot to set up." He continued his walk to the winding staircase.

The council chamber was as wide as the throne room, though not as tall, since it sat beneath. The table was a tiny rectangle in the middle, Esmond's father, King Palmer the Second, swapping the hundred-seat-table with a much more manageable thirty. He believed that no king would ever have need of one hundred councillors, and he was right. Tonight was the biggest council meeting Esmond had endured, a total of fourteen, including himself, to be seated. If Lori, Asher, and Sir Roswell were here, everyone to ever sit at a council table with Esmond would be present.

It took longer than Esmond would have liked for everyone to get settled, some lords not seeing each other for decades, catching up on the missed years. To be fair, many faces Esmond enjoyed seeing for the first time in years too: Tobi Sparks, head of *pennons*, always quick to wear a smile; Elliot Moss, head of development, sharp and considerate, optimisation never far from his mind; Hugo Lane, head of citizen satisfaction, far from a warrior, wearing his fat figure, yet a true thinker for the people. In fact, there wasn't a councillor that Esmond didn't miss. Each and every one of them brought a skill that only they could bring.

"My friends," Esmond eventually stood to interrupt the chatter, a beaming smile on his face, "it is with great gratitude, that I am blessed with such incredible councillors tonight, and I am truly grateful for you all to make it at such short notice. So, before we begin, I'd like to raise a toast," he grinned, holding his goblet of water to the air. He let everyone lift theirs before he continued. "Here's to all of you: the people holding the realm together."

"To the realm!" Sir Orion echoed, raising his goblet.

They drank together, before taking their seats at the large, marble table.

Elder Marcarius cleared his old throat. "Should we begin with the edicts, my king?" he asked, already making himself comfortable enough to fetch the scrolls that told him so.

"Not this time, Marcarius," Esmond decided. "As we all know, the realm is in clear disquiet. Over the last few moons, we've lost strong names like Reynold Lyrderyn, Sigmund Horncurve, Daryl Venulaes, all claimed by the same fate. Furthermore, Sir Devon Thorneton, a long standing and faithful member of my king's guard, was taken from us not even a-"

"Sir Devon is gone?" Thaddeus gasped in disbelief.

"Taken by the same poison that took the others," he nodded. "Until these assassinations are dealt with, I think that it is obvious that we neglect any other advancements; does anyone disagree?"

The room fell silent, the choice showing itself instantly.

Esmond was about to continue, until Wye Vesta put his old arm up. "I don't disagree by any means, my king. These brigands must be stopped, but pushing other matters aside may endanger the realm also."

"I assure you Lord Vesta, if a matter more prominent is brought to our attention, then we will pursue it," Esmond said to the worried lord.

He didn't seem to nod like Esmond thought he would. "I also fear you are with intention to bring these fiends to justice; I believe that pointing fingers and starting wars can only lead to turmoil."

"Ah, you should know, my king, before we continue, more attacks have been reported on areas along the southern coast," Briggs Waker, head of word, chimed in before Wye could continue. "Some of the destinations include: Artis Bay, Sagwhel, Castle Branch, Goattreath, Vaswick..."

"All around the Lagoon," Esmond muttered.

"Attacking from the coast," Galloway Malone pointed out, "these are no mainlanders."

"Definitely of the Archipelago's doing," Elder Marcarius agreed.

"The evidence stacks against them, my lords," Briggs intervened. "Citrine was discovered on multiple bodies from the attack on Goattreath. If I am not mistaken, citrine is the gemstone of the Scorpio."

"Sculptors," Esmond remembered. "If these are coastal attacks, have the Sculptors not spotted ships sailing past the Sangis Waterway?"

"Lord Curtis is likely busy making sure his people are safe; we have received no such word, my king, nor any, come to think of it," Briggs Waker assured.

"Really?" the king winced. "Nothing from Watchpoint Iluro?"

"Lord Curtis doubled the lookouts on the watchpoint after hearing of the attack on Centaur's Lagoon. I assure you, the waters have been silent," Lord Waker confirmed.

Esmond was sure that the Lord of Sangis might have had some intel. Now they were right back to square one.

"Might they have travelled on foot then?" Sir Orion proposed. "We already know that during the ambush on Lord Reynold, they flew no banners. They were disguised."

Thaddeus frowned. "For that many to scathe by unnoticed, they must have had to wear pretty damn convincing disguises."

"Unless they didn't travel conjointly," Elder Marcarius suggested. "Perchance our attackers have planned this for a time."

"They *must* have to form such a sizeable army," said Lord Malone. "Even blind men could see a navy docking on their shores."

"The Venusians have more reason to plan," Elliot Moss muttered from the corner. "It has been thirty years since Cole Scorpius was executed as punishment for the *rebellion*. Perhaps they hatched the plot before Eldric Scorpius's blood was cold."

"We're in too much of a weak position to accuse them," Esmond sighed. "Venusian men line the Taiga coast; if we are to march on the Archipelago, they would break us from within."

"Marching is unwise, my king," Galloway agreed.

"Still," Esmond added, leaning forward, "we outman their armies, no?"

Briggs shook his head. "Impossible to tell, my king. Even *I* don't have eyes on those islands."

Esmond sent an inquisitive look to his head of pennons. "We have almost one hundred and twenty thousand soldiers with the Pole's *pennons* alone," said Tobi Sparks, "even more if we count the north and the west."

"Enough to take them down," Esmond muttered, his fist to his mouth. "My father only needed forty thousand to crush them. If somehow there was a way to root them out of the Pole?" The council traded worried glances as Esmond toyed with the idea. He stroked his beard. He couldn't help but think the Capras might have helped, their home being just off the Taiga coast. Maybe it made sense for the coordinator to send Capricornian men? It could certainly contribute to getting a substantial number of undetected attackers in the Pole. All they needed was one trade boat, carrying poisoned weapons and citrine to plant on the bodies.

He had to shake off the thought; all it did was make him feel negatively towards Galloway. Plus, he couldn't start accusing House Capras out of nowhere; his family were within arm's reach of them. "Elder Marcarius," he said eventually.

"Yes, my king?" Marcarius replied nervously.

"Delmar Khavar is King of the Archipelago, correct?"

"I believe so, your grace."

"Summon him to court," Esmond nodded. "If he is not here by the moon's end..." he sighed, staring at the table, "...gods save him if he doesn't have enough men."

LETA I
-Horse-

It was strange sailing somewhere that wasn't Centaur's Lagoon. It was stranger sailing on a ship that didn't belong to the Centaurs. However unusual, the journey wasn't unpleasant; the vessel was even bordering luxurious. *What a strange life,* she thought.

Leta Centaur had never seen a wood so dark. Her mother had told her it was taiga wood, thanks to the taiga trees that gave the islands their name. It was worked so flawlessly, not a splinter in sight, especially for how large the ship was. It had perfectly smooth wooden masts, with vast black sails beating in the frozen wind. The wooden deck underfoot had the planks perfectly aligned, and a bowsprit leapt out at the front of the boat, the end of the pole sculpted into a fine goat head.

She still hadn't gotten comfortable, or even used to the Capricornian ship crew, even though her own household guard outnumbered them. The guard consisted of eight; they were no knights, but had still sworn to protect like knights would, born and raised in Negalia. The odds of them winning should a battle break out were changing quickly, though, the dark boat leading Leta and her mother straight into the goat's den. Although she was on edge, Leta wasn't scared. It seemed idiotic to her that the Capricornians would murder them now. She knew Fletcher wouldn't hold back on erasing the Capricorn name if he should get word that his sister and mother were slaughtered as guests. That being said, it took Leta a good portion of the journey to come to that conclusion, the uncharted territory of the Capra line being almost as unknown as the Endless Open.

It had been close to two days since they set off, and though bergs of ice recently began to lace the waters, they didn't seem to slow down. The Capricornians sailed without a care past them, even bulldozing through a few smaller ones. Tyran told them not to worry: 'our ships are made to withstand the most traumatic of collisions'. It made Leta wonder. *Would it withstand a trebuchet? A flaming catapult? What about a good anchor swing? We have all three at Fort Deus.*

The evening was growing close, and Leta began to feel exhausted at seeing the same empty expanse of blue peppered with glaciers. Thankfully, she only had to wait a while longer before the shadow of an island crept over the horizon, right before the setting sun. It must have been the island of Seden, since they had passed Refren earlier that morning. Not much seemed to be going on at Refren, Leta gazing at the island through her quarters' window as they passed it. The island wasn't barren, by any means. It was littered with wooden cabins made for housing, shops, and everything you'd need on a secluded island like that. The streets were lifeless though, as if the population slept as a unit. Other than the cabins, no greater structures could be seen. The tallest building was of a watchtower, but that was the greatest extent of Refren's construction.

Seden was another story entirely. They were far from the island, impossible to tell what buildings lay on it, yet silhouettes of great towers and tall trees gingerly revealed themselves. Leta was brought up on childhood stories about the Capricornians being ruthless savages, exiled and hidden on faraway islands. *No savage could build such regal buildings,* she thought. *The stories are lies.* Semira must have been as shocked as her, a gaping mouth stretching her long face out.

The sound of life thriving was prominent from miles away, but as they drew closer to the dock, noise veiled the boat.

"My ladies," Tyran bowed, throwing a dense anchor over the ship, "welcome to Seden."

Leta was the first to step off the boat, landing on the dark wooden dock. Mossy stone took over the ground where the dock ended, some moss even sprawling up to the snug wooden cabins. Tall taiga trees stood all around, the occasional pile of snow falling from the tip as a gust of wind visited. Streetlights of lit lantern candles lined the long streets as herds of people went about their evening life. The Taiga Isles were much colder than Fort Deus, Leta near freezing to death on their voyage, but with the newly found warmth that Seden emitted, began to sweat under the many layers of her cosy, blue dyed furs. She reluctantly took them off, still struck with wonder at the thriving city.

"I can take that, my lady," Tyran offered, swooping the furs before she had a chance to rest them on her arm. "If you would follow me?" he said to the Centaurs, taking lead.

The citizens didn't look any less like the smallfolk in Fort Deus, Leta half expecting the people here to be brawny and feral. They bowed to Tyran as if he was a god upon passing them, dropping what they were doing to fall on their knees, even more so to how people would react to Leta's father strolling through the fort.

"Do you not have horses here?" Semira asked. "I don't see any."

"We would, they're beautiful creatures," Tyran sighed, "but it's too cold for them here. It would cost too much just to keep them warm; we'd much rather spend our time on keeping *people* warm instead."

Leta didn't mind walking. She would do it all the time when she went hunting with Eva, never being able to sneak a horse or two out with them. Still, she missed the animal, always not being too far from one.

It took them no more than an hour to navigate the winding, rocky roads of the island, reaching their destination before the walking became strenuous. They were brought before a gracious castle, with a tower so high, it could be seen from the bottom of the island. It used a lot of wood in its architecture for a castle; a fort built like that would never survive a strong attack on the mainland. That being said, the edges of the steep hill that surrounded the keep would prove difficult for attackers to climb, especially if arrows and barrels rained down on them. Even though they were on a slope, the number of taiga trees didn't seem to wane, some pointing out of the dirt at seemingly impossible angles. The breeze was also cooler up there, the cluster of warmth that was felt at the bottom, staying at the bottom.

It was the first time Leta had seen the sigil of Capra: a brown goat with the tail of an island, atop a background of black. The banners snapped in the wind high on the fort, where the light from inside poured out into the ever-blackening darkness.

The great wooden doors to the mellow keep opened as they approached close enough. On the opposite side stood a man, incredibly tall and sharing the same skin shade as Tyran. He wore a large, green cloak with wool on the inner side, and was dressed in garments made of brown and black leather. On his chin grew a slightly more pruned beard than

Tyran's shaggy one, but it was still impressive.

"Welcome home, my son," the man beamed, embracing Tyran. "Is your news good or ill?"

"Good," Tyran smiled. "Lord Fletcher has agreed to our alliance. He will provide men and resources wherever necessary, as we will for him."

"That is excellent to hear," he replied, grasping Tyran's thick shoulders. His gaze shifted to the Centaurs. "Who might our guests be?"

Tyran turned to them. "Father, I present to you Queen Semira Centaur, and her lady daughter, Princess Leta Centaur."

The man staggered back. He fell to one knee. "It is an honour to receive you, my queen. Stay as long as you wish," he offered warmly. "I would not ask of you to call me a king. My name is Nero, that is all."

"Rise, your grace," Semira chuckled. "We are all urbane here; neither of our titles mean anything past these shores."

"Wisely put, my queen," smiled Nero, "but I will still call you as such." He bowed. "Come, share our meat and mead. Supper is warm."

Brown carpets swallowed the castle floor, the wood-and-stone aesthetic remaining a constant. They were led past a few closed rooms, neither bars nor windows on the doors, Leta itching to have them explored.

Their mess hall was surprisingly larger than Fort Deus's, even though the size of this castle was dwarfed by Leta's home. It looked like food had already been eaten, empty plates littering the large table. Lots of food still sat there, though. Oats and salad separated huge dishes of fresh, half-eaten beef, charred black from the roaring brazier.

"Take a seat," said Nero, "eat as much as you can." He elegantly sank himself at the head of the table, taking a chair slightly larger than the rest.

Leta and her mother were apprehensive to sit down, doing so slowly. "Forgive me, Nero, we do not have food like this up north. Would you...?"

"Ah, yes!" Nero jumped up in his seat. "The kale and beef are grown on our land, expertly steamed and grilled by our chefs. These are cranberries, leeks, and quinoa, fresh in from Boventos. Doubtless you have some of this in the Pole, it might just be differently served here."

"This food is all the way from Heavia?" Semira gasped.

"I'm afraid that, because of our... position, it is either from there or the Archipelago. It just so happens that the Lords of Boventos grow more food than their people can eat."

Lords of Boventos? Leta winced. She was told since she was young that the exiled of Heavia were also savages, even more so than the Capricornians. It was said that the people who lived past the Vetiti Wall were warriors of the jungle, sometimes only carrying their fists into battle and still felling as many as they would with a sword. Athena had told her as such, saying that upon a stay in Lushwood, they were ambushed by Taureans. Although they were quickly shot down by the well defended city, Athena said they ran like they were born running, some even escaping with stolen goods.

Now, Leta couldn't shake the thought of those same animals kicking back and having a civilised cup of tea. It made Leta think. *Maybe to them, we're the savages, our wild armies charging in on horseback, screaming and firing arrows, some even standing to do so.* Even the Horncurve armies could be seen as such, each one of them a brute with giant longswords and painted faces. *No. We can't be barbarians. We settle things with words. We live in fancy castles. We are lords and ladies...* 'Lord of Boventos' rang in her head again. 'King of Seden'. *...But so are they.*

"Leta," Semira said, abruptly snapping her out of thought, "the king asked you a question."

"What?" she uttered, fluttering her eyes.

King Nero chortled. "The food, is it not to your liking? We could send for something else, if it please?"

Leta flinched, her eyes shooting to the steaming food piled on her and Semira's plate. Embarrassment flushed over her. "No. I mean yes. I mean it's ok." She grabbed her fork nervously.

"Lost in thought, were we?" Nero smiled openly. "There must be all sorts of things shooting through that young brain of yours. What do you think of our home?"

"Father, you're interrogating the poor girl," Tyran sighed.

"Your home..." she glanced at her mother, "...isn't what I expected."

Nero held his smile, his teeth hiding behind his lips. He slumped back into his chair. "That's the case from most who come from the north," he sighed, playing with his golden chain that hung heavily around his neck. "Out of all the places of exile, Seden is the last place most pick. It is patent to them that a grander life can be offered at the Archipelago or Heavia. It is the ignorance of what people think this place is that betrays them."

"It's ignorance that betrays most people," Tyran murmured through his teeth, receiving a sharp stare from his father.

"It is easier to travel to the Archipelago or Heavia. This island is very secluded," Semira commented, too familiar with easing dinnertime tension.

"Falsehoods of a rarely seen place are like to be heard more often."

Nero agreed with a single nod. "If it were up to me, we wouldn't be here," he said, standing up. "But that's the hand that has been dealt to us."

"If it were up to Esmond, intentions would be held above crime. It's unfair that you are being punished," Semira affirmed.

Another sigh escaped Nero's tight mouth. "Those birds have long flown," he smiled sadly with his dark eyes. "Esmond is a good king. I hope for our alliance to continue past the attacks." Nero wore a face like he wanted to say more. Leta knew that expression all too well when Hew was forced by their mother to hold his tactless tongue. "Forgive me, your grace, I grow worn from the day. I trust that you and your guard should be found suitable quarters. If anything is required: extra pillow, more candle, what have you, all you need do is shout."

"Thank you, Nero," Semira smiled.

After supper was concluded, they were shown by Tyran to their rooms. "I thought you might want to share my sister's chamber," he offered to Leta as they walked. "I believe she is around your age. Wouldn't hurt to make a new friend."

Befriend those who'd care to do so. "Yeah, I'd like that," she smiled back. Even though she was tasked to, the prospect of making new friends excited Leta. It *was* slightly tainted because of that, but she didn't mind too much.

"Excellent, well this is you then." Tyran opened the creaky door to her chambers. Inside sat a girl on the floor, who seemed to be writing something in a notebook before staggering back. "Princess Leta, this is my sister Kiera, and Kiera, this is Princess Leta."

Kiera was beautiful. She had long brown hair, a similar length to Leta's black. Her ears and neck were chiselled, a constant running down her petite body. Clutching her book close to her chest, she stared at them nervously with her sombre eyes, a shade lighter than her kin.

"Well I'll leave you two to get to know each other then," Tyran grinned on his way out.

"Wait," Kiera whispered sharply. She gestured her brother to come closer, not comfortable with saying what she had to say in front of Leta. It didn't matter, Leta could tell what they said from how their mouths moved. "Is she sleeping here?"

"I thought you might like a new friend."

"We have to share a bed. I don't know her."

"You can get to know her by talking to her."

"I don't want to. I'm fine on my own."

"You can't say no now, she's already here-"

"I could sleep in a different chamber. It's really not a big deal," Leta proposed, silencing the whispers.

They glanced at each other. "Nonsense," Tyran smiled, "tomorrow you'll be the best of friends." He patted his sister on the head before strolling out.

Semira kissed Leta on the forehead. "Goodnight, sweetheart," she said, following Tyran out.

The air seemed colder when everyone but Kiera and Leta had left. Kiera slid back into her huddle on the floor, eyes locked at her feet. Leta looked around the room. It was similar to hers back at Fort Deus, more so if the browns of Capra were replaced by the blues of Centaur. A pile of papers sat in one corner, all faced down. Another corner was filled with screwed or torn-up papers, some of its ink even staining the wooden floor.

"So," Leta said eventually, "I like your room." She edged closer, only to be met with a flinch from Kiera, followed by silence. *Is she shy? She looks a lot older than me.* "What were you writing... before I came in."

Kiera peeled the book from her chest, glancing at her work before pulling it close again. "Nothing,"

It *was* something, the quill she held had fallen out of her hands and rolled next to her feet for a time. *Gods, it's going to be impossible to make her my friend. I'd have better luck courting a brick.*

After Leta's belongings were delivered by her household guard, she slipped into her sleeping silks, all the while Kiera remaining frozen in her position. Occasionally, Leta would catch her adding to what she had written on her notebook, only to freeze and drop her eyes to the floor when she noticed Leta again. By the time Leta had slipped into the king-sized bed, the room was lit only by a single bedside candle, the maids extinguishing the others to prepare the chamber for night. Leta tried to close her eyes, but couldn't keep them shut. She felt guilty that Kiera remained on the floor.

"Are you not coming to bed?" Leta asked.

Although it was difficult to tell due to the dimly lit chamber, it looked like Kiera shook her head, curling up tighter.

Leta sighed, taking a couple of the million pillows that lay at the regal headboard, before placing them on the chilly ground. She curled up atop them, feeling oddly comfortable . She could keep her eyes closed then, only to be reopened by the sound of light footsteps creeping over.

"What are you doing?" Kiera finally asked.

Leta glanced over, Kiera's posture becoming slumped when she was noticed again. "You sleep in the bed. The floor is fine for me."

Kiera held her arm while a small and hidden, yet grateful smile led her face, making dimples hollow out her cheeks. She slipped into the bed in an easier fashion than how she approached Leta.

Leta rolled back over to her pillows, closing her eyes, with a fresh grin of satisfaction. *A smile. That's a start,* she thought, falling asleep.

RILEY II
-Squall-

The journey couldn't have seemed longer. Breaks and pauses were fortunately less frequent than the many that littered their ride down to Fort Deus, but Sigmund's effect on emotion definitely dragged out the journey. That being said, Emily's let the kids run rampant at Merchant's Bay was such a bright one. After that, the three talked and joked with each other as they had always, lifting the spirits of the others. They even seemed to have real conversation for once, which was surprising.

Riley Horncurve knew and empathised with how much everyone wanted to see home again, though, so when the proud city came towering over the morning horizon, the relief could be felt in the mild air. It helped that Selerborn didn't seem any less proud. The gates were ever as grand: a thousand spikes of ram horns shooting up and curling in different directions, all atop a massive portcullis fit to healthily have at least a hundred battering rams go through side-by-side without problems. Ram horns were a feature that continued across the city walls, a form of fortification, impossible for attackers to climb over. Every time Riley saw the city, it felt like more and more horns were a part of it. It didn't shock him, though, Ram's Haven had so many rams and sheep as inhabitants, Riley would wager that the animals outnumbered the people; but that was a brave wager, since Selerborn alone stood at two hundred thousand strong.

Selerborn was a unique city in its build, most cities adopting a traditional layout of a square or a circle, the city of the rams taking a more linear approach. It had an unbroken, straight path down the centre of the city, named the Road of Rams, reaching all the way to the Cenkeep, which, in parts, reached even as far as the Twin River. Riley could see the Cenkeep upon entering the city, ascending on the very edge of the world, a timid, red sun rising from behind it.

The gatekeeper on duty must have been half asleep, taking a while to notice that the giant party entering the city were Horncurves, consequently sending a booming blow on the city horn. Residents tiredly clambered out of their stone homes, a growing crowd gathering around the party. Some cheered, not many though. *Have they not received word? Maybe Esmond didn't want it common knowledge?* It was hard to tell. They were definitely confused. It felt like they had ridden into a different Selerborn. Riley glanced back to his party, all sharing the same worried face in response to the speculative citizens.

"*Where's Sigmund?*" one woman shouted, Riley wincing as he ignored.

Lord Harper Siren came galloping down the gravel road with two guards, stopping before the Horncurves. "Lord Riley," he bowed, out of breath yet hidden well. "I wouldae liked to greet you at the gate. You just slipped by it so quickly."

"Ye did leave the thing totally open. We could have been anyone," Riley responded, lack of jest.

"I'm sorry, my lord. It's been dreadful quiet up here since you left." Lord Harper was fairly young, a few years older than Riley's thirty-four. He had a full head of brown, bushy hair, and faint furrows in his face despite his youth. He wasn't naive though; he must have wanted trouble to leave the gate open. It was strange because Riley always thought Harper seemed like a good leader. *Sigmund trusted him with Selerborn. He wouldn't do that lightly.*

"Ah, don't worry 'bout it," Riley said, kicking his horse back into a trot. "How was my gal?"

"Good." He rotated his mount. "I expected you back sooner."

"Aye," Riley sighed, "so did we." Riley couldn't shake the feeling of eyes judging his every move. He didn't even feel like he could tell the truth about what happened just yet. It was clear that people wouldn't take it well.

"Might I ask why Lord Sigmund is not with you?"

Riley grimaced as the question everyone was thinking surfaced. "*Listen up!*" he thundered, abruptly turning his stallion. "I need you all to come to the Cenkeep. A few things are gonnae change around here."

Luckily, in the brief interaction they had with Thaddeus Centaur, the acting king had gladly provided a wagon for Sigmund's casket, so it wasn't so obvious to the people of Selerborn. Riley felt unwelcomed enough, and for them to know what had happened would only make things worse. He could foresee himself and his party getting mobbed, and it wasn't a notion he wanted to have for much longer.

After a while's ride down the road, the Horncurves arrived at the foot of the keep, letting the stable masters and the servants take the horses and goods. Riley paused for a moment to admire it. If Lunarpass sent shivers down Riley's spine, the Cenkeep did so a thousand times stronger. From where the road ended, two immense staircases split outwards, making a large circle before wrapping back around to the entrance of the keep. He always tried to imagine how Sigmund stormed those massive staircases, accompanied with his militia of just two hundred. *It must have been quite a thing to witness.* More men must have fallen to their death than put to the sword, but still, it was remarkable that Sigmund managed it.

Below, in the large grass circle named the Yard of Heroes, the common people gathered, gazing up and waiting for the announcement. It took a time for Riley to make it up the stairs, but once he did, he immediately placed himself at the head of the podium from where the two cases joined, right before the entrance.

It was the first time in ages that Riley had felt creatures of nervousness wriggle around in his stomach. The people staring up were more intimidating than death itself to him. He cleared his throat, glancing around to spot his brother and Elder Ignatius by his side. They both seemed to be equally as swung by the huge crowd growing at the bottom.

"People of Selerborn," he began, swallowing his nerves. He didn't know how to put it. "There is no easy way to tell you all that Sigmund has left us. I believe there's not a single person here that didn't love the man, no one more than his two sons." Heads fell down, their fears coming true. "He was a strong man; the strongest I knew. He always put his people before himself, and I will vow to give nothing less to you all. As he rests, the torch has been passed to me, and I will do everything I can to keep his memory alive."

The crowd had a mixed response. Some seemed positive, cheering for Sigmund and Riley. Others were still confused, wincing or scowling. *"How didae die?"* one yelled. *"Was he murdered?"* another followed.

"Father... Sigmund had to face punishment for a crime he had committed. A boy had been felled by his hand, and Sigmund was required to pay the price."

"How didae die!?" another yelled, even louder.

"He paid with his head," Riley shouted back, beginning to get frustrated. "King Esmond took it."

The crowd erupted. *"Bloody Centaurs!"* *"Aye, no king of mine!"* *"He was murdered!"*

The louts had voiced their opinion, and Riley was not pleased with it. *Curse me all you like. But curse my king and you can all hang.* "Esmond did what needed to be done to be just. He's not our enemy."

"He's the king! He can do anything!" *"Aye! Killed in cold blood!"*

"It was what Sigmund wanted. Esmond was his friend!" he bawled, beginning to flare up. His mouth said one thing, while his mind thought another. *He was the king. He could have easily saved father if he wanted to.* Riley shook his head. *He had to execute him. It was right.* Emily touched his arm gently. Her eyes screamed for them to leave. He almost turned to walk into the Cenkeep before the furore worsened.

"We need to teach 'em a lesson!" *"Skewer the Centaur for Sigmund!"* *"Aye! The Lord of Selerborn would march on the south at once!"*

"Bloody bampots! We march nowhere! I am the Lord of Selerborn now!" The crowd fell silent. *"It was my blood that ran through his veins, not any of yours, so don't tell me what I should or should not do! Esmond is our king! March south if that makes ye content with yer sorry lives, but know that if you do, you will never be welcomed back through those gates!"* The echo of Riley's voice bounced around the huge city. His heart beat a thousand times a second. He held his poise for an uncomfortable time, before turning around and heading into the Cenkeep. The clamour of curses gradually increased once again as he walked away, muffled out by the keep's door closing behind him. Emily clutched his arm tightly as they walked. He headed straight to the alcohol, not even waiting for the servants to serve the cups before snatching himself a drink. He held his head in his hands as his family gathered. "Marcus, Cadmus, Athena," he mumbled, not looking at them, "you go to your rooms, eh?"

Emily nodded to them, dismissing them. "You did what had to be done," she said, sitting next to him.

"They'll hate me fer it," he sighed.

"Only a few. You're the rightful heir, Riley; most of Selerborn will still stand behind you," Elder Ignatius assured.

"Less so since ya called them bampots," Luther added, joining the others at the table.

"Luther," Emily censured.

"He's right," Riley said, biting his tongue. "There's nae hope of reasonin' with people who only see blood. Love is the last thing I'll get from them."

"I didn't say that," Luther continued. "Once they see yer for Sigmund's son, they'll all respect you, brother. They don't know you like they knew Sigmund. Show them you're a coward, and they'd believe it."

Luther had a look of pity in his eyes, despite his squalor. "A *coward,*" Riley snickered. "Is that what I am for claiming my right? For not committing treason and avenging our father?" He let a moment pass then spoke with less bitterness. "I don't get it. I haven't done anything."

"Come now, you know our folk better than that," Ignatius agreed. "They won't respect a forgiving man. They need a *leader.*"

"What do ye propose, huh?" he snapped. "Marching on the south? Killing all the sheep for sport? How about we try to kill all the Taureans? Gods know father didn't fail at that enough."

"Da' wanted to get back before the Taureans could settle again, before they could take us by surprise," Luther added. "Now would be the perfect time to strike, fast and strong like *he* would have done."

"Bloodshed isn't the only way to command respect," sighed Ignatius.

"Aye, but it seems our option at the moment," Harper jogged in, spattered with fruits and bruises. "It's only getting worse out there."

"The *fucks* wrong with 'em?" Riley slammed his fists on the rocky stone table, almost making them bleed. The room's silence was broken by his voice again. "Harper, you're the head of citizenship, what would ye have me do?"

Lord Siren stuttered. "It would be a tad easier if you hadn't yelled at them... but I think you should just give 'em time. That's their first reaction to the news. It'll blow over," he assured.

"And if it doesn't?" Luther asked sardonically.

Harper hesitated, before pulling out a few crumpled parchments from his belt. "Letters from the south... all screaming one thing: *war, war, war.* More raids are popping up, and some say that the Archipelago is behind 'em. If this is true, and there is a big war in the Pole, the people *definitely* won't respect us if we sit back and do nothing."

Riley shook his head immediately. "We have no part in a southern war; our place is here. They wouldn't fight for Esmond, they *hate* him. Plus, the Archipelago is leagues away. No way can we get our batterin' rams across the water. We take *castles,* not islands," he said, taken aback as his father's words left his mouth.

"I didn't *entirely* mean fighting *for* Esmond." Everyone except Harper looked worried, as if to say *'don't'.* "Look, I know he's your friend, but the people *do* have a point. If he truly loved your father, he wouldae done anythin' to protect him. To be perfectly honest, it probably won't just 'blow over'; a ram has died in a foreign land, and they'll want to see a spill of blood before they deal with that."

"'*The people'* you speak of are nothing more than a radical minority," said Ignatius, angrily. "My lord, if we have any part in this 'war', then it's better to have them on your side first."

"Aye," Luther agreed, sympathetically for once. "Be the lord they need, not the one they want."

"If you're not the ram to lead them, they'll want to choose another who will," Harper assured, his normally strong voice quaking with fear.

His mind was a maze, and he hated it. Riley glanced from one idea to the next, all of them staring back, waiting for his decision. "Leave. I need to think," he sighed, gesturing for his company to exit the room. *What's to stop them from stabbing me in the back if we were to march? And we've just come back, for fucks sake, no way am I marchin' to war so soon.* He tried to think what Sigmund would do. *Maybe I need to be stricter; father showed zero tolerance to disorder. Might that make them hate me even more? 'Be better than me',* his words continued to echo. Whatever he had to do, Riley finally realised he had to lead the storm, as his father had done. The only problem was: he had no idea *where* to lead it.

EVA V
-Youth-

"B oom!" Idris threw his arms in the air excitedly. "I can't get over how good you are!"

Eva Centaur giggled. "It'll help if my arm was healed," she said, strolling confidently to the eighth bunny she had ended.

Idris shook his head, a smile coating his face. "Let's head back now, the folks will be overjoyed with this yield."

She handed the satchel of corpses to him, Idris slinging it over his shoulder. Eva was so happy. She had never been praised so much for her archery, especially from an adult. It was obvious to her that Idris was still wanting to know who she was, as he kept reminding her of his annoyingly correct suspicion that she was highborn, but she had not let him know anything, and he seemed to respect that. Her arm still ached from the gash, sleep being more than uncomfortable since she had to lie in one position, but it had closed up and was restoring really quickly. Idris said that she'd be lucky to get out without a scar, since the knife had cut so deep, but she didn't mind; Idris also said that a scar is the best badge a man could get.

On their way back to the tavern at the Crossroads, they came across a wagon, empty and abandoned. It must have been a trader's wagon, judging by the worn wood. Idris looked over curiously, pulling out a small pouch of coins. "Well, you wanted money," he chuckled.

"No, that's not..." She watched as the coins danced around Idris's hands. "That's dishonest."

He smirked. "I don't recall either of us lying."

Eva shook her head. "Put it back, we're not stealing."

"I agree," he nodded. "We're *not* stealing. We can't be. This cart was dumped here. The person who it belonged to doesn't own it anymore."

"What if you're wrong? They could have just gone for a wander. What if they come back to find all their coin stolen?"

Idris frowned with those dark brows of his. "If we leave it, they'd come back to find it stolen anyway. It's just as likely that one of the drunkards from the tavern come across it, celebrate by wasting it on a few more rounds of ale." He tossed the pouch into Eva's hands. "I'd say it's better in your hands. But it's *your* money. Leave it behind if you want to be *honest.*" Idris slung the corpses back over his shoulder, whistling a tune as he continued their walk down the road. Eva stared at the pouch for a long while. *Better in my hands, yeah,* she thought as she stuffed it into her pocket.

The first time Eva showed her conscious face in the tavern, every eye was locked on her. It terrified her to know what they would do if they caught her alone, but luckily, Idris was an excellent chaperon. The tavern folk loved Eva more as the days went on, buying the girl drinks, and getting her so drunk that she almost couldn't remember the next day. Idris didn't have as many drinks, making sure he was still sober enough to protect her.

The tavern was fairly lively for midday; the roaring of laughter and chatter could be heard miles away. Bards had come and played every night, but at the moment, the music was silent. It was most likely that they were either too inebriated to play, or had travelled elsewhere to play for the Auburn lords.

A cheer met Eva and Idris's arrival, Eva swinging the door open to yell, "lunch has arrived!" Those who could reach patted them on the back as they made their way to the counter.

"Eight today, Fred," Idris smiled, dropping the heavy satchel on the counter.

The bartender raised a brow. "More and more each day; you continue like this and I won't be able to pay you!" he laughed, reaching under the fitment to rummage for money. Fred counted the coins in his palm before placing them on the counter. "There you are, forty-eight coppers."

"Not for me, this time," Idris smiled. "She did all the work."

"Is that so?" Fred asked in astonishment. "Well there you go, little lady. Don't spend 'em all in one place," he chuckled, dropping the coins in Eva's open palm.

She was in awe of the massive amount of money that lay in her hands. Although it was completely dwarfed by the affluent treasury at Fort Deus, Eva couldn't have been prouder, predominantly since it came from *her* own work. If she always knew that bunnies could sell for six coppers each, she would have been the richest girl in the Pole by now.

"Is that enough for you?" Idris smirked.

"More than enough," she grinned, jingling them around in her hands. "I could buy *so* many arrows with this! Or maybe a new satchel? I could definitely get new clothes. And food! I could feed a castle with this much."

Idris laughed at how excited she was. "Amazing," he smiled, scratching the hair under his headband. His expression became strangely solemn. "Before you go on your bender, could I have a word with you alone?"

Eva's smile only half faded, curiosity infecting her brows. She nodded, following him to their room.

He paced around for a time, fumbling with his hands. "Listen, Eva, I wasn't meant to stay here so long. In fact, I was leaving when I found you... and I promised to stay until your arm got better, so... I think it's time... that, um-"

"You want to go home?" Eva asked anxiously.

"I want to stay here. I want to show you to your home so you can find your family again... but I *have* to go home," Idris sighed, sitting on the bed. "I got word a couple of days ago that my father is sick. I overheard some northern folk from Lutum say he might not survive the moon."

"A few days ago?" she gasped. "Why didn't you tell me?"

Idris chuckled. "Because you weren't better."

Eva shook her head. "You nurse me until my arm is better, you protect me from all the drunk tavern people, you sleep on the floor so I can have the bed," she said, starting to tear up, "why?"

Idris walked over and put his hands on her shoulders. "You're not a normal girl. You've made that clear by now. You made that clear when you *somehow* survived five grown men trying to kill you." He chuckled. "I don't doubt you can look after yourself, but behind the bow you're still just a little girl. And I couldn't just leave you." He dropped his arms to his side again. "But I must do this for myself now. My family needs me."

I am family, she felt like saying. "Why are you confused then? Take me with you." She spoke before she thought. *If I go, I might never see home again. I might never see my family again.*

"I feel responsible for you now. I can't take you with me and snatch you away from your family. I would, but I can't. It's not right."

"What's not right? I... left my family. Please, Idris," she begged. "I'd be safer by your side than anywhere else. Like you said, I've already had five men try to kill me, and I wasn't even on my own for a *day*."

Idris paused to think. "Are you sure you want to do this?" he asked eventually. "If I bring you with me, then you'll have to do everything I tell you. I can't promise how well you'll be treated at Lutum. I can't promise if you can safely get back here again."

"I don't *care* how safe I am," she assured. "You told me how great life is when you're not too safe. I want to see the world now. I want to see everything I haven't." Leta's words bounced around in her head: '*When we're old enough*'. She frowned; *I was always old enough.*

Idris sighed, as if to say he regretted telling her that. "You will do everything I ask," he said, staring into her eyes. "If I tell you to run, you will run. If I tell you to hide, you will hide. If I tell you to kill, you will-"

"Kill," she nodded. "I'll do everything you ask of me; I promise."

"The Canicule is a dangerous place, even more so than the Pole." He walked to the window, looking down to the wagons and riders and stablemasters going about their duty. "Ok," he turned. "I'll let you come." Eva ran to him and wrapped her arms around his waist.

The reality of the situation didn't hit her until they were ready to leave. Idris purchased her a beautiful white horse from the stables; it was almost too big to sit on, but Eva loved it all the same. They rode with their minimal luggage, only a few pieces of food and bottles of water attached to the saddle, but Eva felt like they were almost nude. *I'm finally doing it,* she thought excitedly. *I'm finally going out into the world to explore.* Her excitement was somewhat tainted though. *I wonder how father will react to finding my stuff. Would he send out a search party? Would he let mother and everyone else know?* Her heart sank. *Leta knows. What if she tells father about what happened? What if Jovian tells him? What if Galloway tries to kill them for knowing too much?* Suddenly, she was much less comfortable with the decision she had made.

ESMOND VIII
-Fault-

He hoped it wasn't true that they had found an extra suitcase on the spare wagon train. Had it been under any other context, his gut wouldn't have told him to worry. It was probably pessimism talking; it probably just belonged to a squatter. Still, he walked with some pace to where the wagon was taken, closely followed by his squire, Jovian.

"Here it is, my king," Lord Kaleb Shaw, head of the city's garrison said upon entering the tailors.

The case wasn't a case at all; it was more a makeshift bedsheet pouch, bulging with objects of mixed size, and fastened tight as if it had never been touched. *Gods, no. Let it be a squatter, please,* Esmond Centaur prayed, even though there was only one place he knew that had bedsheets like that.

"As soon as I saw it weren't mine, I never touched it, my king," the tailor assured, holding his shaking hands up.

Esmond slowly untied the tight knot of the pouch, letting the crumpled contents spill out. *Eva's clothes. Damn it all.* It had her favourite grey, fur coat, alongside a silver brooch that was given on her latest birthmoon, and her silky leather gloves she loved to hunt in, because the bows at the fort would give her blisters. Underneath, there was a small ball of linen and velvet garments, creased and crumpled. Esmond fell to the nearest chair as a sickness rose to his head.

"What is it, my king?" asked Kaleb.

Esmond shook his head. "It belongs to my daughter, Eva."

Jovian was quick to respond. "How?"

"She begged me not to go," he sighed. *"Gods dammit,* I knew I should have just let her. I knew she would have done it anyway."

"Maybe she's in the city, then?" Jovian asked, panicking. *Jovian, if you know something...*

"Never," Esmond said curiously, "the moment she could come out, she would." The king eyed the boy down. The squire was practically quivering. Esmond startled him as he spoke. "What's wrong, Jovian?"

Jovian's wandering eyes briefly locked with Esmond's before falling again. "I... uh... saw the case when I checked the wagon. I thought I saw something move, but... I'm sorry, it must have been her, it's my fault."

Fool, Esmond sighed. "Don't blame yourself," he said kindly. "Not a word of this travels outside, do you all hear? Chances are, she's in the Pole somewhere. If people find out, then we have no way of keeping her safe."

"Shouldn't we send out a search party, my king?" Kaleb asked.

"No, send a search warrant. The girl sticks out like a sore thumb. Put a description of her and nothing more; Jovian you know her likeness, you go with him. We'll find her sooner if there is a price to be paid."

"And what would that price be?"

Esmond winced. "Let's say... fifty silvers. No. Make it twenty. Too much is suspicious."

Lord Shaw bowed. "Very wise, my king. I will see to Lord Vesta."

As they were walking out, Esmond grew nervous. *What if the Pole thinks she's a bandit? What if they deliver their head instead?* "Make sure it says she is not to be harmed. Often and boldly," he called to them.

Kaleb bowed again. "To your wish, my king."

Esmond sat for a time longer in the tailors, sulking alone with his head in his hands. "Eva, my king. Youngest daughter is it?" the tailor said to him carefully, taking a seat to his side.

The king nodded, not raising his head.

"Ah, don't worry, my king. They always find a way back to you," he assured. "My youngest was taken from me too. *Cruel* gods. She was hungry, you see. Not much money to be made down at Arbor. Wandered too far into the Pole, she did. She were lost for weeks, long enough for me and me wife to give up hope."

"And she came back?"

"Aye," he smiled. "Said she fought off drunken tavern folk and those who wanted to take her in. Not much older than your Eva, she wasn't. She came back when we'd given up on life. It were the happiest I've been in me life. Truth is, I would've never left Arbor if I could. Once you think you've lost someone, you never want 'em to leave your sight again."

Esmond examined the man. Not at all handsome, but he was very lovable. Very fatherly. A rounded belly shaped his waist, and his hands had boils all over from his craft. "Go back to Arbor," Esmond said softly. "Take all the money you need. I'm sure we can find a new master tailor."

The tailor chuckled as he stood, "Too many folk will be let down if I leave, my king. My place is here. Send my earnings back home, I do. Make sure she'll never go hungry again. I only keep enough to eat meself. I'm happy with that."

His positivity made Esmond grin. "What was your name?" He held out his hand.

"Jarrett, if it please," he smiled. "Jarrett Rivers." They shook hands. "She'll come back, my king. They always will."

Esmond was more than ready for something good to happen on his walk back to the inner city. The sight of the comfortable blue silk robes of Elder Marcarius was enough for Esmond to feel content.

"A search warrant, my king?" he asked, worrying. "Who is important enough to yield twenty silvers?"

"How did you know so quickly?" he smiled.

"I caught your squire walking at some haste."

"Why were you looking for my squire?" His grin grew.

"I was looking for *you*," he said harshly. "So, who is this girl?"

The king glanced around the busy crowds, hoping no one was watching. "Eva," he whispered in the elder's ear.

Marcarius's eyes widened. "She's... she's not at the fort? -"

Esmond's explanation was deferred by a ruckus near the lower city square. He shook his head at Marcarius before his attention was pulled toward it. Cursing and shouting could be heard as a man was dragged by two men wearing the oak sigil of Reade. He had a cloth covering his face, but had managed to chew through the gag that bound him. The city's garrison were arguing with the Reade men, telling them to turn around.

"My king!" a third Reade knight called, lack of breath. "My king!"

Esmond walked over. "What's all this about?"

"Apologies, my king," one of the garrison soldiers muttered as he set aside his spear. "We'll have them out of the city in no time."

"Out of the city?" Esmond winced. "They're Madoc Reade's soldiers."

The man's eyes darted about. "They're disrupting the peace, my king."

"Disrupting the peace?" It almost made the king laugh. "What peace? They have a prisoner, you dunce."

He looked to the other garrison men. "The shouting, it's not advo-"

"I part you from Shaw for one second and you all become incompetent," Esmond snickered. "Step aside or I'll have you flogged."

The city's garrison embarrassingly, yet rigidly retreated.

"Our thanks. Lord Madoc Reade sends his felicitations."

"Who is he?" Esmond asked, pointing to the erratic man.

"The bandit, my king. The one who was part of the ambush on Lord Reynold. We found him hiding at Negal Town."

"Is that so?" the king said, a smile spreading out on his face. *And I believed the man an oaf.* He strolled over towards the bandit, still twitching and struggling, limp on one leg. "Show me what's hiding under that mask."

One of the Reade knights that held him took off the cloth, revealing an ugly, plump head, not at all matching his thin stature. He wore a stone grimace, creasing all the cuts and bruises he had on his face. He spat at the king, sending a bloody tooth shooting out his mouth only to reach the king's shoes. The crowds gasped. The king smiled. Esmond walloped him with a punch so hard, even more teeth fell out.

"Good gods, Esmond. Stop," Elder Marcarius said as the king wound up for another. Marcarius was squinting at the bandit. "Show me his face," he ordered, having a Reade knight grab his face to show it to the elder.

"What is it?" Esmond asked, slightly frustrated.

Marcarius eyed him from head to toe. "Manned on the wall, you say?"

"Yes, my lord," nodded the soldier that spoke before.

"What *is* it?" the king asked again, his anger flaring.

The elder wagged his finger, wearing a disgusted face. "This man... this man was on duty when my brother Ulrich and I arrived. No wonder he didn't know who we were. This cretin provoked Lord Sigmund to fury. I believe the name 'sheep' was a common slight, my king."

Esmond cackled loudly. *I knew Sigmund wouldn't attack unprovoked.* "What a day," he said, almost drunkenly. He *was* drunk, though. Drunk with pleasure. "People of Lunarpass," he announced. "The man who stands before you is *not only* the murderer of your first liege lord, Reynold Lyrderyn, but *also* your second, Sigmund 'the Warrior Boy' Horncurve." Most of the crowd were still confused, but some cursed him. "Hereafter, he is charged with treason of the highest degree, and shall be put to death for said crimes." The crowd roared like lions, some booing for the traitor, some cheering for the sentence. "*But...*" Silence flushed over the city again. "Maybe I'm letting him off too lightly, don't you agree?" he asked the public, creating a few 'ayes'. "This man was sent from the *evil* Archipelago to disrupt the king's peace. Should he be let off so easily?"

"*No!*" the crowd yelled, moderately louder.

"He would *kill* any Jupitan he can get his hands on, just like the rest of the attackers. Am I showing him mercy, putting him to a quick death?"

"*Aye!*" the mob roared.

"*Does he deserve a slow death?*"

"*Aye!*"

"*Take him to the stockades, show him no mercy!*"

The horde exploded into chaos, near tearing the man apart as they dragged and flung him about. A huge grin of satisfaction couldn't leave Esmond's face. Even Marcarius approved, smiling as the bandit was carried away. "It might be wise to interrogate him," Marcarius remembered, "see what else he knows about the attacks."

"We will, if he survives the people's wrath," Esmond smiled back. *Hopefully he doesn't.* "Why was it that you were looking for me?"

Marcarius smirked. "Word back from the Archipelago."

Ask and you shall receive, Esmond thought, almost overwhelmed.

"To the King of Jupiter," Marcarius read, as soon as they arrived in his office at the Sphaera. "I received your letter concerning the summoning of King Delmar Khavar, and have acknowledged your intention. I write to you to inform that King Delmar has had no part in the attacks, nor is the man you desire to summon. I am. Give me your word that myself, and the men of my choosing will be safe and protected, and I will give you mine that I will be at the capital by the next moon's end. Signed, Vincent Scorpius, *First Avail* of the king, and Lord of the Stingers." He folded up the parchment and passed it to Esmond.

Very formal, Esmond thought. *Even his handwriting is perfect.* "Grant him passage," he said confidently. "He can bring his escort, if it stops him from pissing his pants."

"Very well," Marcarius nodded, fetching his quill to begin writing.

Esmond sat back in his seat with his hands on the back of his head, finally feeling lively that his best friends were mostly avenged. *We're finally getting somewhere,* he smiled. *Perhaps I won't have to spend long in this wretched city after all.*

LYSSA II
-Cede-

Asher's dreams weren't getting any friendlier. Lyssa Lyrderyn noticed that he was more and more tired every day, a pale colour filling his face, deep lines darkening under his eyes. No one was more scared for him than she was. He would still joke and smile, but it was clear that he hurt underneath. Sometimes, he would avoid sleep entirely, staying up all night rotating the zircon jewels on his bracelet he had got from his sister Leta, staring out into the darkness. Lyssa would be the only one to notice that he was sleeping for most of the time they rode. Uncle Goldwyn would think he got himself a pretty lousy squire if he was caught.

The dream remained all but indifferent. Asher could never react to being cruelly awoken by the feel of knife, only because he would focus on what the seer was saying beforehand. It was like trying to piece a puzzle together, and it wouldn't help that his memory of it was getting increasingly worse. So far, all they had was: 'The Serpent of Stars. It will poison the city, flooded by waters-', and that was the closest thing to a sentence they had come to. They couldn't agree on what or who the serpent was. It could be a person, or an army, or just a stupid snake that had magical powers. Either way, they needed to know while Asher could still handle himself.

That's why Merchant's Bay was such a welcome sight, especially since they had made it in such good time. An early afternoon fell on the trading city, and Lyssa and Asher shared a mutual nervousness about who and what lay there, waiting to take them away.

"Ah, Merchant's Bay," Goldwyn exhaled as he rode on a horse that could barely hold his weight. "Merchant's Bay is the oldest trading city in Austellus," he boasted. "Apart from Lunarpass and Aquamare, of course. Did you know that, Asher?"

Asher weakly shook his head, swaying as if he was going to faint. Lyssa knew he *did* know that. He had to know everything about Austellus when he was the Prince of Caelestia.

"How?" Eleanor asked curiously. "I thought the bay was created by the *Pause?*"

"It was, my sharp niece," he grinned, holding his finger in the air. "But once upon a time, here lay Merchant's City, a twin to Caelestia, founded at the same time. But Merchant's City fell behind, couldn't get as much trade running as Caelestia. So, everyone moved south. Then, the *Pause* happened and destroyed half of Merchant's City, so they rebuilt it to a dock."

"I'm sure everyone is fascinated," Fitz said sarcastically, shooting down the lion's pride.

I'll probably miss him the least, Lyssa thought. There was a time when young Fitzroy was a lovable and fun little cousin to her. She could still remember the merry little toddler running around after her, trying to catch the peridot gem that they would so often steal and almost lose from her father. Lionel was still home back then. In fact, Lyssa would almost *blame* Fitz for turning out the way he did *because* of Lionel. When they were old enough for their voices to break, they would always train with each other, getting better and better each day. From the day Lionel was lost, Fitz stopped laughing and playing all together. All he would ever do, day and night, was train. The fact that he was good at it didn't help him either. By the age twelve, he was the deadliest person in the Canicule. Only gods knew what he could do now. *I wonder if Lionel is the same, if he's still out there.*

A woozy Asher caught Lyssa's eye, struggling to keep up at the back of the trail. "Guys," she muttered, trying to pull the attention of the party.

"Yes," Goldwyn agreed. "Guys were a crucial part in the making of this city, but women were-"

"*Guys!*" she screamed. Lyssa leapt from her horse, catching Asher as he tumbled from his saddle.

"Good gods!" Goldwyn exclaimed.

She shook his lifeless face. "Asher, wake up. Come on."

"Let me see him," Sir Cedric pushed past. He checked Asher's pulse. "It may be a fever; he may not quite be used to the Canicule air."

"Very likely," Goldwyn nodded. "Get the boy some rest."

Oh no, Lyssa thought. *If he's not well enough to sneak away, could we even do it? Please, let him have strength.*

←———————⊟

Asher lay on a featherbed, his skin was white as snow, his long hair laced with sweat, his violent heartbeat *thumping* against the silence of the cabin. Lyssa had been by his side for almost two hours, the uncertainty of tonight making her head churn. *Maybe it's the dream that's making his heart beat so fast.* The thought didn't make her feel any better.

"Come down now, Lyssa. Time for supper," Elayne called up the stairs, no doubt alerting everyone who was staying at the small cabin.

She kissed him on the forehead before descending lethargically. They hadn't started serving the food by the time she arrived at their private mess chamber, which was unexpected. She slipped on a seat in between baby Ayla in her wooden high chair, and Eleanor.

"Lyssa," Eleanor said perkily, "do you like my new dress?"

It was a petite tent dress, dotted with flaming yellow patterns atop a green background. It went well with her gold-and-peridot tiara she always wore. "It's cute," Lyssa smiled as enthusiastically as she could.

"We got something from the markets for you as well, since you weren't coming out," she said, reaching under her stool.

Lyssa was slightly startled when she was passed the small leather container. She unlatched it carefully, revealing a beautiful golden necklace, entwining around fine, deep purple gems, cut into diamond shapes. "Alexandrite?" she recognised immediately.

"It was my choice," Eleanor smiled. "I thought it'd look good on you."

"Why? This must have cost loads," Lyssa winced.

"Don't worry about the cost," Elayne said, a glimmer in her eye.

She blinked in stupor. "I completely forgot, the new moon. I would have put on a dress or something-" she stumbled for words, embarrassed of her dirty orange tunic.

"Relax, girl. We wanted a smile to be put on your face come the turn of the moon," Goldwyn grinned. "Today is no day for woe."

"Thank you, everyone, I don't know what to say."

"Put it on!" Eleanor urged excitedly.

Lyssa did so, not needing any help to tie it around her neck. The jewels almost warmed her.

"Look at that!" Goldwyn chaffed, "it matches your bedclothes!"

She chuckled along with the room's laughter. "Thank you," she said again, hugging her sister.

"Right," the Lord of Ignis clapped. "Time for food."

The servants brought out her favourites: ripe watermelon and tomatoes, alongside salads topped with cheese made by the buffalo near Redmawr. It all tasted amazing. Having to survive on rations and leftovers since Litore had left her taste buds in need of flavour. The night went just as well as they joked and talked for what seemed like forever. It was a shame Asher couldn't spend it with her.

At least he was awake by the time she was at his bedside again. He claimed to feel better, but he had spewed multiple times into the bucket beside him throughout the afternoon. "If you're not completely fine, I think we should wait for tomorrow," Lyssa frowned.

Asher shook his head stubbornly. "Junius said come the *day* we arrive, we must leave. Tomorrow is a different day."

"You have a fever, Asher. What use is it if you keel over and die during the boat ride?"

"Still better than being cursed with this dream for the rest of my days," he sighed.

It was annoying. He was annoying. *Why is he so goddamn attractive?* "Well, please eat something, it'll only get worse if you don't."

Asher disagreed. "Feed a cold, starve a fever. Now can we go yet? I'd rather sneak out while I can still count my fingers."

Lyssa sighed. "Okay. Wait here, I'll make sure it's clear."

It must have been far past midnight. Lyssa could feel the exhaustion weighing her down as she poked her head around the corridors and open rooms of the cabin. It seemed mostly empty, every person staying there likely to be drunk out of their minds. The only sound to be heard was the high tide whooshing in and out of the bay outside.

"Lyssa."

The voice made her jump out of her skin. She whipped around to see Fitz stood there, still awake. "Oh, hey."

"I've been thinking… about everything," he sulked. "About your father, and-"

"Save it, Fitz. I know you were the favourite. I know he always wan-"

"And I've been an asshole to you."

That's not what I expected. It seemed surreal, as if he was reading her thoughts from earlier. "What?" she said. "Have you been drinking?"

"Before Lionel was... we were so close. I think that without him, we just... drifted apart," he groaned, leaning against a wall. "I was so *angry*. All I could think about was how I could end the life of what took him... until I realised, I can't take the life of the desert. It was too late by then. I had a reputation." *He definitely smells of alcohol.*

"That doesn't justify being cruel."

"I know," he said. "I thought I could fill the gap he left by being the best. He just left a gap that was too big."

For that brief moment, he seemed older than he was, rather than younger. "Why are you realising this now?"

"Today you seemed so happy," he said, almost tearing up. "Genuinely happy. The only happiness I've gotten over the past five years was from teasing people, or... knowing I was better than them. I... I just want you to know that I've never hated you, Lyssa. I was jealous of how strong you were when Lionel was lost, and especially when Reynold passed. I'm just..." A tear rolled down his cheek. "I'm just a bad person."

"No, you're not," she said, hugging him. "Bad people don't care about being better. You're only fourteen. You can be any person you want to be."

"You'll have to help me," he sobbed into her shoulder. "I won't be able to alone."

"I... will," she lied, hating herself. They pulled away after a time. "Go on now, go to bed," she said. "There's still a long way back to Ignis."

He nodded, slouching to his room as he wiped the tears from his tired eyes. *Shit,* Lyssa thought as he left. *Just my luck for him to do that to me as I need to leave.* At least she could take comfort from the fact that he was trying to improve himself. *I don't need to help him; he can do it without me.* She had to forget about him to stay sane. She had to forget about-

The thought of them pulled her gaze to the half open door. She saw Eleanor and Ayla snoozing peacefully in their room. She couldn't *just leave*. She crept inside, tears of her own beginning to fabricate. "Eleanor," she said, touching her arm gently.

"Lyssa?" her sister replied in a hoarse voice, rising.

"I'm going away. I don't know when I'll see you again."

"Why?" she asked, rubbing her eyes.

"Because I have to... You mustn't tell anyone." Her dewy-eyed stare broke Lyssa's heart. "I love you," she said, embracing her.

"I love you too," Eleanor murmured deliriously. "Come back soon."

"Make sure you go back to Ignis. Tell Goldwyn not to wait for me." Lyssa said.

Her sister nodded innocently.

"Hey little one," she smiled at Ayla's crib, a tear falling from her face. She kissed her on the forehead, waking her up. "You better be bigger than me next time I see you," she smiled.

Ayla began to cry herself, her wailing growing louder and louder. Lyssa blew one last kiss to Eleanor on her way out, making sure to not be heard by her inevitably woken up mother.

From then on, the adrenaline carried her out. Asher slipped out of the bed, sliding from wall to wall to keep up with the swift lioness. They were only seen by one person: the receptionist, remaining silent as Lyssa urged so by placing a finger on her lips.

The night was strikingly cooler than the stuffy cabin, boiled all day from the warm sun. Lyssa worried if the slick clothes she wore would be enough. It definitely wouldn't be if they were going somewhere east, or even worse, south. She couldn't risk going back now, though. She was sure that whatever ship they boarded would have enough warmth to at least take them wherever they were going alive.

"Do you know where this *boat excursion* is?" Asher asked, hobbling.

"No," Lyssa admitted, even though she took the lead. "I assume by the docks?"

Asher chuckled. "That would make sense."

They walked for a while along the coast, eventually reaching the pier. As they did, Asher mewled sharply, falling to the wooden floor.

"Gods, what is it?" Lyssa rushed towards him, a few paces in front.

"I just saw a seer," he winced, holding his head. "He had a knife."

"What? Where?"

His hand remained glued to his head as he rose. "I don't know, he just flashed before me."

"Said your goodbyes?" A gravelly, young voice hesitated to ask from behind.

"Yeah?" Lyssa said. A shiver shot down her back at the sound of him. *Is he the seer? Is he playing tricks?* Her heart thumped as if trying to escape.

"Good, follow me," he said, looking down.

The boy was difficult to see, but he wore a shaggy, yet short head of muddy blonde hair, all tied underneath a brown cloth. A deep scar cut the right side of his face, almost touching his crystal blue eyes. What he wore underneath his black cloak was concealed, the cloak stretching up and over his head with a hood. He walked in a hurried pace. *Why is my heart beating so fast? I'm not scared of him,* she thought, continuing to examine the boy.

"Sorry, could you slow down, Asher isn't well."

"Don't worry, we're here anyway." He knelt down on the pier edge, grabbing a rope from underneath and pulling a sorry boat to the surface. Lyssa expected a ship. This was barely a raft. The escort hopped in, holding his arms out.

Lyssa followed his steps, until Asher held back her arm. "I don't know about this, Lyssa."

No, not now. We've gotten so far. "What do you mean?"

"I mean..." he sighed, "think about everything you're leaving behind. *We're* leaving behind. We both have families. We both have titles and inheritance. We might lose them for good. We'll stress them to no end."

Lyssa couldn't believe his mind was changed so quickly. "Do you know what will happen if we go to Ignis?" she asked, receiving an ignorant stare from the prince. "I have nothing back there for me." She bared her teeth on the word 'nothing'. "Father is dead; when Fitz gets the throne, his kids will rule, not mine. Everything I could have and want is with *you.*"

"You can still have me at Ignis," he sulked.

"No, I can't!" she cried. "Before I could bloody walk, father wanted me to marry a Horncurve. My uncle would be an idiot to not follow up on that." Another tear rolled down her cheek. "I've already made my choice, Asher," she said softly, placing a hand on his nimble chest.

Asher's pupils expanded as if a demon was cast out of him. *Gods damn him, and his fiery eyes.* Their eyes were locked until Asher leant into a kiss. It made her heart flutter. It made her feel so much safer. If she was scared, she wasn't anymore. "You go first," he said as they pulled away.

She fell into the escort's shaking arms, making the boat rock from side to side as she did so, closely followed by Asher. The escort was quick to start rowing, sailing them out into the Waveless Sea. Before they could change their minds, the land was out of sight.

LETA II
-Unlock-

It wasn't so bad living in Seden. Three days had come and gone and the island almost felt like home to Leta Centaur. Yesterday, she and her mother were given a tour of Equus, what the locals call 'warrior isle'. It definitely lived up to that name, almost every building, keep and castle dedicated to raising and upkeeping fighters. Barracks were never too far from the eye, packed to the brim with spears and swords forged not far from the island. Still, the soldiery was of another story completely. They trained with perfect discipline, the thousands of men acting like a single unit as the military commanders shouted orders. At that point it was decided that they *needed* the Capricornians as allies. If they were to betray, Leta could only hope that Fletcher was training his men just as hard.

When it came to information, Leta was a wordless parchment. It felt like there were no secrets to unveil, every single door that had any chance of holding some, bolted shut, infeasible to open by hand. It seemed impossible to sneak out at night too; if Leta was to even attempt to, an uneasy Kiera would easily spot her.

Luckily, the girl grew more relaxed by the day. She was still nervous around Leta, but at least now she could speak to her. "Hi," she smiled as Leta returned to their chamber. "What did you see today?"

"Insul Tower," Leta said, peeling off her gloves. "It's amazing, you can see everything that's going on in the isles."

"I know, it's incredible. I always go up there." She giggled. "Did you see the crazy farmer?"

"The what?" Leta laughed.

"Gods, I have to show you," Kiera said, rushing out of the room. Leta followed her, looping around the castle and up the island's hills until they were back at the tower. Their steps echoed up the winding stairway as they ran. "There," she said, pointing down to the city.

Leta squinted as the shapes at the bottom of the island took form. Kiera was pointing to a large, sequestered collection of wooden stables and greenhouses. The only soul there was a fat little man walking from building to building. *His walk is a bit funny, but that can't be it.* "He doesn't seem crazy."

"Just wait," Kiera said, excitement ruling her face. "He lets the dogs out about now."

The man was heading to a small house, rumbling with barking. He unlatched the door, causing it to explode as dogs of all sizes ran out, yapping and snarling. *"Come back here, you little shits!"* he yelled, almost falling over. He was trying to stop the excited hounds by throwing his farming equipment at them.

Leta burst into a loud chortle. *"What is he doing?!"*

Kiera's added laughter made a chorus. "One time, I saw him poke his chickens to see if they were still alive. When one of them shit itself with fright, he *threw* the egg at a wall, claiming it was a demon."

Leta couldn't remember the last time she laughed this much. She was weak. Tears of joy filled her eyes.

"He's so *bad* at his job, I honestly don't know how he still has it."

"Me neither," Leta giggled. "Put him on the battlefield and he'll be the last man standing."

"Yeah," Kiera agreed, ridden with chuckling. "They'd all run the other way."

"Wow," she smiled, wiping the tears, "that's hilarious."

"I drew a picture of him. It's not the best, but it's still funny."

"You draw?"

"I'll show you," she grinned, leading the way back. Once back in their solar, Kiera reached for her notebook in her cabinet, placing herself on the floor as she flicked through the pages.

Leta slipped next to her eagerly, only to be met with a cold withdrawal as Kiera held the book to her chest. She was confused. *I thought we were becoming friends?*

"I'm sorry, I..." Kiera's nervous eyes returned. "No one has ever seen these... they're private."

"Oh," Leta muttered. "Well you can trust me, I won't judge."

Kiera bit her cheeks. "Do you promise?"

She nodded innocently, a little hurt that Kiera didn't feel completely comfortable around her. Hesitantly, the girl peeled the book from her chest, revealing an explosion of art on the page. Leta didn't even know it was possible to draw so well. It was a drawing of a boat, the boat Leta had travelled to Seden on. It was done with remarkable detail, even the shadows had their own spot on the page. "You drew this?" she gasped.

"It's bad, I know. I just get bored-"

"I have *never* seen a drawing as good as this." She carefully folded to the next page, as if the pages were of ancient origin. The next picture was of a regal looking city, sand covering the ground with bleached stone buildings. She noticed the gold-and-orange lion sigil of Lyrderyn flapping atop the highest building, even though the lion was slightly fanciful. *"You've* been to Ignis?!"

Kiera seemed to be pleased that Leta thought it was Ignis. "No," she said. "My Aunt Tayla has. She travels. She told me what it looks like."

"Do you want to travel too?" Leta asked, feeling the fine strokes of granite that lay on the page.

"It seems really dangerous," she admitted. "All I want to do is draw."

"You should," Leta smiled. "You're really good at this. I'll take you with me, if father allows it."

She blushed as she tucked her hair behind her ear. "I'd like that."

"Have you drawn anything I've seen? Fort Deus? Lunarpass?"

"You haven't seen Ignis?" she asked, surprised.

"I've never been far past the Negal Wall. The Pole is too dangerous for a little girl like me."

"That's horseshit," she muttered, scrolling through the pages. "You're braver than any girl I've known at fourteen."

They arrived at what seemed like a drawing of Lunarpass. It was remarkable how much detail she got correct: the grotesque, yet beautiful stone pillars, the mixed stone paths made from all sorts of pebbles; so much was wrong, though. "This is amazing," Leta said, "but you got some of the patterns and buildings *way* off. The Sphaera looks perfect though."

"Is it not good?"

"No, it's good. It's really good. It just looks like Lunarpass from the vision of someone who hasn't seen it, which I suppose it is," she said, still in awe of the fine work. "Imagine a city so perfect, that even the birds are afraid to land on the buildings, in case they spoil the harmony. Imagine impossible structures standing everywhere you looked, bending in ways that defied architecture. Even when you see Lunarpass with your own eyes, you still can't believe it's real."

"It sounds incredible," she said sadly.

Leta felt bad for her. "I promise, I'll take you one day. You better take your notebook when we do."

"Okay," she smiled, closing the opus. "Can we do something else now?"

"I *did* notice a lot of the doors had locks on them," Leta smirked playfully, happy with her quick thinking. "Any secrets behind them?"

Kiera grew a mischievous smile of her own. *Perhaps she trusts me after all.* "I sometimes sneak into them. I know the man who holds the keys; he can't stay awake for most of the night."

"When should we go?" she smiled. *I won't be so wordless for long.*

"Are you ready now?" Kiera asked, a few hours later after they had eaten dinner. Today's supper yielded a strange mix of plants and leaves - kale they called it - of which Leta couldn't stand at all. She daren't say that, though, eating as much as her stomach could take without the taste throwing it back up. She couldn't understand how people could *enjoy* that.

"Lead the way," Leta replied. "I can keep up."

It was easy to follow; Leta had become a sneaking professional at Fort Deus. She would often suffer from insomnia, being the lightest sleeper in the family. When she couldn't bear lying in the same bed for any longer, she would sneak out to her special spot and watch the Trader's Sea crash against the rocks of the cliff. Most of the time, the meditative sound of the ocean would send her right to sleep, but if not, it served as a spark that sent her mind into rapture. She would always miss it when she was away.

Because of her proficiency, she was almost tethered to Kiera as they crept along, matching her footsteps perfectly. Kiera went down to a lower layer of the castle, telling Leta to keep watch before returning with a giant ring of keys in her hands. "We have to be really careful," she warned. "Sometimes the doors creak really loudly."

"You open them then," Leta smiled. "I don't trust myself."

The rooms didn't contain what Leta had hoped. To be honest with herself, she didn't know *what* she hoped for. It felt like she expected a juicy mine of information, each door spilling with secrets of dishonesty and treason. In reality, all Leta had seen were concepts and blueprints for designs of boats and houses. Nevertheless, she didn't have to pretend to be fascinated by them. Each of the designs had an overwhelming amount of detail, the kind of meticulousness that made it more of an art piece than a building plan. The architects at Fort Deus weren't nearly as capable, the crammed lower bailey with its tatty houses being enough evidence for that.

She needed something *more* than this - a deep, dark secret perhaps. All that these designs were proving was how impossibly methodical the Capricornians would be to face. She needed to see *letters*, notes of plots and intel coming from the other places of exile. *How can I ask her without giving it away?* "Your people must get a lot of ideas from the other islands," she said. "I've never seen such perfect architecture."

"Actually, most of this comes from within the Three Goats. Jethro Bright he was called: the greatest mind these islands have ever seen. My uncle is named after him. He made most of these designs, until he was killed for going over the border to visit his family at Goattreath."

"Oh, I'm sorry."

"No need to be, you didn't kill him," she smiled, rolling her massive scroll of sketches, before returning it to its home.

Leta reciprocated her smile. "Have *you* been anywhere other than here? Any other place of exile?"

"Nope. I've been here all my life."

She couldn't point towards the topic of the Archipelago any more without it striking attention. If she were to get *any* information before her leave, she'd have to sneak around. There were a lot of keys on the chain, she noticed. *Maybe if I escape in the night, I might be able to find an office or a study of the sort to hold letters.* She observed exactly how Kiera returned the keys to the sleeping man, memorising every move she made. By the time the night grew old, she was ready.

"You can sleep in the bed with me, if you want," Kiera annoyingly offered as Leta tried to get comfortable on the floor.

"No, it's okay," she declined. "I don't sleep that well anyway. I'd probably wake you." *Well I'm not lying.*

"Okay," she grinned. "Goodnight."

As the candle was blown out, Leta could feel her heart beating harshly in the darkness. It was going to be difficult: to sneak out without waking Kiera, to get the chain from the turnkey, to even *find* the room that held the letters without being caught. She had barely any choice, this was the last time she had the chance to.

Getting out was the hardest part. She lay on her pillows for a while, every ten minutes that passed, promising herself that she'd try to escape in the next ten. She eventually picked a time, moving as slow as a raft as she edged towards the door. Getting the keys wasn't so difficult; the man slept like a stone, snoring louder than Leta's soft footsteps. *Where should I go now?* She thought, getting to the head of the staircase, trying her best to mute the noisy keychain. She noticed Nero always heading towards the back of the mess hall every time he prematurely excused himself from suppertime; that would be a good place to start.

There was a locked door when she arrived, but it made her rapid heart sink to also find that none of the keys fitted the mould. She jangled them about for a time, hoping that she had missed one. *Please, please, please.*

"The curiosity of a child," a voice came from behind. "Of such innocence, even if it's not."

A startled Leta swivelled around, hiding the keys with her body. The voice belonged to Tyran. *Dammit. He must have seen me.* "I'm sorry. I was… I was just looking…"

Tyran said nothing as he moved past her, unlocking the room. "Go on, then," he said, swinging the door open gently.

She shook like a string on a lute, slowly entering the study. *He's going to kill me. He's going to kill me.*

He strolled towards a cabinet, opening the draw carefully. "We keep all our letters here, take a look if you'd like."

"How… how did you know?" she stuttered.

Tyran smiled. "It would be unfair to expect trust from those you've fought your whole life, but truly, we have nothing to hide."

She apprehensively edged towards the letters, seeing sigils from all over: Scorpius, Casteron, Hausscier. She didn't see any from Galloway Malone, though. Every letter contained nothing more than gratifications and offers for trade deals. "What was your coalition with Lord Malone about?" she muttered after gaining a bit of confidence.

Tyran sighed as he sat. "We have observed the Dog's Paw for a while. Technically, it is not a place of exile, yet some extremely dangerous people have been brewing plots on those islands. The Helas are who controls them. Our spies report them training and recruiting more and more soldiers. Our coalition with Lord Malone was merely him consenting and assuring that our attack on the Helas would run smoothly. Even if we lost, we both knew that your royal father would never approve of it, and if he spotted our armies out of exile, he would surely turn his displeasure onto us. Lord Malone wouldn't have agreed if we didn't let him know that the Helas were responsible for sinking most of your trade shipments. We intervened, of course, yet I still heard that your home was near starved nonetheless."

It makes too much sense. Gods dammit. What can I believe? "Why are there no letters from Galloway then? We know he wrote to you."

"Because he wished us to burn them upon acquisition," he replied, all too quickly to be a lie. "If your king was to ever find that those letters existed, also finding out that Galloway did this behind his back, he surely would never trust him again."

"You said death is coming for the Centaurs. You said to Lord Malone he could die for something he cared about, and not for the king."

He didn't seem surprised that she knew that. "Death was coming, and still will if we do not take down the Helas. Unlike us, they're *permitted* on the mainland. You'd be surprised how much they've sabotaged already. Devious people. Hungry people. But right now, we must set our sights on the Khavar attack. We can deal with Hela afterwards."

Leta sulked, wanting to deny the newfound trust she had gained for Tyran. "I'm sorry," she said, slipping the last letter back in the draw.

"Not at all. Don't be," Tyran shook his head as he stood. "I admire your search for truth. But I *do* urge you to be more tactful next time; the next person to discover you may not be as kind as I."

ATHENA II
-Augur-

She had missed the lime green grasses and fields of the north. The only thing that kept her stable through her journey was the thought of feeling the tufts once again, to wake up to the sound of thumping ram's hooves as they charged down the fields in the morning, to have the warm, northern sun coat her skin once again. At least she could hear the rams. She gazed out of her bedroom solar, longing to go outside and run among them, but she couldn't. Her father wouldn't allow her, even though the crowds had somewhat cooled down since the uproar upon their return.

As Athena Horncurve stared miserably out her window, she thought about what had torn away at her mind for most of the journey. Strangely, ever since Jugum, neither of her brothers wanted to talk about it, as if they had suddenly forgotten. She wished the same had happened to her. *Someone tried to kill my brother. Someone evil.* Marcus was not like to forget that, *so why is it as if he has? Why was he in that tent? Why was my brother wanted dead? Why was the man selling that... stuff?*

"Lady Athena," a guard knocked on the door, throwing her out of thought, "a visitor has come to see you."

Thank the gods, she thought, *they've answered my prayers.* "Come in!" she called.

The door opened to reveal a slim, black-haired, clean-bearded man. He looked almost like a dream, standing tall in his tailored rags and tunic. "Angelo!" Athena screamed in excitement, running towards his open arms.

"I missed you," he smiled, gripping her tightly. Athena had known Angelo Brysea since she was a little girl. He was an inventor, and an amazing one at that, often entertaining with his next eccentric idea. Although she was first to deny it, her brothers would always tease her for having an infatuation with him. *Yes, he may be handsome, and perfect, but he's twice my age. I'm a princess as well, I can't marry someone lowborn...*

"You're the first person I looked for when we got back," she said. "Where were you?"

"Locked up shop to visit my family in Mea Minor for a moon," he said. "I got the first ship back when I found out you returned."

"You live in Mea Minor? I never knew."

"You never asked," he smirked playfully. "So, my creative consort, are you ready to get on your saddle?"

Athena's smile faded. "I'm not allowed to go out."

"No, you weren't until yours truly swayed your lord father with a certain amount of *charismatic finesse.*"

"Are you serious?"

He grinned. "I've never been more so." He began to skip out before stopping to turn around. "Oh, he did say to wear a cloak or something, he doesn't want you being noticed."

Athena nodded enthusiastically before grabbing a black cloak and following him out. She could still keep up with his quick pace; it was as if nothing had changed. It occurred to her that it didn't matter what she wore, she and Angelo stuck out like black sheep as they charged around Selerborn, jumping and laughing.

They eventually arrived at Angelo's workshop, both of them shy of breath. "I haven't done that run in a while," he chuckled with her as he clumsily fumbled about his tunic to find his keys. "Voila," he said, pushing the door open. "Home."

Athena had to get used to the room once again, always overwhelmed at the sheer number of projects they had completed. The mobiles of makeshift structures hung low from the ceiling, high above the battered-up work desks. All of their many contrivances lay underneath white cloths, pinned to the floor to be hidden from sight. She breathed in deeply so that the smell of dry wood she always loved could enter her lungs.

"So," he smiled, "what ideas have you had while you were away? A southern-inspired device, perhaps? You know, I've really been interested in the south lately. There's so much brown and orange you can play with."

"Actually," she said sadly, taking a seat in a coy manner, "I haven't really had the time to think about *this*."

"*Blasphemy!*" he smiled, seating himself next to her. "So, what's been on your mind, lassie?"

"A lot," she muttered, now that he was closer. "I didn't expect grandpa to pass. I really thought the king would show him mercy."

"The king does what he has to do. No man is above the law," he sighed, not receiving a response from her. "Ah, I'm sorry. I thought there was no point in bringing it up and making you sad."

"No, it's okay," she smiled. "I'm out of sadness."

He sent back a closed smile of his own, peppered with the same modesty. "Truth is, I had really hoped you did have an idea. You know, as... one last project?"

Her pulse skipped a beat. "What do you mean?"

Angelo scratched his beard as he thought of what to say. "It's clear that people aren't exactly... *happy* with your father at the moment. If worse comes to worst, and they rebel, think of who they'd take out first. They're *patriotic* people to say the least. I doubt they would spare a lowborn foreigner like me."

"But the people love you!"

"When I'm not holding a banner," he said, tugging at his barren clothes. "As soon as I pick a side, my head would be off my shoulders faster than a quicksail. Trust me, I'll feel safer and happier with my family."

Athena tried to fight off the tears. "Why did you bother coming back then? Why didn't you stay at home?"

He placed his beloved pocket-sized sketchbook he would always jot in when he had an idea, alongside the keys on the table behind them. "I wanted to say goodbye properly." Athena was still confused, bouncing her eyes between him and the items. "What?" he chuckled at her gormless stare, "they'll be no good in *my* hands when I go back home."

"You're giving them to me?" she realised, almost falling off her stool. "You've taught me everything I know; if you think that notebook would be more useful in my hands then you are out of your mind."

Angelo shook his pretty head, smiling. "My mother always hated what I did. I think it would give her a heart attack if I brought it home with me."

How could anyone hate what you do, she felt like saying. "So, what will you do instead?" She couldn't hide the anger in her voice.

"Probably get a job: become a carpenter or a blacksmith, or both," he chuckled. "I heard about the southern conflicts. If that comes north, then our lords will need all the dirty hands they can get."

"Let me come with you. I can help. We could find a new workshop. Tate Kalyx would look after us, he'd hire us as his personal inventors."

"I touched on that," he smiled still. "Your father wouldn't have it, though. He wants you in arm's reach. To be honest, that's probably better for you."

Tears rolled down Athena's cheeks. It was all so sudden. She wrapped her arms around his waist, pressing her head on his chest. "It won't be the same without you."

"A hazelnut is never the same without its shell," he muttered. "I've always been your shell."

At that point it hit her. She *couldn't* live without him. All of her happiness derived from him. "You can't go. I love you."

Angelo tittered. "Sweet Athena, you're too young to know what love is. One day you'll look back at me, when you've made a fame for yourself, the love of your life by your side, and think of this day as when you began to wander the world yourself. So, smile. You can't be sad over that."

She was staring at the notebook lying on the table as she drenched his shirt with tears. She didn't know what to think.

He took her by the shoulders, positioning her upright. "Listen, I'm going to be right back, because frankly, I am *starving*, and *need* to break my fast. But if I return and you haven't thought of anything, then I swear to the gods I will raze this workshop to the ground."

Athena chuckled, left like that as Angelo dashed out. She thought it would be a cute idea for their last creation with each other to be something to remember each other by, to comfort them when they felt low. It seemed to amuse Angelo, the young architect safe under the idea that this wouldn't be the last time they'd see each other. It didn't bother Athena, though, it was more for her than him.

It was the first time Athena had complete control of a project, covering everything from drawing up the plans to actually making it. Angelo didn't quite share the same vision she had, but at that point, she was driven enough to complete his share of the work also. By the close of the afternoon, they had themselves two wooden box hinges, patterns of constellations acutely embossed in the wood. Inside lay a rotatable, expertly cut white gemstone, reflecting the light in a beautiful way. Athena couldn't have been happier; it was exactly how she hoped.

"They're stunning," said Angelo, eyes lighting up like stars as he flicked away at the gem. "Where did you get diamonds like these?"

"Merchant's Bay," she smiled. "I found a gemcutter, he offered to refine the one I wore on my belt. I didn't know that it would transform the light like that, though."

"Didn't you get that belt for your birthmoon?" he laughed.

"Only cost me a silver," she said. "He had enough gem to cut *two.*"

"Only a silver?!" he laughed harder. "That happens to be a fortune for a poor man like me."

"Here," she grinned, handing him the creation after she tied a leather lace around it.

"A necklace?"

Athena nodded. "For whenever either of us are uninspired."

He put it round his neck, admiring the work. "It's amazing, Athena. I'll never take it off."

"Me neither," she said, hugging him.

After he had left, Athena sat alone in the workshop for a while. She wasn't as sad as she thought she'd be. One hand rested on Angelo's old notebook. There was a nervous energy that ran through her body. It was *her* workshop now. *Her* space, free to do whatever she wanted. But if even Angelo was frightened off by the thought of war, how long she'd have it was uncertain.

ELAYNE I
-Line-

L ady Elayne, I truly think it would be best to leave now. We should
have left days ago."

   "Go without me then!" she roared at Lord Goldwyn. "I'm *not*
leaving without them."

   "Mother, they'll come back, Lyssa told me they will," Eleanor assured,
holding her mother's hands.

   "You *stupid* girl!" she cried. "Why didn't you stop them?"

   Eleanor stared back, blue eyes glistening.

   "Wait, Eleanor, I'm sorry." She winced as her daughter dashed away.

   "We leave at sunrise on the morrow. With or without you," Goldwyn
said in the coldest tone to ever leave his throat.

   She was left alone at her chamber's window, her face damp with the
feel of tears. It was odd to see Fitz share her anguish. The only sound that
filled the morning air of the bay was the *thumping* of katars colliding with
wood, and the constant cry of rage coming from Fitz's mouth. '*You
abandoned me!*' he kept repeating. *She didn't abandon you,* Elayne
Lyrderyn felt like calling down, *you damn well near pushed her away.* She
never really liked Fitz; he was always too big for his boots, always above
everyone else. Thankfully, she never let that be known.

   Thoughts of why and how Lyssa had left were shooting around in her
head like arrows. *Why would she leave? What does Asher have to do with
it? Was it something I did? Did she run away?*

"Lady Elayne," a comfortable voice said from the door.

"Ulrich," she sighed with relief. "Any news?"

He wore a sad, untaught head on his old face as he took a seat next to her. "The receptionist was the only other to see them. He said that they went in quite some haste, as if they were looking for something."

That didn't help. *What were they looking for? Why were they rushing?* She wept a familiar feeling of misery into her hands. "This is exactly what happened to Lionel," she cried. *"Why* does it always happen to me?!"

Elder Ulrich rubbed her tense back gently. "I share your grave grief, my lady, truly. I have lived for over four hundred years. Nothing has been worse than the tragedy of a missing child."

"Don't call it that," she dismissed, waving her hand. "Tragedy implies that they're dead."

"All loss is death until they are found," he said, fondling his great white beard. "Perhaps not for them, if they are still alive, but that doesn't matter if we cannot know. I'm only implying that unknowing..."

The old man fascinated her. Elayne looked to his face, noticing for the first time that he had as many wrinkles of sorrow as laughter. "You must be too familiar with it."

"All too much," he sighed. "I won't give pretext, my lady; it never gets any easier. Other elders shrug off loss like a cough. I never seem to quite get used to it."

"What keeps you going, then? How can you live?"

Ulrich paused to think. "Duty, I suppose. Habit, perhaps?" He felt his golden, silk sleeves. "Truthfully, total loss of will is something I have been close to many an occasion. Though, brother Marcarius has always been there during my lowest. He would always reintroduce me to the fruits of life, the people we could save. He would always pull me out of my pit."

Elayne wiped her tears. "Well you are stronger than I."

"My lady," the elder said softly, placing his soft hands on Elayne's, "would you take a word of advice from a bygone man?"

"Always," she chuckled nasally.

"Brother Marcarius once told me: loss is a terrible thing, but it can never amount to purpose. Volition is the backbone of life. So long as one has a duty to fulfil, a soul to redeem, a joy to feel, a pain to know, then one will never be ready for death. Impoverishment is a similar concept, I believe. So long as one has family, and friends, and possessions around them, then one has never truly lost."

She thought about it for a moment. Her tears dried where they fell. "Thank you, Elder Ulrich."

"Regardless, know that Lyssa is not dead, nor Asher. Chances are, we'd know if they were," he bowed, taking his leave.

He's right. I have a duty to fulfil: the duty of a mother. If I can't trust Lyssa, what's the point? She'll be back soon. She has to be. After a time, she packed what little she had taken out of her case, preparing herself to leave. It took a surprising amount of effort to do so. *I can't fool myself,* she thought, slumping back down. *I need a walk. I need to clear my head.*

Elayne descended the cabin stairs to be met with the party around a small table, largely in silence with occasional chatter. Heading for the exit, she didn't let a word come out of her mouth. "My lady?" Goldwyn said with confusion. "Are you going somewhere?"

"For a walk."

"On your own?" he asked. The benignness of the lord had returned. "It could be dangerous out there."

She sighed. "Fine, Sir Brendan."

Sir Brendan lethargically put down his cup of ale, following Elayne out. The walk on the beach would be so much more relaxing without the steady *clomp* of the burly knight, but she supposed the safety was comforting if anything. It didn't help with taking her mind off things, though. She grew annoyed at every little thing, even the steady rustle of safety that followed her.

Merchant's Bay had seen livelier evenings. The sun was barely out, clouds reaching across the red sky to block it, and the ocean was almost louder than the clamour of trade. Elayne stuck to the coast when the beach ended and the dock began, not wanting to bump into any strangers.

"Where are we headed, my lady?" Sir Brendan asked in his gravelly voice. "Do you not trust the search parties?"

She shrugged. "I just wanted to walk."

"Walking helps," Sir Brendan nodded.

Elayne glanced over to the rough knight. "Tell me a story, Sir Brendan, about yourself. Maybe it'll take my mind off things."

Sir Brendan examined Elayne with half squinted eyes. "The only stories *I* have will depress you, my lady. That seems like the last thing you need right now."

"Depress me, Sir Brendan. Tell a tragedy. I'm doubtful it will make me feel any worse. Who were you before my husband took you in?"

"Tragedy," he sniggered, clearly not sober. His face and grey eyes drooped in response to the word. The knight gritted his teeth, looking around the dim crowds. "I wasn't my own person before I met Lord Reynold; I wasn't anybody. I was a puppet for the cock that brought me into this world."

"Your father?"

"Aye, my *father*. The fucker never liked me, and I never liked him. But he did worse than that. He raised me." His face was sour. "I always wanted to be a knight, as did my older brother, that's why when my father wanted the same thing, he hated me for being shit at fighting. Max was a great fighter. Before long, he served as a first soldier in the capital city's garrison. He wanted higher for himself; he wanted to be in a royal guard to a lord or a king, but to my father, it didn't matter; so long as he was out of Reddust Castle, he may as well have been an anointed knight. As for me, not even peasants would let me defend them. Sometimes my father wouldn't let me eat until I bested one of the guards, which didn't help. I never got any better; I was fighting out of fear... until... your brother visited." He spat. "That day, I embarrassed my family in front of Lord Lyonis. I jumped from my horse during a joust, too afraid that the lance would hurt me. Father was so furious of my failure, he heated irons on a hearth until they burned red-hot. I thought: oh, he'll hit me with it again. It was one of my least favourite punishments, but back then, I thought it was normal. But then he did something that even the cruellest of people would wince at. He had his men hold me down: men I had known since I was born. He took the red-hot irons, and *forced* it so far down my neck I thought I would choke. I felt my voice burn away, along with my throat. The pain... was unimaginable. I almost retched. After that, my voice never healed. People would laugh at me... laugh at the freak child who had the voice of a forty-year-old."

"Gods," Elayne gasped, holding her hands to her mouth.

"Never believed in *gods* after that," he sniggered. "Nor did I believe in letting my father think he won. After that, I fought out of spite, and hatred, and grief. I didn't let any man best me. I used my cursed voice to growl like a lion." He tittered. "It would make them shit themselves. Eventually, I ran away to compete in the Crossroad's open tourney King Esmond held. It was my last chance at a new life. If I had shown my face at Reddust Castle again, I'm sure my father would have skinned it off. Luckily, I didn't have to."

Her husband's actions would always warm her. This was the first time she missed him for them. "You must owe a lot to Reynold, then."

The knight nodded. "I owe my life to Reynold. He was the one who saved it... But it was enough to know that I had achieved a place on a royal guard, far away from my father. It only made it better to know that father despised his Leon blood. That's why we moved south in the first place."

Elayne pulled a lipped smile. "What happened to your brother?"

"He fell off his horse and died a year later. Must have truly been a *tragedy* for my father to be left with his least favourite son."

Elayne tittered. For a time, they walked in silence, before she broke it. "For the record, Sir Brendan," she said, "I think your voice is amazing. I don't think Goldwyn could have a better lion guarding him."

He smiled, looking down to the dock. Sir Brendan Gryfford always seemed like an outsider, as sad as that was. When he was drunk enough to speak about his past, the knight would often go on about how much better his life became when Reynold had taken him to the lion's guard and pulled him away from the Pole. *That all makes sense now.* Elayne could remember his phenomenal performance that day like it was yesterday, Sir Brendan's skill not even comparable to all she had seen since. Clearly, joining the lion's guard changed the knight's life, and it gladdened Elayne.

As they approached the docks, Elayne increasingly saw how irrelevant her worries were. Yes, her eldest had disappeared, but she still had two daughters in arm's reach that she took for granted. Yes, her safety from Reynold had gone, but a righteous king, in Sir Goldwyn, still sat on Ignis' throne. They looked out to the troubled sea, beating the Bay as the tides rolled in. It made her think of Lake Ignis, the peaceful, yet rapid river rushing down the banks just outside of the city. *Home is what I yearn for,* she decided. *Home is what I need.*

Elayne must have been the last person Lord Goldwyn had expected to return with her cases in hand. "I'm ready now, my lord," she said, leaving her bags at the butt of the stairs before dashing up to her children's room.

"What are you doing here?" Eleanor sulked as she arrived. "What do you want with a *stupid* girl."

"This stupid girl is *my* daughter," she smiled, striding closer. "Anyone who has something to say about that will taste the fury of the lioness." She put her arm around her daughter. "I'm sorry, I didn't mean to call you that.

I was upset, and-"

"I know," she muttered. "I'm upset too, because you're right. I *am* stupid for not doing anything."

"Oh, come on, Ellie. What *could* you have done?" she sighed. "We both know that when Lyssa has made her mind up, then there's no changing it."

"It's my fault," she cried. "It's my fault she's gone, it's my fault I told. I can't do anything right."

"Do *not* blame yourself for this," Elayne ordered. "Neither of us know why she left. All we know is that she'll come back, and we're going to have to trust her to."

"I know... but I could have done more."

"Nonsense," she shook her head. "The most you can do now is cheer up. Home is waiting; for all of us."

She skipped away, leaving her daughter in a perplexed state. It took no less than an hour before everyone was ready to depart. The last person they were waiting for was a fiery Fitz, who wouldn't come before some prudent negotiation by his lord father.

Once he did arrive, the party was smooth to transition into its normal trudge. They had not even left Merchant's Bay before Fitz's agitation was prominent.

"Why are *you* so upset," Eleanor asked moodily. "You hated her."

"*Oh, just please shut up!*" he shouted, holding himself back from throwing his katar. He received a swift slap from his mother.

"Stop it," Lady Gina said, angrily.

"Idiot," he muttered under his breath.

Elayne's positive thoughts swiftly faded. She wanted to strangle the boy, but didn't let herself flinch. *A soul to redeem*, she thought.

FELIKS IV
-Toil-

He was not used to the influx of spare time. His position as acting lord was discontinued on his father's awakening, and he suddenly had more than he could handle. Thankfully, Lorimer didn't completely rid Feliks of his power; the bastard was now welcome at council meetings and decision makings of the sort. It seemed like a better situation, since his father would actually *heed* his advice, rather than the councillors second guessing every word Feliks said because of his birthright.

That being said, it didn't bore Feliks any less. His attention span wasn't suited for that type of attendance. He would often drift in and out of conversation, not being able to keep up unless he exerted himself. It wasn't because he was necessarily *bored*, but that he didn't care about queries for lords and ladies, not out of ill intent, but that he couldn't empathise in the slightest. Yes, some highborns around Centaur's Grove would come in and out of Feliks's life from time to time, attending a tourney or a celebration of the like, but he felt that he would be more inclined to help them if he *knew* them. Callum Wells was someone he truly knew, until the Scorpion attack had robbed Feliks of that pleasure too.

He discharged an arrow when the thought of his sister visited again, wishing the target's bullseye was her killer's head. That would have made him happy, for a time; four arrows already lay embedded in the centre. *He deserved worse than death. Killing him wasn't justice.* He nocked another.

Sixteen was the age most believed a boy to become a man, but Feliks didn't feel like a man. The coming of the Thunder Moon was always such an exciting prospect for him, but it seemed like *everything* tainted his birthmoon this year. He *did* look forward to seeing old friends again, but they had all changed; Brandon Snider was as depressed as ever, he wouldn't stop going on about how much of a curse it was to live; he had suffered a deep scar on his left cheek during the raid on the Lagoon, but Feliks saw that as no reason to hate life. Ella Foster was a catalyst of pessimism too; the Scorpions had claimed both her parents during a surprise raid, and now Fort Foster was falling apart because Ella had no idea how to rule. Theo Fox was perhaps the most enjoyable company, but his lack of tolerance had him asleep by the second mug of ale. Any others who had invitations either couldn't come because they saw the journey as too risky, or outright refused. On top of that, he scarcely saw Lori that day either, since the lord was so overburdened by work, it was impossible to spare even a few moments. All things considered, Feliks found himself surprisingly content with the night. After everyone had left, the bastard took to the outskirts of the lagoon, and watched with a skin of ale as night fell. Nothing was more beautiful to him than seeing the blue and green fireflies illuminate the dark lagoon with a thousand stars. Even though he was alone for his name day, as he had been for the past moon, he at least didn't feel lonely that night.

Though, it wasn't like Feliks didn't have his own source of sadness; it just felt that being surrounded by such gloom was overbearing. A gift from his father was a slick jerkin of navy boiled leather, and although Feliks liked it a lot, the only gift he spent the whole day yearning for was to merely see his sister again.

Another arrow flew into the bullseye.

Feliks and the target were the only ones in the small, square courtyard of the castle. It didn't make sense as to why they would even build such a courtyard; most of the Lagoon's knights would train in the barracks of the main city, since the narrow, rickety bridge seemed too much hassle to get some eight thousand soldiers across. It was probably for the best; Feliks enjoyed his privacy, especially when his performance was substandard.

The sound of his father approaching could be heard minutes before he appeared, the steady *clomp* of wood colliding with stone echoing around wherever he visited. Every day Feliks heard the sound, it was welcomely quicker; his father still couldn't completely put his weight on his wounded leg, but it was definitely healing. In this case, it was the empty courtyard where the sound rang, the Lord of the Lagoon eventually joining his son.

His arrival came with laughter, deep and wholesome. Feliks frowned, thinking he'd gone mad. "What's so funny? Why are you laughing?"

"Because life is ridiculous, Feliks, and the sooner you start laughing at it, the less chance it has to hurt you."

The bastard allowed himself to smirk. "Wisdom suits you, father."

"This walking stick makes me look about twenty years older. If I'm to play the role of a magnus, may as well do it right." He grinned before gesturing to the target. "When did you get so bloody good?"

"The time you fell asleep for a moon, don't you remember?" Feliks jested, the dryness of boredom warping his voice.

"Perhaps I should have slept longer; you might've had a chance to become better than me," he smirked.

"Perhaps," he agreed, planting yet another arrow into the centre. "Are you going to tell me why you were *really* laughing or do I have to guess?"

"I told you the truth; life is ridiculous," Lori smiled as he sat on a stone bench. "And I've come to ask something ridiculous of you, Feliks."

"Ask away," Feliks said, plucking arrows one by one from the target.

Lori sighed his smile away, rubbing his freshly-pruned beard. "I don't remember much of my fever dream, but I think the ones now are different."

"Go on…"

He closed his eyes. "Well it's set in Liglock. I know that much because of that great brown bridge. There's a guy who I can't see that talks to me. He says that 'a figure of great import comes in search of your own'. He tells me to 'see them to this place, see them for the surplus of time we need. The king and his serpent shall be unearthed by no other way'."

"The king and his serpent," Feliks repeated, "sounds like a fairytale."

Lori didn't respond to the jest. "By the king it must mean Esmond, but when I ask of the serpent, he goes cuckoo on me. 'The Serpent of Stars', he says, 'It will poison the city'-"

"Flooded by waters," Feliks continued. "Couldn't you have chosen less frightening words to think of?"

"There's more," he said. "Each night I can understand more. 'Flooded by waters as black as night' is what he said."

Feliks was even more confused than before. *Gods, why more?* "What will you do?"

"Probably send one of my own to Liglock," he smirked.

"You really believe it?" Feliks frowned.

"It sounds mad, doesn't it? Doing what a dream tells you," Lori sighed.

"But these are dreams I have *every* night, Feliks, like you said. I don't know what else I can do. There's no harm if it truly *is* nothing."

Feliks nodded, returning his eyes to his arrow-loaded quiver before slinging it over his shoulder again. "Lord Kayden Carr sounds like a good choice. He's already half the way."

"He's not one of my own," Lori grunted, standing, "but you are."

The bastard prematurely let go of an arrow he had nocked. "You want to send *me* to Liglock? Your bastard son."

"Name someone else in this city who is of our kin and I will happily oblige," he grinned. "I thought you'd be happy?"

"No, I am," he shook his head. "I want to. I just can't believe you want *me* to. Why do you trust me all of a sudden?"

"Feliks," Lori said contently, "above all else, you are my son. People may frown on your birth since it was done out of wedlock, but I loved your mother deeply, as I do you."

Feliks squinted suspiciously. Whenever the subject of his birthright came up, Lori would shut himself off, almost embarrassed, coming up with an inventive way to end the conversation. "Who was she?" he muttered.

It looked like it wasn't easy for him to decide what to say. "She was beautiful. She had a... way with words only matched by wordsmiths," Lori smiled, staring at nothing. "I promised her to never tell you *who* she was, but I assure you, son, she is safe, and well, and in a place far from here."

"Why did you promise? Why did she want that for me?"

He chuckled. "Because she shouldn't have made you. She would cut my tongue out for even saying this to you."

Was she highborn? he thought, almost laughing at the notion. "Why are you telling me this now?" he chuckled. "You've waited this long to even mention her."

"Believe it or not, Feliks, being tied up in bedsheets for a fortnight makes you do a lot of thinking. I thought about what I wanted... who I wanted..." he felt the silver pendant around his neck. "She said she wants to meet you one day, 'when you're wise and handsome like his father'. But until that day comes, you are nothing less than my son."

Feliks tried to imagine it, not having much luck. The only thing he truly *wanted* was to not be a bastard, but the fact that *'she shouldn't have made you'* didn't give him much hope. "So, have you figured it out?" he said, picking up the stray arrow he flung. "...about what you want?"

"Right now, for you to go to Liglock would be pretty high on my list."

Feliks chortled. "Fine!" he resigned, dropping his quiver on the floor and marching out the courtyard.

He had his suspicions of who his mother was. When he realised that he would never know, he gave up on guessing. It was apparent to him that he and Vesta were mothered by different women: Vesta inheriting Lorimer's black hair as opposed to Feliks's brown, and his skinny stature going against Vesta's boneless one. Either way, the day he would meet his mother was one he greatly looked forward to, and a day that seemed much more likely for whatever reason. *Safe and well,* he thought happily, *but still far from here.*

It didn't take long for Feliks to prepare. His luggage included a change of clothes, extra arrows and not much more. He had kept a small citrine stone in his chamber since the attack, thinking now as no better time to slot it in his pocket and join him on his journey. *It's probably the kiss of the vectem that is making him have these dreams in the first place.* Cuthbert had said as much before Lori's coma. *Maybe he hasn't completely recovered yet.* Either way, the dream was telling Lori to go to an oddly specific place, for an oddly specific reason. *The delusions of a poisoned man, or a threat bigger than we both think. They're just as likely as each other.* Still, he thought the stone might have something to say towards either of the two circumstances. When he was ready, he met with his father at the great folding drawbridge.

"Nervous?" Lori poked at his son.

Feliks didn't respond. "Who's this?" he said to the brown stallion of his hair colour.

"That *this* is a she, and she will be your company to Liglock."

"Who is *she?*" Feliks corrected himself, feeling her coarse fur.

"Only the swiftest, most loyal mount to graze on this good earth," Lori grinned, petting her. "Her name is Fortune. She is the reason people call me 'Lori the unhorsed'."

"She's *your* joust horse?" Feliks gasped in disbelief.

"Tried and true," he boasted. "Treat her like your child, and she will gallop to the ends of worlds for you. Isn't that right, Fortune?"

The mare snorted as if she heard him.

"The Pole is a dangerous place, Feliks," he said, patting Fortune down before returning his weight on his walking stick. "You know the practise: you see some shady folk, you-"

"Gouge out their eyes for looking at me funny," he jested dryly.

"No," Lori smirked. "You run the other way. No man nor animal can catch up with my Fortune."

"Good," said Feliks, saddling Fortune up. "Are you sure you trust me to go alone?"

"Not entirely," he smiled. "But you're not alone, you have Fortune. My girl is yet to let me down."

Feliks rolled his eyes as he climbed gracefully upon the stallion, having a city guard pass his luggage. Fortune was the comfiest horse he had ever sat on. It was as if her back was moulded for Feliks.

"Don't get yourself killed, bud."

"That probably isn't as high on my list than it is for you, father," he smirked.

"What would be high on your list then?" Lori asked, unsmiling.

Feliks paused to think. "The king and his serpent," he said.

Lori nodded. "I hope you figure it out."

"I will," he promised, kicking Fortune into a trot when the drawbridge was eventually down. He waved back to his father as he was taken away. This was a strange feeling. All alone in the Auburn Pole for the first time. He followed the Centaur's Path with excitement, where it would lead him, he could not tell.

MARCUS II
-Spar-

An inability to sleep was something new for him. Not a night had gone by since Jugum that didn't have Marcus Horncurve lying awake in bed for at least an hour. He hated to think about it, and it was the only thing he could think about. Everything about the past moon made him sad, and that sadness made him angry. Then that anger made him sad again, since being so might send *thousands to the grave.*

Nothing was better at Selerborn, although he hoped everything would be. The uproar from the citizens resonated with Marcus more than he knew it should have, and it didn't help with telling himself that he wanted nothing. *Why am only I thinking about it? How are Cadmus and Athena and Riley so composed? Do they not care about Sigmund?* It made him miss the man more.

Sleep was something of a dream; it was beyond useless trying to get some. Marcus threw his crimson quilt to one side, rubbing his crusty, sleep deprived eyes. Cadmus was still asleep in the other bed, his left arm half hanging over and mouth wide open. His twin stank of alcohol, and that wasn't new. Marcus winced and left their chambers.

The night was later than he thought, as not a single torch was aflame in all the Cenkeep. The rugged stone walls looked different in the Thunder Moon's grey sheen, dark and more beautiful. He wandered to the nearest window and placed his fingers on the facet. Strangely, the air that brushed his hands wasn't chilled like it normally was, but temperate, muggy almost, somewhat like the air around the Ramscar. *That isn't right,* he realised. *Nothing is right.*

He looked out to the city, the slight glimmer of a sun starting to emerge from the horizon, veiled with a breathtaking morning fog. Not even the brothels and inns were awake at this time, which wasn't normal either. Every time Sigmund would wake Marcus and Cadmus before dawn to go hunting, they would pass through the city, and would always hear music or singing or laughter bursting from any and all of the huts. Now, the only thing to accompany the dead of night was the occasional *bahh* of a ram or hoot of a great horned owl.

When he grew tired of listening to the new sounds of nightlife, he continued his stroll through the keep, expecting to find nothing weirder than that. Lo and behold, through the translucent glass of Elder Ignatius's solar, a dim flame glowed into the corridor, bouncing around from within the room. Marcus knocked on the door.

"Yes?" the elder called from inside.

Marcus pushed the door.

"Marcus," Ignatius frowned. "You look dreadful, take a seat."

The Horncurve traipsed to the velvet stool that opposed Ignatius. The scent of spice was in the room, as an essence smoked away from a corner. Dried wax dripped from candles that seemed to be alight all night, and Ignatius's desk was bestrewed with parchments of letters, wax seals, wavering stacks of silver and copper coins, crumbs of dried bread, empty flasks of water... "Why are you up so late?" Marcus asked eventually.

Ignatius smirked and plucked a letter from the heap. He straightened it and cleared his throat. "My Lord Horncurve, we send our deepest condolences in these troubled times. We humbly ask for your good graces today, Lord Riley. Tharnham Keep isn't as grand as it once was; our veteran soldiers have grown aged and ill-suited for battle, and the youth we train have a lack of focus, most turning to thievery and mischief. We Tharnhams have been loyal ever since your legendary father won the throne, and we ask that you would kindly spare soldiers so we can enforce punishment, and feel comfortable with supporting the Horncurve house with fully trained soldiers when the time comes for battle. PS, my sons are anxious to know when we next travel to Heavia. We're in need of a good raid to keep the fingers warm. Yours sincerely, Fionn Tharnham, Lord of Tharnham Keep." He put the letter down. "More than half of these scrolls say the exact same thing."

"About needing soldiers?"

"Soldiers, grain, sheep, wool, steel... about everything under the bloody sun it seems like," he chuckled. "They all think your lord father to be a milksop. They were too afraid to ask Sigmund for... *luxuries*, so perhaps they think they'll have better luck with his son."

"And are they?"

Ignatius chortled. "Gods, no. Stones will crumble before *Lord Mactann* gets extra grain to make his *pigs fatter*. Gods almighty." He continued to chuckle. "Anyway, what can I do for ye, Marcus?"

Marcus looked around nervously a while longer. "Did you mean what you said? About a seer wanting to kill me, because of... what I'll become?"

Ignatius sighed, dropping his gaze. "I wish it wasn't, but that trick you saw with the water and the cloak? That's magic, Marcus: a travel magic long dead and forgotten." He hesitated. "Only *seers* would know any such arts today."

"How do you know?" Marcus pleaded. "Maybe it wasn't a seer at all? Maybe someone learned how to? Maybe it wasn't mag-"

"What do you want me to do?" Ignatius groaned, shrugging.

Marcus swallowed. "Could you... go to the Sanctum?" he asked. "Ask them why, talk to them?"

The elder rubbed his eyes. "You see all this, Marcus?" he asked, waving to the countless scrolls. "Each one of those is either an ally or an enemy. The country is divided, and your father needs me here to decide who we can trust." He sighed. "Have you thought about going yourself?"

Marcus winced. "Father would never let me go."

"Have you asked him?"

"He won't let me," he insisted angrily.

Ignatius took another deep sigh. "Fine," he said. "I'll go as soon as I can, but I have *no idea* when that'll be."

"That's enough," Marcus nodded, standing. He began to walk out.

"Marcus," the elder called softly, stopping the Horncurve's walk. "Get some sleep, eh? You're safe in these walls."

←———◄

Although he was told to, sleep still wasn't something Marcus could achieve. Not even comfort was in reach as he wriggled about for over an hour without finding an agreeable position. What seemed like years passed like years did, and eventually, the sun crept into the Horncurve's room.

Cadmus still wasn't awake, despite dawn coming a while ago. Tired of waiting, Marcus went over to prod his twin, receiving a lifeless groan. Marcus then shook him.

Cadmus winced, holding his head. "Ugh, Marc, let me sleep," he grumbled, turning over.

Marcus frowned. "Cadmus, we train today. Get your lazy ass up."

"I can't," he insisted, "my head hurts too much."

Marcus sighed, giving up on shaking. "That's your own fault."

"Aye... I'll be down soon."

The ram didn't care if he did at that point. His tiredness robbed him of caring. He made his way to the training yard, lagging with lethargy. *Cadmus wouldn't be sleeping still if Sigmund was here. He'd find a way to wake him.* It was too much to think about now. It was too early... though he had been awake for hours.

The training yard wasn't unlike the thousand mornings before: jade grass roughly prickling up from the ground where rams had munched upon, the wooden rafts and beams taking shapes as little huts and stables for weapons and livestock, the wall at the end of the yard descending into a cliff, meeting the Twin River as it marked the end of Selerborn. If not for his constant daunt, the quiet would be blissful. *If it was a seer, surely they'd try again, despite how 'safe' I am in these walls. It wasn't a seer. Someone bad wanted me dead.* He strolled over to the animal pen, taking the first ram to plod over by the giant curved horns. *Who, though? Ignatius thinks it's a seer and he's always right. I know I'm as fucked up in the head as Sigmund.* His face ached from frowning. "What do you think, eh?" he muttered to the ram as it bumped its nose against his palm.

The ram only snorted, probably looking for new food. He was Sigmund's ram, Ragget, the eldest of the whole stock, perhaps even the eldest in the city. Marcus could see why Sigmund favoured him, his giant horns longer than both of Marcus's arms combined. He had a wise beard reaching halfway to the ground, and tired eyes, lost eyes, yet still peaceful and rested. War Rams were creatures that Marcus couldn't wait to adopt and use, even though the way he looked at battle with glittering eyes was slowly transforming into an aberration of himself. *Yet another beautiful thing ruined,* he winced, as a sickness forced him to look elsewhere.

He wandered slowly to the edge of the battlements and sat, carelessly throwing his legs over the edge. From his feet to the ground meant at least a two-hundred-foot fall, but the threat didn't faze him. He closed his eyes and breathed in, absorbing the warm morning sun on his tired face.

Another hour may well have passed before he was joined in the yard, and he opened his eyes to see the sun in a much higher place. *Finally*, he thought. He turned around, jogging down the battlements to fetch his longsword and begin sparring with his brother.

Though, the boy who was there wasn't his brother. He looked about the same age, and had strong Arian features, but still looked foreign. He had short brown hair the colour of ram's horns and dark eyes and brows to match. The only armour he wore were the two thin metal pads that sat upon each shoulder, and underneath, had arms scaled with tight muscles. He sat, blunting his blade with the bottom of his boot. "Ey there, pal," he smirked, "you're up early."

Marcus frowned. "Who are you?"

"Cadell Siren," he smiled, before standing to bow in a burlesque way, "at your service."

"You're Lord Harper's son?"

"Aye, youngest of two," he said, throwing his longsword to his shoulder. "So, I take it you're ready, then? I was half expecting to wait."

"Ready for what?"

"To train."

"I train with my brother."

"You train with me now." A smile played his lips, a smile Marcus didn't like. "I've always wanted to duel a prince."

"Where's Cadmus? He said he was coming."

Cadell shrugged. "Don't know what to tell you, pal. We could keep arguing about who's coming and who's not, but that won't make you any better at fighting."

Marcus squinted. *I'm still better than you*, he felt like saying, but he didn't know that for sure. He sighed, holding his hilt with both hands. "I don't need to be."

Cadell smirked, matching his stance. "Don't you? If I were you, I'd want all the training I could get. The north's getting dangerous, pal."

"Maybe you should go south, then," he replied, edging closer. Slowly, Marcus leant his sword in, effortlessly tapped away by Cadell. He did it again, and that was repelled also. *So, he's not just a bad joke.* Marcus straightened his back, keeping his suspicious eyes locked to Cadell's.

"I could," Cadell admitted, "but then there'd be no one here to help you." This time, Marcus tapped Cadell's sword away, though his prod was almost playful. "Your brother's not coming, Marcus. He's still too drunk."

"I don't need any help."

"Don't you?" Cadell snickered. "Teach me how to train with air and I think both of us would be happier."

Wow, he thinks I'm an idiot, he winced. His grip coiled and tightened like a snake around his hilt. Cadell's face remained smug, and it made Marcus grimace even more. He threw a heavy overhead slash, and it was knocked back. Cadell moved one leg back and pointed his blade. Marcus swung again, a strike from the right, then left, then right, then above, all blocked. He had pushed Cadell halfway across the yard before he was met with a parry, Cadell following up with a weighty right swing that almost sent Marcus off balance. They met eyes again, duelling with stares. Cadell, although panting like Marcus, began to smirk again. *Who does he think he is?* Marcus lunged, pushing the blade against Cadell, and they clashed and stuck. Marcus tensed his muscles as the blunted steel scraped his ears, bringing the blades round several times. Cadell wasn't giving in. He was stronger than he looked. Marcus bared his teeth while Cadell did no more than squint. Cadell won the feat of strength, breaking free of the clash and ramming Marcus with his shoulder. He laughed. "You've got some swings on you, Marc."

"Don't call me that," he frowned. *Only Cadmus calls me that.*

"Have it your way," Cadell chuckled. This time, Cadell attacked, meeting the blades in a wrestle once again. Marcus's arms started to ache from holding, and it became clearer that Cadell was winning. Veins grew from Cadell's arms, and Marcus was slowly pushed down. He released and ducked, sending Cadell's blade slamming to the ground, and swept his longsword to Cadell's arm. Cadell grunted in pain and fell back, grasping his bicep. Standing straight, he lifted his hand to reveal that blood was drawn. He licked his fingers and tittered. "Quite some swings indeed."

Marcus's eyes darted to his sword, a fine line of Cadell's blood stroking the edge. "Shit... I-I didn't mean to..."

"Ah, it happens, pal," Cadell said, shaking his head as he tore some leather from his tunic and wrapped it around the wound. "I say you blunt that blade a bit more next time."

Next time? Marcus didn't like Cadell much, but he was stronger than Cadmus. Plus, it seemed like Cadmus didn't want to show up at all, like he said. "You'd fight me again?"

"'Course I will," Cadell smiled, spitting. "A flea bite, is all." He patted

Marcus on the shoulder before passing his longsword. "I hope you weren't showing all your cards," he smirked, holding his arm as he left.

Nice one, Marcus, he frowned, slotting the two swords to the closest barrel. *You almost fucked that one up too.* He shook his head as he left the yard. Even though he wasn't struck, his arms still throbbed from the exchange. *He's strong,* Marcus thought, not wanting to admit it to his face. *Did Cadmus send him?* They had always been quite close, he knew. Today was the first day Marcus had actually met the boy, so it was strange to him why he'd be sent. Either way, it didn't bother the ram too much; he had gotten a good fight out of it, a good release of his pent-up anger.

His brother wasn't still in bed like he had assumed. Instead, he was racing through a hallway of the Cenkeep, jittering like he had seen a ghost. "There you are," he rushed over, taking Marcus's arm.

"Where were you? I was waiting-"

Cadmus winced. "Ah, sorry, I got distracted." That was when Marcus saw the anguish in his brother's face. "Marc, I've just seen some messed up shit," he whispered.

"W-what do you mean? Where?"

"The Mudstreet, Marc, you won't believe your eyes, I swear."

"The Mudstreet?" Marcus frowned. "We're forbidden to go there, what were you doing?"

Cadmus's head shot to a paranoid amount of directions, beads of sweat on his forehead. "See for yourself," he scowled, dashing away.

EVA VI
-Ruin-

She hoped it would live up to its name. The Ruins of Lignum: once a city high and tall with a thriving population, now a charred-black shadow of its former self. Outlines of what buildings could have been were easy to draw out for Eva Centaur, most of the largest towers still holding half their form. Bits of ash and remnants of humanity still brushed the mild air, and even though the centuries had frozen the grotesque ruins in place, they still decayed at a rate that didn't outpace life.

"I've never quite understood what could devastate a city so badly," Idris said, in awe.

"Alchaesphite," she responded confidently. "It's an explosive made from magic. It burns so hot that it can *melt* stone."

Idris glanced over as they rode, intrigued. "How do you know that?"

"Who *doesn't* know that?" Eva gasped. *"The War of the Wastelands* was only the most *awesome* war to come from Post-Austellus. Led by Archer the Brave, *destroying* Achilles Oquinteus and *all* who rebelled even though they outnumbered him two men to one."

"Seems like quite a hero."

"He was," Eva agreed. "He was the greatest military mind to ever live."

Idris kept the smile on his face as they trotted towards the ruins. "So, how was this *alchaesphite* made? Magic doesn't exist in Post-Austellus."

"No one knows," she admitted. "They mass made it during The Hex War, but they never used it; everyone had their hands on alchaesphite, so if they started using it properly, it probably would have ended the world."

"Well the world *did* near end," Idris pointed out. "I bet *The Great Pause* must have wiped out more people than alchaesphite could."

"Maybe," she said, "but not a lot was needed to completely demolish a city. Most of it was lost in the *Pause*, but some families managed to steal and hide some in mines or in castles that were lucky enough to not fall."

"Wow. Those people must have made a fortune."

Eva nodded. "It's priceless, really. The perfect weapon to win any war."

They approached the dilapidated entrance, the archway completely blown off the top. Eva was leading. "I think we should go around, Eva."

"Do the ruins scare you, Idris?" she chuckled.

"I'm not joking. Squatters and outlaws make this their home."

"Let them look," she said as she trotted onwards, taking in the huge city. Idris sighed as he was made to follow her.

For a time, it was pretty - a dead, grotesque kind of pretty - but still only for a time. A bolas came flying out of nowhere, entangling the legs of the horse Eva rode on. They both tumbled to the floor. Another one was flung, wrapping around Eva's body.

"Eva!" Idris cried, his shout cut short after receiving a bolas of his own around his neck. They were thrown too quickly to react to. They both grunted as they tried to break free of the bind.

Two masked men emerged from the ruins, laughing. "Slow as a cripple," one said. "You'd almost think you two were highborn with those fancy clothes."

"Who's your friend?" the other asked, pressing his dirty boot against Idris's face where he lay.

"Give it a rest," Idris muttered angrily.

"Let us go!" Eva shouted.

"Why? We just captured you," one chuckled.

"It's not like you're valuable when you're free," the other smiled.

"We're *much* more valuable alive," she bargained.

"Go on, then," the man pressing Idris's face down laughed. "We might let him live if you're important enough."

"Stop it!" Idris declared, the best he could with his smushed face. "She doesn't want to tell anyone!"

"Shut it, oldie," the man said, pressing down harder.

"I'm the king's daughter!" she screamed. *"He'll mount both of your heads on spikes if you don't let us go!"*

The ruins fell silent. The men looked at each other. "The fuck are you doing with the king's daughter, Idris?" the idle man said, taking off his mask to reveal a pretty face.

"The fuck *am* I doing with the king's daughter?" he said in disbelief, now that the other man's foot was relieved from his face.

Her heart beat a thousand times a second. "You know each other?"

"You're Eva Centaur?!" Idris repeated, standing.

"My gods," the other man chortled, wiping his weather-beaten face.

"You're lying," the pretty man said.

"The king *did* put out a search warrant for a girl like her," the other said, untying Eva.

"Who are they?" Eva asked Idris.

"Um..." Idris stuttered, not breaking his stare. "Eva, this is my brother, Apollo, and this is my half-brother, Robin. Brothers, this is... Eva Centaur... apparently."

Apollo broke into guffaw. "You didn't know she was a princess?"

"I knew she was highborn. Not *that* highborn," Idris said.

Eva brushed herself off, feeling awkward beyond words.

Robin stroked the back of his young, fair hands against Eva's long, brown hair. "No bloody way."

"*Leave* her," Idris ordered, slapping Robin's arm away. "She's under my protection now."

"How much was the warrant for?" Robin asked Apollo.

"Twenty silvers," he said.

Robin laughed. "We're gonna be rolling in *wad.*"

"No, you can't take me back!" Eva cried.

"You won't be taken back," Idris assured.

Robin winced. "If the king finds out we have his daughter, she'd be right: he'd take our heads off the first chance he gets."

"He won't. I'll tell him you saved me if you bring me with you."

"And when he asks what took so long?" Robin quizzed.

"She's right," Apollo sighed. "Even if we wanted to, we can't take her back. Father needs us."

"Even if you wanted to, you couldn't take me back. I wouldn't come," she said stubbornly.

Robin chuckled, nudging Idris's arm. "She even has the fire of a Centaur. Idris, you're blind for not seeing."

"He *is* blind, but for not spotting us," Apollo giggled. "Nice shot, by the way, right around the neck."

"Thanks," Robin smiled, "it was a pretty big target, to be fair."

"Oh, save it," Idris said, sparking laughter from his brothers. Their banter reminded Eva of home, of Fletcher and Asher and Jovian mocking and joking with each other. If she wasn't in the midst of laughter, she would miss it. Not that she didn't miss her siblings; every moment she could spare a thought for them, the yearn to see them grew. "How did you know we'd come through here?" he asked, remounting his stallion.

"We didn't," Robin smiled, fetching his and Apollo's mounts. "We were about to give up on looking."

Eva knelt down to her white mare, unbinding her.

"Sorry about your pony, Eva... my lady. What should I call her now?" Robin said.

"Just Eva," she said as she had to Idris. "Ladies are stupid."

"Ah, you caught yourself a smart one, Idris," Robin smiled. *"Lads! Lads! Lads!"* he chanted in a silly voice.

"We mustn't tell anyone who she is," Idris affirmed as they rode. "They can't know."

"They can't know that she's the most wanted girl in Austellus?" Apollo added derisively. "Seems like a smart plan."

"Yeah," Robin giggled. "Who is this? Her name's Eva, father. We promise she's not a princess."

Eva chuckled.

"I'm looking at you, Robin," Idris said coldly.

"Thought you were looking forward," he muttered under his breath.

She was quick to draw a liking to Robin, even though she was trussed up by his hand mere moments ago. The more she glanced at him, the more attractive he seemed. His brown hair was a shade brighter than Idris's, and had deep, green eyes, mismatched by Idris and Apollo's hazel. The brothers all looked related: similar in build and strength, prominent jaws, strong noses. Robin definitely looked the most disparate though - along with his eyes and hair, also possessing a lighter shade to his brother's tans.

"So, how did you come across the girl, Idris?" asked Robin. "You kidnap her?"

"No," Idris frowned, grasping his reins.

Robin smirked. "Don't worry, Eva. You can tell us if he's touched you in any way-"

"Oh, come on, Robin, not in front of her," Idris moaned, embarrassed by his half-brother.

"She doesn't seem to mind," he smiled, drawing their attention to a still giggling Eva.

"Idris saved me," Eva said. "He found me after I passed out."

"You were unconscious!" Robin exclaimed. "Idris, brother, you have some explaining to do."

Eva almost fell from her horse with laughter, and she didn't know why. The way Robin spoke tickled her. She replied, not quite after gaining her composure. "I fell off the wagon trail. I fainted after I ran out of water."

"It wasn't *just* water," Idris contested. "She had no food, a huge gash on her arm, and five dead men around her."

Robin surrendered, putting his hands in the air. "I promise we won't touch you, my lady."

"Hang on, how did your father not notice you had fallen off?" Apollo winced, chuckling from Robin's jests.

"He didn't know I was there," Eva admitted. "I snuck on the trail."

"What?!" Idris chuckled, this news new to him also. "Why?"

"He wouldn't let me go," she said. "And I needed to."

"But still, you weren't alone, right?" Apollo continued. "He must have travelled with a party. How come *everyone* happened to pass an unconscious girl without any questions?"

Eva shrugged. "I don't know. My wagon was nearer the back, I guess."

"Well you have more balls than I had at your age," said Robin.

"She's a girl, you idiot," Apollo teased. "She doesn't even have balls."

"Well you never know," Robin said in a bold tone. "Maybe that's the secret: having no balls at all."

"Can we not talk about genitals in front of the Princess of Caelestia?" Idris asked.

"What's wrong, Idris. Have you not got any?" Eva smiled.

Robin burst into a hearty chortle. *"The fall of Idris Equuleus!"* he continued, slapping his knee. Apollo laughed along with him, while Idris only held a playful, yet incredulous smirk.

"Well come on, then," she said as they approached the end of the ruins. "Lutum awaits." She grabbed her reins, booting her horse into a gallop as she took the lead.

FLETCHER III
-Credo-

There's a point when snow becomes a burden to live with: when it gets annoying and cold, whoever having to brace it, wishing it would leave. This point was on the horizon for Fletcher Centaur. When it fell for the first time a few moons ago, it was welcomed with open arms. Everyone in the fort had enjoyed it, even the grave knights and guards breaking a smile to throw a snowball or two. Now, Fletcher sat, sharpening arrows with his warily cold fingers as he wondered how Hew still derived amusement from the white weight.

Keeping watch of Hew in their mother's absence was an easier task than Fletcher thought it would be. He was generally responsible enough to be left to his own devices, normally quite a private boy to begin with. From what Fletcher could tell, Hew enjoyed having his brother watch him rather than Semira, probably because Fletcher was a lot more lenient with him. *He's happy,* Fletcher thought, *no point trying to ruin that with rules.*

It was a while since Fletcher could commit his focus to the making of arrows, the unused stack he reaped standing higher each day. It had almost become an obsession returning, Fletcher wanting every arrow to be more refined than the last. The thought had crossed his mind that his creations would most likely be used to end lives in the future, but he tried not to think of that. It didn't necessarily bother him; *soldiers will have weapons no matter what I do. The least I could do is make sure my arrows are sharp enough to give them quick deaths.* Either way, the craft was more done for the art, not the use.

It seemed like as the days went on, he had more and more time to practise it, since the Negal lords were quick to learn that complaining about a lack of food for the tenth time wouldn't stop their people from starving. It was surprising that food was still an issue, especially since the shipments of increased haul had arrived, and an inflation of people were moving out, up towards the Auburn Pole. Thankfully, that issue should be dealt with, now that the Capras had become allies. Or, at least, Fletcher *hoped* they had, waiting neurotically for his sister and mother's return.

"My lord," Sir Roswell bowed before Fletcher, taking him by surprise as he was knocked out of his thoughts. "A ship at the docks."

He and Hew locked eyes with each other, smiling with excitement before they both darted out of the courtyard. The dock wasn't too far from the fort: down the hill for a mile or two before it stood, placed right next to the Antrum River. It wasn't a particularly fancy dock, Trader's Dock stole all of the dock beauty for the Negal lands, but it was large enough to serve its purpose. That being said, it was embarrassingly overshadowed by the grand Capricornian ship that pulled in.

Leta was the first to jump out, looking as perky as ever. Hew ran over to greet them, clamping himself to her with a big hug.

"How was it?" Fletcher was eager to ask after he hugged his sister.

"I'll tell you later," Leta winked, getting dragged away by Hew because he wanted Leta to see all the new snowmen he had made.

"I see the fort's still standing," Semira observed as she climbed down.

"It's getting easier," he smiled. "Go on, get inside. It must be freezing on that boat." She nodded intently, adjusting her black hair as she followed her children.

"Thank you, Tyran!" Fletcher called as the goat showed his face. "Come down. Spend the night if you will."

"Your offer is gracious, your lordship, but we must be back," he said, scarcely raising his voice. "We never know how far the Khavars are."

"Very well. Have a safe trip back, my lord."

Tyran bowed deeply, before lifting the fat anchor and departing from the dock. *He didn't shed much of a smile,* Fletcher observed. *I hope Leta's news is good.*

<hr/>

A foggy dusk lay on Fort Deus when dinner was served. It wasn't a supper that lasted long, nor one that held much chatter; Leta and Semira scoffed their meals as if it was the first time they had seen food. They seemed to both enjoy the experience of exploring the Three Goats, waffling on about the beautiful lustre that emitted from the city at night, along with how amazing the architecture was. It was evident by their appetite that food wasn't a strong suit, though. Fletcher didn't want to probe them upon arrival, so he let the evening pan out like normal, and decided to wait for the morrow to ask.

At least that was the plan. A more than agitated mind plagued Fletcher as he kept wriggling around in his bed. It wasn't a mind that visited him often, but he couldn't help but bear the thoughts and feelings of the last few moons while they shot around in his head. He decided that learning Leta's verdict might ease him some.

When he discovered that Leta's solar lay empty, he wasn't alarmed. He returned to his chamber to grab a warm cloak and extra furs, before heading outside. The snow that fell in the dead of night was a light one, almost pleasant as the cold fingers brushed against Fletcher's warm face. It piled up to almost ankle height as he left the fort, all that fell *in* the fort having to be shovelled out in order for the soldiers and workers to return to their normal routine. Some of the snow crept in his shoes as he trudged along, tickling his toes.

"I thought I might find you here," Fletcher said as he approached the cliff face.

Leta was sat there, almost startled, wrapped in furs and blankets on a freshly excavated patch of snow. "Oh hi," she smiled. "You want to know my discoveries, I suppose."

Fletcher brushed off snow on the rock next to her. "Actually, I just couldn't sleep."

"Thinking too much?"

He nodded, taking his seat.

"Me too," she said, returning her gaze back to the dark ocean, glimmering under a soft grey moon.

"You first, then," he smirked, nudging her.

She sighed. "They're the same as us, bro. Even for being *savages* born and bred in the wild, us and them are no different. It doesn't make sense why we should draw a barrier and say that they're not allowed to cross it because of something someone did centuries ago."

"Well, ok . . ." Fletcher began to propose, gesturing with his hands. "If you gave each lord of exile the option to: either bend the knee to us and be free of exile, or refuse and remain a *'false kingdom'*, most would either accept and betray us, or decline and stay independent. The world already depicts them as honourless brutes; what's another broken vow to an already destroyed image?"

"But they don't even have that option," she muttered. "The Capras would stay loyal."

"You trust them now?" he asked, not confrontationally.

"Eva got it all wrong," she said, shrugging. "Tyran told me the truth. He said he didn't want to kill *us*. He wanted to take out the Helas. Apparently, they've been responsible for sinking most of our supply ships. Galloway was just making sure that father didn't notice and punish the Capricorns for it."

Fletcher scratched his cheek. The Hela family weren't the friendliest of houses, but he had a hard time believing that the Capras were any friendlier. "And you believe him?"

"It's all too intricate to be a lie," she said confidently.

"They're not idiots; maybe they've planned the lie for a while?"

"It's not a lie," she shook her head, a faint smile playing her lips. "I've lived with Hew for ten years; I know when someone's lying."

Fletcher chuckled. It almost seemed too good to be true: a knight in shining armour dressed as a Capricorn come to save the Negal lands from famine and war. *It wouldn't be that difficult to paint yourself like that.*

"But yeah, you're right," she admitted. "Most of them seem too proud to give up their independence. So, whatever, there's nothing we can do about it… What were you thinking about?"

Fletcher tried to choose from the many thoughts that bounced around. "Everything," he said. He thought back to where the thoughts stemmed from. "On my birthmoon, Asher and I made a toast to change, a leap of life that begins now. I can't help but feel like we were stupid to do so. If I could go back and undo that toast, then I would."

Leta chuckled. "It's not your fault that things have changed so much because you drank to it."

"I know, but before that we were all *happy*," he moaned. "We were all together, as a *family*. Now, father is in Lunarpass, Eva probably is too, Asher is gods know where, and we're stuck watching over a dying fort."

"I can remember pretty clearly you *not* being happy," she smirked. "*All* you and Asher would talk about every day was how much both of you *longed* to see the outside world, calling it a curse to be here."

"Well I still *want* to," he admitted. "Really badly, actually. It just doesn't help stripping me of everything I never knew I'd miss."

"So, if you did leave with Ash to see the world, you wouldn't miss us?"

"I..." Fletcher began, his thoughts stuttering. "I don't know. Probably, yeah."

"Exactly," she said softly. "All of us miss them. Hew asks when Asher's coming back *every day.*"

"I don't know what I want. I don't know who *I* am anymore," he said brushing his hands through his wavy hair. "Not even a week ago I made *arrows* for the first time since the Milk Moon. And yeah, I miss them all, but do I want father to come home? Not really, he *has* to be in Lunarpass right now. Do I want to give up this seat? Not really, people are relying on me now."

"Would you if you could?" she asked.

He honestly didn't know. He *did* enjoy it, when he had things to do.

"I think you want too much, Fletcher," she said. "I didn't bring up Hew to make you feel bad, I just don't think you realise that a lot of what you're looking for doesn't need to be found, like you just said."

Even if she didn't mean to, that made him feel oddly guilty. *Maybe she's right.* "Gods," he spat, planting his head in his palms. "I take it all for granted. You, ma, Hew. One day you could all be torn away from me as easily as the others."

"You don't need us for you to be happy. You don't need us for you to be you," she said, placing her hand on his shoulder. "You're pretty fucked if we go and you don't know *who* you are."

"I *know,* so how do I figure that out?" he asked, frustrated with himself. "How have *you?* I'm a year older than you and I'm off the bloody trail in comparison."

She looked up to the misty stars, holding herself tighter as a cool breeze brushed against them. "You know I can never sleep. I know you see me come out here occasionally to meditate or whatever, but there was a point when I'd come here every night, and just stare at the stars. It was the only thing that made me happy. I had a problem that no one in Austellus could explain to me, and the only thing there to comfort me was the thought of something I couldn't touch, couldn't control, couldn't even *ponder.* It's not for me to determine which stars will go out, or which ones will shoot across the sky, but that doesn't mean I can't watch." Fletcher looked up also. It was beautiful, even though a soft fog hazed the bright lights that shone from the sky. "You can learn a lot about what you want when you recognise that you can't control what you have, when you can only watch things come and go."

"You don't have to watch," Fletcher frowned. "You can *always* work for what you want, whatever that is."

"Then why is father still in Lunarpass?" she smirked. "If he died tomorrow because some assassin stabbed him like Reynold, would that be because you didn't work hard enough?" Fletcher could only wince as everything he thought was being challenged. His eyes were fixed on the sky for a moment before she spoke again. "I'm not a wise, old elder, bro, as much as I'd like to think I am. I don't know how long it'll take for you to figure it out." She pointed up. "But I do know that up there, something has a bigger plan for all of us."

"Gods?"

She sniggered. "You know I don't believe in gods. They seem to me like something man made up to help them sleep at night."

"Maybe you should believe, then," he smirked, "you could use all the sleeping help you could get."

"See?!" she said as she chuckled. "You didn't need to try to be Fletcher Centaur to be an asshole. You just are."

"Hey!" he groaned jokingly, sweeping a handful of snow at his sister.

She brushed the snow off her, all the while holding a smile. "So?" she asked. "What does Fletcher Centaur want?"

He thought about everything they had talked about. The desire to see the world had not left since he sat, but the way Leta looked to the stars inspired him. *But that doesn't mean all things should be predetermined, and you just have to let it happen. Father was adamant that you could change your fate, and he's never wrong. Maybe I have a role to play, bigger than myself... Maybe it's time to lead my own life, and not wait for things to unfold as if they would.* He frowned as an unpleasantly familiar notion popped into his head. "Change," he admitted.

MARCARIUS II
-Call-

M aybe the king needs a change of scroll bearers," the voice of Sir Orion jested, dazedly waking the elder from his kip.

Elder Marcarius ejected up, almost falling from his solar's chair. *I fell asleep.* Beside him sat a legion of unbroken scrolls, seeming to pile higher and higher each day. He glanced outside, expecting to see the lights of day, only to see darkness. "Sir Orion," he stuttered, frantically organising the chaos of scrolls on his desk by sweeping them away with his arm, "what can I do for you, my lord?"

"If it's more apt to visit later, then it's no problem," he offered.

"No, no, not at all," the elder assured. "Please, take a seat."

"Quite the consignment of scrolls," he observed, sitting. "If you had any more, Esmond would work you to death."

Marcarius glanced around. "I did have Lord Waker aiding me, it is his office after all. Though, he seems to have departed."

"Probably to sleep," Orion laughed. "What do the letters concern?"

"All of similar matters," he sighed. "Lords of the Pole appealing for garrison, assurances, protection, what have you. It won't help them; issues breed issues. It's as if they no longer care about the shortage of food."

"Gods," he cursed. "That's an issue I know *too* much about. My old father by law won't shut up about how stocks and remuneration have plummeted in spite of it."

"Lord Ellys has a reason to be," Marcarius chuckled. "Being head of gold during such an ignition of the economy must be a truly stressful feat."

Orion nodded, scratching his stubble beard. "Do you know what caused the low yields?"

"Temperature change," he said, adjusting himself. "I have no knowledge of the current state; I assume things have stabilized. Truth be told, if I didn't have so much work to do, I would pay Elder Solomon a visit in Iustitia. Perhaps the Great Athenaeum too. There is no shortage of ancient tomes of *The Great Pause* in that beast of a library." Although not a lie, when it came to reading, his mind wandered more so to the tomes about serpents, and if they even existed.

"If you want to go, I'd have no problem bearing the burden of your work," Orion offered.

"No, I wouldn't burden you so," he affirmed, fiddling with his scrolls once again. "It is too strenuous of a task. I'll travel once the threats of war have waned."

"Nonsense. Honestly, it's not a trouble for me. You'd think the King's *First Avail* would be assigned more jobs than I have; truly, I'm no more serving than the chalice he drinks from."

Marcarius giggled at his jest. "Thank you, my lord. It would be most mellow of you if you would."

The knight bowed where he sat.

"So, what brings you to my solar at this hour?" the elder asked.

"I'm worried about Esmond," he admitted. "I wanted to know if I wasn't alone in thinking that of late, he's been acting a bit more... I wouldn't say *warmongering...*"

"Tactless perhaps."

"Tactless, yeah," Orion said, snapping his fingers. "The people mostly love him, but the people who don't are sure to make their voices heard, especially since the display of that bandit."

The bandit had its fate met above and beyond what the king intended. After the people tired of throwing fruits, they moved on to stale bread, then rocks, slowly and painfully tearing the man apart. That's what Lord Vesta had told him at least, the elder could barely stomach watching. *We should have questioned him first,* the elder kept telling himself, *we should have learnt what we needed to know about the Archipelago, and not been so impatient for justice.* "I understand your concern," he said, standing to wander towards his open window. "Perhaps the people who desire to keep their harmony reacted distastefully to the display because of the disorder it

Provoked. But we must bear in mind that the king is not tactless by choice. He is doubtless still to suffer from the loss of his lieges, perhaps also in heartache due to the absence of his family."

"In that case, wouldn't it be wise to… second guess decisions, perhaps?"

"Why, do you mistrust him?"

The knight shook his head, smiling. "I've known the man since I was a boy. No way I mistrust him," he assured. "But when it comes to making choices true to himself… I don't think he can, at the moment. His grief is changing him."

Marcarius agreed, nodding. "Do you have something to propose?"

"I wouldn't trust my judgement over yours," he said. "You undoubtedly have much more experience with working untameable kings."

The elder smiled as he thought back. "I've lived to see the likes of Jovian the Second, Fletcher the First. No man knows untameable kings as much as I." A troubled face washed over Marcarius. "Jovian defined untameable…"

Orion winced. "Jovian? Jovian the Cruel? He was a madman!"

"Some would say what Esmond did with that bandit was cruel. It wasn't too dissimilar to what Jovian would have done."

"Jovian killed his younger brother."

The thought of Lori stroked his mind. "Esmond loves Lorimer too much, to be true. But like you said, I have seen this before."

It clearly distressed the knight to hear this. "Gods," he frowned. He nervously grazed his stubble with the back of his hand. "What are we to do, then? What did you do with Jovian?"

"Jovian was never cruel, nor evil," Marcarius admitted. "The days deluded him, though. The pain of loss and power, and the descent to madness can do wicked things to a man. But unfortunately, it's something that we can't help one face. I'd say the only thing we can do is to remind Esmond of his purpose. His willpower for that alone is enough to take him through it. He will soon see clearly, once the clouds of grief pass."

"He won't keep his willpower if the people label him as they did Jovian," Sir Orion averred. "Esmond cares about what they think. If they start to hate him, who has he got to fight for?"

Marcarius sighed, returning to his seat. "You're Esmond's best friend. I've seen him heed your advice at every turn… if you worry for him, let it be known. Advise him. Tell him to be more diplomatic."

The knight sat in a puddle of thought. "Thank you for your wisdom, Elder Marcarius," he eventually bowed. "Good luck on your journey to Iustitia."

"Thank you for your help also," Marcarius smiled. "I'll let Lord Waker know of your role."

His smile was reciprocated with a lipless grin from Sir Orion as he took his leave. Esmond was an enigma, through and through. It must have been tough for Orion to see all of his scruples under such close magnification. *He wouldn't turn out like Jovian, would he?* True, Jovian was like a child in a playground; the last King of Lter had nothing to live for compared to Esmond. He had lost his eldest brother at the young age of nineteen, and that was enough tragedy to trigger his descent... *but so did Esmond.* Esmond was only fifteen when Ivor Centaur vanished from the world. Marcarius hated to think about it: Esmond's legacy to become 'Esmond the Cruel', 'Jovian the Third'. *He's a long way from those titles,* he decided. But living through that once was difficult enough. *The path within one's blood is the path they're doomed to follow.*

<hr/>

The next day arrived in a blink, and Lord Waker was soon to return to Marcarius's solar. "Good morning," the slim, ash-haired man greeted upon entry, bearing a sickly number of scrolls to add to the heap. "Are you... heading somewhere, elder?" he asked, noticing the packed case.

"Fear not," he chuckled. "I am not abandoning you. Sir Orion has offered to cover my share of the work when his duty permits."

"Sir Orion?" Briggs said, surprised. "May I ask where you are destined?"

"Iustitia," he said, continuing to organise the scrolls by family. "A great deal of information regarding the weather and perhaps the serp-" Marcarius remembered himself.

"Serpent?" the head of word smiled with intrigue.

The elder shook his head. "Thinking out loud. It's only a tale."

"Perhaps, but if a serpent is what you seek, then your interests might be piqued by a detour," Briggs smirked, reaching for a key in his cloak to unlock a small box. He fumbled about the box for a time, parting the many scrolls that hid in there. "Only I and the king know of this letter, but it may be more useful for you to know, too," he smiled, holding out a scroll, the first sunbeam of dawn lighting up the broken seal of Centaur's Lagoon.

ATHENA III
-Cabal-

It didn't look right. It still looked *good*; it just wasn't how she remembered it. She knew she could never match its likeness exactly, the Lunar Bells being of such mystical make that it would be a miracle to imitate it. The miniature model was something she wanted to make the moment her eyes lay upon them. Finally, she had more than enough resources and time to do so.

Though, the meaning of the tower had changed to Athena Horncurve. *'The day a serpent kills a ram is the day the great bells of Lunarpass chime for a thirteenth hour'.* It was one of the last things Athena had heard Sigmund say. She flicked the tiny metal bell thirteen times while she leant on her desk, pressing her face with her fist. She wondered if her grandfather even knew what the serpent was. *Maybe it's rebellion? A revolution? It would make sense if it would 'first strike the north'. Why would they use the metaphor of a serpent, though? No snake banner nor sigil sits in Selerborn, or even in Austellus... I think.*

Her stomach grumbled. She looked down to her slimming belly, forgetting how hungry she was. It had been like that every day: she'd wake up, plan a project, and get so immersed in it that food received a loss of priority. Placing her little sculpture among the others, she headed out.

Having the workshop all to herself was really lonely for the first few days Angelo had left, but she was definitely starting to warm up to the room. It was difficult for Athena to see the grand projects that had been left unfinished; the most exciting parts to her weeks had been the finishing touches and testing of Angelo's inventions. There was still a lot that *had* been done, such as the *Otobow:* a handheld ballista that shot arrows with the flick of a finger, the *Chute:* a fabric triangle that Angelo said would slow the fall of anyone, the *Fist:* a device that automated the swing of a hammer. But there was still a lot unfinished that Athena wanted to see work, namely the *Labente*, which Angelo believed could carry the weight of a fully-grown man, and make him *fly*. Once she got deep into making her own structures, however, it bothered her less. She never had the patience, nor the knowledge, nor the discipline to continue the larger scale inventions on her own, but by creating her little trinkets, she could have all the creative liberation she needed while still staying precise.

"Athena," Emily said when her daughter arrived at the mess hall, "we called for you hours ago."

"Sorry," she replied, suddenly aware of her sawdust-infested rags, "I was working."

"Well you can still work, as long as you don't starve yourself."

Athena nodded, eagerly taking a seat. "What are you looking at?" she asked her mother, filling her mouth with bread.

"Your father," she sighed. "It's probably best if you stay inside now."

"What? Why?"

"He's trying to deal with protesters. They've been at it since the morning."

"Protesting about what?"

Emily shrugged. "Can't hear much up here."

Curiosity got the better of Athena after she broke her fast. She disobeyed her mother without a second thought, sneaking out of the Cenkeep in the quickest silent dash she could. It was more than easy to fool the stationed guards. All she had to do was whistle to steal their attention, in turn slipping past them undetected.

The scene in the main street wasn't a pretty one, but luckily wasn't a violent one either. A preacher stood on a fountain, shouting over the masses as he incessantly denied Riley's orders to cease. Her father stood with his ram's guard, looking bored to death. Telling them to stop wasn't working. *Sigmund would have thrown them all into jail by now,* she thought, annoyed with her father. There were a lot of them, but it was possible.

"Please, sir, cease your campaign," Riley said tiredly. "We will go into the eve if we must."

"These are *your* streets, Lord Riley," the preacher observed. "What Lord of Selerborn cannot control his own streets?"

The small crowd of protesters agreed with uproar.

The audacity, Athena thought as she winced.

"Pssst!" a whisper pierced through the noise, *"Athena!"* The voice belonged to Cadmus, crouching behind a stable as he watched the ruckus. Athena crept towards him. *"If they notice you, they'll gut you alive."*

"Saying my name wouldn't get me noticed, would it?" she whispered back sharply. "What are they protesting about?"

"They don't like father," he replied, peeking back. "They want revenge for grandpa. They want someone *stronger* in charge."

"Like who? Surely, they don't mean *him*," she giggled in disbelief. The protester was a skinny little man, similar to Sigmund if he had more muscle.

"They haven't said."

"Where's Marcus?"

"I don't know, let me listen."

"These might be my streets, but it's your time and the people's peace you're interrupting," Riley sighed as he sat on a step.

"Your lord sits down!" the preacher exclaimed. "A lord *worthy* of the seat of Selerborn never seats himself on such stone."

"What the-?" Athena muttered.

"I'm seating myself because you are boring me, sir," Riley said, lighting a chuckle from the neutral crowd. "Now, if you'd please take down your signs and order yer people to stop; I won't ask again."

"He won't ask again!" the preacher chortled. "That is the sign of a *weak* ruler! Sigmund was a strong ruler, but his offspring is sour. Riley Horncurve: the lord who sat."

Riley shrugged to his slumped guards.

Athena tried to dash forward, her arm caught by Cadmus. "Don't," he said.

She didn't care. She was fuming. She jarred his arm away violently as she rushed to the crowds. *"The fuck is wrong with you? What's wrong with all of you?"* she bellowed over the crowds. *"You want Sigmund's way? Well Sigmund would not have left any one of you cunts alive!"* She pointed at her abashed father. *"He* is your lord now, and if your balls are so small that you can't be true northmen and accept that, then I'm sure he'll grant you your wishes and *mount* your heads on the bloody walls!"

"He took Selerborn unwilling to Lord Sigmund!" the preacher

snapped back, his face red. "If this *false king* is worthy of his name, then he would have let us know!"

"*Ye glaikit!*" she yelled, flushing with flare. "You want to know the truth of it? Sigmund pleaded guilty! He admitted to his crimes because he *knew* that his son would rule Selerborn well. He *trusted* you dickheads to *accept* that! Not to *dishonour* what it means to be Arian! You want to betray Esmond and march south? That'll make you no better than the cursed bloody ram!"

The only sound to bounce around the streets of Selerborn was the searing echo of Athena's voice. Every person's jaw was left open. The protesters slowly and embarrassingly retreated to their homes. Riley almost had a proud look on his face as the crowds faded.

"I didn't raise my Athena to use such a vulgar tongue," he smirked, oddly calm. "How much did ye see?"

"All of it," Cadmus chimed in, revealing himself. "Why did you let them do that to you?"

"I couldn't be arsed," their father sighed plainly. "That's the third cabal we've seen since our return."

"You can't let them speak to you like that," Athena agreed.

"Can't control how they speak," he said. "Ignatius says they'll calm down."

"You were made a fool of!" Cadmus insisted.

Riley shrugged. "Then a fool I shall be. Now come to the keep where you're safe."

◆⸺⸺❡

Athena didn't need to be locked up in the Cenkeep for long before she desired escape again. The hour was old, and even though Athena's throat felt like nettles had been dragged through it, her frustration just made her more inspired to create. She had to get to the workshop, and with enough dexterity, it didn't take long. She carefully closed the wooden door of her workshop behind her, making sure to not draw attention in the quiet evening streets.

"Finally," Marcus sighed as she arrived.

She flinched in shock. "You were... how did you get in here-"

"You keep a spare key in between the windowsills."

"Wait, how do you know?"

He grimaced. "Athena, please, I found something. You need to see."

Athena couldn't say another word before her brother grabbed her hand and pulled her out of the hut. They snuck with some pace, relying on the shadows of buildings to conceal them. "Where are we going?" Athena asked, desperately trying to keep up. Marcus didn't reply, keeping his unbroken attention on looking out for people. He led her to Woolton: the Mudstreet most people called it. It was where most of the animals were kept, the stench of excretion never quite evading the main street. They dropped down the hill on the street to approach a small, thatched house in the corner, hugging the city wall. "What were you doing this far in the Mudstreet? We're forbidden to go here," she asked when she could.

"See for yourself," he said, pointing through a hole in the thatch.

"-suited," said a man, secretly speaking to a cult-like circle of listeners.

"We know," one of the listeners agreed, "when has ever a Lord of Selerborn done nothing?"

"It's not *just* nothing," he replied. "It's Lord Riley's *choice* to do nothing, to not kill the king, his *friend*. He's blind to what Esmond did, too busy sucking his cock; it makes the lot of us look weak."

Another man laughed. "You sound like yer father, Fingal."

"My father was made a fool of today," Fingal sighed. "I'm not him."

"Aye, ye better not be," one chuckled. "It'd be the end of us should we ever be scorned by a thirteen-year-old."

"Seems like his daughter's got more balls than him," another added. The group burst into guffaw.

Athena and Marcus glanced at each other, sharing a subtle smirk, though masked in dread.

Fingal didn't join in on the laughter. He continued when they stopped. "So, do you not agree?" he asked. "Lord Sigmund was *our* blood, *our* saviour, the *Warrior Boy* who slew Jaakko Oquinteus sixty years ago. Are we *really* alright with letting Riley do nothing to avenge him?"

Athena had to see the leader. She tried her best to fidget and get a different angle through the thatch. *"Who's Fingal? Do we know him?"*

Marcus shook his head, pressing his ear to the voices as he neurotically looked around.

"Of course we're not-" one replied eventually.

"Good. Then it needs to happen. We need to *stand up*," Fingal insisted.

"The Lord of Selerborn would never listen to lowborn scum," a deep voice complained. "We can't change his mind."

"Would you really call him *our* lord after how he's shamed us?" Fingal asked.

A man laughed. "We don't call you Half-Cut for nothing, Fingal," he said. "You really think *we* could stand a chance against a *kingdom?* Even if we had a *thousand*, we would never make it past the Cenkeep. Riley is the *only* man we can follow."

"There might be someone else," the leader offered. "And we've already seen how he would lead-"

Athena lost her balance, sending an annoyingly loud *rustle* of straw. The leader grabbed a torch, pointing the light at them. Athena could almost get a clear look at the man, but Marcus yanked her away from the hole before she could. They dashed down the streets, shadows hiding them in their black cloaks. She didn't recognise Half-Cut Fingal, neither by face nor by name, but it filled her with dread to recognise who this *'someone else'* was.

ASHER IV
-Disguise-

The Serpent of Stars. It will poison the city, flooded by waters as black as night. It will poison the realms. Each night it became clearer, more vivid. This night, it was clear enough for Asher Centaur to react to the knife. He swivelled around when the wind pushed him back, but in the end, it only made for a null effort. The man reappeared behind him, cutting Asher's throat open like the million dreams before. It was *some* progress at least, and the prince could sense them nearing to a conclusion the closer they made for their destination. The thought of that alone made the uncomfortable wooden raft somewhat bearable, but as he sat, wide awake in his cold sweat, discomfort wasn't rid of him yet.

As for their escort, Asher had never seen the boy sleep. Leo was his name, but the name 'machine' would have been more fitting. He was fairly talkative and caring, always asking if Asher or Lyssa were hungry or in need of anything. Well, he was talkative until the topic of conversation ran into personal life. From what little information he revealed, Asher could construe that Leo was orphaned, left to the world at a young age, and that was about it. The boy was born around Aurdrive Town, explaining his Leon name and accent. In spite of that, him and Lyssa had an instant bond, which was nice to see. Now, he was training to be a seer of Sanctum Amino, which was probably why he was tasked to escort them.

Neither Asher nor Lyssa knew where they were bound, barely even comprehending which way was north, but it was now unmistakable to

Asher where they were, at least. He had his suspicions due to the alien, lime green jungle trees and humid air, but as the unmistakable Enigma Towers crept over the horizon, it was evident that Mea Minor was the radiant city that burst at the foot. *It looks just like the paintings,* he thought, in awe.

"Ok, guys," Leo said, tucking the paddles up into the boat, "you know the drill: keep low, let's not get seen."

Asher had to wake up Lyssa, gently shaking her delicate arms as they both slipped lower into the boat. Leo had prepared them when they passed a fort that must have been Lixhold, because of the Kalyx banners that flew over it, so it wasn't the first time they had to hide from the scouting eyes of a castle. It was more difficult then, since the morning sun lit up the sea, but as they were slipping by Mea Minor, the night was dark and the seas just as black. *This probably won't be half as stressful.*

It looked like Leo was struggling, as he winced and tensed his muscles while trying to move the paddles. "Something wrong?" Asher whispered.

"We're against the current," he grunted. "The sea has never been like this before."

The amount of splashing was bound to be attracting attention. "Do you want me to help?"

Leo shook his head hastily, baring his teeth. The seconds were drawing longer and they weren't going any faster. It didn't take long until the attention of the lookouts was caught. *"You there!"* one called.

The escort tried not to notice, staying down and continuing to row. It worked until a flaming arrow dug into the side of the boat. Leo was quick to break it off, at that point, throwing the paddles down and putting his arms in the air. "Good evening, sir," he smiled. "Is something the matter?"

"Only of your business," he called down, his voice surfing over the sea. "We have no expectation of traders, nor ferries. You lot from Heavia?"

"Heavia!" Leo burst into guffaw. The guard was not amused. "Sorry to bother you, sir. I have two individuals that Lord Todd is expecting." Asher and Lyssa slowly stood.

"Who are they?" he called back, examining the rags Leo had made them wear.

"Afraid I can't tell you that, sir," Leo beamed, "but now that we've established we're not enemies, then we'd be grateful if you'd let us on our way."

The knight looked back, scratching his beard. "Sorry, pal. Without a license, Lord Tate would wish to see you. Please, would you pull over to the docks?"

Leo bit his tongue, sighing. "No problem!" he smiled anyway, doing an amazing job of masking his indignation.

"What now?" Lyssa whispered harshly.

"Play along," Leo said, taking the paddles. "We'll let Tate know that you're old friends of the family, and-"

"We're not lying," Asher contended. "Tell Tate what you told him."

"Tate will ask more questions."

"Then answer them. He's Todd's brother, Leo. I met Todd on the new Rose Moon."

"We can't," Leo began to raise his voice, before catching himself. "We can't tell him; Todd can't know either."

"Todd doesn't know? Where are we going then?"

"Mea, but. . ." he closed his eyes. "Shit, I wasn't meant to tell you that."

"So, Todd *does* know?" Asher asked again, increasingly confused.

Leo had to compose himself, breathing in deeply before resuming rowing. "No one knows. So please, Asher, if you ask about it any more, you'll never find out what your dreams are about."

At the point Asher had more questions than ever, the boat was silenced in the presence of the docks. The setback of being caught only frustrated him more. "Nothing personal, kid," the guard said as he met them, "Lord Tate would just skewer me if I did my job wrong."

"I understand, sir," Leo smiled as he helped Lyssa onto land. "It might even be easier to go by the Enigma Towers to Mea. At least then we wouldn't have to sneak beyond keen eyes such as yours."

The armoured guard chuckled. "If you were to take a ferry, then you wouldn't have to sneak beyond any eyes."

"We might have if we had more time," Leo said. "We embarked at Merchant's Bay, you see."

"Gosh," the guard said, raising his brows, "I bet you're glad you're on land now, then. It's a long way down from here."

The feel of ground *was* refreshing. It wasn't like much activity could be done on a small boat like that, nor much movement for that matter. The streets of Mea Minor were close to dead. It must have been past midnight, since a full blue moon sat straight above, glistening over the weirdly noisy waters. "New moon tonight," Leo observed as they walked.

"The Sturgeon Moon," Asher nodded. "My birthmoon."

Lyssa gasped. "Really?! Why didn't you say?"

His smirk grew. "I forgot."

"Seventeen years old," Lyssa sighed, a smile stretching her face. "You might be getting too old for me, Asher."

"Charming," he smiled, raising his eyebrows. "Is that my gift from you? Insults?"

Lyssa leant in, gently kissing him on the cheek. "Always," she smirked.

"Fat luck that moon is giving for you to run into me," the guard said, a little hesitant.

Asher shrugged. "You're only doing your job."

The guard nodded. "I'm glad you can see that."

Mea Minor's keep was quite a sight; Asher had only seen it in pictures before. It sat not far from the first Enigma Tower, raised high and slim as it felt the sky. Although the keep was meagre in height, it more than made up for in its build. It was a thick block, like a traditional fort tower, apart from the unusual spin of Geminian architecture, as the fort also curved inwards, seemingly to defy physics. It was said that the keep in Mea and Mea Minor once leant on each other for support, but since *The Great Pause* broke them apart, they now stood alone leagues away with the Whitefin Sea to separate them. It certainly wasn't a myth, since Asher could see with his own eyes where the stone had crumbled and broken off, the glimmer of newer replacement stones cutting through the dark.

The only noise in the city came from inside the keep, music and laughter booming into the mild, outside world. The guard led them to a large hall, trashed tables and chairs littering the floors whilst the double doors were wide open. "My lord," the guard bowed, trying his best to be heard over the music.

Tate managed to throw a small white ball into a goblet from across the room and everyone burst into cheer. *"Haha!"* he beamed, punching the air. "Drink up, Lord Doppel. You can't beat the Talyx!"

"I yield!" the man who must have been Lord Doppel smiled, holding up the goblet.

Another guard tapped the slim shoulder of Tate, alerting the lord of their presence. "Visitors!" the young man clapped, jogging over. "Supper has grown cool, but the wine is just as good," he slurred joyfully. "In fact, I believe I heard once that it gets better with time."

The guard smirked. "These are not visitors, my lord. We spotted them just off the coast. They sail on an unlicensed vehicle."

"Oh…" he said, disappointment ringing through his fading grin.

"Well I thank you for bringing them to me, sir. We can never be too safe since those southern attacks rocked the world." Tate stared his dark hazel eyes deep into Asher's, not cracking a smile, until he spoke again. "But you all seem friendly enough. What's your business?"

"With your brother, my lord," Leo stepped forward. "We had hoped it would stay private."

Tate grimaced. "Todd? Why wouldn't he tell me? We could have escorted you."

"He likely didn't have time, my lord," Leo proposed. "Me and my siblings were in quite a hurry to escape our ruined fort down south. When your lord brother visited for the solar celebrations, he offered for us to come to Mea and come into his service. We've not been able to send much warning since barbarians forced us out of our homes." Leo had a unique finesse to his lie, and though it was very convincing to an untrained eye, Asher could see right through it, the boy looking like he was close to bursting with truth.

The Lord of Mea Minor frowned as he tried to fathom the story. "That makes sense, I suppose." He stood, wobbling in thought for a while.

"So, would you let us on our way?"

"No, I'm afraid not," he sighed. "As I said, we need to be careful in times like these." He thought for a moment before drunkenly turning around. "Lord Doppel, write to my b-... good gods," Tate gasped at the sight of the unconscious man. "Fear not, my guests, come the morning I will write to my brother. I'll let him know you're here. What was your name again?"

"Omani," Leo smiled.

"I'll let him know that Omani and his siblings are here. You'll be on your way to Mea come a day or two. Perchance a year or two if I know my brother," Tate laughed, turning to rejoin the party.

"My lord, what is to be done with them?" the guard asked.

"Oh, let them join in," he smiled warmly, "gods know that much thinking needs to be met with more wine."

"They *are* criminals, my lord."

"They *are also* humans that require wine," he insisted. "Find them chambers later. Now we drink."

Tate's hosting was the best Asher had ever witnessed, even outdoing his notoriously wild uncle Lori. The lord was funny and full of wit, despite being so inebriated. Telling him who they were was always annoyingly on the end of Asher's tongue, knowing that the truth would only draw them together. Asher envied Leo's ability to keep it bottled up, also knowing that he could never handle keeping as many secrets as that boy.

Still, nothing tainted the night any more than that. For most of it, he and Lyssa danced along to the bards that played, and chatted when they were too tired to dance any longer. They exclusively talked together until they gravitated to a particularly smiley man, full of stories and ideas.

"Angelo Brysea," the man answered to Asher's question of his name. "I owned a workshop back in Selerborn."

"You must have been pretty famous, then," Asher smiled.

"Infamous, really," Angelo sighed, taking another sip of mead. "They either loved me or hated me there. I had to leave, though. There's some tension with the new lord."

How could anyone hate Riley? Asher thought. During his stay at Fort Deus moons back, his company was great. It made Asher think about what would come of his children. He knew that Fletcher had grown close to the twins while they were there, and same with Eva and Leta to Athena. He hoped, for all their sakes, tension was as far as it would go.

To forget about their worries, they all sang northern songs Asher hardly knew and played games he was useless at deep into the morning, yet Asher was grateful for it nonetheless; this was something they gravely needed.

As the sun poked into the room, and Asher sat on the floor, Lyssa asleep in his arms, most of the room unconscious too, he turned to Leo as the thought of their situation reintroduced itself. "I bet most of the guards are asleep. It'll be a good time to escape."

Leo shook his head, taking the last drop of wine in a skin. "It's too risky," he said tiredly. "With any luck, we'll have permission in a day or two."

"I guess," Asher sighed, leaving a long silence before he spoke again. "Who is Omani, anyway?" he asked, turning to find Leo fast asleep. *Ugh.* That was another thing Asher envied about Leo. The prince sat in the sleeping room, too afraid to close his eyes again.

ELAYNE II
-Bruise-

The road back was kinder since Elder Ulrich's advice and Sir Brendan's story. It was often the most unamiable part of the journey for Elayne Lyrderyn, the Merchant's Road bustling with wagon trails and travellers, while the Golden Road had all that but doubled. That wasn't the case for everyone, though. Fitz and Eleanor would get irritated at every little thing that was out of their control: a merchant bumping them with their massive backpacks, fatigue halting the train, a wheel breaking. Fitz had enough stored up aggression to follow through with the disturbances, quite often snapping at the fault. Eleanor was slower to do so, but Elayne saw that she grew more and more irritated regardless. She didn't like the thought that Fitz had influence over her.

Frustrations aside, the whole party was in dire need of relaxation, so as their home peeked behind Lake Ignis, they partook in a collective sigh of relief. It looked as beautiful as always, the golden lion banners sparkling in the sun as the majestic sandstone buildings sat beside them. She had missed the way the palm trees swayed in the easy wind, and the taste of the fresh coconut water from the fruits they dropped. She had missed her greatest worry being how well fed and happy her family was. No matter how much she lied to herself, the absence of Lyssa took the number one spot now. It felt like life suddenly became duller without her, the energy and kindness she brought leaving a bigger hole than it filled.

Still, it would have been more of a worry if it was Eleanor who vanished instead of her; Lyssa could handle herself. At just eight years old, she had bludgeoned a rattlesnake with a rock as it tried to attack her on the bank of Lake Ignis. That was the moment Elayne realised that Lyssa had been raised a lioness, not a cub. It worried her that Eleanor was on the more defenceless side. Without her big sister to look after her anymore, Elayne was certainly more concerned than usual. Hopefully, Eleanor would replace those shoes for Ayla when she grew old enough to think.

Nevertheless, today, she wasn't letting worry bother her. Today was a day for relaxation. A smile reached her face at the sight of the familiar trade wagons, few in number yet as eminent as always, with their onion-shaped roofs and gold-littered exterior. It was as if the camels around greeted their arrival with nods and grunts as they continued about their business of dragging men and stock about. Though, Elayne had expected to see more, not only camels but people too. Aside from traders, the streets looked like Ignis was in an hour of sleeping, having next to no common man in sight.

Not believing it at first, she then noticed the orange lynx sigil of Lyonis beating on a carriage outside the Ignis Keep, her brother's sigil, *here*. It fluttered in the wind, teasing her, casting a shadow on the coarse-looking yet smooth-feeling sandstone that spanned every wall of the keep. Confusion was followed by fury, yet she remained calm as best she could, even though her face must have flared into a hot red.

"Home, sweet home," Lord Goldwyn smiled, tucking his thumbs into his belt. "Look who has come to visit, too, my Lady Elayne."

She gave the Lord of Ignis her most dry, enthused smile. Her brother waited on the inside, his hawk-like grin spreading across his face at the sight. "Welcome back, my lords, my ladies," he bowed. "I would have waited to visit, but I didn't know when you'd all return."

Goldwyn bellowed with laughter. "Nonsense, make this your home, my lord. You are family." He leaned closer to him. "I wouldn't blame you; I could never quite stand the rock."

Ayden Lyonis only smirked at the jest, turning his attention to Elayne. "You look well, sister," he said, making his pompous stride towards her. "Give me a kiss."

It was awkward and forced, and Ayden knew it. Elayne was thankful it was only a peck on the cheek. She desperately tried to read his grey eyes behind her fake smile, having little luck. Just as she thought of his bastard son, he came, jogging into the room. "Hi, auntie," he smiled.

"Ryan," she sighed, hugging him. She had always liked the boy, which was more than what his father could say for him. He was so sweet, with his ash-black hair and freckled face. When they broke away from the embrace, Elayne instinctively touched his sleeve to reveal yellow and purple bruises coating his forearm. He timidly smiled back as he pulled down his sleeve, with eyes to say: 'don't worry'. It only angered her even more.

"Gods, Fitz," Ryan laughed, "you're going to be taller than me soon."

"No chance of that," Fitz smiled, the first time he had since the Bay. They hugged.

"Ayden, can I speak with you in private?" Elayne asked softly.

"Pray for me," he muttered to Goldwyn as they passed, sparking a guffaw from the lord.

Elayne checked the corridors outside of her chambers close to five times when she had led her brother there. When she was totally sure that the halls were lifeless, she closed the door.

Ayden was pouring himself a goblet of wine. "Is this where you give me my proper welcoming? A hug perhaps, maybe even a-"

She slapped him fiercely. The goblet flew across the room. "What are you doing here?"

He frowned. "That's not the way you should be greeting your beloved brother."

"*What* are you doing here?" she snapped, letting her rage erupt.

Her brother had a confused, yet consistently sly look on his face. It annoyed her even more. "Well... your lord husband is dead, is he not? He took his damn time, but now, all who stands in our way is Lord Goldwyn and his ill son."

"*Our* way? Don't tell me you still have those ambitions," she winced in disgust. "That was almost twenty years ago."

"Don't tell me you've lost them," he said coldly, frowning his eyebrows. "That was the only reason you married that oaf of a lord."

"How can you still be so *naive?*" she snapped back. "Do you really still think it's even possible for our banners to fly over here?"

"Possible?" he echoed. "Now, it's more possible than ever."

He hasn't changed. "You would kill an innocent boy and his father to sit on a sandy chair in the middle of nowhere." She couldn't believe that she was standing up for Fitz.

"You speak of me like a villain. Don't you remember who proposed these thoughts?" he asked, touching her cheek. "Where has your ambition gone, sister? It's unlike you to settle for anything less than we talked of.

Have we not always dreamt of the new empire? Our lineage *pure* with *our* blood." He sighed. "Are your pale offspring to blame? Have you grown to love them?"

"What? I'm their *mother.* How can you-"

He smiled in disbelief. "Gods, it's true. What have the days done to you? Perhaps it was divine intervention that made you lose your eldest. Perhaps the gods are trying to slap some sense into you-"

She slapped him again, this time, so hard, he was knocked to the wall. "You're disgusting."

Ayden said nothing, holding his blushed face.

"What about *Ryan?*" she cried. "What has the boy ever done to you?! Are you really so heartless that you couldn't love your own son?"

He spat. "The only reason the damned boy is alive is because of your inability to see him for who he is. All he's been to me is a waste of food. It would have been much more merciful to blood him early."

"He is a child!"

"He is a *man* and a *bastard.* Any offspring not born by me and you are bastards," he said stubbornly, moving towards her. *Those words came from my mouth,* she thought, wincing. *Insane, witless, adolescent words, but still something that brewed in my head.* She felt sick.

"You're delusional if you think I'd still marry you."

Ayden grabbed her, digging his fingers around her chest and back as if he were handling a sword. "I neither need your hand, nor permission."

"Let go of me!" she screamed, pushing him away. "You're an *animal.*"

"Even if you have lost your desires, it doesn't mean I'll forget mine overnight. I've waited patiently for two decades, and *you* are not the person to take that from me."

"I swear to all the gods," she promised, "lay so much as a finger on my daughters, or Ryan, or Fitz, then I will *burn* your stupid legacy to the ground, and your filthy ambitions with it."

"How?" he smirked.

She yanked a knife from her girdle and dug it into the wooden table.

Ayden let out a subdued laugh. "If you think you can kill me when I'm Lord of Ignis, then you don't know me well enough."

"If you think it's meant for *you,* then you don't know *me* well enough," she hissed, slotting the knife back and storming out of the room.

She couldn't believe his arrogance. *Who does he think he is?* Turning up decades later and expecting nothing to have changed. It was like the

Lynxrock wasn't enough for him, but if being lord of a grand city like that wasn't enough, nothing would be able to appease his appetite. He wanted the whole of the Canicule, and she couldn't see why. Yes, controlling all the major trade, plus King Sol's mines would make you the richest man in Austellus like every Lord of Ignis before. And the land was of an impressive size too. The whole of the desert to do with as you please. *Actually, it might not be so bad.* She hadn't thought of it in so long. She had adopted the lion sigil of Lyrderyn, but it *did* seem sweet to see the lynx of Lyonis fly over Ignis instead.

No. She shook her head. *He needs to leave. He is a vile man.* She hadn't loved Reynold romantically when they married, nor even to his dying day, but they shared a love for their children that made Elayne sick when it was time to see him go. The thought of *anything* bad happening to them wrenched her stomach, the thought of a strong lion as a father not being able to protect his cubs, the thought of them growing up without one. Even Ryan and Fitz; they could both have exciting futures ahead of them. To rob them of that would be despicable. *It's Ayden's fault I thought like that. Without him, I learned to love again. It wasn't my thinking, it was his.* It made her feel weak. *I'm older than him, who am I if I can't think for myself?*

It didn't matter now anyway. Being away from him for so long made her think for herself. Perhaps the desire for power had waned when she adopted the Lyrderyn sigil, when Reynold began to heed her advice, and love her. Something inside of her must have been denying it. *I don't have power anymore. Once Fitz ascends the throne, our family will be wiped out.*

She had to shake off the corrupt thoughts. She had to ground herself. *The past is the past,* she found herself repeatedly thinking, hoping that it hadn't just risen to beat her down once again.

FLETCHER IV
-Onus-

It was change he wanted, and it was change he received; the excess of
snow had near all melted, imports of fresh food from Aquamare left a
much-needed diversion from fish, and Fletcher Centaur felt like his
relationship with everyone was stronger than ever. He would quite often
visit the tavern in the lower bailey in the evening, conversing and jesting
with the people and knights who would visit, and some nights even invite
them for games and drinking in the higher fort. He was more outspoken
generally, and becoming increasingly happier because of it. It felt like he
had finally found himself again.

He had been spending his afternoon with Stig Wynd in his forge, using
the help of the Blackfist to aid him in his craft. The day was chilled and
cloudy, a hesitant rain saturating the frozen orange grass of the huge
courtyard. "That's one thing I would work with if I ever could." Blackfist
was saying. "Magic. Anything you envisage, made quicker than a thought
appearing."

"I guess," Fletcher agreed, dipping another molten arrowhead he had
shaped into cold water. "I imagine it'd be boring after a while, though. If
everything is just made with your mind, there'd be no art to it; no fault."

"Yeah, probably. We'd have to ask a magician to know for sure," he
jested, taking Fletcher's zircon bow in his hands. "So, anyway, do you give
up? I'll tell you if you have."

Fletcher took another glance at the bow, believing he had guessed every element in Austellus. "Go on, then."

"Well you were half right with tin," he smiled, stroking the bow. "It's of an alloy made with tin from the Red Sierra, and a little standard steel. And, of course, the zircon. But the secret ingredient is something called solar flux; that's what makes it so priceless."

"Solar flux?" Fletcher grimaced. "Never heard of it."

Stig chuckled. "Neither had I. This was the first time I used it. Only the best smiths in Lunarpass can even touch the thing."

"Why? What's it made of?"

"Apparently, it's that magic essence stuff inside the solar throne. Solar flux must just be the fancy name those high smiths called it. Your lord father had a batch of it brought here."

Fletcher admired the bow in a new light, not quite believing the whimsical substance was part of the weapon. "Do you still have some?"

"Only of the alloy I made with it. I had to use it as soon as it arrived; the king said it has a life span."

"Really?" Fletcher asked excitedly. "An element that can die?"

Stig nodded, grinning with his bashed teeth. "I reacted the same, my lord. But yes, it has age like us. Some say it also has consciousness."

"Wow," Fletcher sighed with an inspired smile, almost forgetting about his arrowheads, "may I see the alloy?"

"Of course," Blackfist said, placing his hammer down as he searched for the material. He brought out a semi-translucent ingot of a silver sheen, placing it in Fletcher's dirty hands.

"Do you know what you're going to do with it?"

He shrugged. "The king said the extra essence was part of my payment, but I'll probably just end up waiting until he wants a sword or something."

The steel was warm to Fletcher's touch, as if it was freshly forged. A part of him thought it was, that Stig was tricking him once again. He couldn't have been, though; no metal had ever looked so otherworldly. "He wouldn't want a sword," Fletcher smiled. "Make something for yourself."

"I'm not in need of anything, my lord," he smiled, returning the ingot to its home. "Long past are my days of fighting..."

Their conversation was cut short by the hurried presence of Sir Roswell Dart. "Apologies, my lord," he bowed. "Lord Tyran has arrived at the docks."

"So soon?" Fletcher winced, standing. "Bring him to the council chambers."

The young knight nodded and marched away. Fletcher thought it best to fetch his sister too; she would want to hear what he had to say.

Leta wasn't in the courtyard, so Fletcher assumed she'd be in her solar. When he arrived at her chamber to see an empty bed, he sighed at the thought of having to go all the way around to her special place. He had already turned to jog out when he heard the faintest giggle at the end of the hallway. It came from up the stairs, to the blue spire, his parent's room. He slowly pushed the door open, revealing Semira directing Leta's hand around a small canvas. "Am I interrupting something?"

"Oh, hi, Fletch," she giggled, placing her drawing device at the base of the canvas. "Ma was just showing me how to draw."

"Since when did you want to draw?"

"Since when did you want to care?"

You witnessed me wanting to, he almost said.

"What is it, Fletcher?" their mother asked.

"Lord Tyran is back," he said. "I thought you might want to come along and see what he says."

"Already?" Semira gasped, standing from her kneel. "Let's hope it's good news."

Fletcher hovered for a while, watching his sister pick up a quill to resume her work. *Is she ok?* "Leta?"

"I'm fine," she said, "tell me later."

Fletcher nodded, although slightly confused. *Now, I'm the one who distrusts Tyran the most;* Leta seemed to be completely shunned by his alibi. Maybe hearing the tale from the goat's own mouth might change Fletcher's mind, but for now, he stood his ground.

"My lord, welcome," Fletcher smiled warmly as Tyran entered the council chamber. "You're back so soon?"

"I *do* wish it was at my accord, my lord," he sighed after bowing. "But we received ill news that we couldn't not share."

"Well do sit down," Fletcher offered.

"My lord," Sir Roswell bowed, heading out.

"Sir Roswell," Fletcher called, "stay if you'd like."

The knight's gratefulness shone through his face. He bowed and took a seat.

"If I may..." Tyran asked, eager to continue.

"You may," Fletcher smiled, keeping his relaxed posture as he slipped into his seat.

"Apologies that the news is so belated, but our sentries at Equus spotted a Khavar fleet sailing northeast a few days ago."

His stomach sank. *No. Don't come just yet. Not now, when everything's going so well. We're not ready.* He thought he had more time. "You didn't send a raven?" Fletcher asked.

"Forgive me," he bowed apologetically, "I thought it best to bring a garrison with me. Six thousand, if it please."

"How many did you spot?" Semira asked.

"Three hundred ships, my queen. We'd be lucky if they are less than eighteen thousand."

"Even a hundred thousand couldn't fell these walls," Fletcher shrugged. "We'll call our *pennons* up, that'll make nearly forty thousand, right, Sir Roswell?"

"They are not bound for Fort Deus," Tyran claimed.

Shit. "Where, then?"

"We believe either Trader's Dock, or the Deuswater River towards the city."

"The *pennons* won't hear our call if it's their home being attacked, my lord," said Sir Roswell. "Would you like me to ready our men to march?"

"That would be wise," Tyran agreed. "We could keep our garrison here if you'd like."

Yes, march. That would be perfect, wouldn't it? You can cut off our heads before we have a chance to talk back. "Spare your men, Tyran. We march nowhere."

"You intend to stay here?" Semira asked, as if what he said offended her. "Think of all the people who'd lose their homes."

"If they take Deuswater, their reach on the Negal lands would be greater than our own," Sir Roswell agreed.

Fletcher exhaled sedately. *"If* they take Deuswater, their army would be weakened. Where else but here would they march after?"

"That won't stop thousands dying," Semira pleaded. "Deuswater has no walls, sacking the city would be as easy as breathing."

"Then we'll call an evacuation north, let the residents take refuge at the Negal Wall."

"They won't leave," Semira assured, "their homes would be burned."

"Better than their lives."

"My lord," Tyran began, "please, I do believe that marching would be the best course of action. The Venusians have clearly come to pillage. How are you so sure they would march on Fort Deus afterwards?"

I haven't sent the food imports to Deuswater yet, and gold is losing its worth by the day. They're not pillaging, fool. It's a trap. He was so close to bursting as the anger built up inside him. He didn't let it show. To them, he was calm as a horse in a stable. "Thank you for the warning, Lord Tyran," he said eventually, looking at the door.

"My lord..." Tyran begged, before cutting himself off with an angry sigh as he marched out.

"Don't expect your *pennons* to answer if you can't protect their own lands," Semira said when he had left.

"Look, if it were up to me, I would march up with all our force and wipe them out where they dock," he said, letting some of his anger spill, "but it's not, because I still don't trust the man. On the odd chance we *do* win fighting the Khavars north, nothing is stopping the Capricornian garrison from sacking the fort. If that happens, our wounded army would be as meek as lambs. And if we order them all to come with us, and they still betray us, then there would be nowhere better than on a battlefield to take us out. Can't you see how much all of this benefits him?"

Their troubled faces slowly changed as they were rethinking. It annoyed him a little that they didn't trust his judgement in the first place. "Would you at least let me send word to the king?" Sir Roswell asked.

He shook his head. "There's no point troubling him. If the Khavars are dumb enough to march north, then it becomes his problem."

"Damages would be more than expensive if they decide to raze Deuswater," Sir Roswell pointed out. "He'd want to know then. Especially the sect, and the-"

Fletcher sighed. "I hardly have a better option. But what of the fort? What of everyone *here?* Look around, the people have safety."

"This might all be for nothing, Fletcher," Semira said, stroking her black hair. "Tyran's reason is a believable one. Your sister and I trust him. He might not even think to betray us in the first place."

Fletcher bit down on his cheeks and stared at the two coldly. "Never question me in front of him again," he said. "I know what I'm doing."

MARCUS III
-Snap-

D ue to the little sleep he *did* get, waking to a pig snorting his face could well have been the least pleasant awakening to date. Marcus Horncurve rolled away from the hog, burying his face in a mound of shit. *"Egh!"* he leapt back, sweeping it from his face. It made the other pigs stir. Marcus looked around, bewildered, before remembering.

"It's getting way too dangerous now, kids," Riley had said to them all, "you can't keep heading outside the Cenkeep on a whim. A civil war could break out at any moment, and you wouldn't want to be stuck in the middle when it does!"

No one listened. Athena kept creeping out to her workshop, Cadmus kept escaping to the inns and brothels at night, and Marcus was obsessed about this conspiracy circle his twin had discovered. Riley had put out extra guards to stop them, but to no success. Sleeping outside in the pig pen only spared Marcus of penalty, at least for a few more hours.

However uncomfortable it was, it wasn't fruitless; last night, Marcus had got his evidence: a silver, long, twisting ramshorn pin. The sigil of Siren, straight out of Lord Harper's own hand. It fell from him as the turncoat made his way through the Mudstreet, cloaked in a black robe that hid his face. Marcus fondled the pin as he staggered along the streets. *Lord Harper Siren is their new leader, then. He has to be. Why else would he be on this putrid street?* It didn't help with liking Cadell Siren any more; he was Harper's son. They had trained at the break of every day and Marcus was yet to ask him, since there was always so much to learn from him. Yesterday, Siren showed Marcus how he was holding the *Ochs* stance wrongly, a stance the ram never knew *could* be wrong. He was a great teacher, but Marcus wanted to ask today. *If it is Harper who they're turning to, Cadell has to know something too.*

Despite all that, Marcus headed to the hut, hoping to find something that gave him more decisive evidence. The Mudstreet's stench somehow smelt worse in the morning, and Marcus quickly remembered why he hesitated to go. Fortunately, the hut where the conspirators met wasn't too deep, and Marcus remained thankful that no morning eyes watched him slip between the mounds of shit and sludge on route. The aroma of the hut wasn't too different, only that a thin wave of smoke played around the air, a scent as if it wasn't too long ago since the torches had been put out. Marcus would make sure to ration his time there, since Athena was to thank for making the conspirators extra cautious when meetings arose, *but they couldn't have had a meeting that lasted until the morning, could they?* It puzzled Marcus, as last night, the conspirators spoke of matters that conspirators just wouldn't: the state of trade and Ignis, the technicalities that went into feeding sheep, the woollen coats and cloaks that somehow suddenly had a higher supply than demand in the north. Nonetheless, the smell of freshly extinguished candles was undeniable. *Maybe me and Athena misheard. Maybe they were joking.* He had to make sure.

He pushed open the cracked wooden door, probably too forcefully, and was lucky to find no one asleep inside. Marcus wasted no time, thrusting the door backwards as he began to rummage through the hay that filled the room. For the longest time, it seemed like an empty barn, maybe the occasional speck of ash from torches peppered inside the straw, but Marcus didn't want to give up; he had to find *something.*

Before he could, the door flung open. Marcus leapt into a sticky bale of hay. "You *can't* keep dragging me out here, Fingal. *Every time* one of you does, I'm risking my life." The man pulled down his hood. It was Harper. Marcus's heart leapt out of his chest.

"You're risking nothing, milord," Half-Cut Fingal winced. "Who would be listening now? Dawn has barely come."

Harper shook his furrowed face. "Say what you need to, quickly."

Fingal nodded. "I did it, milord. It took bloody long enough, but *seven* of the cabals are behind you now. They see no other to save them."

Harper sighed painfully. "Fully?" he asked. "Men get carried away when blood's already on their hands."

"*Fully*, milord," Fingal assured. "They believe in you, as I do."

"Good," Harper said. "Thank you, Fingal. I owe you a debt."

"You owe me nothing, milord. You promised us *greatness*, and that's all we'll ever need."

Harper nodded nervously. "Okay," he said. "Don't call me back here again. I don't want you to see me until the revolt." Harper was on his way out. *Revolt?* Marcus almost screamed with triumph. *I've got you now.*

"When will it happen, milord?"

For a moment, it seemed as though Harper would actually tell. Marcus clung onto that hope. "We don't decide that," he said, yanking his hood up and leaving.

No, come back. Tell me when. I need to know when you'll attack. He never came back, but still, Marcus could hardly be angry. He knew everything he needed to know. *I've got you now, you traitor.* Though, as he rushed back to the keep, his smile faded with his doubts. *How do I prove it? I can't just show this pin to my father and expect him to believe me... But he's my father, he would take my side through anything, wouldn't he?* He squinted. *Since it is Harper, what does this mean with Cadell? Is he involved? I have to be smart about this.* They were meant to train today, maybe that would create a chance to know for sure.

Sir Egan Brook and Sir Ardin Hawtrey were the two guards who stood by the Cenkeep gate that morning. Marcus let out a huge sigh of relief; they had to be two of the nicest of the guard. *What's with my luck today?*

"Mornin'," Marcus smiled as he skipped up the stairs.

"There ye are!" Sir Egan declared. "Ye know how many men ye father wasted trying to find you?"

"Tell him they weren't good enough," Marcus smirked, allowing his stride to be confident.

"Yer father *did* want to speak to you, lad," Sir Ardin frowned. "I don't think it's good."

"I hope so," he smiled at them, entering the keep. "Have a good duty, lads."

Marcus didn't feel like confronting his father so early; without breakfast, the Lord of Selerborn wasn't a pretty sight. He'd much prefer to have the Siren's company, even though he still had no idea what to say and how to say it.

He couldn't tell why he had as big of a smile on his face as he did, but he didn't care. Lord Dugg Gallach, head of arms, passed him in the hallway, wearing a wince as he always did, and probably more so due to the grin Marcus sent his way. "My lord," he said, continuing his skip like he was a child in a meadow.

The next person he'd see was his brother, sauntering through the crenel as he whistled a tune. "Ay up, Marc," he smiled. "Da' was lookin' for ye."

"He sent you too?" Marcus grimaced, trying to walk past him.

"Mate, you won't *believe* where he's sent me," Cadmus grinned.

Marcus stopped, and frowned. He turned around. "...no way."

Cadmus nodded excitedly. *"Five thousand men,"* he said. "Grandpa never did a raid so big."

Marcus almost fooled himself to grin. "What do you mean sent *you?"*

"It means what I said, Marcus," he smiled, in a way that provoked. "I'm going to Heavia with five thousand men... You shouldn't be so quick to trust people, pal. I didn't think you'd *actually* go to the Mudstreet, thought you were smarter than that."

Marcus didn't know what to say. He found himself gawking like a fish.

"I wouldn't worry about it. Father says it's for your own safety," he nodded, taking too large steps forward. "But 'least yer safe in these walls, eh?" Cadmus patted Marcus on the shoulder, and rotated around casually as a tune came to his whistle once again.

Father would send Cadmus on a raid without me? I've trained with him my whole life! I'm just as good as him! No, I'm better! Now, no part of him wanted to see Riley. *Bugger him!* He kicked the closest barrel on the battlements, sending it rocking.

Marcus couldn't conceal the fury that leaked from his walk. It was the only sound filling the morning air: angry, stubborn steps coming from a pair of thick black boots on stone. Even the chirping birds annoyed him, wishing he had a bow to shoot them from the sky. The recurring thought of Ignatius added to his fury. *Anger will make the seer come again.* He winced. *Fuck the seer. Let him come.*

For a moment, Marcus forgot where he was heading, only to remember when he saw the training yard full with red-cloaked guards. Cadell stood behind them all, shrugging. "I'm sorry, Marcus," he sighed, somehow genuinely.

Fucking perfect. He felt like drawing his sword to fight them all. He almost believed he would. It was only a sparring sword, *but it could do damage.*

"Your father has summoned you, my lord," Sir Raul said, the only ram's guard there, his dark brown cloak different to the other's reds.

"Tell him he can wait," Marcus frowned. "Me and Cadell are busy."

"I can't do that, my lord," Sir Raul smirked. He took one ugly step forward. "Come on," he said, showing the way with his arm.

Marcus clenched his teeth hard, feeling the veins swell from his neck. *Fuck off, will ye? How many bloody men will he send on my case?* He felt like screaming, letting that be known as he cast his sparring sword to the wall, shattering the blade from the guard. He sent a frowning Cadell a loathly look before storming through the castle, to the throne room, all the while cursing and frowning.

"Why did ye do it?!" he shouted at his father on arrival. "To spite me? 'Cus I'll never be as good as yer *perfect son?!*"

Riley winced, shuffling his poise on the horned throne of diamond. "What are you talking about?"

"All my life you have always *promised me* that me and Cadmus would be treated as equals. *You said that,* so *why* does he get to go on raids to Heavia while I'm *stuck* here?!" He bared his teeth. "That's *not* fair."

"I didn't summon you about that," Riley said, his wince not leaving.

Marcus laughed. "Oh, you summoned me because I *slept outside.* Is that why I can't go? Athena and Cadmus sneak out of the keep just as much as me, so that's not a good enough reason. Give me *one good reason* why *I* can't go to Heavia?!"

"You want one good reason?" Riley nodded bitterly, standing up. His steps were slow and strong. "I *forbade* you *one* thing when we came back to Selerborn. *One* thing. Because I care *way too much* for all of you, and the Mudstreet is *way too* dangerous. Tell me *why* I would send you to Heavia if you cannot follow a *basic fucking order!*"

How…? The young ram only just realised his audience: the entire council, including Harper and Ignatius, his mother, sister, even brother, creeping in cautiously, making sure to stay in the corner. Athena had a sheepish look, grasping Emily's arm. "You told him?" Marcus squinted angrily.

"I didn't know what to do," she cried. "I was scared, I knew it was wrong, I-"

"Oh, *boo-hoo,* you were *scared.* I was trying to *save us-*"

"Leave your sister alone, she wants us safe too," Riley bellowed. "The point is: you *defied* my order. You better have a good fucking reason why

you did."

"I do," he nodded, pointing to Lord Harper Siren. "Every night, I saw *his* men plotting to overthrow *you. Every night,* I listened to those scheming bampots!" He reached for the silver Siren pin and tossed it across the throne room. *"There's* your evidence. It was on the *Mudstreet.* Why else would *he* be there? I bet he's behind the protests too. I bet he's behind everything."

For a moment, Marcus thought he had his father convinced, the lord wearing a suspicious frown. Harper strolled over to the pin and picked it up. "I lost this pin three moons ago, my lord," he said to Riley, nodding in response. He turned to Marcus. "Why would you steal it?" he winced. "What have I done to you for you to want an enemy of me so badly?"

Marcus was fed up now. "Oh, don't believe his *bullshit!"* he cried. "He is a *traitor!* Athena, you saw his men in that hut; tell him what he is!"

Athena glanced at Harper nervously. "I-I don't know *whose* men they were. They wanted to support him, but..." Tears filled her soft grey eyes. "Marcus, please stop."

"Cadmus, you saw him too, tell them!"

Cadmus frowned. "I have no idea what you're talking about, Marc."

Understanding crept onto Marcus's face. "You didn't think I'd go? ...you fuckin' asshole. You set this up? You *knew* about the traitors and didn't tell da'?!"

Cadmus stayed quiet. He had a cold look in his eyes.

Marcus groaned and stormed to the door. *Aye, I thought I was smarter than that too. Bloody glaikit. Why can't I trust my own bloody twin?* The tears almost came there and then. *He did this to get to me. He did this so he could be the first, as always. Witness where it gets you, prick.*

"Don't you walk away for me, Marcus!" Riley thundered, a flare in his voice.

Marcus stopped, almost scared to turn around. He did, though, slowly.

"You went to Woolton multiple times, you steal from one of my most trusted councillors and blame him for the city's ills, and when things don't go your way, you turn to your siblings and accuse them too," Riley frowned. "You asked for one reason and you've just given me a mountain."

"I'm not *accusing* anyone!" he cried. *"That man* will backstab you the first chance he g-"

"Shut your mouth!" the Lord of Selerborn boomed. Riley then smiled. "Maybe you were right. Maybe I'm sending your brother and not you

because he's *better.*" Emily tried to touch his arm, but Riley shooed it away. *"Never once* could I compare Cadmus to you. You have *always* been so *arrogant* and *selfish* and you'll *never* change because somehow you *always* get what you want! Let me tell you, Marcus, you might get what you want, but you will *never* get what you need. And I can put up with all of that. I can and I have," he nodded. His face was sorry until it turned sour again. "But you passed your limits when you started to attack your family."

It hurt more than it should have. Marcus could feel his eyes swell up, but no tears fell. "You're not family," he muttered, turning around.

"Marcus, come back," Riley said softly. "Marcus, take that back!" he yelled when he was ignored. *"Marcus!"* he thundered when Marcus was too far into the corridor to turn. His voice bounced from the walls, into Marcus's eyes, making them swell even more.

Don't cry. Don't cry. Men don't cry. He told himself as he arrived at his chambers. He couldn't even *remember* when he cried last. *What will I need?* he thought, already making his mind up. The first thing he grabbed was his edged sword he rode with to and from Fort Deus, slotting it into his baldric. He stuffed extra clothes, cloths, and the two leftover silvers from Merchant's Bay into a little bag and flung it over his shoulder. *I'm not staying here, not with them. Not with people who hate my guts, who don't take my side. Harper can have them all...*

Not wanting any more time wasted, he dashed out to the hall, managing to make it to the kitchen, stealing a few apples for the road before finally escaping. The entrance still had Sir Egan and Sir Ardin posted there, but Marcus had shoved past them with the surprise of a tough shoulder bash. "Hey!" Sir Ardin called. Marcus was halfway down the street before the knight could realise what was happening.

The long, outspread Road of Rams that led to the entrance of Selerborn was close to empty, luckily for Marcus. Almost out of breath, he went straight for the stables, cutting a horse from its ropes before leaping upon it. The stable master must have still been sleeping, the old oaf he was.

"Close the gate!" Sir Ardin yelled when Marcus kicked the horse into gallop, but the meshed gate of ram's horns was too slow to close compared to Marcus's unhesitating hurtle.

At no point during his flight did Marcus have time to cry, only when he passed the gates.

EVA VII
-Force-

Lutum wasn't what she expected. To be fair, she didn't know what she expected. Not even a few days ago did Eva Centaur see and feel the sands of the Canicule for the first time, and after that, the world never stopped changing. *I'm glad I came. I'm glad I get to see it all at last.*

Night after night during their travels, she and Robin would be the last ones to fall asleep, and Idris the first one to rise. She enjoyed talking to Robin, if not for his hysterical humour and energy, for his largely unique outlook. It was similar to Idris's, in that Robin liked to explore too. Robin opened the doors to stories that Idris would not: their exploration of the Archipelago, and Heavia, and even the cursed Deadswood. It inspired Eva. It made her want to go and be free more than ever.

Despite being a bastard, Eva dared to think that Robin was the happiest of the brothers. It made her think of her cousin Feliks, who despised his birthright, or at least, that was what she gathered. He always claimed to not care, but it was evident by the despondent face he pulled every time he glanced at highborn people doing highborn things that he did. It was only ever to uphold image; as soon as the gossiping eyes of the higher lords and ladies had left, Feliks was always included, but it seemed like Feliks didn't feel like any less of an outcast.

"I have three other bastard siblings," Robin was saying one night as they sat on the soft sand, watching the stars glisten from overhead, "and sometimes it seems like I care the least about it."

"What about your birthright?" Eva asked.

"My birthright," he sniggered. "May as well give a blind man a telescope, it would serve the same purpose. Idris gets Lutum after father, then Apollo. Shit, I'd wager my sister Violet would get Lutum before me."

"So, it doesn't bother you?"

"It might if I were in the race; all my life, I've just been part of the crowd," he said, retying his bootlace. "But what about you? Having three brothers and being a girl must make you curse your existence."

She chuckled. "You really think I could rule?"

"No," he smirked, "I think you could lead, though. I bet you could've made it all the way to Fort Lux without my brother slowing you down."

Is he being serious? It was hard to tell. "You don't mean it."

"I do mean it, Eva," he smiled, holding his hands up. "I'm going to have to say a prayer for anyone who gets in your way."

It wasn't what she expected to hear. She suddenly felt deprived of compliments after receiving so many over the past moon. Everyone at home thought she couldn't even lead a horse to the stables. She smiled, coiling around Robin's arm. "You're going to be saying a lot of prayers, then."

As for Apollo, Robin seemed far from related. Under the easy-going, laughable persona he put on, lay a dour brute. The environment in which they were in couldn't bring the side out of Apollo much, but he was always the first fuse to burn out when joking went too far, when they stopped making progress.

Though, progress wasn't something they could be upset with anymore. The sapphire stream that accompanied them on their right curved around the bronze kingdom, hugging the city like an arm. A mix of auburn grass and sandy patches made for an interesting terrain, albeit an annoying terrain as the wind would always toss tiny grains into Eva's eyes and mouth, but that wasn't anything new to bear; the Canicule had done that to her but with twice the intensity, so she didn't really mind it now. Lutum had no walls, which was a surprising enough feature for Deuswater to possess, let alone a kingdom; instead, large pikes and fortifications lined the outskirts, almost primitive-looking despite their pundit make. Oddly, it made the city feel more homely to Eva.

"Good gods, Apollo," Robin gasped, "is that your scope?"

Their attention met a group of children playing with a glistening, golden tube, throwing it about. Fury met Apollo's eyes, grasping his reins as he kicked his horse into gallop.

"Oh, I can't miss this," Robin laughed, chasing after him.

"Ah, there you are, bro," a smug man smiled as they rushed into the city. "Hope you don't mind; the kids wanted a new toy."

"What the fuck, Ivor?" Apollo winced, dismounting and snatching it back.

"Language!" Ivor scolded. "Woah, look at that, Idris, you've brought a girl back. You know, I really thought you were into boys."

"Oh, shut up, Ivor. She's twelve."

"Oh? So, you *are* into boys?" Ivor smiled.

"He didn't say no, did he?" Robin added.

"Speak for yourself, brother," Idris said, grin growing, "you're the one surrounding yourself with kids."

Robin burst into guffaw. "He's right, that's even worse!"

Ivor was speechless, raising his dark, thick eyebrows.

"I'm glad you had fun with the kids," Apollo sighed, a hint of jest returning.

"Okay, you got me," Ivor resigned. "But seriously, what are you doing with her? You kidnap her?"

"Haha!" Robin yelped, swiping his knee. "That's *exactly* what I said!"

"Our bastard's blood strikes again," Ivor smirked, slapping Robin's open hand. "So, spill the beans, Idris the abductor, what's her deal?"

At that point, they had all dismounted and were walking in the same direction. "Her deal is none of your concern. You won't see her around for long."

"Notice as he avoids the question," Ivor said in a snarky manner.

"No, seriously, it's better if you don't know," Robin muttered.

"Oh?" Ivor frowned.

Idris glanced at Eva, worry coating his strapping face. She hardly noticed; she was too awestruck at the strange mix of sandstone and wooden houses, the rags and furs of varying sizes worn by the string of commoners, the great stallions that looked like ants as they whinnied and charged as a swarm in faraway fields. "Where's father? How is he?"

"Not well," a female voice said as she joined the troop, carefully holding a bowl of ground up, green plants.

"Hello to you too, sister," Apollo said.

She rolled her eyes, not even noticing Eva as her swift walk continued. She had a long, black, frayed head of hair, held up with an attempt to tie it. Green eyes like Robin's accompanied her chiselled face, dirty with a dark slush like that of a swamp.

"Where's Violet and Ascella? They're the only ones stopping us from having a full house," Robin smirked.

"Violet's with father, Ascella is in... Aurdrive, I believe," she said.

"Is that for him?" Idris asked, keeping his eyes on the mazer she held.

She nodded. "We heard that you were back today from the scouts. I've just been told to fetch this... It's hemlock."

"Hemlock?" Apollo gasped. "It's *that* bad?"

"He can barely get a full sentence out without coughing up blood," Ivor sighed. "He wanted to see all of us, before he..."

The silence of sorrow washed over the party as they walked. Eva didn't know much about respiratory sickness, such diseases weren't so common in the south, but she *did* know about hemlock. Elder Marcarius ground into her head at the age she could escape the fort never to touch the plant, as she would often scavenge and bring certain ones back with her. He said it was more often than not fatal, so she shared the silence with the Equuleus siblings as if it were her own father.

"Is that enough to kill him, Narcissa?" Idris muttered in a deep tone.

Narcissa nodded, a tear keeping the dirt on her cheek soggy. "It's unfair to keep him alive any longer."

When they spoke of the Lord of Lutum, Eva had assumed they would head all the way to the tall wooden and sandstone keep in the centre of the city, so it surprised her that Ivor and Narcissa led them to a small, planked stable, or at least the shell of one. They were apprehensive about entering, Ivor knocking a few times on the door before slowly opening it.

Trying to sympathise by imagining her father in this situation suddenly became a million times easier when Eva saw the Lord of Lutum lying on the hay bed. Lord Doran Equuleus looked too much like Esmond, and seemed about the same age, too. His beard was well trimmed, and had a body cut like a man who had fought battles every day of his life. Despite this, his face had no shade but pale, some of the blood Ivor had talked about spattered upon his brown garments. He struggled to open his swollen eyes to look upon his children, reaching his arm out to Idris.

"Idris... Apollo... Violet..." he said, with a voice so hoarse that it grazed the air, "I must speak to you three... only you."

The woman who must have been Violet sat beside her father, holding his frail hand. She turned around, looking at her bastard siblings, still not noticing Eva, as Narcissa hadn't.

Robin and Ivor turned and walked out as Eva followed, Narcissa doing so with a delay as she placed the bowl of hemlock at Doran's bedside. When they left the hut, Ivor traipsed away, keeping his head straight. Narcissa took to the stables opposite, petting one of the great stallions that wandered within. Robin and Eva stood together, looking around the grainy city in a similar manner.

After a time, Robin began to creep back to the hut. "What are you doing?" Eva whispered, catching his arm.

"It's about inheritance, it has to be," Robin said. "I want to listen."

"Wouldn't that be wrong?" she frowned.

"It's *my* father dying in there," he shrugged. "I'm his son. Of course it's wrong. Nothing's *right* with me not being able to hear him."

"Why would he send you out, then? He must have done it for a reason." Eva asked, matching his shrug.

"That's what I want to know. Don't you too?" Robin didn't wait for a response. "If you come, you have to be quiet. If not, wait outside."

No, please don't, she thought as she watched him slink around to the alley at the back of the hut. Reluctantly, she followed, joining him in pressing their ears up to the thin planks. Every word seeped through like water through a net. "I am ready, my lord." a posh voice said.

"Who's that?" Eva whispered.

"Layton Giles, father's *First Avail*," Robin whispered back, closing his eyes as he listened.

"You... know what I want, Giles, damn you," Doran groaned.

"Nothing to be changed?" Layton asked.

"No... just write the will," Doran insisted.

"Who will inherit what, then?" Idris asked.

"Slow down, my sons," Doran coughed. "I must... first tell you of what you need to do."

"What we need to do?" Apollo echoed.

"Tell them, would you, Violet?"

Violet sighed. "You two are to lead the armies into war. Father wants us to march on Aurdrive; that's why Ascella is already there."

Robin's eyes widened, as did Eva's.

"*War?* What? Why?" Idris panicked.

"The trade has never been worse," Layton explained. "Come the Hunter's Moon, we might all starve."

"So?" Idris snapped. "This is *rebellion.* Food grows on trees, life doesn't."

"Surely, we shouldn't need to go to that extreme," Apollo agreed.

"It is a necessity for us to survive," Layton insisted. "King Esmond has denied our right to the food trade we have reaped for centuries. When the king doesn't treat us with a fair mind, he is not a king the thousands here should bow to."

"Denied our right?" Idris quizzed. "What were his exact words?"

"He said he couldn't," Violet admitted, "that food yields were at a record low, and receiving our normal share would deprive others."

"Then that is just the case," Apollo said stubbornly. "Taking up arms against Aurdrive is taking up arms against the king. If we do this, we are severing our ties with *any* sort of trade lines."

"The king sits with a surplus of food, fattening his capital, while others starve? That is no king," Layton sighed. "We are to pillage what we can, and raze forts if lords cannot share their private yields."

"You mean kill the lords we've known and protected for centuries?" Idris snapped. "What happens when Esmond marches on us with ten times our force? What happens when the whole Canicule becomes our enemy-?"

"Idris," Doran coughed weakly. "To survive, we must. We don't... have enough food. Please, my sons."

A long silence followed, all the while, Robin's eyes remained firmly fixed on Eva's, analysing her response. The only thing she felt was shock. She didn't care about the act of rebellion against her father, but she cared greatly about seeing Idris and his brothers go into battle... or so that was what she believed. Poisoned memories of Galloway invaded, and worry for her father returned unwillingly. '*Backstabber, meek as a lamb, death is coming for the Centaurs'... Do I have to choose a side?* She didn't know *what* to feel, and that made her feel sick.

Idris sighed slowly. "What do you want me to do?"

"You are to lead an *equo*, my lord, Idris," Layton said. "Two thousand horsemen for you, and each of your brothers. Aurdrive won't have time to prepare, but once they see us, it would be best to attack at every angle of the city."

"Each of his brothers?" Apollo asked. "I am his only brother."

"Esmond was good enough to grant one thing, at least," Layton explained. "All of your bastard siblings have been legitimised by your lord father's wish, Lord Apollo."

Eva could see the shock visibly exit Robin's body as his face loosened into a gasp.

"Legitimised?" Idris choked. "Father, Ivor and Robin are nowhere near serious enough to rule. What made you think this was a good idea?"

Robin leered.

"They have… as much Equuleus blood in them as… you do," Doran stuttered.

"I don't deny that, father," Apollo said, "but to appoint them an *equo* with no such training? Do you know what you're doing? I love them, but they're overgrown boys."

"I agree," said Idris. "We have seasoned chevals that could lead instead. Austyn Chavez? Kieran Byrne?"

"Oh, fuck this," Robin winced, slumping away.

Eva grabbed his arm. "Robin, wait."

"Did you just hear them, Eva?" he whispered harshly. "They think I'm a bloody *child*." He snapped his arm back towards him.

Eva grabbed him again. "Where are you going?"

"Far away from here." She didn't try to grab him for a third time; he seemed set on leaving, wherever that was. It was the first time she saw him like that, and she didn't like it. *Should I stop him? He's an Equuleus now. What if they need him?*

Before she had a chance to make a decision, Idris and Apollo left the hut. "Eva," Idris called softly when he noticed her. "Can I speak with you?"

She didn't protest, following him into an empty, quiet, yet foul smelling stable. Idris prepared himself in a manner that Eva was all too familiar with at this point. "Look, I'm-"

"I heard everything," Eva sulked, slumping down on the dirty hay. "Robin and I were listening."

Idris sighed. "I hope you realise I have no choice."

"Don't you?" Eva asked calmly, holding back tears. "Well I'll make it easy for you; if you go, I go."

He chuckled sadly. "You're not coming with me."

"Then you'll have to stay."

"Eva, I've just lost my father. Please, don't make me lose you too."

"But what if you die? Who will look after me then?" A tear brushed her cheek.

"I promise I won't die if you stay."

"So, you'd leave me here? What happens when my father declares you rebels? Do I become your hostage? What happened to me being *your* responsibility?"

"You *are* my responsibility. That's why I need you to stay here. I need you to be safe."

"Then you have to take me with you!" she cried. *"You're the only one who protects me! I'd be dead without you!"*

"Eva! Gods dammit!" Idris fired back, a voice like thunder. *"If you come with me, you'll worry me to death! No bloody way would I be able to lead an army, let alone go through with the raid. You think I wanted any of this? You think I want anything more than for you to be safe? I'm the Lord of Lutum now, Eva, and if I don't do this, Lutum will be a graveyard!"*

Eva's tears had frozen in place, almost frightened for Idris.

He stood in silence for a time, shaking. His headband shadowed his eyes like a seer. "Do you remember what you promised me the day I allowed you to come with me?"

Eva nodded timidly. "That I'd do anything you tell me to."

"Good," Idris said coldly, turning to the door. "Now, more than ever, I need you to keep that promise. I need you to stay here." He walked out of the stable, leaving Eva in the dark.

Later that evening, Eva had found herself in an odd situation, the same as two moons ago, yet this time, nerves weren't a factor. It felt different, though. It *was* different. It was hatred and treachery that took her from Fort Deus, and it was a love for her new brothers that pulled her from Lutum. When Idris's cohort transitioned into march, Eva was concealed comfortably inside the wagon train that followed, guilt rushing through her as a broken promise stirred around her mind.

ESMOND IX
-Embassy-

Today was the first time in a while he felt his head was on straight. All throughout the last moon, the king was plagued by problems with impossible solutions, all the while being forced to solve them. His country was starving in each direction, and since Esmond Centaur wasn't a mage, controlling crop yields and food consumption came not with his many titles. Bickering came along with the lack of food, Esmond seeing the first fight over a loaf of bread in the city streets a few mornings ago. The wounds weren't severe, bruises and black eyes for the most part, but Esmond knew they'd only escalate. Hopefully, Oberon Trident had heard their plea by now, and had sent food shipments their way. Esmond doubted it, though; *he's probably fallen from one of the crags around Aquamare, for him to send me nothing but silence.*

He didn't enjoy Elder Marcarius abandoning him at such a time either, especially since it was done so without warning. It was Sir Orion who broke the news, but if those same words were to leave the mouth of any other, in that moment, Esmond swore he would have broken that person's nose. Nevertheless, after looking at *why* the elder wanted to leave, it made the king feel more at ease. Coming to a conclusion and a solution of the climate would definitely be more helpful long-term, but for now, Esmond felt like he was alone. At least he had Orion.

All the same, Esmond was positive about the day that lay ahead, a welcome respite from the negativity this moon. He sat alone in his council chamber under the Ulcus Basilica, slumped comfortably on a throne-like chair at the head of the marble table, with nothing more than a jug of wine and two goblets sitting atop it. He had been waiting there for almost an hour, keeping his eyes on the staircase up, all the while having a reflective mind, like the marble that mirrored the light. Oddly, he wasn't nervous. He thought he would be. Today would be a huge step forwards... or backwards. Neither Esmond nor his councillors could tell which.

Before boredom reached, the sharp echo of steps stung the Basilica, slow and confident. The rhythm to their walk was powerful, as if the man who strode was king himself.

His shoes emerged first, his pointed boots reminiscent of a scorpion's tail. A dark red cape came next, dragging elegantly down the winding staircase, becoming its land. Then, the well-cut shape of a chest shone through, puffed and proud, swathed with a careful, dark green robe with clasps of orange citrine. A pointed chin with a sharp grey beard poked from his face, all the while raised higher than his thin neck. His grey beard followed up his face, meeting at the top in a slick head of hair. Finally, the eyes of the scorpion, a heavy green as they pierced through the scattering air, tormented like the rest of his aged face with the years they had seen.

"You're a man of your word, I'll give you that," Esmond said, not flinching. "I half expected you to use the two moons I gave you to raise your armies."

"As are you a man of yours," Vincent Scorpius smirked, peeling his leather gloves from his sculpted hands. "I half expected our royal escorts to murder us where we slept."

"And yet, you trusted me."

Vincent nodded. "And *yet*, you trusted *me*."

A smile played Esmond's lips. The king liked him. "Trust is a strong word for someone whose people are notoriously untrustworthy."

"Then, did you not trust me?" Vincent asked, slowly approaching the marble table.

"I did," Esmond nodded. "Only based on what I know of you."

Vincent wore a smirk as he took his seat opposite to the king. "Perhaps you would like me more if you knew more about me."

Esmond tittered. "I already do."

"Good," he smiled. "At least we know this won't be a mutually unfriendly conversation, then."

The king poured a goblet of wine for himself before sending the jug into surf towards Vincent, not a drop of wine spilling out. "Cheers to that, Lord Vincent."

Vincent poured one for himself as it arrived, holding it up as the king did. They drank together. The Scorpion didn't hesitate to. *That's reckless. What if I'd poisoned it?* "To what do I owe this summons, good King Esmond?" he asked afterwards.

Esmond sighed, pausing for a time. "You lost your eldest in the *rebellion;* my father demanded his head, and for your lives, you gave it." Vincent nodded, dropping his green stare for the first time. "I don't blame you in seeking revenge... the death of Lord Reynold was more than enough damage to avenge him. Though, I do blame you for thinking that the trade of multiple lives for one is fair."

"You think that only my one son died in that war? I admit, I rarely agreed with my father; mad to his dying breath, he was, but he taught me a lot about death... and how it can be used for the payment of others, the payment of *kin.*"

"Your people weren't the only ones to die, either," the king protested, slightly sad that his respect was replaced with a mild anger. "To send more of mine to the grave for reasons they can't even answer for is just wrong."

"Many more Venusians died than mainlanders." He shook his head. "We haven't even begun to claim revenge."

"When will you, then? Do you know exactly how many perished? On each side?" Esmond asked. "To go on attacking our forts and villages for any longer will surely tip the balance of dead to us."

Vincent frowned. "Forgive me, attacks on villages?"

Esmond matched his frown, more struck with irritation than confusion. "Don't claim like you don't know. Citrine was found on the raider's bodies. Their poison is the make of the Archipelago's."

Vincent shook his head, a hint of ire twitching his lip. "Perhaps you are uninformed that citrine has become of invaluable importance ever since the termination of the mining was passed. To throw away what little we have of it would be suicidal."

The king cursed himself for forgetting about that. "The raids weren't at your command?"

He shook his head again.

"They are rebels, then?"

"In the whole Archipelago, only I, and King Delmar have the authority to command troop or envoy movement. Even for a king, Delmar Khavar couldn't hurt a fly. Whoever conducted these attacks has no part in the Archipelago."

Esmond winced. "Then how do you explain the poison? The citrine?"

He shrugged. "I can't. But they're not our units. Believe it or not, that is the truth."

The king sighed, slumping deeper into his chair. He believed him. "Well, clearly you have competition," he muttered. "What exactly do you claim responsibility for?"

Vincent paused to think. "An attempt on Thaddeus Centaur... and Reynold Lyrderyn. I must say, it would have been preferable for the assassins we sent for Reynold to take one of your sons or daughters instead, but I suppose that is the risk of enrolling. It *was* awfully convenient how all of the greatest lords in Austellus were staying at the same place..."

They tried to kill Thaddeus? His blood boiled underneath his calm demeanour. *When was this? Why didn't Thaddeus tell me?* He chewed his cheeks. *And my children, too? If one of them died by his order, there's no way we'd be having this conversation. His house would be too busy burning.* "I respect that honesty," Esmond nodded. "Would you have continued if I didn't summon you?"

"This summons is more than welcome, good King Esmond," he smirked sharply. "It's the last thing we expected from a grieving man."

"Do grieving men have less wits in the Archipelago?" Esmond quipped, squinting at Vincent's piercing green eyes, hoping to get under his skin.

But Vincent was unflinching. "Anger makes men do unfortunate things. Perhaps you'd know more than me in that respect."

He knows about Sigmund. He was having trouble suppressing his rage now. *He would dare prod me in my own halls.* The king ground his teeth. "What do you want to stop this waste of life?"

Vincent inhaled, stood, and began to wander around, admiring the patterns and engravings in the marble walls. "For too long, our family name has been comparable to dirt. Gone are the days when our nation was feared. Common people look at us as just another failed dynasty of exile, judging us with nothing more than our broken history and our forgotten vows."

Esmond examined the lord, stroking the engravings. "If you are asking a pardon from exile, that is something I cannot reimburse."

The Scorpion snickered. "I'm not asking for a pardon of exile. I'm merely asking for what those who know and have seen us already give... Respect."

The king smirked, joining Vincent in his pacing. *"I* respect you."

"That's good," Vincent said, matching his smirk, "but the respect of the king is not the respect of his people. So long as we are depicted as unorthodox savages, a common mainlander would see us as nothing more."

"Controlling my people's minds is a skill I only wish to possess. Do you have something else in mind, apart from impossible sorcery, that is?"

Vincent nodded, not laughing at Esmond's jest. "To regard us as equals. People spit down on us in the position we are now — and I've seen that first hand just by riding through this city. Your people seem to think we're here to slaughter everyone. It was almost as if we were in stockades, asking for fruit to be thrown at us..."

Esmond bit his lip. *That might have been my fault,* he thought, remembering the bandit he had humiliated and accidently condemned to death. "What do you propose, my lord."

He sighed, turning to the king. "I arrived here with my brother by law, Lord Edward Cancer. I ask for you to take him as your own, here in Lunarpass; bring him on your council, heed his advice as much as any other. He will be the voice of the Archipelago, and instead of a place of exile, people will recognise us as a parallel kingdom."

"An embassy? Clever. I like it," Esmond nodded.

"The assassinations on your close ones will cease, and as a gesture of good faith, we will double our security on people leaving our island, just in case your attacks are, in fact, from our home." The Scorpion took one step forward, holding out his hand. "Those are my terms, so, will that be a deal, King Esmond?"

Esmond walked slowly to Vincent, trying to match the lord's power he naturally exuded. Though, it felt unnatural for him. It didn't seem like Lord Scorpius *tried* to come across like that. The king reached out to shake hands, until Vincent retreated it to his side.

"He is the blood of the future," he muttered, now that they were closer. "If he dies, consider our peace to die also."

Vincent put out his hand again, this time, Esmond retreating his.

"If our peace dies, then you'll never have a second chance at it."

A large smirk of respect spread across Vincent's face. And with that, the two men shook hands, sealing said peace.

FELIKS V
-Boon-

Never had he ridden such a graceful mare. Feliks felt like a lord for once when arriving at Liglock, as glances evolved into stares at the auburn stallion. Stable masters jumped at the opportunity to host Fortune; naturally, Feliks only choosing the most luxurious suite for her. He settled with a stable close to the Taiga River, where his father had said the planked bridge lay. The stable master was a retired cheval, first to Feliks's great uncle, King Palmer, which didn't surprise Feliks, as the man had deep scars on his arms and face, and a crooked walk from the years of riding. Ross Byrne was his name. He said he had a son not much older than Feliks, called Kieran and now second cheval to Doran Equuleus in Lutum. Ross didn't like the sultry heats in Lutum, but was happy to send his son to follow in his footsteps when Doran had offered to. That's why, with all of his experience training equestrians, Feliks was surprised when Ross said that Fortune was the most magical horse he had set his eyes on. Still, Feliks was yet to deny her majesty; it was as if even horses bent to her.

Like her namesake, the ride to Liglock was fortunate. Not many encounters were had on the Centaur's path, the few he did have all being pleasant, or familiar faces returning to the Lagoon. To think the Pole was often seen as a wilderness full of cutthroats and savages was just ridiculous.

Although not a kingdom, Liglock was one of the larger cities of the Pole. It had necessities like walls, a fort, services. Business was erupting, but Feliks felt like they should be less relaxed. *If they all saw what happened at the Lagoon, they'd piss themselves at each trader that walked through the gates.* Most of the blame went to Alec Odum, the current, horrendously easy-going Lord of Liglock. In that sense, Feliks could see part of his father in the lord, but the fact that most southern cities had been the target of so many attacks and Lord Alec still wasn't fazed was somewhat unsettling. *Maybe I have a different view since I'm so close to it all. I've seen men die and he hasn't.* The moment the arrow went through his father's leg was when it was no longer safe to be so placid, anywhere in the Pole.

Despite his unlikeable approach, Lord Odum had been very courteous; Lori must have notified him of Feliks's arrival, since not long after he entered the city, a troop greeted him, ready to take him to the fort. Either that, or someone noticed the Centaur sigil embossed on his dark leathers. Feliks could see the disappointment on Alec's face when he was corrected that Feliks was a bastard, not a trueborn. Chambers were still offered to him, but at that point, he decided he'd rather sleep in the city; he had been all too used to sleeping with the pigs anyway, kicked out of Fort Deus's keep and the like when someone *'important'* came to stay. If anything, he preferred it. It gave him a chance to be loosened, the judgement of high eyes always tightening his muscles. Nightlife in Liglock wasn't anything to sneeze at, either. He had a great time the three nights he had already spent drinking and singing familiar southern songs in the taverns. Centaur's Lagoon had its fair share of taverns, but Feliks's face was known all over there. Here, he was nobody, another customer to serve, a man of humble means, a man judged by his person and not his birthright, and he liked it.

Noon on the fourth day had arrived, and Feliks's patience eroded like the river he stared at. *A figure of great import.* He couldn't decide who was important and who wasn't. *'Great import' would be difficult to miss.* He sat on the bank, skimming stones on the shivering Taiga River while he shared Chloe Byrne's company, the daughter and apprentice of Ross.

"What did you say you were waiting for again?" Chloe asked as she fed and groomed Fortune.

Feliks tittered. "Anything at this point."

"Your father can't send you to a place you've rarely been to and expect you to notice when something is different," she said.

"That's why I met you, so you can tell me when something's different," he smirked.

She chuckled. "Sorry to burst your bubble, Liglock has been the same boring city since I was born."

"Good, then you're stuck with me for a lot longer."

"Just because you're pretty, you think I want you here?" she remarked, retying her long, black hair.

"You're hardly protesting."

Chloe smiled offendedly, taking a moment before replying. "I'll throw you out to the dogs when dad isn't looking."

"There's your problem," he sighed curiously, inspecting a fine cut piece of flint he found on the ground, "there aren't any dogs to feed."

"Holy shit," she gasped, dropping a stack of hay.

"What?" he smiled.

"I've never seen an elder before."

Feliks's gaze shot up to the bridge. To his joy, she was right in spotting Elder Marcarius, ocean blue robes glistening in the sun as he trotted into the city. Feliks bolted towards him. "Marcarius! Elder Marcarius!" he called, beaming.

"By gods, if it isn't a Centaur," he smiled. "How fares your lord father, Feliks? I couldn't have been more pleased after learning of his renascence."

"He's getting better," Feliks nodded, letting a smile rule his face from the elder's presence, and the fact he was called a Centaur, though it subdued when he thought of his father. "He still has trouble walking. Cuthbert said he'll never ride like he used to."

"It'll be more of a miracle than it already is if he could. I imagine a lot of the arrow still remains in his leg," Marcarius sighed, dismounting.

"Yeah, Cuthbert also said it would be too dangerous to remove."

Marcarius nodded. "Cuthbert is a wise man. I had actually hoped to-" He cut himself off when he saw Ross waddle out the stable. "Speaking of wise men," he bellowed.

"Elder Marcarius!" he gasped, almost falling over. "What a pleasant surprise."

They shook hands. "Gods, it's been an age since I've seen you."

Ross paused to think. *The Scorpius Rebellion*, if I recall correctly."

"Indeed," the elder nodded, "and what a show you put on. I guarantee, if you'd have stayed on to become King Esmond's first cheval, no man would even think to rebel again."

The retired cheval chuckled. "You flatter me, but gone are my days of fighting. I am grateful enough just to see another day."

"As we all should be," he said sadly. "Nevertheless, you look well; younger, I dare to say."

"Oh, stop," the old man waved his hand, taking Marcarius's horse. "We both know the eldest here." They both laughed as Ross disappeared into his stables.

"Care for a drink, Feliks?" the elder asked.

"If that's where you're going, sure," he smiled.

"Let me teach you the wisest lesson you'll ever learn," Marcarius smirked as they began to walk. "There is not any amount of dilemma that alcohol cannot solve."

Feliks snorted. "I am in awe of your wisdom, Elder Marcarius."

He nodded intently. "Gods, it slipped my mind. My deepest condolences for poor Vesta. Her loss shocked us all."

Feliks sighed, gritting his teeth. Her name still felt like an arrow in the gut. "There's nothing we could have done." *There was plenty I could have done*, but he didn't want to admit that.

"Truly terrible," Marcarius agreed. "How are you doing?"

"Better now you're here," Feliks said with a lipped smile. He thought it best to avoid the question. It hurt too much to think of her. *That's not like you, Feliks, to hide from the truth.* He masked his wince.

"Oh? Were you expecting me?"

"I was expecting '*a figure of great import*,'" Feliks explained. "Who's more important than an elder? A man came to father in a dream. Told him to 'send one of your own' to meet this figure?"

"That was no dream, Feliks," Marcarius said, lack of jest. "Did your lord father describe the man?"

Feliks shook his head.

"Hmph," he sighed, examining the door of a tavern they had halted before. "Still, that was no dream, as that was no man." He pushed the door, revealing a standard afternoon tavern atmosphere of mellow chatter and predrinking for the night. "Two large, please," Marcarius nodded to the man behind the counter.

"At once, my elder," he bowed.

"He was no man?" Feliks asked, wincing. "My father *did* say a guy."

Marcarius frowned. "That's what they want you to believe. Gods know what's under those hoods," he said, staring off into nothing. "Your lord father didn't have a dream because he had a vision. I know it's of their power for the seers of Sanctum Amino to communicate with the weak or dying. Your father was visited by one of the like."

"A seer?" Feliks pouted. "How do you know?"

The elder nodded to the bartender as he brought two giant mugs of ale. "I admit, my knowledge on the subject is limited. I *met* a seer for the first time three moons ago, and still, those creatures are an enigma." They made their way to a table. "But how else would you explain our meeting?" he chuckled. "Plus, Centaur's Lagoon was where I was headed."

"Really?" Feliks smiled excitedly. "The seer said that if I met you here, we'd have the surplus of time we need!"

"And so we do," said Marcarius, reciprocating his smile. "I no longer have to go all that way." This was blowing Feliks's mind. He couldn't fathom how Marcarius remained so relaxed. "Have you brought the stone?"

"I have," Feliks grinned, reaching into his pocket to retrieve an orb of citrine.

Marcarius pinched it away, lifting it to the mellow beam of light that fell through the window. He rotated it and squinted. Eventually he nodded. "Citrine, to be sure. Your father is a smart man." he handed the orb back to Feliks. "What else did this... *seer* say?"

"Just that I should meet you here... 'The king and his serpent will be unearthed by no other way'."

"The serpent," Marcarius repeated, shuddering.

Feliks shrugged, taking a sip. "Perhaps you know more than me."

"An ominous word," Marcarius admitted. "I know much of the physical kind, but I feel that *this* serpent is not of an entity."

"It's not," Feliks agreed. "The Serpent of Stars. It will poison the city, flooded by waters as black as night." He squashed his cheek with his fist, observing the tavern's people. "What kind of living serpent can flood cities?"

"Your father said that."

"How do you know?"

Marcarius smirked, plucking a rolled-up parchment from his robe. "Ravens," he said, before leaning back. "I've heard of this serpent. The King of Light is who will judge," he muttered.

Feliks tapped around the table. "Well, have you brought a shovel? Maybe we can unearth this king and let this nightmare die."

Marcarius only tittered, shaking his head. "Truth be told, I was heading to the Great Athenaeum to learn of this serpent before Lord Waker proposed a detour to Centaur's Lagoon."

"Why?" he asked. "Do you think the serpent and the Scorpions are connected?"

The elder shook his head. "I hadn't proposed that thought, though, it's likely. I was stringing thoughts more so to the acclimatization we've had threats of."

For a moment, Feliks thought he had misheard. "Another *Pause?*" he gasped.

"Or something of the sort," he sighed. "I suppose, *the third Pause* would be incorrect to say. If anything, it would be a... reconstruction."

Feliks tittered, taking a drink. *Gods, so everyone should be much less than placid. The weather will want to kill them as well as Scorpions, soon.* "So, why do you think there's a connection?"

Marcarius shrugged. "Two strongly celestially inclined events so close together? I don't know much of this serpent, but *the Serpent of Stars* sounds fairly otherworldly to me."

The bastard thought it interesting how Marcarius came to that conclusion. He supposed the elder had so much life experience, regardless; anything out of the ordinary would stick out like an arrow from a quiver. *He becomes more fascinating with age*, Feliks thought, noticing that the respect he had for him now wasn't quite as present in Feliks's youth.

"So?" Marcarius asked eventually.

"So, what?" Feliks frowned, confused.

"So, clearly the prophets have a plan for us, bringing us together like this," he smiled. "It seems like the realm doesn't know that those who can solve this mystery and find an antidote for this poison sit a table apart. It seems a shame to go our separate ways now, and finish our business before it begins."

"Books?" Feliks smirked. "I see no better place to start."

ELAYNE III
-Lack-

Humans aren't worthy to share the same earth as elders. To think that the mystery of those people didn't end at their impossibly long lives only made Austellus that much more magical to live in. All her life, she had recognised lynxes as untameable beasts, patrolling the Lynxrock like bloodthirsty scouts, yet as she sat next to a fountain on the Ignis keep's open patio, a small, fully domesticated lynx purred softly on her lap. Una would be seven moons old come the Harvest Moon, the impossible beast a gift from Elder Sol on Ryan Lynx's sixteenth birthmoon. Elayne Lyrderyn practically adopted the cat the moment she set eyes on it. She had never been so close to one, let alone nurse one for most of every day. Despite still being a cub, Una had fangs like daggers and ears like arrowheads, proving uncomfortable, and sometimes dangerous to play with. Though, Elayne could never imagine the cute little cub growing into a deadly beast. Ryan would check in on her occasionally, spending the time he would have spent with Fitz, if the new heir of Ignis didn't receive a new sandstorm of responsibilities that came with his father being the lord.

"I'm glad you have Elder Sol caring for you," Elayne said to him earlier that afternoon. "At least he can be a good father figure to you."

"You don't need to hate your brother, auntie," he smiled. "He might be a bit crazy, but he's harmless."

A bit crazy is an understatement. And harmless is a bigger one. "No child deserves to be treated as you have," she frowned.

Ryan shook his head. "These bruises remind me how bad pain can get. And if I never show how strong I really am, he'll always misjudge me."

When he would mention Ayden, Ryan would never call him by the name 'father', always preferring 'Lord Ayden' or 'your brother'. *Good,* Elayne thought. *He doesn't deserve the title of a father.*

Ayden had been less than outspoken since his arrival. He acted like a shadow, walking proudly down the streets of Ignis as if he already owned them. She could see his thoughts: *You'll soon all bow to me, Ayden the just, a poor lord who's been mistreated his whole life, a lord deprived because of his insatiable appetite.* A frown always came with his presence, even if he had said nothing to cause it. He clearly had no intention of heading back to Lynxrock, but so long as he harmlessly drooled at the throne, she supposed it made no difference. It wasn't like he didn't climb, though; Goldwyn Lyrderyn had appointed the annoyingly furtive man as acting head of *politics*, for the duration of his stay. Elayne liked that - a man scheming to overthrow a lord, given decisive control over the men around him by that same lord. *He can do what he wants. He'll soon realise the consequence of his petty actions.* She didn't care for Goldwyn, but if and when Fitz ascends, *he'll realise, then, he'll be backed into a corner.*

Fortunately, she could keep an eye on him, as Goldwyn appointed her 'Lady Paramount Regent', allowing her to attend council meetings and retain most of the power she had before. Lady Gina didn't mind, as she became the new Lady of Ignis. She was such a sweet woman. Most people, man or woman, in this damned city would snarl at others who stepped on their power, yet Gina shared hers with Elayne with open arms. *Thank the gods she's not on Ayden's hitlist.*

"Lady of mine," Lord Sulwyn Wisp greeted. Elayne was startled, not noticing his silent arrival. "Will you spare your time for a council meeting? Matters are to be discussed, and your word is always valued."

"I'll follow you, my lord," Elayne said, placing Una on her leather bed before standing.

Sulwyn bowed deeply, holding a smile. Everything that man did was done with grace. He would inflate his chest when he walked, keeping his hands in a knot behind his back. His strides were long and silent, much like his way of talking: always above a whisper, yet still with the steady growl of a lion underneath. He wore a humble red cloth from his shoulders to his bare feet, and had a groomed, greasy mane of hair that played with the air. "A lynx within the keep walls is a sight no man can get familiar with," he said as they walked. "I have heard no other gossip from the city."

"I imagine it's getting quite boring for you," she jested dryly, "having the only rumour reach your ears be an old one."

"The results may surprise you, Lady Elayne," Sulwyn smirked. "So long as men have mouths, never will we be void of rumour."

"True," she agreed, "but never will you be void of lies, either."

The head of word tittered gently. "Truths and lies are that of the same breed. So long as men believe one over the other, the *truth* has a loss of importance."

"Not to those who know the truth."

"No," Sulwyn agreed, "but by then, the truth becomes another rumour, and what value would it carry if that rumour has no power?"

A smile pulled Elayne's lips. She had missed the man. Not much was known about Sulwyn Wisp, which was probably how he so effortlessly became head of word. The Wisps themselves were an ancient family, known for their success with magic before the *Pause*. They were so fortunate with the art, that they even rivalled that of Deus Caelestius's powers. Some people believed that the Wisps still practised it, but no one knew for sure. Maybe that was how the man knew everything before it was said. Elayne thought it best if that stayed a mystery.

Their talk had led them to the tall sandstone tower of the council chambers. Most of the council were already there, chatting loudly amongst themselves. "Here you are, Lady Elayne!" Goldwyn boomed from the head of the table. It was odd seeing him on Reynold's chair.

"Where's Elder Ulrich?" she asked, noticing his absence immediately.

"I'll get to that," Goldwyn smirked excitedly, holding his finger up. "Will Jermyn Mayne be joining us, Lord Wisp?"

Sulwyn shook his head. "I'm afraid not. He has been absent all week."

"A shame," Goldwyn frowned, before clapping his hands together. "No matter. If I'm to have your attention, loyal councillors," he smiled, waiting for talk to subside. "I bear exciting news by my lady wife this morning. She is with child. Elder Ulrich says that come the Hunter's Moon, a handsome baby boy will join our family."

The council cheered, bursting into applause. "Congratulations, my lord," James Fysher, Sir Cedric's brother beamed.

Elayne's eyes gravitated to Ayden, who masked his sly face with joy. "Thank you, my lords, thank you," Goldwyn smiled, humbled by the applause. "We will drink later, but now we must discuss." He took his seat.

"Last time we were all here, my beloved brother sat this seat. A lot has happened since then. What issues are in need of our attention first?"

Sulwyn Wisp breathed in to speak, only to be interrupted by Aurelius Kinsey, head of gold and trade. "The trade stands on its last legs, my lord. I knew we were in danger ever since the rumours of low yields spread, but now a paucity of food is of prime concern. We are on the verge of famine."

"Sulwyn, is this true?" Goldwyn asked.

"It is," he sighed lightly. He locked his eyes on Aurelius. "I would have raised an associated issue, if ears would have waited."

"Is there a solution, Lord Kinsey?" Goldwyn asked again, paying no heed to the statement.

"Only temporary ones," he replied. "We can purchase what food we can, but I fear that soon, food will be more valuable than gold."

"And we cannot sustain ourselves?"

"Ignis thrives on trade, my lord. I imagine many kingdoms have the same idea, but if we stop receiving proposals, we won't be able to keep the animals alive, let alone the people."

"A tragedy for Lord Mayne," Elijah Gale muttered, smirking.

"Does that amuse you, Lord Gale?" Aurelius leered.

"Keep this civil, my lords," James Fysher said, scratching his nose. Elijah nodded in response to Aurelius, provoking him.

"There's no point fretting about the weather," Goldwyn sighed, the tension flying past his golden mane. "If it *is* to change, we will have no power. All we can do is advise our people and lower portion sizes."

"My lord, if this becomes common knowledge, theft and crime will increase greatly. Without a head of law, the Canicule could riot," Aurelius Kinsey protested.

"Common knowledge is not what we should battle," Sulwyn smiled, knowingly. "If it is, then we have already lost."

"There may be no head of *law*, but this council is not shy of *enforcement*," James Fysher added, glancing at Cyrus Sand.

"If enforcement is what it comes to, then Ignis won't fall," Cyrus nodded, his craggy face forever in a deep frown. "Regardless, if people are to starve, the crowds will lessen. Only the strong will survive, and strength is what we will need if southern or northern conflicts reach us."

"You think people would fight for us when we deprive them of food?" Elijah winced. "No kingdom would exist if their city turned into a skirmish."

"Lord Gale is right," Goldwyn nodded. "If it becomes that grave, I'm sure evacuations will suffice."

"And if they don't?" Aurelius asked.

Goldwyn shrugged, remaining silent.

"Then it turns into a skirmish," Elayne muttered, reminding them all of her presence.

Lord Goldwyn sighed. "I hope your news, Lord Wisp, is a little more exciting."

"Oh, it will excite Lord Sand, to be sure," he said, passing a roll of parchment to the Lord of Ignis.

Goldwyn gently pulled off the blue seal of Centaur. His eyes followed the words. "Equuleus? Those backstabbing churls!"

"They have taken up arms?" Cyrus asked.

"A host larger by the day," Sulwyn nodded. "They plan to take it to Aurdrive, then to the keeps and towns towards Moat Calor."

"We can't let them do this," James frowned. "If they secure all the food, Lutum will be the kingdom that rules the Canicule. If the people back them, Ignis *will* fall."

"That's why we won't let them do it," Goldwyn said bitterly, scrunching up the paper. "King Esmond has commanded our force to march down and stop them. He has declared Lutum a false kingdom."

"A weed to be torn out before growth... This is a good thing, my lord," Cyrus insisted. "An opportunity for more food, more honours-"

"More death," Goldwyn grunted, gritting his teeth. "We barely have our claws in the sand. A war is just what we need to pull this damned desert apart."

"To refuse would be treason," James sighed.

"We won't refuse," Lord Goldwyn assured as he stood. "Cyrus, James, have the men ready by dusk."

Cyrus nodded, bowing as he stood.

"Our entire force, my lord?" James asked.

"Everyone," Goldwyn nodded. "Thank you, my lords," he said, unenthused. "Soon, this mess will be behind us." He excused the council.

Elayne hadn't quite taken it in. *It must be dire for the Equuleans, of all families, to rebel.* Their loyalty was unparalleled. *What does this mean for the Canicule? What does this mean for me?* She glanced at her brother, who sat alone with her. He wore a smirk like a crow's, looking at the words on the parchment like they were seeds, scattered out for him to peck at.

LYSSA III
-Fervour-

Whatever Leo had done, it worked. They hadn't needed to wait for the second day to come when the twins had given them permission to cross. Though, the same couldn't be said for Leo; he remained a closed story, teething with mystery every chance he had to show his knowledge. It was unlike Lyssa Lyrderyn to not know everything about someone after spending close to a moon with them. She hoped Leo would take the time to eventually talk about himself; her curiosity burnt at the sight of the boy.

Shortly after receiving their pardon, the party of five, with the additions of Drew Ortiz and Evan Stone of the twin's guard, set off to Mea. She had never been on anything like the Enigma Towers' crossing: it was a long, tightly planked wooden bridge, impossible to see the other side due to the thick fog that swallowed it. It was scarcely wide enough for two people to walk side by side, and had round, twisting balustrades, the jungle wood glued together firmly with resin, in parts still sticky to the touch. The crossing was almost one hundred feet off the ground, the Enigma Towers higher still. Ancient houses and inns stood near the great bridge, connected with a rope, and at first glance, seemed to be floating as the wooden beams that stretched down to the Whitefin Sea were swathed in fog. Drew said that once, the entire Kingdom of Mea floated with the bridge, taken up by the clouds and the tall massifs that broke away during The Hex War and the *Pause*. Mea itself wasn't too different to Mea Minor;

appropriately, it looked like a twin.

"Why isn't Lord Todd at Mea, then?" Lyssa asked Drew when he noted Todd's absence.

"He says the crowds lay stress on him," Drew explained. "He thinks of Murberek as respite from that, whilst not forfeiting his responsibilities as Lord of Mea."

The island of Astutus was more exciting to explore than its twin Laetus regardless. On the path to Murberek, mountains surrounded them, shaping a misty valley, whilst jungle trees stood tall in the distance. At almost every view, both Asher and Lyssa would lose their words, gaping at the beauty of the island. The Temple of the Mind they had passed a day ago was enough to make them forget their purpose. It was difficult to see, as the temple stood high, shrouded in fog atop a mountain, but the way the winds wisped around it as if it had character was a magical sight.

"Still, Laetus has its own sort of beauty," Drew disputed, "the Nebulus Plains, the Temple of the Soul, the-"

"I've lived in a desert my whole life, sir," Lyssa giggled. "The sight of a building made of something that isn't sandstone is enough to blow my mind."

"I thought it'd be harder to impress you," Asher smirked, crossing his arms as they walked.

"Obviously not; *you've* managed it," she smiled back.

Ever since the Bay, Asher seemed to be drying of jest, and his optimism with it. Rings as dark as shadows fell from his eyes to coat his pale face, and he would make an effort to keep interactions short, despite how sweet they may be. He was in pain. If it was due to the dreams, or him missing his family, or something else entirely, was difficult to tell. All she hoped was for answers soon; not only for Asher, but for herself too.

Still, the journey hadn't been too uncomfortable. Northern weather was pleasantly surprising to Lyssa. The days were generally muggy and mild, and although a burden to travel in, it wasn't nearly as bad as the sometimes blistering Canicule. *I still have burns from that stupid desert.* Dusk was something Lyssa struggled to get used to, though. It wasn't as cold as the Auburn Pole, but was chilly enough to feel the bugs of frost nip at bare skin. At night, when she felt cooler, she was more thankful than ever to have Asher be a hearth to her.

"Shouldn't be too long now," Evan said that evening before biting into the crouton rations they were given.

"How far away are we?" Leo asked, washing his sweaty face in the river.

"If there wasn't any fog, we'd be able to barely see it," Drew assured. "Five hours, at most."

Leo didn't seem to react to the news, joining the party around the fire as they ate.

"I say, the longer the better," Evan sighed. "Lord Riley sent red alerts to our Lord Todd. As soon as we get there, we'll be sent out to war again."

"Why?" Leo asked. "The Kalyx aren't sworn to Horncurve, are they?"

"No, but if a civil war breaks out, most of their *pennons* would be on one side or the other," Drew said. "Todd is sworn to the king, and we must act as a relief force if the rightful lords should start to fail."

"Plus, most of the Triplex commerce relies on Selerborn standing," Evan nodded. "As much as northerners scare the shit out of me, we need them to stay alive so that we can see tomorrow."

"Stupid," Asher muttered hoarsely, shaking his head.

"What is?" Lyssa asked softly as she held his arm.

"Civil wars," he said. "It's stupid to kill your own men."

"Not if they want to kill you first," Leo said, overhearing.

"Well, if they're *your* men, they shouldn't want to kill you in the first place," Asher replied, leaning back against a rock. "A good leader gives their men a good reason to follow them. If they don't have that, they may as well be slaves."

"It makes no difference for most kings," Drew said, licking his greasy fingers. "Slaves and soldiers look the same to them."

"It makes no difference to *stupid* kings," Asher said coldly.

Evan chuckled. "What do you think of King Esmond, then? Most people either love him or hate him now. Do you think it's wrong for him to deny all these requests for more food?"

"It doesn't sound like he's got much choice," he murmured, eyes turning a darker blue.

"People say he starves Austellus while he feasts in the capital," Drew smiled, closing his eyes. "If that's not the sign of stupid king, I don't know what is."

Asher shook his head, an anger twitching his brow. "He wouldn't do that."

"Let's not talk about politics," Leo interrupted, keeping his eyes locked on the prince. "This journey has been long enough."

The party seemed to agree. "Let's get some rest, then," Drew said, twisting into a comfortable sprawl.

◄———————◄

As the night aged, cool winds rose, and a bright blue moon kissed the darkening sky. For the first time, Asher was the one who slept like a cub, Lyssa unable to as her worries bounced around her mind. The sparkling river was a good thing to look at: constantly changing, reflecting the tall trees and vines around. *My family must have returned to Ignis by now. I wonder how Fitz and Eleanor are doing.* The guilt of abandonment was something she couldn't shake off, as was the loss of home. She *really* liked Asher, but it felt like she had to choose between him and family. *I already have chosen,* she sulked... *And I'd choose the same again, so why am I thinking like this?*

A pair of chilly fingers tapped her shoulder. It was Leo. He held a finger to his lips as he urged Lyssa to come. Asher's limp body fell like a brick as she removed herself from under his arm.

"What is this?" she whispered after Leo had taken her a few yards from the camp.

Leo sighed. "We need to make a decision."

"About what?"

"We shouldn't stop at Murberek," he said, massaging his hands. "I think we can both agree, for Asher's sake, we need to get to where we're headed as soon as possible. And like I said on the boat: Todd doesn't know of my assignment. As soon as he sees you both... well then there's..." he shook his head. "He'll know, for sure."

"Oh," she frowned. "What are the options, then?"

"Well, we can go against instructions and go to Murberek anyway, or we can... kill the guard and run away."

"Kill them?" Lyssa winced. "We shouldn't need to kill them."

"But Lyssa, if they wake up and find us gone, Todd will send a fucking army after us."

Lyssa tittered at the exaggeration before her smile faded. "I don't want to kill them."

"Neither do I, but I don't fancy killing the armed men sent after us either. Asher can barely fight, or run."

"Hm," Lyssa frowned. "On what word is Todd not allowed to know?"

"It doesn't matter what word," Leo sighed. "I've sworn... a lot away to take you and Asher safely with those instructions."

Lyssa blinked. "Fine," she sighed. "We'll leave, but we won't kill them. Let the army chase us." She dashed back to the camp delicately.

Awaking Asher and telling him of the plan was the easy part, as the prince's sleep was light as it was deep. They worried of the next, though.

Slowly rising, it proved difficult to remain silent upon brushing the many ferns and vines that surrounded the camp. They didn't have weapons either. If they were spotted escaping... well, Leo would then have failed what he had sworn.

The mud underfoot had a soft *squelch*, not much louder than movement itself, but enough to raise frets. Leo unhooked the wooden crouton box from a tree, making much hastier steps than Asher and Lyssa's ponderous ones. Drew and Evan fortunately slept like stones, Drew wrapped in a dark blanket, almost invisible, whilst Evan snored overtly, mouth agape.

They followed Leo confidently down the road's slope, tense muscles easing the further they moved away. "Wasn't *that* hard," Leo smiled when he thought they were clear.

"Yeah, but now the armies come," Lyssa sighed.

"Going somewhere?" Drew asked, tired and shabby. He walked from behind a tree in front of them, finding his sword pommel with his palm.

"What are you doing?" Leo gasped, disbelieving.

"Taking a piss, what are you doing?"

"Uhm," Leo stuttered, glancing around. "We... were..."

"I'm gonna give you five seconds to turn around and walk back," Drew ordered, taking one great step towards them. "This doesn't need to be difficult."

"Drew, come on, man, you don't need to do this," Leo said, holding his dirty hands out.

"Two seconds, I'm calling Evan."

"Please, Drew. Don't do this."

"I don't want to, so turn around and walk back."

"I can't, we need to go."

"Have it your way. *Ev-*"

Leo struck the man's face with a stiff fist. "Go! Run!"

"You *fucker!*" Drew winced, holding his bloodied nose.

"Where?" Lyssa cried.

"Just run! I'll catch up." Leo stood his ground while Drew recouped.

Lyssa grabbed Asher's arm, pulling him furiously through the ferns and bushes. The prince didn't seem to know what was going on, eyes and mouth half open, stumbling like a toddler. She glanced back. Leo whipped two small katars from his belt, parrying Drew's first burly slash. *He has katars?!* She noticed, almost tripping. Evan clumsily ran down the hill, unsheathing his sword. He threw a tight overhead thrust, scarcely dodged by Leo. At that point, Lyssa's vision was shielded with leaves. It made her want to slow down so she could see more clearly, but she couldn't. All they could hear in the nighttime valley was the brash grunts and tenacious clattering of weapons, slowly fading as they ran.

FLETCHER V
-Trust-

Deuswater was lost, pillaged and burned to the ground. Fletcher Centaur saw it coming, but he still wasn't sure if Tyran told the truth. At least he knew that they weren't *complete* liars. From what he knew, most locals had peacefully evacuated before the white banner of Khavar came for the city like a rake to soil. Now, by the word of loyal Centaur scouts, they marched south like Fletcher had known they would, mere miles away from his home.

Fort Deus had been preparing all day, armed with last minute training, resistance tactics, weapons, horses, shields. Archers were lined along the fort's battlements, as were a few in the cliff's bunker. Cavalry and foot archers filled the higher and middle bailey, quivering in the frozen winds. A total of seven thousand Centaur men and three thousand Capra men stood in the fort alone, the two thousand from Antrum Lookout and the three thousand left-over Capras dotted outside the fort in *equos* and squadrons. Sir Roswell was right in predicting the other lords of the Negal lands refusing their calls; the five thousand from Deuswater would have helped massively, but all Fletcher could amass by persuading the other strongholds was an extra two thousand, managing two hundred or so per call. He put them to use in the vanguard, just in front of the many cohorts.

As sunset loomed, Fletcher was careful not to share his tactics with Tyran, still not entirely trusting the man. He met with Sir Roswell, Semira, Quintin Baxter, Lord of Antrum Bay, and Kian Weeks, head of the fort's garrison, in secret before he met with the other Negal lords and chevals to draw battle plans.

"We'll have the bulk of our force within the fort for as long as the Khavars are held from advancing past Storm Tower," he was saying, drawing his finger across a map of Fort Deus, spread out across Esmond's office table. "If and when they make it past our vanguard, who will also have the aid of our archers on the tower and the fort, then we will send small brigades of five hundred men to act as relief for our equos and squadrons every so often."

"We won't send relief to help the vanguard?" Quintin asked.

Fletcher shook his head. "If we help the vanguard, we'll push the Khavars back. We need them to come as close as possible, make them think they're making progress, until we send most of our relief force to keep them at bay. Plus, the closer they are, and the sooner their formation breaks, the more likely the archers are to hit their marks."

"How often will we send the brigades?" Kian Weeks asked.

"Whenever they advance, let's say, one hundred feet. Kian, I'll let you take charge of that; I trust you can act on instinct to send brigades if it looks like our outside force is failing."

Kian nodded.

"What if the outside force falls quicker than the reinforcements?" Quintin Baxter asked.

"I'll let you take charge of that, Lord Baxter. If we're throwing away men, then it's your job to sound the retreat back to the fort, where we'll wait for the invasion. They *shouldn't* breach the fort's gates, but if they do, Lord Troy Larton has provided catapults to block up the entrance with stones and seal ourselves in. We *might* last a siege if it comes to it."

The two men analysed the map, nodding, pulling faces of content. *They like the plan*, Fletcher thought, excitedly.

"What of Tyran Capra's forces?" Kian asked.

Fletcher frowned. "I'm gonna try to convince him to join the outside forces. If he *is* to betray us, it'd be better for him to do it outside our walls."

"And if he refuses?" Sir Roswell asked.

"Then..." Fletcher bit his cheeks. "Let's hope it doesn't come to that." He paused for a time. "Other than that, the only way the Khavars can come on land is from the Negal Road, but if we're hit by a surprise naval attack, archers and catapults in the bunker should hopefully be enough to stop them. So, does that sound good, my lords?"

"If I may, my lord," Quintin said, "Fort Deus *is* impenetrable, even more so with Lord Larton's catapults to seal us in. Could we not dispose of aggression entirely? Keep our armies within our walls?"

"Sealing ourselves in is a last resort," Fletcher explained. "I don't know how long we'll last with twenty-five thousand people and no food to feed them. Besides, *equos* belong in the field, where they can ride, not on the walls."

Quintin bowed. "It's bold to assume they'd be provisioned enough for a siege. An excellent plan, my lord."

"Good. Now head on to the council chambers. Tell no one of these tactics. Whatever I say in the meeting doesn't mean anything, ok?"

"As you wish, my lord," Kian bowed, following Quintin out.

"What do you want *me* to do?" Sir Roswell asked when they left.

"Stay with me. If worse comes to worst and they storm the castle, you will organise getaway boats and evacuations from the hidden exit on the Antrum River. If we're lucky, most people can escape safely to Centaur's Lagoon. Otherwise, we'll help the defence of the castle."

"You're going to fight?" Semira gasped.

Fletcher sighed. "If they get past the gates, we're going to have to."

The queen shook her head. "Please be careful."

Sir Roswell Dart had a large grin on his face, tittering. "Look at you now, Fletcher," he smiled, "this strategy is phenomenal."

"I'm glad you think so," Fletcher smirked, before folding up the map. "Come on, then."

It'll be enough to defeat them, he trusted. Though, he didn't expect them to attack on land. He could only assume that those of the Archipelago favoured ships instead, but apparently not. It didn't help that Fletcher had never seen them fight before either. Not even in stories were Cancerians described in battle. But it didn't matter to Fletcher *that* much. *If they can bleed, we can beat them.*

"No," Tyran said during the second meeting, thwarting Fletcher's confidence. "I will not send my men out to die. We are meant to defend the castle together, my lord. You *agreed* to keep my troops as a garrison and *nothing more.*"

"I know, and I'm sorry for not honouring that, my lord," Fletcher said, blushing in front of the many chevals and lords that surrounded the council table. "But for the plan to work, we *need* your men to be there."

"Forgive me, my lord, but it doesn't seem like you *have* much of a plan," Tyran frowned angrily. "The spill of *any* blood is dispensable entirely. Why can't we wait for them to breach the gates, and flood them with our full force? Together."

"This is *our* home we're defending, Lord Tyran," Sir Roswell noted, blades in his eyes. "Twenty-five thousand people live in that lower bailey, and Prince Fletcher is who decides how we defend them, not you."

Tyran squinted at the knight, taking a time before returning his eyes to Fletcher. "I'm giving you most of my army, and that's generous. If you wish to keep them, my lord, then I suggest you don't treat them as *yours.*"

"Just trust him, Fletcher," Semira whispered in his ear.

Just trust him? If he was to betray us, now would be the perfect time to throw him out... And all these people, they'll die if I fail them... Fletcher once knew what he was doing, but not anymore. He took a long sigh. "You're right. I'm sorry, Tyran. I shouldn't have asked that of you."

Tyran closed his eyes, sucking his cheeks. "Not at all, my lord. I'm sorry." He rubbed his eyes. "I'll dedicate half my men to the cause. Three thousand for your use."

Thank the gods. Fletcher couldn't let the relief show. He glanced at Sir Roswell, a face saying: it's better than nothing. "Thank you, my lord. With luck, that will suffice."

Dusk was when they were predicted to arrive, and evening fell like a guillotine. Torches to light up the dark sky had their flames spit and dance around, glistening on the round blue shields and thin steel plate on each man. Fletcher ambled among the units that thronged the fort, patting those he knew on the shoulder. The silence of the fort was strange, unsettling even. The only sound to ring out was the occasional shout or order from chevals or generals, as the rushed rustle of chainmail and clamour of armour and swords had ceased when everyone had taken position.

He made his way up to the battlements, and looked out to the thousands of men that filled the field before him. Never had he felt so tall. *I made this happen*, he smirked. *This is how I become bigger than myself.* He was sure of it. The thought hadn't left Fletcher's mind since he talked with Leta, but now it felt like he had found the answer.

"Are you certain you'll win?" Leta asked earlier, trembling in his chambers as she set her eyes, for the first time, on a Fletcher clad in tight silver-and-blue armour.

"Positive," he sighed, tying a lace on his fingerless gauntlet. "Out there stand the best warriors the Pole will ever see: chevals and riders that have been born mounted on horses."

"We aren't in the Pole," she muttered, hugging a pillow.

Fletcher glared at her. "You know what I mean." He looked back to the mirror. "After the Khavars see the first cheval to stand on his horse while it gallops, they'll scuttle back to the Archipelago with soaked pants."

"But you're outnumbered," Leta frowned. "You said more than eighteen thousand sailed to Deuswater. You barely have seventeen."

"Did you count?"

She picked at the pillow. "I might have eavesdropped."

He shook his head, smiling. "It'd be a different story if we were in an open field, but we're defending. We have high walls, archers, catapults, more horses you'd know what to do with-"

"You'd have thirteen thousand more men if you *were* in an open field," she interrupted.

He paused to sigh. "Yeah, okay, maybe I'm wrong in waiting. Maybe I should've marched up to Deuswater and stopped them while they docked. But I *know* it would have been a trap. I have no reason to trust the Capras."

"You have my word," she winced, standing. "I saw the truth with my own eyes."

Fletcher shrugged. "Maybe."

"Ugh," she groaned bitterly. "It's your fault if our home falls."

After Leta had flounced away, a tart taste was left in Fletcher's mouth. The talk with his brother wasn't any sweeter. Fletcher had told Leta to take care of him during the battle, to keep him safe if they breached the gates, but when Fletcher had met with him after, Hew was about as responsive as a mountain. All he did was stare out of his chamber's window, his eyes following the soldiers marching around the courtyard. "Are you going to be okay?" Fletcher asked, not receiving a reply. "If you're not, and you get frightened or… just find our sister. She'll take care of you." Fletcher thought it pointless to talk to him after that. He didn't even know if his brother took the words in.

It made Fletcher think of his other siblings. *Eva would be in Lunarpass by now, and Asher in Ignis. They were smart to run away.* 'Death is coming for the Centaurs'. He didn't want to think of it, but Tyran's words rang his head like a bell. '*They'll be as meek as lambs*'. Doubt was the last thing he needed right now. He had already come so far in full confidence.

He wished it would begin already, so those thoughts didn't have a chance to brew. Luckily, he didn't have to wait too much longer before the white banners glimmered in the night sky. Each Khavar soldier was plated in shelled armour ranging from deep browns to soft turquoises, rounded, spiked helmets on each of them. Those who looked to be generals had crab arms on their helmets, snapping at the air. Their sheathing was thick and slowing to their already sedate trudge. From this distance, they even *looked* like little crabs marching along. They had massive shields that looked like shells, and huge, brutal, curved swords of varying breadth and size, yet they had no horses, no battering rams, no catapults. "What sort of a siege is this?" Fletcher chuckled to Sir Roswell. Though, Fletcher would give this to them: they were disciplined. No man was ahead or behind the other, and they stopped in sync a few hundred yards away from the Centaur vanguard. They parted to reveal a lone rider, galloping towards Fletcher's army while he held a white flag of submission.

"Bit early to surrender, isn't it?" Sir Roswell smirked.

"They're just *that* scared of us."

The rider continued fearlessly through Fletcher's army. In truth, it was difficult to know whether the flag he held was the flag of yielding or the Khavar sigil, but it mustn't be the latter, since the man hadn't died yet.

"Lord Fletcher!" he bellowed when he was close enough to be heard. *"We don't mean any harm to your people. On our word, we ask that you yield the castle, and no harm will come to them!"*

For a long, cold time, Fletcher eyed the man down. They both stood as still as stone, staring. He eventually replied. *"To whom do I speak?"*

"Julius Khavar, brother to the king, commander of the first contingent. Sent by King Delmar himself on covert orders."

"Esmond is the king here," Fletcher smirked, ruined with a frown. *"Why have you come?"*

"Like I said: to seize you and this outpost. Your people don't need to die."

Fletcher glanced around to the soldiers who stood on the battlements with him, then to the thousands in and around the fort. They all returned his look. *"It's our home you want to seize. Oceans will dry before we yield!"* Centaur men exploded with cheers, shooting their arms up into the air.

Julius was quick to turn his stallion, galloping back as he wore a sour face.

"They want to take our home!" Fletcher thundered, his voice shaking the fort's stone. *"Are we going to let them?"*

"Nay!" his army roared.

"I feel sorry for them, because I don't think they quite understand that. But they'll understand it soon. They'll understand what happens when they march into the Centaur's den. They'll understand what happens when you oppose the king... and when the sun rises on that field, it will shine to see a mountain of broken shells cracked with Centaur swords and arrows."

The fort erupted with cheers.

"Soldiers, are you ready to show them?!"

"Aye!" the land yelled.

"Archers, are you ready to shoot them?!"

"Aye!" the walls yelled.

Huuuuuuuuuuuuuuuuuuu. A warhorn sounded in the distance, soothing and mellow, igniting the Khavar's march.

"For the Pole!" he declared, having his men create a chorus. The outside defence broke into gallop. *"Archers!"* Fletcher echoed down the battlements. *"Nock your damn bows!"* A heartbeat passed. *"Draw!"* The thunder of hooves battled with the progressive *clonk* of heavy armour. Fletcher squinted as the gap between the two armies closed. Another heartbeat. *"Loose!"* Thousands of arrows propelled into the air as one like a swarm of flies: Fletcher's arrows. For a moment, they completely blocked the moon's blue light, before gravity yanked them down in one pull. The Khavars ceased their movement, transforming into a fist of shells. The fist caved in as it became feathered with broken bolts. The Centaur vanguard crumbled as if they had just galloped into a wall. Some tumbled off their horses, flying over the shield wall to be skewered by swords, while some were lucky enough to slow down. Blood spattered across the foremost Khavar shields. Few Khavars fell, but those who did had their position immediately replaced with another oversized shield. *Shit, what are they doing?* Like a hungry turtle, irregular Khavar brands jabbed out of the huge shell, slicing men and horses in two. They began to march again, exposing themselves to a few more successful Centaur riders. *"Nock!"* Fletcher remembered, snapping out of his confusion. *"Draw!"* He glanced at Sir Roswell, wincing as he fondled the hilt of his sword. *"Loose!"* Fletcher ordered, sending another wave to rain on them. They did the same thing: halting all movement to brave the swarm with a wall of shields.

"It's not working," Sir Roswell frowned. "My lord, you can't direct them."

Fletcher agreed, waiting for the Khavars to march again. *"Fire at will!"* he yelled.

That caught them, he saw, as the enemy stuttered to make a shield wall. A lot more attackers fell this time, but every time it seemed like the vanguard broke the Khavar's frontline, another was constructed with ease. They advanced closer and closer to Storm Tower, not because Fletcher's vanguard was defeated, but that most had been unhorsed or had fallen down the hills on either side. The rogue men that climbed back up caught some Khavars by surprise, but not enough to make a difference. The rest were ordered to retreat.

Fletcher's sight caught the first brigade to charge out of the fort. They carried lances and a galloping pace that was absent from the rest of the battle. *Perfect.* They almost made up for the lost men, and their charge was met with a lot more success than the initial, but the Khavar formation would just not break. Arrows continued to whizz past Fletcher's head, a quarter finding their way into enemy chests, and the rest finding thick shields. The fight was brightened with fallen torches, sending smoke and flames into the air as bodies and grass took light.

When the last of the Centaur vanguard had been swept from the battlefield, in charged the equos and squadrons. He had never seen the chevals work their magic before, but the sight was spectacular; the equos hurtled towards the Khavars like waves on a beach, firing a cluster of arrows into the enemy before washing back for another round. The chevals cracked their nine stringed whips around in the air, painting a movement array before their equo copied it. They *were* painters. They continued to sweep like brushes, impossible for the enemy to predict as there wasn't an angle an equo didn't attack from. It was surreal to witness, especially since most of the chevals Fletcher had seen about the fort for most of his life. Amazing as it was, no more arrows were finding their way into Khavar bodies than before, meeting their plated armour if said bolt was *lucky.* It was barely a fair trade, as every Khavar to fall, two Centaurs would get a dart in their neck, or chest, or leg. *Were they darts?* It was hard to tell. They flung some sort of small projectile from within their shield bunker.

The second brigade was released. It helped, but still, the enemy formation refused to break. *The Capricornians could be doing more*, Fletcher frowned as he noticed their poor effort at charging into the fray. Maybe they were just *that* dwarfed in skill compared to the equos. Most of the men in the equos managed to ride in and out of the battle unscathed, but the squadrons and Capricornians seemed quicker and quicker to fall to darts and blades. *I've lost more men by now, for sure.*

"*My lord!*" a voice called from the battlement's exit. It was Quintin Baxter, panting as he dashed up. He held his knees while he caught his breath. "We can't keep sending brigades so small," he panicked. "If you want to break their formation, we'll need our whole force to attack."

"We're losing more men than they are," Fletcher observed calmly, although a steady shake rocked his throat. "If we send them all, we'll have none left to defend."

"Yes, but as you said, if we break their front, it will leave them open for the archers."

Fletcher raked his scalp. "Send half. If their form doesn't break, retreat them immediately."

Quintin nodded, dashing back down.

"This is risky, my lord," Sir Roswell frowned.

"I know," Fletcher sighed.

A blink after Lord Baxter had left, out rode a sickening number of troops. *That's too many*, Fletcher realised, beginning to worry. They closed in on the Khavars, thundering towards their leaden trudge. *This is it. This is either the best, or the worst move of the battle.* Fletcher almost couldn't watch, squinting his eyes. *Clank!* Lances and shields and arrows and bodies rattled accordingly. The Khavar front fell in like dominoes, and the Centaurs ran in, every arrow finding an attacker.

"*Yes!*" Fletcher cheered, a grin on his face.

Screams and yells had doubled. The Khavars were losing more now. The attackers on the front broke into a clunky run, duelling with the defenders for what seemed like the first time. The sound of steel clattering pierced through the air, as the auburn grass turned red. Yet, the Centaurs only got so far. With a click of their claws, the Khavars built another wall, sending those in front to clear the way with mighty swipes that ended horse and Centaur life. They were quick to fall, being blasted with swift arrows, flinging them backwards, but when they fell, all that was left was the same haunting turtle shell.

"*Retreat!*" Quintin sounded from the gate as the wall was rebuilt. By then, darts and swords made it to more Centaurs than arrows to Khavars. Though, it looked like the Khavars had lost more overall.

Salvo's pit and the Antrum River bank had fallen men littered from each army. It was a tussle, impossible to know who was winning due to the dark night and the constant slashing. As for the main Khavar force, they remained composed, advancing dangerously close to the fort.

"Go get ready," Sir Roswell urged, grabbing Fletcher's shoulder. "I'll man the wall."

Fletcher nodded before racing down to the battlements. When he arrived at the gate yard, horses and men scrambled to get back into the fort. It was impossible to move without being shoved or pushed around. He could hardly breathe. It was a panicked, ruched mess, the clatter of men scuttling like rats as they tried to find their defence stances. *"Siege positions!"* and *"Shield wall!"* were commands constantly thrown by the generals. Fletcher hopped on his idle horse, trying his best to not knock over his men as he galloped up the fort.

The upper bailey was all but drained, only containing the occasional knight to gallop down. Fletcher glanced at his brother's window, to see if he was still watching. He wasn't. There wasn't even a light from his chamber. *Oh, gods, has he slipped out?*

A whistle rang through the courtyard, grabbing Fletcher's attention. It was Stig. Fletcher galloped towards him. "Good luck, Centaur," he said, holding out Fletcher's zircon bow.

Fletcher dismounted, taking the bow and quiver. "Thanks, Blackfist," he smiled, hopping back on his horse. "Time to test how good this thing is," he smirked, turning to race out.

Thankfully, upon returning to the gate yard, his troops were a lot more organised. The men had reformed order, a wall of bucklers of their own built safely behind the metal portcullis that separated the two armies. Arrows continued to fly through and from the fort, still mostly to find Khavar shields.

Sir Roswell caught Fletcher's eye, waving his arms around for openings in the enemy's shield wall. The prince ran up to his side again. "They're just standing there," Fletcher winced, looking down at the massive shell at his gates. "Do they not have ladders, siege towers?"

"Doesn't look like it," Sir Roswell frowned. "I don't know *what* they're doing."

The army stepped back slowly from the gates, making concurring grunts with each step they made. *Are they going to charge into the gate?* The Khavar darts stopped firing…

Huuuuuuuuuuuuuuuuuuuu. The same horn that sounded the start of the battle blew. Troy Larton's catapults flung gross boulders, bursting into a thousand pieces as they hit the gate and the walls. It was like they were all on a boat that had just hit land, every man on the battlements swaying in a drunken manner. Fletcher craned his neck to see who fired them. *Why are they firing already?! They haven't breached the gate yet! "Stand down! Stick to the plan!"* More boulders struck. The entrance crumbled, and the Khavars flooded the castle. Mayhem commenced. Fletcher, and everyone on the battlements fell with the wall. All around him, men died; Khavars to arrows, Centaurs to blades, and Capricornians... Fletcher felt sick, especially since he knew it was coming. He first thought *his* men were killing each other, but now he saw. Now he saw whose men manned those catapults. He bared his teeth. *Cowards*, he winced.

Darts flew into the necks of fallen archers around him, waking him abruptly from his rage. He glanced at Sir Roswell, already unloading bolts into the enemy as he blocked the darts with his buckler. *They aren't darts*, he realised, *they're crab claws.* Fletcher stood from the rubble, his head light, causing him to fall again. His fingers were smeared with blood when he tapped his head. His hands were trembling. Men whom he didn't know which side they fought scrambled around him, clashing swords. He stood again, managing to stay up. He pulled an arrow from his quiver, but his shot was weak. It barely came close to an enemy. He shot another; it was weaker. It fell timidly into the dirt. He stumbled to the wall's rubble, feeling the stone. *What is wrong with me?* he winced. He closed his eyes, his thudding heartbeat growing louder than the clangour around him. *I am not dying today. I am Fletcher Centaur. I am not dying today.* He opened his eyes to his zircon bow, the blue jewels reflecting the rippling fire around him. *The blood of the Sagittarius. I am the blood of the Sagittarius. Strength with a bow in hand. My blood is blue. The blood of the Sagittarius. I am Fletcher Centaur. I am the blood of the...*

Like a spell, a blue arrow appeared on his arm. He blinked to believe it. It was the mark of the Sagittarius, and it was on *his* arm, glowing with a radiant shine like the zircon he held. He stood, and in that moment, nerves seemed to disintegrate. It felt like his lungs expanded, the smoke and stifling crowds suddenly becoming painlessly breathable. He began to fire arrows with impossible trajectories, sparking with a blue flame as they flew. He could *feel* his blue blood pumping fiercely around his body, filling his veins with a fiery warmth. He could see, as each and every arrow effortlessly found its way to a new target, tearing through shells and shields with ease. He could hear, as life began to unravel around him by the facile order of his fingertips. In that moment, Fletcher was no boy; he was a bow.

ESMOND X
-Grip-

H e's lying, he has to be," Tobi insisted. "No way could bandits *steal* poison and citrine in such a sum."

"Stranger things have happened," Esmond Centaur said, placing his goblet on the marble table.

"Indeed," Hugo smirked, "like the existence of Lord Edward Cancer."

The room burst into laughter.

"Leave him alone, this place is still foreign to him," the king defended, albeit behind a smirk of his own.

"He told his guard to check if his food was poisoned," Tobi reminded, taking a swig of wine.

"He has a right to be suspicious," Esmond shrugged, "it's not every day you're forced to eat and drink with people who used to be your foes."

"Used to be," Tobi frowned. "Suspicious minds breed fickle souls. If he still can't see us as *allies,* then..."

"He will, in time," Esmond nodded.

"Time we don't have," Sir Orion said grimly. "Not if the country starves to death before he makes up his mind."

Esmond sighed and reached for his goblet, swashing the wine around. He was joined by those he saw as his *'merry'* councillors, the few who always promised a lively time: Tobi Sparks, Hugo Lane, Orion Reade, and Elliot Moss. Though, since Vincent's visit, jesting seemed to be far from everyone's mind. Come to think of it, it had been like that for moons. For too many moons. *Why?* Esmond thought. *We're making so much progress.*

Although not the easiest to settle, Edward, the Venusian embassy, was doing everything he could to become a part of Jupitan life. Not that he needed to try; without his suspicion, Edward was about as lovable and sharp as every councillor around him. Though, with what Tobi had said, that suspicion suddenly seemed larger than it was.

"It's true," Tobi replied eventually. "I really think you should call a meeting, Esmond. We haven't had a *real* one since the Thunder Moon."

"What good would it do?" Esmond winged. "There's nothing *wrong* with the world other than the harvest, and we won't make crops suddenly grow by sitting around a table, aimlessly blathering."

"Nothing wrong? What about Lutum?" Sir Orion frowned.

"The country is starving. They'll do anything to feed themselves," Esmond sighed. "Regardless, I've sent Lord Goldwyn to spurn them."

"It's a large force," Tobi pointed out.

"Lucky if they're subdued," Hugo agreed.

"They won't be the last to arise," Sir Orion muttered.

"Oh, what do you want me to do? Fight human nature?!" Esmond barked, irritation finally stabbing him. "I can't *make* food grow on trees. I can't *make* people eat what I want... I can't do *anything*. I'm a... powerless king." He cast his goblet across the table, defeated. His face felt flushed.

The room was silent.

"Look, can we not talk about it?" Esmond winced weakly. "I can't right now. I summoned you all so we could forget about that."

"He's right," Tobi agreed, filling Esmond's spilled cup. "No point dwelling."

Orion clearly had more to say, but he washed his words down with wine and remained silent.

Like a blight, Darius Boyd, head of arms, marched into the tavern, two scrolls in hand. "My king," he bowed, taut as always.

"What do you want, Boyd?" Esmond asked lightly.

"Word from Selerborn and Ignis, my king," he said.

"And Lord Waker is too busy?" Esmond grimaced.

"It's important, my king. Lord Waker asked me to give them to you."

"Give them here," Sir Orion sighed, standing. He ambled to Darius, plucking the scrolls before nodding for Lord Boyd's leave. He wandered back, slumping into his seat and kicking up his feet. With a *snap*, the red Horncurve seal broke and the letter unravelled. "Oh, gods," Orion sighed.

There had never been so much boredom in the knight's voice. "It's Lord Riley. He needs reinforcements. Can't control his own people."

"*I* can't even control my people," Esmond winced. "Does it say why?"

Orion shook his head. "No, but it's bad. Every day, more riots. He says he fears a civil war."

Esmond frowned. "We can't send troops. We'll need as many as we have when Lunarpass revolts."

"*If* Lunarpass revolts," Orion noted.

"Esmond is right, Orion," Tobi said, "took five of our garrison to stop a tussle the other day. We haven't seen fights as bad since... since ever," he chuckled.

"No, I agree," Sir Orion admitted, "it just seems like Selerborn needs our men *more*."

The king snickered. "Why would you want to help the Horncurves anyway? One happened to kill your eldest son, Orion."

Orion regarded the king with double the scorn. "And paid the price."

"It's not likely our troops would make a difference," Elliot suggested, trying to ease the tension in his relaxed tone. "It'll take most of a moon to make it to Selerborn. By the looks of it, they need men now."

Esmond nodded. "We need to make sure the rebels *know* they're against the crown. That might deter them at the very least. How about we send a spokesperson? Someone to spread fear of the royal army's *wrath.*"

"Better than nothing," Sir Orion agreed, breaking the second seal, the gold lion of Lyrderyn. He scanned the papyrus, eyes widening. His slumped back straightened.

"What is it?" Tobi asked.

"My king, it's..." Orion stuttered.

"Yes?"

"Asher is gone," the knight winced. "With Princess Lyssa, they've... vanished."

His councillors examined Esmond with anxious eyes. *With Princess Lyssa*, he smiled at his cup before raising it and taking a quaff.

"My king?" Hugo frowned.

"Tell Goldwyn he needn't worry," Esmond grinned. "Kings run away all the time..."

"Why is that funny?" Orion asked, wrinkling his brow.

Esmond shook his head, but couldn't shake off his grin.

At that point, Darius Boyd stormed in with more haste than before.

"Back again, Boyd?" Esmond observed lightly.

"You had best come with me, my king," Darius frowned. "It's Lord Edward."

Out of all the things to leave his firm mouth, trouble with their honoured embassy seemed like the worst. Esmond's pride washed from his face like water washes dirt, and he followed Darius out of the tavern.

The day was darkening, and the lunar lights were slowly turning on. The Lunar Tavern was on the edge of the higher city, so fretting wasn't a part of the king's mind as far as the hint of *trouble* was described, but after mounting his horse and following Darius down the streets, it became evident that ruckus belonged to the *lower* city instead.

Esmond thought he had done a good job to appease his people of Edward's role. Silence wasn't normal for announcements like that, but the king trusted them to speak up if they had a problem with it. *Maybe they're speaking up now.* He tightened his grip on the reins. *I can't let them take it out on him. 'If he dies, consider our peace to die also'.*

As they closed in on the crowds, it was surprising that clamour was absent, and instead replaced by a steady, hushed babel. Still, it was a worryingly huge crowd. Traders and citizens at the edge of the throng dropped their fruit baskets and clothes to see what was happening. It was difficult for Esmond to see, even though he was a horse above the league of people.

They galloped down into the lower city, and the crowds were quick enough to notice, and parted like waves; both horses adjusted into a trot as people grew slower to. After a time of scanning, Esmond noticed the inner movement. As they advanced, the crowd's attention pivoted towards the king, and Esmond repaid their confused stares with glances, equally as flummoxed. *At least they're not angry,* he thought.

Edward Cancer was walking as a common man would, admiring the city as the crowds refused to meet his grey eyes. He had fewer guards than normal, armour and weapons non-existent. He smiled when he noticed Esmond. "My king," he bowed, "is everything okay?"

Esmond frowned to a shrugging Darius. "Yes, um…" He looked back to the lean lord. "What are you doing?"

"I thought I'd have a wander, my king," he smiled, strolling slowly.

"…In the lower city… with no guards…"

Edward looked around. "Your people seem friendly enough. I felt like bringing an army with me might frighten them."

Amusement crept onto Esmond's face. *He has balls.* The king squinted. *Is he making a statement, or is he completely oblivious?* It was difficult to tell. "Do you mind if I walk with you?"

"An honour, my king," Edward smiled, falling into step with Esmond. "I don't know how dangerous you think your city is, but… I'd like to think that my extensive time in exile has given me a strong judgement."

"That doesn't paint a very good picture of your home," Esmond noted curiously.

He shook his head. "My home is wonderful. I'm convinced the Belt of Cancer is the most serene place in Austellus." He looked ahead. "I'm talking about the Stingers."

"That's still not a good picture," Esmond said.

"If I had come to paint falsely, then I don't think I'd serve you very well," Edward smiled back.

"I think Lord Vincent would disagree."

"Lord Vincent is not here." Their curious eyes met. His grey eyes were like shells, shielding what he actually felt and thought. Esmond wanted to know more, but it seemed like Lord Edward was already examining the king. "Do you mistrust him?"

"I don't know," Esmond sighed, looking down. "I guess it's the easiest answer not to. Answers are what I need to stay sane right now."

For the first time, a shred of feeling seeped through Edward's eyes. They were sad, sympathetic. "King Delmar couldn't hurt a fly," he said.

"So I've been told," Esmond nodded.

Edward looked around the city for his next words. "I… don't agree with a lot of what Vincent does and thinks, but it's safe to assume he's telling the truth, if that helps."

"That's the annoying thing," Esmond admitted. "I do." He looked to the lord with intrigue. "You don't agree with him?" he asked.

Edward shook his head softly. "He's resentful, jealous, doesn't know when to let things go."

As I saw. "It's good King Delmar has people like you to ground him."

"Had," Edward corrected. "As soon as I spoke a different opinion, I got kicked off the council."

"What?" Esmond winced. "You're the king's brother by law."

Edward nodded, tittering. "And still, I got kicked out."

"You must have had quite an extreme opinion," Esmond suggested.

"No," Edward smirked. "Not even *bickering* is tolerated by King

Delmar." He shook his head. "The truth of it, the king is a puppet for Vincent. He'll skin me for saying it, but it's true. Whatever order the king makes has Vincent's words behind it."

"So, why would you have me trust him?"

Edward pursed his lips. "He's deranged, but he's not a liar. All he cares about is legacy and image. I'm sure he knows that lying would kill that image. If not from me, then from the many who know the truth."

"It won't kill his legacy, though."

Edward shrugged. "Maybe," he said, before stopping to turn around where their paths split. "Well, it was nice talking to you, my king. I'd best make my way back to the Sphaera before it gets dark."

Esmond nodded. "Actually, I was just sharing a few drinks with some of the council. We haven't eaten yet; you could join us if you'd like?"

Edward glanced to the Sphaera. "Umm, today I'll think to pass, my king," he said softly. "I haven't had wine in gods know how long, I wouldn't know how it would rest."

"That's part of the fun, isn't it?" Esmond smirked.

"I'll share mead a later time, my king," Edward smiled. "Definitely later. I enjoy talking to you,"

"As do I," Esmond smiled back. "Then, enjoy your night, Edward."

Edward held his grin and bowed before sauntering away. Seeing Vincent in that new light almost added a skew to Esmond's walk as he trudged back to the Lunar Tavern. *'Whatever order the king makes has Vincent's words behind it'.* That would mean Vincent was responsible for Edward's dismissal, unless Delmar really *was* that stubborn. *Doesn't seem like it. Delmar seems like a pushover.* Esmond snickered. *Why would Vincent do that to Edward?* he frowned. *Does he not trust him? Why would he send an embassy he doesn't trust?* Even though Edward had advised to believe Vincent, the more Esmond thought, the more he felt that belief dwindle like a flame in the wind. *Vincent has nothing to lose by losing someone he distrusts... other than a second chance at peace.*

The chatter in the Lunar Tavern whizzed past Esmond's ears as he slowly returned to his seat. He stared at nothing as his thought carried him.

"You okay, Es?" Orion asked.

"Um, yeah, sure," Esmond nodded, bouncing his eyes around.

"What was that all about?" Tobi asked, giving a nod to the door.

"Oh, nothing," he smirked. "Boyd can be... melodramatic."

"Cheers to that," Tobi grinned, raising his goblet, finding Elliot's to clink with.

"Where's Edward now?" Orion frowned.

"Back at the Sphaera; he didn't want to share our company," Esmond mocked.

"Don't take it personally, my king, I'm sure he hates all of us equally," Hugo smiled, pausing whatever he was writing to speak.

"Or perhaps just you, Hugo," Elliot smirked, sprawled back in his chair, "since you said his existence was *strange*."

Tobi tittered. "Every jape you make is enough for that much, Hugo."

Hugo raised his hands, smiling.

"Are you sure you're ok, my king?" Orion asked again, observing Esmond's stiff face.

Esmond glanced at his *Avail*, then to the others, all sharing a look of slight concern. "Hunger," the king smirked, shaking his head, "the cooks half take a century in this damned place." Sir Orion's face was unchanged. Esmond frowned. "What makes you think I'm not?"

Orion's eyes narrowed. "In all the years I've known you, Esmond, I've never seen you to be a bloody liar." The other's mouths dropped. "Why are you hiding from us? We're your council."

"Hiding what?" Esmond muttered.

"Don't, Esmond," Orion frowned. "You clearly know what happened to Asher. I care for that boy too. And you said earlier 'let's forget about the country' so we can relax, but now you're sulking again…" Orion's face couldn't mask his distress, his dark eyebrows furrowing deep lines that weren't there before. "We're *your* councillors and you're not even allowing us to help; so please, tell us what's wrong."

Esmond took a long sigh. A smile pulled up his face. "Vincent's most likely gaming us, he kicked Edward off his council, so he *clearly* doesn't care about his life as much as he would have me believe, I haven't seen *any* of my family in more than a moon, my closest friends have been *murdered* by order of a man I'm now meant to break bread with, raids by gods know who are still making sure *peace* isn't a luxury anyone can have, and in case you hadn't noticed, those same people are still *starving to death*. Do you want me to write a fucking list or can you remember that next time?"

Sir Orion mouthed words that had no sound. He dropped his gaze.

"Like I said, I summoned you all to forget," Esmond said grimly. "One night where we could all go back to the biggest worry being the temperature of Elder Marcarius's soup." He snickered. "Can I not even have that?" The men stayed quiet. Esmond winced, standing. "Fuck it," he sighed, taking a thick swallow of wine as he strolled hopelessly towards the corner staircase.

No one bothered to chase him, and that was probably for the best. He stood alone on the Lunar Tavern's overly lavish balcony, completed with a golden railing with tips like that of a crown. All his weight was pressed against it as he stared out to the city. The setting sun made it look like Lunarpass was ablaze, a friendly orange painted across the sky. Sun was reflecting off every surface at once: glass domes and sculptures, spire and tower tips, the armour of the city's garrison. It was beautiful, and almost made Esmond forget his situation. He took another swig of wine.

Close to two goblets had been emptied before the king had company again, by no one other than his *First Avail.* Sir Orion mirrored Esmond in drinking, saying nothing to ruin the view.

"Asher let it slip that Hew knew why he was leaving," Esmond said eventually, gluing his eyes to the horizon. "Neither of them told me because I didn't ask, but I gathered that Hew must have seen him and Lyssa one night. I knew what he felt for her; Asher has never been very good at hiding feelings. I found it funny because it was exactly what I did with Semira; I ran away with her too. Like father, like son..."

"How do you know?" Orion frowned.

"I don't," Esmond sighed, drinking again.

Sir Orion tittered. "Makes sense. Asher was always so unruly. It made Jovian jealous, you know."

"Really?" Esmond smirked. "Asher wouldn't stop banging on about how well Jovian dealt with pressure. He would always curse himself for getting flustered."

Orion chuckled, shaking his head. His smile was slow to fade. "Thank you... for telling me."

Esmond only nodded, continuing to sip at his goblet. After a time, he winced. "What do I do?" he sighed. "I have a north on the verge of a civil war, an east on the verge of an uprising, a south on the verge... Is it even a war? I don't know what the fuck I'm against."

"You're not a powerless king, Esmond," Orion said, turning away from the view. "If anything, you have more influence than any king before you." Esmond looked down at the railing, gripping it tighter. Orion placed his hand on Esmond's shoulder, pulling up the king's attention. "Don't waste it by not caring."

Esmond nodded, agreeing.

EVA VIII
-Snare-

Not long had passed before she was caught. She hadn't expected to strike the same luck for a second time, but hoped to all the same. She woke to a rough, steel plated hand shaking her body. "Girl... girl..." the man whispered harshly.

Eva Centaur leapt back, whacking the man with her foot by accident.

"Shit!" he wailed, staggering back, holding his bloodied nose. He drew a sword. "I'll kill you for that, you little squatter!"

"Marvin, calm down!" another guard shouted, holding Marvin's arm. "Look at her, she's frightened."

Marvin's face changed from anger to sorrow. Eva could only imagine how she looked: her eyes as wide as a scared cat's. "What's your name, girl?" Marvin asked, in a wry voice due to his pinched nose.

"E-Eva," she blurted, panicking.

"She looks like a runaway, mate," said the unnamed guard. "Should we take her back to Lady Violet?"

"No, I-I know Idris, please, let me see him-"

"Definitely a runaway," Marvin nodded. "Listen, Eva, I know your first battle is scary, but you're a trainee, and belong in Lady Violet's *equo*."

"No, you don't understand, let me- get off of me! Let go!" The two men pulled her from the carriage, dragging her by the arms. Eva kicked at the air, unable to reach the ground. She bared her teeth. "I'm not a trainee, put me down!"

"This is for your own good, girl. As soon as we get to Aurdrive, you'll be eaten alive if you're in the wrong *equo*," said the other guard.

Her attempts to free herself weren't met with success. She gave up with a moody sigh after she was carried a couple meters from the camp. *Shit. What am I gonna do now?* She didn't even know what she was going to do in the first place, but being thrown into an *equo* didn't help with figuring it out.

Lady Violet looked a lot more beautiful a few days ago; travel did no good for her. She sat alone by a campfire, attacking a charred bunny corpse with dogged bites. Her onyx hair had twice the number of knots, styled fairly in a way that roped down her back. "My lady," Marvin bowed. "We found one of yours in the whetstone carriage."

Violet spun around, grease decorating her cheekbones. She frowned as she examined. "What's your name?" she asked, her breath full of wine.

"Eva," she said, staring into Violet's regal eyes.

She continued to frown, then shook her head. "Thanks." Violet turned to her bunny again.

The men let go of Eva, letting her plunge into the sandy mud. "Don't come back, alright?" said Marvin before leaving.

Eva looked around. Violet was paying her no heed; if she wanted to, she could run back to Idris, to Lunarpass, wherever, no one was stopping her. Tents and smoking fires were littered in clusters around the gritty hills, no more than three guards patrolling each *equo*. The furthest *equo* was as far as the eye could see, a small orange flame in the distance, tall brown Equuleus banners decorating the air like the rest. With help from a breeze, Eva realised how cold she was, her breath and body shaking.

"You'll freeze if you stand there all night," Violet said. "We've never had nights so cold."

Eva nodded, creeping to the furthest log bench from the fire. She observed the other firepits, at least ten girls and boys surrounding each, laughing and conversing and drinking. The smell of food hit the air. Her stomach rumbled.

"Hungry?" Violet asked, smirking, passing a bronzed bunny. Eva savoured each mouthful like it was her first time eating. "How long have you been in that carriage?"

"Since before we left," Eva replied, chunks flying from her mouth. "Those guards are rubbish."

Violet chuckled. "Impressive," she said. "What did I do to make you run away?"

"It's not you," Eva assured, too immersed in her dinner to think of a response.

She only nodded, taking a swig of wine. "I wouldn't care if it was. Most people think it's a joke to see a woman leading an *equo*," she sighed. "I'm not even meant to be here; these people were Robin's until he packed up and left..." She slowly smiled. "That was a massive joke too; 'fear not, Violet, I will always cherish you the most, oh actually, nevermind, let me just legitimise all your siblings'..." She frowned. "Do you know what that means?"

Eva swallowed her morsel. "They can inherit?"

"Oh, they can inherit," she laughed. "I can see father thinking long and hard about the decision." Her face then spoke pain, creases cutting around her pretty eyes. "I was at his bedside every day after he fell ill. I cleaned out his shit, I fetched his meals, I handled his letters, all while Idris and all my other lovely brothers were *gallivanting* about the world. What do they get for abandoning their father at his weakest? Titles, castles, lordships, armies... You know what I get?"

"Nothing?" Eva said, feeling too much pity to have another bite.

"Damn right," she nodded. *"There's* something you shouldn't forget, kid; you see power and prospect together, you've got to take it, and live it. You never know when it's going to be snatched away from you."

Eva frowned with her. "You have an *equo...*"

Violet tittered. "Here," she said, passing her wine skin. "Finish it. Eat what you can. We've got a long day tomorrow."

"Thank you... m-my lady," she remembered.

"Night, Eva," Violet smiled.

◆━━━◆

It didn't take long for Eva not to mind her situation. Riding was more fun than tiring, and she was happy to join Violet's side when she admitted to not having any *equo* training. Her abysmal attempt at the trainee exercises only seemed to further cement that; turns out, being good at archery and riding meant little in the world of high cavalry. In any event, she took the humiliation well. *I'm not here to be judged by a bunch of boring trainees.* All she wanted was to know if Idris would be alright, if they'd win, if they'd get enough food to feed their people. Nothing about *her* safety ever crossed her mind.

She would sleep on the ground every night, just outside Violet's tent. Sometimes the fire would burn long enough to see daylight, but most nights were cold. *This is nothing like the stories,* she thought on one of those nights. *Where are the sweltering heats? The unbreathable sandstorms?* It seemed farfetched to believe it got to that extreme deeper in the desert, a midday sun meeting a mild temperature at best. Either way, the short-sleeved, furless summer clothes Idris had given her were ill-suited for this type of weather. *I want my fur cloaks back,* she thought, consequently thinking of home and her siblings. Guessing what they were doing now was a concept that grew more difficult by the day.

During their journey, they passed many towns, forts, outposts, sometimes even gaining a few horsemen by doing so. Eva didn't understand why they didn't just raid those ones, instead of going all the way to Aurdrive, and Violet explained because they were all under the Equuleus's protection, sworn to them. She said that Lord Humbert Elies, the Lord of Aurdrive Town was sworn to Lyonis, and that Ayden Lyonis had no way of fighting back, since even he couldn't navigate an army through the Red Sierra. "What about the Lyrderyns?" Eva asked, to which Violet replied that 'if the Lyrderyns come marching against Lutum, it would mean the end of the Canicule. We're what they need to stay afloat'. As if it wasn't grave enough already, it suddenly seemed all the more so. Eva didn't want to be watching when the Canicule came to an *end.*

Nonetheless, Eva continued with Violet all the way to Aurdrive. They arrived in the early afternoon, observing the settlement, safely hidden atop and behind the Red Hills. It was *huge*, not alike its name at all since it looked more like a city. It was as compact as could be, most buildings conjoined in some way. There was a spring in the distance, falling into a sparkly river, and the Red Hills hugged the settlement like walls, almost acting like a defence if they weren't being used to conceal the Sagittarian armies. Paired with that, Aurdrive had *actual* walls, for a change, despite it being a stretch to call them that; stones meshed with steel and wood surrounded the town, shooting out thick pikes like the ones in Lutum. The wall was scarcely as tall as a mounted knight. From atop the hills, it almost seemed like a *hurdle.*

Violet was with the other *chevals*, Idris, Apollo, and Ivor, in a tent to draw up battle plans while the armies readied themselves. The *clunk* of greaves and *rattle* of arrows rang all around her as men armed themselves and got into position, and Eva just sat idly, picking at her nails. After a while of sharp stares from sweaty soldiers, she went to pet her horse. The spare gelding had black fur and a thick black forelock, and was the biggest thing Eva had ever sat upon. The Equuleans *must* have done something to them, as the stallions back home were never bred quite as great.

"What's up, Scout?" she smiled as he nuzzled Eva's hand. "What are you thinking about, eh?"

Scout stayed silent, enjoying the feel of Eva's hand. *I wish I could keep you,* she thought, happily, *you're so strong.* His head shot up, snorting at the sound of a thudding gallop. The rider dismounted in front of the red tent, rushing inside. A couple of heartbeats later, out ran the *chevals* calling for battle positions. *"They've seen us!"* Idris bellowed. *"Mount your horses, find your equo!"* People began scrambling, finding their footing, throwing on armour.

Violet ran to the top of the hill, looking down on Aurdrive. Eva met her side.

"They've seen us but they're not attacking," she said. *"Come on, move it!"* She shouted back.

"What are they doing?"

"Preparing." There was a quiver in her voice. "Eva, stay with me."

They couldn't have chosen a more difficult terrain to form an army upon. Eva found it fatiguing enough to concentrate on not colliding with the thousands of horsemen that whizzed by, not that the rough hills helped to see them any better. Nevertheless, the four *equos* somehow formed in a matter of minutes, clustered in huge packs. Idris rode to the front of them all, raising his nine stringed whip high above his head. *"On horseback we drive!"* he yelled.

"On horseback to conquer!" the armies thundered back.

Idris painted a circle with his whip before lashing it to the ground. The *whh-pssssh* that echoed through the hills sent shivers down Eva's spine. In response, the first *equo* charged down. Apollo's was close to follow, his *equo* creating a chorus of thundering hooves. Eva had never seen the oversized beasts break into full gallop before, so witnessing them tear up the soil with each *thud* and with such speed was something magical. Remarkably, despite the steep incline, each horse's footing was so sure as to not trip or fall.

Aurdrive was taken by enough surprise, but by the time the *equos* were halfway down the hill, the defenders had their armies stationed: pikemen and foot soldiers packing close to the miserly wall. They wore sigils Eva somewhat recognised, for whatever reason: a flaming spear in a rugged rock, atop a yellow background. It was more memorable than the Equuleus's mess of brown and orange, horses clashing in mud.

Ivor's *equo* took off, and Violet's was the only one left. "When are you going?" Eva asked.

"I'm hoping we won't have to," she said, nervously shaking her knee.

Movement within the town ceased, the pikemen firmly holding their weapons. Idris's and Apollo's *equos* continued to charge at two different sides, hooting and howling. Idris cracked his whip, making archers at the rear of his *equo* squat on their horses, load their bows, and send arrows flying into enemy soldiers. The Elies had fewer archers, next to none on foot, but had many placed in the numerous archer towers dotted around the town. They began firing as soon as they could, with moderate success. The arrows sent horsemen flying back with extreme velocity, somehow not disrupting the charge of the rest.

What are they going to do? Eva frowned when they didn't slow down, getting dangerously close to the palisade. The fortifications weren't amazing, but were definitely enough to stop them… or so she thought. Much to her amusement, the stallions struck the pikes with such immense strength, they burst open into a hundred splinters of wood. The horses at the front barely received *scratches. How by gods?* she smiled. Once the two sides shattered, the slaughter began. Blood and bodies met the shattered wood and muddy detritus on the ground. Equuleus arrows found the necks of pikemen, and pierced effortlessly through their armour. Eva's eyes kept gravitating towards the flicking whip of Idris Equuleus, still firing his share of arrows. *I've never seen him fight before*, she realised, as the man quickly manoeuvred his horse to kick an enemy in the back.

In rode Ivor's *equo*, and it seemed like the nail in the coffin. The Elies frontline was all but obliterated, and the horses stormed the city like a mass of bugs. Still, there were more Equuleus casualties inside than out; many horsemen had to resort to melee, or received an arrow before they got the chance to… but Idris was completely fine and that was all that mattered.

"*Shit*," Violet spat.

Eva looked to her, then to where she gaped. *Oh, gods.* A pack of lions, ploughing over the horizon line. Golden Lyrderyn banners, glistening and beating in the wind. Fully plated brutes of riders, armed with maces and curved spears and battle axes and cutlasses. The force refused to stop growing.

"We have to go," Violet whispered eventually.

"What?"

"None of my brothers can see the force, we have to go down and warn them." She swallowed. "Eva, you *need* to stay here."

"But-"

"Eva, please." She galloped to the front of the troop. *"Alright, you sorry twats!"* She cracked her whip. *"Get a move on!"* They cheered and broke into charge.

It was too much to process. Eva trotted after them, enough to see what was going on. Each Equuleus death from then on seemed more intense. She would wince at every arrow fired, every blade struck, every horse felled. The Lyrderyns were mostly horseless and clunky, but still charged with haste. Violet's *equo* would make it to the town before them, but to retreat everyone alive seemed like a big ask. *Maybe she doesn't mean to retreat them? Maybe she means to fight?* Eva worried. She looked down to her shaking hands, grasping the reins tightly. *'Eva you need to stay here, please'.* She shook her head. *I can't stay here.* Idris was advancing to the centre of the city, chopping down Elies soldiers with constant overhead hacks. He was oblivious. Oblivious to the horde of lions that charged straight for him. Oblivious of the death that was coming.

Eva winced, and cast Scout into a gallop. *"Idris!"* she screamed, knowing full well he wouldn't hear. The wind attacked her face and swept her hair back. Scout's gallop rumbled through her body. It seemed like her heart beat harder each house Idris rode past. By the time the Lyrderyns were just over halfway down their hill, Violet had reached the city. Her *equo* scattered through the fray, yelling and receiving pikes to their steadfast bucklers. The outer force were quick to win or forfeit their duel to race out, joining the few who heard first. Apollo took notice of the calls, attempting to turn his *equo*. Idris remained oblivious. The Lyrderyns were not thirty seconds away. *No.* Tears shrouded Eva's eyes, swept away by her hand and the wind. Most of Ivor's *equo* was soon safe, far away in the opposite direction from where the Lyrderyns came. Half of Apollo's also seemed fine, only just leaving the city. But Idris… *Gods dammit! "Idris!"* she screamed again as she raced past the fragmented palisade.

She grabbed Violet's attention. *"No!"* she yelled angrily.

Arrows whizzed past Eva's horse and head, but it didn't deter her gallop, nor did it take her attention off Idris. *"Idris!"* she screamed a third time, slowing down as she approached where the fray grew most bloody.

There were yells of pain, grunts from swings, shrieks from horses, screeches from swords. It was enough noise to hurt her ears. It was enough noise to make one deaf, yet Idris heard her call. He turned around, the man highest on his horse. His mud and blood-spattered face creased and dropped in despair. He couldn't stare for long, as he had to split a swordsman who tried to challenge him. Violet grabbed Eva's reins, yanking Scout away from battle. *"No, stop it!"* she cried, leaping from the horse and dodging the Equuleans that were fleeing.

'Idiot', she could see Violet mouth as she turned. Everyone around her was running in some direction. Eva was the only one running in the opposite. It made her lose her breath. There were too many. She was going to be trampled. She closed her eyes, and ran faster. A man *thumped* into her, sending her off course. One rider veered his horse so they wouldn't meet. Another man, this time an Elies soldier, slammed into her, sending her dizzy. Her run then stumbled. She met a fourth, slamming into her stomach and winding her. Her breath had nearly all ran away. She fell to her knees, digging into the mud. The noise around her became faint. Her pain eased. All she felt were tears on her cheeks. *What have I done? I'm such an idiot. I'm dying an idiot.*

An arm clasped her, raising her atop a horse. He joined her. She opened her eyes to see Idris Equuleus, fiercely kicking their stallion into gallop. The noise became loud. Her pain throbbed. They were one of the last riders in the city, charging down men who tried to stop them, racing past arrows before they could hit. Eva looked back, seeing the Lyrderyns sweeping stragglers, filling the red city with gold. Ivor's *equo* was completely out of sight, Apollo's *equo* far up the hills, Violet's lagged behind with Idris's *equo*, saving the wounded and holding back the hungry defenders. The order of the armies was broken. Idris and Eva were at the back of everyone, but were closing in on the flattened wall. They were almost out.

Idris mewled and slouched as an arrow pierced his leg. Eva cried out. A Lyrderyn force swept in front of them, cutting off half of both *equos.*

Another arrow flew into their horse's neck, and they both tumbled to the splintered ground. Idris seized Eva tightly. Lyrderyns careered towards them, holding up thick weapons and sending deep yells into the air. "Why didn't you listen?" Idris wept, clenching Eva's arms tightly enough to burst.

Another arrow careered into Idris's side, and he winced with pain. *"No!"* Eva sobbed, holding him. *"I'm sorry, I'm so sorry! It's all my fault!"*

Idris looked up to her, and slowly placed his trembling hand on her face. "No. *I'm* sorry... I couldn't save you..." He gave a sad smile, and an ugly mace struck the back of his head, sending him flying.

"IDRIS!" she screamed, the sharpest she ever had. She ran to his body. Blood filled his dented skull.

"STOP!" called a man, a moment before the Lyrderyn soldiers turned their maces towards Eva. *"Don't touch her!"*

It was Sir Cedric Fysher. Eva's eyes were almost too flooded to tell who it was. "Eva?" he frowned in disbelief, kneeling next to her. "What the hell are you doing here? Has your father come?" She couldn't respond, holding her face as she cried.

Why do I never listen? He'd be alive if I just fucking listened! This is what I get. This is what I get for being such a bloody idiot.

"Get her to Ignis, now," he said to the men behind. "Before she gets herself killed."

The men nodded and grabbed her. *"No!"* she wailed, grappling onto Idris's leathers. She held on until it tore.

ATHENA IV
-Affray-

It was difficult to get away from an argument. Once she thought one was over, another would start. Not even in her chambers was she free; the shouting seeped through her walls like it was made of paper, seeped through her hands like they didn't exist at all.

"You went too far, Riley! You didn't have to say that!" Emily yelled.

"I said the *truth*. If he can't handle that, he's not a man!"

"If he can't handle that? He's your son! Since when did you become Sigmund?"

"*Don't* talk about my father like that! He was a good man!"

"You hated him and he hated you, don't deny it! Is that *really* what you want for Marcus?"

"Yes! I want him to *thrive*. But he's not gonnae do that if he cries every time reality hits him!"

"Oh, well that's not what you'd have said a moon ago. You pushed him away! He's *always* wanted to go on a raid!"

"After what he did?! You would *really* let him go on a raid if he can't follow orders?"

"No! But I wouldn't scream how incompetent he is in his face either!"

"He needed to hear it! Better me than some stuck-up lord!"

Athena Horncurve anymore couldn't take it. She left her chambers, and the voices grew louder. "Can you *please fucking stop!*" she yelled, louder than both. Her parents froze, staring at her like frightened sheep.

Luther was drinking in the corner, half asleep. "He's gone," she winced. "It's both your faults." As soon as Athena left the room, they started again.

"Ah, nice one, Riley, push away our daughter too."

"What are you talking about? You started all of this!"

"You started it when you didn't take Marcus's side!"

Athena covered her ears again, running away from the voices. *I need my workshop. I need to create.*

Cadmus had left for the raid this morning, and Athena had never missed him more. It was nice having someone to empathise with, despite how sulky and silent he had been since his twin left. It was also strange seeing him sail off down the Twin River, but she preferred him doing what he wanted rather than getting wasted in brothels every night. As for Marcus, she still couldn't believe he was gone. *Give it a day, two days, three*, she thought. Before long, weeks passed like sand through an hourglass. *Could he have really survived out there for so long?* she wondered. For all that Marcus was, he wasn't incapable. He could handle himself, and maybe that was all the hope she needed. Though, that didn't stop her wishing for things to be as they were when Sigmund was still kicking.

"Off again, my lady?" Sir Harold Smyth asked at the Cenkeep gate. He was the eldest in the ram's guard, white whiskers scaling down his body. Riley would normally appoint two of the ram's guard to the duty of guarding the Cenkeep, but Sir Harold was so skilled he would often guard it alone. Come to think of it, Sir Harold was the *only* one on duty since Marcus had left.

"They won't stop arguing," she winced. "Over stupid things as well."

He gave a sullen nod. "Most arguments *are* over stupid things," he said. "My time in Sigmund's ram's guard taught me that."

She smiled for a second. "How would you tame him? Some people say you're the only one who could."

"It's all in emotions, princess; your grandfather was a very emotional man. But the way he showed that to the world, with fury and anger, it disguised him." He shrugged. "Perhaps I'm the only one who saw that."

Athena nodded, thinking about Riley and Emily and Marcus. "More of us should have."

Sir Harold agreed with a grunt. "Don't be long, my lady," he said hesitantly, "I don't like how crowded these streets are."

"I can blend in," she assured, "don't worry."

"Go then. Be quick."

Her workshop was dark, like the midday sky, and hadn't been used in days because she was too frightened to disobey Riley's orders after his outburst. It didn't bother her anymore, though; the more she grew used to her father's consistent yelling, the less threatening it seemed.

When the time came to work, she already knew what she was going to make, taking a thin strip of black steel and dropping it on the table. She had never made a sword before, but had seen her brothers fail at it enough to know what they did wrong. Bending metal was a thing Angelo loved to do too, spending half his time in the corner nudging casts into the tiny kiln. *I wonder how he's doing in Mea Minor? I hope he's still inventing.* She felt the diamond necklace she had made for them both, for a time, forgetting where she was. *A hazelnut without her shell.*

She didn't want a big sword, just a dagger really. Something to keep her safe, if and when she had to protect herself. It was what Cadmus suggested before he left, and it was a good enough idea.

It was a challenge to not burn herself when she took the white-hot blade away from the fire. *It'll be like a mini Shofar*, she thought as her hammer made the black metal take form. *That would be a good story: the warrior girl.* She smiled to herself. The hilt she made from a nice silver-looking alloy, bending the guard downwards until it curved like ram horns around her wrist: the opposite of Shofar. For the pommel, she decided to use her necklace, making sure to keep it mostly intact so she could still flick it and make it spin. The rainbow it made was always pretty, even with the murky sunlight that plagued the day.

As soon as she brushed the finishing touches onto her petite sword, a shout came from outside, louder than the already noisy clamour. She tried to ignore it, but it became more difficult when the crowds grew louder. She stepped up to her window.

To her shock, there was no crowd at all. Not a single person wandered the street. *What? It was booming an hour ago.* She carefully opened the door to her workshop, peering down every alley and lane to find them as lifeless as a ruin. Before she saw *anyone*, she smelt something queer; after the scent took her head up, it was difficult to miss the giant plume of black smoke that accompanied the clouds. Her heart began beating faster than it should have. She followed the scent of burning towards Clyth.

In the middle of the street, next to the burning homes, she saw the crowd, the people of Selerborn. They were surrounding Half-Cut Fingal. The skinny protestor from a moon ago was in his arms, dying, a bloody spear protruding from his stomach. *"NOO!"* Fingal cried again, the only sound to accompany the crackling wood. *"They killed my father! People of Selerborn, can't you see? Our new ram is cursed as the olden! All my father did was express his concerns! I ask you, is that punishable by death?! Our lord sends his garrison to burn our homes, kill our kin, and for what?!"*

Half of the city's garrison *were* there, but they didn't seem guilty. Their spears were brandished, pointed at the crowds. Riley was nowhere in sight. Harper Siren was. One of the garrison called out. *"End this farce now, Fingal. They'll never believe you!"*

"Some still have love for the new lord," Fingal continued yelling as he stood. *"To them I say: how has he bettered your lives? Life was prosperous under Lord Sigmund, aye, he was a legend. But his son is of weakness!"* The skinny man winced. *"Has he avenged his father after he was shamed and murdered in foreign lands? Has he continued Lord Sigmund's many raids that once brought great riches and food into Selerborn? And instead of spurning the disorder in our streets, he makes more by putting our homes to the torch! Is that a Lord of Selerborn we should all bend to?!"*

"Who else is there, Fingal?" one of the crowd asked reluctantly.

"Who else is there?" Fingal turned and pointed to Harper Siren. *"There* stands a man worth fighting for. It's who my father believed in before he was *murdered!* I don't need to tell you how good he is; you've all seen it with yer own eyes when the Horncurves went south. He's a man who puts the people first." *Marcus was right, these are Harper's men,* Athena thought. He made it seem as if he had no part, gawking in the middle as his man praised him. Athena could see straight through it now. *This is way too convenient.*

"If we follow you, will you give us vengeance for Lord Sigmund?" one man from the crowds called.

"I will," Harper nodded. "Esmond is no king of mine."

A lot cheered for that. *Too many.* "Will ye let us raid again, Siren?"

"Of course I bloody will. Raidin' is in our blood."

"This crude age ends now!" Fingal exclaimed, following another cheer. *"Freedom is yours to take, people of Selerborn; raise that man to the diamond throne and choose the side that grants it!"*

One of the city's garrison squawked in pain as a dagger plunged into his neck. The crowd roared, and so began chaos.

Athena had never run quicker in her life. The screams of death and fire faded behind her as she bolted back to her workshop. As she arrived, she grabbed a great wooden plank and lodged it against the door. *No, not now,* she thought when she had time to. Selerborn was used to small uproars and harmless riots over the last few weeks, but never to this scale.

This is it. This is the Civil War. She couldn't decide what to do with herself; her hands shook, and her legs paced; she was led to the window again. The rebels had exploded like a web, sweeping the city's garrison from every direction. Blood sprayed on every swing, every house, every man. Glass grazed Athena's ears as a window was broken on her street. She threw herself back. *Sword. I need the sword.* She ran to the anvil, yanking it to her chest, fixing it to the guard, furiously sharpening it with a whetstone.

Before long, the commotion had arrived at her door. Men rushed back and forth along the street, screaming in pain and yelling in triumph. *Thud!* Her whole workshop shook as the door was battered. *Thud!* She grabbed her new sword and hid in the corner. It almost burnt her hand with how hot it still was, but she was glued to it regardless. *I'm not afraid!* she lied to herself. *Thud! Thud! Come here and you'll wish you hadn't. Thud! Thu-*

A scream of a man sounded the end of the ramming. Athena couldn't sigh, though. It wasn't over. She curled up, letting the tears roll down her face. *Please just stop it. Please stop it. Please...*

An hour may have passed, maybe half that, but Athena felt like moons had. She shook, in the same place she had sat the entire time, her only was company Angelo, in the form of his sprawling inventions. She could still hear the ringing of steel and it had ended ages ago. *It's okay now. Someone has won. My father has, he has to have.*

She carefully left her corner, bearing her sword. The street outside had corpses every few steps. Athena gagged and looked away. *The Cenkeep,* she thought, out of breath. *I need to see who won.*

Afternoon fell by the time she plucked up enough courage to check. She unblocked the door and led herself out, holding her onyx sword closely. At first, it was like there was *no* victory. Never had Selerborn been so quiet, not even when news of Sigmund's death struck it. She followed bodies all the way to the Cenkeep gates, and they didn't stop piling from then on. The stairs seemed twice as large. Her stomach twisted when she saw Sir Harold Smyth, dismembered from an arm with blood leaking from his chest. *Oh, my gods. I spoke to him an hour ago. He was still alive an hour ago.* It happened so fast. So suddenly. She felt the sickness rise through her body. It almost escaped when she saw Siren banners from the castle walls, snapping in the violent wind.

HEW II
-Espy-

A sh was still falling around him. When he'd close his eyes, he would still see the shelled warriors charging through the keep, tearing down the walls, sacking the fort. He wished he had his brother, his mother, his sister, but he knew they wouldn't come back for him, if they were still alive. Hew Centaur was a lone wolf in a dead fort.

As soon as they reached the gates, the young Centaur shot to the mausoleum, hoping his ancestors would keep him safe. He hid himself behind King Thaddeus the Wise, Hew's favourite of all the kings to follow Erland. Thankfully, the Khavars were respectful enough to not pillage the crypts, so Hew was safe during the sack. But now he wished he wasn't.

Leaving the mausoleum was his first challenge, the glass dome roof now a shattered mess on the floor, the arrows now like little blades pointing in different directions. The castle wasn't any better, huge fragments of caved-in walls filling the corridors, making the harsh outside winds see the inside for the first time ever. After that was the worst of sights he had seen: an empty courtyard, grass torn from its roots; an empty middle bailey, once strong walls as protective as leaves, piled like so on the ground; and the lower bailey, over six thousand homes now mounds of ash on the ground, rubble managing to blow about in the wind as if a tornado was moving it. *I hope they didn't kill them all,* Hew thought as he looked over the dead village, *they didn't do anything wrong.*

For a good part of that day, Hew didn't eat; he just followed his frightened gawk around the fort, hoping to find at least one life. He didn't. It smelt like death. When he finally decided to listen to his upset stomach, the kitchens were where he made to. The food he had hoped to find had become ash as well, but there were a few scraps of bread and fruit he could survive on, albeit burnt to a crisp and difficult to eat. That was the first time he cried.

For comfort, he then went to his favourite place, Elder Marcarius's athenaeum, expecting to see it charred black like the rest of the fort. For the most part, it was, age-old tomes ruined with their curled up pages scattered about the floor, but a few remained: The Elder's Gift, a book detailing the ceremony of when the elders received their eternal life from Deus, and the first act they performed - a bond of blood to each gemstone, forever tying the fate of their blood type to each stone. The Wonders Atop the Saturnian Mountains: another non-fiction describing the amusing life of the monks that belonged to the Tantum Monastery, always bound to their faith. And finally, The Aquarian Killer: a tale of an assassin who slew other assassins, or those with the intent to kill. They weren't much, nor were they his favourites, but they were the only things that distracted him from the ruins around him.

Like the three days before, when Hew awoke from his bed of rocks, King Thaddeus, his protector, was looking over him. It took a moment for his head full of dreams to return to his bleak reality. He looked to his three books, wishing he hadn't finished them so quickly. A whistle from the wind brought his head up, a beyond freezing gale making its way through the broken roof. For whatever reason, the fort seemed so much colder generally. *It's because there are no bodies to warm it up*, he thought grimly.

Hew picked himself up, drawing his fur cloak tighter around his body, and headed to the kitchens. He could well have spent a half hour rummaging through black pots and bowls before he decided there was nothing edible left. Some bits of debris he had to look twice at, just to make sure. *I'm going insane*, he frowned to himself. *I need to hunt*, he realised. *I need to catch and cook my own food, like Eva and Fletcher and Asher would.* Not that he knew how to do it; the many books that taught him many fascinating things had failed to teach him how to survive alone in a fort for the first time in his life. But the boy was too hungry to think any differently. *Eva will have a bow, or Fletcher, if they aren't burnt already.*

First, he went to Eva and Leta's shared chambers, only to see a mound of rocks on and around their beds. He tried to navigate through with no luck; the sharp stones that accompanied every step were too painful to bear. Fortunately, Fletcher's room wasn't as difficult to get to. A couple of boulders had to be shunned from the corridor, but for the most part, his brother's chambers were pretty clean. Hew scanned the room, hoping to find a quiver, or a cupboard that wasn't on the floor, or anything really. *Fletcher knew how to make bows. I'm so useless.*

He had nothing to lose by checking the drawers, only time. One out: empty, a third: empty, a fifth: burnt. He followed his bottom to the floor, running his fingers through his curly hair. *This is it;* he felt the tears coming. Hoping his eyes had deceived him, the Centaur looked around once more, to find... letters. Letters engraved in the wall. Squinting and wiping his eyes, Hew edged closer. It was a cobblestone slab, like every other, but this had two small words carved roughly into it. It read: *For Hew.* A blunted rock lay on the floor, as well as a spray of blood. *Oh no.* Hew felt the slab, realising he could wobble it about. He squinted again, using both hands to pull the rock from the wall. Inside lay something silver, glittering in the daylight. To his joy, it was a bow and arrow, but not just any bow: one of intricate make, laced with elegant zircon gems. Hew looked to the stone again, rotating it. The other side read: *Keep it safe,* but it was so sprawled and unclear it could have said anything. *Did he not make it out?* Hew worried. *Did they kill him here?*

A shiver ran down Hew's spine, making him stand. "Thank you, Fletcher," he muttered as he stroked the magical bow. Though, it was only half the battle, he still didn't know how to use the thing.

The outside was much colder than he anticipated. Howling winds almost made him lose balance as he stumbled through the frozen courtyard. *Why is it so cold?* He found himself grimacing. *Leta and mother made it out. I know they did.* He could remember his mother calling for him, her voice booming through the castle walls for no more than a minute. Hew wanted to go to her, but knew he couldn't; it was too late by then. He knew his fate was sealed when he heard the fort's gates collapse.

He scaled the pile of shattered cobble that lay in the gate yard. *At least I don't have to winch it up,* he supposed. He thought he did a good job at ignoring the mass of dead bodies, but every time his eye caught sight of a severed hand, or a leg crushed by a boulder, it made his stomach turn. *Get me out of here,* he winced. The Trado was worse, since no boulders concealed the graveyard. Arrows and claws and spears wedged too far into bodies, stuck out like fangs from a snake, and it was clear where other weapons slashed to end other lives. Some of the sigils Hew recognised: The Lord of Antrum Bay lay with an open throat, bearing the yellow shore sigil of the Baxter family, the Lord of Herst Castle had a crab claw in his neck, his acorn sigil a shredded mess on his plate, the Lord of Larton Keep with his head lopped off, his white horse sigil close to being cloaked in deep red blood. It was the first time he went outdoors since the attack, and he hated it. He closed his eyes and kept walking.

Not too far down the Negal Road did Hew find his first animal: a cluster of rabbits, ears up as they sniffed around the auburn grass. Hew took the bow and nocked an arrow, not quite choosing which one to aim for. He held the arrow for a while before finding one to strike, by which time his fingers shook from the tension. Trusting himself, he released the arrow, but it flew a mile higher than where he wanted it to go. The rabbits scattered away, and Hew's stomach remained hungry. *I didn't want to kill them anyway.* He frowned, marching towards the arrow. *Maybe I could fish. Fishing might be easier,* he thought, frowning at Fletcher's impossibly beautiful zircon bow. *I've fished before,* but with the massive help of his siblings. He decided to carry on, his eyes wide open as he crept further down the road.

He looked up to the lanky orange trees, hoping to find a persimmon that hadn't withered. Though, it wasn't any more fruitful; each piece was brown and ugly, rotten for a long time. A rustle caught his attention: an orange squirrel, gnawing on a shard of bark. *Can I even eat squirrels? Are they poisonous?* He drew his bow, not caring anymore. His fingers were too cold to hold, so he let go as soon as he could, and the arrow, just as he expected, completely missed the squirrel, lodging itself into the trunk. The squirrel scrambled up the branch, letting the wind snatch a bundle of leaves. Hew nocked another arrow, but before he could think to shoot, down fell a perfect, ripe persimmon. A smile tugged at his lips as he grabbed the fruit, sinking his teeth into the soft, juicy skin. *I can't get this lucky every day,* but for now, it filled his slimming belly.

I should probably stay out and learn to hunt, he thought, not quite deciding what to do when he returned. *It's not really home anymore. Why am I going back?* His thoughts didn't stop his legs, though, as they brought him back towards Fort Deus.

Arriving at the gate, as if it were an answer, Hew heard the faint sound of water moving. *The dock,* he realised, holding his cloak tightly as he broke into a sprint. Ice that glazed the ground added slips to Hew's run, especially when he made it further and further down the river bank, but he never lost his footing. Though, it wasn't long before his breath forced him to slow down. *I've never had a breathing attack without mother,* he then realised, *she's saved me every time.* The panic made him breathe faster. *It's okay. People have come back. It's okay.* He started to walk again.

The two boats that had docked were small things: rowing boats, but seeing a cluster of blue Centaur colours that weren't covered in red made Hew's heart flutter. A stocky knight next to the queen tapped her shoulder as he caught sight of Hew.

Semira turned to her son. Her blue eyes glistened and her breath escaped. "Hew."

Hew bolted into her arms, enveloping himself in her blue furs. "You came back."

"Oh, my gods, Hew, you're alright," she said, feeling his curly hair. "You're alright now. You're safe." Hew could feel Semira's heart pumping against his head. He held on tighter. "You're safe now," she kept repeating. "Is your brother with you?" she asked hopefully.

Hew frowned, shaking his head. "He left his bow…"

"So, you've been alone all this time?"

He nodded.

"Oh, you poor thing," she sighed, hugging him again. "You're safe now, I promise."

"We must get moving, my lady. The tides will be dangerous come nightfall," the burly knight said.

"Give me a *fucking* moment, Lukan!" she snapped. Semira's eyes were filled with water. "Your sister is safe too," she nodded. "She's heading to Centaur's Lagoon with Sir Roswell. Your uncle will keep you both safe."

"Are you not coming too?"

"Your brother still might be out there, Hew. I have to find him- I have to try."

Hew nodded again, trying not to cry.

"I'll come back as soon as I can. I promise I will," she said. "Come here." They hugged again. Her onyx hair smelt of home, of safety, a black veil wrapping around him, guiding him. "Guy, Lukan, Addy, stay with me. The men nodded. "You better keep him safe," she said to the other three.

"I'll give my life if I must, my lady," Erik Thyne, Lord of Trader's Dock bowed. His golden beard gave away who he was, the sigil on his arm matching it.

"Why is this happening to us, mummy?" Hew asked, a frown weighing his face down. "Why do we deserve this?"

"There are bad people in this world, Hew. Terrible people," she said. "But I need you to stay strong now. Whenever you're sad, whenever you're scared, think of Elisii, like we always do; think of paradise, a world without bad people, a world with *your* rules."

Hew nodded, wiping his tears. "Please don't stay long," he begged. "He's not in the fort, I know that."

Semira looked at him with helpless eyes. "I love you," she whispered, hugging him for a third time. "I'll come back. I promise."

MARCUS IV
-Distort-

He had ridden for as long as the day had light, his near exhausted mount bringing him to a tiny farming village called Aukfield. The name was familiar to him, but the place wasn't. *I mustn't have come far, then.* However far he'd like to imagine, Selerborn was still only a day's ride away; he couldn't hide there forever. Still, he tried.

It took a week of sowing fields in exchange for a room in a barn for Marcus Horncurve to realise he wasn't happy. The placid life wasn't for him, *but what can I do? If I go back to Selerborn, it would prove Riley right. I would be a failure.* For the first time in a while he yearned for battle, for combat. It was where he felt most alive, and he always knew that. Elder Ignatius was the one who made him think differently, *and for what purpose? If I was to fight, I would fight for my kin, for the glory of my ancestors, for the safety of my people, not to bring fury and anger and hatred into the world.* Regardless, that didn't mask the fury and anger and hatred he had towards Riley for disowning him, Cadmus for cheating him, Athena for exposing him. *I love them,* he kept telling himself when the fire died down, *I always will. I don't want to fight them. I don't need to.*

At least farming alone in a field robbed him of that choice. Staring at soil all day had him thinking about all sorts of futures: *I could start a brotherhood, like the Hounds of Lucewatch, bent to no lord or king, just coexisting. I could start my own dynasty, one more powerful than the one at Selerborn, save enough coin to buy horses, swords.* He had thought a little about going south and bending the knee to someone else, but he could never feel excited about that. He still loved his Arian blood, and that was something he couldn't disown; it was something he *wanted* to fight for. Then again, any thought that involved acceptable truculence had his mind racing, being deprived of it for so long.

It was raining and dark when Marcus met Joras Hopps, knocking at his door, begging for a place to stay. The farmer was old and kind, offering his barn for the first night, and Marcus agreeing to help him the next day, thus bringing the ram so far. Joras had been more than hospitable, sharing his meat and mead with Marcus every night, spare clothes when the fields were soaked and mudded with rain. He claimed to enjoy the company, the man of some sixty years not even having a family to look after him. It made Marcus sad. *I do. I have a family.*

"How did ye sleep, Marcus?" Hopps asked one morning, a smile on his face.

"Well enough," the ram nodded.

"Good," he said. "How about some roasted figs 'fore ye hit the field?"

"Sounds great," Marcus replied, less enthused than he intended.

"Eh, what's on yer mind, lad? Don't like figs?"

"It's not that."

"'Mon then, speak up," Joras insisted, tending to a crackling cooking pot. In any other mind, Marcus's mouth would be watering at the smell.

Marcus hesitated. "Is there... any work around here, you know, that I could do on the side, get a bit of coin?"

"Plannin' on leaving me already?"

Offending the old man was the last thing he wanted. "I don't want to stay here, no."

Joras hummed and paused to think. "I would pay you, the wee bit I have," he nodded. "You've done a lot fer me. But I won't know how much 'till those crops grow."

Marcus smiled. "Thank you," he said. "When will they be ready?"

The farmer chuckled. "Can't rush nature, lad; I don't know, but I've got a good feeling about it. Harvest Moon came a few days ago... gods know there's never been a bad reaping in such a time."

"The Harvest Moon?" Marcus frowned.

Joras glanced up. "Wha's the matter? Looks like you've seen a ghost."

Marcus squinted. *Athena's birthmoon. This is the first year I've not been with her.* "It's nothing," he lied.

Joras nodded, clearly knowing it wasn't nothing.

I wonder if she's happy, if she's safe still. He hoped so, above any spite he bore her. Though, he couldn't pretend he was over it. Whenever the thought of Harper crossed, it felt like a pin had pricked his brain. *He's always been a traitor. Riley is an idiot for not realising that.*

"Aw, pesh," Joras spat, waking Marcus from his daydream, "hide."

"What?" Marcus winced.

Joras was fixed on something outside his window. "Go now, shoo, hide!" The man scuttled to the door, peering through the hatch.

Marcus took himself to a corner, behind a clothed table, just high enough to see the window. Outside rode knights, clad in Selerborn's familiar city's garrison armour, but flying the pennon of Siren. *Shit, he's come to take me back,* Marcus grimaced. "Who claims charge?!" The voice of Raul James bellowed. "Who claims charge?!!" He screamed again when silence was returned. After another while, Sir Raul was handed a torch, the man next to him sparking it alight. *"People of Aukfield, I'll give you one last chance, or tinder will be your answer!"*

Before Marcus had time to stop him, Joras unlatched the wooden door and dashed out. "Wait, no, stop! I am! I am!" Joras was out of breath by the time he made it to the party. "What do you want, sirs? These people are innocent."

A smile stretched across Sir Raul's mouth. He dropped the snapping torch to the ground, his horse extinguishing it with its hoof. "I want the prince," he said coldly. "You know where he went?"

"Prince?" Joras winced. "No princes in these parts."

"He came this way, so I'll ask you again - do you know where he went?"

"I don't," the farmer said angrily, "so go terrorise another village!"

Sir Raul nodded to his men. They dismounted and kicked the farmer down into a seize. Sir Raul followed. *"Agh, let go of me!"* Joras yelled. Marcus could see the whole of Aukfield staring out of their windows.

The knight pulled out a dagger and held it to Joras's arm. "I'm not a patient man," he said. "Do you know where he went?"

Joras frowned. Then he spat. Sir Raul sighed and leant in to cut. *They'd kill him? Those assholes would really kill an unarmed farmer?* Marcus hesitated. *Stop it, Marcus, the man means nothing to you.* He closed his eyes and listened to Joras's cry. It wasn't long before his fury became unbearable.

"Wait!" Marcus yelled, bolting out. *"Don't you fuckin' touch him!"*

Sir Raul looked up. He smiled. His teeth were too big for his face. "Good of you to come, Marcus," he said, sheathing the dagger. Blood was leaking from Joras's wrist, but he didn't seem to care.

"Have you no soul?" Marcus said, squinting hatefully. "These are yer own people."

He seemed to agree. "The Lord of Selerborn has been waiting a while for you."

The knights grabbed Marcus's arms and forced him atop a horse. He was bound to it, but he stayed quiet, as did Joras. The farmer was only frowning at him. "I'm sorry," he whispered.

"Back to your business. Nothing to see," Sir Raul called out. They were quick to start a gallop, and Aukfield was left more tainted than Marcus had found it. *Being caught is less humiliating than coming back*, he thought hopefully as his horse was dragged along. *Maybe my father would be more forgiving.* He doubted that, since he had sent Sir Raul to find him. The man even had a smile on his face for most of the ride. *Suck it up. Enjoy it. It's the last time you will. I'm not getting caught again.*

The ride back to Selerborn was much quicker than the ride to Aukfield, probably because Marcus spent the entire ride thinking of what he was going to say to his father, to Cadmus, to Athena. But when they arrived at the city gates, something felt wrong. Smoke littered the air with charred black homes sitting underneath. The gravel and grass underfoot were soaked with blood, bodies and limbs scattered along the roads. He looked to the banners the party rode with. Then he clocked it. "Riley's not the Lord of Selerborn anymore, is he?" he asked, almost breathlessly.

Sir Raul smiled ruefully, staring into Marcus's eyes. "No, he's not."

Fury was slow to boil inside him. "You *bloody traitor! You were his ram's guard! You swore to the death to defend him! Where is yer fuckin' honour?!*" He started to struggle in his binds.

One of the knights slammed Marcus in the stomach, winding him.

"I've only done what a man needs to do," he said, looking ahead. "You'll learn that soon enough, lad."

Marcus was dizzy; he couldn't respond. Before long, he was thrown off his horse, and found himself staring up at the legs of a man. He was hoisted up. "I'm so sorry," Harper Siren said, sadness in his eyes. He was holding Riley's merlot cloak, shredded and bloodied. By him stood Seathan Blaar, Dugg Gallach, Elder Ignatius; they all wore woeful faces.

Marcus squinted as his vision came back. "What?" he winced. Harper's doorstep was the only one in Selerborn that didn't have bodies on it.

"I couldn't stop them," Harper frowned. "They were so angry... they... they fought each other, and swore and ran... None of us could save them from themselves."

The ram's entire face caved in. *"Liar!!!"* he howled. He was struck across the face, almost to the ground again.

"I don't want to hurt you, Marcus," Harper claimed as blood crept out of Marcus's cracked lip. "Enough terror has taken place... and you have Horncurve blood, you're the future of your family... let me help you. It's what your father would have wanted."

"You *can't* lie to me, Harper! I *saw* your cabals. I *saw* your men plotting to overthrow da'."

Harper nodded, not seeming surprised. "I wanted you to see. To be honest, I was a wee bit startled when you told him."

"He's my father," Marcus winced. "You thought I wouldn't?"

"Aye, but I was wrong," Harper admitted. "Elder Ignatius said to me how much you wanted revenge for Sigmund. Riley would've never given you that justice. I thought their motives would resonate with you." He allowed that to sink in for a moment. "It doesn't matter now anyway. I wanted Cadmus to tell you to go to *Clyth,* to find a *different* cabal. But he betrayed us. He told you to go to the *Mudstreet* instead. He wanted to raid Heavia before you and he knew that going to the Mudstreet would make your da' furious. I don't need to tell you that, though. You know it's true."

He *did* know it was true. Cadmus had told him as such. The rage that bubbled up within was insufferable. Marcus tried with all his force to charge at him. *"I'll kill you! You did this! You killed them!"* He got so close, but was beaten down by the men who held him. He almost coughed blood as he gasped for breath.

"Find him a cell," Harper turned away sadly.

He was dragged away to the dungeons under the Cenkeep, but he hadn't given up on fighting; the boy squirmed like a trapped rat all the way, managing to land elbows and kicks and punches on the guards, swings gradually getting weaker the more beatings he endured. *"You're all traitors!"* he screamed when he was thrown to the pitch-black cell. It was so cold, so empty. He curled up, raising his quivering hands to his arms, clawing at them. *It's not my fault they're dead,* he lied to himself. *I didn't do it. It's not my fault. It's not my fault.*

ELAYNE IV
-Climb-

N o one was surprised when news that Lord Goldwyn had fallen in battle arrived at Ignis. Sulwyn Wisp summoned the council to let everyone know, but they could hardly offer sympathy; almost every member advised Goldwyn *against* leading the vanguard. "Nonsense, I must lead my people, I must inspire them," he insisted, but in actuality inspiring nothing more than a filled grave. That didn't make his death any less tragic though. No one hated Goldwyn, he was good and kind, much like his older brother, and would have made a decent Lord of Ignis if he had a little longer to prove so, but the same couldn't be said for his heir.

"How did he take it?" Elayne Lyrderyn asked as Elder Ulrich plodded onto her balcony.

"I live another day, at the very least," he jested dryly, taking a seat. "He doesn't seem to be affected. He said his father was fat and slow and stupid, and that he should have listened."

"Well he's not wrong," Elayne said, taking a sip of wine.

"No," Ulrich agreed. "Still, it's a shame. Lord Goldwyn had nothing but good intentions."

Elayne nodded. She had no foul memories of the lord. "How is Lady Gina?"

"Grieving, as any widow would," he sighed. "Perhaps you should speak with her? It might do her a service to know she's not alone."

"I've tried," she said. "She wanted to be alone."

"Ah," Ulrich sighed, loosening his posture. "Well, there's no helping those who don't want to be helped."

Elayne returned her gaze to the city. If there were half as many caravans when she returned a moon ago, there were half that again. Lord Aurelius said the '*war*' would have played a part, traders not wanting to make uncertain deals. *Grow up,* Elayne felt like saying, *it's hardly a battle, let alone a war. You don't even know what a war is.* Neither did she, but she wanted to think she could tell when one was happening. From what she knew, most of House Equuleus had been wiped out*, so who else would we have to war with?* Lord Sulwyn contested Aurelius too, claiming that less trade came to Ignis because people had less *to* trade, the supposed *acclimatisation* making food production less fruitful. Regardless, there were too many reasons to keep up with. All Elayne hoped for was that Lyssa was safe and happy, and that Ayden would behave himself, the head of politics thankfully doing just that.

"So, what now?" Elayne asked eventually.

"Fitz is to be crowned later today," Ulrich said. "I can't imagine it to be too extravagant of a ceremony; it seems he wants it over and done with."

Mature of him, she thought for once. "What do you think of him being Lord of Ignis?"

Elder Ulrich looked into her eyes, as if reading her thoughts. "I hope he's not that of what he shows," he said after a time. "A tetchy leader is the last thing we need in this world."

She was glad he thought the same. "Or the first. Riley couldn't hold Selerborn, I'm told. Perhaps a mad leader would have fared differently."

"Mad leaders seldom scare me, it's what they would do that does," he said as he squinted at nothing. "But, alas, perhaps you're right," he smiled as he rose. "My lady." He bowed and took his leave.

Elayne stayed with her thoughts for a while, people watching. *What's the worst thing Fitz could do, really?* She didn't want to answer her own question. *He'll be fifteen soon. What chance does a fifteen-year-old have at pissing off the whole Canicule like he's pissed off everyone he's been around?* She didn't want an answer to that either. *Maybe I'm being too harsh. He'll still only be fifteen,* she decided eventually. *Maybe he'll listen more, unlike his proud father.*

Sun was pouring onto the sandstone when Elayne made it to the open patio. It was bright and warm, making her squint. The gentle rush of water from the sprawling fountain gave her a shiver, if only for a moment, as she heard the faintest sound of running echo from further in the keep. *"Una, come back!"* Ryan was yelling. *I guess she's not totally tame,* Elayne thought with a smile.

Out ran Una, pouncing on Elayne's bare leg. The lynx clung on with all its strength, yet her claws weren't painful at all. Elayne jumped back, beginning to laugh.

"I'm so sorry," Ryan panted as he ran in, wrinkling his forehead and wearing a half smile. "I've been chasing her all morning."

"Locked up in a keep is no place for a lynx," she smirked.

"I know," Ryan nodded, plucking Una from Elayne's leg. "Ayden doesn't want me leaving, though. And Fitz gets antsy if I'm gone too long."

"Antsy?" Elayne frowned.

"He sends guards searching for me, like I've escaped or something," he said. "Is it... because of Lyssa, do you know?"

"Gods know," she sighed. "Leave if you want. You don't belong to anyone."

Ryan's eyes dropped to the ground. Una put a paw on his face. "I know," he said, making a half smile as he glanced up and jogged off.

She wished he would talk more, about what he thought, how he felt. Because he wouldn't, Elayne would always feel sad when the boy was around, even if he was smiling and happy. *Does he have anyone to speak to at the Lynxrock, anyone who'd listen to him?* Elder Sol might, but for all of Elayne's youth, the elder was never at the rock, instead wandering about, scaling the Red Sierra. If he still did that, the time he could spend listening to Ryan's thoughts would be limited, if at all. *I would take him if I could, adopt him,* she thought, even though her heart couldn't take the thought of another child to look after. *I have to know if that's what he wants, though. Perhaps, by some miracle, he's happy at the rock.*

Making her way down towards the throne room, she decided to try once more with Lady Gina, to help her feel positive for the crowning of her son. But as her solar approached, Elayne heard an unfamiliar, smooth tone to her brother's voice coming from within. "If you need anything, anything at all," he was saying, "I am only a call away. I know these are hard times, but us Leons must look after each other."

"Thank you, Lord Lyonis," Gina sniffled. "I couldn't agree more."

He bowed and glided out. Elayne stood at the doorway. He smirked at her. "What are you doing?" she whispered sharply.

"Currying favour," he smiled, leaving before she could retort.

Sly bastard. If she could expose him, she would, but the more it built up, the more she'd seem mad for yelling all the reasons why Ayden was false. She looked to Gina, who was struggling to wipe away tears faster than they fell. *Telling her how she's being used is the last thing she needs.* "My lady?" Elayne asked apprehensively.

"Oh, Elayne," she said softly. "I'm sorry about earlier, I don't do well with stress." She was massaging the small bump on her stomach.

"Don't worry," Elayne smiled. "My brother... he-"

"Was very kind," she nodded. "A family trait."

"Good." Elayne wasn't smiling anymore.

Gina did. "After the coronation, would you ride with me? To Lake Ignis, perhaps, like we always used to. Anywhere but this shit city. I would talk to you when I know no eyes are watching."

"Of course, anything."

Gina stood and took Elayne's hands. "Thank you, Elayne. You're a true friend." She disappeared into the drapes of her wardrobe.

Whatever else Ayden was, he had somehow managed to open Gina up. Elayne didn't know what to feel. She let her legs take her away.

◆————◄

By the time the coronation was upon them, the air had a muggy feel to it. It wasn't unlike the rest of the day, but scalding heat in the late afternoon was a foreign thing to Ignis. Nearly every highborn lord and lady Elayne knew stood in the Ignis keep's throne room, sweating. It even looked like the thick sandstone bricks were sweating as well, the air contorting from the heat. The broad yellow lion pillars that once made the throne room look so huge were twisting too, shaking in the air. Low hanging drapes of orange cloth that swung from the cracked black and golden marble semi-open ceiling looked like flames, spreading across the whole room. It seemed like only the warm mosaic ground stood still, but the flickering light from stained glass made even that look aflame.

Elayne found it funny that everyone's attention was on the heat and not the crowning, even though nothing had happened yet. The dusty old throne of peridot lay at the back, swathed in shadows. The silver iron that poked out of the sandstone chair was once so much more silver, but now had dark muddy rust coating it. *I've only ever seen Reynold sit that seat,* she realised, almost wishing for him to come back. It was like Fitz had skipped a step.

Her daughter found Elayne's side not long after, looking as pretty and petite as ever in the small green dress that seemed to become her favourite since Merchant's Bay. She was with her gang of princess friends, all as beautiful as each other. "There you are," Elayne said. "I sometimes wonder if you're still alive. I never see you anymore, Ellie."

"I've got things to do, mum," Eleanor frowned. "Sights to see, sunlight to enjoy-"

"-Cakes to eat, gossip to indulge in-"

"Mum!" she murmured when her friends began to giggle.

They were new girls, ones Elayne had never seen before, but she gave them no more than a glance. *I shouldn't worry,* she told herself, *she's having fun, and not feeling morose about Lyssa, and that's more than I can do.*

"Where's Fitz?" Eleanor asked innocently.

"Shh, he'll be here soon," Elayne said.

Soon enough, the boy came traipsing into the room with a slump. He looked at no one, only to the ground, and his careful steps. He was dressed in simple clothes: a dark red robe, with a golden belt and two golden clasps on his shoulders matching his wispy hair. Elder Ulrich stood closer to the throne, taking a flamboyant golden crown from a merlot cushion Aurelius Kinsey held. *Where's Gina?* Elayne wondered when Fitz took forever to walk the aisle. People started to get restless, moving about, trying to fan the heat away from themselves. "See where Lady Gina is," she whispered to her closest handmaiden. Raha nodded and dashed out.

Fitz knelt at Ulrich's sandals. "Fitzroy Lyrderyn, son of Goldwyn Lyrderyn, Ignis has passed to you, and with it comes oaths to keep. Would you burden yourself with such ancient oaths, and take the seat that has been bestowed upon you?"

"I will," Fitz nodded, a shake in his voice.

"Would you take your people, young and old, weak and strong, and bring them honour and justice?"

"I will," Fitz repeated.

"Would you, as Lord of Ignis, forsake no mouths, no vows, no life, no blood."

"I will," he then said confidently.

"Rise."

Fitz slowly stood, meeting the eyes of the elder.

"Fitzroy Lyrderyn, I crown you Lord Ruler of Ignis, rightful Lord of the Canicule, and Protector of the Peridot Gem." Ulrich hovered the crown above Fitz's head. His hands were shaking. He began to lower it.

A scream pierced through the castle walls, the scream of Elayne's handmaiden. *"Help! Someone! Come quick!"*

Half of the throne room was still, the other half frowning and wincing. People slowly followed the screams. Elayne was the first in Lady Gina's chambers. She was pale, sprawled out on the floor, dead, a golden goblet in her hand spilling with dark wine.

"NOO!" Fitz yawped as he barged past the crowd. *"Not you too!"* He held his mother's head. *"WHY?!"* The anger trembled his voice. *"Who was it?"* he snapped around to the bystanders. His new crown was already crooked on his head. *"Who killed my mother?!"*

Elayne immediately looked to the deceptively shocked face of her brother. *Now you've done it, Ayden,* she thought. *You've poisoned a mother and her unborn baby; now come the lions.*

ESMOND XI
-Loose-

For the third time, Briggs, it can wait. I don't need more to think about right now."

Lord Waker was struggling to keep up with Esmond Centaur's power walk. "It *can't* wait, my king, please. Just read it."

Semira's letter was sending the king mad. "I will, after the speech, no sooner."

"But Esmond-"

"Are you all set?" Orion asked with a smile at the end of the long marble hallway.

"Just about," Esmond exhaled as he straightened his bronzed cloak.

"Remember: nothing unempathetic. Some of these people's livelihoods will be taken away. They won't take kindly to the wrong words." Sir Orion furrowed his dark brow when he talked. That wasn't something he ever used to do, Esmond couldn't help notice.

The king chuckled. "Nothing unempathetic." He nodded, and tapped his *First Avail's* mailed shoulder before moving aside the cream curtains.

A day had passed since Esmond had called a meeting, and to his relief, as well as quelling his nagging councillors, they had also finally come up with a plan. It wasn't a plan that solved all problems, but it was enough to take steps towards it. He just hoped his people would see it the same way. It was grim enough simply knowing so many people had starved already.

The cheer when the king walked onto the Ulcus Basilica's balcony had once been so great, so loud. He overestimated the response. Still, it was a daunting crowd; he couldn't see where they ended. "People of Lunarpass," he called down, not letting it thwart his confidence. "It's taken a time for me to come before you, I know that. We are struck with an issue so great, that even the best minds will take time to solve it. Still, that doesn't mean we can't. Today will be the first steps we make towards doing so." Another cheer erupted, much louder than the one that greeted his arrival. He held up his palm, quietening it. "So, in case your home is a dungeon, let me be completely honest with what we face." The low murmur of chuckling swept the city. "As we all know, from tales we were taught as children, once the seasons were never still. It would be sunny and warm, then three moons would pass and it would grow colder, then three more moons and *snow* would start to fall. I won't pretend that we might not be going back to that, to a time where the Auburn Pole faced hot summer days as well as cool winter ones. But I also refuse to sit by and watch people I love starve, and struggle to make it through this change."

"Perhaps it would take time for us to adapt, to know where and when to grow food again, but I know we will, we always have. We've survived rebellions, civil wars, *multiple* pauses; What we're facing now is not nearly as bad." He hated to lie, but he hadn't heard back from Elder Marcarius at all. *I'm not lying,* Esmond told himself, *it's just wishful thinking.* "Nevertheless, we all know something needs to be done, while food is something of scarcity. We must all band together and help each other through this, to avoid losing more of those we love."

He paused, expecting the crowd to call out, a lone man challenging his ideas. They were as still as death. It unsettled him. "So, from now on, until we learn how to adapt, a few edicts will be put in place. Firstly, no man, nor woman can *own* large amounts of food henceforward. A warehouse will be built in every city, hamlet, town and castle. *There* will be enough food to feed you all." A hushed babel arose. "Royal guards will be posted at each house; they will make sure you all get your share. Traders and farmers, you need not worry, you will all still receive fixed wages for your yields, but know that if *anyone* is caught hoarding… this is treason. As is theft from the warehouse and theft from others."

Surely now there has to be an outburst. Surely someone is upset with that. Nothing. They only chatted amongst themselves. Theft was never punishable by death before. Esmond knew it wouldn't get rid of crime, though. "These measures are *only* temporary - a safety bunker - as was the

Celestial Complex during the *Pause*. But this is something we have decided *needs* to be done." Still nothing. Complete silence. Esmond nodded to himself contentedly, heading back into the Basilica.

"Well done," Orion said, holding his arms out.

They quickly embraced. "They didn't say anything," Esmond frowned.

"Don't worry, my king," Tobi assured, "we'd know if they disagreed." Esmond nodded. "Then, now we wait."

"Esmond," Briggs Waker said solemnly. He held out the parchment.

Not 'my king'? It normally didn't irk him, but for some reason did now. He scanned the upset face of his head of word, and took the parchment.

My dearest Esmond,

Chances are, you won't get this letter, but if you do, something terrible has happened. We were visited by Lord Tyran Capra of Seden, warning us of a Khavar fleet sailing for the Arrow. Deuswater was razed this morning, and how long Fort Deus has to stand is uncertain. Tyran has offered his forces, but Fletcher distrusts them. We have the numbers as long as Tyran keeps his word. I'm really sorry if this letter ever has to reach you, but you need to know.

I love you, Semira.

Esmond scrunched the letter in his hand as he stared mindlessly into the marble. *My home*, he thought.

"They march north now, my king," Briggs frowned. "They mean to sail up the Negal River and take the Lunar Path here, I believe."

"Fuck what they mean to do, what about my children?"

Lord Waker swallowed nervously, dropping his gaze. "I-"

"Briggs!"

"The rider said Leta should be safe; she sails to the Lagoon with Sir Roswell," he nodded. "But... but Hew and..."

"Yes?"

"Hew and Fletcher have not been found."

Esmond's hands were shaking. He stood in his repressed rage for a while, before turning and marching down the hall. He found Galloway Malone first, grovelling in front of the solar throne. "I'm sorry, my king, I didn't know they would do this, I didn't know-"

"Don't you dare," Esmond said calmly. "Why did you do it?"

The old ram held out his hand. "I *only* bargained with them because the Helas were a threat they offered to take out. They were the ones sinking our cargo ships during the Rose Moon."

"And you didn't tell us?" The king appeared calm somehow, yet he shook in every place that could shake. "Do you know how much time we've wasted trying to figure out who did?"

"If I told you, you'd know," he frowned, "that... that..."

"That you betrayed me?"

Galloway shook his head fiercely. "I would never-"

"What would you call it, treating with turncoats, with *exiles?*"

Lord Malone's eyes were that of a puppy's, sorry and wide, looking as though they would burst into tears at any moment.

"I don't *care* what you did. Get out of this city," Esmond winced as he held himself back. "I never want to see you again."

The king marched out, deciding who to confront next. Footsteps on marble suggested he was being followed, but Esmond didn't care to look. All he saw was red. Red for blood. Red for fire. *They would take my sons away. I understand.* He knew he had to stay calm, he wanted to, he needed to. *They would break the treaty of peace we established when Lord Vincent himself came to the capital. I understand.* His feet took him to his mare, and his mare began to gallop down the lunar streets. *They would take my home away from me while I have no way to defend it, or even know about it. They would deface the Pole with raids and wars for the sake of no one but themselves.* He took grip of his reins, yanking them harder. *They would continue to kill everyone I care about as they have done for moons, while it all goes over me as I'm too stupid to realise.*

The sprawling stairs of the Sphaera were no bigger challenge than the streets to traverse; Esmond forced his stallion to charge up with full speed, knocking men aside, scraping the golden banisters. Echoes of hooves bounced around the large dome louder than they ever had before. And he was still being followed; the hooves made a chorus. Still, he didn't look.

When he arrived at Lord Edward's chambers, he rammed into the door violently, sending the metal bars sweeping into delicate vases, smashing them into a million pieces. Edward flinched from his table. He was writing a letter. "Oh, gods, your grace. I hadn't exp-"

"Do you know about it?" Esmond asked, making a poor effort to contain his anger now. Edward Cancer was gawking. "The *attack* on my *home,* do you know about it?" He marched closer. "Do you know about how your people *killed* my sons, *took* my home, *burned* my country?"

"I don't, your grace, please. Let us figure it out," Edward was backed into a corner, knocking into another pillar, smashing another vase.

Esmond grabbed his throat, pinning him against the wall. "You don't know what your kin have done? Don't lie to me. I've been surrounded by liars; don't think I can't tell you apart by now." He raised the lord, clutching tighter. Edward clawed for his throat. *"Tell me you don't know!"*

"Please," Edward begged hoarsely, as best he could. *"For... peace..."*

Esmond suddenly became conscious of his pounding heartbeat, his trembling hands, his audience of Orion and Jovian and Tobi. He released Edward, and looked away.

Edward gasped for his breath, feeling around his discoloured neck. "I'm so sorry, King Esmond. I know nothing of this, I promise. I'm here to help you. This is King Delmar's doing, if anyone's." He coughed weakly. Esmond bared his teeth. *King Delmar? The man who supposedly couldn't kill a fly. Have I been told a single truth this moon? Wake up, Esmond. The wounds of war are healing...* "Believe me, I am more sorry about your children than anything."

The king twitched and cruelly jabbed his face. Edward's head hit the wall. He fell to the ground. Esmond leapt atop him. *"YOUR KIN!"* he yelled, casting dogged blows to the Cancer's face. *"You killed them! You did this! You and Vincent!"* Tears choked the king's vision, but he could still only see red. *"Aaarrgghhhh!"* He couldn't stop himself, but he didn't want to. *"We agreed for peace! We shook for peace! And you attack my home!"* Hook after fist after pound he kept going. It took way too long to realise what he had done, his peace beaten dark and bloody as it lay dead on the floor.

FELIKS VI
-Hoard-

Riding with Elder Marcarius was leisurely at best. The old man claimed the frequent stops and slow pace were so they could take in the wonders of the Pole, the beauty of the wilderness, but Feliks could hear him panting lightly from his horse the few times he took the lead. If it were down to the bastard, they would have made it to Sangis days ago. Still, he wouldn't have wished for any other company.

They talked of food and ruling and people and riding and fighting, all with far too much enthusiasm. Sometimes Feliks had to remind himself he was speaking to an elder, as Marcarius seemed no less excitable than a child. It was refreshing if anything: to speak to an adult who *wanted* to speak to him, to share company he knew wouldn't judge him, and if he did, for the right reasons only. *A figure of great import,* he smiled to himself.

Without any convictions, Feliks soon recognised how beautiful the Pole truly was. He had never seen the bleak autumness in such a way before. The frosted shards that lay on the orange grass in the morning were that of perfection, twisting as if insects had sculpted them. The Auburn Lake was something Feliks saw every day as it washed into the Lagoon, but never *this* far into the Pole, sweeping bronze leaves in the current as they fell from the tall trees. *I've taken it for granted,* he knew. *It could be all gone one day, withered and dried when the seasons finally change.* Marcarius said it wasn't worth thinking about, that everything dies and all we can do is watch. But he also said there was another cruel kind of beauty to death, one of change, closure, rebirth. Feliks didn't understand. *The dead don't get reborn, else I'd have my sister with me. All that changed from not having her was my happiness, and that's not beautiful.* "The dead don't get reborn," Marcarius agreed, raising more questions than he answered.

A soft sunset glistened over the Waterway when they arrived at Sangis. The city was never how Feliks had imagined; the river's side was almost made entirely of wood, a dark brown timber like that of the orange trees that surrounded the city. Beams of the same planks twisted out to make flickering street lamps, fences, stairs, buildings, joists to hold the dock together. The other half of the city was the opposite, thick boulders of cobblestone that stretched down into the Sangis Waterway, making sturdy buildings, walls, keeps, spires.

Not long after they rode over the first wooden bridge, out galloped a gang of knights from the thick of the lively city. Before them sat a pompous man, his perfect posture even making his stallion look lesser. On each of their dark brown cloaks rippled the silver hammer of Sculptor.

"Elder Marcarius," the man smiled. He seemed more like a boy up close, with his beardless face, his baby cheeks. "We had not received word of your visit. My lord father bids you dine with him."

"Lord Edwin Sculptor," Marcarius nodded. "My, you've grown since I saw you last." Edwin bowed as if it were an achievement. "Lead the way, my lord, we'd be happy to dine."

They hadn't eaten since morning, so they *were* hungry. So much so that Feliks noticed more than he would have, that Sangis *stank* of food. He could smell spices, onions, beef, pork, stews, and even scents he had never smelt before, but smelt good nevertheless. Inside the cobblestone keep, it was no different, only that now he could *see* it all, as the servant brought out countless platters of meat and fruit and bricks of food. *A lot of food for a famine,* Feliks thought distastefully.

After a time of waiting in the lobby, staring at the brown banners that laced the floor and walls, disguising the sound of their rumbling stomachs with coughs, they met Lord Curtis himself. He wore a silk brown cloak with a fur collar that played with his messy brown hair. His lips were plump, his beard stubbled, and he seemed friendly enough. "My lords," Curtis bowed with a smile. "Welcome to Sangis. You have every hospitality of ours for as long as you stay."

Curtis shook the elder's hand. "Fear not, my lord, it won't be for long. We were just passing through."

"You were?" Curtis seemed surprised. "Bound to Iustitia, are you? Oretown? Aquamare? Oh, I apologise, I'm sure it's very confidential."

"Not at all," Marcarius smiled curiously. "You had it right the first guess."

Curtis nodded enthusiastically. "Very well, I won't keep you for too long," he smiled, turning in a way that made them both follow. "I must say, you've come at the *perfect* time. A feast awaits you both. Our yields thanks to the Harvest Moon have left us bounteous."

"So it has," Marcarius agreed, admiring a server rushing past with a thick platter of steak. "We could all use such fortune at times like these."

Lord Sculptor's enthusiasm seemed to plummet with the colour of his face as it flushed a bright red. Curtis was likeable, courteous, kind enough to share his food in the first place, *but still deserves to be embarrassed*. Feliks had seen hunger take its toll first hand at the Lagoon, at Liglock, sweeping over the Pole like a silent assassin. He thought he did a good job at ignoring it, in believing that everything would just as easily return to normal, *but ignoring it isn't mending it*. The thought left a bitter taste in Feliks's mouth.

"We must enjoy what we have, no?" Curtis said eventually. "In a time where it can so easily be torn away from you."

"I couldn't agree more," Marcarius said solemnly.

Silence ruled their walk for the rest of the way to the mess hall, and it seemed none of them minded. The room was a large square, tapestries of sceneries and art drooping high from the stone walls. Curtis led them to the great brown table, already laced with barely touched food and empty plates.

"Had guests already tonight, my lord?" Marcarius asked.

"No guests, only family," he said nervously. "I have an army of nieces and nephews that attack my halls each night."

"As I recall," Marcarius nodded. "They're lucky to have an uncle who would feast them so."

Curtis smiled meekly, a shade of red returning to his face. "Seat yourselves, the road must have starved you both." He made eye contact with Feliks for a brief moment as they all sat. "So, who might your companion be? I don't believe we've met."

"Feliks, my lord," he introduced himself, wanting to leave it at that. "...Lord Lorimer's... bastard son."

There the look was. The look of pity, disappointment, judgment. The look that took a hiatus from Feliks's life for half a moon, making its reintroduction twice as biting.

"He may someday rule the Lagoon in his father's stead," Marcarius said, stealing Curtis's attention. "I saw no one better to aid me."

Curtis gave a sideways look. "Rule, you say?"

"Why not? He's more capable than any highborn lord *I've* ever met."

Lord Sculptor choked on the air. "I mean no disrespect, it's just... To have a... People born-"

Feliks couldn't help but smile. "There's no kinder way of saying 'bastard', my lord. Most people just suck it up and hope I don't get offended." he said dryly. Marcarius was frowning. It was nice seeing the old man defend him.

Curtis's relief came out in a smile of his own. "You can never be too sure. I have a few in my family; they always get offended when they hear someone say it. I can normally get away with calling them 'illegitimate', or 'by-blows', but it all means the same thing, I suppose."

"Right," Feliks nodded. "I can call myself a bird, but that doesn't make me one. Any bastard with half a brain knows that soon enough."

"Feliks." Marcarius continued to frown.

"It's true, Elder Marcarius," Curtis said, chuckling from Feliks's calm inflection. "My nieces are... proud. My nephew, prouder. I admire how you've shouldered it, Feliks. It's not an easy thing to own."

The bastard sent a thin smile back. *It gets boring after a while, pretending that I'm not. All I'm owning is the truth.* "Thank you, my lord."

Curtis nodded in respect. "Well, we'd better dig in before all this food gets cold." He pointed over the platters. "That's a steak stew with some northern seasoning, persimmon roasts fresh from the Pole, cheeses and lamb from the Saturnian Mountains, and those are various breads and grains our chefs have way too much fun crafting," he said, for a time almost seeming overwhelmed by it. "Eat as much as you can, my lords, please."

Marcarius bowed and Feliks smiled, but the bastard still thought it curious how nervous Lord Curtis was. "What happens to the leftovers?"

Curtis glanced around, moving his mouth like a fish. "It will all be eaten," he said defensively. "One way or another..." Feliks kept his blue stare on the flustered lord. *Why is he so uncomfortable?* It was silent for a while.

"Any interesting news, my lord?" Marcarius said to break the unwarranted tension. "Our ears have heard nothing since we left Liglock."

"Now you mention it, we had some interesting intel from Watchpoint Inretio this morning," he nodded, breaking off a piece of bread. "A Casteron fleet was sighted heading east a couple of days ago. I don't suppose you'd know anything about it, Elder Marcarius?"

Marcarius was sipping a bowl of stew. He frowned. "Casteron fleet, you say? Did they not share what business they had?"

"They didn't," Curtis said. "I'm told they were some thirty strong? A sizable fleet, but not enough to take a city."

"True enough, best be sure though. We can never be too careful with Venusians and what they might be planning. Have you sent word to the king?"

"It would be wrong not to."

Marcarius nodded intently. "I don't think we need worry, it's like to be nothing, but we're just as much in the dark as you."

"Honestly, I'd hoped otherwise," Curtis sighed. "What business could *Casterons* have east with such a fleet?"

The elder frowned, laying his cutlery down in favour of some wine. "Blaine Casteron will forever be loyal to Esmond. Their shared time in boyhood has practically made them akin... Perhaps the king needed reinforcements, or had more proposals for the Archipelago. Whatever the reasons, you have naught to guilt over, my lord; Windtune is by far the *least* threatening kingdom, all Venusians considered."

Curtis accepted that, relaxing for the first time as he leant back in his seat. He smiled when he saw Feliks. "Is that to your liking, Feliks? Our cooks rarely have a chance to dabble with lamb."

Grease was running down Feliks's chin, his cheeks, his hands. He gulped his mouthful back. "It's amazing," he said. "I wish more people could taste it."

Curtis dropped his gaze, he fiddled with his brown sleeves. "That which is not eaten shall be tasted by many," he assured.

Feliks was growing tired of the lord's denial. "You wanted a feast, my lord. Why are you so ashamed of that?"

Lord Sculptor was wincing. It seemed like he was looking for another excuse before he sighed and gave up. "Because it's true. Austellus is in famine. People are starving at every stretch of the world and we can gorge ourselves without consequence."

"It's still a consequence if it weighs on you," Feliks frowned, feeling sorry for him. *I know too much about that consequence.* "But why should that matter? It's not like you're responsible... It's not worth turning the colour of an apple every time you're reminded of it."

Marcarius frowned with Feliks, as if it had been on his mind as well. Curtis only shook his head, rubbing his eyes. "You're right, Feliks, but you don't understand," he pleaded. "I have such a large city, such a large family. I do it to keep them happy, to keep them fed." He looked up to them both with sorry ocean eyes. After a time, he cursed under his breath and stood. "You'd best come with me."

They were led back the way they came, through the narrow walled keep and out to the city. The stone dock was less busy than it was earlier as the large, round, orange moon rose in the sky. It was noticeably cooler too, the soft breeze making Feliks shiver. Soon enough, they arrived at a large cobblestone building, a hay roof bursting from the top and two guards posted on the wooden stairs. Curtis nodded and they stepped aside, allowing entry through the creaky door. Inside lay a wealth of food. Stacks and stacks and stacks of grain and bags full of fruit and crates full of meat. Feliks had never seen so much in one place. "There was still plenty of food in the shipments, enough to feed every castle en route, to be sure. We only took a *small* portion from each trade wagon. A tax if you will. When Elder Engelmar came with threats of sparsity, I couldn't help myself. I *had* to know my family would be safe, that my people would be filled come this terrible *Pause*."

"How long have you done it?" Marcarius asked, gaping at the sickening mound of food.

"I've lost count of days," he frowned. "Enough time to regret it greatly." Curtis was sweating like a leaky dam. "But you know my reasons, and you know they aren't false ones. Promise me you'll speak nothing of this. Promise me you won't let the king know."

Marcarius hesitated, still in awe. "Make things right, Lord Sculptor, and we promise our mouths will stay sealed."

RILEY III
-Scatter-

Anger was slow to fill his veins, especially since so much had been exuded over the last few days. "What do you mean you found no one?"

Sir Gerard wasn't fazed. "Don't take it out on me, my lord. The scouts have told me nothing."

Riley Horncurve scratched his thick stubble and sighed. "Then send them out again. Tell them to find my daughter and son. Tell them to stay out until they find *anyone* who would take our side."

Out of all his regrets, leaving Athena at Selerborn during the revolt was the worst of them all. He knew they couldn't have waited, that waiting any longer would mean them getting caught by Sirens, that their escape plan would have fallen apart. If not for her, it would have been perfect; it had *all* gone to plan. It pained him so to have to let go of Sir Harold Smyth too, the old ram being a nostalgic face of home, of safety, but he was insisting. "I'm getting too old fer this shit, Riley," he was saying after Riley had met with his ram's guard, or at least the ones he could trust. "Let me give my life fer this, fer you, fer yer children. I can stall them for as long as you need if they attack. Put me out on duty until they do. Gods know I've been itchin' for battle, one last time."

Part of him hoped Sir Harold lived, that he was spared just for how long he had served and survived, but that hope was a dim one. The Sirens had always been backstabbers. He knew that ever since Marcus had said so.

Emily was picking at her nails nervously when Riley returned to their crimson tent. She looked up with auspicious eyes. Riley shook his head, and she winced.

"You still mad at me?"

His wife sighed, looking up to watch him slowly approach. "I hated fighting with you, you know that? Sometimes it seemed like you meant what you were saying."

"About Marcus?" he asked, taking Emily's hands.

She nodded. "That too. You could have been a lot less harsh."

"I was angry, Emily. Some of it was truth, aye, but I... I thought he could take it." He shook his head. "I'm sorry it's my fault."

Emily frowned and hugged him, gently stroking the back of his dark red hair. "You did what you had to, my love. We'll find them eventually. Athena *and* Marcus. We have to."

Riley agreed, inhaling the scent of Emily's brown hair before pulling away. Her hair reminded him of home, and of Athena, as she had inherited her mother's colour instead of Riley's red. "At least it was believable," he supposed. "If it were any less, Harper might not have bought it."

"Aye," Emily nodded. "You were smart about it; I'll give you that."

The dethroned Lord of Selerborn poured himself and his lady a goblet of wine. Before they could even think for a moment of peace, in came Lady Lili Raing, daughter of the Lord of Salem. "Most the tents are up, m'lord. The men fed and watered."

"Good," Riley nodded. "Have the horses readied, we'll leave within the hour."

She bowed stiffly and left. Riley closed his eyes and drank.

"Are you sure about this, Riley?" Emily asked. "Going so far south before finding them all?"

"I need an army to take back Selerborn," he said. "I'll need a bigger one to hold it. Half of Ram's Haven have turned coat overnight, it seems."

"But won't the Kalyx soldiers be enough? It's a long way to go for a few more men."

"Not just a few more men," he reminded her, "our help is needed." He stood and straightened his boiled leather using a mirror. "It will be weeks until we're ready, perhaps moons, until we have the force and favours, until the Sirens think they're safe enough. Best use that time as we can. Besides, Lord Raing is expecting us."

"He'll understand. Him *and* Lord Beart. It's not too late to go up, to meet with Cadmus now instead of later."

"I promised them war, Emily," he insisted. "And we need the men."

She seemed to accept that, dropping her eyes. "Fine, but I want to stay. Just in case they come back."

Riley nodded. "That's fair," he said. "But *I* want *you* safe." He was heading outside until he stopped himself. Emily hadn't moved, sitting cross legged on a silk chair, frowning. Riley moved to kiss her gently and then marched out.

The Salempath had a sunny day upon it, the lime green jungle trees waving through the light, the great Bullshorn River sparkling like a mass of stars in the distance, the endless pastures of grass swaying calmly in the wind. Salem was upon them, as was Aangmouth, *it makes no sense to go back now.* And to what would they come back to? A ruined Selerborn filled with Siren traitors that had thrice their numbers. Riley's mind wasn't changed, nor would it be. Going south was what he needed to do. Going south was the right thing to do.

Just like Lili had said, all the tents that lay pinned in the ground a few hours ago were now rolled-up into wagons, the only thing left of the encampment being the torn-up ground where the pegs lay. Men were moving hastily all around him, fetching saddles, weapons, horses, hauling sacks of food, locking up the open wagons in the train, and for a moment, Riley was proud. *I've never taken them to war before. Perhaps some have seen raids, but never by my command.* Sigmund would never have it; whenever time came to raid, it would be the Warrior Boy leading the charge. The host Riley had amassed so far wasn't too indifferent to what Sigmund might have taken to Heavia. Nevertheless, a strange feeling kept telling Riley he was less of a leader than his father.

Broken away from the main host, Riley eyed his brother saddling a gelding, looking somewhat lost. He had seemed somewhat lost the entire journey. Riley took towards him. "We're headin' southeast now, mate," he said, "the army's over there."

"Aye, it is," Luther nodded, glancing briefly at his brother.

Riley squinted suspiciously. "Why are ye here then?"

Luther's hazel eyes locked with Riley's. "I don't know why I'm here. I don't know why we're marching. I don't know why you think this plan will work." He continued to tighten his saddle. "We should've never left Selerborn."

"What?" Riley winced, believing he had misheard. "We're alive because of me. If we stayed in the keep, we'd be rotting on spikes."

"If we stayed in the keep, we might have had a chance." Luther wasn't angry, only fatigued.

"We were outnumbered."

"Father was outnumbered."

"We're not Sigmund."

"Aye, we're not," Luther frowned. "That's why you thought it better to play mind games with 'em instead of dealing with them straight, eh? You *knew* they would revolt."

"I knew nothing," Riley contested.

"And you still don't," said Luther. "You could have dealt with the Sirens like father would have, spurned them before they had the thought to rebel, but now the men you're leadin' don't have a fightin' chance in hell to take Selerborn back."

"I had no proof, Luther," Riley sighed angrily. "We had to wait. Half the city was already with Harper, and the other half would've seen me as mad for axing him."

"That's why I thought we would fight *after* the wait, and *defend* the keep, *defend* our home," he snapped, "not use a backdoor to run away like cowards."

"Would you rather be dead?" Riley asked, raising his voice. "That's what it seems like. We would be if we stayed. Harper *knows* the keep, even more than father did."

"Exactly, so why do you think it'd be any easier taking it back?"

"I *don't,*" Riley winced. "But what if I did? What if I took Harper's head? Half the city would still want me off the throne. I need *loyal* men. You don't know how hard it is to rule over men that want you dead."

"Loyalty," he sniggered. "Men won't be loyal to a runaway. You *lost* our home, Riley. You couldn't even keep your kids. I bet Harper has his greasy hands all over Athena."

That felt like a punch in the gut, but he didn't let it show. "You've never shown the slightest care for any of them."

"They're kin, Riley, of course I bloody love them," Luther glared.

Riley looked away as he bit on his cheeks. He had always known that. Even when Luther showed no interest, no support, no love, Riley always knew he did. "I can't turn back time," Riley muttered. "What would you have me do?"

"It's over, brother," Luther said grimly. "I'd leave. I'd set up a life far from here where no one knows my face. Save your kids if you can, but please don't send all these men to the grave for no reason. Don't be an idiot. You can't take Selerborn back."

The would-be Lord of Selerborn squinted in fury. "I *will* take Selerborn back. It's our *home*. It's our *legacy*. And if you're running away from that now, then you're pissing on that legacy."

Luther laughed with contempt, hopped on his gelding and charged to the camp. *"Suicide, this is! Suicide!"* he yelled over the small army. Riley grabbed a horse when one came into reach and galloped after him. *"Go back to your homes! See your families again! You'll be dying for nothing!"* Riley's soldiers were slowly looking up, confused. *"Don't go through with my brother's stupid plan! It'll get you all killed!"*

Riley furiously snatched a warhorn from a lone soldier, and blew as hard as he could. Luther spun around deliriously. *"Go on then! Leave! Piss on your legacy! Us northmen won't forget!"* he screamed, leaping off his horse and unsheathing Shofar. He swung it carelessly as he marched forward. "Get down from that horse, *now*."

His brother scanned Shofar like he had never seen it before, then Riley like he had never seen him before. "This is how you'd have it, eh?"

The Horncurve's tensed arm was shaking, and for a second, he almost dropped the longsword, yet he held on, tightening his grip.

Luther plucked his sword from his scabbard and threw it to the ground. He spat. "Enjoy hell." Tugging at his reins, Luther twisted around and galloped away.

Riley cast Shofar to the dirt. *"Go on, you wean, run! Run back to your tower! Run away, you coward! Don't think you're ever welcome back!"*

ESMOND XII
-Tact-

M arching between the endless ranks of Centaur soldiers didn't make him feel powerful, nor proud, nor kingly, only frustrated that they weren't moving yet. He was due to meet with his councillors, but even that - a prospect which once filled him with such immense relief and closure - felt like an unnecessary chore to him. Maybe it was because Esmond Centaur needed his vengeance and couldn't wait, maybe it was because his tolerance for high lords had lessened the more time he spent in the capital, or maybe it was because his small council had just become four fewer.

It had happened whilst Edward's blood was still wet on the king's fists.

"What the fuck, Esmond?!" Sir Orion knelt, shaking him. "Do you know what you've just done?"

Esmond didn't respond. He swayed lifelessly as he stared at the blood, at his shaking fists, at the beaten skull of Edward Cancer.

Orion stood and began pacing, muttering something under his breath. "What the fuck are you gonna do now?"

"War," he managed to say. "We must war with them. We... must march. They... raze my lands and..."

"Have you gone *insane?!*" his former *First Avail* yelled. "After *so long* trying to make peace? What about your children?"

"The blood of the future," Esmond kept saying, never blinking. "No second chance... something terrible... distrust... peace..."

"I've followed you for years!" Sir Orion cried, with so much emotion that Esmond struggled to comprehend in that moment. "I've followed you through lows, I've followed you through highs. You're completely wrong if you think I'd follow you through madness."

"Madness…" he twitched, tears returning to his dry eyes. "Punishment… laws… be a king…"

"Get your things, Jovian, we're leaving," Orion said. "And you too, Sparks."

Esmond could still remember the alien look Tobi Sparks had on his face as he left, as if he was looking at a monster. *I am,* Esmond knew, left alone in the chamber with a gut-wrenching feeling of fear. But that day was the last time he felt fear.

The council tent looked so much emptier without Sir Orion Reade. As Esmond was gathering the soldiers in Lunarpass, he kept telling himself *he'll come back. He has to. He's the only one to tell me what I need to hear. He's the only one I trust wholly.* Most of a week had passed and the *First Avail* didn't return. Esmond then decided to curse him. *I don't need him to win this war. I don't need him to help me do justice. The traitor knows that just as much as I do.*

But now, with most of his sons dead, the other lost, and no *First Avail* to succeed him, Esmond had no heir. *If I fall in these battles, it'll be the end of the Centaur dynasty.* He couldn't even consider Thaddeus being king. He had always imagined one of his sons on the throne. *There is Sir Roswell.* He was the *Second Avail*, but it was a queer thought seeing him on the throne too. When Esmond gave him that title, he never thought it would come down to inheritance. *As long as I live, it won't.* And Esmond had resolved to live.

Darius Boyd was using his finger to trace a map when Esmond entered. "-and by then, we should be on course to-" He looked up, as did the councillors who came. "My king," he said, and they all bowed. *Missing nine, not four* he remembered when he noticed Thaddeus, Hugo Lane, and Joseph Frost's absence. They had stayed at Lunarpass. He had also almost forgotten Galloway and Marcarius.

"Don't stop," Esmond said, crossing his arms. "Who do we have?"

Briggs Waker hesitated, reaching for a scroll. The head of word clearly didn't seem comfortable in his added title of head of pennons. "Some pennons have refused calls, my king, or are just too far away to meet with our host before the Crossroads. Those who we have, we will meet at Solis

Bridge: the likes of Alec Odum, Jocks Wright, Nate Fuller, Jesse Stods-"

Esmond realised he didn't care who accepted the call. "Who refused the calls?"

Lord Waker seemed to choke on his words. "They... have their reasons, my king."

"Still, I will hear them."

The head of word and pennons blinked nervously, before flipping the papyrus. "Well, Goattreath, Artis Bay, Negal Town, and the Dog's Paw seem to have fallen to Khavars already: I have received no word, not even a refusal, nor have I had replies from the ravens we sent past the Arm of Jupiter." He frowned, glancing at Lord Kaus Jade. "Jade Castle and Fort Diolus would rather protect their holdfasts. You can hardly blame them, my king, Khavars line their outskirts-"

"And who else, Lord Waker? Who *refused?*"

Briggs swallowed deeply. "Brecken Odum, my king. Along with Eduard Starhart and Simon Loost. They're our largest losses."

Good. Then they have chosen their side. Esmond nodded intently. "So be it."

"We still outnumber them, don't we, my lord?" Darius asked.

"Oh, by a landslide, to be sure," Briggs nodded. "Likely they suffered many casualties at..." he glanced at Esmond, "at... New Negalia. We would be a healthy thirty-five thousand when we are due to meet the Khavars at the Crossroads."

"You are certain we'll meet at the Crossroads?" Wye Vesta asked.

Darius nodded. "We must," he said stiffly. "They mean to split up there. We must not let them scatter their pillagers about the Pole."

"Only thirty-five thousand?" Esmond frowned.

Briggs smiled, disbelieving. "That's almost twice their force-"

"We're at war, Lord Waker," the king said coldly. "Do you think I mean to root them out our lands, then forget?"

Every councillor fell still and silent. Ellys Dart looked as if he was about to faint. "You don't mean-"

"After the Crossroads, we march south for the Capras, then we march *east*, to the Archipelago, and we will *burn* every Venusian home until all that sits on those islands is ash and bone. Is there something you don't understand about that? Did I not make that clear when I spoke of *war?*"

Briggs winced. "We'd need the *entire* Pole to stand a chance."

"Good that you're head of *pennons* then, Lord Waker."

Lord Wye Vesta was the only man brave enough to speak up. "What of what we spoke of, my king? I thought we decided that marching was unwise, that they would break us from within?"

Esmond studied the balding man. "Does war sicken you so, Lord Vesta?" he asked. "They are *burning* my country, one keep at a time. I won't *have* one if they continue. How could they *break* us in our home?"

No one replied to that. The king gave sharp glances at his older councillors, those who had been with Esmond for what seemed like forever. They all wore frowns. "Forgive him, my king," said Kaus Jade, "we are all aged, it is true. To see another war unfold..." The bygone man couldn't finish his sentence.

"Go then, all of you, leave," Esmond grimaced. "I don't need old men like you slowing us down. If you wish to take no part then go now, go to your homes, go see your families again." He waited as his councillors gawked. *"Go!"*

Ellys Dart, Wye Vesta, and Kaus Jade scurried out of the room, as fast as their old legs could take them. Esmond sighed as he rubbed his eyes. *Why are these men being so difficult?* "Lord Waker," he said eventually. "I'd take it you haven't written to Centaur's Lagoon?"

"Lord Lorimer is still in a state of recovery, my king," he replied. "I thought it unwise, yes."

"He's the only one who'll understand. Not that any of you have lost children." Esmond smiled. "I bet you all see me as mad."

"You're not mad, my king," Elliot Moss assured. "We are all here to help you."

"As you are," Esmond nodded. "You're all dismissed. Ready the men. Continue our march as soon as we can."

Elliot, Briggs, and Darius bowed and left. *Three left,* Esmond realised, not knowing if he regretted sending the others away. *Three left of my once thriving council.* He was alone in this war, and he knew it... if not for one person...

He took out a parchment and a quill, and began writing.

Brother,

You know what they are. You know what they've done. You know what they've taken. We will meet them at the Sag's Crossroads, and there they will pay. The last time we spoke, you told me what would happen if fate brings swords to our hands. Now the time has come.

LETA III
-Course-

D reams of the battle wouldn't leave her alone, not even for the few hours her insomnia spared her each night. If anything, she was glad they weren't any longer. She dreamt of it all: the piercing sound of warhorns shaking the fort into rubble, the way she would try to help fight, only to have her arms lock up and throw her back whenever she'd try to swing, the way her mother had screamed at her to leave as the people and soldiers of Fort Deus swarmed down the burning Antrum River to the few rowing boats that lay docked. Not even when she was awake could she shake the thought of the cries she heard, the wounds she saw.

Leta Centaur woke after yet another dream of fighting: her arms refusing to swing, her body refusing to move. She gasped and slammed her hands to the wooden row boat, making Sir Roswell jump. "Welcome back, my lady," he tittered nervously.

"Sorry," she winced, holding her head. "Another one."

Sir Roswell nodded silently, elegantly moving the paddles back and forth like he had done for days. Leta would offer to help, but her arms ached after only an hour or two. "You never forget your first battle," he said, frowning to the ocean. "Whether you fought or not."

Leta wanted to forget. "I *wanted* to fight. Like you did."

"You couldn't have," he smiled. "But you're braver than me. I never want to fight." He then chuckled. "Do you think your lord father raised me to *Second Avail* because of my fighting skills?"

"I don't doubt it," she said. "You were better than everyone in the battle. I saw you."

Sir Roswell scanned the horizon, wonder in his blue eyes. "You didn't see your brother then, I take it?"

The princess had to think. "I saw him shouting commands on the battlements. I saw him fetch his bow. I…" Her heart beat faster. "I saw him fall when the wall crumbled…"

The knight shook his head, smiling. "Call me a madman, but your brother summoned *magic* that night," he said.

"Magic?" Leta chuckled. "He's decent with a bow, but…"

"*Magic*," he repeated. "I know it. There were blue flames, Leta, the colour of zircon. The same fire in his eyes, on his fingers. Never, in all my days, have I seen anything like it. Anyone who saw would say the same."

Leta couldn't tell if he was joking or not. It didn't seem like something he would joke about. "Magic," she said again, the word feeling haunted on her tongue. "Are you certain?"

Roswell placed the oars down and put a knuckle to his heart. "On *all* my oaths. Whatever your brother did that night…" he felt the paddles again, smiling. "It wasn't of this world," he decided.

Leta squinted at the ocean, not knowing whether to believe him or not. *Anyone else who saw is most likely dead. But if Fletcher really did do magic, after so long of it not existing…* She sighed. "I hope he's alive."

"He must be," Roswell said softly. "I'd swear on that too, if I knew."

Well that defeats the purpose of swearing, she almost said. It took all that time to realise she was shivering, goosebumps the size of pimples coating her arms. She tugged on the soft furs that lay in the boat, watching the dark, calm Trader's Sea pass her by as she thought.

<hr />

When dawn came, or at least the first lights of dawn, Leta opened her sleepy eyes to the sight of land, and land that was close. So close that by the time she rubbed the crust from her eyes, the boat bumped gently onto it. "Are we here?" she asked hoarsely.

Sir Roswell nodded as he put his finger to his lips. "I saw fires around the Grove," he whispered, "outside the Lagoon. I need to see if it's safe."

"Can I come too?"

The knight glanced around, biting his cheeks. "Stay close," he said, hopping onto the delicate auburn grass. She followed closely.

The air wasn't any warmer than the night, and before long, Leta was shivering again. A thick white mist gripped the auburn trees with cold fingers, extending its reach around their bodies, and around their row boat the further they walked. The soft rustle underfoot wasn't like that of home, Leta realised. Unlike the Negal lands, here had what seemed like an endless amount of flattened leaves, taking up so much ground that even the grass was difficult to see. Each of them made a hard crunch when stepped on, as if they were frozen solid.

Ten crunches later, Sir Roswell held out his arm as he looked down. Leta stopped. "What is it?" she whispered.

"Caltrops," he said, squinting at the leaves. "We need to go back to the boat, try and look for a banner or something."

"In this fog we'll find nothing," she sighed as she followed.

They didn't creep that far back for Sir Roswell to drop his guise and start yelling. *"Hey! Stop! Come back!"* He ran to the bank, as did Leta.

One brutish man of three was towing their raft away on a boat that was slightly bigger. *"Hahaha! Filfy Capras!"* he laughed heartily.

"We're not Capras! We're Centaurs! We're Centaurs!"

The wide-jawed man squinted suspiciously. *"Why you wiv the siege then? You're a filfy Capra! You can't fool me!"*

"They *are* Centaurs, Slabjaw," winced a slender woman next to him. "Look at their coats."

Slabjaw frowned, and thumped the sleeping man behind him. "Keeks, 'these people Centaurs to you?"

Kian Weeks jolted up deliriously, eyeing Roswell and Leta. *"Kian!"* Sir Roswell beamed. *"You're alive! We're here! We made it out! Come back!"*

Slabjaw turned his slabbed jaw towards Kian. "You know 'em?"

A smile spread across Kian's face. It was like he was witnessing a resurrection. "I do," he said quietly, before snapping out of it. "I do know them, I do, turn the boat around!"

Slabjaw frowned and did so, floating the two boats gently back to the bank. Kian leapt off as soon as it landed and embraced Sir Roswell tightly. "Oh, it's so good to see you," he smiled excitedly. "And young Leta too. I didn't think you survived."

"I don't think many did," Sir Roswell said grimly. "But I couldn't be happier to see you, Weeks," he smiled.

"What did that man mean?" Leta asked. "What siege?"

"Shit, get on the boat," Kian frowned, glancing around nervously. "I'll tell you once we're away from here, my lady."

They did so, and the two boats sailed deep into the hazy fog before they spoke again. "I assume you came to meet with Lord Lori?" Kian asked as the boats slowed into a glide.

Sir Roswell nodded. "Is he well?"

"He made it out of the lagoon in time, yes," Kian said, "marching with a host, I don't know where though. A few days later those Capra backstabbers lay down a siege."

Leta bit her lip. *Had they always been turncoats? Or was it Tyran catching me spying that made them change sides? Or Fletcher disregarding them?* She hoped it wasn't either of their faults, but if they always were traitors, it didn't make her feel good to know that she trusted them.

"How long have they been there?" Roswell asked.

Kian shook his head. "Hard to know. Days at least. You're lucky we caught you."

"We're lucky you didn't steal our boat, too," the knight smiled, making Slabjaw look abashed. "Who are your companions?"

"After the battle, the Taigan Midknights found me," he said. "A lot of the survivors we found have been taking refuge at Mount Taigus."

"The Taigan Midknights?" Sir Roswell frowned. "You mean Thyne's outlaws?"

"Hey!" Slabjaw grimaced. "We're no outlaws!"

"Toren is exiled, Slabjaw," the woman sighed. "We *are* outlaws."

Slabjaw pulled a confused face, and shut up.

"I'm Kyna, by the way," she said. Leta smiled at her. She reminded her a lot of Eva, if not for the big forehead and red, tied back hair. But her clothes were definitely something Eva would wear, and the fact her hair was so wiry, looking as though it hadn't been brushed in moons, only added to their semblance.

Supposedly, Leta, although young, was alive when her father sent Toren Thyne into exile, though she could never remember it. It was for some sort of smuggling or piracy, she knew, as Esmond's sole purpose for the longest time was to find 'Toren and his brotherhood of brigands', as he used to call them. He never could. Occasionally, he would catch members of the Midknights sailing among the Taiga Isles. Some he would question, some he would hang, depending on how he judged them. Erik Thyne, the Lord of Trader's Dock, was Toren's brother, and Leta never knew why Esmond didn't see that as suspicious, as a smuggler would be much more successful if the lord of a dock was helping him. *Father is too trusting, just like Fletcher,* even though part of her knew that she was too.

"So, you joined them?" Sir Roswell asked. "The Taigan Midknights?"

"I had no choice, Roswell," Kian sighed. "They razed Fort Deus to the ground. There's nothing for me back there. And to go up to Lunarpass would be suicide. Gods know how many goats and Venusians are lurking between us and the Pole."

Razed to the ground. Leta's stomach sank. The last memory of her home would be of it ablaze, men dying and screaming from within.

"But where will *you* go now?" Kian asked. "You can't wait for the siege to lift. Would you come back to Mount Taigus with us?"

"Is it worth it?" Sir Roswell asked.

Kian smirked and raised his brows. "It's dangerous, but we could use men like you," he said. "We're surrounded by enemies there, I admit. The Helas want us gone, the Capras want us dead, and every bloody noble in the Pole seems to despise us. I imagine you'd want to get away from that."

"We should, yeah," Sir Roswell agreed. "Best to keep the princess safe now that she's out of it."

Leta stayed quiet, not caring if she was near danger or not. "Aquamare might be your best bet then," said Kyna. "I know most of the way; I could take you there. Lord Oberon would keep you both safe. I won't be able to stay, though."

Sir Roswell looked to Leta, his short black hair lifting in the wind. "It'll be safer than that old volcano, I suppose."

Kian nodded and stood, gently rocking the small boat. He held out his arms. "Then I hope to see you soon, friend."

"You too, Weeks," Sir Roswell smiled as they hugged.

"Take care, my lady," Kian bowed to Leta as he and Slabjaw hopped to the second boat. "If you would, tell your lord father not to hang me for joining the Midknights if he should ever find me in the Pole. I'd much rather keep my head for all the years I've served."

"I will. No promises, though," Leta smirked.

The former head of the fort's garrison smiled, and the two boats parted.

ASHER V
-Herald-

A harsh light. A mossy path spiralling down. A seer waiting for him. Asher Centaur had lived this moment so many times that he often forgot it was a dream. In fact, the more they grew closer, the more vivid the dream appeared, and the drearier real life became, both leaving the prince to question whether it *was* a dream or not.

Still, he was ready for what was coming. He knew of the knife that would slash his throat. He knew of the seer who held it. He knew of the windless pressure that would push him back. It was the first time he was conscious of it, *and the first time I'll live instead of die.*

"Prince of Ash is his name," the raspy voiced seer began, "King of Light is his fate."

"Who are you?" Asher asked the light. Even if he thought of something different to say, he would always say the same thing.

"I am none, yet I am some. The serpent that comes is all."

Now the wind starts, he knew, anticipating it a moment before it brushed his arms. "What serpent?"

"The Serpent of Stars. And you must find it, Asher Centaur, as you must find the prince." The wind wasn't as loud as it once was. Every night it became quieter. "For it will poison the city, flooded by waters as black as night. It will poison the realms, infected with discord as cold as winter. It will poison the..." Then the words became unintelligible, drowned by the noisy wind. Asher squinted, trying his best to understand one last word, trying his best to resist the fierce gale. He felt the scrawny hands clutch his arms. *Shit! The man!* He had remembered too late. He closed his eyes and awaited the pain.

"Asher," a soft voice said, pulling him from the dream. "Asher, wake up," she said. "It's time to wake up."

Lyssa was holding out a crouton when Asher opened his eyes deliriously. He frowned, instinctively reaching for his neck, but there was no pain, not there, not anywhere. "Lyssa," he grimaced as his eyes adjusted to the misty daylight. He reeked of sweat.

"How was the dream?" she asked kindly.

Asher shook his head, biting into the crouton. "I didn't understand any more," he croaked.

"I'm sorry," she frowned. "Leo said he heard voices; we should get moving."

The prince nodded, stumbling to his feet and finding the stick he was using to walk. *Did I die or live?* He couldn't remember. He didn't *want* to remember. It took half a minute of standing for him to forget.

Just over a fortnight ago, Asher and Lyssa weren't alone for long before Leo was reunited with them, the blood of Drew Ortiz and Evan Stone still on his hands. Lyssa said nothing, but Asher could still remember the way she stared at the blood-soaked katars, squinting as if she was reading them.

There wasn't much objection once Leo had chosen the mountain path, just in case they *were* hunted, even though that path took thrice the length of the next longest route. Asher could feel the strain on the second day as they ascended closer to the peaks, his legs tensing, his breath leaving him, the wind acting so wildly that one misstep could toss any one of them off the cliff face. "This is better than dealing with every soldier Todd sends in search of us," Leo assured, but it was debatable. Every day would include a strenuous trudge, a small break, pushing on, a break for water, a break for food, a break for sleep, a break for Asher… He hated being so weak. *I'm making this a much longer journey than it needs to be,* he knew. At the very least, they didn't need to make fires, the winds growing warmer and warmer the longer they spent travelling.

After an eternity, they arrived at Caligo, and the small mountainside city proved as luxurious as could be. The party had a featherbed when they stayed in a wooden cabin by the Whitefin River, surrounded by lime jungle trees and peculiarly shaped rocks. Leo paid the owner of the cabin some coin to forget they existed, but once the old man was behind them, they couldn't tell if he'd keep that promise when soldiers came quizzing, *if* soldiers came quizzing. Lyssa wanted to believe that they'd lose their pursuit once they crossed the mountains, but whether they were looking for the trio or not, soldiers were everywhere. It wasn't long before their days became not only a test of stamina, but a test of stealth as well.

Leo was already a good mile ahead before Lyssa and Asher began walking slowly. He was using an old rusted machete to cut away the excessive foliage and jungle leaves, even though these most recent days had seen less of them. Where Leo had found the weapon, neither of them noticed, but they knew better than to ask.

"You're looking better," Lyssa said as she held Asher's arm, helping him walk.

Asher looked to his hand. It was only *slightly* less pale than before. "Better? Impossible," he smirked.

"I beg to differ," she smirked back. "You should consider yourself lucky that it was *me* who came with you, and not some stuck-up highborn lady who faints at the sight of mud."

"Well, you're pretty stuck-up and highborn yourself so I don't know what you're getting at," he jested dryly. Lyssa only laughed. "I *am* lucky," he continued. "I wouldn't have made it so far without you."

Lyssa stared at him with her beautiful blue eyes. "It won't be much longer now."

"We're getting close," Asher agreed. "I can feel it."

It seemed like they had to duck or hide every ten minutes, Leo sending back a signal with his hands to get down. Getting down wasn't the difficult part, as Asher simply fell to his knees; it was getting back up again that proved arduous. Sometimes, it would take ages for Asher to find his dubious footing, but with the help of Lyssa, he would always do so. She would regularly warn him if his foot was about to hit the snare of a vine, or his face a branch of a tree. *She's my guardian, my lioness.* He *needed* one since he couldn't keep his eyes open without long intervals of rest.

◄━━━━━▣

By the time dusk fell and repose was needed, the entire party was drenched in sweat and aching everywhere. Leo had found a deep, rocky river, and fell into it with a sigh as soon as he could. Lyssa lowered Asher gently down next to a jungle tree, splashed her face, and brought a cloth soaked in the cool water for his face. As soon as Asher felt his muscles loosen, Leo came back, drenched and smiling. "How are you both?" he asked as he sat.

"Could be worse," Lyssa supposed, joining the two exhausted boys on the verdant jungle ground.

"It always could be," Leo agreed. "We're not far now, though. Once we're out of this jungle it's only a couple more hills until we reach the Sanct-" he stopped himself, remembering. He winced.

Asher smiled feverishly. His suspicion was confirmed. *Sanctum Amino must also be the place in my dreams.* It seemed eerie to finally put a name to that spectral setting. "We didn't hear anything."

"In any case," their escort continued, reaching into his dusty satchel, "I think we can afford to treat ourselves tonight." He pulled out a drinking skin, grinning ferociously.

"Rum?" Lyssa observed. "You bought *rum* from Caligo?"

"Not rum, Lyssa," he smiled. "It's *much* stronger."

"Oh, no, I can't," Asher frowned with a smile just as big. "As soon as it touches my lips, I'll retch it back up again."

"That's the biggest lie you've ever told," Lyssa said, shaking her head. "The *only* person at Fort Deus who could match you *drink for drink* was Lachlan Casteron, and he was *insane.*"

Asher chuckled, nodding. "I almost couldn't keep up." He glanced at the skin again, smiling. "Fuck it, go on, then."

Leo took a swig, wincing harshly before passing it to Lyssa. "Watch out, it *is really* strong."

"The king always told me that alcohol brings out the truth in men," Asher said as Lyssa drank. "You better watch your tongue, Leo, else your secrets might come spilling out."

Leo held up his hands, still wincing. "I brought this upon myself."

Lyssa wiped her mouth and passed the skin to Asher. The drink burnt his throat; it wasn't like anything he had drunk before. Though, it tasted good, like cherries and sugar and other fruits. Almost immediately, he could feel his head start to sway.

"The king's your father, isn't he?" Leo asked.

Asher nodded, grimacing as he gave the skin back. "The King of Caelestia." He had forgotten how regal the title sounded. "Gave up my claim to that when we came here."

"We'll make it back," Leo disagreed confidently. "You'll still be the heir, won't you?"

The prince dropped his eyes. "Yeah," he muttered. For some reason Asher doubted it. For some reason he wanted to stay here. He glanced at Lyssa's perfect face.

"Oh," Leo smiled, realising. "You don't want to. You *can't.*"

"What?" Asher Centaur was blushing; he could feel it.

Leo laughed. "You may have my secrets by the end of this night, but I have yours as well. No one can know, can they?"

"They could," Lyssa smirked. "But they would be... unhappy."

"You don't have to tell me, I heard at Merchant's Bay," Leo said, shaking off his smile. "Your secrets are safe with me. What will you do, though? Stay here?"

"One step at a time," Asher said. "I won't know what I want until these dreams are sorted." Lyssa didn't add her opinion, keeping her head down. "But what about you, Leo? You're yet to tell us your secrets. You know everything about us and we know nothing about you."

"I wouldn't keep it that way," he said kindly. "But you know a *little.*"

"What, that you were orphaned?" Lyssa added.

Leo nodded reluctantly. "I didn't know my parents for long, no."

"What about after?" Asher asked. "What did you do after your parents died?"

"I travelled," he said, leaning back against the viney trunk of a tree. "Not on purpose, mind you. My legs walked and I followed."

"Have you seen the south then?" Lyssa asked. "The Auburn Pole, the Archipelago?"

Leo smiled and closed his eyes. "Not south. East. To lands you'd never believe exist."

"East?" Lyssa frowned curiously. "You're lying."

"I'm not," he assured. "The Endless Open isn't just an empty desert. Behind it are mountains, and behind those, entire worlds. I've seen cities made of cliff faces, kingdoms that go deep underground, forests that light up with glowing bugs at night, brighter than the day. I've seen men wielding swords the size of chairs, riding elks with great big horns. I'm telling you, those lands are... unbelievable."

"Why haven't you told anyone?" Asher asked as he gawked at the boy.

Leo tittered. "Who could I tell? Who would *believe* me? Anyone who has even *tried* to cross those mountains has ended up dead."

"So many of my *grandfathers* have died trying to figure out those mountains," Lyssa agreed. "How did you do it?"

"I don't know," he smiled, "I just kept walking. I knew if I stopped, I'd die. And I didn't want to die."

"So, why did you come back?" Lyssa asked. "You had *all* the answers over there, no one in Austellus has seen what you've seen. Why give that up and start working for seers?"

"You won't believe this either," he said. "My father came to me in a dream, like a seer came to you, Asher. He looked the same as he did the last time I saw him, but his voice was different; it was old and weak. I didn't know if it was a nightmare until he started telling me to go back, to swear them oaths and play my part... as a son. So, I go to the Sanctum, and... they were there, waiting for me, *expecting* me."

"That's amazing," Lyssa almost slurred, taking a moment before curling herself around Asher's arm. "Maybe we could go east? They'd never find us there."

"Maybe," Asher nodded. He winced and held his head. "Gods, it's hitting me now."

"I'm already flying," Leo beamed, failing to stand, making them laugh.

For the rest of the night they talked about nothing and everything at the same time. Asher could remember slurring old southern songs, badly dancing while doing so, listening intently to Leo's adventures east of the Endless Open, laughing so much that his stomach began to hurt, kissing Lyssa and being inside her long after Leo had fallen asleep. Most of the night remained a blur when he woke the next day, his head pounding like it had been rung with a hammer.

He was the first one to wake up, for once feeling energised, for once not having the dream. He had company, though, in the form of the small zircon bracelet Leta had given him. He thought again about going east with Lyssa, now that he had a clear head. It made him excited. It made him want it now. *But going east would mean saying goodbye to my family forever: to Esmond and Semira and Fletcher and Eva and Hew and Leta.* He didn't feel whole without them. Just missing *one* of them made a huge hole in his chest; he couldn't imagine leaving them *all.*

One step at a time, he reminded himself as the dawn came.

ELAYNE V
-Blade-

Out of every Lord of Ignis, Fitz must have been the first and only one to spend his entire coronation week locked up in his bedroom solar. No one could calm the lion; anyone who dared to enter the den left with their head bitten off. Even Elayne Lyrderyn tried to console her nephew, but she wasn't any more accepted than the others. It was the first time she felt bad for him.

Elayne, Ayden, Fitz, Elder Ulrich, and Sulwyn were the ones guilty of visiting Lady Gina's solar the day she died, or so the servants had told Fitzroy. Elayne thought he would lash out, taking each and every one, bar himself, to hang out in front of the keep for the vultures, but instead, all he did was watch, prowling as if he was hunting for his next meal. It unsettled Elayne, having to endure the daggers Fitz wore in his eyes every time they passed in the hallway. The boy's courtesy was always icy, but he never *hated* anyone. *Anyone who wasn't within his reach, at least.*

Elayne wished to know the answer too; the love she bore for Gina was astronomical compared to the love she bore for any of the slippery lords that were left in Ignis. But even Ayden denied poisoning her. "I promise, Elayne, I did no such thing," he was begging, over and over. "It wasn't me, I *swear*. What reason would I have to lie to you?" *Many,* Elayne thought, but she left it at that, feeling ill at the sight of her brother for any longer.

If she was to believe her brother, they didn't come any closer to an answer; no way would Fitz have poisoned his own mother, especially since he was so angered by her loss; Ulrich was too loyal and had no reason to murder Gina, nor did Sulwyn, but if the head of word was to blame, Elayne thought he would have been more prudent than to gamble with poison. Sulwyn Wisp was a strange man, a mysterious man, but no murderer, and no fool either. That left no one, no suspects that could have carried it out. *That's why it must have been Ayden, no matter what he says. He has everything to gain by slaying the unborn heir.* Still, it was too much of a risk to accuse him. *If he falls, so do I; I have no lions to protect me now.*

"How did you calm him?" Elayne asked Elder Ulrich when Fitz saw sunlight for the first time.

"I didn't," Ulrich shrugged as they walked. "One minute I was alone, the next, he was in my solar, asking me what tasks needed his attention."

The Lady Paramount Regent winced. "And he spoke with no one? No one came to change his mind?"

The elder frowned, shaking his head. "Perhaps he recognised his duty. Everyone does, eventually."

Elayne wanted to believe that. She wanted to believe that the boy had grown up and seen sense. *But he's never been closer to snapping.*

A harsh midday sun scorched Ignis when the heroes of Aurdrive returned, parading through the streets on high horses, flashing shredded Equuleus banners, bowing and catching bouquets as civilians gushed and cheered. Sir Brendan Gryfford was who led the host, remaining still as stone as he rode through the crowds. Behind him was a thick swarm of knights, or soon-to-be knights as Elayne suspected, since it was tradition to give such honours after a battle. Though, it didn't seem like they had even been to a scrap. Less than half wore scrapes and scratches on their armour, on their swords, on their person, and next to none had blood stains on their clothes. Reynold would always tell his wife how war changes men forever, detailing such accounts from the *Scorpius Rebellion. It was either a slaughter, or Reynold completely lied.* But Reynold wasn't a liar. Back then, he would not have had many years over ten. *To a ten-year-old, a cut must seem like a scar.* Elayne took a sip of wine as she watched from her solar's balcony.

A wagon rolled not far between the soldiers, bars on the windows with chained hands trying to reach out. *Prisoners,* Elayne knew, *so they might not have slaughtered everyone.* Cyrus Sand seemed to think the more Equuleus dead, the better: that 'they shan't rebel when numbers don't favour'. *The more dead, the fewer enemies,* Elayne agreed, *but if a desert can't be shared, what more would we own than a heap of sand?* Elijah Gale was the only one from the council sane enough to concur with her.

In due course, Fitz rode out with his guard of two to greet the army. Sir Brendan bowed to him as Sir Cedric and three men Elayne didn't know brought a casket forward. Fitz shifted it opened and looked for no longer than a second before shooing it away. Sir Cedric bowed as well before the Lord of Ignis galloped back to the keep. The rest soon followed.

The Lyrderyns didn't have a mausoleum like the Centaurs or the Tridents had, since bodies rotted quicker in the warmer heat. Sir Goldwyn must have reeked, the men carrying his casket doing well not to wince. They would probably send him off down Lake Ignis tonight before he rotted any more, burn him as they had Reynold and every Lord of Ignis prior to him. It seemed like everything in her life was reminding Elayne of Reynold, and she soon realised she missed him more than ever. "Come back to me," Elayne whispered under her breath as she played with a ring. "Lyssa, come home, keep your mother from going insane. And you, Lionel, if you're out there." She always refused to believe he wasn't.

An hour of warrior watching passed until Elayne had Raha intruding on her. "My lady," she bowed. "Lord Fitz will be going through the honours in the throne room shortly."

"Ok," Elayne nodded, dismissing her. She watched for a while longer, not leaving until the streets were silent once more.

Sunlight was no less brighter in the throne room than the city, the semi-open ceiling letting the light flood onto the throng of highborns and knights atop the mosaic floor. They were all completely still when Elayne snuck in, manoeuvring through the crowds to find Eleanor and Elder Ulrich. All the while, Fitz was knighting a man. "-a loyal servant of Ignis for too long. If you would, I'd also have you on my lion's guard."

"I'll be honoured, my lord. I'll pledge my life to the guard too." The gruff man was on one knee, but he was still taller than Fitz, a step above him. He had huge muscles that his cloths couldn't conceal, and deeply-tanned skin. Aside from his height and muscles, his hair was the most spectacular thing about him, long and brown, easily passing his pectorals, poking out in what must have been six pony tails.

Fitz unsheathed a katar, since he wore no sword, and slid it to the man's shoulder. "Then by the power of this blade and by the witnesses of this court, may you rise as Sir Samson Taheri of the lion's guard."

Samson did so, blocking out the sun for a brief moment, before joining

Sir Cedric, Sir Brendan, and two others beside Fitz. Elayne didn't know where he'd got the other two from, nor did she know their names yet, but they seemed lean and grumpy, never too far from the pommel of their swords. They had been following Fitz around since he was crowned, so they must be of the lion's guard, but Fitz never met with Elayne to confirm that. It seemed like he had met with every councillor *except* Elayne.

"There'll be no more knightings today," he said as he jogged tiredly up to the throne. "Thank you all for your oaths, and your *brave* services, sirs." It was strange seeing Fitz be so diplomatic, daunting almost. "Lord Cyrus Sand," he continued, "step forward, my lord."

Cyrus marched out, falling stiffly to one knee.

"In light of the treachery the Sagittarians have displayed, it's clear to me that Lutum is in need of new rule," he said. "Cyrus Sand, you have been of great help and service over the many years, and, I believe, crucial to our victory at Aurdrive. But your family has no home, no keep, no holdfast. So, as Lord of the Canicule, I would name you Lord of Lutum, and give your line a place in this kingdom once we take it a few moons from now."

The head of military lowered his weathered head. "It would be an honour, my lord," he declared, before shooting up and marching back.

There was a quiet chatter throughout the room. Elayne glanced to Ulrich, who didn't return the look. *Fitz must have consulted with Ulrich before such an edict.* By his placidity, he confirmed it. *Why would he condone taking Lutum, though? It's always been a Sagittarius kingdom.*

"Sir Cedric," Fitz said, quelling the crowd, "you gave me word of prisoners?"

"A prisoner and a guest, my lord," he replied.

"Bring them here," Fitz nodded, looking elsewhere.

The man Sir Cedric brought out had a strong chin with a big nose, a sullen look on his face, dried mud stuck to his cheeks and arms. "Apollo Equuleus, my lord."

"Really?" Fitz smirked, massaging a katar against his cheek. If it were any sharper, it would shave off Fitz's sorry attempt at a beard. "Speak up, then, Apollo. What reason did you have to attack Aurdrive? What reason to go against one of our own?"

"You wouldn't understand, boy," he leered. The Lord of Ignis did no more than a nod for one of his knights to kick Apollo into a kneel.

Fitz stood, sauntering down the throne's steps. "You're not in the place to tell me what I would understand, my lord," he said. "I won't ask again."

Apollo Equuleus locked his hazel eyes on Fitz. His jaw pierced through his cheeks. "We were starving," he said, emotionless. "We wouldn't have lasted past the Hunter's Moon thanks to your *good King Esmond*, denying our right to the food trade, *our* food trade."

"Then you ought to be thanking us," Fitz smirked. "A thinner herd would last longer."

If he were unshackled, Apollo would surely have killed the boy; the look in his eyes was terrifying.

"You *are* aware of your crimes though, I take it?" Fitz asked, spinning the fang-like blade around his fingers as he paced. "The treasons you did to this kingdom, to other kingdoms. You must know your family has no place here after that?"

Apollo said nothing, dropping his eyes to his rusted handcuffs.

"But then what would I do with you? I can hardly ransom you, you're worth nothing to other kingdoms," he said, getting closer to the prisoner. "Nor can I sell you back to your home; your line will cease to exist once we take Lutum."

Apollo spat. "You can bloody well try, boy."

Fitz glanced at the ceiling when he was a step away from the Equuleus. "We will. It's my duty as Lord of Ignis to deliver justice," he smiled, before bending to his ear. "So, this is for my father," he whispered.

A crimson necklace exploded from Apollo's throat, spewing all over Fitz and the mosaic floor. The room gasped. Eleanor clutched her mother's arm. Apollo desperately tried to reach his bloody throat, but his shackles forbade him. Wiping the blood from his katar onto his robes, Fitz then kicked him as if he were a barrel, sending nobles staggering back as Apollo fell in a fountain of red. Ulrich was now a lot less than placid; he looked close to retching.

"Bring the next, Sir Cedric," Fitz said calmly as he returned to his rusty seat.

Sir Cedric only gawked at the blood.

"Sir Cedric?" he was asked again after a time.

The knight hesitantly nodded as Apollo's body was dragged away, a trail of blood left behind him.

"Come on, Eleanor," Elayne winced, trying to escort her daughter away. "You shouldn't see this."

"It's too late," she frowned, staring at the lake of blood.

The next sound to fill the tense hall was the scream of a girl. *"NO!"*

She ran straight for Fitz. *"You killed him!! Why?! Why did you kill him?!"* The two unknown lion's guard grabbed the girl before she reached him.

"Eva," Eleanor said breathlessly, stepping towards her.

Eva Centaur only glanced, tears in her eyes. It looked like she had been sobbing for hours. *"Tell your bastard cousin, Eleanor!"* She kept her hateful eyes on Fitz. *"You killed them! You killed my friends!"*

Fitz seemed to be enjoying this. "Why would traitors be your friends, Eva?"

"They *saved me!"* she cried, *"and you killed them!"*

"We did our duty, princess," he said. "I'll have you know it was *your father* who gave us the order."

"But you didn't have to kill them!" she continued, her voice going hoarse. *"I hope everyone you love dies! I hope they get killed like mine! I hope you can only watch while they're torn away from you!"*

Fitz's smirk dried. "My father died in that battle. He wouldn't have led them to-"

"Good!!" Eva screamed. *"I'm glad we killed him! I'm glad he's rotting in a casket!"* Her voice broke down, and she began to sob.

Fitz stood in fury, clutching his katar. "Maybe I didn't speak loud enough when I killed your Apollo."

Ulrich scampered in front, holding out his hands. "She has King Esmond's own blood, my lord. She does not mean what she says. Put these rebuffs behind you, I beg."

Fitz laughed. "Esmond is a traitor too. What king would deny his people food?" he said. "Samson, move aside my elder."

"Esmond fed us at his table, or would you forget that?" Ulrich said angrily. "My lord, I beg you-" The elder grimaced as Samson's huge hands folded around his lemon robes. "Unhand me!"

"No!" Eleanor cried, running in front of Eva as well. "Don't you *dare* touch her!"

Sir Brendan was who pulled Princess Eleanor back. "Stay back, princess," he said, a shake in his gravelly voice.

Elayne pushed the knight back. "Get off of her!" She then grabbed Eleanor herself, yanking her away.

"Go to hell, *beggar!"* Eva mewled. "You're too stupid to bring me with you."

Fitz's katar flew like an arrow, Eleanor slipped out of Elayne's hands, and a snivelling Eva was saved from the blade that was meant for her.

HEW III
-Devious-

The Dog's Paw seemed much friendlier further away. When Lord Thyne thought it a good idea to dock on the island and get more supplies, the last thing the gang of four expected was to be arrested and taken in by Hela guards. "Nicely done, Erik," Mateo of the fort's garrison moaned while the third cheval gave the Lord of Trader's Dock a dirty look. Hew Centaur felt bad for him. *How could he have known?*

They had their weapons stripped, hands cuffed, boat searched, and were treated like wanted criminals as they were pushed up the small bay they arrived at. Even from there, Hew could see endless columns of green-and-brown-sigiled Hela soldiers lining the inside and outside of the city. They wore thick leather tunics with wolf pelts around their shoulders, and held swords no bigger than daggers. *We could have used them in the battle*, Hew thought as he walked past their static discipline, *It's a good thing we didn't, or there'll be even more knives in our backs.*

The island was that of tall dark taiga trees with a few hills and rocks. Moss seemed to worm through every inch of the city, from the great stone arch that marked the beginning, to the endless streets of cobble houses, to the small but stout keep that lay at the highest elevation. They were marched up the crumbling stairs to meet the lord of the island.

Lord Declan Hela was a smug, tubby man, with greasy hair that made his face look shiny. Hew remembered him from a tourney Esmond had thrown for his thirty-fifth name day five years ago; he never forgot a face, even for how young he might have been. "A Centaur arrives at our shores," Declan smirked when the prisoners were brought before him, digging his fat thumbs into his belt. "My, how you've grown, my boy."

Before Hew could say anything, Erik Thyne spat. "Bloody turncoat," he said sourly. "I never trusted you islanders."

"And right you were to," he smiled. "To survive in times like these, we must *eventually* change our colours. Think of a snake shedding its skin."

"Only honourless brutes like yourself," Yves Larret cursed. The third cheval was aged and receding, no doubt the oldest cheval in Austellus.

"I doubt I'm much of a brute, Larret," he laughed, slapping his belly. "But I wasn't talking to you. How are you, Prince Hew?"

Hew eyed the man, the fat oaf he was. "My father trusted you," he said with a cold, calm voice. "He told me that whenever trouble struck the waters, Lord Declan Hela was the man to fix it. He said he knew no one better to protect the Trader's Sea from criminals and exiles. It looks like you've joined them, my lord."

Declan dropped his eyes, becoming flushed. He waved his hand nervously. "Take them."

Erik was smirking at Hew when they were dragged through the mossy town to the cells. "Unnerved by a boy of ten," he muttered happily to Yves.

It was like they walked into the earth when escorted to the cellar, as they were located just under the hill where the keep stood. It could have been dingier, like the cells at Fort Deus and Fort Angel, but they were unpleasant enough. The sconces that flickered on the cobblestone walls made the room feel warm, despite how bitterly cold it was. Apart from several stinky brown hounds, the four were the only ones in the dusty cellar.

"What now?" Mateo shrugged testily.

"Gods know, boy," Erik sighed, slumping to the floor.

"We were meant to get Prince Hew to Centaur's Lagoon," he panicked. "The queen's going to *kill* us."

"Oh, she'll do more than that," Yves smiled from the floor.

"*Uh?*" Mateo held out his arms, exasperated. One of the tired dogs began whimpering at the panic. "This can't be happening."

Hew was more than unworried, joining the two others on the floor. *Anything's better than trying to live in that hollow of a fort.* He calmly took out the charred leatherback of a burnt book he had found at Fort Deus as he reminded himself. With his nails, he scratched in another I.

"What's that, lad?" Erik asked.

"Nine days," he said, picking the leather. He was counting how long he had lost his home for. There was still plenty of room on the leather. *I wonder if father knows yet, if Asher knows yet.*

From that point onwards, it was difficult to keep track of time. Yves was quick to happily fall asleep, Erik decided to befriend the dogs, Mateo kept pacing around, raking his scalp, and Hew sat and thought and stared at his number of nine. Occasionally, a Hela guard would come to bring them something to eat, and thankfully it wasn't the slightest bit like *prison* food, not that Hew knew what prison food was like. Hew devoured the fresh bread and fish and noodle soups as they came, beyond grateful that he didn't have to find it himself. Three of them were content enough with that, but Mateo Hunt seemed close to breaking the next day.

"What's the point of keeping us here?" he winced, breaking the silence. "Why doesn't he just kill us? It's torture keeping us alive with those *beasts.*"

"Hey," Erik Thyne frowned, petting the hound that lay on his lap. "These are loyal animals."

"We're hostages, not criminals," Yves said. "If Declan wanted us dead, he'd have done it by now."

"Hostages?" Mateo winced. "Are you really mad enough to believe that traitor Declan would *ransom* us to the king?"

"It's not a mad thought," Erik smiled. "Time and time again do lesser men trade highborn prisoners for a bit of coin, a pardon, some steel."

"And you *really* think the king would treat with him?"

"You never know," Erik said. "What do you think, Prince Hew? Would the king buy us back?"

"Of course he would," Hew smirked.

Lord Thyne sent a smug look to Mateo, which seemed to ruffle him even more. The boy returned to his pacing and kept quiet.

<hr>

The nine days had turned into twelve before anything was different. Hew was woken from his soft sleep by muffled shouts from the outside. He frowned and crept tiredly to the cellar's entrance. Following the shouts, came the sound of steel, of greaves marching, of men yelling orders. When the island became louder, the hounds woke too, beginning to whimper and howl. "Shut your dogs up, Thyne," Yves winced, turning over.

Erik was squinting as he sat up, managing to eye Hew. "Something the matter, my lordling?"

"Listen," Hew frowned, pressing his ear to the bars.

The other two did so, eyes slowly widening. "A battle?" Erik asked.

Mateo raced to join Hew at the bars, listening.

The Lord of Trader's Dock was true enough; only once had Hew heard those sounds of marching and arming before, and that wasn't even a fortnight ago. *But who are they fighting? Has father come to save me? How could he know? Has it been more than three days?*

A long silence ensued after a time of panicked rattling, and the only noise to fill the island was the howling of hounds. Soon the dogs were joined by the howling of men, the howling of death that Hew was now way too used to. He felt his breathing hasten. He felt his heart bang faster. He slipped to the floor and thought of Elisii.

"We can't get away from war," Yves said grimly, lying down again.

How Yves managed to fall asleep again was a wonder. The dogs never stopped howling and barking, nor did the screams, the sounds of catapults flinging and swords clashing loudly. Hew had his eyes closed and thought of his tranquil meadow, his perfect world; it was the only thing that fought off memories of the Battle for Fort Deus.

Eventually, with the clamour no quieter than before, a shadow of a figure stole the light from the sconces. It was a man, darting gracefully down the stairs, blood already on his sword. Though, it wasn't like the swords the Helas held. He was dressed in ragged cloths, wrapped tightly underneath his studded leather jerkin. When his face shone in the light, it revealed a dark red cloth of the same make wrapped around his right eye. He smiled crookedly when he saw the prisoners. "What d'we have here?" he said. "This be a day to remember."

"Toren," Erik gasped. He laughed heartily. "By the bloody gods!"

"Anyfin' down there?!" a deep voice boomed down the stairs.

Toren chortled with Erik. *"Oh, you won't believe me, Slabby!"* He fumbled with a set of keys, jamming them into the lock. "Come 'ere, quickly." Mateo shook Yves to wake him. "You're bloody lucky we found you, brother," he smiled.

Brother? That's when Hew realised. *Toren Thyne. He's Toren Thyne. The man father wanted dead for so long has come to save us.* "How?" Erik winced. "How did you know?"

"Shh, we'll talk away from 'ere, come on."

The gang of four followed Toren as he dashed up the stairs. At the top, a big man with the loftiest jaw Hew had ever seen was holding a bunch of weapons, amongst them Fletcher's zircon bow. "Arm yourselves," Toren said, "it's getting bloody out there." Hew snatched the bow back and held it to his chest. *I'll never lose it again, Fletcher. I promise.*

Toren led the charge out of the cellar, and even with Hew's blood pumping fiercely, never had a night been so chilly. In every crack of the city men were fighting, hacking at each other, unloading arrows from the battlements. The gang raced through the streets, tethered to the mossy walls, unspotted, all the while Hew trying to discern a sigil. *Capras*, he saw, knowing the brown colours and chainmail armour all too well. Neither side had much formation; the battle looked like a bar fight. Hew didn't know whether to cheer when a Hela man fell or when a Capra man fell. *They're both traitors. Let them wipe each other out.*

An arrow whizzed past Hew's curly head, digging into the moss on the wall behind. Hew tripped, the zircon bow flying out of his hands. Erik Thyne yanked him up, but Hew broke away, chasing the bow he had thrown a metre behind. He leapt and fell into the dirt, grabbing it with both arms as the foot of the fighting broke out before him. Arrows didn't stop flying. *I'll never lose it again*, he promised once more, wincing as he prepared for an arrow to fly into him. One did, only to become wedged into Erik's fat shield he thrust in front of Hew. "Here, my lordling," he said, holding out his hand.

Toren, Yves, and the thick-jawed man ran towards Hew, swinging at men who dared to get close. They then began running away, and glancing back, Hew saw Toren fell a few more Capras, taking off one's legs and slicing down the others before joining the party.

Homing in on the arched entrance of the city, Yves strung his bow to end some archer's lives by firing arrows into their neck. They fell from the battlements, crushing a few other men. The big-jawed man charged out with no fear, waving his cleaver-like sword as if it were a flag to clear the way. All Hew could focus on was his footing, too scared to fall again, leaping over bodies and swords like they were spikes that would kill him.

As the clangour of battle lulled behind them and the gritty sand met their shoes, the gang sighed with relief, Mateo even falling face-first to the bay. "We're not out yet, boy," Yves groaned, pulling him up with a wince.

Toren dug one foot into the bay, and the other on a rowboat twice the size of the Centaur's raft. "On ye get," he said, nodding. They all did so, making the boat sway as each leapt on.

"You took your time, Toren," smiled one of three men on the boat.

"Took a detour, lad," he said, kicking the boat out to the ocean. Once he was in, he slumped down and sighed, beginning to laugh again. "Jehm, pass us that wine."

"You think you can waltz in out of nowhere and not explain how the hell you found us?" Erik grinned curiously. *"How?"*

"A lot of gold to be made from a man who's more concerned for his life than his purse, brother," he smiled. "We saw the Capras comin'. Soon as they docked, seemed those Hela lot became blind to their treasures."

"Thieving bastard," Erik smiled with him.

"So, you didn't know we were in those cellars?" Yves asked.

Toren shrugged. "How could we 'ave? You should thank those hounds for making such a bloody racket, else we might not've found you." He passed the wineskin to Erik, who took a thick swig. "But that does *us*. Why were you lot there? How d'you let that Declan fucker catch you?"

"That was my fault," Erik admitted. "We're meant to be taking young Hew here to the lagoon."

Toren grew wide eyed. He was the bravest of them all, as he had shown in the battle, but in that moment, he was a child again. "Hew?" he stammered, staring at him. "Centaur?" The leader of the Midknights glanced around nervously. "Oh, gods, what've you done, Erik?"

One of the men chuckled. "Does a boy frighten you so?" he mocked.

"The king frightens me so, Daryn," he snapped. "You know how many Midknights he's left to hang? He's made a bloody trophy of us."

"You saved us," Hew frowned. "I'll tell my father to stop hunting you next time I see him, I promise."

"Aye, you can do that, lad, I'll appreciate it," Toren said, "but it won't erase the last two decades. Nothing against you, little lord, but I can't have you knowing where we stay." He wheeled the raft around with a couple of strong strokes. "Find your boat, Erik, this is where we split."

"Centaurs?" the man with the big jaw clocked. "We saw them Centaurs 'few days ago. The girl with black 'air an' her knight."

"You saw my sister?" Hew grinned hopefully. "She's ok?"

"She wouldn't 'ave been if we didn't warn 'er of the siege."

"Aye, Slabjaw's right," Toren nodded. "The lagoon is under siege. You'll want to head to Aquamare. Think that's where they went anyway."

Erik nodded. "Then that's where we'll go. Thank you, brother. We'd be lost without you."

"Anytime," he said, smiling gratefully. "Just don't get captured again."

FELIKS VII
-Road-

Yeah, but look at what Lunarpass has: the Sphaera, the Solar Auditorium, the Lunar Bells, the Tower of Kings, the Alchemical Forge, the Ulcus Basilica; the *oldest,* most *ancient* buildings in Austellus while the rest of the Pole's just filled with roads and trees." Fortune grunted as Feliks rode her, as if to agree.

Marcarius smirked. "True enough," he said. "Yet some of those roads are just as old." The elder paused before continuing. "In a way, ancient roads are much more beautiful than ancient buildings; buildings will always collapse, lose their integrity, have what made them so astounding, slowly stripped away by the years… Roads are simpler; they are not awe inspiring, nor a huge accomplishment, but their simplicity doesn't take away from their beauty. Roads are ancient civilisations, real people, the feet of young and old, fierce and weak. We all walk the road, yet many people would rather admire that which pleases their eyes, not their thoughts."

Feliks thought for a moment, jarred by the perspective. "People can appreciate both, can they not? Beauty is beauty. Either way, you can't know what people admire, unless you can see into their thoughts. Not even if you have a lifetime of immortality to decide."

Marcarius chuckled. "There are many ways to see into people's thoughts, Feliks. A lifetime of immortality can only help."

"Ways such as?"

The elder shrugged. "Depends on the person, and how they decide to express the truth."

Feliks frowned. "What if they decide to never express the truth?"

"Be it on their soul. They will forever hold their silence."

Seems more trouble than it's worth, keeping secrets. I wonder if father will forever hold his silence about who mothered me. "Is it possible to *always* tell the truth? Holding silence doesn't sound very fun."

Marcarius glanced at him curiously. "You're one of a kind to hope so."

The bastard nodded. "One of a kind to appreciate roads now, at least."

Marcarius chuckled again, shaking his head.

The road they had taken was straining, but far from intolerable. *Spring Road*, travellers called it: a constantly ascending path peppered with jagged rocks and tall alpine trees. They had passed the mining city of Oretown a while back. The place was a pleasant stop: a homely retreat with the same tall trees hugging the walls, the Saturnian Mountains never too far from sight, like all of the Alpinelands. Now that the Spring Road had brought the two so high over those mountains at their leisurely pace, the great city of Iustitia was truly a sight to see. Every building jutted out of a rock, the tallest of which shooting from a summit like a needle. The city spanned multiple mountains, a messy, yet eloquent stretch of cobblestone steps and paths joining each section, winding around the range, shooting up and falling down. Feliks had never seen anything like it. Most buildings were on a stable, albeit treacherous cliff, but some seemed so precarious that even the slightest gust of wind might send the balance astray.

Approaching the colossal city, Feliks found himself thinking of Curtis Sculptor and what he had done, after all, the Lord of Sangis was of Libran heritage, like Iustitia. *He didn't have much choice, or was too tempted by the easy way out, not wanting to see his family suffer.* The bastard could understand that. It was something he could see Esmond or Lori doing just so their children could eat. *But if even Curtis can bring himself to do it - a loyal and trusted lord - how many others will be doing the same? How many lords would be hoarding for themselves so that their kin might eat, and others might not?*

The gossip at an alehouse in Oretown was that King Esmond *outlawed* the owning of food, and the hoarding alike. Feliks hoped it was true, for the sake of the starving. *But if that's the case, how many lords will hang before the seasons change?* Curtis was a good man, a friendly man, and the bastard couldn't bear to see him join them. He had talked with Marcarius at length about it not long after leaving Sangis, and for the most part, the elder agreed with his concerns, all to a sullen nod or a wordless grunt.

A change of seasons wasn't up for debate anymore. The days and nights had never been so bitter, sometimes the nights becoming unbearably so. *It's a ticking clock,* Feliks knew. *Hopefully one that can be broken.* He couldn't even blame the cold on the strange foreign land they were exploring; the Auburn Road had been just as biting, especially so on the path towards Sangis. Granted, Feliks had never travelled *that* path either, but the boy was always conscious of temperature, or so he liked to think. He was excited at the prospect of Iustitia, of finally finding answers to the madness, of unearthing this *serpent* he knew so much yet so little about.

Before they would do so, Marcarius insisted that they pay the Lord of Iustitia a visit, since he'd want to know of their presence. Feliks doubted that. Marcarius had never even met Kenneth Venulaes. "Would he?"

"Would *you* want to know if you were lord?" the elder quipped back. "...of who wandered your streets, highborn and lowborn alike?"

Feliks never troubled himself with such a question; *I would never be a lord, so how can I tell?* "Depends if they've come to kill me."

"It'll be your people you govern over, not your enemies," Marcarius said. "Or so it should be. Current lords have been so eager to forget that."

He couldn't respond to that, keeping his eyes on the steepening path.

The keep couldn't have been higher; it was that needle-like tower Feliks had eyed when they arrived. Along the winding mountain pass stood all sorts of buildings and houses, like a normal city, some even seeming to go *inside* the mountain.

Halfway up, Feliks and Marcarius were escorted by royal guards, sporting the two white feathers atop a pink background: the sigil of Venulaes. They needn't do more than glance at Elder Marcarius's robes to know who he was, and even after they began escorting the two, they barely noticed Feliks's existence. *I would want people to know who I am at first glance.* He didn't think Marcarius knew how lucky he was.

After a tiring climb, the four guards pushed open the keep's dark oaken gates, and waved the two inside. Pink tourmaline sparkled from the throne at the back of the mammoth room, the only bit of colour aside from the long Venulaes banners that fell in every place possible. There were two huge stone arches on either side of the hall, exposed to the mountain wind as it hooted and howled into the room. There was a boy, who must have been Kenneth, talking to a fully armoured knight, feathers prickling out from his collar and shoulder pads. Kenneth himself had a soft, square face, with dimples lining his jaw as he smiled. His hair was short and brown, almost windswept. It didn't take long for his eyes to find his visitors.

"Ah, welcome to Iustitia, my lords," he smiled warmly, sauntering over to them. "How can I help you?"

"My Lord Kenneth," Marcarius smiled, "you look well with your title. It takes a poised man to fill such great halls."

"Thanks to you, I'm sure. Many people thought it folly that I should inherit Iustitia at my age." Even Kenneth only needed to look at Marcarius for no more than a second to know who he was. "I thank you for your condolences regarding my father, too. It meant a great deal to hear that. It's nice to meet you in person to tell you that."

"Nonsense. It was a terrible thing that happened. Lord Daryl was a cogent man."

Kenneth nodded sullenly. "But life goes on." He smiled to Feliks kindly, nodding to him. "What brings you both here?"

"Fear not, we'll be out of your way," Marcarius said. "We seek knowledge from the Great Athenaeum. Very important knowledge."

"Then, by all means, be on your way," Kenneth smiled, backing away. "Iustitia is yours, my lords. Feel at home if you can."

Marcarius bowed deeply, before going back the way they came. "That wasn't so bad, was it?" he asked as they were descending again.

"He seems good-hearted," Feliks nodded. "How old is he?"

"Fifteen, I believe," he said. "A year younger than you, Feliks."

Feliks winced. "And they thought he was *too young* to rule?"

"Esmond didn't." Marcarius was watching the rocky path carefully. "Then again, Esmond was only fifteen himself when he ascended to the solar throne... and he's letting your cousin Fletcher rule at Fort Deus. I don't think the king sees age as that much of an issue."

"Good." Feliks wondered how Fletcher was faring; he was always the kindest of his cousins - not that the others weren't - in that Fletcher always made him feel included. Feliks was a year older than Fletcher too, but he didn't know if that meant he had a better judgement or not. *Of course it doesn't. I haven't been taught anything of ruling. I'm not the son of a king.*

It took much longer for them to get to the Athenaeum than the keep; the great library was a ways south from the rest of the city, in the heart of where the Saturnian Mountains began. They travelled high and low and high again before they could actually see the thing, and it was not at all disappointing. At first glance, one could almost confuse the Great Athenae-

-um *for* a mountain, as the spire-like building twisted to the sky, rooms and sectors reaching out like stony hands trying to grab the air. The base of the Athenaeum had dark green grass all around, the quivering alpine trees hiding most of the bottom if you looked at it from above. But still, from bottom to top, the cobblestone path that led up and down the mountains was clear as day.

Marcarius stopped at the tall, arched entrance, admiring the careful embossing carved into the stone. It wasn't as busy as Feliks thought it would be; only a single person or a couple walked past every thirty seconds or so. "What do we want to find in there?" Feliks asked.

"Answers, hopefully," Marcarius said, like Feliks didn't already know. "This library only truly contains fables and stories, no non-fiction of the sort, I believe. Still, there are an immeasurable number of tomes. With any luck, I'd hope to find some idea of what we face."

No non-fiction. That doesn't sound promising. "What if all the answers we find are part of age-old myths?"

"Then they are part of age-old myths," the elder said, squinting at the wall scribing. "It's better than being ignorant." He took the lead inside.

The first room had no books at all. It was only a short hall of scrolls and paintings, a desk at the back seating a librarian who suspiciously watched those who wandered in and out. The paintings were mostly of landscapes, Feliks noticed, as he eyed the peaks of Iustitia he had just seen, the wonders of Lunarpass, even his home of Centaur's Lagoon; most places he didn't recognise, though. There was what must have been Ignis, the strangely sculpted sandstone buildings across a stretch of sand; there was a building that seemed to be on the same Saturnian Mountains they were on now, but tall and ample, with rounded lanterns falling from the curved green roof; there was a city with two huge bending towers that leant on each other, and a bridge so high it took the clouds, making Feliks shiver to look upon. Most of the rest of the paintings were those of battles with kings he didn't know, and events Feliks must have learned at some point but had forgotten.

"My elder," the librarian bowed, startled by their presence. *That's the third one to know his name in Iustitia alone.* "Welcome to the Great Athenaeum, how can I be of service?"

"To look around, if it's not a trouble," Marcarius smiled.

"Not at all," he said. "Be sure to consult with my colleagues should you need a tome finding."

Marcarius nodded gratefully, leading himself into the library. Feliks's breath left his body when he saw the vast hall of multi-layered shelves packed to the brim with scrolls and books. There were stairs and at least ten shiny silver balconies stretching up to the peak of the building, the stacks of shelves becoming no less common.

"I should hope you know your alphabet, Feliks," the elder smirked, "that's how the books are ordered."

Feliks only smiled at the jest. "Where do we start?"

"I'm going to look for tomes of the *Pause*, or of the like. Perhaps there is something we don't know about the acclimatisation." He glanced at Feliks. "You go where you think is best. I'd suggest you look for serpents, snakes. Perhaps find a connection, what they mean, a symbol, a sign."

Feliks breathed in deeply. "Alright."

"Meet me back here in an hour or two," Marcarius said. "I believe we'll be able to rent out the books we might find."

He nodded and they split.

It was clear almost immediately why Marcarius wanted to look for words starting with C and P, since the books that started with S were at least seven stories high. Feliks's knees ached from the amount of climbing they had already done that day, so they shook by the time he reached the top. He was one of only a few on that floor, probably *because* it was such a climb. Florid and panting, Feliks headed for the shelves.

He spied the first few books that caught his eye: 'Sir Seb and the Giant Gruff', said one, 'The Sebetwane Wine', said another, 'The Second Great Pause', said a third - Feliks took that one. He slotted it under his arm, and kept looking, still not knowing *what* he was looking for. There were so many unrelated ones, of tales and legends that Feliks only needed to glance at to know he wouldn't glean anything from. He must have gone through five or so aisles before he found anything even remotely related to serpents. 'The Servant of Justice', it was called: an old piece of folklore poetry with a stick on the cover, a snake coiling around it. He plucked it out.

"You're new here," said a soft voice.

Feliks turned, startled. He had not heard the girl creep up on him. It was almost haunting how beautiful she was: long white hair with a small nose and neck, fairly slim, and soft, grey, curious eyes. "How do you know?" Feliks asked.

"I don't forget a face," she smirked wickedly. "I wouldn't forget yours."

Feliks glanced around, also smirking. *She's flirting,* he realised. "Is this what you do, then? Go around the Athenaeum annoying people?"

"They usually humour me."

"What if they don't?"

She hid a smile with compressed lips. "Then I won't see their face again." Her grey eyes examined Feliks as if he were a painting. "What's your name?"

"Feliks," he said. "And yours?"

She glanced away from him for the first time. "See you around, Feliks," the girl said, spinning her long grey dress to maunder away.

Feliks couldn't stop gaping. The girl's dress sparkled as she walked. "Wait-" He jogged over, but she was too far gone. When he turned a corner, she had vanished. For the rest of their visit to the Athenaeum, the girl was nowhere in sight.

"My, Feliks," Elder Marcarius smiled when they met in the lobby, "seems like you were fortunate with your finds."

The bastard had found six giant tomes in the end, four of which he didn't know if they were at all relevant; his mind was too occupied with the girl who had just found him. "And you?" he nodded to Marcarius's four. "Did you find what you wanted to?"

"We'll soon see," Marcarius smiled. "I have a feeling luck is on our side today, Feliks."

ATHENA V
-Flock-

L uck was on her side today, as it had been when she spotted her father's Horncurve scouts racing around in the meadow below. Her broken stone tower suddenly felt less lonely; it had been her protection from the Sirens, her shelter from the rain, her home for days, and she was finally rid of it. She placed her thumb and finger in her mouth, and whistled as loud as she could, just how Cadmus used to. The three men glanced at her, and rode their horses over at once.

"My lady," Sir Ardin sighed amiably as she raced out.

Athena Horncurve threw her hands on his stallion. "Is he alive? Did you all make it out?!"

Sir Ardin produced a big grin. "Let's see your father, shall we?"

That was four days ago, and now the city of Salem crept over the horizon, surrounded by hundreds of crimson Horncurve tents. Athena could hardly contain her excitement, unable to stay still without wriggling. She had hoped above everything that Riley was alive, even *believed* it; she refused to let herself think he wasn't. Now she was proven right.

As for her brothers, Athena held on to the hope that they would be in the camp too. *Marcus must have been found, like I was.* But she wasn't so confident about that. Sir Ardin had said during their ride that it had been on his conscience; that it had been "my fault. I should have chased after him, I should have ridden until I couldn't ride anymore." Athena didn't blame him. *Once Marcus has his mind made up, there's no changing it.* She saw that at Merchant's Bay.

There was still hope his twin would make her feel less lonely, *but Cadmus has gone raiding too, the idiot. When he returns, he'll come back to a city full of traitors.* It annoyed her more than it upset her. *What a perfect time to go on a raid.*

Thinking of that made her crack. She threw herself off Sir Ardin's horse as it slowed its gallop, and charged through the red camp. She didn't hear the knight pursuing her.

Athena didn't know which tent was her father's, but she didn't care; she was past caring. She ran headfirst into a few armed men who paced and marched around, cursing as she whizzed past. She was running for ages: over hills and firepits, around wagons and tents, past horses and soldiers. Eventually, as she neared the rear of the camp, there he was. Her father's blood red hair was flicking up with the gusty wind as he stood wordlessly, clad in steel armour, lacking his favourite merlot cloak. It took a moment for him to smile, so struck with shock that he couldn't move. "Athena," he beamed, "my sweet Athena." She leapt into his arms. His heart rang through the armour, as Athena's did. He kissed her over and over again on the head. *"Emily!"* Riley cried with joy, taking Athena's hand. *"Our daughter's home! She came back!"*

Her mother had almost the exact same reaction as Riley, but Athena didn't let it play out again, charging to embrace her, tears filling her eyes. Emily touched her face gently, smiling. "Oh, Athena." They hugged again and didn't let go.

"How by gods did you escape?" Riley asked as he closed the hatch on their tent.

Athena's smile dimmed. "They went to the tavern to get wasted as soon as they took the city. Wasn't much of an *escape.*"

Riley's face collapsed like a building. "You're kidding me," he winced. He turned to Emily. "We could have taken Selerborn back *that night.*"

Emily only pressed her lips together, looking down.

"Where did you go, then?" Riley asked.

"Tempest Tower. The old broken one."

"And how did ye get food?" he winced.

"I hunted."

"With what?"

She reluctantly unsheathed her mini Shofar, the dark grey steel not any foggier than the day she forged it. The diamond glimmered around in the red tent.

Riley smiled sadly as he took and inspected it. He ran his finger along the blade. "You're more like my father's child than I am," he said, feeling the steel.

"Are we gonna march back? Are we gonna take our home back?"

Riley frowned, looking away. "Not me. Your brother will."

"Marcus?" Athena asked excitedly. "He's here?"

Her father swallowed and shook his head. "He's not."

Athena winced. "What do you mean? You sent... Cadmus raiding."

Riley shook his head. "I *said* I sent Cadmus raiding. I said that to Ignatius, to Harper, to the whole of bloody Selerborn. I even believed it myself for a time." He was smirking to himself.

"Cadmus never went to Heavia," Emily added. "Yer father sent him to the Twin Islands to get Kalyx men instead - soldiers he could use to take back Selerborn."

Athena gawked for a while. *He never went raiding? Should I be happy?* She didn't feel happy. "Cadmus is going to retake Selerborn?" she repeated, making sure she hadn't misheard.

"Aye," Riley said confidently.

Athena's wince cut deeper. "How did you know?" she asked. "How did you know Selerborn *needed* to be taken back?"

"Marcus said so, didn't he?"

She hated to think of the day Marcus ran away, but now it sickened her so much more. "You *believed* him?"

"Of course I did," Riley frowned. "He's my son."

Her sickness stirred into anger. "He didn't know that," she said. "You could have just told him. If you did, he'd still be here. Instead, you yelled at him. Instead, you made him believe he was *worthless.*"

Emily took her hands. "Don't be angry, Athena," she said softly. "Your da' did what he had to do. He had to make Harper believe-"

"He didn't have to do that," Athena frowned, yanking her hands away. "You didn't have to call him arrogant and selfish... that he was your *least* favourite child."

"Please, Athena, you've just come back. Let's have some food, eh? You can show us yer new hunting skills."

Athena exhaled hatefully. "And ale to forget about it?" She shook her head, and marched out of the tent. They didn't call after her.

After an age of slogging through the camp, Athena still had no idea where she was going, but neither was she paying attention to that. *Why would Cadmus have more of a chance to take back Selerborn anyway? He's led no attacks.* She was struggling to come to terms with seeing Cadmus on an island treating with lords, and not in a jungle brawling with brutes. *Did da' decide to send him to the Twin Islands before or after Marcus ran away?* After would be worse; *he knew he had fucked up.*

Deviating far from the camp, Athena eventually found the bank of the Bullshorn River. The dark blue water fell from tall mountains that were hazy husks in the distance, and ran as far west as she could see. Before the faded mountains sat Salem, a sprawling city not too different from the one Athena had seen a thousand times. Every time she came here, though, the giant, sharp-edged tower that shot out of the middle of the city seemed taller and taller. It didn't distract her for long, as she returned her aggrieved eyes back to the rushing water.

She picked up a stone and threw it, letting it plop violently into the stream. *Marcus, where are you? Come back, it's not your fault.* A wince covered her mouth. *You're so stupid, Athena. Why did you snitch on him? It's your fault da' was so angry.* She covered her eyes with her palms.

After a time, she heard the gentle sound of chainmail rustling, slowly becoming louder. "Ay up, Athena," the man smiled as he sat beside her. "I thought I saw you storming through the camps."

Athena glanced up to see Sir Gerard Holt, running his fingers through his long brown hair. She looked sadly back to the river.

"I... would say happy birthmoon, but..." He sighed gently. "It hasn't been too happy, has it? Won't soon be over, I suppose."

Athena glanced up again, a smirk tugging at her face. "Not even my parents remembered it was my birthmoon."

Sir Gerard looked towards the city. "Your da's got a lot on his mind."

"He should," Athena mumbled.

Sir Gerard nodded sullenly, using a moment of silence before speaking again. "He's ordered me to take you safely to Mea Minor, to get you to your brother so you're safe when the fighting starts."

"So... I don't get to fight too?" Athena didn't expect a yes.

"No," he said. "At least you'll see Cadmus again before he goes."

Athena agreed. "When can we go?"

"As soon as you're ready."

She stood and brushed herself off. "I'm ready now."

ELAYNE VI
-Abscond-

I should have killed him. The dagger was in her hand, and Fitz was metres away... but she hesitated. *Why did I hesitate?* It cost her everything. She wouldn't hesitate now; she promised herself that the next time she saw that wretched boy, she would bury a knife into his throat, no matter the implications. Elayne Lyrderyn couldn't do that from a cell.

It was all she could think about as she wasted away in the sultry dungeon: the silence that fell in the hall, the dark red blood that seeped out Eleanor's green dress, her cousin's rusty katar rooted into her heart. Madness fell with a violent uproar after Elayne tried to run up to Fitz, but the newly knighted Sir Samson Taheri came in between her and her revenge. She couldn't even remember all the profanities she was yelling at Fitz and his brand-new knight, *Sir Samson Taheri. Stupid, upjumped brute. I'll kill him too if I could.*

She couldn't say what Fitz was going to do with her, even though attempted murder fell under the highest of treasons. *He won't kill me. He doesn't have the guts.* He looked close to retching after Eleanor fell, no less so when he had an incandescent mother springing towards him. *And he's already a kinslayer, what circle of hell is lower than that? If he kills me too, he'll have to find out.*

No one had come to see her since she was imprisoned: not Elder Ulrich, not Ayden, not Sir Brendan, no one. Not even her turnkey would speak to her, avoiding all eye contact when he brought her stale, dry meals.

That was probably because Elayne had managed to bash a rock against his head as she was being dragged away. *I wouldn't speak to them either if they did that to me.* It had swelled into a bright red bump, Elayne could see, and she regretted it. The only other thing she regretted was hesitating. *I won't hesitate again*, she told herself a hundredth time.

She couldn't keep track of time in her cell, not knowing how long had passed, how many nights had fallen, how many tears she had dropped. Crying had stopped a while ago, but Elayne still felt as if the dry geysers around her eyes could erupt at any moment. *What will they do to her? What have they done so far? Have they left her to rot in a stuffy casket like my sweet Reynold? Have they thrown her body into the river?* She winced hatefully... *Would they dare have a funeral without the mother?*

If she knew anything about insanity, Elayne was creeping closer to madness every day; that's what dark cells do; that's what loss does. *I have two children left*, she thought, never distracting herself from her worries, *two lovely children out of four, and they won't even let me see them.* Not that they could let her see Lyssa, since she had abandoned them all, *but what about my sweet Ayla?* Ayla was two years old. It sickened her more than words could say that they would keep a mother from her two-year-old daughter.

She hated herself that she didn't spend much time with Eleanor when they came back to Ignis. *Stupid old hag, too busy grieving over a daughter you haven't lost yet.* She didn't want to forgive herself, but if she'd ever see Ayla or Lyssa again, it wasn't in question whether she would let them out of her sight or not. *I'll protect them with my life, like I should have with Eleanor. I'll kill any man who threatens them, roar at any man who would snarl at them.* She closed her dry eyes as she frowned, and found them wet again. She tried to sleep through it.

"My lady," someone was saying, waking her up. "My lady?"

Elayne opened her eyes to see Elder Ulrich, smiling sadly as a torch burned in his hand. She was light headed with relief. "Ulrich," she sighed, staggering to her knees.

Ulrich let himself into her cage, helping her stand with his gentle hands. "I would have come sooner, but persuading young Fitz has been a difficult task."

"Eleanor..." she said, clutching his hands tightly, "what have they done with her?"

The elder dropped his eyes. "We should be seated, my lady, you look ever-weaker."

Elayne dragged him to the small, round table in the corner that she had never sat on before. "Please, Ulrich. Put a mother's worries to rest."

He licked his lips nervously. "Lord... Fitz couldn't bear the sight of her, my lady." Now, the elder squeezed *her* hands. "Her body was... ordered to be burned."

Her head was light again, but this time it wasn't relief.

"I'm sorry, my lady. I tried to stop him, but..."

Ulrich trailed off as she shook her head, holding out her hand. "I suppose she died for nothing," she said, tears stuttering her speech. "I bet that poor Centaur girl burned with her."

The elder frowned. "You don't know?" he said kindly. "Princess Eva escaped during the chaos. Come nightfall, she was nowhere in Ignis."

"That's for the best," she nodded, wiping her tears. "Fitz won't let her live if he sees her again."

"But for a girl, on her lonesome, in a desert..." Ulrich didn't need to complete that sentence for her to know how it would end.

"What about Ayla? Would they not let me see her at least?"

Ulrich pressed his lips together. "Ayla is safe, I'm tending to her myself. But she will never be happy without her mother."

"Can I not make a two-year-old happy?" she asked again.

The elder shook his head with grief.

"Please, Ulrich, would you not bring me her, smuggle her in? Let me see my last daughter again."

"I am no turncoat, Elayne," he said coldly. "You know what happens if I do."

She nodded as she winced and wept into her palm. Ulrich softly stroked her legs as she did. "What's going to happen to me?" she asked eventually.

"Fitz will see you in two days," he said. The turnkey appeared at the door: waiting, listening. "I don't think he has quite decided what he *should* do with you... but it's... not unlike for you to be spared."

"*Spared*," she smiled hatefully. "He took my daughter away from me. If there's anyone to be spared, it'd be that pale-"

"*Shhhh*," Ulrich frowned, holding a finger to his lips. "Two days, my lady." He clutched her hands again. "Be strong." And he left.

But as Elayne was reunited with her hollow thoughts, she had never felt less strong. *What sort of woman can't protect her own children? A failure of a mother, that's all I am.* She wished for Reynold to rise from the grave and make all right with Ignis once again. *Is this love I bear him, to want him back so badly?*

———◄─────■———

It took a long two days for Elayne to hear her next voice. At first, she thought insanity had taken her, whispering voices in her head, but even the turnkey flinched at the echoes that bounced around in the keep above. It wasn't from the throne room, Elayne knew as much, since the council chambers were so much closer to the dungeons. But it didn't make sense as to why she could hear them, since behind the closed doors of the council chambers, not a sound escaped. "-*presume to walk away! What I've said is final! It's too late!*" The broken adolescent voice made Elayne cringe. She could never hear that voice again without thinking evil things.

"*You don't know how much it hurts!*" a lion roared back. "You don't know how much *heartache* it takes to stick to my honour. You don't know how much it *wounds me* to know that everyone I will ever love will perish before me, and their life will be a mere blink in my own." It took a while for Elayne to recognise Elder Ulrich's voice through his thick, growling rage. "I have thrown away the *very essence* of what it means to be human to *serve the realm.* To stop *idiots* like you from repeating history, and sending *thousands* to their graves." There was a long silence. Elayne could hear her heart thumping. It gave her delight to imagine Fitz's stupefied face. "I have stood by one mad king before…" he grumbled eventually. "…It will *not* happen again."

And that was the last thing she heard for maybe hours, filling her head with all sorts of new questions. *What could Fitz have done to enrage Ulrich so much?* She had never heard the elder in that state before, nor any elder. *Does this mean he's forsworn his vows? Has he betrayed Fitz?* There were so many different emotions shooting around inside her body that she didn't know *what* to feel, or even what those feelings *were*, but then again that wasn't new.

———◄─────■~~———

She was dozing when Ulrich returned, this time rushed and nervous. He didn't give Elayne a chance to say anything before he jammed a key into the lock and flung open the cell door. "Get up," he said, like he was rid of courtesy. "We're leaving."

Elayne's legs wobbled, struggling to hold her weight, but she managed to hobble over to him, squinting at the torchlight. "I heard you," she said hoarsely. "Did Fitz decide to kill me?"

"Worse," Ulrich growled. He threw the torch back to the sconce. On the floor, the turnkey lay dead. "He wants to *war* with Esmond," he winced bitterly. There was a veiny redness in his eyes. "He's proclaimed Ignis an *absolved kingdom*. It's open rebellion. It's folly. He wants to '*restore our great kingdom to what it once was*.'"

Elayne couldn't respond, especially since they went deeper and deeper into the keep, for more ears to hear what they would say. *That is worse*, she thought. *He truly is witless, to defy the king*. Her thoughts immediately went to Elder Marcarius, and how close Ulrich was with him. *That's it, of course. He won't stand to have his greatest friend taken away from him*. But still, never had an elder broken his oath before. '*You know what happens if I do*', Ulrich had said, but she only knew from tales and myths.

Elder Ulrich's power walk was a brittle thing, almost like something was holding him back, though he wasn't stopping himself. Elayne had to spend all her concentration on keeping up with the old man, feeling as if her legs would break at any moment.

They didn't have to speak for her to know they were heading to baby Ayla's nursery. It wouldn't matter if they weren't; she wasn't leaving without her daughter. "Where will we go to?" Elayne asked when the sandstone corridors became smaller.

"Far away from here," he whispered back. "We can never come back, so long as Fitz calls himself a king. To Lunarpass, perhaps."

"Lunarpass," she repeated, not quite comprehending that they were leaving Ignis.

Ayla was sound asleep when Elayne carefully plucked her from her crib, swathing her in soft red blankets and holding her closely. She held her babe to her chest, savouring every little heartbeat she could feel.

"We must be quick," Ulrich said, not carefully. "Is there anything else you need?"

She could feel her wits clouding with adrenaline. "Ryan," she said. "Ryan Lynx, my brother's bastard. And his pet Una."

Ulrich frowned. "Why would you need Ryan?"

She shook her head. "I'm not leaving him here, not in a city full of sadists, not with a father that beats him to bruise. He's too young."

The elder had sorry eyes, still bloodshot from rage. "The boy is no concern of yours."

"He has my blood, Ulrich. He is the son I lost. We're not leaving without him." The tone Elayne used offered no objection. Ulrich sighed and marched out lightly.

By the time they had arrived at Ryan's small guest chambers, Ulrich was shaking testily. He nodded towards the door as he nervously glanced left and right down the moonlit sandstone walls.

Una woke before Ryan did, uncurling her patched, stripy body as her eyes locked onto a creeping Elayne. She was atop the boy, sleeping on his silken sheets. "Ryan, wake up," Elayne whispered, not wanting to get too close to him and his wary lynx. "Ryan."

"Auntie?" he squinted, shooting up like it was his duty to. Una leapt up with him, twirling around his body to find his arm. "You... got out... oh... your daught-"

"Me and Ulrich are leaving," she said, cutting off the stammering boy. "You can't stay here either. Please come with us." Ryan tried to speak, but didn't. Elayne didn't wait for his answer. "Do you want to come?"

Ryan tittered; whether it was through shock or relief or humour, or a mix of the three, Elayne could not say. He dashed lightly over to gather his few belongings, but it was too dark to see what they were. One thing was a sword, Elayne could hear, as the steel made a sharp *shiiing*. Another seemed like clothes, but her heart was pounding too loudly to know for sure. It didn't take long for him to step out of the shadows, nodding as he held his belt full of pouches.

He and Ulrich said nothing to each other when they left the room, if not for their mutual lour. Ulrich nodded and took the lead once again, Una padding softly behind the other three.

Ulrich led them to King Sol's Mines: a vast network of tunnels Elayne knew could lead out of the city, but never dared test. Every guard from the keep to the mines lay dead on the ground, but Elayne did not presume to ask why. One man had an open throat, another a dark wound in his back, another had a battered skull. *Ulrich had help,* she converged, *no way would he himself have killed this many people.*

As they moved further into the stuffy, dark mines, more and more did their nerves take them, turning their creep into a sprint. Elayne's feet stumbled over multiple hefty rocks, making her bare feet bleed a trail behind them. Though, she never felt them hurting.

Ulrich navigated through the tunnels like he had studied them tirelessly, taking sharp turns that wound up and down and left and right. She put all her trust into him knowing the way, and was even foolish enough to believe that they would all make it out unscathed, until the head of citizenship suddenly appeared in front of them.

Elijah Gale wore a sad smile. A torch was crackling in his hand, lighting up the muddy mine and all their faces. "Your party has grown, Ulrich," he smirked.

"My Lord Gale," Ulrich frowned, struggling to stay afoot as he leant against the jagged mine walls and panted.

Elijah seemed afraid of Una as she stalked towards him, but he hid it well. He kept glancing. "Are you sure about this, my elder? Is it worth it? Never has an elder forsaken his vows."

Ulrich squinted hatefully. "Fuck the vows, you've seen what Fitz is. You know what he's done, what he's doing."

Elijah's half smile faded as he glanced at Elayne. "I have."

"Then you *know* we must leave. I will *not* stand beside him while he *tears* our prosperity apart. I will *not* have the blood of innocents on my hands once again."

He frowned. "You *can't* let Fitz find you now, not with all those guards lying dead. But still, vows aren't broken lightly. *Especially* yours."

Ulrich was still panting. "I envy your loyalty, my lord. Not only to us, but also to your duty. I am not befitting of my vows. I never was. But *you are.* You can't let Ignis fall into ruin… that's all a war will bring."

"What hope would I have if you failed? I can control the boy's mind no better than you, Ulrich-"

"*Try*, Elijah," Ulrich begged. "For the millions of people in the Canicule alone. For peace, so that those people may have a life they *deserve.* You're the only chance they've got for it now."

Elijah bit his cheeks. "I'll try for both, I always have, but I can't promise that I can."

The elder frowned. "I know that you could."

He seemed to ponder that thought before he stepped aside, looking away. "I hope the road is kind to you. There should be no more guards hereafter."

"Thank you, my lord," Ulrich said, squeezing Lord Gale's hands, "thank you. Do what I could not."

Elayne had never seen the young man look so sad - he was never too far from a smirk or a smile. She hesitated as the others dashed past him.

"Auntie?" Ryan frowned, noticing she hadn't followed.

"I'm coming," she called back. *Would he care?* she thought when the bastard nodded and continued to run. *Would he be happy that he's finally rid of him?* She realised she didn't care; she wanted to do this for herself. "Elijah, would you do one last thing for me?"

Elijah turned to look at her. "Anything, my lady," he said softly.

Elayne swallowed. *I won't hesitate again.* "It was my brother who poisoned Lady Gina," she said, not confident if it was a lie or not. "Make him pay. Make him hang."

Lord Gale's face remained as still as stone, but his blue eyes were full of stupor as he nodded. "Go, quickly," he said.

ESMOND XII
-Crossroads-

His host seemed to grow larger by the day. Esmond Centaur couldn't even appreciate the nostalgic smell of the auburn trees, the biting cold he was once so used to, the taste of home as outriders brought back fruits and game from the Pole, since the thought of finally getting revenge for what and who he loved was so much sweeter than any tree or nostalgia or piece of fruit. He was ready now, more so than ever, to fight, to claim that revenge. Then again, the king had been more than ready for weeks.

It was a dark brown dusk when he was reunited with his brother Lori, the new Hunter's Moon lighting up his arrival. As soon as Esmond received word, he took to his stallion and galloped out to greet the man.

Lori looked healthier than Esmond had imagined, albeit pale, with dark rings under his eyes. Behind him rode a fat knot of soldiers, donned with a dark steel similar to Esmond's men, holding spears and bucklers and bows and swords, waving the aqueous blue banner that screamed the Centaurs of the Lagoon. *Eight thousand,* Esmond guessed, and hoped. *Lori wants revenge just as much as I do,* he knew, *since he's with his entire host.*

When his brother clumsily dismounted in front of him, they embraced in a tight squeeze. "An army suits you, Esmond. You were never a king to sit by and do nothing."

"Nor was our father. Nor is any Centaur that's to follow us," the king nodded. "It's good to see you, brother."

Lori smiled gratefully.

After his army had settled with Esmond's, and the young lord hobbled over to the king's tent, the two brothers shared a cask of mulled wine. Esmond was studying him dubiously as he tried to navigate about the room. "Are you sure you're well enough to fight?"

Lori sighed as he sat, clutching his wounded leg. "You summoned me, did you not?" he smirked cruelly. "It's my duty to fight."

"It should be your choice to fight," Esmond said, unsmiling.

"It's that too," Lori frowned. "You think my daughter's death hasn't been on my mind for every waking day since the attacks?"

"What else can be?" Esmond frowned.

Lori ground his teeth in a way Esmond had never seen before. "I sometimes dream about the way she died: the ugly dagger to her throat, her gentle blood exploding from her neck, Feliks only being able to watch as she falls to the ground."

No one has made him so angry before, the king realised. *A Lori lack of jest is a terrifying thing.* "They will atone," Esmond said. "Anyone who had a part to play, they will *pay* tomorrow." Vincent said they weren't behind the attacks, but Esmond saw through that now. *I've been played like a lute for too long.*

Lori nodded. "They've killed too many to be safe now." Just like that, when his blue eyes fell back upon his brother, the old Lori returned. "But how have you been, brother? Last time we saw each other, you were deciding whether to kill the Warrior Boy or not. How did that go?"

Esmond hadn't tried to remember Sigmund's face in so long. He almost couldn't. "Didn't get any better from there," Esmond said wryly. "All I've done for the past four moons is say goodbye, it seems." It didn't feel like four moons either; it felt longer. "That's all life comes down to in the end - saying goodbye to everything we've grown to know so well. It took so long to realise it's not worth growing to know anything."

Lori's eyes changed, as if he was looking at a stranger. "All life comes down to? Are you hearing yourself, Esmond? You *always* believed the opposite; I won't believe loss made a pessimist of you. It didn't for me."

"You were close... but now I know there's nothing left to savour. All that matters now is putting an end to everyone who did this to us."

"Does it matter if we don't?" Lori frowned. "We all die, Esmond."

Esmond tittered spitefully. "Not us, if we will it." He licked his lips. "It matters to me if we're still standing when our enemies are rotting in the ground."

"No one can outrun death. Every day we spend in this life is one day closer to it, there's no escaping that," Lori said.

That was when Esmond realised he was looking at a stranger as well. "Don't lecture me on pessimism when you're just as bad, Lori," he said before taking a swig of wine.

"It's not pessimism, it's a fact," Lori smiled, unbelieving. "When have you ever hidden from the truth, brother?"

A moon ago, according to Orion. But Orion was wrong. *He was always wrong.* Esmond bit his cheeks, swallowing another splash of wine. "We're not dying tomorrow."

Lori frowned. "If I did, who would you blame it on?"

In a wave, Esmond felt his head spin. It almost felt like there were tears in his eyes, but he didn't feel like crying. He knew his brother was testing him, yet he answered falsely all the same. "Your... killer... Khavars."

Lori stood and limped over. "You're changed, Esmond," he said, "but you're still in there." He put his coarse hand on Esmond's shoulder. "Tomorrow we will get vengeance. We owe it to our dead as fathers, as kings... but after the fighting, you owe it to yourself to find him again. There's so much left to live for."

Esmond locked his squinting eyes on Lori. The worried Lord of the Lagoon never looked so old, with his long black hair, laughter lines almost eclipsed by lines from fret. "You're talking rubbish," he winced, shaking his head and drinking more wine.

Lori said nothing when he left, if not for that alien look Esmond had last seen Tobi Sparks wear. *I'm the same Esmond,* he frowned when he was alone. *Why does everyone else see someone different?* It made him smile. *I'm not mad. I'm not changed. I'm Esmond Centaur. I am the blood of the Sagittarius. I've always been, and always will be.* He wished to put the war behind him, to go back to simpler days where he would do no more than spend time with his family. But it wasn't behind him; it wouldn't be until Vincent Scorpius and Delmar Khavar and Sir Orion Reade and everyone who had ever wronged him was dead. It helped him sleep to know that tomorrow would be the first day to approach to that: to the deaths of his foes, to the end of his war.

<hr />

Esmond wasn't the first man awake like he thought he would be. As he was making his way to the council tent, he spied many a man pacing, readying themselves, some looking as though they hadn't slept at all. There was a thick white fog that veiled everything, like every morning the Pole had seen before, but Esmond found it strangely comforting, when he normally wouldn't.

All three - now four including Lori - councillors were already inside the tent, looking as if they had been waiting a while. Darius Boyd was sharpening his sword with a whetstone, Lori flicked away at a necklace that hung past his chest, and the other two sat staring into the red of the tent. "Have I kept you waiting?"

No one seemed startled. "We are at your service, my king," Elliot Moss said tiredly.

"It's a tricky thing to sleep before a battle," Darius said, slotting the sword to his sheathe. "I doubt many men slept well."

Esmond swallowed, almost guilty. "Are the men ready?" he asked out of curiosity.

"A command away, my king," Darius nodded. "Would you have them readied?"

"I'm not sure," Esmond said, tapping his fingers on a table, an old map of the Auburn Pole sprawled and pinned across it. "What's the situation?"

"Not any different than what we anticipated," Darius said, joining Esmond at the table. "The Khavars are less than two hours away; we could try and find them, use the morning fogs for a surprise attack like we suggested. Or we could wait here and hold our ground. The choice is yours, my king."

"If that's your counsel, then we'll march," Esmond nodded. He looked to the other three. "You all look as miserable as rain."

"It's a tricky thing to sleep before a battle," Lori repeated dryly. "I doubt many men slept-"

"Thank you, Lori, I may have gathered that," Esmond said. Elliot smirked at the quip. "Are you sure they haven't noticed us, Briggs? A blind man could spot an army as big as ours."

"I wouldn't know if they have, my king," he said, slumped in his chair. "But they don't know these lands. It's not hopeful to say they haven't."

"You're the head of word, Lord Waker, you should know."

Briggs frowned. "Yes," he nodded, "and head of pennons too. I'd best see to your pennons, your grace." He bowed snobbishly and left.

Esmond would have taken that as a slight a few days ago, but he was too happy to let it bother him today. "I'm sure we all have better places to be," Esmond said icily. "We'll march within half the hour." The king stopped himself on his way out. He was going to turn around, perhaps to say goodbye if either of them fell in battle. Something like: *you have all been loyal councillors, loyal friends. If any of you see your last day today, know that I couldn't have chosen anyone better to counsel me.* They had been family for as long as he could remember, friends for even longer, the last few standing of his great council. He could not have known what caused him to keep that to himself.

━━━━━━●～～

A silent swarm, his army advanced. Apart from the steady bristle of horse hoof on frosted orange grass, no one said a word, nor made a sound. It made Esmond smile. With him, the king brought his close to unused bronze sword, along with his favourite twisting wooden bow, a quiver full of arrows, light steel plating that allowed him to easily move around, and his gold and zircon crown he had not taken off since he woke. He normally hated to wear it, but took a liking to it more and more when duty forced him to. It even felt as though Esmond's thoughts were clearer to him with it on. Around him were his king's guard, aside from Sir Connell Atlee, who Esmond had sent with a few outriders to scout ahead.

The fogs had not faded much by the time Sir Connell came galloping softly back to Esmond. "They're marching," he said, out of breath, "full host, two miles perhaps, maybe more."

"Very well," Esmond nodded, glancing at Lori. "Sir Ellis, Sir Robert, tell the chevals. We're to get into formation and hold until they arrive. Tell them to make it heaviest on the flanks. They're to wait for the first crack before we charge." Two miles was a long way away, Esmond couldn't have said why he still whispering.

The two knights nodded and galloped away down the ranks. By the time they rode back, Esmond's army had split into two sectors of thick columns, stretching so far that the white mist and the dark trees cloaked their greatness, with a tiny equo vanguard in the middle. The king looked upon what he could see of his army, and many seemed closed to retching, unprepared, sleep deprived, but thankfully most of all, powerful; most sat high on horses, behind a seasoned cheval, under dark blue banners. Esmond was content as they waited. Whatever army the Khavars had brought, Esmond's was stronger. Darius had said so. "We have the numbers, we know the lands, we have the discipline. We'll destroy them like a rake destroys dirt."

It was impossible to tell how far the Khavars were, but Esmond was still counting away the minutes, trusting his instinct to sound the ambush. He could barely make out the Sag's Crossroads, knowing it was such since there was only one place in Austellus where the Lunar Path exploded outwards like that. *Trees are our lives,* he knew, remembering what Elliot had said, *as long as we stick to them, and stay off the road, we'll survive.*

Eventually, he could vaguely hear the unmistakable *clunk, clunk, clunk* that only an army could make. That was when his heartbeat began to climb. It grew louder and louder and louder, but still, the only thing anyone could see was a sea of whiteness swirling around in the wind. *Clunk, clunk, clunk, clunk.* Esmond squinted while he waited, and waited, and waited. Multiple times did Sir Arter Whyte tap his shoulder to nod, but multiple times did Esmond shake his head because his instincts told him otherwise. *Clunk, clunk, clunk, clunk, clunk.* All that mattered was the endless white, and what it told the king. It told the king to wait, so he waited. *Clunk, clunk.*

Suddenly, the feeling came to him. *This is it.* He nodded to Lord Jocks Wright, and the first cheval didn't hesitate to swing around his nine stringed whip and bring it down to make a harsh *crack.* *"CHAAAARRGGE!"* one man yelled in the silence, and the Auburn Pole rang aloud with the sound of whips and hooves and cries.

As they tore through the white sea, the mesh of green and orange and white that was the Khavar army appeared to them, and just as quickly did the equos begin to hail them with arrows. The arrows flew like deadly birds through clouds, impossible to react to. *Like a rake destroys dirt.* Esmond even *felt* like a rake as he unloaded bolts into his discomposed enemies; they scattered back and continued to fall. He wished he could focus more on the killing, but half his energy was used trying to dodge the lanky trees scattered in front of them. *Trees are our lives,* he tittered breathlessly.

After they charged by maybe a tenth of the crab army, a deep *huuuuuuuuuu* shook the forest, and they all scuttled out of formation like the crabs they were. They used their curved swords and shields to fearfully hack away at the horses that ran past. Horses fell, and Centaurs died, but so did Khavars.

Far ahead of him, he saw a rider charge into a tree, speared by a branch. Closer than that, a horse tumbled into a group of Khavars, and another Khavar used his cutlass to chop away one stallion's four legs in one swipe.

Behind *and* in front, unhorsed Centaurs unsheathed their swords to fight away the horde of crabs. Next to him, Sir Ellis kicked away a swordsman who tried to leap on his horse. Esmond started to feel his fingers lock up, but he didn't slow down his tenacious firing.

Every new Khavar soldier to appear from the whiteness seemed to be just as startled as the last. Neither could the fortified ones save themselves, as their towering shields could only protect them from one angle, and arrows were flying everywhere.

It took a while for Esmond to realise that they weren't *just* an army, but a *weapon*, with huge siege towers and tall ladders that lay on the ground, splintered to pieces as hooves thundered atop. *They meant to besiege the Pole, raze every fort from here to Lunarpass*, he thought, scarcely believing. *What by gods made them think they could?* He laughed at that. He laughed at the endless Khavars that lay planted with arrows. He laughed at the Venusian blood that sprayed up in the air to mingle with the dirt and the parting fog. Sir Robert Hyll glanced over with a concerned face, somehow hearing the king's hysterics over the rumbling and crashing and bawling of war. Esmond only nodded and lopped at the throat of a running soldier.

Soon, Khavars stopped appearing, and their bruised column found the end of the army. In response, Lord Wright let his whip fly once again, and the Centaurs rotated to charge head-on to the crabs, back the way they had come. That was when riding became difficult: Esmond was thankfully not at the front, not having to bear the impact as they ploughed through the Khavar ranks. Still, galloping over the fallen soldiers and their oversized weapons almost sent the king and his mare flying multiple times. The *crunch* that sounded for every shield and body his horse pounded upon sent tingles through Esmond's spine.

He was almost careless when dealing with his arrows now, not slowing his fire when so many others had. Some Centaurs in front of him snapped their heads back when his arrow would fly past them, but by then Esmond had already loaded another.

All around him, Khavars tried their hand at dismounting the king, but before they could even get close, a member of his guard would *always* ride them down. Sir Arter had fallen himself, Esmond saw, the knight at the rear of the army hacking away at challengers. Esmond wasn't able to react to a spear one threatened to throw before Sir Ellis chopped it and the bearer in two, and one Khavar got dangerously close before Sir Connell's arrow flew into his neck. *I'd be dead without them*, he knew, but that didn't dampen his recklessness.

They may have been in the very heart of the battle before Esmond's horse keeled over a body. *"ESMOND!"* Lori screamed, leaping after him. Esmond winced and braced as he rolled. He stopped next to a dying Centaur, clawing at his bloody throat. The king staggered to his feet as fast as he could, and found himself afoot with his guard surrounding him, protecting him. He wiped the mud from his eyes, straightened his crown, and yelled as he charged. He chopped down his first man easily. The second held a fat shield up, but a few heavy blows made it drop.

"Esmond!" his brother called again. Esmond duelled his way to the voice. *You're a bloody idiot, Lori.* He winced as a cutlass slashed just under his eye, but didn't hesitate to cut out the stomach of the Khavar who did it. He leapt for his bow - or was it his bow? he couldn't tell - when he and his guard had more breathing room, and sent arrows flying at any man who was running towards him, whether he could tell if it was an enemy or not.

As he charged through the crowds, Esmond found his brother sparring with maybe three Khavars. The king immediately dispatched one with an arrow. The second was ridden down by a cheval, and the third was Lori's doing. After the crab fell, Lori winced and grabbed his leg, using his sword for balance.

"Don't worry, brother, I'm here," Esmond said, pulling Lori's arm around his shoulders.

Lori smiled tiredly. "It's happening, Esmond. We're doing it."

"Yes. And we still are," Esmond grunted as he swept his blade at a charging man. Despite his worry, the king couldn't help but smile with his brother. "Are you well to fight? Do you need aid?"

Lori shook his head stupidly, pushing himself away from Esmond. "I'm always well to fight."

"But your leg... you jumped off your horse."

Lori had a wicked smile. "And you fell."

Esmond grimaced as he watched his brother hobble over to his next kill. *I shouldn't have summoned him. It'll be a miracle if he keeps what strength he has.* He let his breathing steady before he found his bow again. He looked back for his guard. *"Where's Sir Connell?"*

Sir Ellis Lovell whipped around frantically, hopping over two bodies to reach the king. "He was here a second ago," he said breathlessly.

"Sir Warrick?"

"He fell while we charged. He took an arrow for you-" Ellis had to briefly break away his attention to parry a Khavar blade and stab its wielder.

"Sir Warrick's dead?" Esmond winced, disbelieving. *He sacrificed himself and I didn't even realise. The great Sir Warrick Mayne. Oldest in the guard. Killed by Khavars.* He let his hatred build when Sir Ellis nodded, turning to jump over a fallen horse to fiercely hack away at more bodies.

The next Khavar he found was particularly strong, and they both blocked and swung for ages until an arrow flew out of nowhere to end his life. The king felt like the strongest man on the field when he fell. He plunged his sword into another's shoulder, and turned around quick enough to parry one more. He and Sir Robert double teamed one man with two blades, the two of them disarming him with ease. Sir Robert only then seemed to notice the whopping arrow that was wedged in his arm. The big man just broke it in half and continued fighting. Esmond had to smile.

He wanted to have an overview of the battle, to know how many Khavars were left, to know how many had fallen, but they never seemed to stop appearing through the fog or from behind a tree. At least he knew that the bulk of them lay broken on the floor, since Esmond couldn't seem to step anywhere without knocking a body or a weapon. *How does it feel, Vincent? To have your men butchered by us? This is what it means to break a peace treaty, viper-*

"Aggghhhhhhhhh.!!!"

The scream was distinctive. Esmond felt his stomach twist. *"Lori?!"* He ran over. His king's guard followed.

Lorimer was struggling against a tree as he tried to shuffle away from a Khavar. He was disarmed. A spear was lodged in his good leg. The Khavar reared back his thick sword, and swiped at Lori with all his might, cutting through his armour like a knife through butter. His chest split open from a crimson line. Esmond cast his sword to the soldier, with a force so strong that it could have brought down castles. The Khavar staggered backward, dying instantly.

Esmond stumbled next to Lori, catching him as he fell. "I've lost my leg, Esmond. I'm legless." Lori smiled. "I might... need that aid now."

"We'll get you out," Esmond nodded, unable to take his eyes away from the infinite blood that darkened the orange grass, the deep gash that exposed Lori's stuttering chest, the fat spear protruding from his leg. "You'll be fine, brother. We'll go back to Lunarpass, we'll share a barrel of wine with our cousin for our victory, it'll all be o-"

"The last thing I... want to hear as I go are more lies," he winced. "My brother... was the Esmond who could tell the truth."

Esmond tried to hold back the tears, but it only made his vision blurrier. "No," he said. "I forbid you to die."

"I've already cheated death once, Esmond," he frowned, a pale colour flushing over him. "Let me die for something I'm... proud of."

Esmond shook his head. "We were meant to show Austellus why we... No, stay with me, *please*."

"Look around, brother," he said, taking an eternity to twist his head, "we *have* shown them. I promised we would." His brother smiled kindly, before grimacing with pain. "My... scabbard." Esmond reached inside and pulled out a rolled-up scroll. "I was meant to give it to you... before."

"What is it?"

"You'll... see." Lori jerked away to cough up blood. "It's... the last thing I want... the *only* thing I want... Promise me you'll do what that letter says. Promise me *as* Esmond. *As* my brother."

"I *promise* you, little brother," he winced. "But please don't leave me alone in this world."

"Another lie," he grunted. "You'll never... be alone, Esmond." He exhaled contently.

"*Who is there left?!*" Esmond wailed. "*There's no one! I have no one! Brother, please!*" Lorimer didn't blink again. "Lori?" The king hoped otherwise for a long while... but hope was no use. His last brother was dead.

Esmond ran his fingers through Lori's black hair. He gripped it so hard he could have pulled it out from the root, but he didn't care. He rocked back and forth as he pulled his brother's head to his chest, letting the tears fall down his face. It was all his fault. No doubt the noise from the war he started drowned out his cry.

FELIKS VIII
-Bond-

H e woke up gasping. Feliks knew it was a dream, but the pain had never felt more real. He felt his chest, making sure there wasn't a tear across it, and then his leg, just in case he did in fact have a spear poking out of it. He could only sigh with relief when he found out there wasn't. But still, it was unsettling how vividly he could remember it: the war around him, men dying at every sight, his uncle Esmond, who had a seeping red gash under his eye, rushing towards him, shouting words in a language he couldn't understand. *Only a dream*, he reminded his lightheaded self, *you're alive, don't worry.* It made him think of the dreams his father was having back at the Lagoon. *Does he still suffer them?* Feliks thought. If he did, the bastard felt sorrier for him, now more than ever.

Not wanting to think about dreams any longer, Feliks forced himself out the featherbed, and made his way down the royal mountainside tavern. "You're up early, Feliks," Marcarius observed as the boy joined his small corner table.

"Bad dream," Feliks winced, rubbing his eyes.

Elder Marcarius had a tome out and his reading glasses on. It seemed like he was inseparable from books since their visit to the Athenaeum, but so was Feliks. "Good that you're up then," he nodded. "Might be you're just hungry."

"So hungry," Feliks agreed, getting up to make his way to the innkeep.

As he waited for his food, his mind wandered to the girl he had met at the Athenaeum. He hadn't told Marcarius, *but how could I? What am I meant to say? That I met the strangest girl in all of Austellus... with those deep grey eyes... haunting, curious grey eyes.* Work was the only thing he could do to take his mind off her; whenever he stopped, she was all he would think about. *Who was she? Why was she there? Why did she talk to me? Was she flirting with me in the first place? Where is she now?* He knew it was stupid, putting a girl he had just met at the forefront of his mind, before matters like *the serpent* and *the Pause*, but thoughts of her still came, involuntarily or not. *What does it matter? She's gone. Focus on why you're here, Feliks.*

That being said, the books he had taken were of far less help than he would have liked. The tomes on the *Pause* couldn't have been more vague about *how* and *why* it happened; many of them just had small excerpts from people who had survived, detailing how they miraculously braved through brutal sandstorms, blistering blizzards, incredible winds that lifted and shook buildings and sometimes even the sea. "A *Pause* that we might face won't be nearly as bad. I wouldn't worry," Marcarius said. Still, Feliks would imagine, and wonder if he would be safe at the Lagoon, or if it would break in half and lift up into the sky like so many other islands.

Perhaps the most useful tome was the cryptic 'Servant of Justice' Feliks had found just before he met the girl. It *was* a poem, like Feliks had suspected. He might have known it once before, but when he read it aloud to Elder Marcarius, it felt like new text to him:

> 'Long since has passed for healing,
> Never more so for he who would restore death,
> For death was all they saw, and the life he brought was not.
> He was slain in spite of that,
> Banished by Jupiter from belief and the tale,
> An incomplete kingdom without, but a weeping kingdom with.
> Long would he not coexist,
> Never more so for his sons, his kin,
> For a race to not belong was something men would not forgive.
> They thought their days were numbered,
> Until a just man was born to them,
> He swore to deliver that of which they were so misguided to misgive.
> Long did he take to conquer,

Never was he more judged by gods, by men,
For I serve only justice, the just man said, never knowing what it meant.
Eighty-eight were owed to him,
By right of steel and blood,
But the pacts of dying men would send bias where they could.
Long since has passed for justice,
Never more so for the serpent and its bearer,
For the just man to rule the stars, and for no one else to know.'

'Never more so for the serpent and its bearer' was what had Marcarius clueing. But it wasn't like he could glean anything from that or the rest either. "It's an old poem, old enough for its author to be lost to history."

"How long ago, do you know?" Feliks asked.

Marcarius sighed unknowingly. "The Ancient Era, easily."

"And you weren't around to know back then?"

"The *cheek*," Marcarius scolded with a smirk. "I have not even seen five hundred years, I'll have you know."

It wasn't much, but it was still progress, not that more fiction and poetry could help with understanding *who* this *bearer of serpents* was. In any case, Feliks had written the poem down on some papyrus just in case they would one day come to understand it.

As Feliks returned to Marcarius's corner table, holding a plate full of oats and almonds with an apple on the side, the elder looked as though he had gone through most of the book. *How can someone read that fast?* he thought. "So, did you meet with Elder Solomon yesterday?"

"I did," Marcarius nodded, somehow continuing to read. "It was as we suspected," he said. "Temperatures are falling: slowly, but falling nonetheless. They're the lowest they've been for centuries."

"Could he not tell you anything new, then?" Feliks asked with a mouth half full of apple.

"Only that my brother fares dreadfully under pressure," he said.

Feliks tittered and swallowed. "Are elders *really* brothers? I've always wondered."

Marcarius lowered his glasses. "I must have stern words with your lord father, for you to not know of the Elder's Gift."

"I know of the Elder's Gift," Feliks smirked.

Marcarius stared nostalgically into the empty tavern, spare of a knight or two breaking their fast. "We're not *family*, as other people would describe. We share no blood, no, only that of what spilled during our bond, during our accepting of duty."

"I suppose it'd be a bit more complicated if you were," he nodded. "Did you have *any* family?"

"Well yes, Feliks, no man can be born without parents," the elder said dryly.

"Brothers, I mean," Feliks smiled, "and sisters and cousins."

"No, but I don't envy you," Marcarius said happily. "We elders are fathers to the realm; we have millions of children to look after."

"That's different, though."

"Not as much as you'd think," the elder smiled. "What runs through my veins is the very same as every Centaur, and Reade, and Equuleus. You are all my kin, whether I like it or not."

"Even me?"

"You are a Sagittarius, are you not?"

Feliks had to smile. He much preferred looking at who he was in that way, and not through the bastardised lens of royalty and men who made up the rules. *In blood, I'm not a bastard. I never was. I never will be. I am the blood of the Sagittarius.* For once, he felt whole.

The man Kenneth Venulaes was talking to when they had arrived, Sir Lamont Chaney, carefully came into the tavern. The feathers on his spaulders gently floated about as he walked. "My lords," he bowed. "If it's not a trouble, Lord Kenneth would like to break fast with you."

"Not a trouble at all, Sir Lamont," Marcarius smiled, closing his tome. "Lead the way, my lord."

It wasn't the best of days for Iustitia; it wasn't as windy as when they arrived, but across the mountain range loomed huge silver clouds, threatening to burst into rain at any second. Though, all Feliks felt on his brown hair was the occasional spit. Even with the potentially dangerous weather, Feliks enjoyed the city, and the sights it had to offer, the mountains it had to scale, the history it had to discover.

The two followed Lamont to the *Aquila:* the needle-like keep where the throne of tourmaline sat. The keep was mostly the same as they first had seen it, only that massive, thick grey banners stretched across the two stone arcs on either side, probably to shield from the oncoming rain. Lord Kenneth was standing by one arc, peering down to the mountains below. "My lords," he smiled as they entered. "It's good of you to join me."

"Couldn't well refuse to break fast with the Lord of Iustitia," Marcarius said.

Kenneth blushed. "Come, that hike must have starved you both."

They followed him past the throne into a back room, and after a couple of steps entered a wide stone mess hall with stuttering heights and high windows. Food had been set, but it was not much different to what Feliks had already been eating at the tavern. "Help yourselves, my lords," Kenneth said, "we haven't enough people to feed up here."

"Does your family not keep company of you, Kenneth?" Marcarius asked as he sat.

"They do, but lower down," he nodded, "my siblings are too lazy to climb this high, I'm afraid. My mother, Lady Rosanna, was the only one who would, but since... Daryl's passing... she hasn't... had the time to."

"Doesn't it get lonely?" Feliks asked, reminded of the family he had at the lagoon, and lack thereof.

Kenneth smiled and shook his head. "I have no reason to be." He took a swig of water. "I can't fake a smile, though; I've had some grim news from the Pole. I thought it best to tell you in person."

If Marcarius was going to eat, he wasn't anymore; he placed a fork down. "Esmond?"

Kenneth sighed and nodded. "It concerns him. It's ill done of me to mention it before you've eaten."

"What's happened?" Marcarius insisted.

The boy looked like he didn't want to continue. "We had a raven come at dawn. The king has... declared war on the Archipelago."

If Marcarius was eating, he'd have choked. *"War?!"* He frowned and rubbed his eyes. "Oh, Esmond, you fool."

"If sources can be trusted, he was last marching south with a full host to battle," Kenneth sighed.

"To *battle?"* Marcarius's frown cut deeper. He stood abruptly. "I need to be there. He needs me." The elder ran his hand down his face. "Feliks, we have to go. I must get you home."

"That might be a bit tricky," Kenneth winced. "I'm sorry, Feliks, but Centaur's Lagoon has been besieged as well. Unless you go back with an army bigger than ours, you can't go home."

"Can't we?" Feliks said breathlessly. "...take your army?"

Kenneth sighed sadly. "It's the Venusians we're warring with, Feliks. I can't abandon my people, not with the Archipelago so close."

Marcarius was just as wordless as the bastard. "Gods," he cursed. "Then you have to come with me, Feliks. Come, let's get our things." The elder bowed to Kenneth. "Thank you, my lord, for your hospitality and roof. I'm sorry we have to leave so suddenly."

Kenneth nodded, standing as well. "I can offer a small escort, just in case you find trouble on the road."

"That would be valued," Marcarius bowed again, marching out.

As the elder panicked to pack the little stuff they had come with, Feliks was given time to think about what was happening. It unsettled him to imagine the lagoon, enemies all around, his father trapped inside. *It's good that I left*, he thought, *that way I could come back with an army. I could lift the siege myself.* Then he remembered. *But who would follow me? I'm a bastard. Bastards don't lead armies.* That only left him one choice. He felt the need to distance himself from his home, from his father. "Are you ready now, Feliks?" Marcarius asked when he had made up his mind.

Feliks sighed. "I don't think I can come. I don't think I want to."

Marcarius looked at him like he had lost his wits. "What's wrong?"

"Well, I would go home if I could, but..." Feliks shook his head. "I know we're not anywhere close, but as long as I'm here, I want to figure out this bloody serpent and what it means. I'm sure Lori would prefer that. He hoped I'd figure it out."

"I can't leave you here," Marcarius squinted.

Feliks tittered. "Why not? I'm closer to home here than I am with Esmond."

"You'll need to be even closer if a war is what we face," he said. "I'll allow you to stay, but at least go to Aquamare like I intended. You'll be safer there, and *closer* still."

"What will I find in Aquamare?"

"An observatory. And in it, what you desire:" Marcarius said, "Truth."

LETA IV
-Refuge-

Mountains were all she could see from the coast, towering high in a scattered rocky bluff. Kyna had to row their small wooden boat deep down the strait before anything more than a house belonging to the great city of Aquamare appeared. Still, the city was a lot higher than them, and only the peaks of towers and spires poked out between the mountains.

"This isn't the way people normally come, is it?" Leta Centaur observed as they serpentined past the tiny rocky islands.

"Clever," Kyna smirked. "No, not normally."

It made sense that she didn't want to be seen. Leta had to keep reminding herself that Kyna was an outlaw. It had been so easy to forget, since she had been so quiet, *and so... un-outlaw-like.* "How do you know the way so well, then? Do you come here often?"

Kyna never stopped smirking. "Aquamare is my home. My family live here."

Leta frowned. "So, you have to sneak in this way every time you want to visit?"

She nodded sullenly. "It's better than not being able to see them at all."

"Don't you mind it?" Leta continued curiously. "Do you regret it, what you did? What *did* you do to become an outlaw?"

"My lady," Sir Roswell cut in, "I'm sure the last thing our focused escort needs right now is an interrogation."

"It's quite alright, Sir Roswell," she laughed. "I did bad things, Leta. I pissed off people I shouldn't have pissed off." Her red hair lifted as she shrugged. "And I paid for it."

Leta felt sorry for her. *Paid how? By not being able to reliably see her family again? That isn't justice, whatever she may have done.* Kyna didn't seem like the type of person capable of doing wrong, doing *bad things*. But neither did Nero and Tyran Capra, who had welcomed Leta and her mother into their home, just to backstab them mercilessly a moon and a half later. She didn't feel like talking after remembering that.

For the longest time, the gentle splash of water against their boat was the only sound to float along the lake, but soon voices joined the splashing. Kyna's eyes widened. "Get down," she whispered, yanking the oars into the boat.

"Well, it depends if you want to involve yourself in that. I doubt many Venusians would want to trouble themselves with trying their hand at the Saturnian Mountains." It was a man's voice.

"It might be I don't have much of a choice, especially when King Esmond comes," said another man. "I'll give you this: the boy is capable, more so than I thought. How many people were *grieving* over the fact that someone so young would rule Iustitia?"

"Too many. They'll know better now, though." There was a small splash after he replied, followed by a curse.

"I should hope so. They've never been too-"

"Why are we hiding?" Leta whispered. "Do you know them?"

"*Shhh,*" Kyna frowned.

In an instant, the voices had stopped. Leta's stomach was caught in her throat. There was a long silence before they were heard again. "Perhaps we shouldn't be talking politics out in the open like this. Voices travel further over water, I hear."

"I hear the same," the man chuckled. "But who would do such a thing as listen without us knowing? Might they be scared of us? I've never considered us particularly *scary.*"

"Ah, some people have strange fears, brother, but who would do such a thing indeed? I feel as though our home isn't as private as it once was."

"Oh, undoubtedly. There's always trouble on these waters; especially where the *lake falls.*"

Kyna winced. "You didn't have to," she called out.

There was a small silence again, and the two men emerged from the jutting rocks. They definitely seemed like brothers, both sharing a short, ghostly white head of hair. They were both built well too: broad but slim, one wearing humble turquoise rags and a belt while the other, a slightly chubbier man, wore tight leathers embossed with a sigil Leta had never seen before. The slimmer one had a smile on his face, and leant easily against the rusted bronze trident he held. "Lady Lakefall," he said. "I was wondering when I'd see you again."

"No one calls me that anymore."

"No one calls you that but it's still your name." Both men were smiling, but the man with the trident had a particularly wicked smirk. "We'll never forget who we are, will we, Kyna?"

"You're an asshole," she said scathingly. "I'm not even here for me."

"I can see that," he said, nodding to her company.

"Um, we don't want trouble, friend," Sir Roswell said carefully. "We've come from Fort Deus; we were hoping to be received by the Lord of Aquamare?"

The same man nodded with a smile. "Come ashore and be received, then." He slipped away behind the rocks.

Kyna was wearing a bitter face as she took to rowing again.

"I'm sorry, Kyna," Leta frowned. "I didn't think they'd hear."

"Don't worry, it's fine," she sighed. "Will you both be ok from here?"

"I think so," Sir Roswell nodded, stepping onto a bay full of pebbles and stones. "Thank you, my lady. It's been kind of you to take us."

Kyna only nodded as she rowed back the way they'd come.

Leta felt bad. She was curious what they were talking about, how they knew each other. *Lady Lakefall.* The name felt familiar enough, but she couldn't decide where from. She couldn't imagine Kyna being a lady, just as she couldn't imagine her sister Eva being one either.

"She didn't want to stick around?" asked the man with the trident as he joined them on the tiny bay. "I'm almost offended."

"She... said she couldn't stay," Sir Roswell said.

"No," he agreed. "So, who might you both be? It's been a while since we've had Centaurs this far west."

"I'm sorry, I can't tell you," Sir Roswell frowned. "Is the Lord of Aquamare coming? Lord... Oberon?"

"The Lord of Aquamare?" he smirked. "You're looking at him."

Sir Roswell's handsome face went red. "...Oberon Trident."

"That's me," Oberon smiled. "The fat one behind me is my brother,

Lord Gwydon Trident."

"I'm not fat," Gwydon protested calmly.

"He's not fat," Leta added.

Gwydon Trident smiled and bowed.

"As you say," Oberon said, using his trident to turn around and take the lead. "Still, how am I to receive you if I don't know your names?"

The three followed as he navigated along the rocky river bank. "My apologies, my lord. My name is Sir Roswell Dart, the King's *Second Avail*. And this is his daughter, Princess Leta."

Oberon abruptly stopped twizzling his trident. He raised a brow. "Princess Leta," he repeated, inspecting her. "You don't say?"

"We had nowhere else to go," Sir Roswell frowned. "Centaur's Lagoon has been besieged, Lunarpass is leagues away... we were told the safest place was here."

Oberon turned and started walking again. "Whoever told you that wasn't wrong, unfortunately."

"What's going on?" Sir Roswell continued. "Are the Capras warring?"

"You haven't heard?" Gwydon asked sadly. He continued when the knight shook his head. "It's not the Capras, it's the king, King Esmond. He's declared on all of exile, it seems."

"The... Archipelago too?" Sir Roswell was pale.

"The Archipelago most of all," Gwydon nodded.

Leta had only heard stories of the Archipelago, and none of them were good. She remembered seeing Blaine Casteron and his two eldest sons when they stayed at Fort Deus, and when it came to feast for Fletcher's birth day. *Does that include them? Are the people we feasted now our enemies?*

"For how long?" Sir Roswell asked eventually.

"Not long after the Harvest Moon came," Gwydon said.

"That was ages ago," Sir Roswell winced.

"When was it that Fort Deus fell?" Oberon asked. Somehow, a salmon had appeared on the end of his trident, wriggling about helplessly as the Lord of Aquamare poked at it. Leta hadn't even heard the water splash.

"Late Sturgeon Moon, I thought."

"Late Sturgeon Moon," Leta nodded. "I remember the moon being blue."

"You've been asea quite a while, then," Oberon said curiously. "You're welcome here, though. Any friend of Esmond is a friend of mine."

"Thank you, my lord," Sir Roswell said as courteously as he could. He had a nervous skew to his walk, as if he wanted to pee really badly. "So, what's happened since then? Since the... declaration?"

"A battle," said Gwydon. "A victory for the crown, but still a battle. They met with most of the Khavar army before either had the chance to disperse. *The Battle of the Crossroads,* I hear it called."

"How many losses?" Sir Roswell continued to quiz nervously.

"We don't know," Gwydon admitted.

"Where is the king going now?"

"Back to Lunarpass, I believe."

There was a long silence after that. It was difficult not to concentrate on the ever-changing rocky terrain around them, but Leta still found herself wincing. *Father's been in a battle. He's killed men with a sword and bow like Fletcher did.* She couldn't imagine it. She couldn't even imagine *Fletcher* killing men, even though Sir Roswell had told her he had, *and had done so really well apparently.*

"It's a terrible thing, war," Oberon said eventually, plucking the scales off the fish he had skewered. "But like you said, you're safe now. You're far away from death here." He didn't pause for long before attempting to lighten the mood. "I imagine so long on that ship would have made you both an appetite. Care for a fish, my lady?" he asked, moving the trident to her face.

"It's raw," Leta said.

"Which makes it better," he said, carving out a chunk and throwing it into his mouth. Leta expected him to wince, but he seemed to be *enjoying* it. "We have cooked food in the city, if you insist."

Leta's titter evolved into a chuckle. *Small wonder Sir Roswell confused him for just a normal fisherman.* She was struggling to see him on a throne.

It didn't take long before Leta's worry for war and her father were completely forgotten, mainly due to their rocky trek finally reaching the entrance to the city. The lake they had sailed in on exploded outward into canals and rocky waterfalls and wooden water wheels. The entire city was built atop and around it, multiple layers of rocky patio acting as walkways, docks, tunnels, and bridges. Moss spread where it could: in between the cracks of stone on mountains, massifs, and even on the already dark pine trees. Almost every part of the lake had long, thin row boats sailing atop it, with long flat lead roofs and a dark red and orange interior to match.

Aquamare's architecture was of another world entirely, most houses seeming to have a roof above a roof above a roof, all twisting up like some god had pinched it. Even Seden couldn't compare to Aquamare's fine wooden cabins, pulled together with lead beams and soft blue lanterns. Those same lanterns were littered across the entire city, giving it a blue hue that cut through the mist. Within them, it wasn't fire, but *water* frolicking around in the way fire burns. Leta had to look twice at each one she passed, just to make sure her eyes weren't deceiving her. It seemed to amuse Oberon how in awe she was.

She could see where they were headed right away, as the keep must have been the grandest looking building. It was above a rocky waterfall, stretching across the rocks for as far as twenty normal houses side-by-side would. Smooth towers and spires made of stone protruded from the castle, twisting and reaching to the sky, outsizing the trees around it.

The entrance was over a large bridge, with fat stone pillars and those same magical blue lanterns posted on every side. Turquoise banners rubbed against the castle walls, of the same sigil Gwydon bore on his leather jerkin: a block of waves with a trident shooting through the middle.

It was as if they had walked into a different kingdom when they entered the castle, with its own web of stone streets and royal markets, filled with merchants and fishermen and farmers. They couldn't get away from the water lanterns, it seemed, their blue sheen echoing on every wall and person and animal. The walls and buildings were tall, taller than Fort Deus, yet the streets seemed more spacious, with wide open battlements and walkways full of breadth.

The keep was no less spectacular, the thin building towering over the rest of the city, complete with the same multi-layered pointed roof that was seen so often throughout Aquamare. The two men guarding the entrance seemed surprised to see Lord Oberon, but stepped aside as they came regardless.

"We don't have many visitors here," Oberon said. "Fat and ritzy traders for the most part." He smiled to Leta. "I'm sure my children will rejoice to have someone like-"

"Father!" a boy screamed. Leta's heart fluttered. It sounded like Hew.

Oberon was chuckling as the child ran up to hug him. "Hello," he said. "Have you been getting into trouble?"

"Y-yes," he beamed.

"Good lad," Oberon nodded, ruffling the boy's shaggy ash hair the way Esmond ruffled Hew's. "Behold my youngest son, the brave Oswin. Friends have come to stay, Oswin."

When Oswin saw Leta and her knight, it didn't take long for his smile to return. He darted towards her, and wrapped his arms around Leta's waist. "H-h-hello!"

Leta chuckled. "Hi."

He smiled at Sir Roswell and ran away.

"And there he goes," Oberon said dolorously. "Follow me, I'll show you to your chambers."

It wasn't Hew. You're dreaming, Leta. For some reason that made her miss him more. She held faith that her youngest brother was still alive, somehow surviving the fight and its aftermath, finding an escape boat like her. *They couldn't have killed a boy of ten,* she thought. *No one is that cruel.* But cruelty had been more salient than ever the past few moons.

She scarcely noticed the large stone hallways and stunning river views as she thought about her family. Thinking about Hew made her miss them all; Asher on his great *quest* at Ignis, Fletcher for the leader he had been and the safety he had given at Fort Deus, and Eva, the idiot, over in Lunarpass with father. *Well, not anymore if he's gone to war.* She missed Eva the most. Eva always needed her older sister. *She did want to be rid of home,* Leta thought grimly. It made her titter. *Now we are. We're half a world away from each other, and half a world more from home.*

"This'll be you, then," Oberon said, nodding to a huge square room with six doors on the sides. "Pick any room, they're all empty, as far as I know." He had already begun walking away. "I'm not entirely sure you are who you say, but no matter. You are welcome until I am proved wrong."

"Thank you, my lord," Sir Roswell bowed, slightly confused.

Oberon only smiled, twizzling his trident around as he left.

And the knight and the princess were alone again. "War," Sir Roswell said, wandering to brood over the lakes. He still had a bitter wince on his face. "I still don't want to believe it."

Leta frowned. "You should be with him, with my father."

He sighed, and turned his head. "Who would look after you then?"

She hadn't considered. "Myself?"

The knight smiled sadly. "The king has better men than me around him. I just... wish he wasn't so bloody far away."

The gentle sound of the lakes was tranquillising, much more so than Fort Deus. That might help Leta sleep for once. "How long will we stay here, Sir Roswell?"

"I wish I could know, Leta," he said. "I wish I could know."

ASHER VI
-Divination-

Ohne step at a time, Asher Centaur and his two lions traversed the beautiful cobblestone path, smothered with moss and veiled in mist. They had arrived. The road had been long and tiring and almost too much sometimes, *but now we're finally here. We're where I've been a thousand times in my head, allegedly.* And to Asher's dismay, Sanctum Amino was more than unchanged from the version in his dreams.

"Are you ok?" Lyssa asked for the fourth time that day as she touched their linked arms.

Asher nodded, but against his will; he was far from ok. The dizziness that swayed his head made each step more difficult than the last, and Asher could *feel* his blood nervously rush around his body. He wanted to retch, but nothing would ever come up. He wanted to fall, but Lyssa was practically carrying him. He had nowhere to go but forward, forward to the Sanctum, forward to his fate, whatever that was.

Whenever he tried to think of anything other than the seers, or if Leo and Lyssa would try to make conversation that didn't relate to them, Asher found that it wasn't long before his mind collapsed and his thoughts were invaded again. It had been getting worse every day, maybe because they were drawing closer, maybe because the prince's willpower was draining like a dry lake. But still, it didn't take all of his wits to feel that an end of it was near.

He felt suffocated, possibly down to the humid air, or the high misty valley, or something else entirely. "We're almost there, Asher," Leo said, trying to encourage his staggering walk. "We're so close, hang in there, brother." *I can barely hang on to my thoughts, Leo*, he felt like snapping, before he forgot why that angered him.

Every day of their journey had blurred into one for Asher. It didn't help that every night was impossible to tell apart either, since his recurring dream made each one identical. Leo claimed that they left Merchant's Bay three moons ago, to which Asher replied: "What's a Merchant's Bay?" The prince scarcely believed that he knew that man for three moons. That could almost be a hundred days if the stars played it kindly. Surely, if a hundred days had passed, Asher would've known the man better. "We *do* know him," Lyssa claimed. "He told us how he got here, what he's done, how he's done it. Don't you remember?" He didn't. The most vivid thing he remembered was the dream.

There were things each day that stuck out to him, namely when he'd see the dark brown trail they were following, or when he'd get to sink his teeth into a half-cooked boar or snake Leo had managed to hunt, or when he felt Lyssa's soft lips against his; *especially* when he felt that. Each event seemed nostalgic to the prince, as if he had lived them all before, but Asher wasn't convinced. Lyssa said they did, and they had done, many times. She seemed wounded enough to be telling the truth.

Occasionally, Asher would remember small details, like why they were walking, and what hunger felt like, and that he actually *did* adore Lyssa, calling her *my guardian* and *a lioness* and *my shield* in his head, but those thoughts were too few to know if they were true. From fear of saying anything that *wasn't* true, Asher held his tongue most days. But now, with Sanctum Amino a handful of hills away, it felt amazing that Asher might finally be rid of that burden.

The three paused to catch their breath when they scaled the first peak of the valley, and to take in the last stretch. Lyssa's mouth dropped after a time of panting. "Leo... do you see that?" she shivered.

Asher could barely see anything but fog. "What... is it?"

Leo was wincing. "That's not meant to happen."

Asher squinted again, trying his hardest to see. It was like they were camouflaged, but he eventually saw: dead seers, scattered along the mossy green valley, their dark cloaks torn, their frail bodies rotting. "It looks like they tried to run away," Lyssa said.

"Running away," Leo repeated, "that seems like a good idea."

"Shut up, Leo," Lyssa frowned, "we're not going back now."

Leo was forced to follow her and a crippled Asher. When they passed the bodies, it didn't *smell* like they were dead, but no man alive could stay so still. Leo stopped to check one for breathing, and felt nothing. "Who could have done this?" Lyssa asked with disgust.

"More like *what* could have done this," Leo frowned, taking the lead.

It seemed like whenever Asher would blink, he moved forward a dozen steps without knowing. That didn't make time pass any faster, though. Sometimes, it even felt like they were going backwards. He almost did when they climbed up the rocky stairs to the final peak. "What's wrong, Asher?" Lyssa asked.

The prince was frozen, an uncomfortable familiarity churning his stomach. Down the stairs they had to descend, Asher saw: the rounded stone floor surrounded by harsh yet delicate mossy cliffs, the smooth water sitting as still as death within the strange engravings, the scraggy pillars around the airy waterfalls that seemed to mean so much and so little at once. "You recognise it?" Leo asked.

Asher nodded.

Leo replied with a nod as well. "It doesn't look any less dreamy with your own eyes, does it?"

"Are we here?" Lyssa asked, baffled at what Asher knew was Sanctum Amino.

"We are," Leo said with a smile, performing a well-deserved back stretch. "Are you ready then, Asher? This is as far as we can take you."

"Why?" Lyssa protested. "Do you think he can walk down those stairs alone? He can't even walk on flatland without stumbling around."

Leo didn't respond, keeping his eyes on Asher. "It's ok, Lyss," Asher uttered weakly. "I can do it."

She frowned at him before reluctantly letting go, and Asher began to follow the stairs down. It was a struggle to look back, but he did anyway, Lyssa and Leo wearing almost identical, worried yet hopeful faces. He turned forward again, grabbing each smooth warm piece of stone as they came for his balance.

If Asher had fallen asleep, he wouldn't have known, nor would he know if he had woken up. Words couldn't describe how bizarre he felt: in a state between wakefulness and sleep, in a place he was only familiar with in his dreams. But it was also like he couldn't think straight, as if his thoughts had a stammer, as if his memory was jumbled. He *felt* how familiar the place was, but never remembered seeing it, or how he saw it. Every few steps he'd wonder where he was, how he got there.

"*ASHER!*" Lyssa screamed.

She had noticed he had fallen before he did. The prince's foot had rolled off a pebble, and he tumbled down to the lower set of steps. A sharp pain shot through his spine, but to him it was almost dull, numb. "I'm okay!" he called up as best he could, pushing up from the ground to continue his stagger along the cliff face.

At the bottom, there was no light like in his dream, and a hooded person stood in place of the silhouette. It took a while for Asher to realise what it was. The seer stepped towards him. "Prince of Ash is his name," he said in a raspy tone. "King of Light is his fate."

Asher felt his heart thudding tenaciously. *I'm here. It's happening.* He had lived this moment a thousand times, *so why am I so scared?* "Who are you?" he heard himself say.

"I am none, yet I am some. The serpent that comes is all."

Asher was shivering and sweating and squinting all at once. "What serpent?"

"The Serpent of Stars. And you must find him, Asher Centaur, as you must find the prince. For it will poison the city, flooded by waters as black as night. It will poison the realms, infected with discord as cold as winter. It will poison the light, laced with death that will leave life wilted." The seer's dark mouth twisted into a frown. "Do not let yourself be fooled, Asher Centaur. Do not let anyone befall their spell; for a completed kingdom of stars is something many a man would find beguiling."

His own mind came flooding back to him. *The Serpent of Stars. The King of Light. The Prince of Ash. A completed kingdom. I must find them, but where do I start? How do I start? What are these titles? Leave life wilted; the serpent's a killer. The serpent's going to kill. The king's peace; he wants me to keep it.*

He could finally understand, even if he didn't. The words were imprinted in Asher's mind, and questions shook his thoughts, even though he wasn't awake enough to ask them. He finally knew what he needed to know moons after it had begun plaguing him, even if it meant taking his attention away from the killer behind.

The seer staggered back with horror, as did Asher. The prince whipped around, but the hooded man had already grabbed him. He didn't have the energy to struggle. *I forgot?! How?!* He had never hated himself more.

Asher shut his eyes fearfully, his pain soon to be relieved. The knife pressed against his neck. *This is how I die. This has always been how I die. My dream was a vision, and I saw my own blood. I'm sorry father. I'm sorry Fletcher, and Lyssa. I had one job: to remember, and I failed. Now this all means nothing.*

But then... nothing itself. Asher awoke to his senses by his thumping heart. His lioness was behind him, a bloody rock in her hand. The man and his knife were dead on the floor, a crater in his head. Lyssa dropped the rock from her shaking hand.

"Lyssa," he said, holding his breath. He had seen his death every night, but he had never seen his lioness too. *My guardian. My shield.* "I love you," Asher exhaled, his life flashing before his eyes.

ATHENA VI
-Touch-

S he regretted not saying goodbye. She regretted it as soon as she and Sir Gerard Holt set sail down the Bullshorn River. It didn't make her any less angry with them, but even the gruff knight didn't know when they'd see them again. "Where is he taking the armies?" Athena Horncurve had asked him as she brooded on the boat.

Sir Gerard shrugged. "South. Your da' always liked being vague."

"You're part of his ram's guard. Didn't he tell you where?"

"I don't think he's told much to anyone since Sigmund died." The knight frowned. "He's not helping himself. Most brave men think they can bottle it up and deal with it."

"No one can," she decided. Not even Sigmund, as Sir Harold had said. The Warrior Boy was the bravest man Athena knew.

"Aye, no one can. Not even brave men." Sir Gerard pondered the oars as he rowed. He sighed. "It's always worth saying goodbye, though, even if you know you'll see them again."

She always believed Riley would be old and grey by the time he died, as old and grey as Sigmund was. She never wanted to believe otherwise. Her optimism about that was dwindling slowly. She had seen her grandfather's head lopped off, men dead and dying en masse on the streets of Selerborn, Siren banners battling with the wind as they flew from the Cenkeep, a host of unimaginable size at her father's back, all of which were the *opposite* of what she ever expected. *I should have said goodbye.*

Gerard told her about what her uncle had done, what he had almost caused. It made Athena wince. Luther had always been the more confrontational of the two brothers, the more stubborn. *The younger child always gets away with more*, she thought. Athena was living proof of that. *Or maybe it's because I'm a girl.* Either way, her uncle had abandoned them when he was needed most. She didn't want to forgive that, not yet.

Ten days of rough rowing did they have to endure before finally seeing the city of Mea Minor. Athena had never spent so long on a boat before. The city was unmistakable to her, with Kurvam Keep bending up into the sky, its twin long lost in the larger city of Mea, and a while after when one of the Enigma Towers revealed itself to her. Countless times had she wandered the streets of both Mea and Mea Minor, with their identical scattered homes on high and low hills, appearing to float if the soft white fogs ever graced the day. Sadly, it was a harsh midday sun that fell on the Twin Islands when they rowed into the docks.

There was a stream of boats with varying sizes sailing to and from the city, littering the maze-like wooden docks with men and women of all looks and accents. Athena had expected to see half as many, maybe a third. "Why are there so many people?"

"They're traders, I'm guessing," Sir Gerard said, a half-wince tugging at his lips.

"But the other docks are for traders," she said confidently, "the ones facing Mea."

"Aye, you might be right," he frowned.

I am right. She remembered the day vividly when her grandfather was fined for docking at the wrong one. Well, *almost* fined. It took a long stare and a shouting match for Sigmund to have the poor docker boy in tears.

They gently bumped against the outskirts, and Sir Gerard tied their boat to a pilling. A small fat man waltzed up to them. "License, please."

"License?" Sir Gerard growled with a thick northern accent. "Since when have ye needed a license to own a boat?"

"Part of the Twin's new initiative," he said wearily. "It's not really *new*, Todd and Tate have just been too lazy to follow it through, or forgot. Now we *have* to be more vigilant, though, with King Esmond's new laws."

"What new laws?"

"Gods, you *have* been living under a rock, haven't you? He's outlawed the owning of food. It's to help with the famine."

Athena and her knight glanced at each other.

"If you haven't got a license, I'll have to take you to Lord Tate."

"Take us, by all means," Sir Gerard sighed. "But we're here for Lord Cadmus, not him. His sister's come."

The fat man only needed to blink at Sir Gerard's fiery Horncurve sigil on his breastplate for his eyes to widen. "Shit, I thought you were traders. My apologies, follow me."

They were escorted through the maze of streets, past the throngs of traders, by the foot of the hills. Athena could scarcely take in the city fully, since the harsh midday sun made her break into a sweat after a time of walking. Eventually, they arrived at the main dock, an inordinate amount of ships and galleys choking the Whitefin Sea. There were twice as many ships here than at the other docks, mostly with huge yellow sails, but there were some white, a few greens, and most importantly, crimson. Horncurve crimson. Athena knew these weren't humble traders, but warriors. She could see as much as hundreds of men marched about moving armour, fetching arrows, caring to the ships. *My brother's new army,* she thought.

She found Cadmus in a tower just off the coast, sharing the company of four young lords as they looked at a map. "My lord, your sister," the escort said.

Cadmus's head shot up. Only a moon had passed, but he looked so much older. His scarlet hair was freshly cut, windswept in the way Riley wore. "My lords," he said, not taking his eyes off Athena.

Not a second after the four left did the two charge towards each other. Athena squeezed him as tightly as she could. "You found me," he smirked.

Athena punched him. "I hate you so much. Why didn't you tell me?"

Cadmus frowned. "How could I have? Harper was always listening." A smile led his face when he eyed the sword that hung from Athena's belt. "I see you took my advice."

Athena beamed and unsheathed her blade.

Cadmus chuckled, stroking his fingers along the steel. "It looks like Shofar."

"I meant it to."

Cadmus nodded. "That's pretty good, sis."

Athena agreed. "Better than what you could do."

Her brother's smile dried. "Ey, watch yerself. I might have not seen you in a moon but don't think I won't hesitate to chuck ye out this window."

"I've been dancing with death all moon, Cad," she said grimly.

He frowned again, more deeply this time. "It's happened, then?"

Athena didn't need an explanation to know what he meant. She nodded. "I was at the workshop."

"Oh, Athena, you weren't," he winced. "How did ye get out?"

"I didn't until it was over," she said. "Sir Harold died. They lopped off his arm."

Cadmus cursed and turned to the window. "But you found da'?"

"He found me," she wandered over to join him. The view showed the entire dock, a perfect place for a commander to watch over his army.

Cadmus shook his head. "I said to da', even before he decided to send me here: *'kill 'em now, save us the hassle, be done with it'.* He never listened, diddae?"

Athena snickered. "I'd be impressed if you can think of a Horncurve who listened to *anyone.*"

Her brother chuckled, but quickly grew sombre. "Aye, look where it gets you, though. Grandpa listened the least and lost his head for it."

Da's not Sigmund, she wanted to say, *he died stupidly,* but she didn't want to delude herself from Riley's mistakes either. "Marcus didn't come back," she said. "If he has, Harper's taken him."

Cadmus was silent for a while. "All those men down there have pledged to fight for me, for us. Once we take Selerborn back, we'll find him."

Athena thought back to the day he left. It didn't make her wince any less. "But he was angry at you the day he snapped," she frowned. "He said 'you set this up'. He said you knew about the cabals."

Cadmus's hazel eyes stared into Athena's grey, before he broke away to look down on the dock again. He sighed like it pained him to be reminded. "I knew fuck all, I just wanted to raid. Cadell told me it'd be a good jape to get Marcus to go to the Mudstreet, a good ploy for da' to favour me for Heavia, since I overheard he wanted to go again. I knew da' would be angry at him, but..."

"Not as much as he was," she gleaned. "Who's Cadell?"

"Cadell Siren. Harper's son. I should have bloody known," he winced. "I'll kill that bastard the first chance I get. He did this as much as I."

Athena sighed. "You're an idiot, Cadmus."

"I know. It was stupid," he said in an irritated tone. "All I thought about was getting to go to Heavia first. I wanted to be *better* than him for once. I know we joke a lot about how cocky he is, no more than you and ma' tease me, but I take it on the chin. I don't think Marcus does, but he still has a better reason to be cocky. He's *always* been the best."

Athena frowned. "He thinks the same of you."

"I doubt it."

"Yeah?" she smiled. "For being twins, you two are so damn out of touch sometimes. He *definitely* thinks that."

"If he *really* thinks that, then why is he so adamant about trying to prove how much better he is?"

"I don't know, why are you?" Cadmus looked away and flushed a deep red. It seemed like he couldn't decide what to say. "You owe it to Marcus to tell him the truth."

"What good would it do?" Cadmus winged.

"He's our brother, Cadmus," she frowned. "After what we did to him, it's the first thing he deserves. *None* of us took his side the day he left."

"But that was all an act. So was da' gettin' angry to some extent."

"How would *Marcus* know that?" Athena winced. Her brother didn't respond again. "He'll still be angry with you."

"He ditched us, Athena. *I'll* still be angry with *him*." Cadmus took his map and left the room sullenly.

Sir Gerard was waiting outside. "Did you hear?" Athena asked.

The knight nodded. "You said the right things, princess."

Athena sighed and started down the tower stairs. *What is it with boys, always wanting to have the last say, always needing to clash heads?* It had happened to Luther when he abandoned them, to Sigmund as he sealed his fate, to Riley as he became so hellbent on his *masterplan*, incidentally losing Marcus. And now to Cadmus, as he tries and fails to be the bigger twin. "Sometimes, being strong isn't winning all your battles, but knowing when you've lost." That was what Sigmund had told her, ultimately not following through when the time came to back down. *None of them will ever back down. It'll kill them all. Then it'll just be me and ma'.*

She and Sir Gerard walked around the docks for an hour before Cadmus's fleet was ready to sail. The docks were all but empty, only for a few dockers, the soldiers that were clambering about a time ago now safely ordered within the war galleys. Cadmus himself was before a Horncurve ship, shaking hands with a slim, brown-haired, brown-eyed man. They stopped talking when Athena and Sir Gerard approached.

"You'll win, won't you?" Athena asked.

Cadmus chuckled. "With all these men? Of course we will."

"How? No one's ever taken Selerborn from outside her walls."

Cadmus had a great smirk. "Lord Dugg may be on our side," he said. "Harper believes differently. As head of arms, perhaps Harper'll trust him to control some of the guards on the walls, the gates, the forces..."

"Dugg Gallach?" she asked, turning her mouth. "I wouldn't trust that man. He never smiles."

"You know how fuckin' tall Selerborn's walls are?" he smiled. "We have *no* chance of getting in without him."

Athena had no mind for war or planning of the like. "If you say so."

Cadmus smiled sadly. "What will you do now?"

"Wait 'till you win?"

He tittered. "And if I don't?"

"Well, you just said you would."

Cadmus examined her. "Athena, this is Lord Tate, Tate Kalyx. I trust you'll keep her safe?"

Tate smiled kindly. "Of course," he said. "I have a niece about your age in Mea. She'd be delighted to meet you."

"Hey, don't let her get too comfortable," Cadmus said, "she won't want to come back."

"We'll see," Athena said.

Her brother pointed at Gerard. "You too, Sir Gerard. Keep her safe."

The knight smirked. "I've been keeping Horncurves safe since before ye were born, Cadmus. Don't you worry about it."

"What would it matter, Cadmus?" she smiled. "I can keep myself safe now. Have you forgotten?"

Cadmus tittered, glancing at the dark sword that fell from her belt. "No," he said.

After a heartbeat or two, they embraced each other tightly. Athena could no longer squeeze her brother's body, his steel plate veiling him like a wall. Still, she held on for as long as she could. When they broke away, there was a tear in his eye, before he wiped it. "Wish me luck."

Athena smiled. "You're doing what grandpa did sixty years ago. Luck is in yer blood."

"Aye," he smiled.

Cadmus looked down on them once he climbed onto the ship. He smiled, and it slowly floated away. Athena clutched Sir Gerard's arm as she watched her brother sail to battle.

LETA V
-Shiver-

Exploring her new temporary home was the first thing Leta Centaur wanted to do. That was always the case when she visited somewhere new. The first thing she did when visiting Seden was explore. The first time she saw Deuswater and the Negal Wall, she could remember running around the streets and towers, exploring with Fletcher and Asher. She even believed that the first thing she did in this world was explore the fort she was born in. *A fort that's now rubble.* That's why calling Aquamare a *temporary* home was a queer thing. *I guess Lunarpass is my home now?* she thought, *that's where father is, and Eva.* Nothing was more of a home than Fort Deus, though. She needed to explore to think of something else.

It didn't feel like she and Sir Roswell had been at Aquamare for a week already, but being on a rowboat for an entire moon made days feel like minutes. They had been exploring every day, and the city would never get less enchanting, with its constant stream of traders, soothing blue lanterns that decorated everywhere and anywhere, its tranquil lakes and waterfalls that actually granted Leta some sleep for once, as she had predicted. Nothing was more tranquil than being safe at home, though.

Oberon Trident and his brother were never in the *Ardus Keep,* as everyone seemed to call it; they would always be off talking with common folk, or fishing like Leta and Sir Roswell had found them. It was Oberon's wife, Lady Lysanda who was always at the keep, who sat the throne of amethyst and held the amethyst trident, who seemed to have all the power and control when Oberon was gallivanting about with the fish.

Lysanda was nice enough. She would break fast and dine with them every day. Her silvery-grey eyes were something Leta found mesmerizing, and she had a faded brown length of hair which was almost the opposite of her family's white. "If you want something to do today, I heard the halfway stars have just become visible," she was saying at breakfast. "You could go to the observatory, and see them with the best scope in Austellus, if you wish."

So that's where Sir Roswell and the princess were going. Leta would always look at stars from Fort Deus. She would go out so often, that when moons came and went, she would remember which stars came at which moon. She could never put names to them, though, only shapes, and *feelings*, which she was aware was a stupid thing to measure with. It excited her to finally learn what she already knew.

Lady Lysanda continued by saying they'd not only be able to gaze at stars from the observatory, but also that "it's home to the largest non-fiction collection in all of Austellus."

"Non-fables? All the good stuff is in fiction," Leta complained to Sir Roswell. "What would I want to do with non-fables?"

"Truth," he shrugged.

The observatory was a majestic thing to look at. For the longest time concealed by mountains and trees, the great glass dome appeared to them from what seemed like a puff of smoke. The glass was lined with golden rims, and had balconies and sections underneath where people laughed and conversed and read. It was impossible to not notice the giant shining tube that projected out of the building, ending with a bulbous glass eye that stared at the sky. *Why would you ever need a scope so big?* She always thought the scope at Deuswater was huge enough. *This is just showing off.*

Lady Lysanda wasn't jesting about it being the *largest non-fiction collection in Austellus*. Inside the building was a sprawling hexagon of a room, with stacks of shelves so high that no one could realistically expect to reach the top without one of the fifty-foot ladders the librarians were shifting about. *Unless you were a mountain,* Leta smiled, *a mountain could reach that high.* The floor was a crimson carpet, complementing the glass and gold walls that reflected and echoed the cloudy, miserable day across the observatory. Come to think of it, she had seen nought of an 'observatory' so far. Leta tittered. "They should have just called it 'mostly a library and maybe a little bit an observatory'."

That made Sir Roswell smile. "It seems only midday. It'll be hours yet until we can see the stars."

"Are we waiting here, then?"

"If only we had books to help pass the time," Sir Roswell smirked. "Perhaps you'll learn something, princess."

Leta didn't have the will to object. She never had any energy in the first half of the day. Regardless, even if she had, reading was fun to her. Out of all her siblings, only her brother Hew read more than her, that being easy to know since the other three had never touched a book. It would be one of the things she would do when her insomnia would visit. For a long while, she would take books out to read on her special rock by the Endless Moat, as that was her favourite place to spend her sleepless nights, eventually stopping when a sudden gust of wind stole her copy of 'The Kingmaker's Squire', sending it into the Trader's Sea. Elder Marcarius panicked a few days later, searching every crevice of the fort that would be impossible to hide such a book in the first place. Leta was too embarrassed to admit what she did, and too young to appreciate the truth. *I'll never see my special rock again*, she thought sadly. *It's not there anymore for when I'm lonely.*

Her hand stroked many tomes as she walked along, hoping that one would grab her interest. None did. Sir Roswell seemed to be happy, plucking out any and every tome to briefly flick through. Leta found the people wandering about more interesting, some of wizened age with twisting walking canes, lords and ladies dressed in robes who held their heads high, lowborn men and women in their humble cloth.

Over a waist-high pier full of books, Leta spied a boy who was browsing intently, a deep frown on his face. He was a handsome boy, with shaggy brown hair, blue eyes, a scruff of half a beard. Something about him was eerily nostalgic. He caught Leta staring when he glanced over, and she pretended she was looking at a book. Leta tried to keep stealing looks, and caught him glancing again, at her *and* at her knight. On his third glance, the boy's mouth dropped. "Oh, my gods," he exhaled. "Leta? Sir Roswell?"

Her heart stopped. It took a while for Leta to realise where she had seen that face before. "What the fuck?" she gasped. "Feliks?! What are you doing here?"

Feliks shook his head and shrugged. "Gods know."

"My, you're a man grown now, Feliks," Sir Roswell observed.

"I try to be, Sir Roswell," he quipped. "Come here, Leta, it's been ages since I've seen you." They rushed around the pier and hugged.

"I didn't know if it was you for sure," Leta said.

"You didn't know if it was me at all," he smirked.

"Well, the last time I saw you, you were like… twelve? You've changed, Feliks."

Feliks seemed hung up on that. "Yeah," he said sullenly. "Is everyone else with you?"

Leta's smile faded. "It's just us," she said. "Fort Deus was attacked."

"By whom?" Feliks asked darkly.

Leta glanced around. "Venusians. They came two moons ago."

Feliks didn't seem surprised. "Is everyone okay?"

The Centaur didn't have an answer for that. "We haven't found Fletcher, or Hew. Mother hasn't come back yet. Asher and Esmond and Eva are all away, so I guess they're okay."

Feliks nodded. "I heard your brother had the castle."

"We've had worse rulers," Leta japed.

Her cousin smiled, before frowning. "Centaur's Lagoon was raided by them as well. Do you know what they did to Vesta?"

She didn't want to ask after seeing the anguish on his face. "What?"

"They slit her throat open, right in front of me. I couldn't do anything. I was leading the defence and I couldn't even save her."

Leta felt sick. She knew Vesta so well. All she could think about was them laughing together, as they always would. Vesta had the prettiest laugh. She couldn't laugh anymore with an open neck. "I'm… so sorry," she said. "She didn't deserve a death like that."

"No," he sighed. "You're the closest thing to a sister I have now. You won't be going anytime soon, will you?"

She glanced at Sir Roswell. "I don't think so. Now that father's at war, I don't think there are many safe places left in the Pole."

Feliks nodded. "We're safe here. No Scorpion can reach this high."

Leta frowned. "Scorpion?"

The bastard pulled a confused face. "Yeah?"

"You weren't attacked by Khavars?"

"The Scorpions must have been behind ours. We found their citrine, their poisons…"

"We found their poisons over at Fort Deus too," she winced. *"Lord Reynold died* because of it."

"Are you serious?" Feliks frowned bitterly.

"Why are both of you so surprised?" Sir Roswell smirked grimly. "The entire Archipelago is against us. They'd be stupid not to work together."

"Not the *entire* Archipelago. It can't be," Feliks protested. "The Casterons are sworn to Esmond, aren't they?"

"They're sworn to both" Sir Roswell said. "They've also said vows to the Khavars, too, I believe. If a war is between them and the crown, they'd have to pick a side."

Feliks frowned. "Why would they pick the losing side?"

"Well, Khavars are closer to them than the king," Sir Roswell admitted. "It's whether you'd rather betray the man on your doorstep or the man a world away."

Before Feliks could think of an answer, two Trident guards ambushed them. "My lady," one bowed stiffly. "Your brother has just arrived at the docks."

That was the news she needed to hear. She lost her breath as she exhaled, and bolted excitedly out of the observatory. She barely even knew where the docks were.

When she eventually found them, sure enough, her brother was standing there, accompanied by Lord Erik Thyne, Cheval Yves Larret, and a garrison boy Leta recognised the face of but could not remember the name. They were talking with Lady Lysanda. Leta ran towards her brother.

"Hew!" she cried. Hew turned his tired head around slowly, but it lit up when he saw his sister. Leta slammed into him, hugging tightly. She clutched his thick, curly hair. He had many layers of clothes on, all of different widths and size. "I thought you were gone."

"I-I thought y-you were!" he smiled.

"You're shivering," Leta frowned, "what's wrong?"

"My princess," Erik Thyne bowed. "It's good to see you again. Your brother caught a chill on the water. He's been struggling to warm up."

"He needs rest, princess," Lady Lysanda urged as she placed a delicate hand on her shoulder. "We'll take your brother to the keep, give him some food, some warmth. We wouldn't want you getting the same chill."

Leta nodded sadly, glancing at her pale ghost of a little brother. *How did he survive?* She wanted to know so badly. They took the boy away.

She was left frowning for a while, muddled with so many different emotions at once. *It's a curable chill. It has to be.* Her brother *did* seem like a ghoul, but she couldn't believe that a mere *cold wind* would claim a Centaur's life. *But he's here. I should be happier, shouldn't I?*

She found Sir Roswell and Feliks half-way back to the Ardus Keep.

The knight was smiling until he saw Leta's frown. "How is he?"

"He's sick," Leta said. "They're taking him to the keep. He came with Lord Erik and Cheval Yves."

"Finally, some more Centaurs," Sir Roswell sighed. "May I have leave to talk to them, my lady?"

Leta chuckled tiredly. "You don't need to ask."

Sir Roswell smiled and bowed, taking his leave.

Her cousin was staring into the distance. "It's good that you're here too," she said awkwardly. "I was scared of being alone for much longer."

Feliks glanced at her with a sad smile, and went back to his brooding.

"What's wrong?" Leta frowned.

He tensed his jaw. "Sir Roswell is right, isn't he? The Casterons wouldn't side with a king half a world away, especially since the Archipelago is already teething with kings."

Leta stared at his blue eyes. "What's happened?"

Feliks sighed. "Curtis Sculptor said he spotted their fleet sailing towards the capital."

"How many?"

"Thirty," Feliks admitted. "Not enough to take a city, we can hope."

ESMOND XIV
-Drum-

The fleet was large enough to take the city. Unmanned, Lunarpass was about as protected as a man in a lion's cage. King Esmond Centaur had received the news that the Casterons had sacked his capital as he approached it, *after* he had sent most of his army to regroup and retake lands, *after* he had trekked with his remaining troops over the Lunar Hills, *after* he had buried his brother in the Sag's Crossroads. *There's nowhere else to bury him*, not with Fort Deus destroyed, and most likely, the mausoleum with it. Still, whether it was because Esmond had to bury his younger brother himself, knowing that he caused it, or because Lorimer couldn't rest with his ancestors, the king couldn't put how queer he felt into words. *You were right, Lori. The blame is on me.*

Esmond had *only* one thousand men. *Only* one thousand out of the thirty-five he had at *The Battle of the Crossroads.* He had sent Lord Ramon Kramer and Sir Arter White and five thousand men to lift the siege on Centaur's Lagoon, Lord Nate Fuller with eight thousand to retake Goattreath, Negal Town, and any captured keep in the Sagswood, and most importantly, Lord Alec Odum with fifteen thousand - including most of Lunarpass's city's garrison - to sail to the Three Goats, and wipe out the Capras once and for all. The rest, Esmond had dismissed, to regroup at their homes, to gather strength before they all marched west to deal with the Archipelago. That left him with *only* one thousand.

In a perfect world, Esmond would wait to recapture Lunarpass, to have

ANTONI KRUPSKI

455

more than *only* one thousand men. But he had only known about the sacking for a few hours, and the Piscean army stood leagues away, their would-be battlefield to separate them, threatening to chase after the Centaurs if they ran. Running was pointless, and not only because it would waste time; Esmond didn't want to find out how his exhausted, battle-worn army would fare with fleeing back over the enervating Lunar Hills.

In truth, the king wasn't shocked. Another day, another time, and perhaps he would have been, but not after he had lost his *entire* family. When the Centaur scout came back with the news, Esmond was crushed with an overpowering feeling of apathy. And now that he saw the armies of Casteron lined outside his city, ready to kill all of his men, that feeling of apathy was far from gone, but was also accompanied by something new, something *contradictory:* fear. Esmond wasn't ready to face it.

"What are your orders, my king?" Darius Boyd asked.

Esmond didn't reply. He wondered if Blaine Casteron was a part of the force, or even behind its appearance. *'The last time we will meet as allies'* he had said at Fort Deus. *Is this where we meet, to settle our lives? For him to settle mine, rather?*

After what Lori had said, Esmond soon realised how tired he was from lying. He could tell them apart now: which were lies to himself and which weren't. *It's my fault my men died,* he knew, *dragging them into a war they didn't sign up for. It's my fault they'll die today. It's my fault my family is split and mostly dead. It's my fault my country is burning. It's my fault I was stupid enough to not take the signs and spurn this war before it began. Death is no less what I deserve.* So, in that sense, he almost welcomed the Casteron army. *But what can I do about all of this? A bad king: this is what I am now, and we're all dying today. There's no chance of being someone else now.*

A tall man with scaly burgundy armour had ridden out under a white flag of peace. "King Esmond!" he called when he was close enough. "I am Lord Julian Shell, brother by law to Lord Blaine Casteron!" Esmond didn't reply. "We have your city, and thrice your men, King Esmond! Lay down your arms and your army and there need not be bloodshed!"

The wind was quite loud, as were the few Centaur banners that the wind attacked. Julian Shell could barely hold his white flag up. Esmond cared more about the wind than the words that just came out of Julian's mouth. Apathetically, the king strung his bow and fired. Julian Shell fell from his horse with an arrow in his neck.

The confused Casteron force was almost amusing to Esmond. They couldn't decide what to do. Each of them were clad in armour that looked like fish scales: a rainbow of blues and greens in the distance. The armour was familiar to Esmond, as he had seen so much of it when he was fostered at the Tusks. The weapons were familiar too, most Pisceans holding spears with curved heads, which Esmond never understood the point of, the rest with a variety of queer looking swords and cutlasses. "Esmond, that was a white flag of submission," Elliot Moss panicked.

"It's red now," he said, almost forgetting about the man he just killed.

It doesn't feel good to kill people. That was another truth he could tell himself. He had learnt that at *The Battle of the Crossroads*, when all the men he was slaying wasn't enough to fill the hole in his heart, the hole where his family had been, where his friends had been, where his home and power had been. *Would it even feel good to kill Vincent, or Orion?* His immediate thought was yes, but he grew more unsure the more he thought. *They're not suffering if they die. Not as they've made me suffer.* But something told him that *torture* wouldn't fill the hole in his heart either. *Only my death would relieve that, so why am I frightened?* "No one can outrun death," Lori told him again.

"My king," Darius pressed.

Esmond looked up to see the Casteron force charging, galloping to the music of a deep war horn he had scarcely heard. He closed his eyes and felt the wind on his neck. The wind was nice.

"What are your orders, my king? We need orders," Darius repeated, raising his voice.

He turned to look at his head of arms. It was a long look. Darius's eyes searched the king, but Esmond didn't reply. His death was here. He wanted to face it with dignity. The king walked forward slowly. *No one can outrun death.*

"*My king! We need orders!*" Darius cried.

Esmond kept walking. He walked far enough away from his army for them to not see the water that was blurring his eyes. The thunder of boots was getting closer and louder.

"*My king!*" Darius yelled a final time, before giving up. "*Spears! Frontline!*"

The king didn't think death would scare him. It never had before. But the tears streaking down his face was truth that it did. "I've outrun it for so long. I don't want to die, Lori," he confessed to the wind. "I want to change. I want to live long enough to see truth through." The wind replied with the only low moan it could reply with, and Esmond's fears weren't put to rest. *I am alone in this war, if not for one person. And I've put that one person to death.* "I only wanted... to be just. Is that a lie, brother? Is that not what a king should be?"

He trembled when he realised he was talking to thin air, and dropped to his knees, feeling the cold orange grass brush against his legs. The Casterons grew ever-closer, yelling for the honour of their lords and their families. *What honour do I have now, with all the good men I've killed? What house is mine to keep, that's not a pile of rubble and flame? What family have I not lost?* The king touched his crown, ready to take it off...

Before he could, his ears pricked up at the sound of a pipe. A high pipe. A *northern* pipe.

The Casteron charge slowed into halt, and the soldiers were even more confused than before.

All alone, the piper revealed himself on the highest Lunar Hill. He wore his bagpipes like it was armour, and held a single note for longer than normal lungs should manage. He was joined by the sound of drums. *Boooom bom, boooom bom, boooom bom.* First one, then two, then three, all the while getting faster and faster. Soon it was impossible to tell how many drums blared between the hills. It could have been hundreds. It could have been thousands. *BOOOM BOM, BOOOM BOM, BOOOM BOM.* They shook the ground. They shook the wind.

The single piper was then killed by a Piscean arrow, his note ending, but not the music; the hills exploded with music.

A man galloped into view: one with blood-red hair, sat proudly atop a hazel horse as he unsheathed a dark black sword. *"CHARGE!"* Riley Horncurve yelled, somehow louder than the ensemble of drums. The Lunar Hills cried a flood of northmen.

Esmond's heart couldn't take much more. It thumped along with the war drums. He tittered to see the wave of crimson charging down, the son of Sigmund leading the storm with Shofar in hand. Then he chuckled. *He answered the call when I didn't, when I couldn't.* Before long, the king was laughing. He was dizzy when he ran back to his horse. It took a moment to remember how to ride. *"I thought I'd brought you all to your deaths!"* Esmond cried as he galloped along his army. The king held out his arms and smiled. *"I don't think we're dying today!"*

His men roared back in cheer.

The king veered his horse and charged. His one thousand men followed behind in chorus. For a while, the Casterons stood still as stone, soiling their breeches in unison, until they turned and scattered as the Khavars had. *Thrice my numbers,* Esmond laughed. *Threaten me not on my own land, cowards.*

Esmond could *smell* the fear when his two armies closed on the Pisceans. It was a fear much greater than he had just experienced. *You've given me my chance, Lori, I won't waste it,* the king thought, stringing his bow to better his odds.

THE WARRIOR BOY
-A Curved Horn-

Against the cold, dark sky ahead of dawn, his ships looked like a pack of crimson sharks gliding gracefully down the Twin River. He was amazed at how silent ships could be if men paddled the water with a little more grace. Silence was what they needed to take Selerborn by surprise.

The time of day was on their side too, as not even a crescent of a sun was born into it yet. To him, there was no other time. Dawn was always when his grandfather Sigmund would wake him up to train. Dawn was when he learned everything there was to learn about swordsmanship and fighting. Dawn was when he and his twin brother would spar loudly in the training yard, somehow not waking up the whole of Selerborn. Dawn was when he'd seen his first taste of battle, as a dagger was plunged into Reynold Lyrderyn's stomach and he was made to cut down a bandit. Dawn was when Cadmus Horncurve felt most alive.

He held on excitedly to a thick wooden mast as a shadow of Selerborn crept into view. *Home. My home. My city*, he thought. *"Prepare to land,"* he whispered to his crew. His Arian men nodded and sent silent signals to the other captains.

He thought time and time again over the last moon about retaking the heart of the north, but now it was finally happening. He thought Riley had gone mad when he told Cadmus that it was what he needed to do. *But da' was right*, the Horncurve saw, as the yellow Siren banners added the only bit of colour to a dark, sleeping Selerborn. It was a pity, because Cadmus always admired the Sirens; Cadell was a good friend, and Harper a good leader. Regardless, admiration comes to an end with betrayal, for him, for anyone.

Cadmus felt a shiver down his back as his ships slowed and grazed against the muddy river bank. *Whatever happens today, we'll be in the history books. I'll be alongside Sigmund with every proceeding battle for Selerborn.* That made him smile. *I hope I make you proud, grandpa,* he whispered. *I hope I make a story worth telling, as the Warrior Boy had.*

The ships barely grazed to a halt before the soldiers hastily threw anchors over, leaping off the boat. No one uttered a sound, but the clatter of armour as each one landed made Cadmus wince.

Tate's Kalyx soldiers were many compared to the Horncurves, so they were definitely needed; at Mea Minor, Cadmus had upgraded his 'raiding party' to an army. *I just hope they can fight.* Not only the Geminian men, but the Arians as well. *And listen. And plan.* He knew nothing and little about the generals who led his contingents. As for the Arian generals, there was Ruairi Raidarms, who was famed in Selerborn for never missing a raid in his life, Lord Fionn Tharnham's two sons, Lou and Struan Tharnham, and Oisean Peuter, Lord of Diamondstream. They all seemed to be capable fighters, but apart from Ruairi, it looked as if they had never even *seen* an army, let alone *led* one. Though, Cadmus could hardly blame them for being flustered. A moon ago they thought they were pawns in a raid against Heavia; now they were generals in an army ready to besiege a city.

The plan was to have Struan and Oisean stay near the river, to climb over the walls and flank the Sirens from Fricum Street and Corum Street. The remainder of the army was to storm the main gate, the *only* gate. That was where Lord Dugg Gallach came into play; if the head of arms hadn't turned coat yet, he would order the great gate to be opened as soon as he spied the armies docking. Harper was fond of keeping the gate open, Cadmus could remember from when they returned from Fort Deus, but still, winching open the gate at this time of morning could only be suspicious. *I hope he makes it.*

Selerborn's walls were their only friend as his armies made their way to the gate; they hugged them like a hand hugs a sword, only existing in its shadow. It wasn't long before Cadmus started to worry about the idea, as the city was vast, and it was a tall order to get his army to the other side unnoticed. Still, tall orders weren't impossible ones, and a sleeping

Selerborn remained oblivious as the armies got into position.

Father said there would be guards, that there would be men manned and ready to kill on the battlements. Did he lie to make me more cautious? It wasn't unlike Riley to do so, but an entire strategy could change by having that information. The walls *were* monumentally tall, so it might just be that they were far enough away to not be heard. Regardless, Cadmus led his army with caution.

Cadmus's heart was beating like a blacksmith's hammer by the time they arrived at the gate. He spied the first few men of his army on the other side, clutching their weapons and baring their teeth. Most of his host was there. It would have been perfect had the gates been open. The massive portcullis was still wedged deeply into the mud.

"What do we do now?" Lou Tharnham whispered.

"Wait," Cadmus said, squinting. He wouldn't believe Dugg would betray them. *Perhaps he hasn't seen us?*

The Horncurve didn't have to hold his breath for long before he heard voices from atop the battlements. "From Lord Harper. You sure?"

"You sure?" the voice of Dugg repeated. "You're talking to a lord, not a common peasant. You shan't address me as such. Remember yer place and open this damn gate."

"Y-yes milord," the other replied. *"OPEN THE GATES!"*

A few seconds passed before the deep-rooted chains began to moan and the gate slowly lifted. They needed a dozen men to winch open such an enormous gate, Cadmus could recall. Not that he could see a dozen; he could see nothing this close to the walls.

It would always take a long time for the gate to open, but Cadmus was getting more impatient the longer he waited. He tapped his foot doggedly. *Come on*, he whispered under his breath. It was less than halfway open by the time they heard voices again.

"That's enough, tie it down!" Dugg urged.

"TIE IT DOWN!" the other man repeated.

Cadmus heard galloping from the distance. A long silence fell. Then he heard death; a man on the battlements was slaying the gatekeepers. *"CLOSE THEM! CLOSE THEM-"* he heard a gatekeeper yell before it was cut short, presumably by a sword.

BOOOooooooooooooo! A deep warhorn rumbled the twilight sky.

The head of arms appeared on the battlement's edge.

"Cadmus! Get out! Ru-" Dugg Gallach's eyes widened as a sword

emerged from his belly. Harper Siren pushed his sword free, and Dugg's lifeless body tumbled from the wall, crunching mere feet before the army.

"Cut the ropes! Siege positions!" Harper yelled, puffing on the warhorn again before disappearing from the battlements.

Cadmus unsheathed his sword. *"Keep it open! Storm the streets!"*

His army yelled and hooted in response, and they funnelled into the city. At least, funnelling in before the giant portcullis abruptly slammed into the dirt, decapitating those who were underneath like a guillotine. *"Get to the cranes! Now!"* Cadmus ordered.

Luckily, no Siren men were on the Road of Rams yet, only on the battlements as Riley had said. Cadmus's northmen stormed through the towers to get to them. Dead men plummeted inches away as they fell down the winding stairs. Cadmus was at the forefront of the charge, behind a couple of warriors, so he only had to slice his sword through the collarbone of one Siren before sending him down the steps. Most were smart enough to wait on the battlements.

When they arrived at the top, the Horncurve who opened the door was perforated by ten arrows at once. The archers couldn't reload quickly enough to stop the one behind slicing them down, though. Cadmus followed his northmen left along the battlements, towards the winches.

The gatekeepers were still there, trembling as the Horncurves charged towards them. *Shit. How are we to open the gates with the ropes cut?* Cadmus himself drove a sword into one of them. After slaying him, the young ram grabbed the nearest shoulder he could. "We have to get this gate open. Use your men to lift it."

Lou Tharnham nodded briskly. *"Lift the gate!"* he yelled, ushering the men who were flooding up the tower steps. *"Grab a chain and pull!"*

Cadmus joined in the effort, grabbing one of the many jagged chains that a few minutes ago had been roped to the hoist. It didn't feel like he was helping, as the gate barely rose, but he pulled with all his might, all the same. *"By my call!"* he yelled. *"Heave! Heave! Heave!"* It took only a few moments to establish a rhythm. His men barked *"Heave!"* in return, and each time, the gate rose maybe two inches.

Cadmus let go of the chain and grabbed Lou's shoulder again. "Lou, whatever you do, keep this gate open. Charge the battlements after. We need them clear."

Lou nodded. "Good luck, Cadmus. *By my call!"* he yelled. *"Heave! Heave! Heave!"*

The Horncurve trusted and left the Tharnham, as he dashed back down the winding steps of the tower. By the time he was at the gate again, it had been raised just below head height. *"Come through! Come through!"* he urged the soldiers that stood on the other side. All at once, one by one, his army ducked under the gate and resumed to flood the city. *"Storm the streets! Come on!"* he yelled again after he glanced back at the Siren host that charged down the Road of Rams.

Harper wasn't leading them, as far as Cadmus could glean. *Coward.* Regardless, they came mounted on horses and rams, and Cadmus's host was all but afoot. They could either brace the charge, or meet them swords ablaze. There was only one choice for a Horncurve. *"Charge!"* Cadmus screamed, holding up his sword.

His army roared back, and all around him, Selerborn awoke to a thunder of footsteps and hooves. Mud flew up from the road as the northmen ploughed it apart. The two hosts clashed like two storms meeting, both charges coming to a complete halt as everyone on either frontline was skewered or squashed or ridden over. Cadmus parried a horseman's blade, and stabbed the horse in the neck. He tumbled down for his army to devour.

Horses meant nothing when they couldn't charge, and soon, most of them had fled or began to rear on their hind legs as the Horncurves drowned them. *"Don't stop! Charge!"* Cadmus yelled as he thrust his longsword into a Siren's chest. It was onerous to get past the Horncurve men in front of him; they just would not die.

Cadmus had to climb upon a dead man upon a dead horse, upon some more dead men to see what was happening. If northmen used bows more than swords, he would be a dead man right now too. One man tried to climb up his hill, but Cadmus eyed him and chopped him down with two strokes. He was hardly tiring. His beating heart gave him power.

Soon, he saw what he wanted to see, their destination: the high and mighty Cenkeep, with its multi-layered cut battlements, and towers of curved horns. The sight of it filled Cadmus with so much drive, he leapt back into the fray without so much as a flinch, plunging his longsword into a man's shoulder.

When Harper's main host fell, the risk had all but gone. A few Siren stragglers occasionally rode out from the keep or street to try and fell one last Horncurve, but to no avail. The warhorn Harper had blown undoubtedly woke the entirety of Selerborn, so Cadmus thought a few locals would have something to say about their home being invaded once again, but few fought. In fact, the few who *did* leave their huts and houses *joined* the Horncurve force. Cadmus acknowledged each one with a smile and a nod.

The gates to the Cenkeep were easier to pass through than he could have thought. Harper had done a terrific job of destroying it during his revolt, so it seemed. It was only made easier when they met Oisean's and Struan's contingents. Cadmus and his men scaled up the sprawling steps to the castle, cutting down any last man brave enough to make a stand. He wasn't even acknowledging the men he killed anymore. He was blind to it. All he could see was the Cenkeep.

The entrance to the Cenkeep didn't require any force to breach either; Harper had already done them the favour and battered the door down. That made Cadmus smile. *Your betrayal might have brought you glory, Siren, but it brings you down just as much.*

He found the man in the throne room, as he thought he would. The diamond throne glistened like stars at the back, yet no one sat it. There were a few hundred Horncurves in the room. There were less than a quarter in Sirens. Cadmus had won.

"Cadmus," Harper Siren said softly. He didn't seem like a man ready for defeat, but didn't seem like a man who wanted to continue fighting either. His sword was sheathed. "Nicely done. You have me outwitted."

"Outwitted. Outnumbered. What made you think you could win?"

Harper sighed. "You can never win in this world, Cadmus. You'll realise that if you ever sit this seat: that someone always wants to cast you down, to take what you hold dear."

"I've won. You've lost. It's *my* seat. There's nothing more to it. Have your men lay down your arms."

"I won't," he said sadly. "You're not the Lord of Selerborn yet. You need to challenge his claim."

Cadmus squinted. "You pretentious twat." He pointed his sword at the false lord. "How *dare* you sit my father's seat, and pretend you earned it. Unsheathe your sword. I challenge you with every bone in my body."

Harper didn't reach for it; it remained safely in his scabbard. "You *may* soon challenge me, but you have to say it properly first. You have to *challenge* the Lord of Selerborn. You have to *challenge* his claim."

"Get off your high horse, Harper. You're not the *bloody* Lord of Selerborn."

"True as that may be, I don't make up the rules, Cadmus."

"Fine," Cadmus said bitterly. "I challenge the bloody Lord of Selerborn. I challenge his *false claim*."

Harper nodded sullenly. "As you wish." He stepped back.

From beside the shadowed diamond throne, Cadmus heard footsteps, slow and clumsy. Steel screeched uncomfortably against the stone floor as a sword was dragged along. Then, even from the inky shadows, Cadmus recognised his messy red locks: the locks of a Horncurve, of his brother, of his twin... *of the Lord of Selerborn.* His heart sank.

There was no white left in Marcus's eyes, only a dark bloody crimson like his hair. It looked as if he had been flayed, yet his skin was intact. He had pimples on his face, scratches on his arms, pale skin that even the moonlight was afraid of. At first, it seemed like there were huge round bruises under his eyes, but no bruise could ever be so dark. Cadmus scowled, feeling sick to see his brother like this. "What's he done to you?"

"Nothing worse than what da's done... than what you've done." Marcus's voice was stuttered and broken, as if he was on the verge of tears. If he'd cried any tears, they had long since dried.

Cadmus winced. "What?" It was more out of confusion than it was a question.

Marcus frowned bitterly. "Do you not understand?"

Cadmus could only laugh. "You think I would? Put down your sword, Marc, what are you doing?"

"I'm doing *something*," he said, remaining far from his brother's jest. "That's more than what da' did. That was more than what the *north* did when Esmond lopped off Sigmund's head."

"Sigmund's got nothing to do with this."

Marcus snickered. "Why do you think you're having to retake Selerborn in the first place?"

Cadmus truly thought he was jesting now too. "Oh, put it off, Marc. You know who did this. Esmond had no part."

"I'm not joking," he insisted. "Da' was an idiot, but only half as dumb as you."

Cadmus frowned. "Excuse me?"

"Heavia?" he winced. With that word, his broken voice morphed into an angry one. "The north's pulling herself apart, the man who *murdered* our grandfather is still safe and sound in his capital, and when we *needed* you the most, when enemies were on our doorstep ready to kill us, you jaunted off to *Heavia?!*"

"I never went to Heavia," Cadmus said. "I went to *Mea.* I went to get *troops* we could take back Selerborn with. Ask any man behind me."

"Bullshit. I know when you're lying, brother," Marcus squinted.

Cadmus tittered. "Clearly not."

"Even if you aren't, you still weren't here," he said with a distasteful frown. "Mother and father and Athena, they're all dead now. They're all dead and you weren't here to fight with them. To fight *for* them."

"Well neither were *you.* You *ran away* because you couldn't take a wee bit of reproval," he snapped back. Cadmus couldn't believe this. *This is Harper's doing. It has to be.* "But it doesn't matter, they're *not* dead. Mother and father are towards Salem way, Athena is safe on the-"

"*I know when you're lying!*" he screamed, clutching his sword.

Cadmus examined Harper. He still had a sullen look on his face for some reason. *Why? This is what you wanted, isn't it? To turn brother against brother with lies and torture.* "Look at him. You're giving him what he wants. *He's* the enemy, Marc, not me."

"He could have helped us, Cadmus. He wants a free north just as much as us, and now we have it. His knee is bent and I'm his king."

Cadmus used all his strength to keep his rage down. *His knee is bent?* "He's been feeding you shite and you know it."

Marcus shrugged. "It doesn't matter now, does it?"

"'Course it matters. Whatever that bastard has put into your head-"

"Not that." He lifted his resting sword to stroke the blade. "You challenged my claim. Doesn't matter what I believe if I'm dead. Nothing matters when we fight."

"I challenged *him! Harper!* The man who *burnt* our home! Don't be so *stupid,* brother!"

"*Stupid?*" Marcus scowled. "That's always what you've thought, isn't it? You and Riley." He drew closer. "*Stupid* and *arrogant* and *lesser* and *selfish* and *weaker* and-"

"I've never thought that. Father's never thought that. He knew Harper was watching, he was *pretending* to-"

"*BULLSHIT!! YOU ALWAYS HAVE!!*" He charged forward sporadically, and the sword came crashing overhead. Cadmus barely parried. Another two slashes came from either side, as fast as snakes biting. Cadmus leapt away. Marcus staggered forward.

Cadmus didn't stop to catch his breath. "I've *never* thought that! *Listen to me!* You've *always* been better, Marcus. I didn't *let you win* all the duels we've had-"

"LIAR!!" Marcus lurched forward again, and the blades continued to ring with relentless *clangs*. His brother was faster with every swing. He was hesitating less and less. *"MOTHER AND FATHER AND ATHENA AND ME! YOU'VE KILLED US ALL!!"*

"He isn't-" It took all of Cadmus's concentration to volley his brother's unflagging swings. He dodged away again, and Marcus's sword slammed against the ground. *"Marcus, stop it! Father's not dead! Mother's not dead! Athena's not dead! We're all safe right now but you!"*

Marcus winced and charged again. *Clang, Clank, Clang, Clang, Clang, Clank, Shhhink.* Cadmus's arms were tiring and he hadn't even swung yet. He leapt away when he could. Marcus staggered forward, this time falling.

"FIGHT ME, YOU COWARD!" he screamed, thumping his chest like an angry gorilla. *"FIGHT BACK!"*

Cadmus shook his head. "I'm not fighting you, Marcus."

"You've fought me every day of your *bloody life*."

"Never with an edged blade."

"Aye, that was the mistake." The hateful squint Marcus held was just as wounding as an edged blade.

"You don't mean it," Cadmus said. "You're my brother. You *know* I'd kill for you... I know you'd kill for me."

Marcus sucked in his lips. *"aaaAAAGGHH!!!"* The blades clashed again. *Clank, Clang.* The third swing made Cadmus duck, as it flew where his neck had been. That was a mistake Marcus always made when they trained. That was a mistake that always guaranteed a loss. That mistake was an opening to end this duel, but Cadmus didn't take it.

Marcus almost caught him when he tried to dodge away again, but luckily, Cadmus's sword was facing down to block. *"I'm not fighting you, Marcus. I won't!"*

"DO IT! KILL ME! TAKE THE BLOODY THRONE YOU WANT SO BADLY! YOU'VE ALWAYS WANTED ME DEAD!"

"I'VE NEVER WANTED THAT! LISTEN TO YOURSELF!"

"STOP LYING!!" Clank, Clank, Clang, Clank. *"You made me go to the Mudstreet!"* Marcus yelled, slowing his swings. *"You lost our home! You cheated me! All so you could fucking raid?! All so you could be better! Tell me that's not a lie! Tell me you didn't want to go to Heavia!"*

It only took a split second of hesitation...

He saw the blood before he felt the pain; Horncurve blood on a Horncurve blade. Cadmus grabbed the edge, not quite believing it was plunged through his heart. The rising sun made it glow a fiery orange as the crimson crept down the sword, through his fingers. He fell backwards. His brother caught him.

Marcus was just as shocked. His face broke and he began to weep. "I was... wrong," Cadmus uttered weakly.

"No," he said, orange tears streaking down his face. "No, you were *meant to kill me! Why didn't you fight back?!*"

It hurt too much to say words. *Because I didn't think you would have,* he wanted to say, but all it amassed to was a few wordless grunts. *Not you. Not my brother. Not my twin.* "I... thought... you wouldn't..."

Tears were streaming down Marcus's face. His eyes were becoming even redder. "That's the problem. You're always wrong," he sobbed again, closing his eyes. "You should have let me die."

Cadmus felt his life leaving him, fleeing him. Marcus let go.

He took the blade that had just slain his brother, and winced at the blood. Never had he cried so much. He was writhing in pain, clutching the sword, shaking his head. Marcus then lifted the sword and attempted to impale himself with it. Blood crept out of his stomach as he slowly drove the tip in with his trembling hands. Cadmus couldn't lament for long... not after he closed his eyes.

FLETCHER VI
-Compromised-

He had seen darkness for so long that it was almost frightening every time light poured into his cell. Frightening as it was, the light always promised something good: such as food, or company, even though said *company* - an ugly gaoler who always seemed in a rush - never said a word to him. This time was different, though.

Fletcher Centaur desperately tried to rub his eyes. It would have been easier if his chains weren't so tight. Red marks cut deep into his wrists from where he tried to resist, and later, simply move. It didn't help that the man who came to see him was the man he despised most in this world.

"My prince," Tyran Capra greeted, inclining his head. "Are you not eating?" he asked awkwardly. "You look... thin."

Fletcher felt the daggers in his eyes thrusting into Tyran's. "I wonder why?" he said hoarsely.

"We have... tried for this to be comfortable for you. I hope you know this."

I know nothing of the sort. Which part of it was meant to be comfortable? The way you helped butcher my men and my people? The way you imperilled my family forever? The way you backstabbed us in favour of some Venusian scum? Hopefully the stare Fletcher sent his way was enough to tell him all of that. He was too weary to speak.

Tyran sighed. "You're only a boy, Fletcher. You don't deserve what's happened to you."

Fletcher winced as best he could. "So, if I were older, I would deserve it more?"

The Capricorn frowned and looked away. "Any man in your place would have been an obstacle. I bear you no ill will."

Fletcher looked down to the stony floor he was so used to staring at. "Did you lie about everything?"

Tyran met his eyes again. "I lied about nothing, Fletcher. Not to you, nor your sister." He revealed a set of keys and began to unlock his cell.

Lied about nothing? What about keeping a simple bloody alliance? The keys were more important to Fletcher in that moment than saying that, though. "What are you doing?"

"A visitor will be here soon," he said sadly. "He wishes to dine with you."

Fletcher's legs were trembling when he stood, even more so when he tried to walk. Tyran had brought a soldier to help guide Fletcher's chains along. *He doesn't want to get his hands dirty.* That made him smile. *Yet he has the filthiest hands in the realm.*

Luckily, the mess hall wasn't too far from where the cells were, and Fletcher only had to stumble over a hill or two, and through a few stone hallways filled with brown carpets before arriving. King Nero Capra was already there, sat upon a golden chair at the head of the table that looked like a throne compared to the rest. "My prince," he bowed. "I'm glad you could join us."

Fletcher said nothing. He was taken to a seat, and had his chains unbolted. The first thing he touched was the fork next to his plate. *They've blunted it,* he noticed. He smirked. *Do I pose so much of a threat for them to fear me with a fork?* Regardless, it didn't matter; there were close to ten guards present, each ready to cut Fletcher down if he was to make a move. *I'm not that stupid, Tyran, don't worry.*

Nero cleared his throat. "The last guests we had in these halls were your sister and lady mother," he said proudly. "They took quite a liking to the kale. Have some, if you'd like."

Fletcher paid him no heed. He poked the blunted fork end into his thumb.

It was a while before Nero spoke again. He was probably expecting an answer. "We had some good news for your family this dawn, my lord," he said. "Your father, the king, has fought two battles, and won. He defeated Khavars at the Crossroads, Casterons at the Lunar Hills to retake the capital... I'd wager Esmond become a hero before this war is done."

That was the first time Fletcher set his eyes on him, on his honest brown eyes, on his well pruned beard, on the excessive amount of furs he wore that almost made the tall man look fat. The King of the Three Goats smiled kindly. Fletcher went back to staring at nothing. *The Khavars are dead. Good. At least Esmond could do what his stupid son couldn't.*

"My lords," a guard said as he marched in. Tyran and Nero stood abruptly, bowing their heads. "I have the honour to present to you, Prince Lomax Khavar, son and heir of King Delmar."

In sauntered the prince. He was a pale man, tall and lanky. He had big hands, and most other features small, Fletcher noticed immediately. The Centaur always wanted big hands; big hands work steel better. The prince's brow leapt from his face, and his eyes were a sea of ocean blue. On his head, he had a clot of dark brown hair, and wore a crown so small, it looked like one of Eva's old tiaras. Behind him were a block of Khavar guards, wearing the hefty shell armour Fletcher was all too familiar with. "My lords," he smiled. Everyone in the room was bowing to him save Fletcher; Fletcher was still playing with his blunted fork.

"It's good to see you again, my prince," Tyran said kindly.

Lomax nodded, glancing at Fletcher with a smile. "Oh, you needn't all bow for so long. Your necks must ache by now."

"Take a seat, if you would, my prince," Nero smiled. "Supper is fresh."

"My lord is too kind," Prince Lomax said, strolling to sit the side no one sat.

The two Capras couldn't stop glancing at the throng of guards Lomax had brought. It was more than double theirs. "If... you are concerned for your safety, my lord, know that words cannot describe how welcome you are in our home," Nero said.

Lomax turned to admire his guards. "If I were concerned for my safety, I would have brought more men than this," he smiled. "May I be frank, Lord Nero?" The Khavar didn't wait for a yes. "My father, the king, isn't very happy with you. Lord Vincent isn't very happy with you either. In fact, I would go as far as to say that your actions these past moons have *angered* them."

Nero choked on his words. "A-angered them? Forgive me, my lord, I do not understand."

"You understand well enough," he said, so calmly it was almost chilling. "You wanted our aid to destroy the Centaurs, to destroy Fort

Deus," he continued, glancing at Fletcher, "so you could be a part of our empire, void of any... complications. We would be happy to aid you again, my lords, only that... this time was a mistake." Lomax studied their faces, but the Capricornians only gawked. "After we sent our fleet your way, Lord Vincent was in the capital, treating with the king. They agreed to a *treaty of peace*." He studied their faces again. "Tell me, how could we have sent word of this *treaty*, when our fleet had already sailed so far away, *days* from taking Fort Deus? You made us break a vow they didn't know existed."

"M-my lord, how could we have known?" Nero frowned.

"You couldn't have, and that's not your fault," he admitted kindly. "But Vincent seems to think otherwise."

"But Vincent is wrong. It's *not* our fault," Tyran protested.

"It is, in ways you couldn't have known," Lomax said. "We knew a war would follow Fort Deus, and were prepared for it. We didn't prepare to march north so soon, though. Still, when our armies heard about the broken peace treaty, *more than half* abandoned us. *More than half.*" He frowned. "The Centaurs slaughtered us at the Crossroads, and now we have scarce men to fight with."

"You have our men, my lord, always," Nero panicked. "Take as many as you need-"

"If it was my choice, I would. But I'm young and dumb and must listen to my elders; Lord Vincent called it *unwise* to continue working with men who had already compromised us," Lomax said. "And unwiser still to keep them alive... Forgive me if you can. We thank you for your many years of service, my lords."

Tyran Capra was the first to move, and the first to freeze. A Khavar guard thrust a sword into his back. He let out a cry of pain and fell. Another appeared behind Nero's throne and opened his throat, turning the king's many furs a dark red. Fletcher handled his blunted fork stressfully. The others duelled for a while, but it wasn't long before the Capra guards were overpowered and butchered by Khavar swords. The cries died with the last Capra, and Fletcher found himself alone with the crabs.

Lomax Khavar hadn't moved at all. "Given what they did to you, I thought you might appreciate to see, Prince Fletcher," he said, before standing to stroll out.

The Khavars grabbed Fletcher's arms. His blunted fork clattered on the ground.

Fletcher felt like retching, and he didn't know why. The Centaur couldn't count on two hands how many times he had thought about Tyran and his men dying when he was confined in his cell. *No less killed by the man whose fault this was in the first place.*

The Khavars led Fletcher out of the castle, and a rough wind smacked him in the face. Even so, it was nice to feel nature again. It would have been nicer to go at his own pace, though, and not urged along by more enemies. Fletcher found that funny. *I've escaped one cell to find another.* In truth, he didn't know what they'd do to him, but a cell seemed like the safest wager. *That's just what happens when you have turncoat allies. They'll all kill each other before they have a chance to war the enemy.* That was funny too. *No wonder it's taken the Archipelago so long to raise arms.*

Lomax peered back as they walked. He didn't stop. "What's so funny?" he asked with a smirk of his own.

Fletcher held his tongue and concentrated on not tripping over the rocks and pebbles that threatened to turn his staggering walk into a failed one. *He's more of a friend than the Capras, to free me so valiantly,* he smiled. Fletcher examined the man. *Prince Lomax Khavar. Son of King Delmar... Heir to the Archipelago?* It just occurred to him how important this man was. *That's why they were so scared. If and when Delmar dies, Lomax will be the man who rules exile.* If and when Esmond dies, Asher would be the man who rules Austellus. Fletcher never saw his brother in that light, as a powerful man, but he supposed he was too. *King Asher Centaur.* Esmond had always been king, so the thought seemed queer.

Still, it troubled him. *The future King of the Archipelago has me prisoner. And the future might come sooner than it would if there's as much treachery on the islands as here.* He winced. *King Lomax Khavar. He's the true enemy.*

"You can't win this war," Fletcher told the future king.

He smiled at the Centaur. "Where would that be written, my prince?"

"My father has ten times your men."

"And we have a Centaur. Tell me, which is more valuable?"

Lomax's constant smirk annoyed him. "Men. They win wars, not boys." Anyway, it was Fletcher's time to smirk. "My father slaughtered you at the Hills. He won the heart of Austellus back."

"He slaughtered me, did he? I believe I'm still alive," Lomax said. *It's a game to him.* "Why would you think our two thousand would stand a fighting chance in hell against fifty-some, however many your father had?"

"You sent two thousand to sack a city?" Fletcher tittered tiredly. "No wonder it got snatched back so easily. I've known better sackings in a bakery."

"The fools must have thought they stood a chance on the battlefield," he said. "But I agree, two thousand is too few to sack a city."

Fletcher smiled. "And you thought you could?"

"Did I say that?" he chuckled. "Might be we never meant to *sack* it."

The Centaur winced. "There were two thousand. You just said you needed men. You sent two thousand for a *jolly?*"

"We sent two thousand for a *city,*" he smiled. It was a great white smile. "The *great city of Lunarpass.* We had to make it look convincing. Too few pose *no* threat to sack."

Now, this Prince Lomax was speaking gibberish. "What do you mean *convincing?*"

"I already said," he claimed, "we were never meant to *hold* it. Be it the heart of Austellus; what good is a heart that can't beat?"

Fletcher felt stupid from not understanding his mind games. "Why send your soldiers in the first place, then?"

Lomax smirked a final time. "There's no need to ask *why,* Prince Fletcher. Your father has already made his choices. We might make it to Lunarpass in time, but it doesn't matter if we don't. . ." He looked out to the sea. "The entire Auburn Pole will see the show."

ESMOND XV
-Paroxysm-

Tonight were the celebrations. They had won a great victory at the hands of the Horncurves yesterday, and never had a chance to carouse afterwards. Too many complications went into retaking a 'sacked' city, although, most of those complications merely consisted of removing the dead from the Hills and the city itself. They had found the bodies of Hugo Lane and Joseph Frost, but Thaddeus Centaur was never found, neither dead nor alive. *My council of three remains three,* the king thought. Still, tonight they could *finally* celebrate, and perhaps for the last time in a while. But as he looked upon his city from his solar in the Sphaera, King Esmond Centaur wasn't a part of that time.

Most of the day he brooded about his brother. *If he were here, we'd be celebrating.* Esmond told him as much at the Crossroads, but that ended up being another lie. The king saw what Lori meant now. *Everything I've told myself and others the past few moons have been falsehoods. Why was I blind to that? I've never let myself believe my own lies before.* It made him feel powerless. *Orion said I'm not a powerless king, yet I've never felt more so. I pushed him away because of lies to myself as well.*

The rest of the day he had spent planning his war, his march. The will to see Vincent dead didn't fuel him as much as it had done in the past. Esmond couldn't even feel *affected* about it. He had stronger feelings of wanting Vincent dead way back when Reynold was murdered, when they didn't even know it was Vincent's doing. *But that was long ago. That was when my kingdom wasn't in shambles. When my family were all safe and happy in one place. When food was in such abundance, we could afford to feast every night during the Solar Celebrations. When I had friends and allies and power which I have no more.* After all that had happened, killing Vincent now seemed like another chore. *My desires have become duty, and my duties have become desire.*

Esmond watched his city grow livelier and livelier the lower the sun fell, and the higher the two-day-old Frost Moon rose. He could see the multitude of soldiers he had allowed to carouse in the Lunar Tavern multiply in number, and hear the songs and laughter start to engulf Lunarpass. *They deserve it,* he thought with a smile, *they fought well.*

"You've been in that bloody room for hours, Esmond," a friendly northern voice sang through the door.

Esmond strolled over and opened it. Riley Horncurve had two cups in hand, and a flagon of wine. "This bloody room needs me here," the king smirked, returning to his balcony.

Riley led himself to a table to fill the two goblets. "Ah, to plan yer war? It almost slipped my mind," he japed. "What's the plan, then? What's happenin' next?"

"The Venusian Archipelago," he said mockingly. "All our hosts will meet at Sangis. From there, we'll sail." *Straight for the heart: The Stingers.*

"Ye barely won this battle, Esmond," Riley tittered, arriving at his side and offering the king a goblet, "you gonnae steal my men for yer war even longer?"

"I owe it to my people," the king said sullenly. "I dragged them into this war. What sort of king would I be if I don't save them from it?"

"I was joking," Riley claimed. "Still, you're *doing* something. Last time we met, you were saying how you never do enough."

Esmond nodded. "And now I've done *too* much."

Riley shook his head. "There's no such thing," he said, holding out his cup. They clinked glasses and drank.

The wine was sweet, and almost went to Esmond's head. He hadn't had strong alcohol in a while. "I'm... sorry I couldn't honour your plea a few moons back. We needed men in Lunarpass. It would've taken them too long to get to Selerborn anyway."

"Ah, don't worry about it, I understand. Lord Waker has told me all about the trouble you've had here," he said. "Selerborn was as good as lost when Sigmund died. Half the people wanted *you* dead."

Esmond smiled. "I'm glad you didn't give them what they wanted."

"I was close to, you know," he frowned. "It's the most frustrating thing in the world when the only options you have would cripple you more in some other way."

"Is that all my death would be to you? A crippling?"

Riley smirked playfully. "Might be it would."

The king chuckled. "I agree. It *is* the most frustrating thing. That's been in my thoughts for moons now," he sighed. "If you protect the rich, you forsake the poor. If you enforce order, you strip freedom. If you act on war, you endanger the innocent... If *just* is what a king needs to be, why does it feel like I betrayed the entire north with that stupid execution?"

The Horncurve bit his lip. "You don't need to convince me how hard of a choice that was for you," he said kindly. "I could see it when you swung this sword." Shofar still looked strange on Sigmund's son's belt.

"I mean, that thing is pretty heavy," Esmond jested.

Riley chortled loudly.

The king smiled and continued when the laughing stopped. "So, what will you do, after the war?"

He had to think. "Cadmus would have Selerborn back by now..." The ram scratched his crimson beard. "Don't know. Might stay a while. I'm no good with northmen. My kids have always known them better. They probably learned from Sigmund, sad as that is; I learned nothing from that old goat."

"Know them better?"

"Aye, it was Marcus who tipped me off about the plotting behind my back. If it wasn't for him, I'd be dead. And you too," he shook his head with a smile. "There were *nine* different cabals, all plotting different treasons. *Nine* of them. If they didn't all rally behind that sneaky fucker Harper, they might have all done us a favour and killed each other before they could march south."

"What could a single cabal do against the crown?" Esmond smirked.

"Exactly," Riley said. "With Harper dead, and no one to follow, they'll split back into their sorry cabals again. If Cadmus was to act as if, say, he *supported* these cabals, one by one, he could send them south to their deaths and no one would know."

Esmond tittered. "That's *good,*" he said. "But what if one of these cabals was to succeed? You'd have slain your king."

"I guess I would have," Riley smiled, sipping his wine.

Esmond chuckled, before turning his head to brood on his city again. "You should be there. You're the Lord of Selerborn, not Cadmus."

"Aye, but like I said, northmen aren't fer me," he frowned. "If these last moons haven't proved that, I dinnae what will. I even lost my *brother* when I did something I thought was right. With Ignatius, my kids'll do a better job than me, for sure."

Esmond examined his hazel eyes. "What about southerners?"

"Your people might be a bit different than what they're used to up north," he said, amusement thick in his voice.

"Not them. You."

Riley's proud, playful demeanour shattered in front of him. "I don't understand."

"The King's *First Avail* is a very important man," Esmond said. "His ears, his mind, his heir, his tongue for when he can't talk for himself. He's crucial to any reign... and *my First Avail* abandoned me-"

"Oh, no, I can't-"

"You can. You have," he continued. "You saved me when no one else did. That's a debt I can never repay. Last time I saw you, I told you that friendship holds these kingdoms together. A friendship between the north and the south."

Riley's dark eyes looked close to tears. "Would you, truly?"

"I am," he nodded, trying not to laugh at his confounded reaction.

Riley's pupils scattered, dodging eye contact. He slowly knelt in front of the king. "You... honour me, my king."

"Be my eyes when I can't see, my heir when there is none, my king, should I ever fall," Esmond said. He had only said those words twice before. "Rise, Lord Horncurve. Rise as my *First Avail*."

Riley Horncurve did so. He was trembling. He embraced the king tightly. Esmond didn't expect that. When they pulled away, the ram was beaming. "Come on. We're celebrating. We've got too much to drink to."

Esmond pulled back. "Oh, no, I can't," he smiled. "My head must be clear... the war-"

"Oh, listen to yerself, you miserable wean!" Riley insisted. "My first counsel, as your *First Avail*, is that tonight, we drink ourselves into an early grave. He who defies counsel will not have it for long, King Esmond."

Esmond laughed, and resigned. "Then that is what we'll do."

"Aye, it is," Riley agreed, shoving the king out of his solar.

Many a man was already drunk by the time they arrived at the Lunar

Tavern. Some were mid song: a cluster of musicians and soldiers in the corner. Few were dancing, most were laughing and drinking and passionately yelling, a good amount were with women they romanced in various ways, and some were already asleep, thrown to the side of the tavern to make room for the conscious people. The atmosphere made Esmond happy. It always did. *I should have come sooner.*

Gradually, men started to notice them. *"Long live the king!"* a man cheered, raising his cup. That pulled more attention to the two of them. "The king's here," Esmond could hear another say. "Shhhh."

Esmond smiled. *"Why have you stopped?!"* he asked. *"Get to the bar! Drinks are on me!"*

The tavern suddenly became twice as vital. Everyone whooped and slapped the king's back excitedly as he made his way through, and the tavern fell back into an effusive and loud chatter, littered with laughter.

Darius Boyd was the first face to recognise. "King Esmond, it's good to see you join us," the head of arms said. "We won a great battle yesterday."

Esmond simpered. "I'm sorry to have scared you beforehand, Boyd. The victory wasn't mine."

Darius pulled a face. "Me? Scared? Never!"

"He was pissing his breeches. I saw the puddle." Elliot Moss appeared from the crowd.

Esmond laughed. Darius glanced around, flushed.

"The victory *was* yours, Esmond," Elliot continued. "The Crossroads was all but you."

"For better *and* for worse," the king sighed. "I'm sorry you both had to see me at my lowest."

"War does that," Elliot said eventually. "You're the best king we could hope for."

The king grinned. "Since when did my Lord Moss become so couthly?"

Elliot raised his eyebrows. "Am I? Oh, I forget myself. You're a joke of one, in truth," he smiled back.

Esmond laughed at the delivery. "Likewise, though, truly," he said. "I couldn't wish for better councillors."

They both smiled. "To the realm," Darius said, raising his cup.

Not long after, Esmond spied Briggs Waker. He was drinking with Sir Robert Hyll and Sir Ellis Lovell in a quiet corner, observing the lunar life

"Is that water in those cups?" he asked his king's guard distastefully.

"Drink slows reactions, my king," Sir Robert said.

"We're not in a battle any more, Sir Robert," Esmond smiled. "And you still have that wound to heal. Go. Drink. Both of you. I command it. There were no better men on the field at the Crossroads!"

With that, the two knights sent each other a mischievous look. They bowed and sauntered off to the bar.

"Briggs," Esmond greeted.

The head of word and pennons inclined his head. "My king," he said.

"I dislike strife," the king said, taking a seat next to him, "however impossible that may be to believe... I'm sorry, Lord Waker, I shouldn't have put so much pressure on you. Being the head of word is difficult enough a task."

Briggs seemed taken aback by the apology. "It... is a difficult time, my king. And our council grows smaller every day. I understand our burden."

"My burden, more like," he sighed. "Vows haven't stopped people from leaving me before."

Lord Waker searched the king's eyes. "You know we'd never do that. I said my vows with the intention to serve you until my last breath, as have the others."

Esmond was suspicious. "You *really* still believe in me? After I murdered Lord Edward? After I forsook my council? After I yanked my brother into a war he had no chance of surviving?"

"Until our last breath," he repeated. "The worst is behind us, I assure you. What I *believe* in, is a better future led by the king whom I serve. It's not right for your past to haunt you."

"I hope so," Esmond smiled. "Thank you, Briggs."

Briggs Waker nodded. He held up his goblet. "To the realm, my king."

Esmond shook his head. "I've already drunk to that," he said, raising his cup too. "To a better future."

Lord Waker smiled, and they drank.

"Esmond!" Riley called from across the room. *"Come 'ere!"*

The ram was with the musicians, as well as his two ram's guard, Sir Ardin and Sir Egan, and it didn't take long for half the tavern to become a choir. They sang with heart such classics as *'He Who Escaped', 'Two Armies to One', 'The Arm of Jupiter', 'The Blue Fire of King Archer', 'A Bow in Hand', 'A Drink, Perhaps', 'Five Good Men'* and *'The Maid of Mea'* - Esmond sang that one the loudest - it was his brother's favourite.

They even sang *'The Warrior Boy'*, and for a time, the tavern became Selerborn, thundering with northern drums and thick accents. It even made *Esmond* feel patriotic, and he hadn't an ounce of northern in him.

"I still can't believe what you've made me," Riley said to him after. "This is a dream, I'm convinced."

"It's no dream, Riley," Esmond grimaced. "I've done terrible things, and thought a great deal worse," he said. "I was so full of hate. You're the man to help me, to ground me, I'm sure of it."

"You wouldn't need me," Riley disagreed.

"I can't help myself," Esmond admitted. He felt the tears coming. He fought them back. "My brother... died because of me. My last brother. My family too. Every time I act on what I think is right, it's the ones I love most who are killed and lost."

"Can you tell right from wrong?" Riley asked. "Clearly you still can. If you were *truly* lost, nothing would matter to you."

"But... I can't-"

"No, listen to me," Riley insisted, almost slurring. "My da' came 'round in the end. He was lost for so long, but still, he died content. I lost the north, my home, and when I go back, I'll have it again. Time will find a way to make things better, Esmond. It always does."

Esmond smiled sadly at his *First Avail*. "This is why you're the one to help me."

Riley had dew in his eyes again. He shook his head and squeezed Esmond's shoulder. Before another word could come out of him, the Horncurve leapt atop a table. *"Your attention, all of you!"* he yelled, shaking a chandelier to add music to his announcement.

"Riley! Riley! Riley!" the mass of soldiers began to chant.

The former Lord of Selerborn raised his hand, and they all quietened. *"We've won a great victory, a great battle!"* he proclaimed. *"Every one of you played a part, and should be proud for it. But you should also be proud of this man here, because behind every great battle is a great king who led it!"* He raised his cup. *"To the king! To Esmond the Fearless!"*

Fearless. Never has there been a more apt name. That made Esmond smile. *I was preparing to die before you came to save me.* Regardless, his men cheered and drank all the same, as if they'd forgotten that, or maybe not even known. *"A speech!"* one man yelled.

"Aye, a speech, your grace!" another added.

"Speech!" Briggs Waker smiled.

Elliot began the chant. *"Speech! Speech! Speech!"* The rest of the army slowly joined in.

Esmond was amazed to see how many wanted to hear him speak. *They love me*, he thought, as if he had forgotten. They always loved him. *Why? They couldn't have had a worse king if they tried.*

"Speech! Speech! Speech!" The Lunar Tavern continued to hoot.

"Very well!" the king yelled, raising his cup and standing on a table. His army cheered. He waited for them to calm down and quieten. "There was a time when being given the chance to speak would just be an opportunity to talk about myself," he jested. "But we all know that war is so much bigger than that, and doubtless there should be people with us tonight, drinking with us, celebrating with us, but have had that chance robbed from them." All the smiles in the tavern had died. Some soldiers looked more distraught than others. "But I can't pretend that wasn't expected," he continued, grinding his teeth passionately. "Every man who has died so far, did so for a purpose, and I say this as not *only* a king, but as a *brother*, and a *father*, and a *husband* - since we serve said purpose together, each one of those fallen souls was a part of us. Mark my words, more parts will follow. War will wash over Austellus like a tsunami of poisoned water. Until we are completely rid of enemies, I can't promise safety. I don't say this to lessen our victory; each victory is a *triumph!"* His men cheered. "…but remember that flames follow a spark… and flames will follow the spark we put-"

BWOOM. There was a deep rumble. Then another. Then another, twice as loud.

"-out," the king finished.

It sounded like the ground had awoken, releasing a fiery demon, or a volcano of chaos. The ancient marble around them trembled with each *BOOM. BOOOOM BOM. VOOOMP. BRRRUMP…*

A soldier bolted into the tavern. *"ALCHAESPHITE! RUN!"*

The Lunar Tavern erupted with screams and panic. Still, no number of yells were louder than the deafening *VOOOOMP. BOOOM.*

Esmond found himself frozen as his men ran and pushed and fell around him. *BOOOOM. VRRRUUMP.* Eventually, the king staggered through the chaos to the stairs. *The balcony. I need to see. BOOOM.* Dust fell from the ceiling. Candles fell from their tables. Glass shattered from far away windows. Screams drenched the city. *VOOOOMP. BOOOOOM.*

Esmond Centaur lost his breath at what he saw. For a moment, he thought the sun had returned. Buildings were exploding with great orange flames that punched the dark sky. It was a chain of death, destroying homes and taverns, then the towers next to them, then the closest armouries and stables. Not even the fastest of horses could outrun it. People tried, Esmond could see, but the flames caught up, burning them, scorching them, killing them. The fire burned so hot, metals and rocks were *melting* into a river of molten alloys before it had a chance to shatter. The Alchemical Forge burst outwards in a mountain of fire. The Tower of Kings broke and toppled, crushing a thousand other buildings with it. The flames were swallowing the great city, and creeping closer and closer like a wave, *like a tsunami. You're kidding me,* was the only thing Esmond could think.

Apathetically, Esmond found his crown, and pulled it off. It clattered on the ground, rolling along the balcony. He breathed in deeply, and his tired hands found the golden railings.

The king couldn't look away. If it wasn't his city burning, his people dying, it would have been a beautiful sight: an ocean of orange that snapped and crackled and wrapped around towers with tight fingers, turning them into fragments with a single squeeze. It swept forwards and sideways and upwards until no city could be seen. Soon, Esmond could feel the heat on his face, on his hands. All he could do was watch as his city burned, as his people died, as the flames consumed his skin.

EPILOGUE

I t's happened. We've done it. We've actually done it." The mark on his arm was so fresh, blood crept out when he touched it.

Ulrich stared at the gash. "I can't believe it either," he smiled. "Stab me. I want to see if it works."

"*Stab* you?" Marcarius winced. "You're an idiot, you know that?"

"We're *immortal* now, Marcarius," the young lion beamed. "We *can't* die. Don't you understand?"

"I understand," Marcarius smiled back as he made laps around his marble solar. "But stabbing you would kill you, fool. Deus said we're not invincible."

"We're *close* though," he insisted. "Do you know what this means?" He didn't wait for an answer. "We'll be alive to see the end of time, to see kings rise and fall, to see empires evolve and crumble-"

"*So long as we uphold our vows,*" Marcarius reminded. "That was the cost."

"It's not much of a cost, if you ask me," said Ulrich. "Yes, we said a few vows to serve. So be it. We'll serve."

Marcarius frowned. "It goes deeper than that. You know it does."

"What are you saying?" Ulrich challenged. "That I'd break them?"

Marcarius couldn't form words. He looked out of the lattice window, with its perfect view of the rounded hall where they had just bled.

"If anyone's already doomed, it's you," the lion winced, watching a beautiful lady hold up her skirt as she ran across the dome. Her black hair danced behind her. "You're meant to uphold vows to your liege *as well.*"

He couldn't rebuke that. It was true. He had wronged Lord Ahearn Centaur like no other. As if she was summoned by thought, in ran Lady Celosia. "So, it's happened?" she beamed after shutting the door. "Are you finally immortal?"

"You shouldn't be here," Marcarius said gruffly, biting his cheeks as her hands found his chest and his manhood began to stiffen.

"I shouldn't be anywhere near you, Marcarius," she whispered in his ear. "Not after all the things you've done to me." She kissed him passionately.

Ulrich had half an eye open. "Should I leave?" he asked cholerically. "Do you need to be alone?"

Marcarius backed away. It was difficult to; Celosia's lips were always so soft. "No, you shouldn't, Ulrich. You're right. We need to stop this, Celosia. We can't do this anymore."

Lady Celosia's big, deep blue eyes broke Marcarius's heart. "What's changed?"

"I've said my vows now," Marcarius said, walking to the window. He felt uncomfortable looking at her. "Part of this is to obey and serve your husband, my liege. I can't do that with you in my bed."

Celosia followed him to the window. "You said your vows to Ahearn years ago," she said. "Why is this suddenly wrong?"

"It's not *suddenly* wrong, it was *always* wrong," Marcarius snapped. He sighed and rubbed his eyes. "I'm bound by blood to serve now, Celosia. If we break that vow, I've lost my place in the world."

"Serve who?" she asked calmly. "I'm a Centaur now too. Both of my parents had the blood of the Sagittarius."

Marcarius looked to Ulrich for guidance. He was only frowning. "You're not the liege, my lady. Our people don't follow you."

"I can be," she insisted. "I can for you."

"You can try. But even trying would get you killed."

"Not if I'm smart."

Marcarius chuckled. "If you're smart, it'll get *me* killed for knowing about it."

"You don't need to know. Men can be killed, unlike you. As can my husband."

Marcarius tittered against his chagrin. He cupped her hands in his. *"Please,* Celosia. Don't make this harder than it needs to be. I never *could* be yours. You can't make it work. Commit treason and we're both accursed. I couldn't live with myself if I lost you just because you tried."

A tear trickled down her face. Her hands slipped out of his, and she left.

Marcarius sighed and fell back into a chair. "'If anyone's already doomed'," he winced tiredly. "Thank you, Ulrich."

Despite Ulrich's stubborn face, his eyes were sympathetic. "What do you want me to say? That it would have worked? Someone would have found out eventually..."

Marcarius shook his head as he stared into nothing.

Ulrich approached nervously, placing a hand on Marcarius's shoulder. "Hey, forget about her. We can't have you miserable for the feast later on."

He could barely think about the feast right now. "What if she was?"

The lion retreated his hand. "What?"

"What if she *was* the liege?" he asked. "What if she took up arms? Would I have to serve Lord Ahearn or her? Or both? Or have I broken my vows already by falling for her so stupidly?"

"Are you going to ask the king?"

"Of course not," he winced.

"Then you'll never know. Forget about her."

"Oh, stop it, Ulrich," Marcarius winged. "It's a *genuine* question."

Ulrich hesitated. "One that you're considering?" he asked. "Because if you are, then it's my duty to-"

"Must I consider carrying out every question I ask?" the Sagittarian scowled. "Ulrich, I just sent her away. I just cast the one person I care most about in this world out of my life, perhaps for good! And do you know why? Because of *duty*. Because we have *influence* now. And it's a problem when we don't even know where that duty lies." The rebuke came harder than intended. Ulrich shrank slowly. "I'm sorry, I-"

"It's fine," Ulrich said. He thought for a moment. His new lemon robes folded under him as he sat. "I can't say. I don't know," he continued. "If you're having to ask, Deus wasn't clear enough about them."

Marcarius furrowed his dark, black eyebrows. "We'd need to know. It can go deeper than that," he said. "What if Lord Ahearn decides to war with Deus? What if Erik Lyrderyn does? Who do we serve?"

"That's the second time you've said 'it can go deeper' today. You're paranoid, Marcarius," Ulrich loured. "No one would ever war with Deus."

"Likelihood has nothing to do with it." Marcarius said. "It's a big deal,

Ulrich. We lose our lives if we forsake our vows."

"And some people lose their lives by falling down some stairs," he said dryly. "What of it?"

Marcarius clenched his jaw. "You're right," he said, "but there's no harm in knowing." He stood and looked out the lattice again. "Anyway, where's Yuval and Sage? Weren't they meeting us before the feast?"

Ulrich examined Marcarius for a long while as they waited. He was pacing around the room. "Marcarius," he said eventually, "your mind is still on it." The lion stood and stopped him walking. "Forget about her. Forget about vows. Remember them tomorrow, if you must, but tonight is meant to be a *celebration;* the *last* time we are able to celebrate our lives as *men*, the *last* time we can drink and jest with our brothers. You can't do that with a troubled mind."

"It's not troubling me," Marcarius said icily. "I'd know my choice if it happens."

Ten minutes passed before Yuval and Sage arrived at Marcarius's solar. "Took your bloody time," Ulrich smirked as he opened the door.

"We're sorry, we forgot," Yuval said like a child giddy on too much sugar. "I just can't believe what we've done."

Sage was the calmer of the two. "I would have come sooner, but our new brother was too excited. He couldn't hold his tongue for much longer."

"You've told people?" Marcarius asked as he led them out the solar and closed the door.

Yuval shrugged. "A... fair few."

"A fair *many*," Sage corrected. The other two groaned jokingly.

"Look, how could I *not?*" Yuval asked. "We're *immortal*. No man should have so much power."

"You think Deus prances around, boasting of how much power he has?" Sage asked.

"I wasn't *boasting*. That's not what I said."

"As you say, brother," Ulrich chuckled. "How drunk are we getting Solomon tonight?"

"Nonoperatively drunk," Sage said, "as we all should be."

"That's a thought," Yuval said, like he had just discovered the cure for eremus disease. "Mortal men die after too much drink. What of us?"

"You can be our experiment, Yuval," Sage smirked.

"No, stop it. I'm being serious," he groaned. Yuval's eye caught

Marcarius as he stared at the main stone doors to the king's chambers. "Brother, what's wrong?" he asked.

By that point, the other two seemed curious too. *Not like I'd lie anyway.* "I'll catch you all up. I need to have a word with Deus."

"Ok," Sage said, continuing to walk. Yuval turned and followed slowly. Ulrich lingered with an unforgiving look.

Marcarius breathed in deeply as he made his way up the rounded steps. No guards stood outside the great, intricately carved door of rock. No one had to, since only Marcarius's new brothers were allowed in the Doenum to begin with. He hesitated before pressing his hand on the rock. The pulsating green magic prickled his palm. "Come in," Deus said from the other side. Marcarius opened the stone door.

The room was lavish, yet humble, the marble and gold of the Caelestius sigil being a constant, with light grey stones, smooth and jagged alike, to break them up. In truth, it wasn't much different to the servant's chambers, only that Marcarius's solar had far fewer golden candles and a few more looking glasses. Though, the extra space that Deus had wouldn't go amiss.

Deus Caelestius didn't appear like a king, or a saviour, or a great magnus. He was a skinny man, with dark black hair that never seemed to age or recede. None of Deus seemed to age. He was a forty-six-year-old in a twenty-year-old's body. Marcarius felt older, and he was only twenty-seven himself. The only thing that gave a hint of Deus's age was the ever-deepening field of lines on his forehead.

He was at the rear of his chamber, cleansing his hands in a golden trough before drying them with the air. "Marcarius," he smiled kindly, "how may I be of service?"

Being in his king's presence still made Marcarius's heart thump. "I... Me and Ulrich were discussing the vows, what they meant. I was... hoping to learn truly."

"Of course," the king said. "What is it that troubles you, my archer?"

Marcarius hated how worry could be read in his face. "The vows said we owe allegiance to our lieges, but also serve under you."

"Not specifically, but yes," Deus said, entwining his hands in front of him as he so often did. "Your liege represents your race, what they stand for, who they follow. You're to serve them, but above all, counsel them. Counsel *is* your service. You're my peacekeepers, Marcarius."

"Yes, but... still under *your* rule," Marcarius said. "You're the king. All men must serve you."

Deus shrugged. "Am I a king whilst I wear no crown?"

Marcarius half squinted. "Is this a trick?"

Deus chuckled gently. "Scepticism is becoming of you, Marcarius. Fear not what choices you may make during your watch. There is no wrong choice made with a good heart."

"But I *do* fear," Marcarius frowned. "I essentially serve two kings."

"As do two kings serve *you*," Deus smirked. "Whatever order we may command of you, you still have the will of a servant to judge."

"What if I can't judge?" he asked. "What if there is no right decision. What if no good heart can be found in either?"

Deus's colourful eyes inspected his new servant. He said nothing, if not with his eyes.

Marcarius took the silence as his cue. "If. . . I should ever be put against you-"

Deus shook his head. "That would never happen-"

"*If* it should," he continued. "Whose side should I take? Our saviour's or my people's?"

Deus never blinked. "Let's hope it doesn't come to that."

TO BE CONTINUED IN:
'A GALE OF VIRTUE'

APPENDIX

Kingdoms and their Courts
Timeline of Notable Events
Terms and Titles
Centaur Dynasty

The Centaurs of Lunarpass
And Sagittarian natives
'Our Arrows Pierce'

A dynasty founded by Erland the Escaper in 163 AP, the Centaurs have ruled over the lands of Austellus for hundreds of years. Although the kings of Austellus are *of* Lunarpass, the opposite couldn't be further from the truth, as Centaurs often see their old kingdom of Negalia as their true home, consequently abiding or even ruling at the heart, Fort Deus. With their equos and chevals and askew customs regarding ruling, it's undeniable that the Centaurs have had a lasting impact on the new world.

> KING ESMOND CENTAUR, King of Jupiter, ruler of fires, Protector of the Auburn Pole, holder of the Zircon Crown, 14th King of Post-Austellus,
> -his wife, QUEEN SEMIRA, maiden name Jade, daughter of Kaus Jade,
> -their children:
>> -ASHER, eldest son, heir to the zircon throne, heir to the solar throne, sixteen,
>> -FLETCHER, a boy of fourteen,
>> -LETA, eldest daughter, fourteen,
>> -EVA, youngest daughter, twelve,
>> -HEW, youngest son, ten,
> -his siblings:
>> -{IVOR}, eldest brother, king before Esmond, renounced his claim, last seen at Sagwhel, presumed dead,
>> -LORIMER, called Lori, youngest brother, Lord of Centaur's Lagoon,

-his bastard son, FELIKS SAGITTA, fifteen years of age,

-his bastard daughter, VESTA SAGITTA, ten,

-HOPE JADE, sister by law, daughter of Kaus Jade, Lady of Jade Castle,

-his council:

-SIR ORION READE, Esmond's First Avail,

-his father, LORD MADOC READE, commander of Fort Angel,

-his wife, {EMMA DART}, died at childbirth,

-his eldest son, ISBEN, Madoc's squire, nineteen,

-his son, JOVIAN, Esmond's squire, sixteen,

-SIR ROSWELL DART, Esmond's Second Avail, brother to Emma Dart,

-THADDEUS CENTAUR, cousin to Esmond and Lori, Acting King of Lunarpass,

-ELDER MARCARIUS, Sagittarius representative at the Solar Auditorium,

-ELLYS DART, father of Roswell Dart and Emma Dart, head of gold and events,

-WYE VESTA, head of law,

-GALLOWAY MALONE, head of war, former member of Sigmund's ram's guard,

-KAUS JADE, head of trade, father of Semira and Hope,

-HUGO LANE, head of citizen satisfaction, stationed at Lunarpass,

-ELLIOT MOSS, head of development, stationed at Lunarpass,

-DARIUS BOYD, head of arms, stationed at Lunarpass,

-TOBI SPARKS, head of pennons and the city's garrison, stationed at Lunarpass,

-JOSEPH FROST, head of labour, stationed at Lunarpass,

-BRIGGS WAKER, head of word, stationed at Lunarpass,

-his king's guard:

-SIR CONNELL ATLEE, of the king's guard,

-SIR ELLIS LOVELL, of the king's guard,

-SIR ARTER WHYTE, of the king's guard,

-SIR ROBERT HYLL, of the king's guard,

-SIR WARRICK MAYNE, of the king's guard, brother to Jermyn Mayne,

-SIR DEVON THORNETON, of the king's guard,

-at Fort Deus:

-KIAN WEEKS, head of the fort's garrison,

-LUKAN THITE, first cheval,

-NATHAN RISLEY, second cheval,

-YVES LARRET, third cheval,

-GUY LACE, teacher and carer,

-MATEO HUNT, of the fort's garrison,

-ADDY RORE, of the fort's garrison,

-STIG 'BLACKFIST' WYND, master of arms, royal blacksmith,

-at Centaur's Lagoon:

-ALCHEMIST CUTHBERT OF REDMAWR, principal advisor to Lorimer,

-OLIVER PATEL, politics advisor to Lorimer,

-AUSTIN LOTT, military advisor to Lorimer,

-KAYDEN CARR, citizen advisor to Lorimer,

-CALLUM WELLS, of the city's garrison, Feliks's friend,

-OLLIE WEBB, of the city's garrison,

-BRANDON SNIDER, of the city's garrison,

-ELLA FOSTER, Lady of Fort Foster,

-THEO FOX, squire to Kayden Carr, Feliks's friend,

-at Lunarpass:

-KALEB SHAW, head of the city's garrison,

-JARRETT RIVERS, master tailor,

-his daughter, CHESNA,

-BARTLE FIREHANDS, head of the Alchemical Forge,

-ODDE SITLACK, head of the docks,

-ESMOUR TRAIN, master cheval,

-pennons of note: (Arms rounded to nearest 100)

-ALEC ODUM, Lord of Liglock, (7,000),

-his brother BRECKEN, Lord of Boneholde,

(5,000),
-RAMON KRAMER, Lord of Sagwhel, (5,000),
-BRODY ORR, Lord of Artis Bay, (3,000),
-AARON TREATH, Lord of Goattreath, (4,000),
-THOMAS BRANCH, Lord of Castle Branch, (3,000),
-QUINTIN BAXTER, Lord of Antrum Bay, (2,000),
-DECLAN HELA, Lord of The Dog's Paw, (6,000),
-JOCKS WRIGHT, Lord of Arbor, (5,000),
-JESSE STODSEA, Lord of Brunnock, (4,000),
-CAELON DIOLUS, Lord of Fort Diolus, (3,500),
-EDUARD STARHART, Lord of Starhold, (4,500),
-SIMON LOOST, Lord of Wilton Fort, (4,000),
-NATE FULLER, Lord of Solis Bridge, (6,000),
-HOPE JADE, Lady of Jade Castle, (3,500),
-lesser pennons:
-RYAN HERST, Lord of Herst Fort, (200),
-TROY LARTON, Lord of Larton Keep, (150),
-ERIK THYNE, Lord of Trader's Dock, (300),
-his brother TOREN, exiled to Mount Taigus
for piracy, leader of the 'Taigan Midknights',
-his gang of *known* outlaws:
-DARYN SHYST,
-PORL 'SLABJAW'
WATTS,
-JEHM INCIR,
-KYNA LAKEFALL,
-WATTIE WILL,
-SARM FOSTER, Lord of Fort Foster, (100),
-his daughter, LADY ELLA,
-DANE ASHEYE, Warden of the Diolus Isles, (200),

Sagittarian natives: Asheye, Atlee, Auber, Auriga, Baxter, Boyd, Branch, Byrne, Carr, Centaur, Chavez, Dart, Diolus, Dow, Drury, Equuleus, Firehands, Fogg, Foster, Fox, Frost, Fuller, Giles, Hela, Herfast, Herst, Hunt, Jade, Khan, Knighton, Kramer, Lace, Lane, Larret, Larton, Lott, Lovell, Monoceros, Orion, Orr, Pegasus, Reade, Risley, Rore, Sagitta, Shaw, Shyst, Sitlack, Snider, Sparks, Starhart, Stike, Thite, Thorneton, Thyne, Train, Vesta, Waywood, Webb, Weeks, Wells, Whyte, Wright, Wynd, Wyvil,

THE TEN KINGDOMS
The kingdoms pledged and bent to the crown

The Lyrderyns of Ignis
And Leon natives
'The Gold Roars'

Matching the time of the Centaur's rule, the Lyrderyns rule over the desolate deserts of the Canicule. They are by far the richest family, being at the source of the trade in all of Austellus. Ruling above the buried empire of Lter, Lyrderyns have managed to rebuild what the seasons felled bigger and better.

REYNOLD LYRDERYN, Lord of Ignis, Liege of Jupiter, holder of the Peridot Gem,
-his wife, LADY ELAYNE, maiden name Lyonis,
-their children:
>-LYSSA, eldest daughter, sixteen,
>-{LIONEL}, heir to Ignis, only twelve when lost in the desert; presumed dead,
>-ELEANOR, a girl of twelve,
>-AYLA, youngest daughter, two years of age,
-his brothers:
>-SIR GOLDWYN, his younger brother, Reynold's First Avail,
>>-his wife, GINA, sister by law to Reynold,
>>-his son, FITZROY, called Fitz, fourteen,
>-AYDEN LYONIS, brother by law, Lord of Lynxrock, brother to Lady Elayne,
>>-his bastard son, RYAN LYNX, sixteen,
-his council:
>-ELDER ULRICH, Leo representative at the Solar Auditorium,

-JAMES FYSHER, head of pennons, brother to Sir Cedric,

-AURELIUS KINSEY, head of gold and trade,

-CYRUS SAND, head of military,

-JERMYN MAYNE, head of the city's garrison, brother to Sir Warrick Mayne,

-SULWYN WISP, head of word,

-ELIJAH GALE, head of citizenship,

-his lion's guard:

-SIR CEDRIC FYSHER, of the lion's guard,

-SIR BRENDAN GRYFFORD, of the lion's guard, son of Galvin Gryfford,

-at Ignis:

-EHSHAN GRYNN, head of the city's garrison,

-SAMSON TAHERI, a mercenary,

-pennons of note: (Arms rounded to nearest 100)

-JENSON KLINE, Lord of Goldspine Watch, (2,000),

-OSMYD SHYNE, Lord of Sabulo Holdfast, (4,000),

-SATTAR TYMOS, Lord of Bloodstones, (1,100),

-LEYLI ROSEYE, Lady of Redmawr, (4,600),

-JAPHAR VYMER, Lord Moat Calor, (3,700),

-KNAVE FARYD, Lord of Litore, (5,300),

-GODE YELLOWSTRAND, Lord of Merchant's Bay, (7,000),

-ERFYN IREONS, Warden of Desert's End, (4,500),

-DARYA DEADSWOOD, Lady of Chartree, (2,600),

-LANCYL GREENYR, Lord of Fort Palm, (2,200),

-ARYF RAYZE, Lord of Rusted Leaf, (900),

-HASAN EYSAND, Lord of Slipstorm, (5,200),

-PETYR IFLOT, Lord of Rynworth Fast, (3,400),

Leon natives: Alper, Andromeda, Brassie, Brazier, Cassiopeia, Cephus, Deadswood, Elies, Eysand, Fornax, Golding, Greenyr, Gryfford, Grynn, Henlye, Hizdir, Iflot, Ireons, Kinsey, Kline, Leafer, Leo, Lynx, Lyonis, Lyrderyn, Mayne, Mesut, Meryck, Mustafa, Obson, Oken, Phoenix, Pyne, Ratan, Rayze, Sand, Sevki, Shyne, Smoker, Tansal, Trevyt, Trone, Tulon, Tymos, Vymer, Wisp, Wrenne, Yellowstrand,

The Horncurves of Selerborn
And Arian natives
'Leading the Storm'

Possibly one of the newest families to rise, the Horncurves are prominent for usurping the last Oquinteus and restoring order to the north after their exile. After Sigmund took the throne, they were pardoned and raised to lordship. Being a strong branch from the old blood of Aries, the Horncurves have done everything in their power to hold on to that origin, often causing unwanted wars and even more unwanted deaths.

      SIGMUND HORNCURVE, Lord of Selerborn, holder of the Diamond Horn,
      -his wife, {LADY SCARLETT}, maiden name Hastem, fell in battle at Heavia,
      -their children:
            -RILEY, eldest son, heir to Selerborn,
            -his wife, LADY EMILY, maiden name Lynch,
            -their children:
                  -CADMUS, a twin to Marcus, sixteen,
                  -MARCUS, a twin to Cadmus, sixteen,
                  -ATHENA, only daughter, thirteen,
            -LUTHER, Lord of Serpent's Tower, younger brother,
      -his council:
            -RILEY HORNCURVE, Sigmund's First Avail,
            -ELDER IGNATIUS, Aries representative at the Solar Auditorium,
            -SIR THIRSTON WILES, commander of the military,
            -HARPER SIREN, head of citizenship, Acting Lord of

Selerborn,
>-his eldest son, BRYAN,
>-his youngest son, CADELL,
-SEATHAN BLAR, head of trade,
-DUGG GALLACH, head of arms,
-his ram's guard:
>-SIR ARDIN HAWTREY, of the ram's guard,
>-SIR GERARD HOLT, of the ram's guard,
>-SIR HAROLD SMYTH, of the ram's guard,
>-SIR EGAN BROOK, of the ram's guard,
>-SIR RAUL JAMES, of the ram's guard,
-at Selerborn:
>-ARRAN GIBBS, head of the city's garrison,
>-RUAIRI 'RAIDARMS' JECKSON, master armourer,
>-ANGELO BRYSEA, inventor, Athena's tutor,
-at Serpent's Tower:
>-VOLUSIA NARSES, said to be a witch,
>-FINLAY KNOX, master of ships,
-pennons of note: (Arms rounded to nearest 100)
>-AILIG RAING, Lord of Salem, (7,500),
>>-LILI, daughter of Ailig,
>-IAIN BEART, Lord of Aangmouth, (7,800),
>-ROB AMBORSAN, Warden of Fort Flum, (5,200),
>-BEARN BARAN, Lord of Lushwood, (6,100),
>-PARLAN LOGLACH, Lord of Ramsport, (3,400),
>-DANIEL CAMSHON, Lord of Brumstone, (4,100),
>-OISEAN PEUTER, Lord of Diamondstream, (2,400),
>-SEALON MACTANN, Lord of Fort Lux, (1,500),
>-FIONN THARNHAM, Lord of Tharnham Keep, (3,900),
>>-LOU, son of Fionn,
>>-STRUAN, son of Fionn,
>-ANGUS DINN, Warden of Jugum, (700),

Arian natives: Ara, Amborsan, Baran, Beart, Blar, Bootes, Borealis, Brook, Camshon, Dinn, Draco, Gallach, Gibbs, Hastem, Hawtrey, Holt, Horncurve, James, Jeckson, Knox, Loglach, Lynch, Mactann, Malone, Pavo, Peuter, Perseus, Raing, Siren, Smyth, Tharnham, Trotter, Wiles, Will,

The Kalyx of Mea
And Geminian natives
'Of Two Minds'

Unlike other families, Kalyx, and all rulers of Gemini, keep to their roots and elect two kings or queens rather than one. Typically, the rulers are legitimate twins at birth: so much so, that the youngest ever rulers were both 3 years of age. This superstitious behaviour has been detrimental to the peace of the Twin Islands, sometimes having the thrones passed to a family that have skewed morals.

TODD KALYX AND TATE KALYX, Lord(s) of the Twin Islands, Liege(s) of Mercury, holder(s) of the Twinned Alexandrite, ruler(s) of air,
-their siblings:
      -ELENA KALYX, sister,
      -her bastard daughter, SKYLA APUS, thirteen years,
-Todd's council:
      -HAMAR DUFOLD, First Avail to Todd,
      -ELDER YUVAL, Gemini representative at the Solar Auditorium,
      -SEER JUNIUS, Soothsayer, the leading seer,
      -RONAN HOOD, head of trade,
      -HUXLEY GERBOLD, head of pennons,
      -SEB VALTER, head of defence,
-Tate's council:
      -GALEN DOPPEL, First Avail to Tate, brother to Clarke Doppel,
      -MASO MERYCK, head of events,

-LEW FOLKER, head of citizenship,
-FLYNN LITTEL, head of feasts and wine, appointed
by Tate as a jape.
-their twin's guard:
-SIR QUINN FAIRMAN, of the twin's guard,
-BRUNE STIKE, of the twin's guard,
-CORBIN HAWK, of the twin's guard,
-JOCE LERYX, of the twin's guard,
-DREW ORTIZ, of the twin's guard,
-EVAN STONE, of the twin's guard,
-at Murberek:
-CLERIC CALLAN, temple of the mind,
-BRADLEY BRANES, head of the city's garrison,
-at Mea Minor:
-CLERIC ARCHER, temple of the soul,
-CRAIG ANCHOR, dockmaster, named Bluntmouth,
-at Mea:
-ARIA WILSIN, innkeep at the Twin's Pleasure,
-pennons of note: (Arms rounded to nearest 100)
-JALEN BHOSHA, Lord of Geminport, (2,000),
-ABEL POX, Warden of Fort Nebula, (5,500),
-BEN RINNIP, Lord of Caligo, (2,700),
-JUNE LARNER, Lady of Whitefin Bay, (4,600),
-CIAN LYNCH, Warden of Lixhold, uncle of Lady
Emily Horncurve, (5,700),
-WILDER KNOCKFIELD, Lord of Fort Praes, (500),
-TEDDIE BLACK, Lord of Cautus, (7,000),
-MACK SHIELDS, Lord of the Lonely Tree, (4,300),
-LYALL KHAN, Lord of Tanin Toar, (700),
-TOMLIN SADYX, Lord of Garley Fort, (1,900),
-PIPER FALLS, Lady of Craigleth, (400),
-MATTHEW BARQUE, Lord of Kirkleck, (600),
-HANNA DISDANCE, Lady of Faerdham, (700),

Geminian natives: Apus, Bhosha, Black, Branes, Brysea, Chamaeleon,
Columba, Crux, Disdance, Doppel, Dufold, Fairman, Folker, Gerbold,
Hawk, Kalyx, Knockfield, Larner, Leryx, Littel, Musca, Ortiz, Pox, Rinnip,
Sadyx, Shields, Stone, Valter, Vulpecula, Watts, Wilsin,

The Tridents of Aquamare
And Aquarian natives
'Whether Water to Bend'

The mystical Trident family are based in the south of the Saturnian Mountains, being the kings of the rock even as far back as before the pause. It is said that they have the ability to manipulate water, always granting the greatest yield of fish and food in all of Austellus. Their capital of Aquamare was said to be raised from nothing and no one but a fisherman and his trident.

OBERON TRIDENT, Lord of the Shattered Trident,
-his wife, LADY LYSANDA, maiden name Neola, holder of the Amethyst Trident,
-their children:
>-CELESTE, eldest daughter, eighteen,
>-KIEL, eldest son, fourteen, heir to the Shattered Trident,
>-OSWIN, youngest son, ten,
-Oberon's bastard son, STERLING CETUS, a boy of fifteen,
-GWYDON, his elder brother, denied the throne and passed it to Oberon, now Oberon's First Avail,
-his council:
>-ELDER SAGE, Aquarius representative at the Solar Auditorium,
>-KAI CYNDER, head of pennons,
>-ARWIN LANBY, head of trade,
>-NORMAN KINWICH, head of the city's garrison,
-their bearer's guard:

-THOM PUCK, of the bearer's guard,
-HAGEN CETUS, of the bearer's guard, a bastard,
-SIR HARTWIG CATER, of the bearer's guard,
-TILL TROTTER, of the bearer's guard,
-at Aquamare:
-WILMAR OF GALEHEART, master farmhand,
-LOTHAR SALTER, chief of the canals,
-AUBREY STRATH, mistress of the Observatory,
-at the Shattered Trident:
-CLERIC BALTHASAR, priest, water arts guru,
-his chief student, WALO,
-GURU LOMAN, trident arts guru,
-GURU TAGGART, spear arts guru,
-pennons of note: (Arms rounded to nearest 100)
-CARLA GELDWINE, Lady of Situla, (4,000),
-GOSWIN GRAVES, Lord of Fort Harbere, (4,500),
-EIKE TAVERNER, Warden of Fluo Keep, (6,200),
-ASHWIN FISKE, Lord of Castlecross, (3,200),
-SIR WILMAR BEKKER, Lord of Orris, (6,100),
-EGON LISPE, Lord of Halton, (2,000),
-EBBA WAYWOOD, Lady of Brasstal, (1,600),
-FALKO DRAWL, Lord of Aspach Keep, (5,200),
-MANFRED FLEEDON, Lord of Southbay, (800),
-HENRY BACKUS, Lord of Drogstone, (2,100),
-ELRIC MYNYDDTHWAITE, Warden of
Wintersdam, (6,900),
-KURT SMOKER, Lord of Smoker's Holdfast,
(8,900),
-LUDWIG CROCKHELM, Lord of Waterkee, (900),
-ULRICH OTTMAR, Lord of Fort Longrey, (3,400),

Aquarian natives: Anchor, Antilia, Backus, Beele, Blaknall, Cater, Cetus, Corvus, Crockhelm, Cynder, Drawl, Eridanus, Falls, Fleedon, Gale, Geldwine, Graves, Kinwich, Lakefall, Laken, Lanby, Lispe, Mynyddthwaite, Neola, Ottmar, Puck, Salter, Stodsea, Strath, Taverner, Trident, Tucana,

The Venulaes of Iustitia
And Libran natives
'Judgement Fairs'

Located on the harsh landscapes of the Saturnian Mountains, the Venulaes have a knack for keeping things gracious. Although they threaten little, they are still a house to be feared, knowing that the past kings of Iustitia would have stopped at nothing to deliver justice.

DARYL VENULAES, Lord of Iustitia, Liege of Saturn, holder of the Tourmaline Gem,
-his wife, LADY ROSANNA, maiden name Till,
-their children:
    -KENNETH, eldest son, fifteen years of age, heir to Iustitia,
    -JUSTUS, son, of fourteen years,
    -SHERYL, only daughter, twelve,
    -VERRELL, youngest son, ten,
-his brother:
    -{KEVIN}, threw himself from the Aquila at age twenty,
        -his widow, ESTELLE, maiden name Didier,
-his council:
    -SIR LAMONT CHANEY, First Avail to Daryl,
    -ELDER SOLOMON, Libra representative at the Solar Auditorium,
    -CLARKE DOPPEL, head of word, brother to Galen Doppel,
    -NATHANIAL GARDET, head of trade,
    -ELISE BACH, head of pennons,

-THOMAS LOWELL, head of citizenship,

-ARNEST APPEL, head of guards,

-at the Tantum Monastery:

-MASTER HERLE, master of the monastery,

-REMON LEPUS, chief acolyte, a bastard,

-TASSIN CYRIELLE, apprentice acolyte,

-ALCESTE NEE, bookkeeper,

-CLERIC SABRINA, priest and warrior,

-SEER TYONIUS, not of Sanctum Amino; claims to be a seer of his own methods,

-pennons of note: (Arms rounded to nearest 100)

-LUQUIN CORBIS, Lord of Fort Pondus, (2,700),

-OCEANE LOUPE, Lady of Civitas, (6,300),

-her son, AXEL, a boy too young to rule,

-MATTHAS BRUNT, Warden of Judicium, (3,000),

-TIEBALD CASTEX, Lord of Fort Creo, (7,500),

-HELIES FRESNEL, Lord of Arkdale, (2.400),

-ARTUS MAITRE, Lord of Frisen Keep, (2,600),

-SYLVESTRE LAZARD, Lord of Moat Stilio, (4,000),

-LOYS MALLET, Lord of Oretown, (1,500),

-OMER CHARRIER, Lord of Templebay, (2,600),

-ALEXA SERRE, Lady of Westreen, (3,800),

-JUNIEN VIDAL, Lord of Lorveil, (1,700),

-GILBERT BRAZIER, Lord of Erthal Keep, (2,300),

-LORENS SEYERS, Lord of Barlon Peak, (700),

-MILO HALPHER, Lord of Fellbrook, (1,300),

-GARIN MARE, Lord of Baerston's Hearth, (4,000),

-FREDRIS HACKET, Lord of Fort Wextry, (3,200),

-HARALT CORBERT, Lord of Kinhal Peak, (1,200),

-LISA VYMONT, Lady of Hallcross, (500),

Libran natives: Appel, Aquila, Ayde, Bach, Brunt, Burke, Camelopardus, Castex, Chaney, Charrier, Corbert, Corbis, Cyrielle, Derring, Didier, Dumont, Dyel, Estney, Fiske, Fresnel, Gardet, Grus, Hacket, Halpher, Incir, Irons, Lazard, Lepus, Loupe, Lowell, Lupus, Maitre, Mallet, Mare, Nee, Odum, Paston, Patel, Quincy, Sculptor, Seeder, Seyers, Serre, Stoke, Till, Valles, Venulaes, Vidal, Vymont, Waker,

The Casterons of Windtune
And Piscean natives
'Fish Always Swim'

The Venusian Archipelago can be a place of deceit and lies. As for the Casterons, compassion comes first in their nature. Judging from their history, a house must perform a great deal of cruelty before they are looked down upon by a Casteron. Surrounded by frozen waters, the Casterons, for the most part, have been the uncontested kings and queens of the Tusks for thousands of years.

BLAINE CASTERON, Lord of the Tusks, holder of the Aquamarine Gem,
-his wife, LADY IVETTE, maiden name Shell,
-their children:
>-LACHLAN, eldest son, sixteen, heir to the Tusks,
>-MAXWELL, a boy of fifteen,
>-CLEMENT, a boy of fourteen,
>-MERYL, eldest daughter, eleven,
>-FAE, youngest daughter, ten, twin to Finn,
>-FINNEGAN, called Finn, youngest son, ten, twin to Fae,
-his siblings:
>-ROSEMARY, called Rose, sister to Blaine,
>-JULIAN, brother by law,
>-LAWLER, brother by law,
-his council:
>-JULIAN SHELL, Blaine's First Avail,
>-DON GOFRAID, head of pennons,

-ELDER COLBERT, Pisces representative at the solar auditorium,
-PILIB ODHA, head of ships,
-EANAN CINNE, head of trade,
-his brother, TIERNAN CINNE, head of word,
-his pikesguard:
    -SIR MICHAN FOLAIN, of the pikesguard,
    -SIR AGASTAS TOGG, of the pikesguard,
    -DAGHAN DEIN, of the pikesguard,
    -EILIS FLAIT, of the pikesguard,
-pennons of note: (Arms rounded to nearest 100)
    -FITHEAL COSGAIR, Lord of Forsten, (2,300),
    -LONAN MAGHNUS, Lord of Kipway, (1,500),
    -OISIN CUIRC, Lord of Bloomswood Rock, (2,400),
    -TASSACH EATH, Lord of Oxmar Reef, (1,100),
    -ROSNIN LIATHAN, Lady of Taefa, (900),
    -COMAN SALMO, Lord of Westrick, (400),
    -FLANN PEATAIN, Lord of Fort Cobalt, (2,600),
    -EAMON DONNACH, Lord of Brightpool, (1,400),
    -DUFACH SILURUS, Lord of Thorlorn Dock, (800),
    -CRIO MERENA, Lord of Eel's Skerry, (2,900),
    -NAITHI PISTRIS, Warden of Darwon, (500),
    -ART SCOMBER, Lord of Moaning Rock, (600),
    -GILLEY BURBOT, Lord of Boxrose Bay, (1,300),
    -LACHTIN AODHA, Lord of Teal Islet, (300),
    -BRAN KRAITH, Lord of Frozenfall, (4,200),
    -AILIN FEARGHALL, Lord of Lilydore, (700),

Piscean natives: Aodha, Austrinis, Barque, Bekker, Burbot, Casteron, Cinne, Cosgair, Cuirc, Cygnus, Dein, Donnach, Dorado, Eath, Fearghall, Flait, Folain, Fysher, Gill, Gofraid, Kraith, Liathan, Maghnus, Merena, Odha, Peatrain, Pistris, Pyxis, Reticulum, Rivers, Roseye, Salmo, Scomber, Silurus, Till, Togg, Volans,

The Equuleus of Lutum
Of Sagittarian amalgamation
'On Horseback We Drive'

A distant branch of the Sagittarius, the Equuleus have had an unbroken faith with the Centaurs since long before the pause. Having Lutum located on the very edge of where the Canicule starts has proven a difficult place to live, yet this robust kingdom has managed to thrive, mainly from the Lake Ignis trade route delivering priceless supplies.

DORAN EQUULEUS, Lord of Lutum, holder of the Tanzanite Reins,
-his wife, {LADY CAMILLA}, maiden name Dive, passed of natural cause,
-their children:
-VIOLET, eldest offspring,
-IDRIS, eldest son, heir to Lutum,
-APOLLO, youngest legitimate son,
-Doran's numerous bastards:
-IVOR SAGITTA,
-NARCISSA SAGITTA,
-ASCELLA SAGITTA,
-ROBIN SAGITTA,
-his council:
-LAYTON GILES, Doran's First Avail,
-REMON DOW, head of trade,
-SAERUS PYNE, head of the city's garrison,
-MYCHAELL LAKEN, head of word,
-EVERYD BRASSIE, head of gold,

-at Lutum:

      -ELDER TOXOTES, called 'Elder Headcase', lives in his library, refuses to give counsel, said to have gone mad from his immortality,

      -AUSTYN CHAVEZ, first cheval,

      -KIERAN BYRNE, second cheval,

            -his father, ROSS BYRNE, first cheval to Palmer II, living in Liglock,

            -his sister, CHLOE BYRNE,

      -TYBOST OKEN, horsemaster and breeder,

      -SIR POWELL WRENNE, head of arms,

-pennons of note: (Arms rounded to nearest 100)

      -BLAIVE WYVIL, Warden of Dunshoals, (8,000),

      -PIERS FOGG, Warden of Fort Foxstrake, (6,700),

      -ELLING OBSON, Warden of Greysea Keep, (5,800),

      -ANTHONY TREVYT, Warden of Litdun Peaks, (6,200),

      -SIR JOHEN KNIGHTON, Warden of Brinkshold, (9,500),

      -KLEEVE GOLDING, Warden of Ashgrove, (7,500),

The Sculptors of Sangis
Of Libran amalgamation
'Hammers of Steel'

Famed for their thriving economy, this ancient branch of the Libra have been the kings of southern commerce since long before the Pause. The Sangis Waterway, which before the Pause wasn't a waterway at all but a river, only helped continue their reign, as a natural dock was born of Sangis, and the Sculptors were quick to reconquer the southern commerce of Austellus.

CURTIS SCULPTOR, Lord of Sangis, holder of the Platinum Coin,
-his wife, LADY OLIVIA, maiden name Stoke,
-their son, EDWIN, only child, heir to Sangis,
-his siblings:
>-DARREL, eldest brother,
>>-his wife, RACHEL, of House Irons,
>>-his daughter, AVELINE,
>>-his son, JULIEN, eighteen,
>-KATT QUINCY, eldest sister,
>>-her husband, OSBERT, of the Quincy family,
>>-her bastard son, EMERY LEPUS,
>>-her bastard daughter, LISA LEPUS, twenty,
>>-her bastard daughter, GRACE LEPUS, eighteen,
>>-her trueborn son, ALBERT, ten,
>-FLEUR VALLES, youngest sister,
>>-her husband, RICHER, of the Valles family,
>>-her son, BENADIN, sixteen,

-her son, OLIVER, fourteen,

-her daughter, SUZO, eleven,

-GERALD, brother,

-his wife, YVANNE, maiden name Auber,

-his son, NIEL, eleven,

-his daughter, ZOE, nine,

-his daughter, ADE, Zoe's twin,

-his hammer's guard:

-ESDRAS RISLEY, of the hammer's guard, father to Nathan Risley,

-SIR OCTAVIAN BLAKNALL, of the hammer's guard,

-LUKE SEEDER, of the hammer's guard,

-GARROT PASTON, of the hammer's guard,

-MARTIN BEELE, of the hammer's guard,

-his council:

-ELDER ENGELMAR, second Libra representative at the Solar Auditorium, head of trade,

-OSMUNT DYEL, head of law, brother to Widmunt,

-his brother, WIDMUNT, watchmaster,

-his brother, LAURUNT, Warden of the Dam,

-PIERIN BURKE, head of ships,

-ADAM DUMONT, head of coin,

-pennons of note: (Arms rounded to nearest 500)

-DAUBENY DRURY, Lord of Hydwick, (4,000),

-GABRIEL HERFAST, Lord of Vaswick, (6,000),

-GIPP ESTNEY, Lord of Somerdock, (4,500),

-BERTOL AYDE, Lord of Penny Harbour, (3,000),

-SIR AVERY DERRING, Warden of Kitsvale, (5,000),

The Lyonis of Lynxrock
Of Leon amalgamation
'Prowling High'

A fairly new power to rise in the Canicule, not much is known about the Lyonis family. The current Lord of Lynxrock, Ayden Lyonis, has made controversial political moves to enhance both his power and his status, one of those moves being to wed his sister to the Lord of Ignis, Lord Reynold Lyrderyn, securing a powerful bond between the two kingdoms. Though, without a legitimate heir, nor a wife to show for, it seems this house's name has numbered days.

AYDEN LYONIS, Lord of Lynxrock,
> -his bastard child RYAN LYNX, sixteen,
-his siblings:
> -LADY ELAYNE, maiden name Lyonis, wed to Reynold Lyrderyn,
> -REYNOLD LYRDERYN, brother by law, Lord of Ignis,
-his council:
> -ELDER SOL, second Leo representative at the Solar Auditorium,
> -AMEER LEAFER, head of defence,
> -SYMYAK RATAN, head of law,
> -OSMAN ALPER, head of trade,
-his lynx's guard:
> -JAE HIZDIR, of the lynx's guard,
> -ETHYN TULON, of the lynx's guard,
> -DEVEN MUSTAFA, of the lynx's guard,

-at Lynxrock:

 -SIR VOSSO SEVKI,

-pennons of note: (Arms rounded to nearest 100)

 -GALVIN GRYFFORD, Lord of Reddust Castle,
 father of Sir Brendan Gryfford, (3,400),
 -HUMBERT ELIES, Lord of Aurdrive Town, (2,500),
 -DALTON HENLYE, Lord of Damastar, (800),
 -KEENAN TANSAL, Lord of Samabair Hills, (4,100),
 -TYREK MESUT, Lord of Fort Ziden, (4,200),
 -DENZYL TRONE, Lord of Mount Nuzdith, (2,800),

THE FALSE KINGDOMS
The independent kingdoms raised in the lands of exile

The Khavars of Ortus Isle
And Cancerian natives
'Not Without Claws'

Once a peasant family with no wealth or heritage, the Khavars have recently climbed to become the undisputed behemoths of the Venusian Archipelago. The Khavars have bent powerful lords to rally by their side and married into great bloodlines, making them able to seize the power of the entire Archipelago in a single click of their claws.

> DELMAR KHAVAR, King of the Venusian Archipelago, Lord of the Crab Belt, holder of the Ruby Shell,
> -his wife LADY NYDIA, maiden name Cancer,
> -their children:
>> -LOMAX, eldest son, a boy of nineteen, heir to the Archipelago,
>>> -his betrothed, LADY SOPHIA, of maiden name Scorpius, daughter of Vincent,
>> -MARK, a boy of seventeen,
>> -DYLAN, a boy of fifteen,
>> -HARRIET, eldest daughter, a girl of ten,
>> -CARLIN, a boy of seven,
>> -LUNA, a girl of five,
> -his siblings:
>> -JULIUS, eldest brother to Delmar,
>> -EDWARD, brother by law, maiden name Cancer, brother to Nydia,
> -his council:
>> -VINCENT SCORPIUS, Delmar's First Avail,

-ELDER EZEKIEL, Scorpius representative at the Solar Auditorium,
-ELDER JERICHO, Cancer representative at the Solar Auditorium,
-FRANCO BOTIN, head of ships,
-KEVIN TACK, head of trade,
-LUZ VERELA, head of word,
-MARCO FAWCETT, head of pennons.
-his crab's guard:
    -CADBY KLARK, of the crab's guard,
    -ABBOT TASSIS, of the crab's guard,
    -DAMIAN BALO, of the crab's guard,
    -JOAQUIN PADDLE, of the crab's guard,
-pennons of note: (Arms rounded to nearest 100)
    -LAUTARO ZORITA, Lord of Bloodmoon Isle, (4,100),
    -HADWIN SAEZ, Lord of Trimea, (1,500),
    -STEFANO VEXX, Lord of Fort Sedito, (1,900),
    -RYLAND CHANE, Lord of Turtle's Reef, (2,100),
    -ROBERT FROMIR, Lord of Syvya Isle, (6,100),
    -DUNTON KEIC, Lord of Nirtia, (2,600),
    -JAVIER YMO, Lord of Burclave, (500),
    -SPALDER EDJJ, Lord of Hospirm Rock, (900),
    -DELVIN SAZALLA, Warden of Fort Carabus, (1,500),
    -KERWIN ROUCKO, Lord of Korgos, (2,200),
    -VANCE MANDRED, Lord of Palecraw, (800),
    -LYNDON GALLO, Lord of the Isle of Gales, (1,000),

Cancerian natives: Balo, Botin, Cancer, Carina, Chane, Delphinus, Edjj, Fawcett, Fromir, Gallo, Khavar, Kiec, Klark, Lacerta, Mandred, Octans, Paddle, Puppis, Roucko, Saez, Sazalla, Scutum, Tack, Tassis, Vela, Verela, Vexx, Ymo, Zorita,

The Scorpius of the Stingers
And Scorpion natives
'Stingers of Mars'

Infamous for the many revolts conducted since The Great Pause, one shudders at the thought of crossing a Scorpion. Although often being the bunt of ridicule due to their countless failed rebellions, those who actually encounter the Scorpius know that they are a house to be feared. Proud down to their last breath, no matter how much mockery they endure, they'll never back down from a fight. In most cases, the mocking only fuels revenge.

VINCENT SCORPIUS, Lord of the Stingers, First Avail to King Delmar Khavar, holder of the Citrine Gem,
-his wife, LADY LEILA, maiden name Vemn,
-their children:
> -LADY SOPHIA, betrothed to Lomax, eldest child,
> -{COLE}, executed by Palmer II as punishment of a rebellion,
> -RAYNER, a boy of eighteen,
> -GRIFFITH, a boy of fifteen,
> -ERAN, youngest son, a boy of twelve,
-his siblings:
> -{TYCHO}, eldest brother, fell in The Battle of the Auburn Pole,
> -{RAYNER}, older brother, fell while attacking Fort Deus in the Scorpius Rebellion,
> -CYAMUS, younger brother, shipmaster,
> -ASTRID, only sister, widow of two,
>> -her first husband, {PHILO VICTINUS},

-her second husband, {EUSTACH SYLLIA},
-QUINTIS, his youngest brother,
-his scorpion's guard:
-TITUS NARSES, of the scorpion's guard,
-LENNOX SAYE, of the scorpion's guard,
-his one and only advisor, ELDER EZEKIEL, Scorpius
representative at the Solar Auditorium,
-pennons of note: (Arms rounded to nearest 100)
-GALLUS ARKEN, Lord of Arkencliff, (5,200),
-PETRUS SYLLIA, Lord of Nova Isle, younger brother
of Eustach Syllia, (3,100),
-AUGUST SORIO, Lord of Aricia, (2,600),
-FLEANCE BASSUS, Lord of Ostium, (2,800),
-THEO REMMUS, Lord of Dyrrachium Dock, (800),
-AULUS VICTINUS, Lord of Fort Victory, first son of
Philo Victinus, (1,900),
-LYCO VESNIUS, Lord of Cyrene, (700),
-KANE PETRI, Lord of Basilia Isle, (3,400),
-VIRIDIA LEPTIS, Lady of Lutestream, (1,000),
-SIMO MARSUS, Lord of Acrae Isle, (300),
-LUCIA CELSUS, Lady of Gades, (600),
-BALLIO PRICIAN, Lord of Virrial Isle, (3,700),
-STAPH LAEKA, Lord of Aesis Key, (2,000),
-KAESO SOUL, Lord of Soul's Palace, (1,600),
-TULLIA AFER, Lady of Siscia, (2,700),
-PAEG PASTOR, Lord of Pharos Isle, (1,500),
-HARPAX SERVANT, Lord of Fort Syrack, (1,300),

Scorpion natives: Afer, Arken, Australe, Bassus, Berenices, Celsus, Crater,
Hydra, Laeka, Leptis, Marsus, Narses, Pastor, Petri, Pictor, Prician,
Remmus, Saye, Scorpius, Servant, Sorio, Soul, Syllia, Triagulum, Vemn,
Vesnius, Victinus,

The Capras of Seden
And Capricornian natives
'Made of Kings'

The Kingdom of Seden is a mystery to most men, the three islands that make up the kingdom being so far out of reach, that they can only be found if someone is searching for them. Located near the bottom of the known world, The Three Goats became a popular destination for runaway people of exile, their time alone and undisturbed allowing the islands to flourish into a proud kingdom.

NERO CAPRA, King of the Three Goats, holder of the Garnet Horn, Lord of Fort Lytia,
-his wife, IRMA, maiden name Gill,
-their children:
      -TYRAN, eldest son, nineteen, heir to Seden,
      -CLINT, youngest son, sixteen,
      -KIERA, only daughter, thirteen,
-his siblings:
      -CIARA, eldest sibling to Nero,
      -TALYA, sister to Nero,
      -OREA, youngest sister to Nero,
      -JETHRO, of the Gill family, brother by law to Nero,
-his council:
      -GABRIAN SPEYER, Nero's First Avail,
      -ELDER ALDOUS, Capricorn representative at the Solar Auditorium,
      -MARVIN AMOS, head of trade,
      -EVRI TZUR, head of ships,

-ARLIN GOODMAN, head of arms,
-JERED SPECTOR, head of citizenship,
-pennons of note: (Arms rounded to nearest 100)
-YONAN GOLD, Lord of Midian Dock, (1,600),
-ESDRAS WALEY, Lord of Fort Nimrod, (200),
-JACK GEIGER, Lord of Sodom Bay, (1,000),
-IVRI ADLER, Lord of Gallile Pass, (1,500),
-BERTIN ADIEL, Lord of Fort Lustre, (400),
-JAMON BRAFF, Lord of Opis Hill, (800),
-XIMUN WOOLF, Lord of Fort Shiloh, (200),
-ARIANE FLEISHER, Lady of Ramath Woods, (300),
-NESSLE DATZ, Lord of Fort Tyre, (700),
-LURIA BRASKE, Lord of Braskrock, (600),
-YITZ GRENNER, Lord of Fort Etham, (900),
-LARISSA PIRBRIGHT, Lady of Hebryn Bay, (2,100),

Capricornian natives: Adiel, Adler, Amos, Australis, Braff, Braske, Caelum,
Capra, Datz, Fleisher, Geiger, Gold, Goodman, Grenner, Hood, Moss,
Norma, Pirbright, Spector, Speyer, Tzur, Ursa, Waley, Woolf,

The Haussciers of Boventos
And Taurean natives
'What's Ours is Ours'

Defending their reign as kings of the jungle from countless Arian raids, the Haussciers have much and more to show for how to raise a thriving kingdom. They have abided in the prolific forests of Heavia for as long as even before their exile, using their time in banishment to only grow wealthier and wealthier.

GODRED HASSCIER, King of Heavia, holder of the Emerald Horn,
-his wife, BRITH, maiden name Rocker,
-their children:
  -AELWIN, only son, heir to Boventos,
  -ESTRITH, eldest daughter, eighteen,
  -HAYLEY, daughter, sixteen,
  -FREA, youngest daughter, ten,
-his older brother, {DUNSTAN}, slain by Horncurves,
-his sister, ESTRID,
  -her husband, CYNFERTH, of House Woodward,
-his younger brother, {OSWIN}, slain by Horncurves,
-his council:
  -SWITHUN TRANTER, Godred's First Avail,
  -ELDER LYMAN, Taurus representative at the Solar Auditorium,
  -CYNRIC SUDGHYLL, head of defence,
  -OSGOOD THATCHER, head of word,
  -BRYNSTAN SHEPSHAW, head of trade,

        -ALCRED LANGPOOL, head of coin,
        -SABERT SPITTLE, chief smuggler,
    -pennons of note: (Arms rounded to nearest 100)
              -FREOMUND REDMAN, Lord of Cornhold, (4,000),
              -ODARD HAMMER, Lord of Hammer's Holdfast,
              (2,500),
              -TATING SKINNER, Lord of Llyncheth, (3,600),
              -DUNSTAN HAYZE, Lord of Fort Hayze, (3,100),
              -AEGEN COTTS, Lord of Silvertoft, (2,700),
              -WALDEN KINSWICK, Lord of Strathport, (2,100),
              -KENALD WARF, Lord of Windcoom Docks, (900),
              -WIGSTON SKULLY, Lord of Fort Skully, (800),
              -ULFRIC FALCONER, Lord of Gerrit, (600),
              -CYNE STONIER, Lord of Achleigh, (1,200),
              -ORDRIC KELLOG, Warden of Dungarth Castle,
              (2,400),
              -EALH NAYLOR, Lord of Fort Finstow, (1,300),
              -ALLRIC KEY, Lord of Vadir's Temple, (3,000),
              -SAYWIN LISTER, Lord of Winkirk, (1,800),
              -SPERLING TARBOR, Warden of Fort Porthea,
              (2,400),

Taurean natives: Canis, Cotts, Falconer, Hammer, Hayze, Hausscier, Hercules, Kellog, Key, Kinswick, Langpool, Lister, Naylor, Redman, Rocker, Sextans, Shepshaw, Skinner, Skully, Spittle, Stonier, Sudghyll, Tarbor, Taurus, Thatcher, Tranter, Venatici, Warf, Woodward,

TIMELINE OF NOTABLE EVENTS
(After Pause)

THE GREAT PAUSE - A catastrophic celestial event, sending the seasons into perpetual stillness, summoning natural disasters such as tsunamis, blizzards, sandstorms, hurricanes, earthquakes, tearing Austellus in half, 0 AP,

DEUS'S SALVATION - The eventual fabrication of the Celestial Complex, made with magic by Deus Caelestius, served as a bunker for those who could make it during *The Great Pause*, 1 AP,

THE ELDER'S GIFT - A magical act where Deus Caelestius made fifteen pledged servants *elders*, granting them eternal life so long as they upheld their vows, 25 AP,

ERLAND'S ESCAPE - A silent uprising led by Erland the Escaper, leading his men and those who would come out of the Celestial Complex against Deus Caelestius's orders, united *The Eight Kingdoms* under one crown, 163 AP – 165 AP,

THE RISE OF LTER – The acknowledgement and conquest of the Centaur Empire, universally deeming the Great City of Lter as the capital of Austellus, the purging of dissent to uphold peace and power by Archer I Centaur, 183 AP – 196 AP,

THE FALL OF LTER – Also known as the Collapse of the Eight Kingdoms, old and new kingdoms begin to claim independence from Jovian II Centaur, causing conflict and civil war, 262 AP – 278 AP,

THE OQUINTEUS REBELLION - A revolt led by Percival Oquinteus, overthrowing Deus Caelestius and instating Percival as the ruler of the Celestial Complex, continued by his son, Achilles Oquinteus, once escaping from the Complex, subdued following a defeat in *The Battle of the Wastelands*, 276 AP - 279 AP,

THE SECOND PAUSE - An event only half as ruinous as *The Great Pause*, following *The Oquinteus Rebellion*, a notable occurrence being the burial of the Centaur capital of Lter, creating the Canicule, 278 AP,

THE WAR OF THE WASTELANDS - A conflict between Archer III Centaur, and Achilles Oquinteus, reaching its apex at *The Battle of the Wastelands*, where the Oquinteus army fell, 279 AP,

THE GREAT EXILE - An act issued by Esmond II Centaur, exiling those who were pledged to Achilles Oquinteus during *The War of the Wastelands*, subsequently having *The Nine Kingdoms* established under one crown, 318 AP,

SIGMUND'S UPRISING - A revolt led by Sigmund Horncurve, overthrowing Jaakko Oquinteus to become Lord of Selerborn, subsequently being pardoned by Palmer II Centaur in 385 AP, establishing Selerborn as part of *The Ten Kingdoms* under one crown, 368 AP,

THE SCORPIUS REBELLION - A revolt led by Eldric Scorpius, attempting to take the solar throne and free themselves of exile, subdued following a defeat by Palmer II Centaur during *The Battle of The Auburn Pole*, 400 AP – 405 AP,

TERMS AND TITLES

ELDER - One who is magically infused with eternal life, sworn to Deus Caelestius to protect the realms of men, receiving their power during *The Elder's Gift*,

FIRST AVAIL - Primary councillor, Acting King/Lord upon absence, inherits King/Lords' seat if there are no heirs,

SECOND AVAIL - Same as the *First Avail*, but next in line,

CHEVAL - Horse riders, trainers, warriors, and keepers of the highest calibre, normally in control of an *Equo*,

GURU - A teacher and master of a particular martial art or skill, a custom originating in the Kingdom of Aquamare,

EQUO - A categorisation of trained cavalry units, normally upheld by a *Cheval*, a specialised unit of Sagittarian origin,

CITY'S GARRISON - A patrol of soldiers taking turns to protect a city, normally a quarter of the city's total soldiery, suited with specialty weapons,

PENNON - A house with armed units sworn to another, to be called upon when assistance is required,

BIRTHMOON - The moon in which one is born in, a celebration of the moon rather than the day, as moons have a mutable amount of days, making one's *birth day* sometimes missed,

BIRTH DAY - The day in which one is born, not as commonly celebrated as *birthmoons*, but is if said day arrives amongst nobles,

THE CENTAUR DYNASTY
(After Pause)

A dynasty founded by Erland the Escaper in 163 AP, the Centaurs have ruled over the lands of Austellus for hundreds of years. As Erland received his namesake, escaping from the Celestial Complex, people began to flock behind him, choosing him as their leader not for his ambition of being king, but his ambition of leading a new world. Thus, Erland paved the path for his ancestors to travel.

163-179	ERLAND I	Named Erland the Escaper, led the families of Centaur, Lyrderyn, Casteron, Khavar, Lynx, Pegasus, Sagitta, and Equuleus out of the Complex,
179-215	ARCHER I	Son of Erland, named the Pioneer, led his people across The Arm of Jupiter, raised the Great City of Lter,
215-216	ESMOND I	Son of Archer, named the Sickly, died of eremus disease while venturing east,
216-227	JOVIAN I	Brother of Archer, named the Just,
227-250	THADDEUS I	Son of Jovian, named the Wise,
250-261	ARCHER II	Son of Thaddeus, named the Strong,
261-264	PALMER I	Son of Archer, named the Untimely, died to a snake bite,
264-278	JOVIAN II	Brother of Palmer, named the Cruel, died in The Second Great Pause, buried with the Empire of Lter,
278-300	ARCHER III	Son of Jovian, named the Brave, won The War of the Wastelands, constructed the Solar Auditorium,
300-318	ESMOND II	Son of Archer, named the Sharer of Lands, constructed the Negal Wall, responsible for The Great Exile,
318-345	FLETCHER I	Son of Esmond, named the Maker of

		Weapons,
345-404	PALMER II	Son of Fletcher, named the Keeper of Peace, unexiled the Aries, won The Scorpius Rebellion.
404-405	IVOR I	Son of Palmer, named the Lost King, fled after renouncing his claim, last seen at Sagwhel, presumed dead.
405-XXX	ESMOND III	Brother of Ivor, only fifteen when he inherited the throne,

Marking Esmond's coronation, there has been a total of fourteen Kings of Post-Austellus.

Claimants in order After Esmond III

ASHER CENTAUR, legitimate heir, eldest son, living at Fort Deus,

FLETCHER CENTAUR, second son, living at Fort Deus,

HEW CENTAUR, third son, living at Fort Deus,

LORIMER CENTAUR, younger brother, Lord of Centaur's Lagoon,

THADDEUS CENTAUR, cousin, Acting King of Lunarpass,

ORION READE, First Avail, living at Fort Deus,

ROSWELL DART, Second Avail, living at Fort Deus,

ABOUT THE AUTHOR & OTHER STUFF

There was a time when being given the chance to speak would just be an opportunity to talk about myself... and that time is still now. My name is Antoni and I'm not really an author. Well, unless I am now. Nor did I have any aspiration to be, not since I was *very* young. But that was before I had the pleasure of a series called A Song of Ice and Fire.

There's something about George's realistic, gritty, punishing, vast style of storytelling that I found so interesting. As soon as I finished binging the show for the first time, it took me a good couple of days until I told myself I needed more of that shit. Clearly, the most logical thing to do from there was to undertake the world of Austellus, of which is way too huge from what I could actually handle, and the perfect spawn of many headaches. But we're here, it's done, and because there was so much freedom and indulgence in writing something so huge, those headaches were more than worth it.

What I'm trying to say is a thank you to George, and everyone who had a part in bringing it to life on the big screen. Thank you for inspiring me to pour two years, and many years to come, of my life into something I've grown to love so much.

That being said, it's only about a third of my life that fantasy has a hold of. Another huge time sink is music, and with that comes a whole novel more of inspirations that won't fit on this page. But what I *can* fit on this page is a shameless plug telling you that all my stuff can be followed if you search for Antoni Krupski on YouTube, Instagram, Spotify, iTunes, and whatever music distributor you prefer to listen on.

I've somehow made this relevant as I've written and recorded a 24-track album about this book and this world, called 'The Auburn Pole'. Hopefully, it'll make the series richer, and if not, it wouldn't hurt to have a few more bangers on your playlist. ~They perhaps might even have a few hints and secrets of An Age of Stars' future as well hehe.

Printed in Great Britain
by Amazon